THE
ESSENTIAL
STEINBECK

THE ESSENTIAL STEINBECK

~

THE GRAPES OF WRATH

CANNERY ROW

OF MICE AND MEN

TORTILLA FLAT

SEAFARER BOOKS • NEW YORK

SEAFARER BOOKS
a Division of Penguin Books USA Inc.
375 Hudson Street
New York, New York 10014

Published by Seafarer Books, a Division of Penguin Books USA Inc.

First Seafarer Printing, August 1994

The Grapes of Wrath
First published in the United States of America by The Viking Press Inc., 1939
Copyright John Steinbeck, 1939
Copyright renewed John Steinbeck, 1967

Cannery Row
First published in the United States of America by
The Viking Press Inc., 1945
Copyright John Steinbeck, 1945
Copyright renewed Elaine Steinbeck, John Steinbeck IV and
Thom Steinbeck, 1973

Of Mice and Men
First published in the United States of America by
Covici, Friede, Inc., 1937
Published by The Viking Press Inc., 1938
Copyright John Steinbeck, 1937
Copyright renewed John Steinbeck, 1965

Tortilla Flat
First published in the United States of America by
Covici, Friede, Inc., 1935
Published by The Viking Press Inc., 1938
Copyright John Steinbeck, 1935
Copyright renewed John Steinbeck, 1963

PUBLISHER'S NOTE:
These are works of fiction. Names, characters, places, and incidents either are the
product of the author's imagination or are used fictitiously, and any resemblance
to actual persons, living or dead, events, or locales is entirely coincidental.

THE
ESSENTIAL
STEINBECK

THE
GRAPES
OF
WRATH

To CAROL *who willed this book.*
To TOM *who lived it.*

1

To the red country and part of the gray country of Oklahoma, the last rains came gently, and they did not cut the scarred earth. The plows crossed and recrossed the rivulet marks. The last rains lifted the corn quickly and scattered weed colonies and grass along the sides of the roads so that the gray country and the dark red country began to disappear under a green cover. In the last part of May the sky grew pale and the clouds that had hung in high puffs for so long in the spring were dissipated. The sun flared down on the growing corn day after day until a line of brown spread along the edge of each green bayonet. The clouds appeared, and went away, and in a while they did not try any more. The weeds grew darker green to protect themselves, and they did not spread any more. The surface of the earth crusted, a thin hard crust, and as the sky became pale, so the earth became pale, pink in the red country and white in the gray country.

In the water-cut gullies the earth dusted down in dry little streams. Gophers and ant lions started small avalanches. And as the sharp sun struck day after day, the leaves of the young corn became less stiff and erect; they bent in a curve at first, and then, as the central ribs of strength grew weak, each leaf tilted downward. Then it was June, and the sun shone more fiercely. The brown lines on the corn leaves widened and moved in on the central ribs. The weeds frayed and edged back toward their roots. The air was thin and the sky more pale; and every day the earth paled.

In the roads where the teams moved, where the wheels milled the ground and the hooves of the horses beat the ground, the dirt crust broke and the dust formed. Every moving thing lifted the dust into the air: a walking man lifted a thin layer as high as his waist, and a wagon lifted the dust as high as the fence tops, and an automobile boiled a cloud behind it. The dust was long in settling back again.

When June was half gone, the big clouds moved up out of Texas and the Gulf, high heavy clouds, rain-heads. The men in the fields looked up at the clouds and sniffed at them and held wet fingers up to sense the wind. And the horses were nervous while the clouds were up. The rain-heads dropped a little spattering and hurried on to some other country. Behind them the sky was pale again and the sun flared. In the dust there were drop craters where the rain had fallen, and there were clean splashes on the corn, and that was all.

A gentle wind followed the rain clouds, driving them on northward, a wind that softly clashed the drying corn. A day went by and the wind increased, steady, unbroken by gusts. The dust from the roads fluffed up and spread out and fell on the weeds beside the fields, and fell into the fields a little way. Now the wind grew strong and hard and it worked at the rain crust in the corn fields. Little by little the sky was darkened by the mixing dust, and the wind felt over the earth, loosened the dust, and carried it away. The wind grew stronger. The rain crust broke and the dust lifted up out of the fields and drove gray plumes into the air like sluggish smoke. The corn threshed the wind and made a dry, rushing sound. The finest dust did not settle back to earth now, but disappeared into the darkening sky.

The wind grew stronger, whisked under stones, carried up straws and old leaves, and even little clods, marking its course as it sailed across the fields. The air and the sky darkened and through them the sun shone redly, and there was a raw sting in the air. During a night the wind raced faster over the land, dug cunningly among the rootlets of the corn, and the corn fought the wind with its weakened leaves until the roots were freed by the prying wind and then each stalk settled wearily sideways toward the earth and pointed the direction of the wind.

The dawn came, but no day. In the gray sky a red sun appeared, a dim red circle that gave a little light, like dusk; and as that day advanced, the dusk slipped back toward darkness, and the wind cried and whimpered over the fallen corn.

Men and women huddled in their houses, and they tied handkerchiefs over their noses when they went out, and wore goggles to protect their eyes.

When the night came again it was black night, for the stars cound not pierce the dust to get down, and the window lights could not even spread beyond their own yards. Now the dust was evenly mixed with the air, an emulsion of dust and air. Houses were shut tight, and cloth wedged around doors and windows, but the dust came in so thinly that it could not be seen in the air, and it settled like pollen on the chairs and tables, on the dishes. The prople brushed it from their shoulders. Little lines of dust lay at the door sills.

In the middle of that night the wind passed on and left the land quiet. The dust-filled air muffled sound more completely than fog does. The people, lying in their beds, heard the wind stop. They awakened when the rushing wind was gone. They lay quietly and listened deep into the stillness. Then the roosters

crowed, and their voices were muffled, and the people
stirred restlessly in their beds and wanted the morning. They knew it would take a long time for the dust
to settle out of the air. In the morning the dust hung
like fog, and the sun was as red as ripe new blood. All
day the dust sifted down from the sky, and the next
day it sifted down. An even blanket covered the earth.
It settled on the corn, piled up on the tops of the fence
posts, piled up on the wires; it settled on roofs, blan-
keted the weeds and trees.

The people came out of their houses and smelled
the hot stinging air and covered their noses from it.
And the children came out of the houses, but they did
not run or shout as they would have done after a rain.
Men stood by their fences and looked at the ruined
corn, drying fast now, only a little green showing
through the film of dust. The men were silent and they
did not move often. And the women came out of the
houses to stand beside their men—to feel whether this
time the men would break. The women studied the
men's faces secretly, for the corn could go, as long as
something else remained. The children stood near by,
drawing figures in the dust with bare toes, and the
children sent exploring senses out to see whether men
and women would break. The children peeked at the
faces of the men and women, and then drew careful
lines in the dust with their toes. Horses came to the
watering troughs and nuzzled the water to clear the
surface dust. After a while the faces of the watching
men lost their bemused perplexity and became hard
and angry and resistant. Then the women knew that
they were safe and that there was no break. Then they
asked, What'll we do? And the men replied, I don't
know. But it was all right. The women knew it was all
right, and the watching children knew it was all right.
Women and children knew deep in themselves that no
misfortune was too great to bear if their men were
whole. The women went into the houses to their work,

and the children began to play, but cautiously at first. As the day went forward the sun became less red. It flared down on the dust-blanketed land. The men sat in the doorways of their houses; their hands were busy with sticks and little rocks. The men sat still—thinking—figuring.

2

A huge red transport truck stood in front of the little roadside restaurant. The vertical exhaust pipe muttered softly, and an almost invisible haze of steel-blue smoke hovered over its end. It was a new truck, shining red, and in twelve-inch letters on its sides—OKLAHOMA CITY TRANSPORT COMPANY. Its double tires were new, and a brass padlock stood straight out from the hasp on the big back doors. Inside the screened restaurant a radio played, quiet dance music turned low the way it is when no one is listening. A small outlet fan turned silently in its circular hole over the entrance, and flies buzzed excitedly about the doors and windows, butting the screens. Inside, one man, the truck driver, sat on a stool and rested his elbows on the counter and looked over his coffee at the lean and lonely waitress. He talked the smart listless language of the roadsides to her. "I seen him about three months ago. He had a operation. Cut somepin out. I forget what." And she—"Doesn't seem no longer ago than a week I seen him myself. Looked fine then. He's a nice sort of a guy when he ain't stinko." Now and then the flies roared softly at the screen door.

The coffee machine spurted steam, and the waitress, without looking, reached behind her and shut it off.

Outside, a man walking along the edge of the highway crossed over and approached the truck. He walked slowly to the front of it, put his hand on the shiny fender, and looked at the *No Riders* sticker on the windshield. For a moment he was about to walk on down the road, but instead he sat on the running board on the side away from the restaurant. He was not over thirty. His eyes were very dark brown and there was a hint of brown pigment in his eyeballs. His cheek bones were high and wide, and strong deep lines cut down his cheeks, in curves beside his mouth. His upper lip was long, and since his teeth protruded, the lips stretched to cover them, for this man kept his lips closed. His hands were hard, with broad fingers and nails as thick and ridged as little clam shells. The space between thumb and forefinger and the hams of his hands were shiny with callus.

The man's clothes were new—all of them, cheap and new. His gray cap was so new that the visor was still stiff and the button still on, not shapeless and bulged as it would be when it had served for a while all the various purposes of a cap—carrying sack, towel, handkerchief. His suit was of cheap gray hardcloth and so new that there were creases in the trousers. His blue chambray shirt was stiff and smooth with filler. The coat was too big, the trousers too short, for he was a tall man. The coat shoulder peaks hung down on his arms, and even then the sleeves were too short and the front of the coat flapped loosely over his stomach. He wore a pair of new tan shoes of the kind called "army last," hobnailed and with half-circles like horseshoes to protect the edges of the heels from wear. This man sat on the running board and took off his cap and mopped his face with it. Then he put on the cap, and by pulling started the future ruin of the

visor. His feet caught his attention. He leaned down
and loosened the shoelaces, and did not tie the ends
again. Over his head the exhaust of the Diesel engine
whispered in quick puffs of blue smoke.

The music stopped in the restaurant and a man's
voice spoke from the loudspeaker, but the waitress
did not turn him off, for she didn't know the music
had stopped. Her exploring fingers had found a lump
under her ear. She was trying to see it in a mirror
behind the counter without letting the truck driver
know, and so she pretended to push a bit of hair to
neatness. The truck driver said, "They was a big
dance in Shawnee. I heard somebody got killed or
somepin. You hear anything?" "No," said the waitress, and she lovingly fingered the lump under her
ear.

Outside, the seated man stood up and looked over
the cowl of the truck and watched the restaurant for a
moment. Then he settled back on the running board,
pulled a sack of tobacco and a book of papers from his
side pocket. He rolled his cigarette slowly and perfectly, studied it, smoothed it. At last he lighted it and
pushed the burning match into the dust at his feet.
The sun cut into the shade of the truck as noon
approached.

In the restaurant the truck driver paid his bill and
put his two nickels' change in a slot machine. The
whirling cylinders gave him no score. "They fix 'em so
you can't win nothing," he said to the waitress.

And she replied, "Guy took the jackpot not two
hours ago. Three-eighty he got. How soon you gonna
be back by?"

He held the screen door a little open. "Week-ten
days," he said. "Got to make a run to Tulsa, an' I
never get back soon as I think."

She said crossly, "Don't let the flies in. Either go
out or come in."

"So long," he said, and pushed his way out. The

screen door banged behind him. He stood in the sun, peeling the wrapper from a piece of gum. He was a heavy man, broad in the shoulders, thick in the stomach. His face was red and his blue eyes long and slitted from having squinted always at sharp light. He wore army trousers and high laced boots. Holding the stick of gum in front of his lips he called through the screen, "Well, don't do nothing you don't want me to hear about." The waitress was, turned toward a mirror on the back wall. She grunted a reply. The truck driver gnawed down the stick of gum slowly, opening his jaws and lips wide with each bite. He shaped the gum in his mouth, rolled it under his tongue while he walked to the big red truck.

The hitch-hiker stood up and looked across through the windows. "Could ya give me a lift, mister?"

The driver looked quickly back at the restaurant for a second. "Didn' you see the *No Riders* sticker on the win'shield?"

"Sure—I seen it. But sometimes a guy'll be a good guy even if some rich bastard makes him carry a sticker."

The driver, getting slowly into the truck, considered the parts of this answer. If he refused now, not only was he not a good guy, but he was forced to carry a sticker, was not allowed to have company. If he took in the hitch-hiker he was automatically a good guy and also he was not one whom any rich bastard could kick around. He knew he was being trapped, but he couldn't see a way out. And he wanted to be a good guy. He glanced again at the restaurant. "Scrunch down on the running board till we get around the bend," he said.

The hitch-hiker flopped down out of sight and clung to the door handle. The motor roared up for a moment, the gears clicked in, and the great truck moved away, first gear, second gear, third gear, and then a high whining pick-up and fourth gear. Under the clinging

man the highway blurred dizzily by. It was a mile to
the first turn in the road, then the truck slowed down.
The hitch-hiker stood up, eased the door open, and
slipped into the seat. The driver looked over at him,
slitting his eyes, and he chewed as though thoughts
and impressions were being sorted and arranged by his
jaws before they were finally filed away in his brain.
His eyes began at the new cap, moved down the new
clothes to the new shoes. The hitch-hiker squirmed his
back against the seat in comfort, took off his cap, and
swabbed his sweating forehead and chin with it.
"Thanks, buddy," he said. "My dogs was pooped out."

"New shoes," said the driver. His voice had the
same quality of secrecy and insinuation his eyes had.
"You oughtn' to take no walk in new shoes—hot
weather."

The hiker looked down at the dusty yellow shoes.
"Didn't have no other shoes," he said. "Guy got to
wear 'em if he got no others."

The driver squinted judiciously ahead and built up
the speed of the truck a little. "Goin' far?"

"Uh-uh! I'd a walked her if my dogs wasn't pooped
out."

The questions of the driver had the tone of a subtle
examination. He seemed to spread nets, to set traps
with his questions. "Lookin' for a job?" he asked.

"No, my old man got a place, forty acres. He's a
cropper, but we been there a long time."

The driver looked significantly at the fields along
the road where the corn was fallen sideways and the
dust was piled on it. Little flints shoved through the
dusty soil. The driver said, as though to himself, "A
forty-acre cropper and he ain't been dusted out and he
ain't been tractored out?"

" 'Course I ain't heard lately," said the hitch-hiker.

"Long time," said the driver. A bee flew into the
cab and buzzed in back of the windshield. The driver
put out his hand and carefully drove the bee into an

air stream that blew in out of the window. "Croppers going fast now," he said. "One cat' takes and shoves ten families out. Cat's all over hell now. Tear in and shove the croppers out. How's your old man hold on?" His tongue and his jaws became busy with the neglected gum, turned it and chewed it. With each opening of his mouth his tongue could be seen flipping the gum over.

"Well, I ain't heard lately. I never was no hand to write, nor my old man neither." He added quickly, "But the both of us can, if we want."

"Been doing a job?" Again the secret investigating casualness. He looked out over the fields, at the shimmering air, and gathering his gum into his cheek, out of the way, he spat out the window.

"Sure have," said the hitch-hiker.

"Thought so. I seen your hands. Been swingin' a pick or an ax or a sledge. That shines up your hands. I notice all stuff like that. Take a pride in it."

The hitch-hiker stared at him. The truck tires sang on the road. "Like to know anything else? I'll tell you. You ain't got to guess."

"Now don't get sore. I wasn't gettin' nosy."

"I'll tell you anything. I ain't hidin' nothin'."

"Now don't get sore. I just like to notice things. Makes the time pass."

"I'll tell you anything. Name's Joad, Tom Joad. Old man is ol' Tom Joad." His eyes rested broodingly on the driver.

"Don't get sore. I didn't mean nothin'."

"I don't mean nothin' neither," said Joad. "I'm just tryin' to get along without shovin' nobody around." He stopped and looked out at the dry fields, at the starved tree clumps hanging uneasily in the heated distance. From his side pocket he brought out his tobacco and papers. He rolled his cigarette down between his knees, where the wind could not get at it.

The driver chewed as rhythmically, as thoughtfully,

as a cow. He waited to let the whole emphasis of the
preceding passage disappear and be forgotten. At last,
when the air seemed neutral again, he said, "A guy
that never been a truck skinner don't know nothin'
what it's like. Owners don't want us to pick up nobody. So we got to set here an' just skin her along 'less
we want to take a chance of gettin' fired like I just
done with you."

" 'Preciate it," said Joad.

"I've knew guys that done screwy things while
they're drivin' trucks. I remember a guy use' to make
up poetry. It passed the time." He looked over secretly
to see whether Joad was interested or amazed. Joad
was silent, looking into the distance ahead, along the
road, along the white road that waved gently, like a
ground swell. The driver went on at last, "I remember
a piece of poetry this here guy wrote down. It was
about him an' a couple other guys goin' all over the
world drinkin' and raisin' hell and screwin' around. I
wisht I could remember how that piece went. This guy
had words in it that Jesus H. Christ wouldn't know
what they meant. Part was like this: 'An' there we
spied a nigger, with a trigger that was bigger than a
elephant's proboscis or the whanger of a whale.' That
proboscis is a nose-like. With a elephant it's his
trunk. Guy showed me in a dictionary. Carried that
dictionary all over hell with him. He'd look in it while
he's pulled up gettin' his pie an' coffee." He stopped,
feeling lonely in the long speech. His secret eyes
turned on his passenger. Joad remained silent. Nervously the driver tried to force him into participation.
"Ever know a guy that said big words like that?"

"Preacher," said Joad.

"Well, it makes you mad to hear a guy use big words.
'Course with a preacher it's all right because nobody
would fool around with a preacher anyway. But this guy
was funny. You didn't give a damn when he said a big
word 'cause he just done it for ducks. He wasn't puttin'

on no dog." The driver was reassured. He knew at least that Joad was listening. He swung the great truck viciously around a bend and the tires shrilled. "Like I was sayin'," he continued, "guy that drives a truck does screwy things. He got to. He'd go nuts just settin' here an' the road sneakin' under the wheels. Fella says once that truck skinners eats all the time—all the time in hamburger joints along the road."

"Sure seem to live there," Joad agreed.

"Sure they stop, but it ain't to eat. They ain't hardly ever hungry. They're just goddamn sick of goin'—get sick of it. Joints is the only place you can pull up, an' when you stop you got to buy somepin so you can sling the bull with the broad behind the counter. So you get a cup a coffee and a piece pie. Kind of gives a guy a little rest." He chewed his gum slowly and turned it with his tongue.

"Must be tough," said Joad with no emphasis.

The driver glanced quickly at him, looking for satire. "Well, it ain't no goddamn cinch," he said testily. "Looks easy, jus' settin' here till you put in your eight or maybe your ten or fourteen hours. But the road gets into a guy. He's got to do somepin. Some sings an' some whistles. Company won't let us have no radio. A few takes a pint along, but them kind don't stick long." He said the last smugly. "I don't never take a drink till I'm through."

"Yeah?" Joad asked.

"Yeah! A guy got to get ahead. Why, I'm thinkin' of takin' one of them correspondence school courses. Mechanical engineering. It's easy. Just study a few easy lessons at home. I'm thinkin' of it. Then I won't drive no truck. Then I'll tell other guys to drive trucks."

Joad took a pint of whisky from his side coat pocket. "Sure you won't have a snort?" His voice was teasing.

"No, by God. I won't touch it. A guy can't drink liquor all the time and study like I'm goin' to."

Joad uncorked the bottle, took two quick swallows,

recorked it, and put it back in his pocket. The spicy hot smell of the whisky filled the cab. "You're all wound up," said Joad. "What's the matter—got a girl?"

"Well, sure. But I want to get ahead anyway. I been training my mind for a hell of a long time"

The whisky seemed to loosen Joad up. He rolled another cigarette and lighted it. "I ain't got a hell of a lot further to go," he said.

The driver went on quickly, "I don't need no shot," he said. "I train my mind all the time. I took a course in that two years ago." He patted the steering wheel with his right hand. "Suppose I pass a guy on the road. I look at him, an' after I'm past I try to remember ever'thing about him, kind a clothes an' shoes an' hat, an' how he walked an' maybe how tall an' what weight an' any scars. I do it pretty good. I can jus' make a whole picture in my head. Somtimes I think I ought to take a course to be a fingerprint expert. You'd be su'prised how much a guy can remember."

Joad took a quick drink from the flask. He dragged the last smoke from his raveling cigarette and then, with callused thumb and forefinger, crushed out the glowing end. He rubbed the butt to a pulp and put it out the window, letting the breeze suck it from his fingers. The big tires sang a high note on the pavement. Joad's dark quiet eyes became amused as he stared along the road. The driver waited and glanced uneasily over. At last Joad's long upper lip grinned up from his teeth and he chuckled silently, his chest jerked with the chuckles. "You sure took a hell of a long time to get to it, buddy."

The driver did not look over. "Get to what? How do you mean?"

Joad's lips stretched tight over his long teeth for a moment, and he licked his lips like a dog, two licks, one in each direction from the middle. His voice became harsh. "You know what I mean. You give me a goin'-over when I first got in. I seen you." The driver looked straight ahead, gripped the wheel so tightly that the pads of his palms bulged, and the backs of his hands paled. Joad continued, "You know where I come from." The driver was silent. "Don't you?" Joad insisted.

"Well—sure. That is—maybe. But it ain't none of my business. I mind my own yard. It ain't nothing to me." The words tumbled out now. "I don't stick my nose in nobody's business." And suddenly he was silent and waiting. And his hands were still white on the wheel. A grasshopper flipped through the window and lighted on top of the instrument panel, where it sat and began to scrape its wings with its angled jumping legs. Joad reached forward and crushed its hard skull-like head with his fingers, and he let it into the wind stream out the window. Joad chuckled again while he brushed the bits of broken insect from his fingertips. "You got me wrong, mister," he said. "I ain't keepin' quiet about it. Sure I been in McAlester. Been there four years. Sure these is the clothes they give me when I come out. I don't give a damn who knows it. An' I'm goin' to my ole man's place so I don't have to lie to get a job."

The driver said, "Well—that ain't none of my business. I ain't a nosy guy."

"The hell you ain't," said Joad. "That big old nose of yours been stickin' out eight miles ahead of your face. You had that big nose goin' over me like a sheep in a vegetable patch."

The driver's face tightened. "You got me all wrong—" he began weakly.

Joad laughed at him. "You been a good guy. You give me a lift. Well, hell! I done time. So what! You want to know what I done time for, don't you?"

"That ain't none of my affair."

"Nothin' ain't none of your affair except skinnin' this here bull-bitch along, an' that's the least thing you work at. Now look. See that road up ahead?"

"Yeah."

"Well, I get off there. Sure, I know you're wettin' your pants to know what I done. I ain't a guy to let you down." The high hum of the motor dulled and the song of the tires dropped in pitch. Joad got out his pint and took another short drink. The truck drifted to a stop where a dirt road opened at right angles to the highway. Joad got out and stood beside the cab window. The vertical exhaust pipe puttered up its barely visible blue smoke. Joad leaned toward the driver. "Homicide," he said quickly. "That's a big word—means I killed a guy. Seven years. I'm sprung in four for keepin' my nose clean."

The driver's eyes slipped over Joad's face to memorize it. "I never asked you nothin' about it," he said. "I mind my own yard."

"You can tell about it in every joint from here to Texola." He smiled. "So long, fella. You been a good guy. But look, when you been in stir a little while, you can smell a question comin' from hell to breakfast. You telegraphed yours the first time you opened your trap." He spatted the metal door with the palm of his hand. "Thanks for the lift," he said. "So long." He turned away and walked into the dirt road.

For a moment the driver stared after him, and then he called, "Luck!" Joad waved his hand without looking around. Then the motor roared up and the gears clicked and the great red truck rolled heavily away.

3

The concrete highway was edged with a mat of tangled, broken, dry grass, and the grass heads were heavy with oat beards to catch on a dog's coat, and foxtails to tangle in a horse's fetlocks, and clover burrs to fasten in sheep's wool; sleeping life waiting to be spread and dispersed, every seed armed with an appliance of dispersal, twisting darts and parachutes for the wind, little spears and balls of tiny thorns, and all waiting for animals and for the wind, for a man's trouser cuff or the hem of a woman's skirt, all passive but armed with appliances of activity, still, but each possessed of the anlage of movement.

The sun lay on the grass and warmed it, and in the shade under the grass the insects moved, ants and ant lions to set traps for them, grasshoppers to jump into the air and flick their yellow wings for a second, sow bugs like little armadillos, plodding restlessly on many tender feet. And over the grass at the roadside a land turtle crawled, turning aside for nothing, dragging his high-domed shell over the grass. His hard legs and yellow-nailed feet threshed slowly through the grass, not really walking, but boosting and dragging his shell along. The barley beards slid off his shell, and the clover burrs fell on him and rolled to the ground. His horny beak was partly open, and his fierce, humorous eyes, under brows like fingernails, stared straight ahead. He came over the grass leaving a beaten trail behind him, and the hill, which was the highway embankment, reared up ahead of him. For a moment he stopped, his head held high. He blinked and looked up and down. At last he started to climb the embankment. Front clawed feet reached forward but did not touch. The hind feet kicked his shell along, and it scraped on the grass, and on the gravel. As the embankment grew steeper and steeper, the more frantic were the efforts of the land turtle. Pushing hind legs strained and slipped, boosting the shell along, and the horny head protruded as far as the neck could stretch. Little by little the shell slid up the embankment until at last a parapet cut straight across its line of march, the shoulder of the road, a concrete wall four inches high. As though they worked independently the hind legs pushed the shell against the wall. The head upraised and peered over the wall to the broad smooth plain of cement. Now the hands, braced on top of the wall, strained and lifted, and the shell came slowly up and rested its front end on the wall. For a moment the turtle rested. A red ant ran into the shell, into the soft skin inside the shell, and suddenly head and legs snapped in, and the armored tail clamped in sideways. The red ant was crushed between body and legs. And one head of wild oats was clamped into the shell by a front leg. For a long moment the turtle lay still, and then the neck crept out and the old humorous frowning eyes looked about and the legs and tail came out. The back legs went to work, straining like elephant legs, and the shell tipped to an angle so that the front legs could not reach the level cement plain. But higher and higher the hind legs boosted it, until at last the center of balance was reached, the front tipped down, the front legs scratched at the pavement, and it was up.

But the head of wild oats was held by its stem around the front legs.

Now the going was easy, and all the legs worked, and the shell boosted along, waggling from side to side. A sedan driven by a forty-year-old woman approached. She saw the turtle and swung to the right, off the highway, the wheels screamed and a cloud of dust boiled up. Two wheels lifted for a moment and then settled. The car skidded back onto the road, and went on, but more slowly. The turtle had jerked into its shell, but now it hurried on, for the highway was burning hot.

And now a light truck approached, and as it came near, the driver saw the turtle and swerved to hit it. His front wheel struck the edge of the shell, flipped the turtle like a tiddly-wink, spun it like a coin, and rolled it off the highway. The truck went back to its course along the right side. Lying on its back, the turtle was tight in its shell for a long time. But at last its legs waved in the air, reaching for something to pull it over. Its front foot caught a piece of quartz and little by little the shell pulled over and flopped upright. The wild oat head fell out and three spearhead seeds stuck in the ground. And as the turtle crawled on down the embankment, its shell dragged dirt over the seeds. The turtle entered a dust road and jerked itself along, drawing a wavy shallow trench in the dust with its shell. The old humorous eyes looked ahead, and the horny beak opened a little. His yellow toe nails slipped a fraction in the dust.

4

When Joad heard the truck get under way, gear climbing up to gear and the ground throbbing under the rubber beating of the tires, he stopped and turned about and watched it until it disappeared. When it was out of sight he still watched the distance and the blue air-shimmer. Thoughtfully he took the pint from his pocket, unscrewed the metal cap, and sipped the whisky delicately, running his tongue inside the bottle neck, and then around his lips, to gather in any flavor that might have escaped him. He said experimentally, "There we spied a nigger—" and that was all he could remember. At last he turned about and faced the dusty side road that cut off at right angles through the fields. The sun was hot, and no wind stirred the sifted dust. The road was cut with furrows where dust had slid and settled back into the wheel tracks. Joad took a few steps, and the flour-like dust spurted up in front of his new yellow shoes, and the yellowness was disappearing under gray dust.

He leaned down and untied the laces, slipped off first one shoe and then the other. And he worked his damp feet comfortably in the hot dry dust until little spurts of it came up between his toes, and until the skin on his feet tightened with dryness. He took off his

coat and wrapped his shoes in it and slipped the
bundle under his arm. And at last he moved up the
road, shooting the dust ahead of him, making a cloud
that hung low to the ground behind him.

The right of way was fenced, two strands of barbed
wire on willow poles. The poles were crooked and
badly trimmed. Whenever a crotch came to the proper
height the wire lay in it, and where there was no
crotch the barbed wire was lashed to the post with
rusty baling wire. Beyond the fence, the corn lay
beaten down by wind and heat and drought, and the
cups where leaf joined stalk were filled with dust.

Joad plodded along, dragging his cloud of dust behind him. A little bit ahead he saw the high-domed
shell of a land turtle, crawling slowly along through
the dust, its legs working stiffly and jerkily. Joad
stopped to watch it, and his shadow fell on the turtle.
Instantly head and legs were withdrawn and the short
thick tail clamped sideways into the shell. Joad picked
it up and turned it over. The back was brown-gray,
like the dust, but the underside of the shell was
creamy yellow, clean and smooth. Joad shifted his
bundle high under his arm and stroked the smooth
undershell with his finger, and he pressed it. It was
softer than the back. The hard old head came out and
tried to look at the pressing finger, and the legs waved
wildly. The turtle wetted on Joad's hand and struggled
uselessly in the air. Joad turned it back upright and
rolled it up in his coat with his shoes. He could feel it
pressing and struggling and fussing under his arm. He
moved ahead more quickly now, dragging his heels a
little in the fine dust.

Ahead of him, beside the road, a scrawny, dusty
willow tree cast a speckled shade. Joad could see it
ahead of him, its poor branches curving over the way,
its load of leaves tattered and scraggly as a molting
chicken. Joad was sweating now. His blue shirt darkened down his back and under his arms. He pulled at

the visor cap and creased it in the middle, breaking its cardboard lining so completely that it could never look new again. And his steps took on new speed and intent toward the shade of the distant willow tree. At the willow he knew there would be shade, at least one hard bar of absolute shade thrown by the trunk, since the sun had passed its zenith. The sun whipped the back of his neck now and made a little humming in his head. He could not see the base of the tree, for it grew out of a little swale that held water longer than the level places. Joad speeded his pace against the sun, and he started down the declivity. He slowed cautiously, for the bar of absolute shade was taken. A man sat on the ground, leaning against the trunk of the tree. His legs were crossed and one bare foot extended nearly as high as his head. He did not hear Joad approaching, for he was whistling solemnly the tune of "Yes, Sir, That's My Baby." His extended foot swung slowly up and down in the tempo. It was not dance tempo. He stopped whistling and sang in an easy thin tenor:

> "Yes, sir, that's my Saviour,
> Je—sus is my Saviour,
> Je—sus is my Saviour now.
> On the level
> 'S not the devil,
> Jesus is my Saviour now."

Joad had moved into the imperfect shade of the molting leaves before the man heard him coming, stopped his song, and turned his head. It was a long head, bony, tight of skin, and set on a neck as stringy and muscular as a celery stalk. His eyeballs were heavy and protruding; the lids stretched to cover them, and the lids were raw and red. His cheeks were brown and shiny and hairless and his mouth full—humorous or sensual. The nose, beaked and hard, stretched the skin so tightly that the bridge showed white. There was no perspiration on the face, not even on the tall pale forehead. It was an abnormally high forehead, lined with delicate blue veins at the temple. Fully half of the face was above the eyes. His stiff gray hair was mussed back from his brow as though he had combed it back with his fingers. For clothes he wore overalls and a blue shirt. A denim coat with brass buttons and a spotted brown hat creased like a pork pie lay on the ground beside him. Canvas sneakers, gray with dust, lay near by where they had fallen when they were kicked off.

The man looked at Joad. The light seemed to go far into his brown eyes, and it picked out little golden specks deep in the irises. The strained bundle of neck muscles stood out.

Joad stood still in the speckled shade. He took off his cap and mopped his wet face with it and dropped it and his rolled coat on the ground.

The man in the absolute shade uncrossed his legs and dug with his toes at the earth.

Joad said, "Hi. It's hotter'n hell on the road."

The seated man stared questioningly at him. "Now ain't you young Tom Joad—ol' Tom's boy?"

"Yeah," said Joad. "All the way. Goin' home now."

"You wouldn' remember me, I guess," the man said. He smiled and his full lips revealed great horse teeth. "Oh, no, you wouldn't remember. You was always too busy pullin' little girls' pigtails when I give you the Holy Sperit. You was all wropped up in yankin' that pigtail out by the roots. You maybe don't recollect, but I do. The two of you come to Jesus at once 'cause of that pigtail yankin'. Baptized both of you in the irrigation ditch at once. Fightin' an' yellin' like a couple a cats."

Joad looked at him with drooped eyes, and then he laughed. "Why, you're the preacher. You're the preacher. I jus' passed a recollection about you to a guy not an hour ago."

"I was a preacher," said the man seriously. "Reverend Jim Casy—was a Burning Busher. Used to howl out the name of Jesus to glory. And used to get an irrigation ditch so squirmin' full of repented sinners half of 'em like to drownded. But no more," he sighed. "Just Jim Casy now. Ain't got the call no more. Got a lot of sinful idears—but they seem kinda sensible."

Joad said, "You're bound to get idears if you go thinkin' about stuff. Sure I remember you. You use ta give a good meetin'. I recollect one time you give a whole sermon walkin' around on your hands, yellin' your head off. Ma favored you more than anybody. An' Granma says you was just lousy with the spirit." Joad dug at his rolled coat and found the pocket and brought out his pint. The turtle moved a leg but he wrapped it up tightly. He unscrewed the cap and held out the bottle. "Have a little snort?"

Casy took the bottle and regarded it broodingly. "I ain't preachin' no more much. The sperit ain't in the people much no more; and worse'n that, the sperit ain't in me no more. 'Course now an' again the sperit gets movin' an' I rip out a meetin', or when folks set out food I give 'em a grace, but my heart ain't in it. I on'y do it 'cause they expect it."

Joad mopped his face with his cap again. "You ain't too damn holy to take a drink, are you?" he asked.

Casy seemed to see the bottle for the first time. He tilted it and took three big swallows. "Nice drinkin' liquor," he said.

"Ought to be," said Joad. "That's fact'ry liquor. Cost a buck."

Casy took another swallow before he passed the bottle back. "Yes, sir!" he said. "Yes, sir!"

Joad took the bottle from him, and in politeness did not wipe the neck with his sleeve before he drank. He squatted on his hams and set the bottle upright against his coat roll. His fingers found a twig with which to draw his thoughts on the ground. He swept the leaves

from a square and smoothed the dust. And he drew
angles and made little circles. "I ain't seen you in a
long time," he said.

"Nobody seen me," said the preacher. "I went off
alone, an' I sat and figured. The sperit's strong in me,
on'y it ain't the same. I ain't so sure of a lot of things."
He sat up straighter against the tree. His bony hand
dug its way like a squirrel into his overall pocket,
brought out a black, bitten plug of tobacco. Carefully
he brushed off bits of straw and gray pocket fuzz before he bit off a corner and settled the quid into his
cheek. Joad waved his stick in negation when the plug
was held out to him. The turtle dug at the rolled coat.
Casy looked over at the stirring garment. "What you
got there—a chicken? You'll smother it."

Joad rolled the coat up more tightly. "An old
turtle," he said. "Picked him up on the road. An old
bulldozer. Thought I'd take 'im to my little brother.
Kids like turtles."

The preacher nodded his head slowly. "Every kid got
a turtle some time or other. Nobody can't keep a turtle
though. They work at it and work at it, and at last one
day they get out and away they go—off somewheres. It's
like me. I wouldn' take the good ol' gospel that was just
layin' there to my hand. I got to be pickin' at it an'
workin' at it until I got it all tore down. Here I got the
sperit sometimes an' nothin' to preach about. I got the
call to lead the people, an' no place to lead 'em."

"Lead 'em around and around," said Joad. "Sling
'em in the irrigation ditch. Tell 'em they'll burn in hell
if they don't think like you. What the hell you want to
lead 'em someplace for? Jus' lead 'em." The straight
trunk shade had stretched along the ground. Joad
moved gratefully into it and squatted on his hams and
made a new smooth place on which to draw his
thoughts with a stick. A thick-furred yellow shepherd
dog came trotting down the road, head low, tongue
lolling and dripping. Its tail hung limply curled, and it

panted loudly. Joad whistled at it, but it only dropped
its head an inch and trotted fast toward some definite
destination. "Goin' someplace," Joad explained, a
little piqued. "Goin' for home maybe."

The preacher could not be thrown from his subject.
"Goin' someplace," he repeated. "That's right, he's
goin' someplace. Me—I don't know where I'm goin'.
Tell you what—I use ta get the people jumpin' an'
talkin' in tongues, an' glory-shoutin' till they just fell
down an' passed out. An' some I'd baptize to bring 'em
to. An' then—you know what I'd do? I'd take one of
them girls out in the grass, an' I'd lay with her. Done
it ever' time. Then I'd feel bad, an' I'd pray an' pray,
but it didn't do no good. Come the nex' time, them an'
me was full of the sperit, I'd do it again. I figgered
there just wasn't no hope for me, an' I was a damned
ol' hypocrite. But I didn't mean to be."

Joad smiled and his long teeth parted and he licked
his lips. "There ain't nothing like a good hot meetin'
for pushin' 'em over," he said. "I done that myself."

Casy leaned forward excitedly. "You see," he cried,
"I seen it was that way, an' I started thinkin'." He
waved his bony big-knuckled hand up and down in a
patting gesture. "I got to thinkin' like this—'Here's me
preachin' grace. An' here's them people gettin' grace
so hard they're jumpin' an' shoutin'. Now they say
layin' up with a girl comes from the devil. But the
more grace a girl got in her, the quicker she wants to
go out in the grass'. An' I got to thinkin' how in hell,
s'cuse me, how can the devil get in when a girl is so
full of the Holy Sperit that it's spoutin' out of her nose
an' ears. You'd think that'd be one time when the devil
didn't stand a snowball's chance in hell. But there it
was." His eyes were shining with excitement. He
worked his cheeks for a moment and then spat into the
dust, and the gob of spit rolled over and over, picking
up dust until it looked like a round dry little pellet.
The preacher spread out his hand and looked at his

palm as though he were reading a book. "An' there's me," he went on softly. "There's me with all them people's souls in my han'—responsible an' feelin' my responsibility—an' ever' time, I lay with one of them girls." He looked over at Joad and his face looked helpless. His expression asked for help.

Joad carefully drew the torso of a woman in the dirt, breasts, hips, pelvis. "I wasn't never a preacher," he said. "I never let nothin' get by when I could catch it. An' I never had no idears about it except I was goddamn glad when I got one."

"But you wasn't a preacher," Casy insisted. "A girl was just a girl to you. They wasn't nothin' to you. But to me they was holy vessels. I was savin' their souls. An' here with all that responsibility on me I'd just get 'em frothin' with the Holy Sperit, an' then I'd take 'em out in the grass."

"Maybe I should of been a preacher," said Joad. He brought out his tobacco and papers and rolled a cigarette. He lighted it and squinted through the smoke at the preacher. "I been a long time without a girl," he said. "It's gonna take some catchin' up."

Casy continued, "It worried me till I couldn't get no sleep. Here I'd go to preachin' and I'd say, 'By God, this time I ain't gonna do it.' And right while I said it, I knowed I was."

"You should a got a wife," said Joad. "Preacher an' his wife stayed at our place one time. Jehovites they was. Slep' upstairs. Held meetin's in our barnyard. Us kids would listen. That preacher's missus took a god-awful poundin' after ever' night meetin'."

"I'm glad you tol' me," said Casy. "I use to think it was jus' me. Finally it give me such pain I quit an' went off by myself an' give her a damn good thinkin' about." He doubled up his legs and scratched between his dry dusty toes. "I says to myself, 'What's gnawin' you? Is it the screwin'?' An' I says, 'No, it's the sin.' An' I says, 'Why is it that when a fella ought to be just

about mule-ass proof against sin, an' all full up of
Jesus, why is it that's the time a fella gets fingerin' his
pants buttons?' " He laid two fingers down in his palm
in rhythm, as though he gently placed each word there
side by side. "I says, 'Maybe it ain't a sin. Maybe it's
just the way folks is. Maybe we been whippin' the hell
out of ourselves for nothin'.' An' I thought how some
sisters took to beatin' theirselves with a three-foot shag
of bobwire. An' I thought how maybe they liked to hurt
themselves, an' maybe I liked to hurt myself. Well, I
was layin' under a tree when I figured that out, and I
went to sleep. And it come night, an' it was dark when
I come to. They was a coyote squawkin' near by. Before I knowed it, I was sayin' out loud, 'The hell with
it! There ain't no sin and there ain't no virtue. There's
just stuff people do. It's all part of the same thing.
And some of the things folks do is nice, and some ain't
nice, but that's as far as any man got a right to say.' "
He paused and looked up from the palm of his hand,
where he had laid down the words.

Joad was grinning at him, but Joad's eyes were
sharp and interested, too. "You give her a goin'-over,"
he said. "You figured her out."

Casy spoke again, and his voice rang with pain and
confusion. "I says, 'What's this call, this sperit?' An' I
says, 'It's love. I love people so much I'm fit to bust,
sometimes.' An' I says, 'Don't you love Jesus?' Well, I
thought an' thought, an' finally I says, 'No, I don't
know nobody name' Jesus. I know a bunch of stories,
but I only love people. An' sometimes I love 'em fit to
bust, an' I want to make 'em happy, so I been preachin' somepin I thought would make 'em happy.' An'
then—I been talkin' a hell of a lot. Maybe you wonder
about me using bad words. Well, they ain't bad to me
no more. They're jus' words folks use, an' they don't
mean nothing bad with 'em. Anyways, I'll tell you one
more thing I thought out; an' from a preacher it's the

most unreligious thing, and I can't be a preacher no
more because I thought it an' I believe it."

"What's that?" Joad asked.

Casy looked shyly at him. "If it hits you wrong,
don't take no offense at it, will you?"

"I don't take no offense 'cept a bust in the nose,"
said Joad. "What did you figger?"

"I figgered about the Holy Sperit and the Jesus
road. I figgered, 'Why do we got to hang it on God or
Jesus? Maybe,' I figgered, 'maybe it's all men an' all
women we love; maybe that's the Holy Sperit—the
human sperit—the whole shebang. Maybe all men got
one big soul ever'body's a part of.' Now I sat there
thinkin' it, an' all of a suddent—I knew it. I knew it so
deep down that it was true, and I still know it."

Joad's eyes dropped to the ground, as though he
could not meet the naked honesty in the preacher's
eyes. "You can't hold no church with idears like that,"
he said. "People would drive you out of the country
with idears like that. Jumpin' an' yellin'. That's what
folks like. Makes 'em feel swell. When Granma got to
talkin' in tongues, you couldn't tie her down. She
could knock over a full-growed deacon with her fist."

Casy regarded him broodingly. "Somepin I like to
ast you," he said. "Somepin that been eatin' on me."

"Go ahead. I'll talk, sometimes."

"Well"—the preacher said slowly—"here's you that
I baptized right when I was in the glory roof-tree. Got
little hunks of Jesus jumpin' outa my mouth that day.
You won't remember 'cause you was busy pullin' that
pigtail."

"I remember," said Joad. "That was Susy Little.
She bust my finger a year later."

"Well—did you take any good outa that baptizin'?
Was your ways better?"

Joad thought about it. "No-o-o, can't say as I felt
anything."

"Well—did you take any bad from it? Think hard."

Joad picked up the bottle and took a swig. "They wasn't nothing in it, good or bad. I just had fun." He handed the flask to the preacher.

He sighed and drank and looked at the low level of the whisky and took another tiny drink. "That's good," he said. "I got to worryin' about whether in messin' around maybe I done somebody a hurt."

Joad looked over toward his coat and saw the turtle, free of the cloth and hurrying away in the direction he had been following when Joad found him. Joad watched him for a moment and then got slowly to his feet and retrieved him and wrapped him in the coat again. "I ain't got no present for the kids," he said. "Nothin' but this ol' turtle."

"It's a funny thing," the preacher said. "I was thinkin' about ol' Tom Joad when you come along. Thinkin' I'd call in on him. I used to think he was a godless man. How is Tom?"

"I don' know how he is. I ain't been home in four years."

"Didn't he write to you?"

Joad was embarrassed. "Well, pa wasn't no hand to write for pretty, or to write for writin'. He'd sign up his name as nice as anybody, an' lick his pencil. But Pa never did write no letter. He always says what he couldn't tell a fella with his mouth wasn't worth leanin' on no pencil about."

"Been out travelin' around?" Casy asked.

Joad regarded him suspiciously. "Didn' you hear about me? I was in all the papers."

"No—I never. What?" He jerked one leg over the other and settled lower against the tree. The afternoon was advancing rapidly, and a richer tone was growing on the sun.

Joad said pleasantly, "Might's well tell you now an' get it over with. But if you was still preachin' I wouldn't tell, fear you get prayin' over me." He drained the last of the pint and flung it from him, and the flat brown bottle skidded lightly over the dust. "I been in McAlester them four years."

Casy swung around to him, and his brows lowered so that his tall forehead seemed even taller. "Ain't wantin' to talk about it, huh? I won't ask you no questions, if you done something bad——"

"I'd do what I done—again," said Joad. "I killed a guy in a fight. We was drunk at a dance. He got a knife in me, an' I killed him with a shovel that was layin' there. Knocked his head plumb to squash."

Casy's eyebrows resumed their normal level. "You ain't ashamed of nothin' then?"

"No," said Joad, "I ain't. I got seven years, account of he had a knife in me. Hot out in four—parole."

"Then you ain't heard nothin' about your folks for four years?"

"Oh, I heard. Ma sent me a card two years ago, an' las' Christmus Granma sent a card. Jesus, the guys in the cell block laughed! Had a tree an' shiny stuff looks like snow. It say in po'try:

" 'Merry Christmus, purty child,
    Jesus meek an' Jesus mild,
    Underneath the Christmus tree
    There's a gif' for you from me.'

I guess Granma never read it. Prob'ly got it from a drummer an' picked out the one with the mos' shiny stuff on it. The guys in my cell block goddamn near died laughin'. Jesus Meek they called me after that. Granma never meant it funny; she jus' figgered it was so purty she wouldn' bother to read it. She lost her glasses the year I went up. Maybe she never did find 'em."

"How they treat you in McAlester?" Casy asked.

"Oh, awright. You eat regular, an' get clean

clothes, and there's places to take a bath. It's pretty nice some ways. Makes it hard not havin' no women." Suddenly he laughed. "They was a guy paroled," he said. " 'Bout a month he's back for breakin' parole. A guy ast him why he bust his parole. 'Well, hell,' he says. 'They got no conveniences at my old man's place. Got no 'lectric lights, got no shower baths. There ain't no books, an' the food's lousy.' Says he come back where they got a few conveniences an' he eats regular. He says it makes him feel lonesome out there in the open havin' to think what to do next. So he stole a car an' come back." Joad got out his tobacco and blew a brown paper free of the pack and rolled a cigarette. "The guy's right, too," he said. "Las' night, thinkin' where I'm gonna sleep, I got scared. An' I got thinkin' about my bunk, an' I wonder what the stir-bug I got for a cell mate is doin'. Me an' some guys had a strang band goin'. Good one. Guy said we ought to go on the radio. An' this mornin' I didn' know what time to get up. Jus' laid there waitin' for the bell to go off."

Casy chuckled. "Fella can get so he misses the noise of a saw mill."

The yellowing, dusty, afternoon light put a golden color on the land. The cornstalks looked golden. A flight of swallows swooped overhead toward some waterhole. The turtle in Joad's coat began a new campaign of escape. Joad creased the visor of his cap. It was getting the long protruding curve of a crow's beak now. "Guess I'll mosey along," he said. "I hate to hit the sun, but it ain't so bad now."

Casy pulled himself together. "I ain't seen ol' Tom in a bug's age," he said. "I was gonna look in on him anyways. I brang Jesus to your folks for a long time, an' I never took up a collection nor nothin' but a bite to eat."

"Come along," said Joad. "Pa'll be glad to see you. He always said you got too long a pecker for a preacher." He picked up his coat roll and tightened it snugly about his shoes and turtle.

Casy gathered in his canvas sneakers and shoved his bare feet into them. "I ain't got your confidence," he said. "I'm always scared there's wire or glass under the dust. I don't know nothin' I hate so much as a cut toe."

They hesitated on the edge of the shade and then they plunged into the yellow sunlight like two swimmers hastening to get to shore. After a few fast steps they slowed to a gentle, thoughtful pace. The cornstalks threw gray shadows sideways now, and the raw smell of hot dust was in the air. The corn field ended and dark green cotton took its place, dark green leaves through a film of dust, and the bolls forming. It was spotty cotton, thick in the low places where water had stood, and bare on the high places. The plants strove against the sun. And distance, toward the horizon, was tan to invisibility. The dust road stretched out ahead of them, waving up and down. The willows of a stream lined across the west, and to the northwest a fallow section was going back to sparse brush. But the smell of burned dust was in the air, and the air was dry, so that mucus in the nose dried to a crust, and the eyes watered to keep the eyeballs from drying out.

Casy said, "See how good the corn come along until the dust got up. Been a dinger of a crop."

"Ever' year," said Joad. "Ever' year I can remember, we had a good crop comin', an' it never come. Grampa says she was good the first five plowin's, while the wild grass was still in her." The road dropped down a little hill and climbed up another rolling hill.

Casy said, "Ol' Tom's house can't be more'n a mile from here. Ain't she over that third rise?"

"Sure," said Joad. " 'Less somebody stole it, like Pa stole it."

"Your pa stole it?"

"Sure, got it a mile an' a half east of here an' drug
it. Was a family livin' there, an' they moved away.
Grampa an' Pa an' my brother Noah like to took the
whole house, but she wouldn' come. They only got part
of her. That's why she looks so funny on one end.
They cut her in two an' drug her over with twelve head
of horses and two mules. They was goin' back for the
other half an' stick her together again, but before they
got there Wink Manley come with his boys and stole
the other half. Pa an' Grampa was pretty sore, but a
little later them an' Wink got drunk together an'
laughed their heads off about it. Wink, he says his
house is at stud, an' if we'll bring our'n over an' breed
'em we'll maybe get a litter of crap houses. Wink was
a great ol' fella when he was drunk. After that him an'
Pa an' Grampa was friends. Got drunk together ever'
chance they got."

"Tom's a great one," Casy agreed. They plodded
dustily on down to the bottom of the draw, and then
slowed their steps for the rise. Casy wiped his forehead with his sleeve and put on his flat-topped hat
again. "Yes," he repeated, "Tom was a great one. For
a godless man he was a great one. I seen him in
meetin' sometimes when the sperit got into him just a
little, an' I seen him take ten-twelve foot jumps. I tell
you when ol' Tom got a dose of the Holy Sperit you got
to move fast to keep from gettin' run down an'
tromped. Jumpy as a stud horse in a box stall."

They topped the next rise and the road dropped into
an old water-cut, ugly and raw, a ragged course, and
freshet scars cutting into it from both sides. A few
stones were in the crossing. Joad minced across in his
bare feet. "You talk about Pa," he said. "Maybe you
never seen Uncle John the time they baptized him over
to Polk's place. Why, he got to plungin' an' jumpin'.
Jumped over a feeny bush as big as a piana. Over he'd
jump, an' back he'd jump, howlin' like a dog-wolf in

moon time. Well, Pa seen him, an' Pa, he figgers he's
the bes' Jesus-jumper in these parts. So Pa picks out a
feeny bush 'bout twicet as big as Uncle John's feeny
bush, and Pa lets out a squawk like a sow litterin'
broken bottles, an' he takes a run at that feeny bush
an' clears her an' bust his right leg. That took the
sperit out of Pa. Preacher wants to pray it set, but Pa
says, no, by God, he'd got his heart full of havin' a
doctor. Well, they wasn't a doctor, but they was a travelin' dentist, an' he set her. Preacher give her a prayin'
over anyways."

They plodded up the little rise on the other side of
the water-cut. Now that the sun was on the wane some
of its impact was gone, and while the air was hot, the
hammering rays were weaker. The strung wire on
crooked poles still edged the road. On the right-hand
side a line of wire fence strung out across the cotton
field, and the dusty green cotton was the same on both
sides, dusty and dry and dark green.

Joad pointed to the boundary fence. "That there's
our line. We didn't really need no fence there, but we
had the wire, an' Pa kinda liked her there. Said it give
him a feelin' that forty was forty. Wouldn't of had the
fence if Uncle John didn' come drivin' in one night
with six spools of wire in his wagon. He give 'em to Pa
for a shoat. We never did know where he got that
wire." They slowed for the rise, moving their feet in
the deep soft dust, feeling the earth with their feet.
Joad's eyes were inward on his memory. He seemed to
be laughing inside himself. "Uncle John was a crazy
bastard," he said. "Like what he done with that
shoat." He chuckled and walked on.

Jim Casy waited impatiently. The story did not continue. Casy gave it a good long time to come out.
"Well, what'd he do with that shoat?" he demanded at
last, with some irritation.

"Huh? Oh! Well, he killed that shoat right there,

an' he got Ma to light up the stove. He cut out pork chops an' put 'em in the pan, an' he put ribs an' a leg in the oven. He et chops till the ribs was done, an' he et ribs till the leg was done. An' then he tore into that leg. Cut off big hunks of her an' shoved 'em in his mouth. Us kids hung around slaverin', an' he give us some, but he wouldn' give Pa none. By an' by he et so much he throwed up an' went to sleep. While he's asleep us kids an' Pa finished off the leg. Well, when Uncle John woke up in the mornin' he slaps another leg in the oven. Pa says, 'John, you gonna eat that whole damn pig?' An' he says, 'I aim to, Tom, but I'm scairt some of her'll spoil 'fore I get her et, hungry as I am for pork. Maybe you better get a plate an' gimme back a couple rolls of wire.' Well, sir, Pa wasn't no fool. He jus' let Uncle John go on an' eat himself sick of pig, an' when he drove off he hadn't et much more than half. Pa says, 'Whyn't you salt her down?' But not Uncle John; when he wants pig he wants a whole pig, an' when he's through, he don't want no pig hangin' around. So off he goes, and Pa salts down what's left."

Casy said, "While I was still in the preachin' sperit I'd a made a lesson of that an' spoke it to you, but I don't do that no more. What you s'pose he done a thing like that for?"

"I dunno," said Joad. "He jus' got hungry for pork. Makes me hungry jus' to think of it. I had jus' four slices of roastin' pork in four years—one slice ever' Christmas."

Casy suggested elaborately, "Maybe Tom'll kill the fatted calf like for the prodigal in Scripture."

Joad laughed scornfully. "You don't know Pa. If he kills a chicken most of the squawkin' will come from Pa, not the chicken. He don't never learn. He's always savin' a pig for Christmas and then it dies in September of bloat or somepin so you can't eat it. When Uncle John wanted pork he et pork. He had her."

They moved over the curving top of the hill and saw the Joad place below them. And Joad stopped. "It ain't the same," he said. "Looka that house. Somepin's happened. They ain't nobody there." The two stood and stared at the little cluster of buildings.

5

The owners of the land came onto the land, or more often a spokesman for the owners came. They came in closed cars, and they felt the dry earth with their fingers, and sometimes they drove big earth augers into the ground for soil tests. The tenants, from their sun-beaten dooryards, watched uneasily when the closed cars drove along the fields. And at last the owner men drove into the dooryards and sat in their cars to talk out of the windows. The tenant men stood beside the cars for a while, and then squatted on their hams and found sticks with which to mark the dust.

In the open doors the women stood looking out, and behind them the children—corn-headed children, with wide eyes, one bare foot on top of the other bare foot, and the toes working. The women and the children watched their men talking to the owner men. They were silent.

Some of the owner men were kind because they hated what they had to do, and some of them were angry because they hated to be cruel, and some of them were cold because they had long ago found that one could not be an owner unless one were cold. And all of them were caught in something larger than themselves. Some of them hated the mathematics that drove them, and some were afraid, and some worshiped the mathematics because it provided a refuge from thought and from feeling. If a bank or a finance company owned the land, the owner man said, the Bank—or the Company—needs—wants—insists—must have—as though the Bank or the Company were a monster, with thought and feeling, which had ensnared them. These last would take no responsibility for the banks or the companies because they were men and slaves, while the banks were machines and masters all at the same time. Some of the owner men were a little proud to be slaves to such cold and powerful masters. The owner men sat in the cars and explained. You know the land is poor. You've scrabbled at it long enough, God knows.

The squatting tenant men nodded and wondered and drew figures in the dust, and yes, they knew, God knows. If the dust only wouldn't fly. If the top would only stay on the soil, it might not be so bad.

The owner men went on leading to their point: You know the land's getting poorer. You know what cotton does to the land; robs it, sucks all the blood out of it.

The squatters nodded—they knew, God knew. If they could only rotate the crops they might pump blood back into the land.

Well, it's too late. And the owner men explained the workings and the thinkings of the monster that was stronger than they were. A man can hold land if he can just eat and pay taxes; he can do that.

Yes, he can do that until his crops fail one day and he has to borrow money from the bank.

But—you see, a bank or a company can't do that, because those creatures don't breathe air, don't eat side-meat. They breathe profits; they eat the interest on money. If they don't get it, they die the way you die without air, without side-meat. It is a sad thing, but it is so. It is just so.

The squatting men raised their eyes to understand. Can't we just hang on? Maybe the next year will be a good year. God knows how much cotton next year. And with all the wars—God knows what price cotton will bring. Don't they make explosives out of cotton? And uniforms? Get enough wars and cotton'll hit the ceiling. Next year, maybe. They looked up questioningly.

We can't depend on it. The bank—the monster has to have profits all the time. It can't wait. It'll die. No, taxes go on. When the monster stops growing, it dies. It can't stay one size.

Soft fingers began to tap the sill of the car window, and the hard fingers tightened on the restless drawing sticks. In the doorways of the sun-beaten tenant houses, women sighed and then shifted feet so that the one that had been down was now on top, and the toes working. Dogs came sniffing near the owner cars and wetted on all four tires one after another. And chickens lay in the sunny dust and fluffed their feathers to get the cleansing dust down to the skin. In the little sties the pigs grunted inquiringly over the muddy remnants of the slops.

The squatting men looked down again. What do you want us to do? We can't take less share of the crop— we're half starved now. The kids are hungry all the time. We got no clothes, torn an' ragged. If all the neighbors weren't the same, we'd be ashamed to go to meeting.

And at last the owner men came to the point. The tenant system won't work any more. One man on a tractor can take the place of twelve or fourteen families. Pay him a wage and take all the crop. We have to do it. We don't like to do it. But the monster's sick. Something's happened to the monster.

But you'll kill the land with cotton.

We know. We've got to take cotton quick before the land dies. Then we'll sell the land. Lots of families in the East would like to own a piece of land.

The tenant men looked up alarmed. But what'll happen to us? How'll we eat?

You'll have to get off the land. The plows'll go through the dooryard.

And now the squatting men stood up angrily. Grampa took up the land, and he had to kill the Indians and drive them away. And Pa was born here, and he killed weeds and snakes. Then a bad year came and he had to borrow a little money. An' we was born here. There in the door—our children born here. And Pa had to borrow money. The bank owned the land then, but we stayed and we got a little bit of what we raised.

We know that—all that. It's not us, it's the bank. A bank isn't like a man. Or an owner with fifty thousand acres, he isn't like a man either. That's the monster.

Sure, cried the tenant men, but it's our land. We measured it and broke it up. We were born on it, and we got killed on it, died on it. Even if it's no good, it's still ours. That's what makes it ours—being born on it, working it, dying on it. That makes ownership, not a paper with numbers on it.

We're sorry. It's not us. It's the monster. The bank isn't like a man.

Yes, but the bank is only made of men.

No, you're wrong there—quite wrong there. The bank is something else than men. It happens that every man in a bank hates what the bank does, and yet the bank does it. The bank is something more than men, I tell you. It's the monster. Men made it, but they can't control it.

The tenants cried, Grampa killed Indians, Pa killed snakes for the land. Maybe we can kill banks—they're worse than Indians and snakes. Maybe we got to fight to keep our land, like Pa and Grampa did.

And now the owner men grew angry. You'll have to go.

But it's ours, the tenant men cried. We——

No. The bank, the monster owns it. You'll have to go.

We'll get our guns, like Grampa when the Indians came. What then?

Well—first the sheriff, and then the troops. You'll be stealing if you try to stay, you'll be murderers if you kill to stay. The monster isn't men, but it can make men do what it wants.

But if we go, where'll we go? How'll we go? We got no money.

We're sorry, said the owner men. The bank, the fifty-thousand-acre owner can't be responsible. You're on land that isn't yours. Once over the line maybe you can pick cotton in the fall. Maybe you can go on relief. Why don't you go on west to California? There's work there, and it never gets cold. Why, you can reach out anywhere and pick an orange. Why, there's always some kind of crop to work in. Why don't you go there? And the owner men started their cars and rolled away.

The tenant men squatted down to their hams again to mark the dust with a stick, to figure, to wonder. Their sunburned faces were dark, and their sun-whipped eyes were light. The women moved cautiously out of the doorways toward their men, and the children crept behind the women, cautiously, ready to run. The bigger boys squatted beside their fathers, because that made them men. After a time the women asked, What did he want?

And the men looked up for a second, and the smolder of pain was in their eyes. We got to get off. A tractor and a superintendent. Like factories.

Where'll we go? the women asked.

We don't know. We don't know.

And the women went quickly, quietly back into the houses and herded the children ahead of them. They knew that a man so hurt and so perplexed may turn in anger, even on people he loves. They left the men alone to figure and to wonder in the dust.

After a time perhaps the tenant man looked about—
at the pump put in ten years ago, with a goose-neck
handle and iron flowers on the spout, at the chopping
block where a thousand chickens had been killed, at
the hand plow lying in the shed, and the patent crib
hanging in the rafters over it.

The children crowded about the women in the
houses. What we going to do, Ma? Where we going to
go?

The women said, We don't know, yet. Go out and
play. But don't go near your father. He might whale
you if you go near him. And the women went on with
the work, but all the time they watched the men squatting in the dust—perplexed and figuring.

The tractors came over the roads and into the fields,
great crawlers moving like insects, having the incredible strength of insects. They crawled over the ground,
laying the track and rolling on it and picking it up.
Diesel tractors, puttering while they stood idle; they
thundered when they moved, and then settled down to
a droning roar. Snub-nosed monsters, raising the dust
and sticking their snouts into it, straight down the
country, across the country, through fences, through
dooryards, in and out of gullies in straight lines. They
did not run on the ground, but on their own roadbeds.
They ignored hills and gulches, water courses, fences,
houses.

The man sitting in the iron seat did not look like a
man; gloved, goggled, rubber dust mask over nose and
mouth, he was part of the monster, a robot in the seat.
The thunder of the cylinders sounded through the
country, became one with the air and the earth, so that
earth and air muttered in sympathetic vibration. The
driver could not control it—straight across country it
went, cutting through a dozen farms and straight back.
A twitch at the controls could swerve the cat', but the

driver's hands could not twitch because the monster
that built the tractor, the monster that sent the tractor
out, had somehow got into the driver's hands, into his
brain and muscle, had goggled him and muzzled
him—goggled his mind, muzzled his speech, goggled
his perception, muzzled his protest. He could not see
the land as it was, he could not smell the land as it
smelled; his feet did not stamp the clods or feel the
warmth and power of the earth. He sat in an iron seat
and stepped on iron pedals. He could not cheer or
beat or curse or encourage the extension of his power,
and because of this he could not cheer or whip or
curse or encourage himself. He did not know or own or
trust or beseech the land. If a seed dropped did not
germinate, it was nothing. If the young thrusting plant
withered in drought or drowned in a flood of rain, it
was no more to the driver than to the tractor.

He loved the land no more than the bank loved the
land. He could admire the tractor—its machined surfaces, its surge of power, the roar of its detonating
cylinders; but it was not his tractor. Behind the tractor
rolled the shining disks, cutting the earth with blades—
not plowing but surgery, pushing the cut earth to the
right where the second row of disks cut it and pushed it
to the left; slicing blades shining, polished by the cut
earth. And pulled behind the disks, the harrows combing with iron teeth so that the little clods broke up and
the earth lay smooth. Behind the harrows, the long
seeders—twelve curved iron penes erected in the foun-
dry, orgasms set by gears, raping methodically, raping
without passion. The driver sat in his iron seat and he
was proud of the straight lines he did not will, proud of
the tractor he did not own or love, proud of the power he
could not control. And when that crop grew, and was
harvested, no man had crumbled a hot clod in his
fingers and let the earth sift past his fingertips. No man
had touched the seed, or lusted for the growth. Men ate
what they had not raised, had no connection with the

bread. The land bore under iron, and under iron gradually died; for it was not loved or hated, it had no prayers or curses.

At noon the tractor driver stopped sometimes near a tenant house and opened his lunch: sandwiches wrapped in waxed paper, white bread, pickle, cheese, Spam, a piece of pie branded like an engine part. He ate without relish. And tenants not yet moved away came out to see him, looked curiously while the goggles were taken off, and the rubber dust mask, leaving white circles around the eyes and a large white circle around nose and mouth. The exhaust of the tractor puttered on, for fuel is so cheap it is more efficient to leave the engine running than to heat the Diesel nose for a new start. Curious children crowded close, ragged children who ate their fried dough as they watched. They watched hungrily the unwrapping of the sandwiches, and their hunger-sharpened noses smelled the pickle, cheese, and Spam. They didn't speak to the driver. They watched his hand as it carried food to his mouth. They did not watch him chewing; their eyes followed the hand that held the sandwich. After a while the tenant who could not leave the place came out and squatted in the shade beside the tractor.

"Why, you're Joe Davis's boy!"

"Sure," the driver said.

"Well, what you doing this kind of work for—against your own people?"

"Three dollars a day. I got damn sick of creeping for my dinner—and not getting it. I got a wife and kids. We got to eat. Three dollars a day, and it comes every day."

"That's right," the tenant said. "But for your three dollars a day fifteen or twenty families can't eat at all. Nearly a hundred people have to go out and wander on the roads for your three dollars a day. Is that right?"

And the driver said, "Can't think of that. Got to think of my own kids. Three dollars a day, and it comes every day. Times are changing, mister, don't you know? Can't make a living on the land unless you've got two, five, ten thousand acres and a tractor. Crop land isn't for little guys like us any more. You don't kick up a howl because you can't make Fords, or because you're not the telephone company. Well, crops are like that now. Nothing to do about it. You try to get three dollars a day someplace. That's the only way."

The tenant pondered. "Funny thing how it is. If a man owns a little property, that property is him, it's part of him, and it's like him. If he owns property only so he can walk on it and handle it and be sad when it isn't doing well, and feel fine when the rain falls on it, that property is him, and some way he's bigger because he owns it. Even if he isn't successful he's big with his property. That is so."

And the tenant pondered more. "But let a man get property he doesn't see, or can't take time to get his fingers in, or can't be there to walk on it—why, then the property is the man. He can't do what he wants, he can't think what he wants. The property is the man, stronger than he is. And he is small, not big. Only his possessions are big—and he's the servant of his property. That is so, too."

The driver munched the branded pie and threw the crust away. "Times are changed, don't you know? Thinking about stuff like that don't feed the kids. Get your three dollars a day, feed your kids. You got no call to worry about anybody's kids but your own. You get a reputation for talking like that, and you'll never get three dollars a day. Big shots won't give you three dollars a day if you worry about anything but your three dollars a day."

"Nearly a hundred people on the road for your three dollars. Where will we go?"

"And that reminds me," the driver said, "you better get out soon. I'm going through the dooryard after dinner."

"You filled in the well this morning."

"I know. Had to keep the line straight. But I'm going through the dooryard after dinner. Got to keep the lines straight. And—well, you know Joe Davis, my old man, so I'll tell you this. I got orders wherever there's a family not moved out—if I have an accident—you know, get too close and cave the house in a little—well, I might get a couple of dollars. And my youngest kid never had no shoes yet."

"I built it with my hands. Straightened old nails to put the sheathing on. Rafters are wired to the stringers with baling wire. It's mine. I built it. You bump it down—I'll be in the window with a rifle. You even come too close and I'll pot you like a rabbit."

"It's not me. There's nothing I can do. I'll lose my job if I don't do it. And look—suppose you kill me? They'll just hang you, but long before you're hung there'll be another guy on the tractor, and he'll bump the house down. You're not killing the right guy."

"That's so," the tenant said. "Who gave you orders? I'll go after him. He's the one to kill."

"You're wrong. He got his orders from the bank. The bank told him, 'Clear those people out or it's your job.'"

"Well, there's a president of the bank. There's a board of directors. I'll fill up the magazine of the rifle and go into the bank."

The driver said, "Fellow was telling me the bank gets orders from the East. The orders were, 'Make the land show profit or we'll close you up.'"

"But where does it stop? Who can we shoot? I don't aim to starve to death before I kill the man that's starving me."

"I don't know. Maybe there's nobody to shoot. Maybe the thing isn't men at all. Maybe, like you said, the property's doing it. Anyway I told you my orders."

"I got to figure," the tenant said. "We all got to figure. There's some way to stop this. It's not like lightning or earthquakes. We've got a bad thing made by men, and by God that's something we can change." The tenant sat in his doorway, and the driver thundered his engine and started off, tracks falling and curving, harrows combing, and the phalli of the seeder slipping into the ground. Across the dooryard the tractor cut, and the hard, foot-beaten ground was seeded field, and the tractor cut through again; the uncut space was ten feet wide. And back he came. The iron guard bit into the house-corner, crumbled the wall, and wrenched the little house from its foundation so that it fell sideways, crushed like a bug. And the driver was goggled and a rubber mask covered his nose and mouth. The tractor cut a straight line on, and the air and the ground vibrated with its thunder. The tenant man stared after it, his rifle in his hand. His wife was beside him, and the quiet children behind. And all of them stared after the tractor.

6

The Reverend Casy and young Tom stood on the hill and looked down on the Joad place. The small unpainted house was mashed at one corner, and it had been pushed off its foundations so that it slumped at an angle, its blind front windows pointing at a spot of sky well above the horizon. The fences were gone and the cotton grew in the dooryard and up against the house, and the cotton was about the shed barn. The outhouse lay on its side, and the cotton grew close against it. Where the dooryard had been pounded hard by the bare feet of children and by stamping horses' hooves and by the broad wagon wheels, it was cultivated now, and the dark green, dusty cotton grew. Young Tom stared for a long time at the ragged willow beside the dry horse trough, at the concrete base where the pump had been. "Jesus!" he said at last. "Hell musta popped here. There ain't nobody livin' there." At last he moved quickly down the hill, and Casy followed him. He looked into the barn shed, deserted, a little ground straw on the floor, and at the mule stall in the corner. And as he looked in, there was a skittering on the floor and a family of mice faded in under the straw. Joad paused at the entrance to the tool-shed leanto, and no tools were there—a broken plow point, a mess of hay wire in the corner, an iron wheel from a hayrake and a rat-gnawed mule collar, a flat gallon oil can crusted with dirt and oil, and a pair of torn overalls hanging on a nail. "There ain't nothin' left," said Joad. "We had pretty nice tools. There ain't nothin' left."

Casy said, "If I was still a preacher I'd say the arm of the Lord had struck. But now I don't know what happened. I been away. I didn't hear nothin'." They walked toward the concrete well-cap, walked through cotton plants to get to it, and the bolls were forming on the cotton, and the land was cultivated.

"We never planted here," Joad said. "We always kept this clear. Why, you can't get a horse in now without he tromps the cotton." They paused at the dry watering trough, and the proper weeds that should grow under a trough were gone and the old thick wood of the trough was dry and cracked. On the well-cap the bolts that had held the pump stuck up, their threads rusty and the nuts gone. Joad looked into the tube of the well and spat and listened. He dropped a clod down the well and listened. "She was a good well," he said. "I can't hear water." He seemed reluctant to go to the house. He dropped clod after clod down the well. "Maybe they're all dead," he said. "But somebody'd told me. I'd a got word some way."

"Maybe they left a letter or something to tell in the house. Would they of knowed you was comin' out?"

"I don' know," said Joad. "No, I guess not. I didn' know myself till a week ago."

"Le's look in the house. She's all pushed out a shape. Something knocked the hell our of her." They walked slowly toward the sagging house. Two of the supports of the porch roof were pushed out so that the roof flopped down on one end. And the house-corner was crushed in. Through a maze of splintered wood the room at the corner was visible. The front door hung open inward, and a low strong gate across the front door hung outward on leather hinges.

Joad stopped at the step, a twelve-by-twelve timber. "Doorstep's here," he said. "But they're gone—or Ma's dead." He pointed to the low gate across the front door. "If Ma was anywheres about, that gate'd be shut an' hooked. That's one thing she always done—seen that gate was shut." His eyes were warm. "Ever since the pig got in over to Jacobs' an' et the baby. Milly Jacobs was jus' out in the barn. She come in while the pig was still eatin' it. Well, Milly Jacobs was in a family way, an' she went ravin'. Never did get over it. Touched ever since. But Ma took a lesson from it. She never lef' that pig gate open 'less she was in the house herself. Never did forget. No—they're gone—or dead." He climbed to the split porch and looked into the kitchen. The windows were broken out, and throwing rocks lay on the floor, and the floor and walls sagged steeply away from the door, and the sifted dust was on the boards. Joad pointed to the broken glass and the rocks. "Kids," he said. "They'll go twenty miles to bust a window. I done it myself. They know when a house is empty, they know. That's the fust thing kids do when folks move out." The kitchen was empty of furniture, stove gone and the round stovepipe hole in the wall showing light. On the sink shelf lay an old beer opener and a broken fork with its wooden handle gone. Joad slipped cautiously into the room, and the floor groaned under his weight. An old copy of the Philadelphia *Ledger* was on the floor against the wall, its pages yellow and curling. Joad looked into the bedroom—no bed, no chairs, nothing. On the wall a picture of an Indian girl in color, labeled Red Wing. A bed slat leaning against the wall, and in one corner a woman's high button shoe, curled up at the toe and broken over the instep. Joad picked it up and looked at it. "I remember this," he said. "This was Ma's. It's

all wore out now. Ma liked them shoes. Had 'em for
years. No, they've went—an' took ever'thing.''

The sun had lowered until it came through the angled end windows now, and it flashed on the edges of
the broken glass. Joad turned at last and went out and
crossed the porch. He sat down on the edge of it and
rested his bare feet on the twelve-by-twelve step. The
evening light was on the fields, and the cotton plants
threw long shadows on the ground, and the molting
willow tree threw a long shadow.

Casy sat down beside Joad. "They never wrote you
nothin'?" he asked.

"No. Like I said, they wasn't people to write. Pa
could write, but he wouldn'. Didn't like to. It give him
the shivers to write. He could work out a catalogue
order as good as the nex' fella, but he wouldn' write no
letters just for ducks." They sat side by side, staring
off into the distance. Joad laid his rolled coat on the
porch beside him. His independent hands rolled a
cigarette, smoothed it and lighted it, and he inhaled
deeply and blew the smoke out through his nose.
"Somepin's wrong," he said. "I can't put my finger on
her. I got an itch that somepin's wronger'n hell. Just
this house pushed aroun' an' my folks gone."

Casy said, "Right over there the ditch was, where I
done the baptizin'. You wasn't mean, but you was
tough. Hung onto that little girl's pigtail like a bulldog. We baptize' you both in the name of the Holy
Ghos', and still you hung on. Ol' Tom says, 'Hol' 'im
under water.' So I shove your head down till you start
to bubblin' before you'd let go a that pigtail. You
wasn't mean, but you was tough. Sometimes a tough
kid grows up with a big jolt of the sperit in him."

A lean gray cat came sneaking out of the barn and
crept through the cotton plants to the end of the porch.
It leaped silently up to the porch and crept low-belly
toward the men. It came to a place between and behind the two, and then it sat down, and its tail

stretched out straight and flat to the floor, and the last inch of it flicked. The cat sat and looked off into the distance where the men were looking.

Joad glanced around at it. "By God! Look who's here. Somebody stayed." He put out his hand, but the cat leaped away out of reach and sat down and licked the pads of its lifted paw. Joad looked at it, and his face was puzzled. "I know what's the matter," he cried. "That cat jus' made me figger what's wrong."

"Seems to me there's lots wrong," said Casy.

"No, it's more'n jus' this place. Whyn't that cat jus' move in with some neighbors—with the Rances. How come nobody ripped some lumber off this house? Ain't been nobody here for three-four months, an' nobody's stole no lumber. Nice planks on the barn shed, plenty good planks on the house, winda frames—an' nobody's took 'em. That ain't right. That's what was botherin' me, an' I couldn't catch hold of her."

"Well, what's that figger out for you?" Casy reached down and slipped off his sneakers and wriggled his long toes on the step.

"I don' know. Seems like maybe there ain't any neighbors. If there was, would all them nice planks be here? Why, Jesus Christ! Albert Rance took his family, kids an' dogs an' all, into Oklahoma City one Christmus. They was gonna visit with Albert's cousin. Well, folks aroun' here thought Albert moved away without sayin' nothin'—figgered maybe he got debts or some woman's squarin' off at him. When Albert come back a week later there wasn't a thing lef' in his house—stove was gone, beds was gone, winda frames was gone, an' eight feet of plankin' was gone off the south side of the house so you could look right through her. He come drivin' home just as Muley Graves was goin' away with the doors an' the well pump. Took Albert two weeks drivin' aroun' the neighbors' 'fore he got his stuff back."

Casy scratched his toes luxuriously. "Didn't nobody

give him an argument? All of 'em jus' give the stuff up?"

"Sure. They wasn't stealin' it. They thought he lef' it, an' they jus' took it. He got all of it back—all but a sofa pilla, velvet with a pitcher of an Injun on it. Albert claimed Grampa got it. Claimed Grampa got Injun blood, that's why he wants that pitcher. Well, Grampa did get her, but he didn't give a damn about the pitcher on it. He jus' liked her. Used to pack her aroun' an' he'd put her wherever he was gonna sit. He never would give her back to Albert. Says, 'If Albert wants this pilla so bad, let him come an' get her. But he better come shootin', 'cause I'll blow his goddamn stinkin' head off if he comes messin' aroun' my pilla.' So finally Albert give up an' made Grampa a present of that pilla. It give Grampa idears, though. He took to savin' chicken feathers. Says he's gonna have a whole damn bed of feathers. But he never got no feather bed. One time Pa got mad at a skunk under the house. Pa slapped that skunk with a two-by-four, and Ma burned all Grampa's feathers so we could live in the house." He laughed. "Grampa's a tough ol' bastard. Jus' set on the Injun pilla an' says, 'Let Albert come an' get her. Why,' he says, 'I'll take that squirt and wring 'im out like a pair of drawers.' "

The cat crept close between the men again, and its tail lay flat and its whiskers jerked now and then. The sun dropped low toward the horizon and the dusty air was red and golden. The cat reached out a gray questioning paw and touched Joad's coat. He looked around. "Hell, I forgot the turtle. I ain't gonna pack it all over hell." He unwrapped the land turtle and pushed it under the house. But in a moment it was out, headed southwest as it had been from the first. The cat leaped at it and struck at its straining head and slashed at its moving feet. The old, hard, humorous head was pulled in, and the thick tail slapped in

under the shell, and when the cat grew tired of waiting
for it and walked off, the turtle headed on southwest
again.

Young Tom Joad and the preacher watched the
turtle go—waving its legs and boosting its heavy, high-
domed shell along toward the southwest. The cat crept
along behind for a while, but in a dozen yards it
arched its back to a strong taut bow and yawned, and
came stealthily back toward the seated men.

"Where the hell you s'pose he's goin'?" said Joad.
"I seen turtles all my life. They're always goin' someplace. They always seem to want to get there." The
gray cat seated itself between and behind them again.
It blinked slowly. The skin over its shoulders jerked
forward under a flea, and then slipped slowly back.
The cat lifted a paw and inspected it, flicked its claws
out and in again experimentally, and licked its pads
with a shell-pink tongue. The red sun touched the
horizon and spread out like a jellyfish, and the sky
above it seemed much brighter and more alive than it
had been. Joad unrolled his new yellow shoes from his
coat, and he brushed his dusty feet with his hand
before he slipped them on.

The preacher, staring off across the fields, said,
"Somebody's comin'. Look! Down there, right through
the cotton."

Joad looked where Casy's finger pointed. "Comin'
afoot," he said. "Can't see 'im for the dust he raises.
Who the hell's comin' here?" They watched the figure
approaching in the evening light, and the dust it
raised was reddened by the setting sun. "Man," said
Joad. The man drew closer, and as he walked past
the barn, Joad said, "Why, I know him. You know
him—that's Muley Graves." And he called, "Hey,
Muley! How ya?"

The approaching man stopped, startled by the call,
and then he came on quickly. He was a lean man,

rather short. His movements were jerky and quick. He carried a gunny sack in his hand. His blue jeans were pale at knee and seat, and he wore an old black suit coat, stained and spotted, the sleeves torn loose from the shoulders in back, and ragged holes worn through at the elbows. His black hat was as stained as his coat, and the band, torn half free, flopped up and down as he walked. Muley's face was smooth and un-wrinkled, but it wore the truculent look of a bad child's, the mouth held tight and small, the little eyes half scowling, half petulant.

"You remember Muley," Joad said softly to the preacher.

"Who's that?" the advancing man called. Joad did not answer. Muley came close, very close, before he made out the face. "Well, I'll be damned," he said. "It's Tommy Joad. When'd you get out, Tommy?"

"Two days ago," said Joad. "Took a little time to hitch-hike home. An' look here what I find. Where's my folks, Muley? What's the house all smashed up for, an' cotton planted in the dooryard?"

"By God, it's lucky I come by!" said Muley. " 'Cause ol' Tom worried himself. When they was fixin' to move I was settin' in the kitchen there. I jus' tol' Tom I wan't gonna move, by God. I tol' him that, an' Tom says, 'I'm worryin' myself about Tommy. S'pose he comes home an' they ain't nobody here. What'll he think?' I says, 'Whyn't you write down a letter?' An' Tom says, 'Maybe I will. I'll think about her. But if I don't, you keep your eye out for Tommy if you're still aroun'.' 'I'll be aroun',' I says. 'I'll be aroun' till hell freezes over. There ain't nobody can run a guy by name of Graves outa this country.' An' they ain't done it, neither."

Joad said impatiently, "Where's my folks? Tell about you standin' up to 'em later, but where's my folks?"

"Well, they was gonna stick her out when the bank

come to tractorin' off the place. Your grampa stood out
here with a rifle, an' he blowed the headlights off that
cat', but she come on just the same. Your grampa
didn't wanta kill the guy drivin' that cat', an' that was
Willy Feeley, an' Willy knowed it, so he jus' come on,
an' bumped the hell outa the house, an' give her a
shake like a dog shakes a rat. Well, it took somepin
outa Tom. Kinda got into 'im. He ain't been the same
ever since."

"Where is my folks?" Joad spoke angrily.

"What I'm tellin' you. Took three trips with your
Uncle John's wagon. Took the stove an' the pump an'
the beds. You should a seen them beds go out with all
them kids an' your granma an' grampa settin' up against
the headboard, an' your brother Noah settin' there
smokin' a cigareet, an' spittin' la-de-da over the side of
the wagon." Joad opened his mouth to speak. "They're
all at your Uncle John's," Muley said quickly.

"Oh! All at John's. Well, what they doin' there?
Now stick to her for a second, Muley. Jus' stick to her.
In jus' a minute you can go on your own way. What
they doin' there?"

"Well, they been choppin' cotton, all of 'em, even
the kids an' your grampa. Gettin' money together so
they can shove on west. Gonna buy a car and shove on
west where it's easy livin'. There ain't nothin' here.
Fifty cents a clean acre for choppin' cotton, an' folks
beggin' for the chance to chop."

"An' they ain't gone yet?"

"No," said Muley. "Not that I know. Las' I heard
was four days ago when I seen your brother Noah out
shootin' jackrabbits, an' he says they're aimin' to go in
about two weeks. John got his notice he got to get off.
You jus' go on about eight miles to John's place.
You'll find your folks piled in John's house like
gophers in a winter burrow."

"O.K." said Joad. "Now you can ride on your own
way. You ain't changed a bit, Muley. If you want to

tell about somepin off northwest, you point your nose straight southeast."

Muley said truculently, "You ain't changed neither. You was a smart-aleck kid, an' you're still a smart aleck. You ain't tellin' me how to skin my life, by any chancet?"

Joad grinned. "No, I ain't. If you wanta drive your head into a pile of broken glass, there ain't nobody can tell you different. You know this here preacher, don't you, Muley? Rev. Casy."

"Why, sure, sure. Didn't look over. Remember him well." Casy stood up and the two shook hands. "Glad to see you again," said Muley. "You ain't been aroun' for a hell of a long time."

"I been off a-askin' questions," said Casy. "What happened here? Why they kickin' folks off the lan'?"

Muley's mouth snapped shut so tightly that a little parrot's beak in the middle of his upper lip stuck down over his under lip. He scowled. "Them sons-a-bitches," he said. "Them dirty sons-a-bitches. I tell ya, men, I'm stayin'. They ain't gettin' rid a me. If they throw me off, I'll come back, an' if they figger I'll be quiet underground, why, I'll take couple-three of the sons-a-bitches along for company." He patted a heavy weight in his side coat pocket. "I ain't a-goin'. My pa come here fifty years ago. An' I ain't a-goin'."

Joad said, "What's the idear of kickin' the folks off?"

"Oh! They talked pretty about it. You know what kinda years we been havin'. Dust comin' up an' spoilin' ever'thing so a man didn't get enough crop to plug up an ant's ass. An' ever'body got bills at the grocery. You know how it is. Well, the folks that owns the lan' says, 'We can't afford to keep no tenants.' An' they says, 'The share a tenant gets is jus' the margin a profit we can't afford to lose.' An' they says, 'If we put all our lan' in one piece we can jus' hardly make her pay.' So they tractored all the tenants off a the lan'.

All 'cept me, an' by God I ain't goin'. Tommy, you know me. You knowed me all your life."

"Damn right," said Joad, "all my life."

"Well, you know I ain't a fool. I know this land ain't much good. Never was much good 'cept for grazin'. Never should a broke her up. An' now she's cottoned damn near to death. If on'y they didn' tell me I got to get off, why, I'd prob'ly be in California right now a-eatin' grapes an' a-pickin' an orange when I wanted. But them sons-a-bitches says I got to get off—an', Jesus Christ, a man can't, when he's tol' to!"

"Sure," said Joad. "I wonder Pa went so easy. I wonder Grampa didn' kill nobody. Nobody never tol' Grampa where to put his feet. An' Ma ain't nobody you can push aroun', neither. I seen her beat the hell out of a tin peddler with a live chicken one time 'cause he give her a argument. She had the chicken in one han', an' the ax in the other, about to cut its head off. She aimed to go for that peddler with the ax, but she forgot which hand was which, an' she takes after him with the chicken. Couldn' even eat that chicken when she got done. They wasn't nothing but a pair a legs in her han'. Grampa throwed his hip outa joint laughin'. How'd my folks go so easy?"

"Well, the guy that come aroun' talked nice as pie. 'You got to get off. It ain't my fault.' 'Well,' I says, 'whose fault is it? I'll go an' I'll nut the fella.' 'It's the Shawnee Lan' an' Cattle Company. I jus' got orders.' 'Who's the Shawnee Lan' an' Cattle Company?' 'It ain't nobody. It's a company.' Got a fella crazy. There wasn't nobody you could lay for. Lot a the folks jus' got tired out lookin' for somepin to be mad at—but not me. I'm mad at all of it. I'm stayin'."

A large red drop of sun lingered on the horizon and then dripped over and was gone, and the sky was brilliant over the spot where it had gone, and a torn cloud, like a bloody rag, hung over the spot of its going. And dusk crept over the sky from the eastern

horizon, and darkness crept over the land from the
east. The evening star flashed and glittered in the
dusk. The gray cat sneaked away toward the open barn
shed and passed inside like a shadow.

Joad said, "Well, we ain't gonna walk no eight
miles to Uncle John's place tonight. My dogs is burned
up. How's it if we go to your place, Muley? That's on'y
about a mile."

"Won't do no good." Muley seemed embarrassed.
"My wife an' the kids an' her brother all took an' went
to California. They wasn't nothin' to eat. They wasn't
as mad as me, so they went. They wasn't nothin' to eat
here."

The preacher stirred nervously. "You should of went
too. You shouldn't of broke up the fambly."

"I couldn'," said Muley Graves. "Somepin jus'
wouldn' let me."

"Well, by God, I'm hungry," said Joad. "Four solemn years I been eatin' right on the minute. My guts is
yellin' bloody murder. What you gonna eat, Muley?
How you been gettin' your dinner?"

Muley said ashamedly, "For a while I et frogs an'
squirrels an' prairie dogs sometimes. Had to do it. But
now I got some wire nooses on the tracks in the dry
stream brush. Get rabbits, an' sometimes a prairie
chicken. Skunks get caught, an' coons, too." He
reached down, picked up his sack, and emptied it on
the porch. Two cottontails and a jackrabbit fell out and
rolled over limply, soft and furry.

"God Awmighty," said Joad, "it's more'n four years
sence I've et fresh-killed meat."

Casy picked up one of the cottontails and held it in
his hand. "You sharin' with us, Muley Graves?" he
asked.

Muley fidgeted in embarrassment. "I ain't got no
choice in the matter." He stopped on the ungracious
sound of his words. "That ain't like I mean it. That
ain't. I mean"—he stumbled—"what I mean, if a

fella's got somepin to eat an' another fella's hungry—
why, the first fella ain't got no choice. I mean, s'pose
I pick up my rabbits an' go off somewheres an' eat
'em. See?"

"I see," said Casy. "I can see that. Muley sees
somepin there, Tom. Muley's got a-holt of somepin,
an' it's too big for him, an' it's too big for me."

Young Tom rubbed his hands together. "Who got a
knife? Le's get at these here miserable rodents. Le's
get at 'em."

Muley reached in his pants pocket and produced a
large horn-handled pocket knife. Tom Joad took it
from him, opened a blade, and smelled it. He drove
the blade again and again into the ground and smelled
it again, wiped it on his trouser leg, and felt the edge
with his thumb.

Myley took a quart bottle of water out of his hip
pocket and set it on the porch. "Go easy on that there
water," he said. "That's all there is. This here well's
filled in."

Tom took up a rabbit in his hand. "One of you go
get some bale wire outa the barn. We'll make a fire
with some a this broken plank from the house." He
looked at the dead rabbit. "There ain't nothin' so
easy to get ready as a rabbit," he said. He lifted the
skin of the back, slit it, put his fingers in the hole,
and tore the skin off. It slipped off like a stocking,
slipped off the body to the neck, and off the legs to
the paws. Joad picked up the knife again and cut off
head and feet. He laid the skin down, slit the rabbit
along the ribs, shook out the intestines onto the skin,
and then threw the mess off into the cotton field. And
the clean-muscled little body was ready. Joad cut off
the legs and cut the meaty back into two pieces. He
was picking up the second rabbit when Casy came
back with a snarl of bale wire in his hand. "Now
build up a fire and put some stakes up," said Joad.
"Jesus Christ, I'm hungry for these here creatures!"

He cleaned and cut up the rest of the rabbits and
strung them on the wire. Muley and Casy tore
splintered boards from the wrecked house-corner and
started a fire, and they drove a stake into the ground
on each side to hold the wire.

Muley came back to Joad. "Look out for boils on
that jackrabbit," he said. "I don't like to eat no jackrabbit with boils." He took a little cloth bag from his
pocket and put it on the porch.

Joad said, "The jack was clean as a whistle—Jesus
God, you got salt too? By any chance you got some
plates an' a tent in your pocket?" He poured salt in his
hand and sprinkled it over the pieces of rabbit strung
on the wire.

The fire leaped and threw shadows on the house,
and the dry wood crackled and snapped. The sky was
almost dark now and the stars were out sharply. The
gray cat came out of the barn shed and trotted miaow-
ing toward the fire, but, nearly there, it turned and
went directly to one of the little piles of rabbit entrails
on the ground. It chewed and swallowed, and the entrails hung from its mouth.

Casy sat on the ground beside the fire, feeding it
broken pieces of board, pushing the long boards in as
the flame ate off their ends. The evening bats flashed
into the firelight and out again. The cat crouched back
and licked its lips and washed its face and whiskers.

Joad held up his rabbit-laden wire between his two
hands and walked to the fire. "Here, take one end,
Muley. Wrap your end around that stake. That's good,
now! Let's tighten her up. We ought to wait till the
fire's burned down, but I can't wait." He made the
wire taut, then found a stick and slipped the pieces of
meat along the wire until they were over the fire. And
the flames licked up around the meat and hardened
and glazed the surfaces. Joad sat down by the fire, but
with his stick he moved and turned the rabbit so that it
would not become sealed to the wire. "This here is a

party," he said. "Salt, Muley's got, an' water an' rabbits. I wish he got a pot of hominy in his pocket. That's all I wish."

Muley said over the fire, "You fellas'd think I'm touched, the way I live."

"Touched, nothin'," said Joad. "If you're touched, I wisht ever'body was touched."

Muley continued, "Well, sir, it's a funny thing. Somepin went an' happened to me when they tol' me I had to get off the place. Fust I was gonna go in an' kill a whole flock a people. Then all my folks all went away out west. An' I got wanderin' aroun'. Jus' walkin' aroun'. Never went far. Slep' where I was. I was gonna sleep here tonight. That's why I come. I'd tell myself, 'I'm lookin' after things so when all the folks come back it'll be all right.' But I knowed that wan't true. There ain't nothin' to look after. The folks ain't never comin' back. I'm jus' wanderin' aroun' like a damn ol' graveyard ghos'."

"Fella gets use' to a place, it's hard to go," said Casy. "Fella gets use' to a way a thinkin', it's hard to leave. I ain't a preacher no more, but all the time I find I'm prayin', not even thinkin' what I'm doin'."

Joad turned the pieces of meat over on the wire. The juice was dripping now, and every drop, as it fell in the fire, shot up a spurt of flame. The smooth surface of the meat was crinkling up and turning a faint brown. "Smell her," said Joad. "Jesus, look down an' jus' smell her!"

Muley went on, "Like a damn ol' graveyard ghos'. I been goin' aroun' the places where stuff happened. Like there's a place over by our forty; in a gully they's a bush. Fust time I ever laid with a girl was there. Me fourteen an' stampin' an' jerkin' an' snortin' like a buck deer, randy as a billygoat. So I went there an' I laid down on the groun', an' I seen it all happen again. An' there's the place down by the barn where Pa got gored to death by a bull. An' his blood is right in that

groun', right now. Mus' be. Nobody never washed it
out. An' I put my han' on that groun' where my own
pa's blood is part of it." He paused uneasily. "You
fellas think I'm touched?"

Joad turned the meat, and his eyes were inward.
Casy, feet drawn up, stared into the fire. Fifteen feet
back from the men the fed cat was sitting, the long gray
tail wrapped neatly around the front feet. A big owl
shrieked as it went overhead, and the firelight showed
its white underside and the spread of its wings.

"No," said Casy. "You're lonely—but you ain't
touched."

Muley's tight little face was rigid. "I put my han'
right on the groun' where that blood is still. An' I seen
my pa with a hole through his ches', an' I felt him
shiver up against me like he done, an' I seen him kind
of settle back an' reach with his han's an' his feet. An'
I seen his eyes all milky with hurt, an' then he was
still an' his eyes so clear—lookin' up. An' me a little
kid settin' there, not cryin' nor nothin', jus' settin'
there." He shook his head sharply. Joad turned the
meat over and over. "An' I went in the room where Joe
was born. Bed wasn't there, but it was the room. An'
all them things is true, an' they're right in the place
they happened. Joe come to life right there. He give a
big ol' gasp an' then he let out a squawk you could
hear a mile, an' his granma standin' there says, 'That's
a daisy, that's a daisy,' over an' over. An' her so proud
she bust three cups that night."

Joad cleared his throat. "Think we better eat her
now."

"Let her get good an' done, good an' brown, awmost
black," said Muley irritably. "I wanta talk. I ain't
talked to nobody. If I'm touched, I'm touched, an' that's
the end of it. Like a ol' graveyard ghos' goin' to neighbors' houses in the night. Peters', Jacobs', Rance's,
Joad's; an' the houses all dark, standin' like miser'ble
ratty boxes, but they was good parties an' dancin'. An'

there was meetin's and shoutin' glory. They was weddin's, all in them houses. An' then I'd want to go in
town an' kill folks. 'Cause what'd they take when they
tractored the folks off the lan'? What'd they get so their
'margin a profit' was safe? They got Pa dyin' on the
groun', an' Joe yellin' his first breath, an' me jerkin'
like a billy goat under a bush in the night. What'd they
get? God knows the lan' ain't no good. Nobody been
able to make a crop for years. But them sons-a-bitches
at their desks, they jus' chopped folks in two for their
margin a profit. They jus' cut 'em in two. Place where
folks live is them folks. They ain't whole, out lonely on
the road in a piled-up car. They ain't alive no more.
Them sons-a-bitches killed 'em." And he was silent,
his thin lips still moving, his chest still panting. He
sat and looked down at his hands in the firelight. "I—I
ain't talked to nobody for a long time," he apologized
softly. "I been sneakin' aroun' like a ol' graveyard
ghos'."

Casy pushed the long boards into the fire and the
flames licked up around them and leaped up toward
the meat again. The house cracked loudly as the
cooler night air contracted the wood. Casy said quietly, "I gotta see them folks that's gone out on the
road. I got a feelin' I got to see them. They gonna need
help no preachin' can give 'em. Hope of heaven when
their lives ain't lived? Holy Sperit when their own
sperit is downcast an' sad? They gonna need help.
They got to live before they can afford to die."

Joad cried nervously, "Jesus Christ, le's eat this
meat 'fore it's smaller'n a cooked mouse! Look at her.
Smell her." He leaped to his feet and slid the pieces of
meat along the wire until they were clear of the fire.
He took Muley's knife and sawed through a piece of
meat until it was free of the wire. "Here's for the
preacher," he said.

"I tol' you I ain't no preacher."

"Well, here's for the man, then." He cut off

another piece. "Here, Muley, if you ain't too god-damn upset to eat. This here's jackrabbit. Tougher'n a bull-bitch." He sat back and clamped his long teeth on the meat and tore out a great bite and chewed it. "Jesus Christ! Hear her crunch!" And he tore out another bite ravenously.

Muley still sat regarding his meat. "Maybe I oughtn' to a-talked like that," he said. "Fella should maybe keep stuff like that in his head."

Casy looked over, his mouth full of rabbit. He chewed, and his muscled throat convulsed in swallowing. "Yes, you should talk," he said. "Sometimes a sad man can talk the sadness right out through his mouth. Sometimes a killin' man can talk the murder right out of his mouth an' not do no murder. You done right. Don't you kill nobody if you can help it." And he bit out another hunk of rabbit. Joad tossed the bones in the fire and jumped up and cut more off the wire. Muley was eating slowly now, and his nervous little eyes went from one to the other of his companions. Joad ate scowling like an animal, and a ring of grease formed around his mouth.

For a long time Muley looked at him, almost timidly. He put down the hand that held the meat. "Tommy," he said.

Joad looked up and did not stop gnawing the meat. "Yeah?" he said, around a mouthful.

"Tommy, you ain't mad with me talkin' about killin' people? You ain't huffy, Tom?"

"No," said Tom. "I ain't huffy. It's jus' somepin that happened."

"Ever'body knowed it was no fault of yours," said Muley. "Ol' man Turnbull said he was gonna get you when ya come out. Says nobody can kill one a his boys. All the folks hereabouts talked him outa it, though."

"We was drunk," Joad said softly. "Drunk at a

dance. I don' know how she started. An' then I felt that knife go in me, an' that sobered me up. Fust thing I see is Herb comin' for me again with his knife. They was this here shovel leanin' against the schoolhouse, so I grabbed it an' smacked 'im over the head. I never had nothing against Herb. He was a nice fella. Come a-bullin' after my sister Rosasharn when he was a little fella. No, I liked Herb."

"Well, ever'body tol' his pa that, an' finally cooled 'im down. Somebody says they's Hatfield blood on his mother's side in ol' Turnbull, an' he's got to live up to it. I don't know about that. Him an' his folks went on to California six months ago."

Joad took the last of the rabbit from the wire and passed it around. He settled back and ate more slowly now, chewed evenly, and wiped the grease from his mouth with his sleeve. And his eyes, dark and half closed, brooded as he looked into the dying fire. "Ever'body's goin' west," he said. "I got me a parole to keep. Can't leave the state."

"Parole?" Muley asked. "I heard about them. How do they work?"

"Well, I got out early, three years early. They's stuff I gotta do, or they send me back in. Got to report ever' so often."

"How they treat ya there in McAlester? My woman's cousin was in McAlester an' they give him hell."

"It ain't so bad," said Joad. "Like ever'place else. They give ya hell if ya raise hell. You get along O.K. les' some guard get it in for ya. Then you catch plenty hell. I got along O.K. Minded my own business, like any guy would. I learned to write nice as hell. Birds an' stuff like that, too; not just word writin'. My ol' man'll be sore when he sees me whip out a bird in one stroke. Pa's gonna be mad when he sees me do that. He don't like no fancy stuff like that. He don't even like word writin'. Kinda scares 'im, I guess. Ever' time Pa seen writin', somebody took somepin away from 'im.''

"They didn' give you no beatin's or nothin' like that?"

"No, I jus' tended my own affairs. 'Course you get goddamn good an' sick a-doin' the same thing day after day for four years. If you done somepin you was ashamed of, you might think about that. But, hell, if I seen Herb Turnbull comin' for me with a knife right now, I'd squash him down with a shovel again."

"Anybody would," said Muley. The preacher stared into the fire, and his high forehead was white in the settling dark. The flash of little flames picked out the cords of his neck. His hands, clasped about his knees, were busy pulling knuckles.

Joad threw the last bones into the fire and licked his fingers and then wiped them on his pants. He stood up and brought the bottle of water from the porch, took a sparing drink, and passed the bottle before he sat down again. He went on, "The thing that give me the mos' trouble was, it didn' make no sense. You don't look for no sense when lightnin' kills a cow, or it comes up a flood. That's jus' the way things is. But when a bunch of men take an' lock you up four years, it ought to have some meaning. Men is supposed to think things out. Here they put me in, an' keep me an' feed me four years. That ought to either make me so I won't do her again or else punish me so I'll be afraid to do her again"—he paused—"but if Herb or anybody else come for me, I'd do her again. Do her before I could figure her out. Specially if I was drunk. That sort of senseless-ness kind a worries a man."

Muley observed, "Judge says he give you a light sentence 'cause it wasn't all your fault."

Joad said, "They's a guy in McAlester—lifer. He studies all the time. He's sec'etary of the warden—

writes the warden's letters an' stuff like that. Well, he's
one hell of a bright guy an' reads law an' stuff like that.
Well, I talked to him one time about her, 'cause he
reads so much stuff. An' he says it don't do no good to
read books. Says he's read ever'thing about prisons
now, an' in the old times; an' he says she makes less
sense to him now than she did before he starts readin'.
He says it's a thing that started way to hell an' gone
back, an' nobody seems to be able to stop her, an' nobody got sense enough to change her. He says for God's
sake don't read about her because he says for one thing
you'll jus' get messed up worse, an' for another you
won't have no respect for the guys that work the
gover'ments."

"I ain't got a hell of a lot of respec' for 'em now,"
said Muley. "On'y kind of gover'ment we got that leans
on us fellas is the 'safe margin a profit.' There's one
thing that got me stumped, an' that's Willy Feely—
drivin' that cat', an' gonna be a straw boss on lan' his
own folks used to farm. That worries me. I can see
how a fella might come from some other place an' not
know no better, but Willy belongs. Worried me so I
went up to 'im and ast 'im. Right off he got mad. 'I got
two little kids,' he says. 'I got a wife an' my wife's
mother. Them people got to eat.' Gets madder'n hell.
'Fust an' on'y thing I got to think about is my own
folks,' he says. 'What happens to other folks is their
look-out,' he says. Seems like he's 'shamed, so he gets
mad."

Jim Casy had been staring at the dying fire, and his
eyes had grown wider and his neck muscles stood
higher. Suddenly he cried, "I got her! If ever a man
got a dose of the sperit, I got her! Got her all of a
flash!" He jumped to his feet and paced back and
forth, his head swinging. "Had a tent one time.
Drawed as much as five hundred people ever'night.
That's before either you fellas seen me." He stopped

and faced them. "Ever notice I never took no collections when I was preachin' out here to folks—in barns
an' in the open?"

"By God, you never," said Muley. "People around
here got so use' to not givin' you money they got to
bein' a little mad when some other preacher come
along an' passed the hat. Yes, sir!"

"I took somepin to eat," said Casy. "I took a pair a
pants when mine was wore out, an' a ol' pair a shoes
when I was walkin' through to the groun', but it wasn't
like when I had the tent. Some days there I'd take in
ten or twenty dollars. Wasn't happy that-a-way, so I
give her up, an' for a time I was happy. I think I got
her now. I don' know if I can say her. I guess I won't
try to say her—but maybe there's a place for a preacher. Maybe I can preach again. Folks out lonely on the
road, folks with no lan', no home to go to. They got to
have some kind of home. Maybe—" He stood over the
fire. The hundred muscles of his neck stood out in
high relief, and the firelight went deep into his eyes
and ignited red embers. He stood and looked at the
fire, his face tense as though he were listening, and
the hands that had been active to pick, to handle, to
throw ideas, grew quiet, and in a moment crept into
his pockets. The bats flittered in and out of the dull
firelight, and the soft watery burble of a night hawk
came from across the fields.

Tom reached quietly into his pocket and brought out
his tobacco, and he rolled a cigarette slowly and
looked over it at the coals while he worked. He ignored the whole speech of the preacher, as though it
were some private thing that should not be inspected.
He said, "Night after night in my bunk I figgered how
she'd be when I come home again. I figgered maybe
Grampa or Granma'd be dead, an' maybe there'd be
some new kids. Maybe Pa'd not be so tough. Maybe
Ma'd set back a little an' let Rosasharn do the work. I

knowed it wouldn't be the same as it was. Well, we'll sleep here I guess, an' come daylight we'll get on to Uncle John's. Leastwise I will. You think you're comin' along, Casy?"

The preacher still stood looking into the coals. He said slowly, "Yeah, I'm goin' with you. An' when your folks start out on the road I'm goin' with them. An' where folks are on the road, I'm gonna be with them."

"You're welcome," said Joad. "Ma always favored you. Said you was a preacher to trust. Rosasharn wasn't growed up then." He turned his head. "Muley, you gonna walk on over with us?" Muley was looking toward the road over which they had come. "Think you'll come along, Muley?" Joad repeated.

"Huh? No. I don't go no place, an' I don't leave no place. See that glow over there, jerkin' up an' down? That's prob'ly the super'ntendent of this stretch a cotton. Somebody maybe seen our fire."

Tom looked. The glow of light was nearing over the hill. "We ain't doin' no harm," he said. "We'll jus' set here. We ain't doin' nothin'."

Muley cackled. "Yeah! We're doin' somepin jus' bein' here. We're trespassin'. We can't stay. They been tryin' to catch me for two months. Now you look. If that's a car comin' we go out in the cotton an' lay down. Don't have to go far. Then by God let 'em try to fin' us! Have to look up an' down ever' row. Jus' keep your head down."

Joad demanded, "What's come over you, Muley? You wasn't never no run-an'-hide fella. You was mean."

Muley watched the approaching lights. "Yeah!" he said. "I was mean like a wolf. Now I'm mean like a weasel. When you're huntin' somepin you're a hunter, an' you're strong. Can't nobody beat a hunter. But when you get hunted—that's different. Somepin happens to you. You ain't strong; maybe you're fierce, but you ain't strong. I been hunted now for a long time. I ain't a hunter no more. I'd maybe shoot a fella in the dark, but I don't maul nobody with a fence stake no more. It don't do no good to fool you or me. That's how it is."

"Well, you go out an' hide," said Joad. "Leave me an' Casy tell these bastards a few things." The beam of light was closer now, and it bounced into the sky and then disappeared, and then bounced up again. All three men watched.

Muley said, "There's one more thing about bein' hunted. You get to thinkin' about all the dangerous things. If you're huntin' you don't think about 'em, an' you ain't scared. Like you says to me, if you get in any trouble they'll sen' you back to McAlester to finish your time."

"That's right," said Joad. "That's what they tol' me, but settin' here restin' or sleepin' on the groun'—that ain't gettin' in no trouble. That ain't doin' nothin' wrong. That ain't like gettin' drunk or raisin' hell."

Muley laughed. "You'll see. You jus' set here, an' the car'll come. Maybe it's Willy Feeley, an' Willy's a deputy sheriff now. 'What you doin' trespassin' here?' Willy says. Well, you always did know Willy was full a crap, so you says, 'What's it to you?' Willy gets mad an' says, 'You get off or I'll take you in.' An' you ain't gonna let no Feeley push you aroun' 'cause he's mad an' scared. He's made a bluff an' he got to go on with it, an' here's you gettin' tough an' you got to go through—oh, hell, it's a lot easier to lay out in the cotton an' let 'em look. It's more fun, too, 'cause they're mad an' can't do nothin', an' you're out there a-laughin' at 'em. But you jus' talk to Willy or any boss, an' you slug hell out of 'em an' they'll take you in an' run you back to McAlester for three years."

"You're talkin' sense," said Joad. "Ever' word you

say is sense. But, Jesus, I hate to get pushed around! I lots rather take a sock at Willy."

"He got a gun," said Muley. "He'll use it 'cause he's a deputy. Then he either got to kill you or you got to get his gun away an' kill him. Come on, Tommy. You can easy tell yourself you're foolin' them lyin' out like that. An' it all just amounts to what you tell yourself." The strong lights angled up into the sky now, and the even drone of a motor could be heard. "Come on, Tommy. Don't have to go far, jus' fourteen-fifteen rows over, an' we can watch what they do."

Tom got to his feet. "By God, you're right!" he said. "I ain't got a thing in the worl' to win, no matter how it comes out."

"Come on, then, over this way." Muley moved around the house and out into the cotton field about fifty yards. "This is good," he said, "Now lay down. You on'y got to pull your head down if they start the spotlight goin'. It's kinda fun." The three men stretched out at full length and propped themselves on their elbows. Muley sprang up and ran toward the house, and in a few moments he came back and threw a bundle of coats and shoes down. "They'd of taken 'em along just to get even," he said. The lights topped the rise and bore down on the house.

Joad asked, "Won't they come out here with flashlights an' look aroun' for us? I wisht I had a stick."

Muley giggled. "No, they won't. I tol' you I'm mean like a weasel. Willy done that one night an' I clipped 'im from behint with a fence stake. Knocked him colder'n a wedge. He tol' later how five guys come at him."

The car drew up to the house and a spotlight snapped on. "Duck," said Muley. The bar of cold white light swung over their heads and crisscrossed the field. The hiding men could not see any movement, but they heard a car door slam and they heard voices. "Scairt to get in the light," Muley whispered. "Once-

twice I've took a shot at the headlights. That keeps
Willy careful. He got somebody with 'im tonight".
They heard footsteps on wood, and then from inside
the house they saw the glow of a flashlight. "Shall I
shoot through the house?" Muley whispered. "They
couldn't see where it come from. Give 'em somepin to
think about."

"Sure, go ahead," said Joad.

"Don't do it," Casy whispered. "It won't do no good.
Jus' a waste. We got to get thinkin' about doin' stuff
that means somepin."

A scratching sound came from near the house. "Puttin' out the fire," Muley whispered. "Kickin' dust over
it." The car doors slammed, the headlights swung
around and faced the road again. "Now duck!" said
Muley. They dropped their heads and the spotlight
swept over them and crossed and recrossed the cotton
field, and then the car started and slipped away and
topped the rise and disappeared.

Muley sat up. "Willy always tries that las' flash. He
done it so often I can time 'im. An' he still thinks it's
cute."

Casy said, "Maybe they left some fellas at the
house. They'd catch us when we come back."

"Maybe. You fellas wait here. I know this game."
He walked quietly away, and only a slight crunching
of clods could be heard from his passage. The two
waiting men tried to hear him, but he had gone. In a
moment he called from the house, "They didn't leave
nobody. Come on back." Casey and Joad struggled up
and walked back toward the black bulk of the house.
Muley met them near the smoking dust pile which had
been their fire. "I didn' think they'd leave nobody," he
said proudly. "Me knockin' Willy over an' takin' a shot
at the lights once-twice keeps 'em careful. They ain't
sure who it is, an' I ain't gonna let 'em catch me. I
don't sleep near no house. If you fellas wanta come

along, I'll show you where to sleep, where there ain't nobody gonna stumble over ya."

"Lead off," said Joad. "We'll folla you. I never thought I'd be hidin' out on my old man's place."

Muley set off across the fields, and Joad and Casy followed him. They kicked the cotton plants as they went. "You'll be hidin' from lots of stuff," said Muley. They marched in single file across the fields. They came to a water-cut and slid easily down to the bottom of it.

"By God, I bet I know," cried Joad. "Is it a cave in the bank?"

"That's right. How'd you know?"

"I dug her," said Joad. "Me an' my brother Noah dug her. Lookin' for gold we says we was, but we was jus' diggin' caves like kids always does." The walls of the water-cut were above their heads now. "Ought to be pretty close," said Joad. "Seems to me I remember her pretty close."

Muley said, "I've covered her with bresh. Nobody couldn't find her." The bottom of the gulch leveled off, and the footing was sand.

Joad settled himself on the clean sand. "I ain't gonna sleep in no cave," he said. "I'm gonna sleep right here." He rolled his coat and put it under his head.

Muley pulled at the covering brush and crawled into his cave. "I like it in here," he called. "I feel like nobody can come at me."

Jim Casy sat down on the sand beside Joad.

"Get some sleep," said Joad. "We'll start for Uncle John's at daybreak"

"I ain't sleepin'," said Casy. "I got too much to puzzle with." He drew up his feet and clasped his legs. He threw back his head and looked at the sharp stars. Joad yawned and brought one hand back under his head. They were silent, and gradually the skitter-

ing life of the ground, of holes and burrows, of the
brush, began again; the gophers moved, and the rabbits crept to green things, the mice scampered over
clods, and the winged hunters moved soundlessly
overhead.

7

In the towns, on the edges
of the towns, in fields, in vacant lots, the used-car
yards, the wreckers' yards, the garages with blazoned
signs—Used Cars, Good Used Cars. Cheap transportation, three trailers. '27 Ford, clean. Checked cars,
guaranteed cars. Free radio. Car with 100 gallons of
gas free. Come in and look. Used Cars. No overhead.

A lot and a house large enough for a desk and chair
and a blue book. Sheaf of contracts, dog-eared, held
with paper clips, and a neat pile of unused contracts.
Pen—keep it full, keep it working. A sale's been lost
'cause a pen didn't work.

Those sons-of-bitches over there ain't buying. Every
yard gets 'em. They're lookers. Spend all their time
looking. Don't want to but no cars; take up your time.
Don't give a damn for your time. Over there, them two
people—no, with the kids. Get 'em in a car. Start 'em
at two hundred and work down. They look good for one
and a quarter. Get 'em rolling. Get 'em out in a jalopy.
Sock it to 'em! They took our time.

Owners with rolled-up sleeves. Salesmen, neat,
deadly, small intent eyes watching for weaknesses.

Watch the woman's face. If the woman likes it we
can screw the old man. Start 'em on that Cad'. Then

you can work 'em down to that '26 Buick. 'F you start on the Buick, they'll go for a Ford. Roll up your sleeves an' get to work. This ain't gonna last forever. Show 'em that Nash while I get the slow leak pumped up on that '25 Dodge. I'll give you a Hymie when I'm ready.

What you want is transportation, ain't it? No baloney for you. Sure the upholstery is shot. Seat cushions ain't turning no wheels over.

Cars lined up, noses forward, rusty noses, flat tires. Parked close together.

Like to get in to see that one? Sure, no trouble. I'll pull her out of the line.

Get 'em under obligation. Make 'em take up your time. Don't let 'em forget they're takin' your time. People are nice, mostly. They hate to put you out. Make 'em put you out, an' then sock it to 'em.

Cars lined up, Model T's, high and snotty, creaking wheel, worn bands. Buicks, Nashes, De Sotos.

Yes, sir. '22 Dodge. Best goddamn car Dodge ever made. Never wear out. Low compression. High compression got lots of sap for a while, but the metal ain't made that'll hold it for long. Plymouths, Rocknes, Stars.

Jesus, where'd that Apperson come from, the Ark? And a Chalmers and a Chandler—ain't made 'em for years. We ain't sellin' cars—rolling junk. Goddamn it, I got to get jalopies. I don't want nothing for more'n twenty-five, thirty bucks. Sell 'em for fifty, seventy-five. That's a good profit. Christ, what cut do you make on a new car? Get jalopies. I can sell 'em fast as I get 'em. Nothing over two hundred fifty. Jim, corral that old bastard on the sidewalk. Don't know his ass from a hole in the ground. Try him on that Apperson. Say, where is that Apperson? Sold? If we don't get some jalopies we got nothing to sell.

Flags, red and white, white and blue—all along the curb. Used Cars. Good Used Cars.

Today's bargain—up on the platform. Never sell it. Makes folks come in, though. If we sold that bargain at that price we'd hardly make a dime. Tell 'em it's jus' sold. Take out that yard battery before you make delivery. Put in that dumb cell. Christ, what they want for six bits? Roll up your sleeves—pitch in. This ain't gonna last. If I had enough jalopies I'd retire in six months.

Listen, Jim, I heard that Chevvy's rear end. Sounds like bustin' bottles. Squirt in a couple quarts of sawdust. Put some in the gears, too. We got to move that lemon for thirty-five dollars. Bastard cheated me on that one. I offer ten an' he jerks me to fifteen, an' then the son-of-a-bitch took the tools out. God Almighty! I wisht I had five hundred jalopies. This ain't gonna last. He don't like the tires? Tell 'im they got ten thousand in 'em, knock off a buck an' a half.

Piles of rusty ruins against the fence, rows of wrecks in back, fenders, grease-black wrecks, blocks lying on the ground and a pig weed growing up through the cylinders. Brake rods, exhausts, piled like snakes. Grease, gasoline.

See if you can't find a spark plug that ain't cracked. Christ, if I had fifty trailers at under a hundred I'd clean up. What the hell is he kickin' about? We sell 'em, but we don't push 'em home for him. That's good! Don't push 'em home. Get that one in the Monthly, I bet. You don't think he's a prospect? Well, kick 'im out. We got too much to do to bother with a guy that can't make up his mind. Take the right front tire off the Graham. Turn that mended side down. The rest looks swell. Got tread an' everything.

Sure! There's fifty thousan' in that ol' heap yet. Keep plenty oil in. So long. Good luck.

Lookin' for a car? What did you have in mind? See anything attracts you? I'm dry. How about a little snort a good stuff? Come on, while your wife's lookin' at that La Salle. You don't want no La Salle. Bearings shot.

Uses too much oil. Got a Lincoln '24. There's a car. Run forever. Make her into a truck.

Hot sun on rusted metal. Oil on the ground. People are wandering in, bewildered, needing a car.

Wipe your feet. Don't lean on that car, it's dirty. How do you buy a car? What does it cost? Watch the children, now. I wonder how much for this one? We'll ask. It don't cost money to ask. We can ask, can't we? Can't pay a nickel over seventy-five, or there won't be enough to get to California.

God, if I could get a hundred jalopies. I don't care if they run or not.

Tires, used, bruised tires, stacked in tall cylinders; tubes, red, gray, hanging like sausages.

Tire patch? Radiator cleaner? Spark intensifier? Drop this little pill in your gas tank and get ten extra miles to the gallon. Just paint it on—you got a new surface for fifty cents. Wipers, fan belts, gaskets? Maybe it's the valve. Get a new valve stem. What can you lose for a nickel?

All right, Joe. You soften 'em up an' shoot 'em in here. I'll close 'em, I'll deal 'em or I'll kill 'em. Don't send in no bums. I want deals.

Yes, sir, step in. You got a buy there. Yes, sir! At eighty bucks you got a buy.

I can't go no higher than fifty. The fella outside says fifty.

Fifty. Fifty? He's nuts. Paid seventy-eight fifty for that little number. Joe, you crazy fool, you tryin' to bust us? Have to can that guy. I might take sixty. Now look here, mister, I ain't got all day. I'm a business man but I ain't out to stick nobody. Got anything to trade?

Got a pair of mules I'll trade.

Mules! Hey, Joe, hear this? This guy wants to trade mules. Didn't nobody tell you this is the machine age? They don't use mules for nothing but glue no more.

Fine big mules—five and seven years old. Maybe we better look around.

Look around! You come in when we're busy, an' take up our time an' then walk out! Joe, did you know you was talkin' to pikers?

I ain't a piker. I got to get a car. We're goin' to California. I got to get a car.

Well, I'm a sucker. Joe says I'm a sucker. Says if I don't quit givin' my shirt away I'll starve to death. Tell you what I'll do—I can get five bucks apiece for them mules for dog feed.

I wouldn't want them to go for dog feed.

Well, maybe I can get ten or seven maybe. Tell you what we'll do. We'll take your mules for twenty. Wagon goes with 'em, don't it? An' you put up fifty, an' you can sign a contract to send the rest at ten dollars a month.

But you said eighty.

Didn't you never hear about carrying charges and insurance? That just boosts her a little. You'll get her all paid up in four-five months. Sign your name right here. We'll take care of ever'thing.

Well, I don't know——

Now, look here. I'm givin' you my shirt, an' you took all this time. I might a made three sales while I been talkin' to you. I'm disgusted. Yeah, sign right there. All right, sir. Joe, fill up the tank for this gentleman. We'll give him gas.

Jesus, Joe, that was a hot one! What'd we give for that jalopy? Thirty bucks—thirty-five wasn't it? I got that team, an' if I can't get seventy-five for that team, I ain't a business man. An' I got fifty cash an' a contract for forty more. Oh, I know they're not all honest, but it'll surprise you how many kick through with the rest. One guy come through with a hundred two years after I wrote him off. I bet you this guy sends the money. Christ, if I could only get five hundred jalopies! Roll up your sleeves, Joe. Go out an' soften 'em, an' send 'em in to me. You get twenty on that last deal. You ain't doing bad.

Limp flags in the afternoon sun. Today's Bargain. '29 Ford pickup, runs good.

What do you want for fifty bucks—a Zephyr?

Horsehair curling out of seat cushions, fenders battered and hammered back. Bumpers torn loose and hanging. Fancy Ford roadster with little colored lights at fender guide, at radiator cap, and three behind. Mud aprons, and a big die on the gear-shift lever. Pretty girl on tire cover, painted in color and named Cora. Afternoon sun on the dusty windshields.

Christ, I ain't had time to go out an' eat! Joe, send a kid for a hamburger.

Spattering roar of ancient engines.

There's a dumb-bunny lookin' at that Chrysler. Find out if he got any jack in his jeans. Some a these farm boys is sneaky. Soften 'em up an' roll 'em in to me, Joe. You're doin' good.

Sure, we sold it. Guarantee? We guaranteed it to be an automobile. We didn't guarantee to wet-nurse it. Now listen here, you—you bought a car, an' now you're squawkin'. I don't give a damn if you don't make payments. We ain't got your paper. We turn that over to the finance company. They'll get after you, not us. We don't hold no paper. Yeah? Well you jus' get tough an' I'll call a cop. No, we did not switch the tires. Run 'im outa here, Joe. He bought a car, an' now he ain't satisfied. How'd you think if I bought a steak an' et half an' try to bring it back? We're runnin' a business, not a charity ward. Can ya imagine that guy, Joe? Say—looka there! Got a Elk's tooth! Run over there. Let 'em glance over that '36 Pontiac. Yeah.

Square noses, round noses, rusty noses, shovel noses, and the long curves of streamlines, and the flat surfaces before streamlining. Bargains Today. Old monsters with deep upholstery—you can cut her into a truck easy. Two-wheel trailers, axles rusty in the hard afternoon sun. Used Cars. Good Used Cars. Clean, runs good. Don't pump oil.

Christ, look at 'er! Somebody took nice care of 'er.

Cadillacs, La Salles, Buicks, Plymouths, Packards, Chevvies, Fords, Pontiacs. Row on row, headlights glinting in the afternoon sun. Good Used Cars.

Soften 'em up, Joe. Jesus, I wisht I had a thousand jalopies! Get 'em ready to deal, an' I'll close 'em.

Goin' to California? Here's jus' what you need. Looks shot, but they's thousan's of miles in her.

Lined up side by side. Good Used Cars. Bargains. Clean, runs good.

8

The sky grayed among the stars, and the pale, late quarter-moon was insubstantial and thin. Tom Joad and the preacher walked quickly along a road that was only wheel tracks and beaten caterpillar tracks through a cotton field. Only the unbalanced sky showed the approach of dawn, no horizon to the west, and a line to the east. The two men walked in silence and smelled the dust their feet kicked into the air.

"I hope you're dead sure of the way," Jim Casy said. "I'd hate to have the dawn come and us be way to hell an' gone somewhere." The cotton field scurried with waking life, the quick flutter of morning birds feeding on the ground, the scamper over the clods of disturbed rabbits. The quiet thudding of the men's feet in the dust, the squeak of crushed clods under their shoes, sounded against the secret noises of the dawn.

Tom said, "I could shut my eyes an' walk right there. On'y way I can go wrong is think about her. Jus' forget about her, an' I'll go right there. Hell, man, I was born right aroun' in here. I run aroun' here when I was a kid. They's a tree over there—look, you can jus' make it out. Well, once my old man hung up a dead coyote in that tree. Hung there till it was all sort of melted, an' then dropped off. Dried up, like. Jesus, I hope Ma's cookin' somepin. My belly's caved."

"Me too," said Casy. "Like a little eatin' tobacca? Keeps ya from gettin' too hungry. Been better if we didn' start so damn early. Better if it was light." He paused to gnaw off a piece of plug. "I was sleepin' nice."

"That crazy Muley done it," said Tom. "He got me clear jumpy. Wakes me up an' says, ' 'By, Tom. I'm goin' on. I got places to go.' An' he says, 'Better get goin' too, so's you'll be offa this lan' when the light comes.' He's gettin' screwy as a gopher, livin' like he does. You'd think Injuns was after him. Think he's nuts?"

"Well, I dunno. You seen that car come las' night when we had a little fire. You seen how the house was smashed. They's somepin purty mean goin' on. 'Course Muley's crazy, all right. Creepin' aroun' like a coyote; that's boun' to make him crazy. He'll kill somebody purty soon an' they'll run him down with the dogs. I can see it like a prophecy. He'll get worse an' worse. Wouldn' come along with us, you say?"

"No," said Joad. "I think he's scared to see people now. Wonder he come up to us. We'll be at Uncle John's place by sunrise." They walked along in silence for a time, and the late owls flew over toward the barns, the hollow trees, the tank houses, where they hid from daylight. The eastern sky grew fairer and it was possible to see the cotton plants and the graying earth. "Damn' if I know how they're all sleepin' at Uncle John's. He on'y got one room an' a cookin' leanto, an' a little bit of a barn. Must be a mob there now."

The preacher said, "I don't recollect that John had a fambly. Just a lone man, ain't he? I don't recollect much about him."

"Lonest goddamn man in the world," said Joad. "Crazy kind of son-of-a-bitch, too—somepin like

Muley, on'y worse in some ways. Might see 'im anywheres—at Shawnee, drunk, or visitin' a widow
twenty miles away, or workin' his place with a lantern.
Crazy. Ever'body thought he wouldn't live long. A lone
man like that don't live long. But Uncle John's older'n
Pa. Jus' gets stringier an' meaner ever' year. Meaner'n
Grampa."

"Look a the light comin'," said the preacher. "Sil-
very-like. Didn' John never have no fambly?"

"Well, yes, he did, an' that'll show you the kind a
fella he is—set in his ways. Pa tells about it. Uncle
John, he had a young wife. Married four months. She
was in a family way, too, an' one night she gets a pain
in her stomick, an' she says, 'You better go for a
doctor.' Well, John, he's settin' there, an' he says,
'You just got a stomickache. You et too much. Take a
dose a pain killer. You crowd up ya stomick an' ya get
a stomickache,' he says. Nex' noon she's outa her
head, an' she dies at about four in the afternoon."

"What was it?" Casy asked. "Poisoned from somepin she et?"

"No, somepin jus' bust in her. Ap—appendick or
somepin. Well, Uncle John, he's always been a easy-
goin' fella, an' he takes it hard. Takes it for a sin. For
a long time he won't have nothin' to say to nobody.
Just walks aroun' like he don't see nothin', an' he
prays some. Took 'im two years to come out of it, an'
then he ain't the same. Sort of wild. Made a damn
nuisance of hisself. Ever'time one of us kids got worms
or a gutache Uncle John brings a doctor out. Pa finally
tol' him he got to stop. Kids all the time gettin' a
gutache. He figures it's his fault his woman died.
Funny fella. He's all the time makin' it up to somebody—givin' kids stuff, droppin' a sack a meal on
somebody's porch. Give away about ever'thing he got,
an' still he ain't very happy. Gets walkin' around alone
at night sometimes. He's a good farmer, though. Keeps
his lan' nice."

"Poor fella," said the preacher. "Poor lonely fella. Did he go to church much when his woman died?"

"No, he didn'. Never wanted to get close to folks. Wanted to be off alone. I never seen a kid that wasn't crazy about him. He'd come to our house in the night sometimes, an' we knowed he come 'cause jus' as sure as he come there'd be a pack a gum in the bed right beside ever' one of us. We thought he was Jesus Christ Awmighty."

The preacher walked along, head down. He didn't answer. And the light of the coming morning made his forehead seem to shine, and his hands, swinging beside him, flicked into the light and out again.

Tom was silent too, as though he had said too intimate a thing and was ashamed. He quickened his pace and the preacher kept step. They could see a little into gray distance ahead now. A snake wriggled slowly from the cotton rows into the road. Tom stopped short of it and peered. "Gopher snake," he said. "Let him go." They walked around the snake and went on their way. A little color came into the eastern sky, and almost immediately the lonely dawn light crept over the land. Green appeared on the cotton plants and the earth was gray-brown. The faces of the men lost their grayish shine. Joad's face seemed to darken with the growing light. "This is the good time," Joad said softly. "When I was a kid I used to get up an' walk around by myself when it was like this. What's that ahead?"

A committee of dogs had met in the road, in honor of a bitch. Five males, shepherd mongrels, collie mongrels, dogs whose breeds had been blurred by a freedom of social life, were engaged in complimenting the bitch. For each dog sniffed daintily and then stalked to a cotton plant on stiff legs, raised a hind foot ceremoniously and wetted, then went back to smell. Joad and the preacher stopped to watch, and suddenly Joad laughed joyously. "By God!" he said. "By God!" Now all dogs met and hackles rose, and they stood stiffly,

each waiting for the others to start a fight. One dog
mounted and, now that it was accomplished, the others
gave way and watched with interest, and their tongues
were out, and their tongues dripped. The two men
walked on. "By God!" Joad said. "I think that up-dog
is our Flash. I thought he'd be dead. Come, Flash!"
He laughed again. "What the hell, if somebody called
me, I wouldn't hear him neither. 'Minds me of a story
they tell about Willy Feeley when he was a young
fella. Willy was bashful, awful bashful. Well, one day
he takes a heifer over to Graves' bull. Ever'body was
out but Elsie Graves, and Elsie wasn't bashful at all.
Willy, he stood there turnin' red an' he couldn't even
talk. Elsie says, 'I know what you come for; the bull's
out in back a the barn.' Well, they took the heifer out
there an' Willy an' Elsie sat on the fence to watch.
Purty soon Willy got feelin' purty fly. Elsie looks over
an' says, like she don't know, 'What's a matter,
Willy?' Willy's so randy he can't hardly set still. 'By
God,' he says, 'by God, I wisht I was a-doin' that!'
Elsie says, 'Why not, Willy? It's your heifer.' "

The preacher laughed softly. "You know," he said,
"it's a nice thing not bein' a preacher no more. Nobody
use' ta tell stories when I was there, or if they did I
couldn' laugh. An' I couldn' cuss. Now I cuss all I
want, any time I want, an' it does a fella good to cuss
if he wants to."

A redness grew up out of the eastern horizon, and
on the ground birds began to chirp, sharply. "Look!"
said Joad. "Right ahead. That's Uncle John's tank.
Can't see the win'mill, but there's his tank. See it
against the sky?" He speeded his walk. "I wonder if
all the folks are there." The hulk of the tank stood
above a rise. Joad, hurrying, raised a cloud of dust
about his knees. "I wonder if Ma——" They saw the
tank legs now, and the house, a square little box,
unpainted and bare, and the barn, low-roofed and
huddled. Smoke was rising from the tin chimney of the

house. In the yard was a litter, piled furniture, the blades and motor of the windmill, bedsteads, chairs, tables. "Holy Christ, they're fixin' to go!" Joad said. A truck stood in the yard, a truck with high sides, but a strange truck, for while the front of it was a sedan, the top had been cut off in the middle and the truck bed fitted on. And as they drew near, the men could hear pounding from the yard, and as the rim of the blinding sun came up over the horizon, it fell on the truck, and they saw a man and the flash of his hammer as it rose and fell. And the sun flashed on the windows of the house. The weathered boards were bright. Two red chickens on the ground flamed with reflected light.

"Don't yell," said Tom. "Let's creep up on 'em, like," and he walked so fast that the dust rose as high as his waist. And then he came to the edge of the cotton field. Now they were in the yard proper, earth beaten hard, shiny hard, and a few dusty crawling weeds on the ground. And Joad slowed as though he feared to go on. The preacher, watching him, slowed to match his step. Tom sauntered forward, sidled embarrassedly toward the truck. It was a Hudson Super-Six sedan, and the top had been ripped in two with a cold chisel. Old Tom Joad stood in the truck bed and he was nailing on the top rails of the truck sides. His grizzled, bearded face was low over his work, and a bunch of six-penny nails stuck out of his mouth. He set a nail and his hammer thundered it in. From the house came the clash of a lid on the stove and the wail of a child. Joad sidled up to the truck bed and leaned against it. And his father looked at him and did not see him. His father set another nail and drove it in. A flock of pigeons started from the deck of the tank house and flew around and settled again and strutted to the edge to look over; white pigeons and blue pigeons and grays, with iridescent wings.

Joad hooked his fingers over the lowest bar of the truck side. He looked up at the aging, graying man on the truck. He wet his thick lips with his tongue, and he said softly, "Pa."

"What do you want?" old Tom mumbled around his mouthful of nails. He wore a black, dirty slouch hat and a blue work shirt over which was a buttonless vest; his jeans were held up by a wide harness-leather belt with a big square brass buckle, leather and metal polished from years of wearing; and his shoes were cracked and the soles swollen and boat-shaped from years of sun and wet and dust. The sleeves of his shirt were tight on his forearms, held down by the bulging powerful muscles. Stomach and hips were lean, and legs, short, heavy, and strong. His face, squared by a bristling pepper and salt beard, was all drawn down to the forceful chin, a chin thrust out and built out by the stubble beard which was not so grayed on the chin, and gave weight and force to its thrust. Over old Tom's unwhiskered cheek bones the skin was as brown as meerschaum, and wrinkled in rays around his eye-corners from squinting. His eyes were brown, black-coffee brown, and he thrust his head forward when he looked at a thing, for his bright dark eyes were failing. His lips, from which the big nails protruded, were thin and red.

He held his hammer suspended in the air, about to drive a set nail, and he looked over the truck side at Tom, looked resentful at being interrupted. And then his chin drove forward and his eyes looked at Tom's face, and then gradually his brain became aware of what he saw. The hammer dropped slowly to his side, and with his left hand he took the nails from his mouth. And he said wonderingly, as though he told himself the fact, "It's Tommy——" And then, still informing himself, "It's Tommy come home." His mouth opened again, and a look of fear came into his eyes. "Tommy," he said softly, "you ain't busted out? You ain't got to hide?" He listened tensely.

"Naw," said Tom. "I'm paroled. I'm free. I got my

papers." He gripped the lower bars of the truck side
and looked up.

Old Tom laid his hammer gently on the floor and
put his nails in his pocket. He swung his leg over the
side and dropped lithely to the ground, but once beside his son he seemed embarrassed and strange.
"Tommy," he said, "we are goin' to California. But we
was gonna write you a letter an' tell you." And he
said, incredulously, "But you're back. You can go
with us. You can go!" The lid of a coffee pot slammed
in the house. Old Tom looked over his shoulder. "Le's
supprise 'em," he said, and his eyes shone with excitement. "Your ma got a bad feelin' she ain't never
gonna see you no more. She got that quiet look like
when somebody died. Almost she don't want to go to
California, fear she'll never see you no more." A stove
lid clashed in the house again. "Le's supprise 'em,"
old Tom repeated. "Le's go in like you never been
away. Le's jus' see what your ma says." At last he
touched Tom, but touched him on the shoulder, timidly, and instantly took his hand away. He looked at
Jim Casy.

Tom said, "You remember the preacher, Pa. He
come along with me."

"He been in prison too?"

"No, I met 'im on the road. He been away."

Pa shook hands gravely. "You're welcome here,
sir."

Casy said, "Glad to be here. It's a thing to see when
a boy comes home. It's a thing to see."

"Home," Pa said.

"To his folks," the preacher amended quickly. "We
stayed at the other place last night."

Pa's chin thrust out, and he looked back down the
road for a moment. Then he turned to Tom. "How'll we
do her?" he began excitedly. "S'pose I go in an' say,
'Here's some fellas want some breakfast,' or how'd it

be if you jus' come in an' stood there till she seen you?
How'd that be?" His face was alive with excitement.

"Don't le's give her no shock," said Tom. "Don't
le's scare her none."

Two rangy shepherd dogs trotted up pleasantly, until they caught the scent of strangers, and then they
backed cautiously away, watchful, their tails moving
slowly and tentatively in the air, but their eyes and
noses quick for animosity or danger. One of them,
stretching his neck, edged forward, ready to run, and
little by little he approached Tom's legs and sniffed
loudly at them. Then he backed away and watched Pa
for some kind of signal. The other pup was not so
brave. He looked about for something that could honor-
ably divert his attention, saw a red chicken go mincing
by, and ran at it. There was the squawk of an outraged
hen, a burst of red feathers, and the hen ran off,
flapping stubby wings for speed. The pup looked
proudly back at the men, and then flopped down in the
dust and beat its tail contentedly on the ground.

"Come on," said Pa, "come on in now. She got to
see you. I got to see her face when she sees you. Come
on. She'll yell breakfast in a minute. I heard her slap
the salt pork in the pan a good time ago." He led the
way across the fine-dusted ground. There was no porch
on this house, just a step and then the door; a chopping block beside the door, its surface matted and soft
from years of chopping. The graining in the sheathing
wood was high, for the dust had cut down the softer
wood. The smell of burning willow was in the air, and,
as the three men neared the door, the smell of frying
side-meat and the smell of high brown biscuits and the
sharp smell of coffee rolling in the pot. Pa stepped up
into the open doorway and stood there blocking it with
his wide short body. He said, "Ma, there's a coupla
fellas jus' come along the road, an' they wonder if we
could spare a bite."

Tom heard his mother's voice, the remembered

cool, calm drawl, friendly and humble. "Let 'em come," she said. "We got a'plenty. Tell 'em they got to wash their han's. The bread is done. I'm jus' takin' up the side-meat now." And the sizzle of the angry grease came from the stove.

Pa stepped inside, clearing the door, and Tom looked in at his mother. She was lifting the curling slices of pork from the frying pan. The oven door was open, and a great pan of high brown biscuits stood waiting there. She looked out the door, but she saw only a dark figure outlined by the bright yellow sunlight. She nodded pleasantly. "Come in," she said. "Jus' lucky I made plenty bread this morning."

Tom stood looking in. Ma was heavy, but not fat; thick with child-bearing and work. She wore a loose Mother Hubbard of gray cloth in which there had once been colored flowers, but the color was washed out now, so that the small flowered pattern was only a little lighter gray than the background. The dress came down to her ankles, and her strong, broad, bare feet moved quickly and deftly over the floor. Her thin, steel-gray hair was gathered in a sparse wispy knot at the back of her head. Strong, freckled arms were bare to the elbow, and her hands were chubby and delicate, like those of a plump little girl. She looked out into the sunshine. Her full face was not soft; it was controlled, kindly. Her hazel eyes seemed to have experienced all possible tragedy and to have mounted pain and suffering like steps into a high calm and a superhuman understanding. She seemed to know, to accept, to welcome her position, the citadel of the family, the strong place that could not be taken. And since old Tom and the children could not know hurt or fear unless she acknowledged hurt and fear, she had practiced denying them in herself. And since, when a joyful thing happened, they looked to see whether joy was on her, it was her habit to build up laughter out of inadequate materials. But better than joy was calm. Imperturbability could be depended upon. And from her great and humble position in the family she had taken dignity and a clean calm beauty. From her position as healer, her hands had grown sure and cool and quiet; from her position as arbiter she had become as remote and faultless in judgment as a goddess. She seemed to know that if she swayed the family shook, and if she ever really deeply wavered or despaired the family would fall, the family will to function would be gone.

She looked out into the sunny yard, at the dark figure of a man. Pa stood near by, shaking with excitement. "Come in," he cried. "Come right in, mister." And Tom a little shamefacedly stepped over the doorsill.

She looked up pleasantly from the frying pan. And then her hand sank slowly to her side and the fork clattered to the wooden floor. Her eyes opened wide, and the pupils dilated. She breathed heavily through her open mouth. She closed her eyes. "Thank God," she said. "Oh, thank God!" And suddenly her face was worried. "Tommy, you ain't wanted? You didn' bust loose?"

"No, Ma. Parole. I got the papers here." He touched his breast.

She moved toward him lithely, soundlessly in her bare feet, and her face was full of wonder. Her small hand felt his arm, felt the soundness of his muscles. And then her fingers went up to his cheek as a blind man's fingers might. And her joy was nearly like sorrow. Tom pulled his underlip between his teeth and bit it. Her eyes went wonderingly to his bitten lip, and she saw the little line of blood against his teeth and the trickle of blood down his lip. Then she knew, and her control came back, and her hand dropped. Her breath came out explosively. "Well!" she cried. "We come mighty near to goin' without ya. An' we was wonderin' how in the worl' you could ever find us." She picked up the fork and combed the boiling grease and brought out a dark curl of crisp pork. And she set the pot of tumbling coffee on the back of the stove.

Old Tom giggled, "Fooled ya, huh, Ma? We aimed to fool ya, and we done it. Jus' stood there like a hammered sheep. Wisht Grampa'd been here to see. Looked like somebody'd beat ya between the eyes with a sledge. Grampa would a whacked 'imself so hard he'd a throwed his hip out—like he done when he seen Al take a shot at that grea' big airship the army got. Tommy, it come over one day, a half a mile big, an' Al get the thirty-thirty and blazes away at her. Grampa yells, 'Don't shoot no fledglin's, Al; wait till a growed-up one goes over,' an' then he whacked 'imself an' throwed his hip out."

Ma chuckled and took down a heap of tin plates from a shelf.

Tom asked, "Where is Grampa? I ain't seen the ol' devil."

Ma stacked the plates on the kitchen table and piled cups beside them. She said confidentially, "Oh, him an' Granma sleeps in the barn. They got to get up so much in the night. They was stumblin' over the little fellas."

Pa broke in, "Yeah, ever' night Grampa'd get mad. Tumble over Winfield, an' Winfield'd yell, an' Grampa'd get mad an' wet his drawers, an' that'd make him madder, an' purty soon ever'body in the house'd be yellin' their head off." His words tumbled out between chuckles. "Oh, we had lively times. One night when ever'body was yellin' an' a-cussin', your brother Al, he's a smart aleck now, he says, 'Goddamn it, Grampa, why don't you run off an' be a pirate?' Well, that made Grampa so goddamn mad he went for his gun. Al had ta sleep out in the fiel' that night. But now Granma an' Grampa both sleeps in the barn."

Ma said, "They can jus' get up an' step outside when they feel like it. Pa, run on out an' tell 'em Tommy's home. Grampa's a favorite of him."

"A course," said Pa. "I should of did it before." He went out the door and crossed the yard, swinging his hands high.

Tom watched him go, and then his mother's voice called his attention. She was pouring coffee. She did not look at him. "Tommy," she said hesitantly, timidly.

"Yeah?" His timidity was set off by hers, a curious embarrassment. Each one knew the other was shy, and became more shy in the knowledge.

"Tommy, I got to ask you—you ain't mad?"

"Mad, Ma?"

"You ain't poisoned mad? You don't hate nobody? They didn' do nothin' in that jail to rot you out with crazy mad?"

He looked sidewise at her, studied her, and his eyes seemed to ask how she could know such things. "No-o-o," he said. "I was for a little while. But I ain't proud like some fellas. I let the stuff run off'n me. What's a matter, Ma?"

Now she was looking at him, her mouth open, as though to hear better, her eyes digging to know better. Her face looked for the answer that is always concealed in language. She said in confusion, "I knowed Purty Boy Floyd. I knowed his ma. They was good folks. He was full a hell, sure, like a good boy oughta be." She paused and then her words poured out. "I don' know all like this—but I know it. He done a little bad thing an' they hurt 'im, caught 'im an' hurt him so he was mad, an' the nex' bad thing he done was mad, an' they hurt 'im again. An' purty soon he was mean-mad. They shot at him like a varmint, an' he shot back, an' then they run him like a coyote, an' his a-snappin' an' a-snarlin', mean as a lobo. An' he was mad. He wasn't no boy or no man no more, he was jus' a walkin' chunk a mean-mad. But the folks that knowed him didn' hurt 'im. He wasn' mad at them. Finally they run him down an' killed 'im. No matter how they say it in the paper how he was bad—that's how it was." She paused and she licked her dry lips, and her whole face was an aching question. "I got to know, Tommy. Did they hurt you so much? Did they make you mad like that?"

Tom's heavy lips were pulled tight over his teeth. He looked down at his big flat hands. "No," he said. "I ain't like that." He paused and studied the broken nails, which were ridged like clam shells. "All the time in stir I kep' away from stuff like that. I ain' so mad."

She sighed, "Thank God!" under her breath.

He looked up quickly. "Ma, when I seen what they done to our house——"

She came near to him then, and stood close; and she said passionately, "Tommy, don't you go fightin' 'em alone. They'll hunt you down like a coyote. Tommy, I got to thinkin' an' dreamin' an' wonderin'. They say there's a hun'erd thousand of us shoved out. If we was all mad the same way, Tommy—they wouldn't hunt nobody down——" She stopped.

Tommy, looking at her, gradually drooped his eyelids, until just a short glitter showed through his lashes. "Many folks feel that way?" he demanded.

"I don' know. They're jus' kinda stunned. Walk aroun' like they was half asleep."

From outside and across the yard came an ancient creaking bleat. "Pu-raise Gawd fur vittory! Pu-raise Gawd fur vittory!"

Tom turned his head and grinned. "Granma finally heard I'm home. Ma," he said, "you never was like this before!"

Her face hardened and her eyes grew cold. "I never had my house pushed over," she said. "I never had my fambly stuck out on the road. I never had to sell—ever'thing—Here they come now." She moved back to the stove and dumped the big pan of bulbous biscuits on two tin plates. She shook flour into the deep grease to make gravy, and her hand was white with flour. For a moment Tom watched her, and then he went to the door.

Across the yard came four people. Grampa was ahead, a lean, ragged, quick old man, jumping with quick steps and favoring his right leg—the side that came out of joint. He was buttoning his fly as he came, and his old hands were having trouble finding the buttons, for he had buttoned the top button into the second buttonhole, and that threw the whole sequence off. He wore dark ragged pants and a torn blue shirt, open all the way down, and showing long gray underwear, also unbuttoned. His lean white chest, fuzzed with white hair, was visible through the opening in his underwear. He gave up the fly and left it open and fumbled with the underwear buttons, then gave the whole thing up and hitched his brown suspenders. His was a lean excitable face with little bright eyes as evil as a frantic child's eyes. A cantankerous, complaining, mischievous, laughing face. He fought and argued, told dirty stories. He was as lecherous as always. Vicious and cruel and impatient, like a frantic child, and the whole structure overlaid with amusement. He drank too much when he could get it, ate too much when it was there, talked too much all the time.

Behind him gobbled Granma, who had survived only because she was as mean as her husband. She had held her own with a shrill ferocious religiosity that was as lecherous and as savage as anything Grampa could offer. Once, after a meeting, while she was still speaking tongues, she fired both barrels of a shotgun at her husband, ripping one of his buttocks nearly off, and after that he admired her and did not try to torture her as children torture bugs. As she walked she hiked her Mother Hubbard up to her knees, and she bleated her shrill terrible war cry: "Pu-raise Gawd fur vittory."

Granma and Grampa raced each other to get across the broad yard. They fought over everything, and loved and needed the fighting.

Behind them, moving slowly and evenly, but keeping up, came Pa and Noah—Noah the first-born, tall and strange, walking always with a wondering look on his face, calm and puzzled. He had never been angry in his life. He looked in wonder at angry people, wonder and uneasiness, as normal people look at the insane. Noah moved slowly, spoke seldom, and then so slowly that people who did not know him often thought him stupid. He was not stupid, but he was strange. He had little pride, no sexual urges. He worked and slept in a curious rhythm that nevertheless sufficed him. He was fond of his folks, but never showed it in any way. Although an observer could not have told why, Noah left the impression of being misshapen, his head or his body or his legs or his mind; but no misshapen member could be recalled. Pa thought he knew why Noah was strange, but Pa was ashamed, and never told. For on the night when Noah was born, Pa, frightened at the spreading thighs, alone in the house, and horrified at the screaming wretch his wife had become, went mad with apprehension. Using his hands, his strong fingers for forceps, he had pulled and twisted the baby. The midwife, arriving late, had found the baby's head pulled out of shape, its neck stretched, its body warped; and she had pushed the head back and molded the body with her hands. But Pa always remembered, and was ashamed. And he was kinder to Noah than to the others. In Noah's broad face, eyes too far apart, and long fragile jaw, Pa thought he saw the twisted, warped skull of the baby. Noah could do all that was required of him, could read and write, could work and figure, but he didn't seem to care; there was a listlessness in him toward things people wanted and needed. He lived in a strange silent house and looked out of it through calm eyes. He was a stranger to all the world, but he was not lonely.

The four came across the yard, and Grampa demanded, "Where is he? Goddamn it, where is he?"

And his fingers fumbled for his pants button, and forgot and strayed into his pocket. And then he saw Tom standing in the door. Grampa stopped and he stopped the others. His little eyes glittered with malice. "Lookut him," he said. "A jailbird. Ain't been no Joads in jail for a hell of a time." His mind jumped. "Got no right to put 'im in jail. He done just what I'd do. Sons-a-bitches got no right." His mind jumped again. "An' ol' Turnbull, stinkin' skunk, braggin' how he'll shoot ya when ya come out. Says he got Hatfield blood. Well, I sent word to him. I says, 'Don't mess around with no Joad. Maybe I got McCoy blood for all I know.' I says, 'You lay your sights anywheres near Tommy an' I'll take it an' I'll ram it up your ass,' I says. Scairt 'im, too."

Granma, not following the conversation, bleated, "Pu-raise Gawd for vittory."

Grampa walked up and slapped Tom on the chest, and his eyes grinned with affection and pride. "How are ya, Tommy?"

"O.K." said Tom. "How ya keepin' yaself?"

"Full a piss an' vinegar," said Grampa. His mind jumped. "Jus' like I said, they ain't a gonna keep no Joad in jail. I says, 'Tommy'll come a-bustin' outa that jail like a bull through a corral fence.' An' you done it. Get outa my way, I'm hungry." He crowded past, sat down, loaded his plate with pork and two big biscuits and poured the thick gravy over the whole mess, and before the others could get in, Grampa's mouth was full.

Tom grinned affectionately at him. "Ain't he a heller?" he said. And Grampa's mouth was so full that he couldn't even splutter, but his mean little eyes smiled, and he nodded his head violently.

Granma said proudly, "A wicketer, cussin'er man never lived. He's goin' to hell on a poker, praise Gawd! Wants to drive the truck!" she said spitefully. "Well, he ain't goin' ta."

Grampa choked, and a mouthful of paste sprayed into his lap, and he coughed weakly.

Granma smiled up at Tom. "Messy, ain't he?" she observed brightly.

Noah stood on the step, and he faced Tom, and his wide-set eyes seemed to look around him. His face had little expression. Tom said, "How ya, Noah?"

"Fine," said Noah. "How a' you?" That was all, but it was a comfortable thing.

Ma waved the flies away from the bowl of gravy. "We ain't got room to set down," she said. "Jus' get yaself a plate an' set down wherever ya can. Out in the yard or someplace."

Suddenly Tom said, "Hey! Where's the preacher? He was right here. Where'd he go?"

Pa said, "I seen him, but he's gone."

And Granma raised a shrill voice, "Preacher? You got a preacher? Go get him. We'll have a grace." She pointed at Grampa. "Too late for him—he's et. Go git the preacher."

Tom stepped out on the porch. "Hey, Jim! Jim Casy!" he called. He walked out in the yard. "Oh, Casy!" The preacher emerged from under the tank, sat up, and then stood up and moved toward the house. Tom asked, "What was you doin', hidin'?"

"Well, no. But a fella shouldn' butt his head in where a fambly got fambly stuff. I was jus' settin' a-thinkin'."

"Come on in an' eat," said Tom. "Granma wants a grace."

"But I ain't a preacher no more," Casy protested.

"Aw, come on. Give her a grace. Don't do you no harm, an' she likes 'em." They walked into the kitchen together.

Ma said quietly, "You're welcome."

And Pa said, "You're welcome. Have some breakfast."

"Grace fust," Granma clamored. "Grace fust."

Grampa focused his eyes fiercely until he recognized Casy. "Oh, that preacher," he said. "Oh, he's all right. I always liked him since I seen him—" He winked so lecherously that Granma thought he had spoken and retorted, "Shut up, you sinful ol' goat."

Casy ran his fingers through his hair nervously. "I got to tell you, I ain't no preacher no more. If me jus' bein' glad to be here an' bein' thankful for people that's kind and generous, if that's enough—why, I'll say that kinda grace. But I ain't a preacher no more."

"Say her," said Granma. "An' get in a word about us goin' to California." The preacher bowed his head, and the others bowed their heads. Ma folded her hands over her stomach and bowed her head. Granma bowed so low that her nose was nearly in her plate of biscuit and gravy. Tom, leaning against the wall, a plate in his hand, bowed stiffly, and Grampa bowed his head sidewise, so that he could keep one mean and merry eye on the preacher. And on the preacher's face there was a look not of prayer, but of thought; and in his tone not supplication, but conjecture.

"I been thinkin'," he said. "I been in the hills, thinkin' almost you might say like Jesus went into the wilderness to think His way out of a mess of troubles."

"Pu-raise Gawd!" Granma said, and the preacher glanced over at her in surprise.

"Seems like Jesus got all messed up with troubles, and He couldn't figure nothin' out, an' He got to feelin' what the hell good is it all, an' what's the use fightin' an' figurin'. Got tired, got good an' tired, an' His sperit all wore out. Jus' about come to the conclusion, the hell with it. An' so He went off into the wilderness."

"A—men," Granma bleated. So many years she had timed her responses to the pauses. And it was so many years since she had listened to or wondered at the words used.

"I ain't sayin' I'm like Jesus," the preacher went on.

"But I got tired like Him, an' I got mixed up like Him, an' I went into the wilderness like Him, without no campin' stuff. Nighttime I'd lay on my back an' look up at the stars; morning I'd set an' watch the sun come up; midday I'd look out from a hill at the rollin' dry country; evenin' I'd foller the sun down. Sometimes I'd pray like I always done. On'y I couldn' figure what I was prayin' to or for. There was the hills, an' there was me, an' we wasn't separate no more. We was one thing. An' that one thing was holy."

"Hallelujah," said Granma, and she rocked a little, back and forth, trying to catch hold of an ecstasy.

"An' I got thinkin', on'y it wasn't thinkin', it was deeper down than thinkin'. I got thinkin' how we was holy when we was one thing, an' mankin' was holy when it was one thing. An' it on'y got unholy when one mis'able little fella got the bit in his teeth an' run off his own way, kickin' an draggin' an' fightin'. Fella like that bust the holiness. But when they're all workin' together, not one fella for another fella, but one fella kind of harnessed to the whole shebang—that's right, that's holy. An' then I got thinkin' I don't even know what I mean by holy." He paused, but the bowed heads stayed down, for they had been trained like dogs to rise at the "amen" signal. "I can't say no grace like I use' ta say. I'm glad of the holiness of breakfast. I'm glad there's love here. That's all." The heads stayed down. The preacher looked around. "I've got your breakfast cold," he said; and then he remembered. "Amen," he said, and all the heads rose up.

"A—men," said Granma, and she fell to her breakfast, and broke down the soggy biscuits with her hard old toothless gums. Tom ate quickly, and Pa crammed his mouth. There was no talk until the food was gone, the coffee drunk; only the crunch of chewed food and the slurp of coffee cooled in transit to the tongue. Ma watched the preacher as he ate, and her eyes were questioning, probing and understanding. She watched him as though he were suddenly a spirit, not human any more, a voice out of the ground.

The men finished and put down their plates, and drained the last of their coffee; and then the men went out, Pa and the preacher and Noah and Grampa and Tom, and they walked over to the truck, avoiding the litter of furniture, the wooden bedsteads, the windmill machinery, the old plow. They walked to the truck and stood beside it. They touched the new pine side-boards.

Tom opened the hood and looked at the big greasy engine. And Pa came up beside him. He said, "Your brother Al looked her over before we bought her. He says she's all right."

"What's he know? He's just a squirt," said Tom.

"He worked for a company. Drove truck last year. He knows quite a little. Smart aleck like he is. He knows. He can tinker an engine, Al can."

Tom asked, "Where's he now?"

"Well," said Pa, "he's a-billygoatin' aroun' the country. Tom-cattin' hisself to death. Smart-aleck sixteen-year-older, an' his nuts is just a-eggin' him on. He don't think of nothin' but girls and engines. A plain smart aleck. Ain't been in nights for a week."

Grampa, fumbling with his chest, had succeeded in buttoning the buttons of his blue shirt into the buttonholes of his underwear. His fingers felt that something was wrong, but did not care enough to find out. His fingers went down to try to figure out the intricacies of the buttoning of his fly. "I was worse," he said happily. "I was much worse. I was a heller, you might say. Why, they was a camp meetin' right in Sallisaw when I was a young fella a little bit older'n Al. He's just a squirt, an' punkin-soft. But I was older. An' we was to this here camp meetin'. Five hundred folks there, an' a proper sprinklin' of young heifers."

"You look like a heller yet, Grampa," said Tom.

"Well, I am, kinda. But I ain't nowheres near the fella I was. Jus' let me get out to California where I can pick me an orange when I want it. Or grapes. There's a thing I ain't never had enough of. Gonna get me a whole big bunch a grapes off a bush, or whatever, an' I'm gonna squash 'em on my face an' let 'em run offen my chin."

Tom asked, "Where's Uncle John? Where's Rosasharn? Where's Ruthie an' Winfield? Nobody said nothin' about them yet."

Pa said, "Nobody asked. John gone to Sallisaw with a load a stuff to sell: pump, tools, chickens, an' all the stuff we brung over. Took Ruthie an' Winfield with 'im. Went 'fore daylight."

"Funny I never saw him," said Tom.

"Well, you come down from the highway, didn' you? He took the back way, by Cowlington. An' Rosasharn, she's nestin' with Connie's folks. By God! You don't even know Rosasharn's married to Connie Rivers. You 'member Connie. Nice young fella. An' Rosasharn's due 'bout three-four-five months now. Swellin' up right now. Looks fine."

"Jesus!" said Tom. "Rosasharn was just a little kid. An' now she's gonna have a baby. So damn much happens in four years if you're away. When ya think to start out west, Pa?"

"Well, we got to take this stuff in an' sell it. If Al gets back from his squirtin' aroun', I figgered he could load the truck an' take all of it in, an' maybe we could start out tomorra or day after. We ain't got so much money, an' a fella says it's damn near two thousan' miles to California. Quicker we get started, surer it is we get there. Money's a-dribblin' out all the time. You got any money?"

"On'y a couple a dollars. How'd you get money?"

"Well," said Pa, "we sol' all the stuff at our place, an' the whole bunch of us chopped cotton, even Grampa."

"Sure did," said Grampa.

"We put ever'thing together—two hundred dollars. We give seventy-five for this here truck, an' me an' Al cut her in two an' built on this here back. Al was gonna grind the valves, but he's too busy messin' aroun' to get down to her. We'll have maybe a hundred an' fifty when we start. Damn ol' tires on this here truck ain't gonna go far. Got a couple of wore out spares. Pick stuff up along the road, I guess."

The sun, driving straight down, stung with its rays. The shadows of the truck bed were dark bars on the ground, and the truck smelled of hot oil and oilcloth and paint. The few chickens had left the yard to hide in the tool shed from the sun. In the sty the pigs lay panting, close to the fence where a thin shadow fell, and they complained shrilly now and then. The two dogs were stretched in the red dust under the truck, panting, their dripping tongues covered with dust. Pa pulled his hat low over his eyes and squatted down on his hams. And, as though this were his natural position of thought and observation, he surveyed Tom critically, the new but aging cap, the suit, and the new shoes.

"Did you spen' your money for them clothes?" he asked. "Them clothes are jus' gonna be a nuisance to ya."

"They give 'em to me," said Tom. "When I come out they give 'em to me." He took off his cap and looked at it with some admiration, then wiped his forehead with it and put it on rakishly and pulled at the visor.

Pa observed, "Them's a nice-lookin' pair a shoes they give ya."

"Yeah," Joad agreed. "Purty for nice, but they ain't no shoes to go walkin' aroun' in on a hot day." He squatted beside his father.

Noah said slowly, "Maybe if you got them sideboards all true on, we could load up this stuff. Load her up so maybe if Al comes in——"

"I can drive her, if that's what you want," Tom said. "I drove truck at McAlester."

"Good," said Pa, and then his eyes stared down the road. "If I ain't mistaken, there's a young smart aleck draggin' his tail home right now," he said. "Looks purty wore out, too."

Tom and the preacher looked up the road. And randy Al, seeing he was being noticed, threw back his shoulders, and he came into the yard with a swaying strut like that of a rooster about to crow. Cockily, he walked close before he recognized Tom; and when he did, his boasting face changed, and admiration and veneration shone in his eyes, and his swagger fell away. His stiff jeans, with the bottoms turned up eight inches to show his heeled boots, his three-inch belt with copper figures on it, even the red arm bands on his blue shirt and the rakish angle of his Stetson hat could not build him up to his brother's stature; for his brother had killed a man, and no one would ever forget it. Al knew that even he had inspired some admiration among boys of his own age because his brother had killed a man. He had heard in Sallisaw how he was pointed out: "That's Al Joad. His brother killed a fella with a shovel."

And now Al, moving humbly near, saw that his brother was not a swaggerer as he had supposed. Al saw the dark brooding eyes of his brother, and the prison calm, the smooth hard face trained to indicate nothing to a prison guard, neither resistance nor slavishness. And instantly Al changed. Unconsciously he became like his brother, and his handsome face brooded, and his shoulders relaxed. He hadn't remembered how Tom was.

Tom said, "Hello, Al. Jesus, you're growin' like a bean! I wouldn't of knowed you."

Al, his hand ready if Tom should want to shake it, grinned self-consciously. Tom stuck out his hand and Al's hand jerked out to meet it. And there was liking between these two. "They tell me you're a good hand with a truck," said Tom.

And Al, sensing that his brother would not like a boaster, said, "I don't know nothin' much about it."

Pa said, "Been smart-alecking aroun' the country. You look wore out. Well, you got to take a load of stuff into Sallisaw to sell."

Al looked at his brother Tom. "Care to ride in?" he said as casually as he could.

"No, I can't," said Tom. "I'll help aroun' here. We'll be—together on the road."

Al tried to control his question. "Did—did you bust out? Of jail?"

"No," said Tom. "I got paroled."

"Oh." And Al was a little disappointed.

9

In the little houses the tenant people sifted their belongings and the belongings of their fathers and of their grandfathers. Picked over their possessions for the journey west. The men were ruthless because the past had been spoiled, but the women knew how the past would cry to them in the coming days. The men went into the barns and the sheds.

That plow, that harrow, remember in the war we planted mustard? Remember a fella wanted us to put in that rubber bush they call guayule? Get rich, he said. Bring out those tools—get a few dollars for them. Eighteen dollars for that plow, plus freight—Sears, Roebuck.

Harness, carts, seeders, little bundles of hoes. Bring 'em out. Pile 'em up. Load 'em in the wagon. Take 'em to town. Sell 'em for what you can get. Sell the team and the wagon, too. No more use for anything.

Fifty cents isn't enough to get for a good plow. That seeder cost thirty-eight dollars. Two dollars isn't enough. Can't haul it all back—Well, take it, and a bitterness with it. Take the well pump and the harness. Take halters, collars, hames, and tugs. Take the little glass brow-band jewels, roses red under glass.

Got those for the bay gelding. 'Member how he lifted his feet when he trotted?

Junk piled up in a yard.

Can't sell a hand plow any more. Fifty cents for the weight of the metal. Disks and tractors, that's the stuff now.

Well, take it—all junk—and give me five dollars. You're not buying only junk, you're buying junked lives. And more—you'll see—you're buying bitterness. Buying a plow to plow your own children under, buying the arms and spirits that might have saved you. Five dollars, not four. I can't haul 'em back—Well, take 'em for four. But I warn you, you're buying what will plow your own children under. And you won't see. You can't see. Take 'em for four. Now, what'll you give for the team and wagon? Those fine bays, matched they are, matched in color, matched the way they walk, stride to stride. In the stiff pull—straining hams and buttocks, split-second timed together. And in the morning, the light on them, bay light. They look over the fence sniffing for us, and the stiff ears swivel to hear us, and the black forelocks! I've got a girl. She likes to braid the manes and forelocks, puts little red bows on them. Likes to do it. Not any more. I could tell you a funny story about that girl and that off bay. Would make you laugh. Off horse is eight, near is ten, but might of been twin colts the way they work together. See? The teeth. Sound all over. Deep lungs. Feet fair and clean. How much? Ten dollars? For both? And the wagon—Oh, Jesus Christ! I'd shoot 'em for the dog feed first. Oh, take 'em! Take 'em quick, mister. You're buying a little girl plaiting the forelocks, taking off her hair ribbon to make bows, standing back, head cocked, rubbing the soft noses with her cheek. You're buying years of work, toil in the sun; you're buying a sorrow that can't talk. But watch it, mister. There's a premium goes with this pile of junk and the bay horses—so beautiful—a packet of bitterness to grow in your house and to flower, some day. We could have saved you, but you cut us down, and soon you will be cut down and there'll be none of us to save you.

And the tenant men came walking back, hands in their pockets, hats pulled down. Some bought a pint and drank it fast to make the impact hard and stunning. But they didn't laugh and they didn't dance. They didn't sing or pick the guitars. They walked back to the farms, hands in pockets and heads down, shoes kicking the red dust up.

Maybe we can start again, in the new rich land—in California, where the fruit grows. We'll start over.

But you can't start. Only a baby can start. You and me—why, we're all that's been. The anger of a moment, the thousand pictures, that's us. This land, this red land, is us; and the flood years and the dust years and the drought years are us. We can't start again. The bitterness we sold to the junk man—he got it all right, but we have it still. And when the owner man told us to go, that's us; and when the tractor hit the house, that's us until we're dead. To California or any place—every one a drum major leading a parade of hurts, marching with our bitterness. And some day— the armies of bitterness will all be going the same way. And they'll all walk together, and there'll be a dead terror from it.

The tenant men scuffed home to the farms through the red dust.

When everything that could be sold was sold, stoves and bedsteads, chairs and tables, little corner cupboards, tubs and tanks, still there were piles of possessions; and the women sat among them, turning them over and looking off beyond and back, pictures, square glasses, and here's a vase.

Now you know well what we can take and what we can't take. We'll be camping out—a few pots to cook and wash in, and mattresses and comforts, lantern and buckets, and a piece of canvas. Use that for a tent. This kerosene can. Know what that is? That's the stove. And clothes—take all the clothes. And—the rifle? Wouldn't go out naked of a rifle. When shoes and clothes and food, when even hope is gone, we'll have the rifle. When grampa came—did I tell you?— he had pepper and salt and a rifle. Nothing else. That goes. And a bottle for water. That just about fills us. Right up the sides of the trailer, and the kids can set in the trailer, and granma on a mattress. Tools, a shovel and saw and wrench and pliers. An ax, too. We had that ax forty years. Look how she's wore down. And ropes, of course. The rest? Leave it—or burn it up.

And the children came.

If Mary takes that doll, that dirty rag doll, I got to take my Injun bow. I got to. An' this roun' stick—big as me. I might need this stick. I had this stick so long—a month, or maybe a year. I got to take it. And what's it like in California?

The women sat among the doomed things, turning them over and looking past them and back. This book. My father had it. He liked a book. *Pilgrim's Progress.* Used to read it. Got his name in it. And his pipe—still smells rank. And this picture—an angel. I looked at that before the fust three come—didn't seem to do much good. Think we could get this china dog in? Aunt Sadie brought it from the St. Louis Fair. See? Wrote right on it. No, I guess not. Here's a letter my brother wrote the day before he died. Here's an old-time hat. These feathers—never got to use them. No, there isn't room.

How can we live without our lives? How will we know it's us without our past? No. Leave it. Burn it.

They sat and looked at it and burned it into their memories. How'll it be not to know what land's outside the door? How if you wake up in the night and know— and *know* the willow tree's not there? Can you live without the willow tree? Well, no, you can't. The willow tree is you. The pain on that mattress there—that dreadful pain—that's you.

And the children—if Sam takes his Injun bow an' his long roun' stick, I get to take two things. I choose the fluffy pilla. That's mine.

Suddenly they were nervous. Got to get out quick now. Can't wait. We can't wait. And they piled up the goods in the yards and set fire to them. They stood and watched them burning, and then frantically they loaded up the cars and drove away, drove in the dust. The dust hung in the air for a long time after the loaded cars had passed.

10

When the truck had gone, loaded with implements, with heavy tools, with beds and springs, with every movable thing that might be sold, Tom hung around the place. He mooned into the barn shed, into the empty stalls, and he walked into the implement leanto and kicked the refuse that was left, turned a broken mower tooth with his foot. He visited places he remembered—the red bank where the swallows nested, the willow tree over the pig pen. Two shoats grunted and squirmed at him through the fence, black pigs, sunning and comfortable. And then his pilgrimage was over, and he went to sit on the doorstep where the shade was lately fallen. Behind him Ma moved about in the kitchen, washing children's clothes in a bucket; and her strong freckled arms dripped soapsuds from the elbows. She stopped her rubbing when he sat down. She looked at him a long time, and at the back of his head when he turned and stared out at the hot sunlight. And then she went back to her rubbing.

She said, "Tom, I hope things is all right in California."

He turned and looked at her. "What makes you think they ain't?" he asked.

"Well—nothing. Seems too nice, kinda. I seen the han'bills fellas pass out, an' how much work they is, an' high wages an' all; an' I seen in the paper how they want folks to come an' pick grapes an' oranges an' peaches. That'd be nice work, Tom, pickin' peaches. Even if they wouldn't let you eat none, you could maybe snitch a little ratty one sometimes. An' it'd be nice under the trees, workin' in the shade. I'm scared of stuff so nice. I ain't got faith. I'm scared somepin ain't so nice about it."

Tom said, "Don't roust your faith bird-high an' you won't do no crawlin' with the worms."

"I know that's right. That's Scripture, ain't it?"

"I guess so," said Tom. "I never could keep Scripture straight sence I read a book name' *The Winning of Barbara Worth.*"

Ma chuckled lightly and scrunged the clothes in and out of the bucket. And she wrung out overalls and shirts, and the muscles of her forearms corded out. "Your Pa's pa, he quoted Scripture all the time. He got it all roiled up, too. It was the *Dr. Miles' Almanac* he got mixed up. Used to read ever' word in that almanac out loud—letters from folks that couldn't sleep or had lame backs. An' later he'd give them people for a lesson, an' he'd say, 'That's a par'ble from Scripture.' Your Pa an' Uncle John troubled 'im some about it when they'd laugh." She piled wrung clothes like cord wood on the table. "They say it's two thousan' miles where we're goin'. How far ya think that is, Tom? I seen it on a map, big mountains like on a post card, an' we're goin' right through 'em. How long ya s'pose it'll take to go that far, Tommy?"

"I dunno," he said. "Two weeks, maybe ten days if we got luck. Look, Ma, stop worryin'. I'm a-gonna tell you somepin about bein' in the pen. You can't go thinkin' when you're gonna be out. You'd go nuts. You got to think about that day, an' then the nex' day, about the ball game Sat'dy. That's what you got to do.

Ol' timers does that. A new young fella gets buttin' his head on the cell door. He's thinkin' how long it's gonna be. Whyn't you do that? Jus' take ever' day."

"That's a good way," she said, and she filled up her bucket with hot water from the stove, and she put in dirty clothes and began punching them down into the soapy water. "Yes, that's a good way. But I like to think how nice it's gonna be, maybe, in California. Never cold. An' fruit ever'place, an' people just bein' in the nicest places, little white houses in among the orange trees. I wonder—that is, if we all get jobs an' all work—maybe we can get one of them little white houses. An' the little fellas go out an' pick oranges right off the tree. They ain't gonna be able to stand it, they'll get to yellin' so."

Tom watched her working, and his eyes smiled. "It done you good jus' thinkin' about it. I knowed a fella from California. He didn't talk like us. You'd of knowed he come from some far-off place jus' the way he talked. But he says they's too many folks lookin' for work right there now. An' he says the folks that pick the fruit live in dirty ol' camps an' don't hardly get enough to eat. He says wages is low an' hard to get any."

A shadow crossed her face. "Oh, that ain't so," she said. "Your father got a han'bill on yella paper, tellin' how they need folks to work. They wouldn't go to that trouble if they wasn't plenty work. Costs 'em good money to get them han'bills out. What'd they want to lie for, an' costin' 'em money to lie?"

Tom shook his head. "I don't know, Ma. It's kinda hard to think why they done it. Maybe—" He looked out at the hot sun, shining on the red earth.

"Maybe what?"

"Maybe it's nice, like you says. Where'd Grampa go? Where'd the preacher go?"

Ma was going out of the house, her arms loaded high with the clothes. Tom moved aside to let her pass. "Preacher says he's gonna walk aroun'. Grampa's asleep here in the house. He comes in here in the day an' lays down sometimes." She walked to the line and began to drape pale blue jeans and blue shirts and long gray underwear over the wire.

Behind him Tom heard a shuffling step, and he turned to look in. Grampa was emerging from the bedroom, and as in the morning, he fumbled with the buttons of his fly. "I heerd talkin'," he said. "Sons-a-bitches won't let a ol' fella sleep. When you bastards get dry behin' the ears, you'll maybe learn to let a ol' fella sleep." His furious fingers managed to flip open the only two buttons on his fly that had been buttoned. And his hand forgot what it had been trying to do. His hand reached in and contentedly scratched under the testicles. Ma came in with wet hands, and her palms puckered and bloated from hot water and soap.

"Thought you was sleepin'. Here, let me button you up." And though he struggled, she held him and buttoned his underwear and his shirt and his fly. "You go aroun' a sight," she said, and let him go.

And he spluttered angrily, "Fella's come to a nice— to a nice—when somebody buttons 'em. I want ta be let be to button my own pants."

Ma said playfully, "They don't let people run aroun' with their clothes unbutton' in California."

"They don't, hey! Well, I'll show 'em. They think they're gonna show me how to act out there? Why, I'll go aroun' a-hangin' out if I wanta!"

Ma said, "Seems like his language gets worse ever' year. Showin' off, I guess."

The old man thrust out his bristly chin, and he regarded Ma with his shrewd, mean, merry eyes. "Well, sir," he said, "we'll be a-startin' 'fore long now. An', by God, they's grapes out there, just a-hangin' over inta the road. Know what I'm a-gonna do? I'm gonna pick me a wash tub full of grapes, an' I'm gonna set in 'em, an' scrooge aroun', an' let the juice run down my pants."

Tom laughed. "By God, if he lives to be two hundred you never will get Grampa house broke," he said. "You're all set on goin', ain't you, Grampa?"

The old man pulled out a box and sat down heavily on it. "Yes, sir," he said. "An' goddamn near time, too. My brother went on out there forty years ago. Never did hear nothin' about him. Sneaky son-of-a-bitch, he was. Nobody loved him. Run off with a single-action Colt of mine. If I ever run across him or his kids, if he got any out in California, I'll ask 'em for that Colt. But if I know 'im, an' he got any kids, he cuckoo'd 'em, an' somebody else is a-raisin' 'em. I sure will be glad to get out there. Got a feelin' it'll make a new fella outa me. Go right to work in the fruit."

Ma nodded. "He means it, too," she said. "Worked right up to three months ago, when he throwed his hip out the last time."

"Damn right," said Grampa.

Tom looked outward from his seat on the doorstep. "Here comes that preacher, walkin' aroun' from the back side a the barn."

Ma said, "Curiousest grace I ever heerd, that he give this mornin'. Wasn't hardly no grace at all. Jus' talkin', but the sound of it was like a grace."

"He's a funny fella," said Tom. "Talks funny all the time. Seems like he's talkin' to hisself, though. He ain't tryin' to put nothin' over."

"Watch the look in his eye," said Ma. "He looks baptized. Got that look they call lookin' through. He sure looks baptized. An' a-walkin' with his head down, a-starin' at nothin' on the groun'. There *is* a man that's baptized." And she was silent, for Casy had drawn near the door.

"You gonna get sun-shook, walkin' around like that," said Tom.

Casy said, "Well, yeah—maybe." He appealed to them all suddenly, to Ma and Grampa and Tom. "I got to get goin' west. I got to go. I wonder if I kin go along with you folks." And then he stood, embarrassed by his own speech.

Ma looked to Tom to speak, because he was a man, but Tom did not speak. She let him have the chance that was his right, and then she said, "Why, we'd be proud to have you. 'Course I can't say right now; Pa says all the men'll talk tonight and figger when we gonna start. I guess maybe we better not say till all the men come. John an' Pa an' Noah an' Tom an' Grampa an' Al an' Connie, they're gonna figger soon's they get back. But if they's room I'm pretty sure we'll be proud to have ya."

The preacher sighed. "I'll go anyways," he said. "Somepin's happening. I went up an' I looked, an' the houses is all empty, an' the lan' is empty, an' this whole country is empty. I can't stay here no more, I got to go where the folks is goin'. I'll work in the fiel's, an' maybe I'll be happy."

"An' you ain't gonna preach?" Tom asked.

"I ain't gonna preach."

"An' you ain't gonna baptize?" Ma asked.

"I ain't gonna baptize. I'm gonna work in the fiel's, in the green fiel's, an' I'm gonna be near to folks. I ain't gonna try to teach 'em nothin'. I'm gonna try to learn. Gonna learn why the folks walks in the grass, gonna hear 'em talk, gonna hear 'em sing. Gonna listen to kids eatin' mush. Gonna hear husban' an' wife a-poundin' the mattress in the night. Gonna eat with 'em an' learn." His eyes were wet and shining. "Gonna lay in the grass, open an' honest with anybody that'll have me. Gonna cuss an' swear an' hear the poetry of folks talkin'. All that's holy, all that's what I didn' understan'. All them things is the good things."

Ma said, "A-men."

The preacher sat humbly down on the chopping block beside the door. "I wonder what they is for a fella so lonely."

Tom coughed delicately. "For a fella that don't preach no more," he began.

"Oh, I'm a talker!" said Casy. "No gettin' away from that. But I ain't preachin'. Preachin' is tellin' folks stuff. I'm askin' 'em. That ain't preachin', is it?"

"I don't know," said Tom. "Preachin's a kinda tone a voice, an' preachin's a way a lookin' at things. Preachin's bein' good to folks when they wanna kill ya for it. Las' Christmus in McAlester, Salvation Army come an' done us good. Three solid hours a cornet music, an' we set there. They was bein' nice to us. But if one of us tried to walk out, we'd a-drawed solitary. That's preachin'. Doin' good to a fella that's down an' can't smack ya in the puss for it. No, you ain't no preacher. But don't you blow no cornets aroun' here."

Ma threw some sticks in the stove. "I'll get you a bite now, but it ain't much."

Grampa brought his box outside and sat on it and leaned against the wall, and Tom and Casy leaned back against the house wall. And the shadow of the afternoon moved out from the house.

In the late afternoon the truck came back, bumping and rattling through the dust, and there was a layer of dust in the bed, and the hood was covered with dust, and the headlights were obscured with a red flour. The sun was setting when the truck came back, and the earth was bloody in its setting light. Al sat bent over the wheel, proud and serious and efficient, and Pa and Uncle John, as befitted the heads of the clan, had the honor seats beside the driver. Standing in the truck bed, holding onto the bars of the sides, rode the others, twelve-year-old Ruthie and ten-year-old Winfield, grime-faced and wild, their eyes tired but excited, their fingers and the edges of their mouths black and sticky from licorice whips, whined out of their father in town. Ruthie, dressed in a real dress of pink

muslin that came below her knees, was a little serious
in her young-ladiness. But Winfield was still a trifle of
a snot nose, a little of a brooder back of the barn, and
an inveterate collector and smoker of snipes. And
whereas Ruthie felt the might, the responsibility,
and the dignity of her developing breasts, Winfield
was kid-wild and calfish. Beside them, clinging lightly
to the bars, stood Rose of Sharon, and she balanced,
swaying on the balls of her feet, and took up the road
shock in her knees and hams. For Rose of Sharon was
pregnant and careful. Her hair, braided and wrapped
around her head, made an ash-blond crown. Her
round soft face, which had been voluptuous and inviting a few months ago, had already put on the barrier of
pregnancy, the self-sufficient smile, the knowing per-
fection-look; and her plump body—full soft breasts
and stomach, hard hips and buttocks that had swung
so freely and provocatively as to invite slapping and
stroking—her whole body had become demure and
serious. Her whole thought and action were directed
inward on the baby. She balanced on her toes now, for
the baby's sake. And the world was pregnant to her;
she thought only in terms of reproduction and of
motherhood. Connie, her nineteen-year-old husband,
who had married a plump, passionate hoyden, was still
frightened and bewildered at the change in her; for
there were no more cat fights in bed, biting and
scratching with muffled giggles and final tears. There
was a balanced, careful, wise creature who smiled
shyly but very firmly at him. Connie was proud and
fearful of Rose of Sharon. Whenever he could, he put
a hand on her or stood close, so that his body touched
her at hip and shoulder, and he felt that this kept a
relation that might be departing. He was a sharp-
faced, lean young man of a Texas strain, and his pale
blue eyes were sometimes dangerous and sometimes
kindly, and sometimes frightened. He was a good hard
worker and would make a good husband. He drank

enough, but not too much; fought when it was required of him; and never boasted. He sat quietly in a gathering and yet managed to be there and to be recognized.

Had he not been fifty years old, and so one of the natural rulers of the family, Uncle John would have preferred not to sit in the honor place beside the driver. He would have liked Rose of Sharon to sit there. This was impossible, because she was young and a woman. But Uncle John sat uneasily, his lonely haunted eyes were not at ease, and his thin strong body was not relaxed. Nearly all the time the barrier of loneliness cut Uncle John off from people and from appetites. He ate little, drank nothing, and was celibate. But underneath, his appetites swelled into pressures until they broke through. Then he would eat of some craved food until he was sick; or he would drink jake or whisky until he was a shaken paralytic with red wet eyes; or he would raven with lust for some whore in Sallisaw. It was told of him that once he went clear to Shawnee and hired three whores in one bed, and snorted and rutted on their unresponsive bodies for an hour. But when one of his appetites was sated, he was sad and ashamed and lonely again. He hid from people, and by gifts tried to make up to all people for himself. Then he crept into houses and left gum under pillows for chidren; then he cut wood and took no pay. Then he gave away any possession he might have: a saddle, a horse, a new pair of shoes. One could not talk to him then, for he ran away, or if confronted hid within himself and peeked out of frightened eyes. The death of his wife, followed by months of being alone, had marked him with guilt and shame and had left an unbreaking loneliness on him.

But there were things he could not escape. Being one of the heads of the family, he had to govern; and now he had to sit on the honor seat beside the driver.

The three men on the seat were glum as they drove

toward home over the dusty road. Al, bending over the wheel, kept shifting eyes from the road to the instrument panel, watching the ammeter needle, which jerked suspiciously, watching the oil gauge and the heat indicator. And his mind was cataloguing weak points and suspicious things about the car. He listened to the whine, which might be the rear end, dry; and he listened to tappets lifting and falling. He kept his hand on the gear lever, feeling the turning gears through it. And he had let the clutch out against the brake to test for slipping clutch plates. He might be a musking goat sometimes, but this was his responsibility, this truck, its running, and its maintenance. If something went wrong it would be his fault, and while no one would say it, everyone, and Al most of all, would know it was his fault. And so he felt it, watched it, and listened to it. And his face was serious and responsible. And everyone respected him and his responsibility. Even Pa, who was the leader, would hold a wrench and take orders from Al.

They were all tired on the truck. Ruthie and Winfield were tired from seeing too much movement, too many faces, from fighting to get licorice whips; tired from the excitement of having Uncle John secretly slip gum into their pockets.

And the men in the seat were tired and angry and sad, for they had got eighteen dollars for every movable thing from the farm: the horses, the wagon, the implements, and all the furniture from the house. Eighteen dollars. They had assailed the buyer, argued; but they were routed when his interest seemed to flag and he told them he didn't want the stuff at any price. Then they were beaten, believed him, and took two dollars less than he had first offered. And now they were weary and frightened because they had gone against a system they did not understand and it had beaten them. They knew the team and the wagon were worth much more. They knew the buyer man would get much more, but they didn't know how to do it. Merchandising was a secret to them.

Al, his eyes darting from road to panel board, said, "That fella, he ain't a local fella. Didn' talk like a local fella. Clothes was different, too."

And Pa explained, "When I was in the hardware store, I talked to some men I know. They say there's fellas comin' in jus' to buy up the stuff us fellas got to sell when we get out. They say these new fellas is cleaning up. But there ain't nothin' we can do about it. Maybe Tommy should of went. Maybe he could of did better."

John said, "But the fella wasn't gonna take it at all. We couldn' haul it back."

"These men I know told about that," said Pa. "Said the buyer fellas always done that. Scairt folks that way. We jus' don' know how to go about stuff like that. Ma's gonna be disappointed. She'll be mad an' disappointed."

Al said, "When ya think we're gonna go, Pa?"

"I dunno. We'll talk her over tonight an' decide. I'm sure glad Tom's back. That makes me feel good. Tom's a good boy."

Al said, "Pa, some fellas was talkin' about Tom, an' they says he's parole'. An' they says that means he can't go outside the State, or if he goes, an' they catch him, they send 'im back for three years."

Pa looked startled. "They said that? Seem like fellas that knowed? Not jus' blowin' off?"

"I don' know," said Al. "They was just a-talkin' there, an' I didn't let on he's my brother. I jus' stood an' took it in."

Pa said, "Jesus Christ, I hope that ain't true! We need Tom. I'll ask 'im about that. We got trouble enough without they chase the hell out of us. I hope it ain't true. We got to talk that out in the open."

Uncle John said, "Tom, he'll know."

They fell silent while the truck battered along. The engine was noisy, full of little clashings, and the brake rods banged. There was a wooden creaking from the wheels, and a thin jet of steam escaped through a hole in the top of the radiator cap. The truck pulled a high whirling column of red dust behind it. They rumbled up the last little rise while the sun was still half-face above the horizon, and they bore down on the house as it disappeared. The brakes squealed when they stopped, and the sound printed in Al's head—no lining left.

Ruthie and Winfield climbed yelling over the side walls and dropped to the ground. They shouted, "Where is he? Where's Tom?" And then they saw him standing beside the door, and they stopped, embarrassed, and walked slowly toward him and looked shyly at him.

And when he said, "Hello, how you kids doin'?" they replied softly, "Hello! All right." And they stood apart and watched him secretly, the great brother who had killed a man and been in prison. They remembered how they had played prison in the chicken coop and fought for the right to be prisoner.

Connie Rivers lifted the high tail-gate out of the truck and got down and helped Rose of Sharon to the ground; and she accepted it nobly, smiling her wise, self-satisfied smile, mouth tipped at the corners a little fatuously.

Tom said, "Why, it's Rosasharn. I didn' know you was comin' with them."

"We was walkin'," she said. "The truck come by an' picked us up." And then she said, "This is Connie, my husband." And she was grand, saying it.

The two shook hands, sizing each other up, looking deeply into each other; and in a moment each was satisfied, and Tom said, "Well, I see you been busy."

She looked down. "You do not see, not yet."

"Ma tol' me. When's it gonna be?"

"Oh, not for a long time! Not till nex' winter."

Tom laughed. "Gonna get 'im bore in a orange

ranch, huh? In one a them white houses with orange trees all aroun'."

Rose of Sharon felt her stomach with both her hands. "You do not see," she said, and she smiled her complacent smile and went into the house. The evening was hot, and the thrust of light still flowed up from the western horizon. And without any signal the family gathered by the truck, and the congress, the family government, went into session.

The film of evening light made the red earth lucent, so that its dimensions were deepened, so that a stone, a post, a building had greater depth and more solidity than in the daytime light; and these objects were curiously more individual—a post was more essentially a post, set off from the earth it stood in and the field of corn it stood out against. And plants were individuals, not the mass of crop; and the ragged willow tree was itself, standing free of all other willow trees. The earth contributed a light to the evening. The front of the gray, paintless house, facing the west, was luminous as the moon is. The gray dusty truck, in the yard before the door, stood out magically in this light, in the overdrawn perspective of a stereopticon.

The people too were changed in the evening, quieted. They seemed to be a part of an organization of the unconscious. They obeyed impulses which registered only faintly in their thinking minds. Their eyes were inward and quiet, and their eyes, too, were lucent in the evening, lucent in dusty faces.

The family met at the most important place, near the truck. The house was dead, and the fields were dead; but this truck was the active thing, the living principle. The ancient Hudson, with bent and scarred radiator screen, with grease in dusty lobules at the worn edges of every moving part, with hub caps gone and caps of red dust in their places—this was the new hearth, the living center of the family; half passenger car and half truck, high-sided and clumsy.

Pa walked around the truck, looking at it, and then he squatted down in the dust and found a stick to draw with. One foot was flat to the ground, the other rested on the ball and slightly back, so that one knee was higher than the other. Left forearm rested on the lower, left, knee; the right elbow on the right knee, and the right fist cupped for the chin. Pa squatted there, looking at the truck, his chin in his cupped fist. And Uncle John moved toward him and squatted down beside him. Their eyes were brooding. Grampa came out of the house and saw the two squatting together, and he jerked over and sat on the running board of the truck, facing them. That was the nucleus. Tom and Connie and Noah strolled in and squatted, and the line was a half-circle with Grampa in the opening. And then Ma came out of the house and Granma with her, and Rose of Sharon behind, walking daintily. They took their places behind the squatting men; they stood up and put their hands on their hips. And the children, Ruthie and Winfield, hopped from foot to foot beside the women; the children squidged their toes in the red dust, but they made no sound. Only the preacher was not there. He, out of delicacy, was sitting on the ground behind the house. He was a good preacher and knew his people.

The evening light grew softer, and for a while the family sat and stood silently. Then Pa, speaking to no one, but to the group, made his report. "Got skinned on the stuff we sold. The fella knowed we couldn't wait. Got eighteen dollars only."

Ma stirred restively, but she held her peace.

Noah, the oldest son, asked, "How much, all added up, we got?"

Pa drew figures in the dust and mumbled to himself for a moment. "Hunderd fifty-four," he said. "But Al here says we gonna need better tires. Says these here won't last."

This was Al's first participation in the conference. Always he had stood behind with the women before.

And now he made his report solemnly. "She's old an'
she's ornery," he said gravely. "I gave the whole thing
a good goin'-over 'fore we bought her. Didn' listen to
the fella talkin' what a hell of a bargain she was. Stuck
my finger in the differential and they wasn't no
sawdust. Opened the gear box an' they wasn't no
sawdust. Test' her clutch an' rolled her wheels for
line. Went under her an' her frame ain't splayed none.
She never been rolled. Seen they was a cracked cell in
her battery an' made the fella put in a good one. The
tires ain't worth a damn, but they're a good size. Easy
to get. She'll ride like a bull calf, but she ain't shootin'
no oil. Reason I says buy her is she was a pop'lar car.
Wreckin' yards is full a Hudson Super-Sixes, an' you
can buy parts cheap. Could a got a bigger, fancier car
for the same money, but parts too hard to get, an' too
dear. That's how I figgered her anyways." The last was
his submission to the family. He stopped speaking and
waited for their opinions.

Grampa was still the titular head, but he no longer
ruled. His position was honorary and a matter of custom. But he did have the right of first comment, no
matter how silly his old mind might be. And the squatting men and the standing women waited for him.
"You're all right, Al," Grampa said. "I was a squirt
jus' like you, a-fartin' aroun' like a dog-wolf. But when
they was a job, I done it. You've growed up good." He
finished in the tone of a benediction, and Al reddened
a little with pleasure.

Pa said, "Sounds right-side-up to me. If it was
horses we wouldn' have to put the blame on Al. But
Al's the on'y automobile fella here."

Tom said, "I know some. Worked some in McAlester. Al's right. He done good." And now Al was rosy
with the compliment. Tom went on, "I'd like to say—
well, that preacher—he wants to go along." He was
silent. His words lay in the group, and the group was
silent. "He's a nice fella," Tom added. "We've

knowed him a long time. Talks a little wild sometimes, but he talks sensible." And he relinquished the proposal to the family.

The light was going gradually. Ma left the group and went into the house, and the iron clang of the stove came from the house. In a moment she walked back to the brooding council.

Grampa said, "They was two ways a thinkin'. Some folks use' ta figger that a preacher was poison luck."

Tom said, "This fella says he ain't a preacher no more."

Grampa waved his hand back and forth. "Once a fella's a preacher, he's always a preacher. That's somepin you can't get shut of. They was some folks figgered it was a good respectable thing to have a preacher along. Ef somebody died, preacher buried 'em. Weddin' come due, or overdue, an' there's your preacher. Baby come, an' you got a christener right under the roof. Me, I always said they was preachers *an'* preachers. Got to pick 'em. I kinda like this fella. He ain't stiff."

Pa dug his stick into the dust and rolled it between his fingers so that it bored a little hole. "They's more to this than is he lucky, or is he a nice fella," Pa said. "We got to figger close. It's a sad thing to figger close. Le's see, now. There's Grampa an' Granma—that's two. An' me an' John an' Ma—that's five. An' Noah an' Tommy an' Al— that's eight. Rosasharn an' Connie is ten, an' Ruthie an Winfiel' is twelve. We got to take the dogs 'cause what'll we do else? Can't shoot a good dog, an' there ain't nobody to give 'em to. An' that's fourteen."

"Not countin' what chickens is left, an' two pigs," said Noah.

Pa said, "I aim to get those pigs salted down to eat on the way. We gonna need meat. Carry the salt kegs right with us. But I'm wonderin' if we can all ride, an' the preacher too. An' kin we feed an extra mouth?" Without turning his head, he asked, "Kin we, Ma?"

Ma cleared her throat. "It ain't kin we? It's will we?" she said firmly. "As far as 'kin,' we can't do nothin', not go to California or nothin'; but as far as 'will,' why, we'll do what we will. An' as far as 'will'— it's a long time our folks been here and east before, an' I never heerd tell of no Joads or no Hazletts, neither, ever refusin' food an' shelter or a lift on the road to anybody that asked. They's been mean Joads, but never that mean."

Pa broke in, "But s'pose there just ain't room?" He had twisted his neck to look up at her, and he was ashamed. Her tone had made him ashamed. "S'pose we jus' can't all get in the truck?"

"There ain't no room now," she said. "There ain't room for more'n six, an' twelve is goin' sure. One more ain't gonna hurt; an' a man, strong an' healthy, ain't never no burden. An' any time when we got two pigs an' over a hunderd dollars, an' we wonderin' if we kin' feed a fella—" She stopped, and Pa turned back, and his spirit was raw from the whipping.

Granma said, "A preacher is a nice thing to be with us. He give a nice grace this morning."

Pa looked at the face of each one for dissent, and then he said, "Want to call 'im over, Tommy? If he's goin', he ought ta be here."

Tom got up from his hams and went toward the house, calling, "Casy—oh, Casy!"

A muffled voice replied from behind the house. Tom walked to the corner and saw the preacher sitting back against the wall, looking at the flashy evening star in the light sky. "Calling me?" Casy asked.

"Yeah. We think long as you're goin' with us, you ought to be over with us, helpin' to figger things out."

Casy got to his feet. He knew the government of families, and he knew he had been taken into the family. Indeed his position was eminent, for Uncle John moved sideways, leaving space between Pa and himself for the preacher. Casy squatted down like the others, facing Grampa enthroned on the running board.

Ma went into the house again. There was a screech of a lantern hood and the yellow light flashed up in the dark kitchen. When she lifted the lid of the big pot, the smell of boiling side-meat and beet greens came out the door. They waited for her to come back across the darkening yard, for Ma was powerful in the group.

Pa said, "We got to figger when to start. Sooner the better. What we got to do 'fore we go is get them pigs slaughtered an' in salt, an' pack our stuff an' go. Quicker the better, now."

Noah agreed, "If we pitch in, we kin get ready tomorrow, an' we kin go bright the nex' day."

Uncle John objected, "Can't chill no meat in the heat a the day. Wrong time a year for slaughterin'. Meat'll be sof' if it don' chill."

"Well, le's do her tonight. She'll chill tonight some. Much as she's gonna. After we eat, le's get her done. Got salt?"

Ma said, "Yes. Got plenty salt. Got two nice kegs, too."

"Well, le's get her done, then," said Tom.

Grampa began to scrabble about, trying to get a purchase to arise. "Gettin' dark," he said. "I'm gettin' hungry. Come time we get to California I'll have a big bunch of grapes in my han' all the time, a-nibblin' off it all the time, by God!" He got up, and the men arose.

Ruthie and Winfield hopped excitedly about in the dust, like crazy things. Ruthie whispered hoarsely to Winfield, "Killin' pigs *and* goin' to California. Killin' pigs *and* goin'—all the same time."

And Winfield was reduced to madness. He stuck his finger against his throat, made a horrible face, and wobbled about, weakly shrilling, "I'm an ol' pig. Look! I'm an ol' pig. Look at the blood, Ruthie!" And he staggered and sank to the ground and waved arms and legs weakly.

But Ruthie was older, and she knew the tremendousness of the time. "*And* goin' to California," she said again. And she knew this was the great time in her life so far.

The adults moved toward the lighted kitchen through the deep dusk, and Ma served them greens and sidemeat in tin plates. But before Ma ate, she put the big round wash tub on the stove and started the fire to roaring. She carried buckets of water until the tub was full, and then around the tub she clustered the buckets, full of water. The kitchen became a swamp of heat, and the family ate hurriedly, and went out to sit on the doorstep until the water should get hot. They sat looking out at the dark, at the square of light the kitchen lantern threw on the ground outside the door, with a hunched shadow of Grampa in the middle of it. Noah picked his teeth thoroughly with a broom straw. Ma and Rose of Sharon washed up the dishes and piled them on the table.

And then, all of a sudden, the family began to function. Pa got up and lighted another lantern. Noah, from a box in the kitchen, brought out the bow-bladed butchering knife and whetted it on a worn little Carborundum stone. And he laid the scraper on the chopping block, and the knife beside it. Pa brought two sturdy sticks, each three feet long, and pointed the ends with the ax, and he tied strong ropes, double half-hitched, to the middle of the sticks.

He grumbled, "Shouldn't of sold those singletrees— all of 'em."

The water in the pots steamed and rolled.

Noah asked, "Gonna take the water down there or bring the pigs up here?"

"Pigs up here," said Pa. "You can't spill a pig and scald yourself like you can hot water. Water about ready?"

"Jus' about," said Ma.

"Aw right. Noah, you an' Tom an' Al come along. I'll carry the light. We'll slaughter down there an' bring 'em up here."

Noah took his knife, and Al the ax, and the four men moved down on the sty, their legs flickering in the lantern light. Ruthie and Winfield skittered along, hopping over the ground. At the sty Pa leaned over the fence, holding the lantern. The sleepy young pigs struggled to their feet, grunting suspiciously. Uncle John and the preacher walked down to help.

"All right," said Pa. "Stick 'em, an' we'll run 'em up and bleed an' scald at the house." Noah and Tom stepped over the fence. They slaughtered quickly and efficiently. Tom struck twice with the blunt head of the ax; and Noah, leaning over the felled pigs, found the great artery with his curving knife and released the pulsing streams of blood. Then over the fence with the squealing pigs. The preacher and Uncle John dragged one by the hind legs, and Tom and Noah the other. Pa walked along with the lantern, and the black blood made two trails in the dust.

At the house, Noah slipped his knife between tendon and bone of the hind legs; the pointed sticks held the legs apart, and the carcasses were hung from the two-by-four rafters that stuck out from the house. Then the men carried the boiling water and poured it over the black bodies. Noah slit the bodies from end to end and dropped the entrails out on the ground. Pa sharpened two more sticks to hold the bodies open to the air, while Tom with the scrubber and Ma with a dull knife scraped the skins to take out the bristles. Al brought a bucket and shoveled the entrails into it, and dumped them on the ground away from the house, and two cats followed him, mewing loudly, and the dogs followed him, growling lightly at the cats.

Pa sat on the doorstep and looked at the pigs hanging in the lantern light. The scraping was done now,

and only a few drops of blood continued to fall from
the carcasses into the black pool on the ground. Pa got
up and went to the pigs and felt them with his hand,
and then he sat down again. Granma and Grampa went
toward the barn to sleep, and Grampa carried a candle
lantern in his hand. The rest of the family sat quietly
about the doorstep, Connie and Al and Tom on the
ground, leaning their backs against the house wall,
Uncle John on a box, Pa in the doorway. Only Ma and
Rose of Sharon continued to move about. Ruthie and
Winfield were sleepy now, but fighting it off. They
quarreled sleepily out in the darkness. Noah and the
preacher squatted side by side, facing the house. Pa
scratched himself nervously, and took off his hat and
ran his fingers through his hair. "Tomorra we'll get
that pork salted early in the morning, an' then we'll get
the truck loaded, all but the beds, an' nex' morning off
we'll go. Hardly is a day's work in all that," he said
uneasily.

Tom broke in, "We'll be moonin' aroun' all day,
lookin' for somepin to do." The group stirred uneasily.
"We could get ready by daylight an' go," Tom suggested. Pa rubbed his knee with his hand. And the
restiveness spread to all of them.

Noah said, "Prob'ly wouldn't hurt that meat to get
her right down in salt. Cut her up, she'd cool quicker
anyways."

It was Uncle John who broke over the edge, his
pressures too great. "What we hangin' aroun' for? I
want to get shut of this. Now we're goin', why don't we
go?"

And the revulsion spread to the rest. "Whyn't we
go? Get sleep on the way." And a sense of hurry crept
into them.

Pa said, "They say it's two thousan' miles. That's a
hell of a long ways. We oughta go. Noah, you an' me
can get that meat cut up an' we can put all the stuff in
the truck."

Ma put her head out of the door. "How about if we forgit somepin, not seein' it in the dark?"

"We could look 'round after daylight," said Noah. They sat still then, thinking about it. But in a moment Noah got up and began to sharpen the bow-bladed knife on his little worn stone. "Ma," he said, "git that table cleared." And he stepped up to a pig, cut a line down one side of the backbone and began peeling the meat forward, off the ribs.

Pa stood up excitedly. "We got to get the stuff together," he said. "Come on, you fellas."

Now that they were committed to going, the hurry infected all of them. Noah carried the slabs of meat into the kitchen and cut it into small salting blocks, and Ma patted the coarse salt in, laid it piece by piece in the kegs, careful that no two pieces touched each other. She laid the slabs like bricks, and pounded salt in the spaces. And Noah cut up the side-meat and he cut up the legs. Ma kept her fire going, and as Noah cleaned the ribs and the spines and leg bones of all the meat he could, she put them in the oven to roast for gnawing purposes.

In the yard and in the barn the circles of lantern light moved about, and the men brought together all the things to be taken, and piled them by the truck. Rose of Sharon brought out all the clothes the family possessed: the overalls, the thick-soled shoes, the rubber boots, the worn best suits, the sweaters and sheepskin coats. And she packed these tightly into a wooden box and got into the box and tramped them down. And then she brought out the print dresses and shawls, the black cotton stockings and the children's clothes—small overalls and cheap print dresses—and she put these in the box and tramped them down.

Tom went to the tool shed and brought what tools were left to go, a hand saw and a set of wrenches, a hammer and a box of assorted nails, a pair of pliers and a flat file and a set of rat-tail files.

And Rose of Sharon brought out the big piece of tarpaulin and spread it on the ground behind the truck. She struggled through the door with the mattresses, three double ones and a single. She piled them on the tarpaulin and brought arm-loads of folded ragged blankets and piled them up.

Ma and Noah worked busily at the carcasses, and the smell of roasting pork bones came from the stove. The children had fallen by the way in the late night. Winfield lay curled up in the dust outside the door; and Ruthie, sitting on a box in the kitchen where she had gone to watch the butchering, had dropped her head back against the wall. She breathed easily in her sleep, and her lips were parted over her teeth.

Tom finished with the tools and came into the kitchen with his lantern, and the preacher followed him. "God in a buckboard," Tom said, "smell that meat! An' listen to her crackle."

Ma laid the bricks of meat in a keg and poured salt around and over them and covered the layer with salt and patted it down. She looked up at Tom and smiled a little at him, but her eyes were serious and tired. "Be nice to have pork bones for breakfas'," she said.

The preacher stepped beside her. "Leave me salt down this meat," he said. "I can do it. There's other stuff for you to do."

She stopped her work then and inspected him oddly, as though he suggested a curious thing. And her hands were crusted with salt, pink with fluid from the fresh pork. "It's women's work," she said finally.

"It's all work," the preacher replied. "They's too much of it to split it up to men's or women's work. You got stuff to do. Leave me salt the meat."

Still for a moment she stared at him, and then she poured water from a bucket into the tin wash basin and she washed her hands. The preacher took up the blocks of pork and patted on the salt while she watched him. And he laid them in the kegs as she had. Only when he had finished a layer and covered it carefully and patted down the salt was she satisfied. She dried her bleached and bloated hands.

Tom said, "Ma, what stuff we gonna take from here?"

She looked quickly about the kitchen. "The bucket," she said. "All the stuff to eat with: plates an' the cups, the spoons an' knives an' forks. Put all them in that drawer, an' take the drawer. The big fry pan an' the big stew kettle, the coffee pot. When it gets cool, take the rack outa the oven. That's good over a fire. I'd like to take the wash tub, but I guess there ain't room. I'll wash clothes in the bucket. Don't do no good to take little stuff. You can cook little stuff in a big kettle, but you can't cook big stuff in a little pot. Take the bread pans, all of 'em. They fit down inside each other." She stood and looked about the kitchen. "You jus' take that stuff I tol' you, Tom. I'll fix up the rest, the big can a pepper an' the salt an' the nutmeg an' the grater. I'll take all that stuff jus' at the last." She picked up a lantern and walked heavily into the bedroom, and her bare feet made no sound on the floor.

The preacher said, "She looks tar'd."

"Women's always tar'd," said Tom. "That's just the way women is, 'cept at meetin' once an' again."

"Yeah, but tar'der'n that. Real tar'd, like she's sick-tar'd."

Ma was just through the door, and she heard his words. Slowly her relaxed face tightened, and the lines disappeared from the taut muscular face. Her eyes sharpened and her shoulders straightened. She glanced about the stripped room. Nothing was left in it except trash. The mattresses which had been on the floor were gone. The bureaus were sold. On the floor lay a broken comb, an empty talcum powder can, and a few dust mice. Ma set her lantern on the floor. She reached behind one of the boxes that had served as chairs and brought out a stationery box, old and soiled and cracked at the corners. She sat down and opened the box. Inside were letters, clippings, photographs, a pair of earrings, a little gold signet ring, and a watch chain braided of hair and tipped with gold swivels. She touched the letters with her fingers, touched them lightly, and she smoothed a newspaper clipping on which there was an account of Tom's trial. For a long time she held the box, looking over it, and her fingers disturbed the letters and then lined them up again. She bit her lower lip, thinking, remembering. And at last she made up her mind. She picked out the ring, the watch charm, the earrings, dug under the pile and found one gold cuff link. She took a letter from an envelope and dropped the trinkets in the envelope. She folded the envelope over and put it in her dress pocket. Then gently and tenderly she closed the box and smoothed the top carefully with her fingers. Her lips parted. And then she stood up, took her lantern, and went back into the kitchen. She lifted the stove lid and laid the box gently among the coals. Quickly the heat browned the paper. A flame licked up and over the box. She replaced the stove lid and instantly the fire sighed up and breathed over the box.

Out in the dark yard, working in the lantern light, Pa and Al loaded the truck. Tools on the bottom, but handy to reach in case of a breakdown. Boxes of clothes next, and kitchen utensils in a gunny sack; cutlery and dishes in their box. Then the gallon bucket tied on behind. They made the bottom of the load as even as possible, and filled the spaces between boxes with rolled blankets. Then over the top they laid the mattresses, filling the truck in level. And last they spread the big tarpaulin over the load and Al made holes in the edge, two feet apart, and inserted little ropes, and tied it down to the side-bars of the truck.

"Now, if it rains," he said, "we'll tie it to the bar

above, an' the folks can get underneath, out of the wet. Up front we'll be dry enough."

And Pa applauded. "That's a good idear."

"That ain't all," Al said. "First chance I git I'm gonna fin' a long plank an' make a ridge pole, an' put the tarp over that. An' then it'll be covered in, an' the folks'll be outa the sun, too."

And Pa agreed, "That's a good idear. Whyn't you think a that before?"

"I ain't had time," said Al.

"Ain't had time? Why, Al, you had time to coyote all over the country. God knows where you been this las' two weeks."

"Stuff a fella got to do when he's leavin' the country," said Al. And then he lost some of his assurance. "Pa," he asked. "You glad to be goin', Pa?"

"Huh? Well—sure. Leastwise—yeah. We had hard times here. 'Course it'll be all different out there— plenty work, an' ever'thing nice an' green, an' little white houses an' oranges growin' aroun'."

"Is it all oranges ever'where?"

"Well, maybe not ever'where, but plenty places."

The first gray of daylight began in the sky. And the work was done—the kegs of pork ready, the chicken coop ready to go on top. Ma opened the oven and took out the pile of roasted bones, crisp and brown, with plenty of gnawing meat left. Ruthie half awakened, and slipped down from the box and slept again. But the adults stood around the door, shivering a little and gnawing at the crisp pork.

"Guess we oughta wake up Granma an' Grampa," Tom said. "Gettin' along on toward day."

Ma said, "Kinda hate to, till the las' minute. They need the sleep. Ruthie an' Winfield hardly got no real rest neither."

"Well, they kin all sleep on top a the load," said Pa. "It'll be nice an' comf'table there."

Suddenly the dogs started up from the dust and listened. And then, with a roar, went barking off into the darkness. "Now what in hell is that?" Pa demanded. In a moment they heard a voice speaking reassuringly to the barking dogs and the barking lost its fierceness. Then footsteps, and a man approached. It was Muley Graves, his hat pulled low.

He came near timidly. "Morning, folks," he said.

"Why, Muley." Pa waved the ham bone he held. "Step in an' get some pork for yourself, Muley."

"Well, no," said Muley. "I ain't hungry, exactly."

"Oh, get it, Muley, get it. Here!" And Pa stepped into the house and brought out a hand of spareribs.

"I wasn't aiming to eat none a your stuff," he said. "I was jus' walkin' aroun', an' I thought how you'd be goin', an' I'd maybe say good-by."

"Goin' in a little while now," said Pa. "You'd a missed us if you'd come an hour later. All packed up—see?"

"All packed up." Muley looked at the loaded truck. "Sometimes I wisht I'd go an' fin' my folks."

Ma asked, "Did you hear from 'em out in California?"

"No," said Muley, "I ain't heard. But I ain't been to look in the post office. I oughta go in sometimes."

Pa said, "Al, go down, wake up Granma, Grampa. Tell 'em to come an' eat. We're goin' before long." And as Al sauntered toward the barn, "Muley, ya wanta squeeze in with us an' go? We'd try to make room for ya."

Muley took a bite of meat from the edge of a rib bone and chewed it. "Sometimes I think I might. But I know I won't," he said. "I know perfectly well the las' minute I'd run an' hide like a damn ol' graveyard ghos'."

Noah said, "You gonna die out in the fiel' some day, Muley."

"I know, I thought about that. Sometimes it seems pretty lonely, an' sometimes it seems all right, an' sometimes it seems good. It don't make no difference. But if ya come acrost my folks—that's really what I come to say—if ya come on any my folks in California, tell 'em I'm well. Tell 'em I'm doin' all right. Don't let on I'm livin' this way. Tell 'em I'll come to 'em soon's I git the money."

Ma asked, "An' will ya?"

"No," Muley said softly. "No, I won't. I can't go away. I got to stay now. Time back I might of went. But not now. Fella gits to thinkin', an' he gits to knowin'. I ain't never goin'."

The light of the dawn was a little sharper now. It paled the lanterns a little. Al came back with Grampa struggling and limping by his side. "He wasn't sleepin'," Al said. "He was settin' out back of the barn. They's somepin wrong with 'im."

Grampa's eyes had dulled, and there was none of the old meanness in them. "Ain't nothin' the matter with me," he said. "I jus' ain't a-goin'."

"Not goin'?" Pa demanded. "What you mean you ain't a-goin'? Why, here we're all packed up, ready. We got to go. We got no place to stay."

"I ain't sayin' for you to stay," said Grampa. "You go right on along. Me—I'm stayin'. I give her a goin'-over all night mos'ly. This here's my country. I b'long here. An' I don't give a goddamn if they's oranges an' grapes crowdin' a fella outa bed even. I ain't a-goin'. This country ain't no good, but it's my country. No, you all go ahead. I'll jus' stay right here where I b'long."

They crowded near to him. Pa said, "You can't, Grampa. This here lan' is goin' under the tractors. Who'd cook for you? How'd you live? You can't stay here. Why, with nobody to take care of you, you'd starve."

Grampa cried, "Goddamn it, I'm an ol' man, but I can still take care a myself. How's Muley here get along? I can get along as good as him. I tell ya I ain't goin', an' ya can lump it. Take Granma with ya if ya want, but ya ain't takin' me, an' that's the end of it."

Pa said helplessly, "Now listen to me, Grampa. Jus' listen to me, jus' a minute."

"Ain't a-gonna listen. I tol' ya what I'm a-gonna do."

Tom touched his father on the shoulder. "Pa, come in the house. I wanta tell ya somepin." And as they moved toward the house, he called, "Ma—come here a minute, will ya?"

In the house one lantern burned and a plate of pork bones was still piled high. Tom said, "Listen, I know Grampa got the right to say he ain't goin', but he can't stay. We know that."

"Sure he can't stay," said Pa.

"Well, look. If we got to catch him an' tie him down, we li'ble to hurt him, an' he'll git so mad he'll hurt himself. Now we can't argue with him. If we could get him drunk it'd be all right. You got any whisky?"

"No," said Pa. "There ain't a drop a whisky in the house. An' John got no whisky. He never has none when he ain't drinkin'."

Ma said, "Tom, I got a half a bottle soothin' sirup I got for Winfiel' when he had them earaches. Think that might work? Use ta put Winfiel' ta sleep when his earache was bad."

"Might," said Tom. "Get it, Ma. We'll give her a try anyways."

"I threw it out on the trash pile," said Ma. She took a lantern and went out, and in a moment she came back with a bottle half full of black medicine.

Tom took it from her and tasted it. "Don' taste bad," he said. "Make up a cup of black coffee, good an' strong. Le's see—says one teaspooon. Better put in a lot, coupla tablespoons."

Ma opened the stove and put a kettle inside, down next to the coals, and she measured water and coffee into it. "Have to give it to 'im in a can," she said. "We got the cups all packed."

Tom and his father went back outside. "Fella got a right to say what he's gonna do. Say, who's eatin' spareribs?" said Grampa.

"We've et," said Tom. "Ma's fixin' you a cup a coffee an' some pork."

He went into the house, and he drank his coffee and ate his pork. The group outside in the growing dawn watched him quietly, through the door. They saw him yawn and sway, and they saw him put his arms on the table and rest his head on his arms and go to sleep.

"He was tar'd anyways," said Tom. "Leave him be."

Now they were ready. Granma, giddy and vague, saying, "What's all this? What you doin' now, so early?" But she was dressed and agreeable. And Ruthie and Winfield were awake, but quiet with the pressure of tiredness and still half dreaming. The light was sifting rapidly over the land. And the movement of the family stopped. They stood about, reluctant to make the first active move to go. They were afraid, now that the time had come—afraid in the same way Grampa was afraid. They saw the shed take shape against the light, and they saw the lanterns pale until they no longer cast their circles of yellow light. The stars went out, few by few, toward the west. And still the family stood about like dream walkers, their eyes focused panoramically, seeing no detail, but the whole dawn, the whole land, the whole texture of the country at once.

Only Muley Graves prowled about restlessly, looking through the bars into the truck, thumping the spare tires hung on the back of the truck. And at last Muley approached Tom. "You goin' over the State line?" he asked. "You gonna break your parole?"

And Tom shook himself free of the numbness. "Jesus

Christ, it's near sunrise," he said loudly. "We got to get goin'." And the others came out of their numbness and moved toward the truck.

"Come on," Tom said. "Let's get Grampa on." Pa and Uncle John and Tom and Al went to the kitchen where Grampa slept, his forehead down on his arms, and a line of drying coffee on the table. They took him under the elbows and lifted him to his feet, and he grumbled and cursed thickly, like a drunken man. Out the door they boosted him, and when they came to the truck Tom and Al climbed up, and, leaning over, hooked their hands under his arms and lifted him gently up, and laid him on top of the load. Al untied the tarpaulin, and they rolled him under and put a box under the tarp beside him, so that the weight of the heavy canvas would not be upon him.

"I got to get that ridge pole fixed," Al said. "Do her tonight when we stop." Grampa grunted and fought weakly against awakening, and when he was finally settled he went deeply to sleep again.

Pa said, "Ma, you an' Granma set in with Al for a while. We'll change around so it's easier, but you start out that way." They got into the cab, and then the rest swarmed up on top of the load. Connie and Rose of Sharon, Pa and Uncle John, Ruthie and Winfield, Tom and the preacher. Noah stood on the ground, looking up at the great load of them sitting on top of the truck.

Al walked around, looking underneath at the springs. "Holy Jesus," he said, "them springs is flat as hell. Lucky I blocked under 'em."

Noah said, "How about the dogs, Pa?"

"I forgot the dogs," Pa said. He whistled shrilly, and one bouncing dog ran in, but only one. Noah caught him and threw him up on the top, where he sat rigid and shivering at the height. "Got to leave the other two," Pa called. "Muley, will you look after 'em some? See they don't starve?"

"Yeah," said Muley. "I'll like to have a couple dogs. Yeah! I'll take 'em."

"Take them chickens, too," Pa said.

Al got into the driver's seat. The starter whirred and caught and whirred again. And then the loose roar of the six cylinders and a blue smoke behind. "So long, Muley," Al called.

And the family called, "Good-by, Muley."

Al slipped in the low gear and let in the clutch. The truck shuddered and strained across the yard. And the second gear took hold. They crawled up the little hill, and the red dust arose about them. "Chr-ist, what a load!" said Al. "We ain't makin' no time on this trip."

Ma tried to look back, but the body of the load cut off her view. She straightened her head and peered straight ahead along the dirt road. And a great weariness was in her eyes.

The people on top of the load did look back. They saw the house and the barn and a little smoke still rising from the chimney. They saw the windows reddening under the first color of the sun. They saw Muley standing forlornly in the dooryard looking after them. And then the hill cut them off. The cotton fields lined the road. And the truck crawled slowly through the dust toward the highway and the west.

11

The houses were left vacant on the land, and the land was vacant because of this. Only the tractor sheds of corrugated iron, silver and gleaming, were alive; and they were alive with metal and gasoline and oil, the disks of the plows shining. The tractors had lights shining, for there is no day and night for a tractor and the disks turn the earth in the darkness and they glitter in the daylight. And when a horse stops work and goes into the barn there is a life and a vitality left, there is a breathing and a warmth, and the feet shift on the straw, and the jaws champ on the hay, and the ears and the eyes are alive. There is a warmth of life in the barn, and the heat and smell of life. But when the motor of a tractor stops, it is as dead as the ore it came from. The heat goes out of it like the living heat that leaves a corpse. Then the corrugated iron doors are closed and the tractor man drives home to town, perhaps twenty miles away, and he need not come back for weeks or months, for the tractor is dead. And this is easy and efficient. So easy that the wonder goes out of work, so efficient that the wonder goes out of land and the working of it, and with the wonder the deep understanding and the relation. And in the tractor man there grows the contempt that comes only to a stranger who has little understanding and no relation. For nitrates are not the land, nor phosphates; and the length of fiber in the cotton is not the land. Carbon is not a man, nor salt nor water nor calcium. He is all of these, but he is much more, much more; and the land is so much more than its analysis. The man who is more than his chemistry, walking on the earth, turning his plow point for a stone, dropping his handles to slide over an outcropping, kneeling in the earth to eat his lunch; that man who is more than his elements knows the land that is more than its analysis. But the machine man, driving a dead tractor on land he does not know and love, understands only chemistry; and he is contemptuous of the land and of himself. When the corrugated iron doors are shut, he goes home, and his home is not the land.

The doors of the empty houses swung open, and drifted back and forth in the wind. Bands of little boys came out from the towns to break the windows and to pick over the debris, looking for treasures. And here's a knife with half the blade gone. That's a good thing. And—smells like a rat died here. And look what Whitey wrote on the wall. He wrote that in the toilet at school, too, an' teacher made 'im wash it off.

When the folks first left, and the evening of the first day came, the hunting cats slouched in from the fields and mewed on the porch. And when no one came out, the cats crept through the open doors and walked mewing through the empty rooms. And then they went back to the fields and were wild cats from then on, hunting gophers and field mice, and sleeping in ditches in the daytime. When the night came, the bats, which had stopped at the doors for fear of light, swooped into the houses and sailed about through the empty rooms, and in a little while they stayed in dark room corners during the day, folded their wings high, and hung head-down among the rafters, and the smell of their droppings was in the empty houses.

And the mice moved in and stored weed seeds in corners, in boxes, in the backs of drawers in the kitchen. And weasels came in to hunt the mice, and the brown owls flew shrieking in and out again.

Now there came a little shower. The weeds sprang up in front of the doorstep, where they had not been allowed, and grass grew up through the porch boards. The houses were vacant and a vacant house falls quickly apart. Splits started up the sheathing from the rusted nails. A dust settled on the floors, and only mouse and weasel and cat tracks disturbed it.

On a night the wind loosened a shingle and flipped it to the ground. The next wind pried into the hole where the shingle had been, lifted off three, and the next, a dozen. The midday sun burned through the hole and threw a glaring spot on the floor. The wild cats crept in from the fields at night, but they did not mew at the doorstep any more. They moved like shadows of a cloud across the moon, into the rooms to hunt the mice. And on windy nights the doors banged, and the ragged curtains fluttered in the broken windows.

12

Highway 66 is the main migrant road. 66—the long concrete path across the country, waving gently up and down on the map, from the Mississippi to Bakersfield—over the red lands and the gray lands, twisting up into the mountains, crossing the Divide and down into the bright and terrible desert, and across the desert to the mountains again, and into the rich California valleys.

66 is the path of a people in flight, refugees from dust and shrinking land, from the thunder of tractors and shrinking ownership, from the desert's slow northward invasion, from the twisting winds that howl up out of Texas, from the floods that bring no richness to the land and steal what little richness is there. From all of these the people are in flight, and they come into 66 from the tributary side roads, from the wagon tracks and the rutted country roads. 66 is the mother road, the road of flight.

Clarksville and Ozark and Van Buren and Fort Smith on 64, and there's an end of Arkansas. And all the roads into Oklahoma City, 66 down from Tulsa, 270 up from McAlester, 81 from Wichita Falls south, from Enid north. Edmond, McLoud, Purcell, 66 out of Oklahoma City; El Reno and Clinton, going west on

66. Hydro, Elk City, and Texola; and there's an end to
Oklahoma. 66 across the Panhandle of Texas. Sham-
rock and McLean, Conway and Amarillo, the yellow.
Wildorado and Vega and Boise, and there's an end of
Texas. Tucumcari and Santa Rosa and into the New
Mexican mountains to Albuquerque, where the road
comes down from Santa Fe. Then down the gorged Rio
Grande to Los Lunas and west on 66 again to Gallup,
and there's the border of New Mexico.

And now the high mountains. Holbrook and Wins-
low and Flagstaff in the high mountains of Arizona.
Then the great plateau rolling like a ground swell.
Ashfork and Kingman and stone mountains again,
where water must be hauled and sold. Then out of
the broken sun-rotted mountains of Arizona to the
Colorado, with green reeds on its banks, and that's
the end of Arizona. There's California just over the
river, and a pretty town to start it. Needles, on the
river. But the river is a stranger in this place. Up
from Needles and over a burned range, and there's
the desert. And 66 goes on over the terrible desert,
where the distance shimmers and the black center
mountains hang unbearably in the distance. At last
there's Barstow, and more desert until at last the
mountains rise up again, the good mountains, and 66
winds through them. Then suddenly a pass, and below the beautiful valley, below orchards and vineyards and little houses, and in the distance a city.
And, oh, my God, it's over.

The people in flight streamed out on 66, sometimes
a single car, sometimes a little caravan. All day they
rolled slowly along the road, and at night they stopped
near water. In the day ancient leaky radiators sent up
columns of steam, loose connecting rods hammered
and pounded. And the men driving the trucks and the
overloaded cars listened apprehensively. How far between towns? It is a terror between towns. If something
breaks—well, if something breaks we camp right here

while Jim walks to town and gets a part and walks back and—how much food we got?

Listen to the motor. Listen to the wheels. Listen with your ears and with your hands on the steering wheel; listen with the palm of your hand on the gear shift lever; listen with your feet on the floor boards. Listen to the pounding old jalopy with all your senses; for a change of tone, a variation of rhythm may mean—a week here? That rattle—that's tappets. Don't hurt a bit. Tappets can rattle till Jesus comes again without no harm. But that thudding as the car moves along—can't hear that—just kind of feel it. Maybe oil isn't gettin' someplace. Maybe a bearing's startin' to go. Jesus, if it's a bearing, what'll we do? Money's goin' fast.

And why's the son-of-a-bitch heat up so hot today? This ain't no climb. Le's look. God Almighty, the fan belt's gone! Here, make a belt outa this little piece a rope. Le's see how long—there. I'll splice the ends. Now take her slow—slow, till we can get to a town. That rope belt won't last long.

'F we can on'y get to California where the oranges grow before this here ol' jug blows up. 'F we on'y can.

And the tires—two layers of fabric worn through. On'y a four-ply tire. Might get a hunderd miles more outa her if we don't hit a rock an' blow her. Which'll we take—a hunderd, maybe, miles, or maybe spoil the tube? Which? A hunderd miles. Well, that's somepin you got to think about. We got tube patches. Maybe when she goes she'll only spring a leak. How about makin' a boot? Might get five hunderd more miles. Le's go on till she blows.

We got to get a tire, but, Jesus, they want a lot for an ol' tire. They look a fella over. They know he got to go on. They know he can't wait. And the price goes up.

Take it or leave it. I ain't in no business for my health. I'm here a-sellin' tires. I ain't givin' 'em away.

I can't help what happens to you. I got to think what happens to me.

How far's the nex' town?

I seen forty-two cars a you fellas go by yesterday. Where you all come from? Where all of you goin'?

Well, California's a big State.

It ain't that big. The whole United States ain't that big. It ain't that big. It ain't big enough. There ain't room enough for you an' me, for your kind an' my kind, for rich and poor together all in one country, for thieves and honest men. For hunger and fat. Whyn't you go back where you come from?

This is a free country. Fella can go where he wants.

That's what *you* think! Ever hear of the border patrol on the California line? Police from Los Angeles— stopped you bastards, turned you back. Says, if you can't buy no real estate, we don't want you. Says, got a driver's license? Le's see it. Tore it up. Says you can't come in without no driver's license.

It's a free country.

Well, try to get some freedom to do. Fella says you're jus' as free as you got jack to pay for it.

In California they got high wages. I got a han'bill here tells about it.

Baloney! I seen folks comin' back. Somebody's kiddin' you. You want that tire or don't ya?

Got to take it, but, Jesus, mister, it cuts into our money! We ain't got much left.

Well, I ain't no charity. Take her along.

Got to, I guess. Let's look her over. Open her up, look a' the casing—you son-of-a-bitch, you said the casing was good. She's broke damn near through.

The hell she is. Well—by George! How come I didn' see that?

You did see it, you son-of-a-bitch. You wanta charge us four bucks for a busted casing. I'd like to take a sock at you.

Now keep your shirt on. I didn' see it, I tell you. Here—tell ya what I'll do. I'll give ya this one for three-fifty.

You'll take a flying jump at the moon! We'll try to make the nex' town.

Think we can make it on that tire?

Got to. I'll go on the rim before I'd give that son-of-a-bitch a dime.

What do ya think a guy in business is? Like he says, he ain't in it for his health. That's what business is. What'd you think it was? Fella's got— See that sign 'longside the road there? Service Club. Luncheon Tuesday, Colmado Hotel? Welcome, brother. That's a Service Club. Fella had a story. Went to one of them meetings an' told the story to all them business men. Says, when I was a kid my ol' man give me a haltered heifer an' says take her down an' git her serviced. An' the fella says, I done it, an' ever' time since then when I hear a business man talkin' about service, I wonder who's gettin' screwed. Fella in business got to lie an' cheat, but he calls it somepin else. That's what's important. You go steal that tire an' you're a thief, but he tried to steal your four dollars for a busted tire. They call that sound business.

Danny in the back seat wants a cup of water.

Have to wait. Got no water here.

Listen—that the rear end?

Can't tell.

Sound telegraphs through the frame.

There goes a gasket. Got to go on. Listen to her whistle. Find a nice place to camp an' I'll jerk the head off. But, God Almighty, the food's gettin' low, the money's gettin' low. When we can't buy no more gas—what then?

Danny in the back seat wants a cup of water. Little fella's thirsty.

Listen to that gasket whistle.

Chee-rist! There she went. Blowed tube an' casing all to hell. Have to fix her. Save that casing to make boots, cut 'em out an' stick 'em inside a weak place.

Cars pulled up beside the road, engine heads off, tires mended. Cars limping along 66 like wounded things, panting and struggling. Too hot, loose connections, loose bearings, rattling bodies.

Danny wants a cup of water.

People in flight along 66. And the concrete road shone like a mirror under the sun, and in the distance the heat made it seem that there were pools of water in the road.

Danny wants a cup of water.

He'll have to wait, poor little fella. He's hot. Nex' service station. *Service* station, like the fella says.

Two hundred and fifty thousand people over the road. Fifty thousand old cars—wounded, steaming. Wrecks along the road, abandoned. Well, what happened to them? What happened to the folks in that car? Did they walk? Where are they? Where does the courage come from? Where does the terrible faith come from?

And here's a story you can hardly believe, but it's true, and it's funny and it's beautiful. There was a family of twelve and they were forced off the land. They had no car. They built a trailer out of junk and loaded it with their possessions. They pulled it out to the side of 66 and waited. And pretty soon a sedan picked them up. Five of them rode in the sedan and seven on the trailer, and a dog on the trailer. They got to California in two jumps. The man who pulled them fed them. And that's true. But how can such courage be, and such faith in their own species? Very few things would teach such faith.

The people in flight from the terror behind—strange things happen to them, some bitterly cruel and some so beautiful that the faith is refired forever.

13

The ancient overloaded Hudson creaked and grunted to the highway at Sallisaw and turned west, and the sun was blinding. But on the concrete road Al built up his speed because the flattened springs were not in danger any more. From Sallisaw to Gore is twenty-one miles and the Hudson was doing thirty-five miles an hour. From Gore to Warner thirteen miles; Warner to Checotah fourteen miles; Checotah a long jump to Henrietta—thirty-four miles, but a real town at the end of it. Henrietta to Castle nineteen miles, and the sun was overhead, and the red fields, heated by the high sun, vibrated the air.

Al, at the wheel, his face purposeful, his whole body listening to the car, his restless eyes jumping from the road to the instrument panel. Al was one with his engine, every nerve listening for weaknesses, for the thumps or squeals, hums and chattering that indicate a change that may cause a breakdown. He had become the soul of the car.

Granma, beside him on the seat, half slept, and whimpered in her sleep, opened her eyes to peer ahead, and then dozed again. And Ma sat beside

Granma, one elbow out the window, and the skin reddening under the fierce sun. Ma looked ahead too, but
her eyes were flat and did not see the road or the
fields, the gas stations, the little eating sheds. She did
not glance at them as the Hudson went by.

Al shifted himself on the broken seat and changed
his grip on the steering wheel. And he sighed, "Makes
a racket, but I think she's awright. God knows what
she'll do if we got to climb a hill with the load we got.
Got any hills 'tween here an' California, Ma?"

Ma turned her head slowly and her eyes came to
life. "Seems to me they's hills," she said. " 'Course I
dunno. But seems to me I heard they's hills an' even
mountains. Big ones."

Granma drew a long whining sigh in her sleep.

Al said, "We'll burn right up if we got climbin' to
do. Have to throw out some a' this stuff. Maybe we
shouldn' a brang that preacher."

"You'll be glad a that preacher 'fore we're through,"
said Ma. "That preacher'll help us." She looked ahead
at the gleaming road again.

Al steered with one hand and put the other on the
vibrating gear-shift lever. He had difficulty in speaking. His mouth formed the words silently before he
said them aloud. "Ma—" She looked slowly around at
him, her head swaying a little with the car's motion.
"Ma, you scared a goin'? You scared a goin' to a new
place?"

Her eyes grew thoughtful and soft. "A little," she
said. "Only it ain't like scared so much. I'm jus' a
settin' here waitin'. When somepin happens that I got
to do somepin—I'll do it."

"Ain't you thinkin' what's it gonna be like when we
get there? Ain't you scared it won't be nice like we
thought?"

"No," she said quickly. "No, I ain't. You can't do
that. I can't do that. It's too much livin' too many
lives. Up ahead they's a thousan' lives we might live,

but when it comes, it'll on'y be one. If I go ahead on all of 'em, it's too much. You got to live ahead 'cause you're so young, but—it's jus' the road goin' by for me. An' it's jus' how soon they gonna wanta eat some more pork bones." Her face tightened. "That's all I can do. I can't do no more. All the rest'd get upset if I done any more'n that. They all depen' on me jus' thinkin' about that."

Granma yawned shrilly and opened her eyes. She looked wildly about. "I got to get out, praise Gawd," she said.

"First clump a brush," said Al. "They's one up ahead."

"Brush or no brush, I got to git out, I tell ya." And she began to whine, "I got to git out. I got to git out."

Al speeded up, and when he came to the low brush he pulled up short. Ma threw the door open and half pulled the struggling old lady out beside the road and into the bushes. And Ma held her so Granma would not fall when she squatted.

On top of the truck the others stirred to life. Their faces were shining with sunburn they could not escape. Tom and Casy and Noah and Uncle John let themselves wearily down. Ruthie and Winfield swarmed down the side-boards and went off into the bushes. Connie helped Rose of Sharon gently down. Under the canvas, Grampa was awake, his head sticking out, but his eyes were drugged and watery and still senseless. He watched the others, but there was little recognition in his watching.

Tom called to him, "Want to come down, Grampa?"

The old eyes turned listlessly to him. "No," said Grampa. For a moment the fierceness came into his eyes. "I ain't a-goin', I tell you. Gonna stay like Muley." And then he lost interest again. Ma came back, helping Granma up the bank to the highway.

"Tom," she said. "Get that pan a bones, under the canvas in back. We got to eat somepin." Tom got the pan and passed it around, and the family stood by the roadside, gnawing the crisp particles from the pork bones.

"Sure lucky we brang these along," said Pa. "Git so stiff up there can't hardly move. Where's the water?"

"Ain't it up with you?" Ma asked. "I set out that gallon jug."

Pa climbed the sides and looked under the canvas. "It ain't here. We must a forgot it."

Thirst set in instantly. Winfield moaned, "I wanta drink. I wanta drink." The men licked their lips, suddenly conscious of their thirst. And a little panic started.

Al felt the fear growing. "We'll get water the first service station we come to. We need some gas too." The family swarmed up the truck sides; Ma helped Granma in and got in beside her. Al started the motor and they moved on.

Castle to Paden twenty-five miles and the sun passed the zenith and started down. And the radiator cap began to jiggle up and down and steam started to whish out. Near Paden there was a shack beside the road and two gas pumps in front of it; and beside a fence, a water faucet and a hose. Al drove in and nosed the Hudson up to the hose. As they pulled in, a stout man, red of face and arms, got up from a chair behind the gas pumps and moved toward them. He wore brown corduroys, and suspenders and a polo shirt; and he had a cardboard sun helmet, painted silver, on his head. The sweat beaded on his nose and under his eyes and formed streams in the wrinkles of his neck. He strolled toward the truck, looking truculent and stern.

"You folks aim to buy anything? Gasoline or stuff?" he asked.

Al was out already, unscrewing the steaming radiator cap with the tips of his fingers, jerking his hand away to escape the spurt when the cap should come loose. "Need some gas, mister."

"Got any money?"

"Sure. Think we're beggin'?"

The truculence left the fat man's face. "Well, that's all right, folks. He'p yourself to water." And he hastened to explain. "Road is full a people, come in, use water, dirty up the toilet, an' then, by God, they'll steal stuff an' don't buy nothin'. Got no money to buy with. Come beggin' a gallon gas to move on."

Tom dropped angrily to the ground and moved toward the fat man. "We're payin' our way," he said fiercely. "You got no call to give us a goin'-over. We ain't asked you for nothin'."

"I ain't," the fat man said quickly. The sweat began to soak through his short-sleeved polo shirt. "Jus' he'p yourself to water, and go use the toilet if you want."

Winfield had got the hose. He drank from the end and then turned the stream over his head and face, and emerged dripping. "It ain't cool," he said.

"I don' know what the country's comin' to," the fat man continued. His complaint had shifted now and he was no longer talking to or about the Joads. "Fifty-six cars a folks go by ever' day, folks all movin' west with kids an' househol' stuff. Where they goin'? What they gonna do?"

"Doin' the same as us," said Tom. "Goin' someplace to live. Tryin' to get along. That's all."

"Well, I don' know what the country's comin' to. I jus' don' know. Here's me tryin' to get along, too. Think any them big new cars stops here? No, sir! They go on to them yella-painted company stations in town. They don't stop no place like this. Most folks stop here ain't got nothin'."

Al flipped the radiator cap and it jumped into the air with a head of steam behind it, and a hollow bubbling sound came out of the radiator. On top of the truck, the suffering hound dog crawled timidly to the edge of the load and looked over, whimpering, toward the water. Uncle John climbed up and lifted him down by the scruff of the neck. For a moment the dog staggered on stiff legs, and then he went to lap the mud under the faucet. In the highway the cars whizzed by, glistening in the heat, and the hot wind of their going fanned into the service-station yard. Al filled the radiator with the hose.

"It ain't that I'm tryin' to git trade outa rich folks," the fat man went on. "I'm jus' tryin' to git trade. Why, the folks that stops here begs gasoline an' they trades for gasoline. I could show you in my back room the stuff they'll trade for gas an' oil: bed an' baby buggies an' pots an' pans. One family traded a doll their kid had for a gallon. An' what'm I gonna do with the stuff, open a junk shop? Why, one fella wanted to gimme his shoes for a gallon. An' if I was that kinda fella I bet I could git——" He glanced at Ma and stopped.

Jim Casy had wet his head, and the drops still coursed down his high forehead, and his muscled neck was wet, and his shirt was wet. He moved over beside Tom. "It ain't the people's fault," he said. "How'd you like to sell the bed you sleep on for a tankful of gas?"

"I know it ain't their fault. Ever' person I talked to is on the move for a damn good reason. But what's the country comin' to? That's what I wanta know. What's it comin' to? Fella can't make a livin' no more. Folks can't make a livin' farmin'. I ask you, what's it comin' to? I can't figure her out. Ever'body I ask, they can't figure her out. Fella wants to trade his shoes so he can git a hunderd miles on. I can't figure her out." He took off his silver hat and wiped his forehead with his palm. And Tom took off his cap and wiped his forehead with it. He went to the hose and wet the cap through and squeezed it and put it on again. Ma worked a tin cup out through the side bars of the truck, and she took water to Granma and to Grampa on top of the load. She stood on the bars and handed the cup to Grampa, and he wet his lips, and then shook his head and refused more. The old eyes looked up at Ma in pain and bewilderment for a moment before the awareness receded again.

Al started the motor and backed the truck up to the gas pump. "Fill her up. She'll take about seven," said Al. We'll give her six so she doesn't spill none."

The fat man put the hose in the tank. "No, sir," he said. "I jus' don't know what this country's comin' to. Relief an' all."

Casy said, "I been walkin' aroun' in the country. Ever'body's askin' that. What we comin' to? Seems to me we don't never come to nothin'. Always on the way. Always goin' and goin'. Why don't folks think about that? They's movement now. People movin'. We know why, an' we know how. Movin' 'cause they got to. That's why folks always move. Movin' 'cause they want somepin better'n what they got. An' that's the on'y way they'll ever git it. Wantin' it an' needin' it, they'll go out an' git it. It's bein' hurt that makes folks mad to fightin'. I been walkin' aroun' the country, an' hearin' folks talk like you."

The fat man pumped the gasoline and the needle turned on the pump dial, recording the amount. "Yeah, but what's it comin' to? That's what I want ta know."

Tom broke in irritably, "Well, you ain't never gonna know. Casy tries to tell ya an' you jest ast the same thing over. I seen fellas like you before. You ain't askin' nothin'; you're jus' singin' a kinda song. 'What we comin' to?' You don' wanta know. Country's movin' aroun', goin' places. They's folks dyin' all aroun'. Maybe you'll die pretty soon, but you won't know nothin'. I seen too many fellas like you. You don't want to know nothin'. Just sing yourself to sleep with a song—'What we comin' to?'" He looked at the gas pump, rusted and old, and at the shack behind it, built of old lumber, the nail holes of its first use still showing through the paint that had been brave, the brave yellow paint that had tried to imitate the big company stations in town. But the paint couldn't cover the old nail holes and the old cracks in the lumber, and the paint could not be renewed. The imitation was a failure and the owner had known it was a failure. And inside the open door of the shack Tom saw the oil barrels, only two of them, and the candy counter with stale candies and licorice whips turning brown with age, and cigarettes. He saw the broken chair and the fly screen with a rusted hole in it. And the littered yard that should have been graveled, and behind, the corn field drying and dying in the sun. Beside the house a little stock of used tires and retreaded tires. And he saw for the first time the fat man's cheap washed pants and his cheap polo shirt and his paper hat. He said, "I didn't mean to sound off at ya, mister. It's the heat. You ain't got nothin'. Pretty soon you'll be on the road yourse'f. And it ain't tractors'll put you there. It's them pretty yella stations in town. Folks is movin'," he said ashamedly. "An' you'll be movin, mister."

The fat man's hand slowed on the pump and stopped while Tom spoke. He looked worriedly at Tom. "How'd you know?" he asked helplessly. "How'd you know we was already talkin' about packin' up an' movin' west?"

Casy answered him. "It's ever'body," he said. "Here's me that used to give all my fight against the devil 'cause I figgered the devil was the enemy. But they's somepin worse'n the devil got hold a the country, an' it ain't gonna let go till it's chopped loose. Ever see one a them Gila monsters take hold, mister? Grabs hold, an' you chop him in two an' his head hangs on. Chop him at the neck an' his head hangs on. Got to take a screw-driver an' pry his head apart to git him loose. An' while he's layin' there, poison is drippin' an' drippin' into the hole he's made with his teeth." He stopped and looked sideways at Tom.

The fat man stared hopelessly straight ahead. His

hand started turning the crank slowly. "I dunno what we're comin' to," he said softly.

Over by the water hose, Connie and Rose of Sharon stood together, talking secretly. Connie washed the tin cup and felt the water with his finger before he filled the cup again. Rose of Sharon watched the cars go by on the highway. Connie held out the cup to her. "This water ain't cool, but it's wet," he said.

She looked at him and smiled secretly. She was all secrets now that she was pregnant, secrets and little silences that seemed to have meanings. She was pleased with herself, and she complained about things that didn't really matter. And she demanded services of Connie that were silly, and both of them knew they were silly. Connie was pleased with her too, and filled with wonder that she was pregnant. He liked to think he was in on the secrets she had. When she smiled slyly, he smiled slyly too, and they exchanged confidences in whispers. The world had drawn close around them, and they were in the center of it, or rather Rose of Sharon was in the center of it with Connie making a small orbit about her. Everything they said was a kind of secret.

She drew her eyes from the highway. "I ain't very thirsty," she said daintily. "But maybe I *ought* to drink."

And he nodded, for he knew well what she meant. She took the cup and rinsed her mouth and spat and then drank the cupful of tepid water. "Want another?" he asked.

"Jus' a half." And so he filled the cup just half, and gave it to her. A Lincoln Zephyr, silvery and low, whisked by. She turned to see where the others were and saw them clustered about the truck. Reassured, she said, "How'd you like to be goin' along in that?"

Connie sighed, "Maybe—after." They both knew what he meant. "An' if they's plenty work in California, we'll git our own car. But them"—he indicated the disappearing Zephyr—"them kind costs as much as a good size house. I ruther have the house."

"I like to have the house *an'* one a them," she said. "But 'course the house would be first because—" And they both knew what she meant. They were terribly excited about the pregnancy.

"You feel awright?" he asked.

"Tar'd. Jus' tar'd ridin' in the sun."

"We *got* to do that or we won't never get to California."

"I know," she said.

The dog wandered, sniffing, past the truck, trotted to the puddle under the hose again and lapped at the muddy water. And then he moved away, nose down and ears hanging. He sniffed his way among the dusty weeds beside the road, to the edge of the pavement. He raised his head and looked across, and then started over. Rose of Sharon screamed shrilly. A big swift car whisked near, tires squealed. The dog dodged helplessly, and with a shriek, cut off in the middle, went under the wheels. The big car slowed for a moment and faces looked back, and then it gathered greater speed and disappeared. And the dog, a blot of blood and tangled, burst intestines, kicked slowly in the road.

Rose of Sharon's eyes were wide. "D'you think it'll hurt?" she begged. "Think it'll hurt?"

Connie put his arm around her. "Come set down," he said. "It wasn't nothin'."

"But I felt it hurt. I felt it kinda jar when I yelled."

"Come set down. It wasn't nothin'. It won't hurt." He led her to the side of the truck away from the dying dog and sat her down on the running board.

Tom and Uncle John walked out to the mess. The last quiver was going out of the crushed body. Tom took it by the legs and dragged it to the side of the road. Uncle John looked embarrassed, as though it were his fault. "I ought ta tied him up," he said.

Pa looked down at the dog for a moment and then he turned away. "Le's get outa here," he said. "I don' know how we was gonna feed 'im anyways. Just as well, maybe."

The fat man came from behind the truck. "I'm sorry, folks," he said. "A dog jus' don' last no time near a highway. I had three dogs run over in a year. Don't keep none, no more." And he said, "Don't you folks worry none about it. I'll take care of 'im. Bury 'im out in the corn field."

Ma walked over to Rose of Sharon, where she sat, still shuddering, on the running board. "You all right, Rosasharn?" she asked. "You feelin' poorly?"

"I seen that. Give me a start."

"I heard ya yip," said Ma. "Git yourself laced up, now."

"You suppose it might of hurt?"

"No," said Ma. " 'F you go to greasin' yourself an' feelin' sorry, an' tuckin' yourself in a swalla's nest, it might. Rise up now, an' he'p me get Granma comf'table. Forget that baby for a minute. He'll take care a hisself."

"Where is Granma?" Rose of Sharon asked.

"I dunno. She's aroun' here somewheres. Maybe in the outhouse."

The girl went toward the toilet, and in a moment she came out, helping Granma along. "She went to sleep in there," said Rose of Sharon.

Granma grinned. "It's nice in there," she said. "They got a patent toilet in there an' the water comes down. I like it in there," she said contentedly. "Would of took a good nap if I wasn't woke up."

"It ain't a nice place to sleep," said Rose of Sharon, and she helped Granma into the car. Granma settled herself happily. "Maybe it ain't nice for purty, but it's nice for nice," she said.

Tom said, "Le's go. We got to make miles."

Pa whistled shrilly. "Now, where'd them kids go?" He whistled again, putting his fingers in his mouth.

In a moment they broke from the corn field, Ruthie ahead and Winfield trailing her. "Eggs!" Ruthie cried. "I got sof' eggs." She rushed close, with Winfield close behind. "Look!" A dozen soft, grayish-white eggs were in her grubby hand. And as she held up her hand, her eyes fell upon the dead dog beside the road. "Oh!" she said. Ruthie and Winfield walked slowly toward the dog. They inspected him.

Pa called to them. "Come on, you, 'less you want to git left."

They turned solemnly and walked to the truck. Ruthie looked once more at the gray reptile eggs in her hand, and then she threw them away. They climbed up the side of the truck. "His eyes was still open," said Ruthie in a hushed tone.

But Winfield gloried in the scene. He said boldly, "His guts was just strowed all over—all over"—he was silent for a moment—"strowed—all—over," he said, and then he rolled over quickly and vomited down the side of the truck. When he sat up again his eyes were watery and his nose running. "It ain't like killin' pigs," he said in explanation.

Al had the hood of the Hudson up, and he checked the oil level. He brought a gallon can from the floor of the front seat and poured a quantity of cheap black oil into the pipe and checked the level again.

Tom came beside him. "Want I should take her a piece?" he asked.

"I ain't tired," said Al.

"Well, you didn' get no sleep las' night. I took a snooze this morning. Get up there on top. I'll take her."

"Awright," Al said reluctantly. "But watch the oil gauge pretty close. Take her slow. An' I been watchin' for a short. Take a look at the needle now an' then. 'F she jumps to discharge, it's a short. An' take her slow, Tom. She's overloaded."

Tom laughed. "I'll watch her," he said. "You can res' easy."

The family piled on top of the truck again. Ma settled herself beside Granma in the seat, and Tom took his place and started the motor. "Sure is loose," he said, and he put it in gear and pulled away down the highway.

The motor droned steadily and the sun receded down the sky in front of them. Granma slept steadily, and even Ma dropped her head forward and dozed. Tom pulled his cap over his eyes to shut out the blinding sun.

Paden to Meeker is thirteen miles, Meeker to Harrah is fourteen miles; and then Oklahoma City—the big city. Tom drove straight on. Ma waked up and looked at the streets as they went through the city. And the family, on top of the truck, stared about at the stores, at the big houses, at the office buildings. And then the buildings grew smaller and the stores smaller. The wrecking yards and hot-dog stands, the out-city dance halls.

Ruthie and Winfield saw it all, and it embarrassed them with its bigness and its strangeness, and it frightened them with the fine-clothed people they saw. They did not speak of it to each other. Later—they would, but not now. They saw the oil derricks in the town, on the edge of the town; oil derricks black, and the smell of oil and gas in the air. But they didn't exclaim. It was so big and so strange it frightened them.

In the street Rose of Sharon saw a man in a light suit. He wore white shoes and a flat straw hat. She touched Connie and indicated the man with her eyes, and then Connie and Rose of Sharon giggled softly to themselves, and the giggles got the best of them. They covered their mouths. And it felt so good that they looked for other people to giggle at. Ruthie and Winfield saw them giggling and it looked such fun that they tried to do it too—but they couldn't. The giggles wouldn't come. But Connie and Rose of Sharon were breathless and red with stifling laughter before they could stop. It got so bad that they had only to look at each other to start over again.

The outskirts were wide spread. Tom drove slowly and carefully in the traffic, and then they were on 66—the great western road, and the sun was sinking on the line of the road. The windshield was bright with dust. Tom pulled his cap lower over his eyes, so low that he had to tilt his head back to see out at all. Granma slept on, the sun on her closed eyelids, and the veins on her temples were blue, and the little bright veins on her cheeks were wine-colored, and the old brown marks on her face turned darker.

Tom said, "We stay on this road right straight through."

Ma had been silent for a long time. "Maybe we better fin' a place to stop 'fore sunset," she said. "I got to get some pork a-boilin' an' some bread made. That takes time."

"Sure," Tom agreed. "We ain't gonna make this trip in one jump. Might's well stretch ourselves."

Oklahoma City to Bethany is fourteen miles.

Tom said, "I think we better stop 'fore the sun goes down. Al got to build that thing on the top. Sun'll kill the folks up there."

Ma had been dozing again. Her head jerked upright. "Got to get some supper a-cookin'," she said. And she said, "Tom, your pa tol' me about you crossin' the State line——"

He was a long time answering. "Yeah? What about it, Ma?"

"Well, I'm scairt about it. It'll make you kinda runnin' away. Maybe they'll catch ya."

Tom held his hand over his eyes to protect himself from the lowering sun. "Don't you worry," he said. "I figgered her out. They's lots a fellas out on parole an' they's more goin' in all the time. If I get caught for anything else out west, then they got my pitcher an'

my prints in Washington. They'll sen' me back. But if
I don't do no crimes, they won't give a damn."

"Well, I'm a-scairt about it. Sometimes you do a
crime, an' you don't even know it's bad. Maybe they
got crimes in California we don't even know about.
Maybe you gonna do somepin an' it's all right, an' in
California it ain't all right."

"Be jus' the same if I wasn't on parole," he said.
"On'y if I get caught I get a bigger jolt'n other folks.
Now you quit a-worryin'," he said. "We got plenty to
worry about 'thout you figgerin' out things to worry
about."

"I can't he'p it," she said. "Minute you cross the
line you done a crime."

"Well, tha's better'n stickin' around Sallisaw an'
starvin' to death," he said. "We better look out for a
place to stop."

They went through Bethany and out on the other
side. In a ditch, where a culvert went under the road,
an old touring car was pulled off the highway and a
little tent was pitched beside it, and smoke came out
of a stove pipe through the tent. Tom pointed ahead.
"There's some folks campin'. Looks like as good a
place as we seen." He slowed his motor and pulled to
a stop beside the road. The hood of the old touring car
was up, and a middle-aged man stood looking down at
the motor. He wore a cheap straw sombrero, a blue
shirt, and a black, spotted vest, and his jeans were
stiff and shiny with dirt. His face was lean, the deep
cheek-lines great furrows down his face so that his
cheek bones and chin stood out sharply. He looked up
at the Joad truck and his eyes were puzzled and angry.

Tom leaned out of the window. "Any law 'gainst
folks stoppin' here for the night?"

The man had seen only the truck. His eyes focused
down on Tom. "I dunno," he said. "We on'y stopped
here 'cause we couldn't git no further."

"Any water here?"

The man pointed to a service-station shack about a quarter of a mile ahead. "They's water there they'll let ya take a bucket of."

Tom hesitated. "Well, ya 'spose we could camp down 'longside?"

The lean man looked puzzled. "We don't own it," he said. "We on'y stopped here 'cause this goddamn ol' trap wouldn' go no further."

Tom insisted. "Anyways you're here an' we ain't. You got a right to say if you wan' neighbors or not."

The appeal to hospitality had an instant effect. The lean face broke into a smile. "Why, sure, come on off the road. Proud to have ya." And he called, "Sairy, there's some folks goin' to stay with us. Come on out an' say how d'ya do. Sairy ain't well," he added. The tent flaps opened and a wizened woman came out—a face wrinkled as a dried leaf and eyes that seemed to flame in her face, black eyes that seemed to look out of a well of horror. She was small and shuddering. She held herself upright by a tent flap, and the hand holding onto the canvas was a skeleton covered with wrinkled skin.

When she spoke her voice had a beautiful low timbre, soft and modulated, and yet with ringing overtones. "Tell 'em welcome," she said. "Tell 'em good an' welcome."

Tom drove off the field and brought his truck into the field and lined it up with the touring car. And people boiled down from the truck; Ruthie and Winfield too quickly, so that their legs gave way and they shrieked at the pins and needles that ran through their limbs. Ma went quickly to work. She untied the three-gallon bucket from the back of the truck and approached the squealing children. "Now you go git the water—right down there. Ask nice. Say, 'Please, kin we git a bucket a water?' and say, 'Thank you.' An' carry it back together helpin', an' don't spill none. An' if you see stick wood to burn, bring it on." The children stamped away toward the shack.

By the tent a little embarrassment had set in, and social intercourse had paused before it started. Pa said, "You ain't Oklahomy folks?"

And Al, who stood near the car, looked at the license plates. "Kansas," he said.

The lean man said, "Galena, or right about there. Wilson, Ivy Wilson."

"We're Joads," said Pa. "We come from right near Sallisaw."

"Well, we're proud to meet you folks," said Ivy Wilson. "Sairy, these is Joads."

"I knowed you wasn't Oklahomy folks. You talk queer, kinda—that ain't no blame, you understan'."

"Ever'body says words different," said Ivy. "Arkansas folks says 'em different, and Oklahomy folks says 'em different. And we seen a lady from Massachusetts, an' she said 'em differentest of all. Couldn' hardly make out what she was sayin'."

Noah and Uncle John and the preacher began to unload the truck. They helped Grampa down and sat him on the ground and he sat limply, staring ahead of him. "You sick, Grampa?" Noah asked.

"You goddamn right," said Grampa weakly. "Sicker'n hell."

Sairy Wilson walked slowly and carefully toward him. "How'd you like ta come in our tent?" she asked. "You kin lay down on our mattress an' rest."

He looked up at her, drawn by her soft voice. "Come over now," she said. "You'll git some rest. We'll he'p you over."

Without warning Grampa began to cry. His chin wavered and his old lips tightened over his mouth and he sobbed hoarsely. Ma rushed over to him and put her arms around him. She lifted him to his feet, her broad back straining, and she half lifted, half helped him into the tent.

Uncle John said, "He must be good an' sick. He ain't never done that before. Never seen him blubberin' in my life." He jumped up on the truck and tossed a mattress down.

Ma came out of the tent and went to Casy. "You been aroun' sick people," she said. "Grampa's sick. Won't you go take a look at him?"

Casy walked quickly to the tent and went inside. A double mattress was on the ground, the blankets spread neatly; and a little tin stove stood on iron legs, and the fire in it burned unevenly. A bucket of water, a wooden box of supplies, and a box for a table, that was all. The light of the setting sun came pinkly through the tent walls. Sairy Wilson knelt on the ground, beside the mattress, and Grampa lay on his back. His eyes were open, staring upward, and his cheeks were flushed. He breathed heavily.

Casy took the skinny old wrist in his fingers. "Feeling kinda tired, Grampa?" he asked. The staring eyes moved toward his voice but did not find him. The lips practiced a speech but did not speak it. Casy felt the pulse and he dropped the wrist and put his hand on Grampa's forehead. A struggle began in the old man's body, his legs moved restlessly and his hands stirred. He said a whole string of blurred sounds that were not words, and his face was red under the spiky white whiskers.

Sairy Wilson spoke softly to Casy. "Know what's wrong?"

He looked up at the wrinkled face and burning eyes. "Do you?"

"I—think so."

"What?" Casy asked.

"Might be wrong. I wouldn' like to say."

Casy looked back at the twitching red face. "Would you say—maybe—he's workin' up a stroke?"

"I'd say that," said Sairy. "I seen it three times before."

From outside came the sounds of camp-making, wood chopping, and the rattle of pans. Ma looked through the flaps. "Granma wants to come in. Would she better?"

The preacher said, "She'll jus' fret if she don't."

"Think he's awright?" Ma asked.

Casy shook his head slowly. Ma looked quickly down at the struggling old face with blood pounding through it. She drew outside and her voice came through. "He's awright, Granma. He's jus' takin' a little res'."

And Granma answered sulkily. "Well, I want ta see him. He's a tricky devil. He wouldn't never let ya know." And she came scurrying through the flaps. She stood over the mattress and looked down. "What's the matter'th you?" she demanded of Grampa. And again his eyes reached toward her voice and his lips writhed. "He's sulkin'," said Granma. "I tol' you he was tricky. He was gonna sneak away this mornin' so he wouldn't have to come. An' then his hip got a-hurtin'," she said disgustedly. "He's jus' sulkin'. I seen him when he wouldn't talk to nobody before."

Casy said gently, "He ain't sulkin', Granma. He's sick."

"Oh!" She looked down at the old man again. "Sick bad, you think?"

"Purty bad, Granma."

For a moment she hesitated uncertainly. "Well," she said quickly, "why ain't you prayin'? You're a preacher, ain't you?"

Casy's strong fingers blundered over to Grampa's wrist and clasped around it. "I tol' you, Granma. I ain't a preacher no more."

"Pray anyway," she ordered. "You know all the stuff by heart."

"I can't," said Casy. "I don't know what to pray for or who to pray to."

Granma's eyes wandered away and came to rest on

Sairy. "He won't pray," she said. "D'I ever tell ya how
Ruthie prayed when she was a little skinner? Says,
'Now I lay me down to sleep. I pray the Lord my soul
to keep. An' when she got there the cupboard was
bare, an' so the poor dog got none. Amen.' That's jus'
what she done." The shadow of someone walking between the tent and the sun crossed the canvas.

Grampa seemed to be struggling; all his muscles
twitched. And suddenly he jarred as though under a
heavy blow. He lay still and his breath was stopped.
Casy looked down at the old man's face and saw that it
was turning a blackish purple. Sairy touched Casy's
shoulder. She whispered, "His tongue, his tongue, his
tongue."

Casy nodded. "Get in front a Granma." He pried
the tight jaws apart and reached into the old man's
throat for the tongue. As he lifted it clear, a rattling
breath came out, and a sobbing breath was indrawn.
Casy found a stick on the ground and held down the
tongue with it, and the uneven breath rattled in and
out.

Granma hopped about like a chicken. "Pray," she
said. "Pray, you. Pray, I tell ya." Sairy tried to hold
her back. "Pray, goddamn you!" Granma cried.

Casy looked up at her for a moment. The rasping
breath came louder and more unevenly. "Our Father
who art in Heaven, hallowed be Thy name———"

"Glory!" shouted Granma.

"Thy kingdom come, Thy will be done—on earth—
as it is in Heaven."

"Amen."

A long gasping sigh came from the open mouth, and
then a crying release of air.

"Give us this day—our daily bread—and forgive
us—" The breathing had stopped. Casy looked down
into Grampa's eyes and they were clear and deep and
penetrating, and there was a knowing serene look in
them.

"Hallelujah!" said Granma. "Go on."

"Amen," said Casy.

Granma was still then. And outside the tent all the noise had stopped. A car whished past on the highway. Casy still knelt on the floor beside the mattress. The people outside were listening, standing quietly intent on the sounds of dying. Sairy took Granma by the arm and led her outside, and Granma moved with dignity and held her head high. She walked for the family and held her head straight for the family. Sairy took her to a mattress lying on the ground and sat her down on it. And Granma looked straight ahead, proudly, for she was on show now. The tent was still, and at last Casy spread the tent flaps with his hands and stepped out.

Pa asked softly, "What was it?"

"Stroke," said Casy. "A good quick stroke."

Life began to move again. The sun touched the horizon and flattened over it. And along the highway there came a long line of huge freight trucks with red sides. They rumbled along, putting a little earthquake in the ground, and the standing exhaust pipes sputtered blue smoke from the Diesel oil. One man drove each truck, and his relief man slept in a bunk high up against the ceiling. But the trucks never stopped; they thundered day and night and the ground shook under their heavy march.

The family became a unit. Pa squatted down on the ground, and Uncle John beside him. Pa was the head of the family now. Ma stood behind him. Noah and Tom and Al squatted, and the preacher sat down, and then reclined on his elbow. Connie and Rose of Sharon walked at a distance. Now Ruthie and Winfield, clattering up with a bucket of water held between them, felt the change, and they slowed up and set down the bucket and moved quietly to stand with Ma.

Granma sat proudly, coldly, until the group was formed, until no one looked at her, and then she lay down and covered her face with her arm. The red sun set and left a shining twilight on the land, so that faces were bright in the evening and eyes shone in reflection of the sky. The evening picked up light where it could.

Pa said, "It was in Mr. Wilson's tent."

Uncle John nodded. "He loaned his tent."

"Fine friendly folks," Pa said softly.

Wilson stood by his broken car, and Sairy had gone to the mattress to sit beside Granma, but Sairy was careful not to touch her.

Pa called, "Mr. Wilson!" The man scuffed near and squatted down, and Sairy came and stood beside him. Pa said, "We're thankful to you folks."

"We're proud to help," said Wilson.

"We're beholden to you," said Pa.

"There's no beholden in a time of dying," said Wilson, and Sairy echoed him, "Never no beholden."

Al said, "I'll fix your car—me an' Tom will." And Al looked proud that he could return the family's obligation.

"We could use some help." Wilson admitted the retiring of the obligation.

Pa said, "We got to figger what to do. They's laws. You got to report a death, an' when you do that, they either take forty dollars for the undertaker or they take him for a pauper."

Uncle John broke in, "We never did have no paupers."

Tom said, "Maybe we got to learn. We never got booted off no land before, neither."

"We done it clean," said Pa. "There can't be no blame be laid on us. We never took nothin' we couldn' pay; we never suffered no man's charity. When Tom here got in trouble we could hold up our heads. He only done what any man would a done."

"Then what'll we do?" Uncle John asked.

"We go in like the law says an' they'll come out for him. We on'y got a hundred an' fifty dollars. They take forty to bury Grampa an' we won't get to California—or else they'll bury him a pauper." The men stirred restlessly, and they studied the darkening ground in front of their knees.

Pa said softly, "Grampa buried his pa with his own hand, done it in dignity, an' shaped the grave nice with his own shovel. That was a time when a man had the right to be buried by his own son an' a son had the right to bury his own father."

"The law says different now," said Uncle John.

"Sometimes the law can't be foller'd no way," said Pa. "Not in decency, anyways. They's lots of times you can't. When Floyd was loose an' goin' wild, law said we got to give him up—an' nobody give him up. Sometimes a fella got to sift the law. I'm sayin' now I got the right to bury my own pa. Anybody got somepin to say?"

The preacher rose high on his elbow. "Law changes," he said, "but 'got to's' go on. You got the right to do what you got to do."

Pa turned to Uncle John. "It's your right too, John. You got any word against?"

"No word against," said Uncle John. "On'y it's like hidin' him in the night. Grampa's way was t'come out a-shootin'."

Pa said ashamedly, "We can't do like Grampa done. We got to get to California 'fore our money gives out."

Tom broke in, "Sometimes fellas workin' dig up a man an' then they raise hell an' figger he been killed. The gov'ment's got more interest in a dead man than a live one. They'll go hell-scrapin' tryin' to find out who he was and how he died. I offer we put a note of writin' in a bottle an' lay it with Grampa, tellin' who he is an' how he died, an' why he's buried here."

Pa nodded agreement. "Tha's good. Wrote out in a nice hand. Be not so lonesome too, knowin' his name is there with 'im, not jus' a old fella lonesome underground. Any more stuff to say?" The circle was silent.

Pa turned his head to Ma. "You'll lay 'im out?"

"I'll lay 'im out," said Ma. "But who's to get supper?"

Sairy Wilson said, "I'll get supper. You go right ahead. Me an' that big girl of yourn."

"We sure thank you," said Ma. "Noah, you get into them kegs an' bring out some nice pork. Salt won't be deep in it yet, but it'll be right nice eatin'."

"We got a half sack a potatoes," said Sairy.

Ma said, "Gimme two half-dollars." Pa dug in his pocket and gave her the silver. She found the basin, filled it full of water, and went into the tent. It was nearly dark in there. Sairy came in and lighted a candle and stuck it upright in a box and then she went out. For a moment Ma looked down at the dead old man. And then in pity she tore a strip from her own apron and tied up his jaw. She straightened his limbs, folded his hands over his chest. She held his eyelids down and laid a silver piece on each one. She buttoned his shirt and washed his face.

Sairy looked in, saying, "Can I give you any help?"

Ma looked slowly up. "Come in," she said. "I like to talk to ya."

"That's a good big girl you got," said Sairy. "She's right in peelin' potatoes. What can I do to help?"

"I was gonna wash Grampa all over," said Ma, "but he got no other clo'es to put on. An' 'course your quilt's spoilt. Can't never get the smell a death from a quilt. I seen a dog growl an' shake at a mattress my ma died on, an' that was two years later. We'll wrop 'im in your quilt. We'll make it up to you. We got a quilt for you."

Sairy said, "You shouldn't talk like that. We're proud to help. I ain't felt so—safe in a long time. People needs—to help."

Ma nodded. "They do," she said. She looked long into the old whiskery face, with its bound jaw and silver eyes shining in the candlelight. "He ain't gonna look natural. We'll wrop him up."

"The ol' lady took it good."

"Why, she's so old," said Ma, "maybe she don't even rightly know what happened. Maybe she won't really know for quite a while. Besides, us folks takes a pride holdin' in. My pa used to say, 'Anybody can break down. It takes a man not to.' We always try to hold in." She folded the quilt neatly about Grampa's legs and around his shoulders. She brought the corner of the quilt over his head like a cowl and pulled it down over his face. Sairy handed her half-a-dozen big safety pins, and she pinned the quilt neatly and tightly about the long package. And at last she stood up. "It won't be a bad burying," she said. "We got a preacher to see him in, an' his folks is all aroun'." Suddenly she swayed a little, and Sairy went to her and steadied her. "It's sleep——" Ma said in a shamed tone. "No, I'm awright. We been so busy getting ready, you see."

"Come out in the air," Sairy said.

"Yeah, I'm all done here." Sairy blew out the candle and the two went out.

A bright fire burned in the bottom of the little gulch. And Tom, with sticks and wire, had made supports from which two kettles hung and bubbled furiously, and good steam poured out under the lids. Rose of Sharon knelt on the ground out of range of the burning heat, and she had a long spoon in her hand. She saw Ma come out of the tent, and she stood up and went to her.

"Ma," she said. "I got to ask."

"Scared again?" Ma asked. "Why, you can't get through nine months without sorrow."

"But will it—hurt the baby?"

Ma said, "They used to be a sayin', 'A chile born outa sorrow'll be a happy chile.' Isn't that so, Mis' Wilson?"

"I heard it like that," said Sairy. "An' I heard the other: 'Born outa too much joy'll be a doleful boy.'"

"I'm all jumpy inside," said Rose of Sharon.

"Well, we ain't none of us jumpin' for fun," said Ma. "You jes' keep watchin' the pots."

On the edge of the ring of firelight the men had gathered. For tools they had a shovel and a mattock. Pa marked out the ground—eight feet long and three feet wide. The work went on in relays. Pa chopped the earth with the mattock and then Uncle John shoveled it out. Al chopped and Tom shoveled, Noah chopped and Connie shoveled. And the hole drove down, for the work never diminished in speed. The shovels of dirt flew out of the hole in quick spurts. When Tom was shoulder deep in the rectangular pit, he said, "How deep, Pa?"

"Good an' deep. A couple feet more. You get out now, Tom, and get that paper wrote."

Tom boosted himself out of the hole and Noah took his place. Tom went to Ma, where she tended the fire. "We got any paper an' pen, Ma?"

Ma shook her head slowly. "No-o. That's one thing we didn' bring." She looked toward Sairy. And the little woman walked quickly to her tent. She brought back a Bible and a half pencil. "Here," she said. "They's a clear page in front. Use that an' tear it out." She handed book and pencil to Tom.

Tom sat down in the firelight. He squinted his eyes in concentration, and at last wrote slowly and carefully on the end paper in big clear letters: "This here is William James Joad, dyed of a stroke, old old man. His fokes bured him becaws they got no money to pay for funerls. Nobody kilt him. Jus a stroke an he dyed." He stopped. "Ma, listen to this here." He read it slowly to her.

"Why, that soun's nice," she said. "Can't you stick on somepin from Scripture so it'll be religious? Open up an' git a-sayin' somepin outa Scripture."

"Got to be short," said Tom. "I ain't got much room lef' on the page."

Sairy said, "How 'bout 'God have mercy on his soul'?"

"No," said Tom. "Sounds too much like he was hung. I'll copy somepin." He turned the pages and read, mumbling his lips, saying the words under his breath. "Here's a good short one," he said. " 'An' Lot said unto them, Oh, not so, my Lord.' "

"Don't mean nothin'," said Ma. "Long's you're gonna put one down, it might's well mean somepin."

Sairy said, "Turn to Psalms, over further. You kin always get somepin outa Psalms."

Tom flipped the pages and looked down the verses. "Now here *is* one," he said. "This here's a nice one, just blowed full a religion: 'Blessed is he whose transgression is forgiven, whose sin is covered.' How's that?"

"That's real nice," said Ma. "Put that one in."

Tom wrote it carefully. Ma rinsed and wiped a fruit jar and Tom screwed the lid down tight on it. "Maybe the preacher ought to wrote it," he said.

Ma said, "No, the preacher wasn't no kin." She took the jar from him and went to the dark tent. She unpinned the covering and slipped the fruit jar in under the thin cold hands and pinned the comforter tight again. And then she went back to the fire.

The men came from the grave, their faces shining with perspiration. "Awright," said Pa. He and John and Noah and Al went into the tent, and they came out carrying the long, pinned bundle between them. They carried it to the grave. Pa leaped into the hole and received the bundle in his arms and laid it gently down. Uncle John put out a hand and helped Pa out of the hole. Pa asked, "How about Granma?"

"I'll see," Ma said. She walked to the mattress and looked down at the old woman for a moment. Then she went back to the grave. "Sleepin'," she said. "Maybe she'll hold it against me, but I ain't a-gonna wake her up. She's tar'd."

Pa said, "Where at's the preacher? We oughta have a prayer."

Tom said, "I seen him walkin' down the road. He don't like to pray no more."

"Don't like to pray?"

"No," said Tom. "He ain't a preacher no more. He figgers it ain't right to fool people actin' like a preacher when he ain't a preacher. I bet he went away so nobody wouldn' ast him."

Casy had come quietly near, and he heard Tom speaking. "I didn' run away," he said. "I'll he'p you folks, but I won't fool ya."

Pa said, "Won't you say a few words? Ain't none of our folks ever been buried without a few words."

"I'll say 'em," said the preacher.

Connie led Rose of Sharon to the graveside, she reluctant. "You got to," Connie said. "It ain't decent not to. It'll jus' be a little."

The firelight fell on the grouped people, showing their faces and their eyes, dwindling on their dark clothes. All the hats were off now. The light danced, jerking over the people.

Casy said, "It'll be a short one." He bowed his head, and the others followed his lead. Casy said solemnly, "This here ol' man jus' lived a life an' just died out of it. I don' know whether he was good or bad, but that don't matter much. He was alive, an' that's what matters. An' now he's dead, an' that don't matter. Heard a fella tell a poem one time, an' he says 'All that lives is holy.' Got to thinkin', an' purty soon it means more than the words says. An' I wouldn't pray for a ol' fella that's dead. He's awright. He got a job to do, but it's all laid out for 'im an' there's on'y one way to do it. But us, we got a job to do, an' they's a thousan' ways, an' we don' know which one to take. An' if I was to pray, it'd be for the folks that don' know which way to turn. Grampa here, he got the easy straight. An' now cover 'im up an let 'im get to his work." He raised his head.

Pa said, "Amen," and the others muttered, "Amen." Then Pa took the shovel, half filled it with dirt, and spread it gently into the black hole. He handed the shovel to Uncle John, and John dropped in a shovelful. Then the shovel went from hand to hand until every man had his turn. When all had taken their duty and their right, Pa attacked the mound of loose dirt and hurriedly filled the hole. The women moved back to the fire to see to supper. Ruthie and Winfield watched, absorbed.

Ruthie said solemnly, "Grampa's down under there." And Winfield looked at her with horrified eyes. And then he ran away to the fire and sat on the ground and sobbed to himself.

Pa half filled the hole, and then he stood panting with the effort while Uncle John finished it. And John was shaping up the mound when Tom stopped him. "Listen," Tom said. " 'F we leave a grave, they'll have it open in no time. We got to hide it. Level her off an' we'll strew dry grass. We got to do that."

Pa said, "I didn't think a that. It ain't right to leave a grave unmounded."

"Can't he'p it," said Tom. "They'd dig 'im right up, an' we'd get it for breakin' the law. You know what I get if I break the law."

"Yeah," Pa said. "I forgot that." He took the shovel from John and leveled the grave. "She'll sink, come winter," he said.

"Can't he'p that," said Tom. "We'll be a long ways off by winter. Tromp her in good, an' we'll strew stuff over her."

When the pork and potatoes were done the families sat about on the ground and ate, and they were quiet, staring into the fire. Wilson, tearing a slab of meat with his teeth, sighed with contentment. "Nice eatin' pig," he said.

"Well," Pa explained, "we had a couple shoats, an' we thought we might's well eat 'em. Can't get nothin' for them. When we get kinda use' ta movin' an' Ma can set up bread, why, it'll be pretty nice, seein' the country an' two kegs a' pork right in the truck. How long you folks been on the road?"

Wilson cleared his teeth with his tongue and swallowed. "We ain't been lucky," he said. "We been three weeks from home."

"Why, God Awmighty, we aim to be in California in ten days or less."

Al broke in, "I dunno, Pa. With that load we're packin', we maybe ain't never gonna get there. Not if they's mountains to go over."

They were silent about the fire. Their faces were turned downward and their hair and foreheads showed in the firelight. Above the little dome of the firelight the summer stars shone thinly, and the heat of the day was gradually withdrawing. On her mattress, away from the fire, Granma whimpered softly like a puppy. The heads all turned in her direction.

Ma said, "Rosasharn, like a good girl go lay down with Granma. She needs somebody now. She's knowin', now."

Rose of Sharon got to her feet and walked to the mattress and lay beside the old woman, and the murmur of their soft voices drifted to the fire. Rose of Sharon and Granma whispered together on the mattress.

Noah said, "Funny thing is—losin' Grampa ain't made me feel no different than I done before. I ain't no sadder than I was."

"It's just the same thing," Casy said. "Grampa an' the old place, they was jus' the same thing."

Al said, "It's a goddamn shame. He's been talkin' what he's gonna do, how he's gonna squeeze grapes over his head an' let the juice run in his whiskers, an' all stuff like that."

Casy said, "He was foolin', all the time. I think he knowed it. An' Grampa didn' die tonight. He died the minute you took 'im off the place."

"You sure a that?" Pa cried.

"Why, no. Oh, he was breathin'," Casy went on, "but he was dead. He was that place, an' he knowed it."

Uncle John said, "Did you know he was a-dyin'?"

"Yeah," said Casy. "I knowed it."

John gazed at him, and a horror grew in his face. "An' you didn' tell nobody?"

"What good?" Casy asked.

"We—we might of did somepin."

"What?"

"I don' know, but——"

"No," Casy said, "you couldn' a done nothin'. Your way was fixed an' Grampa didn' have no part in it. He didn' suffer none. Not after fust thing this mornin'. He's jus' stayin' with the lan'. He couldn' leave it."

Uncle John sighed deeply.

Wilson said, "We hadda leave my brother Will." The heads turned toward him. "Him an' me had forties side by side. He's older'n me. Neither one ever drove a car. Well, we went in an' we sol' ever'thing. Will, he bought a car, an' they give him a kid to show 'im how to use it. So the afternoon 'fore we're gonna start, Will an' Aunt Minnie go a-practicin'. Will, he comes to a bend in the road an' he yells 'Whoa' an' yanks back, an' he goes through a fence. An' he yells 'Whoa, you bastard' an' tromps down on the gas an' goes over into a gulch. An' there he was. Didn't have nothing more to sell an' didn't have no car. But it were his own damn fault, praise God. He's so damn mad he won't come along with us, jus' set there a-cussin' an' a-cussin'."

"What's he gonna do?"

"I dunno. He's too mad to figger. An' we couldn'

wait. On'y had eighty-five dollars to go on. We couldn'
set an' cut it up, but we et it up anyways. Didn' go a
hunderd mile when a tooth in the rear end bust, an'
cost thirty dollars to get her fix', an' then we got to get
a tire, an' then a spark plug cracked, an' Sairy got
sick. Had ta stop ten days. An' now the goddamn car
is bust again, an' money's gettin' low. I dunno when
we'll ever get to California. 'F I could on'y fix a car,
but I don' know nothin' about cars."

Al asked importantly, "What's the matter?"

"Well, she jus' won't run. Starts an' farts an' stops.
In a minute she'll start again, an' then 'fore you can git
her goin', she peters out again."

"Runs a minute an' then dies?"

"Yes, sir. An' I can't keep her a-goin' no matter
how much gas I give her. Got worse an' worse, an' now
I cain't get her a-movin' a-tall."

Al was very proud and very mature, then. "I think
you got a plugged gas line. I'll blow her out for ya."

And Pa was proud too. "He's a good hand with a
car," Pa said.

"Well, I'll sure thank ya for a han'. I sure will.
Makes a fella kinda feel—like a little kid, when he
can't fix nothin'. When we get to California I aim to
get me a nice car. Maybe she won't break down."

Pa said, "When we get there. Gettin' there's the
trouble."

"Oh, but she's worth it," said Wilson. "Why, I seen
han'bills how they need folks to pick fruit, an' good
wages. Why, jus' think how it's gonna be, under them
shady trees a-pickin' fruit an' takin' a bite ever' once
in a while. Why, hell, they don't care how much you
eat 'cause they got so much. An' with them good
wages, maybe a fella can get hisself a little piece a
land an' work out for extra cash. Why, hell, in a
couple years I bet a fella could have a place of his
own."

Pa said, "We seen them han'bills. I got one right here." He took out his purse and from it took a folded orange handbill. In black type it said, "Pea Pickers Wanted in California. Good Wages All Season. 800 Pickers Wanted."

Wilson looked at it curiously. "Why, that's the one I seen. The very same one. You s'pose—maybe they got all eight hunderd awready?"

Pa said, "This is jus' one little part a California. Why, that's the secon' biggest State we got. S'pose they did get all them eight hunderd. They's plenty places else. I rather pick fruit anyways. Like you says, under them trees an' pickin' fruit—why, even the kids'd like to do that."

Suddenly, Al got up and walked to the Wilsons' touring car. He looked in it for a moment and then came back and sat down.

"You can't fix her tonight," Wilson said.

"I know. I'll get to her in the morning."

Tom had watched his young brother carefully. "I was thinkin' somepin like that myself," he said.

Noah asked, "What you two fellas talkin' about?"

Tom and Al were silent, each waiting for the other. "You tell 'em," Al said finally.

"Well, maybe it's no good, an' maybe it ain't the same thing Al's thinking. Here she is, anyways. We got a overload, but Mr. an' Mrs. Wilson ain't. If some of us folks could ride with them an' take some a their light stuff in the truck, we wouldn't break no springs an' we could git up hills. An' me an' Al both knows about a car, so we could keep that car a-rollin'. We'd keep together on the road an' it'd be good for ever'body."

Wilson jumped up. "Why, sure. Why, we'd be proud. We certainly would. You hear that, Sairy?"

"It's a nice thing," said Sairy. "Wouldn' be a burden on you folks?"

"No, by God," said Pa. "Wouldn't be no burden at all. You'd be helpin' us."

Wilson settled back uneasily. "Well, I dunno."

"What's a matter, don' you wanta?"

"Well, ya see—I on'y got 'bout thirty dollars lef', an' I won't be no burden."

Ma said, "You won't be no burden. Each'll help each, an' we'll all git to California. Sairy Wilson he'ped lay Grampa out," and she stopped. The relationship was plain.

Al cried, "That car'll take six easy. Say me to drive, an' Rosasharn an' Connie and Granma. Then we take the big light stuff an' pile her on the truck. An' we'll trade off ever' so often." He spoke loudly, for a load of worry was lifted from him.

They smiled shyly and looked down at the ground. Pa fingered the dusty earth with his fingertips. He said, "Ma favors a white house with oranges growin' around. They's a big pitcher on a calendar she seen."

Sairy said, "If I get sick again, you got to go on an' get there. We ain't a-goin' to burden."

Ma looked carefully at Sairy, and she seemed to see for the first time the pain-tormented eyes and the face that was haunted and shrinking with pain. And Ma said, "We gonna see you get through. You said yourself, you can't let help go unwanted."

Sairy studied her wrinkled hands in the firelight. "We got to get some sleep tonight." She stood up.

"Grampa—it's like he's dead a year," Ma said.

The families moved lazily to their sleep, yawning luxuriously. Ma sloshed the tin plates off a little and rubbed the grease free with a flour sack. The fire died down and the stars descended. Few passenger cars went by on the highway now, but the transport trucks thundered by at intervals and put little earthquakes in the ground. In the ditch the cars were hardly visible under the starlight. A tied dog howled at the service station down the road. The families were quiet and sleeping, and the field mice grew bold and scampered about among the mattresses. Only Sairy Wilson was awake. She stared into the sky and braced her body firmly against pain.

14

The western land, nervous under the beginning change. The Western States, nervous as horses before a thunder storm. The great owners, nervous, sensing a change, knowing nothing of the nature of the change. The great owners, striking at the immediate thing, the widening government, the growing labor unity; striking at new taxes, at plans; not knowing these things are results, not causes. Results, not causes; results, not causes. The causes lie deep and simple—the causes are a hunger in a stomach, multiplied a million times; a hunger in a single soul, hunger for joy and some security, multiplied a million times; muscles and mind aching to grow, to work, to create, multiplied a million times. The last clear definite function of man—muscles aching to work, minds aching to create beyond the single need—this is man. To build a wall, to build a house, a dam, and in the wall and house and dam to put something of Manself, and to Manself take back something of the wall, the house, the dam; to take hard muscles from the lifting, to take the clear lines and form from conceiving. For man, unlike any other thing organic or inorganic in the universe, grows beyond his work, walks up the stairs of his concepts, emerges ahead of his accomplish-

ments. This you may say of man—when theories
change and crash, when schools, philosophies, when
narrow dark alleys of thought, national, religious, economic, grow and disintegrate, man reaches, stumbles
forward, painfully, mistakenly sometimes. Having
stepped forward, he may slip back, but only half a
step, never the full step back. This you may say and
know it and know it. This you may know when the
bombs plummet out of the black planes on the market
place, when prisoners are stuck like pigs, when the
crushed bodies drain filthily in the dust. You may
know it in this way. If the step were not being taken, if
the stumbling-forward ache were not alive, the bombs
would not fall, the throats would not be cut. Fear the
time when the bombs stop falling while the bombers
live—for every bomb is proof that the spirit has not
died. And fear the time when the strikes stop while the
great owners live—for every little beaten strike is
proof that the step is being taken. And this you can
know—fear the time when Manself will not suffer and
die for a concept, for this one quality is the foundation
of Manself, and this one quality is man, distinctive in
the universe.

The Western States nervous under the beginning
change. Texas and Oklahoma, Kansas and Arkansas,
New Mexico, Arizona, California. A single family
moved from the land. Pa borrowed money from the
bank, and now the bank wants the land. The land
company—that's the bank when it has land—wants
tractors, not families on the land. Is a tractor bad? Is
the power that turns the long furrows wrong? If this
tractor were ours it would be good—not mine, but
ours. If our tractor turned the long furrows of our land,
it would be good. Not my land, but ours. We could
love that tractor then as we have loved this land when
it was ours. But this tractor does two things—it turns

the land and turns us off the land. There is little difference between this tractor and a tank. The people are driven, intimidated, hurt by both. We must think about this.

One man, one family driven from the land; this rusty car creaking along the highway to the west. I lost my land, a single tractor took my land. I am alone and I am bewildered. And in the night one family camps in a ditch and another family pulls in and the tents come out. The two men squat on their hams and the women and children listen. Here is the node, you who hate change and fear revolution. Keep these two squatting men apart; make them hate, fear, suspect each other. Here is the anlage of the thing you fear. This is the zygote. For here "I lost my land" is changed; a cell is split and from its splitting grows the thing you hate— "We lost *our* land." The danger is here, for two men are not as lonely and perplexed as one. And from this first "we" there grows a still more dangerous thing: "I have a little food" plus "I have none." If from this problem the sum is "We have a little food," the thing is on its way, the movement has direction. Only a little multiplication now, and this land, this tractor are ours. The two men squatting in a ditch, the little fire, the side-meat stewing in a single pot, the silent, stone-eyed women; behind, the children listening with their souls to words their minds do not understand. The night draws down. The baby has a cold. Here, take this blanket. It's wool. It was my mother's blanket— take it for the baby. This is the thing to bomb. This is the beginning—from "I" to "we."

If you who own the things people must have could understand this, you might preserve yourself. If you could separate causes from results; if you could know that Paine, Marx, Jefferson, Lenin, were results, not causes, you might survive. But that you cannot know. For the quality of owning freezes you forever into "I," and cuts you off forever from the "we."

The Western States are nervous under the beginning change. Need is the stimulus to concept, concept to action. A half-million people moving over the country; a million more restive, ready to move; ten million more feeling the first nervousness.

And tractors turning the multiple furrows in the vacant land.

15

Along 66 the hamburger stands—Al & Susy's Place—Carl's Lunch—Joe & Minnie—Will's Eats. Board-and-bat shacks. Two gasoline pumps in front, a screen door, a long bar, stools, and a foot rail. Near the door three slot machines, showing through glass the wealth of nickels three bars will bring. And beside them, the nickel phonograph with records piled up like pies, ready to swing out to the turntable and play dance music. "Ti-pi-ti-pi-tin," "Thanks for the Memory," Bing Crosby, Benny Goodman. At one end of the counter a covered case; candy cough drops, caffeine sulphate called Sleepless, No-Doze; candy, cigarettes, razor blades, aspirin, Bromo-Seltzer, Alka-Seltzer. The walls decorated with posters, bathing girls, blondes with big breasts and slender hips and waxen faces, in white bathing suits, and holding a bottle of Coca-Cola and smiling—see what you get with a Coca-Cola. Long bars, and salts, peppers, mustard pots, and paper napkins. Beer taps behind the counter, and in back the coffee urns, shiny and steaming, with glass gauges showing the coffee level. And pies in wire cages and oranges in pyramids of four. And little piles of Post Toasties, corn flakes, stacked up in designs.

The signs on cards, picked out with shining mica: Pies Like Mother Used to Make. Credit Makes Enemies, Let's Be Friends. Ladies May Smoke But Be Careful Where You Lay Your Butts. Eat Here and Keep Your Wife for a Pet. IITYWYBAD?

Down at one end the cooking plates, pots of stew, potatoes, pot roast, roast beef, gray roast pork waiting to be sliced.

Minnie or Susy or Mae, middle-aging behind the counter, hair curled and rouge and powder on a sweating face. Taking orders in a soft low voice, calling them to the cook with a screech like a peacock. Mopping the counter with circular strokes, polishing the big shining coffee urns. The cook is Joe or Carl or Al, hot in a white coat and apron, beady sweat on white forehead, below the white cook's cap; moody, rarely speaking, looking up for a moment at each new entry. Wiping the griddle, slapping down the hamburger. He repeats Mae's orders gently, scrapes the griddle, wipes it down with burlap. Moody and silent.

Mae is the contact, smiling, irritated, near to outbreak; smiling while her eyes look on past—unless for truck drivers. There's the backbone of the joint. Where the trucks stop, that's where the customers come. Can't fool truck drivers, they know. They bring the customers. They know. Give 'em a stale cup a coffee an' they're off the joint. Treat 'em right an' they come back. Mae really smiles with all her might at truck drivers. She bridles a little, fixes her back hair so that her breasts will lift with her raised arms, passes the time of day and indicates great things, great times, great jokes. Al never speaks. He is no contact. Sometimes he smiles a little at a joke, but he never laughs. Sometimes he looks up at the vivaciousness in Mae's voice, and then he scrapes the griddle with a spatula, scrapes the grease into an iron trough around the plate. He presses down a hissing hamburger with his spatula. He lays the split buns on the plate to toast and heat. He gathers up stray onions from the plate and heaps them on the meat and presses them in with the spatula. He puts half the bun on top of the meat, paints the other half with melted butter, with thin pickle relish. Holding the bun on the meat, he slips the spatula under the thin pad of meat, flips it over, lays the buttered half on top, and drops the hamburger on a small plate. Quarter of a dill pickle, two black olives beside the sandwich. Al skims the plate down the counter like a quoit. And he scrapes his griddle with the spatula and looks moodily at the stew kettle.

Cars whisking by on 66. License plates. Mass., Tenn., R.I., N.Y., Vt., Ohio. Going west. Fine cars, cruising at sixty-five.

There goes one of them Cords. Looks like a coffin on wheels.

But, Jesus, how they travel!

See that La Salle? Me for that. I ain't a hog. I go for a La Salle.

'F ya goin' big, what's a matter with a Cad'? Jus' a little bigger, little faster.

I'd take a Zephyr myself. You ain't ridin' no fortune, but you got class an' speed. Give me a Zephyr.

Well, sir, you may get a laugh outa this—I'll take a Buick-Puick. That's good enough.

But, hell, that costs in the Zephyr class an' it ain't got the sap.

I don' care. I don' want nothin' to do with nothing of Henry Ford's. I don' like 'im. Never did. Got a brother worked in the plant. Oughta hear him tell.

Well, a Zephyr got sap.

The big cars on the highway. Languid, heat-raddled ladies, small nucleuses about whom revolve a thousand accouterments: creams, ointments to grease themselves, coloring matter in phials—black, pink, red, white, green, silver—to change the color of hair, eyes, lips, nails, brows, lashes, lids. Oils, seeds, and pills to make the bowels move. A bag of bottles, syringes, pills, powders, fluids, jellies to make their sexual intercourse safe, odorless, and unproductive. And this apart from clothes. What a hell of a nuisance!

Lines of weariness around the eyes, lines of discontent down from the mouth, breasts lying heavily in little hammocks, stomach and thighs straining against cases of rubber. And the mouths panting, the eyes sullen, disliking sun and wind and earth, resenting food and weariness, hating time that rarely makes them beautiful and always makes them old.

Beside them, little pot-bellied men in light suits and panama hats; clean, pink men with puzzled, worried faces, with restless eyes. Worried because formulas do not work out; hungry for security and yet sensing its disappearance from the earth. In their lapels the insignia of lodges and service clubs, places where they can go and, by a weight of numbers of little worried men, reassure themselves that business is noble and not the curious ritualized thievery they know it is; that business men are intelligent in spite of the records of their stupidity; that they are kind and charitable in spite of the principles of sound business; that their lives are rich instead of the thin tiresome routines they know; and that a time is coming when they will not be afraid any more.

And these two, going to California; going to sit in the lobby of the Beverly-Wilshire Hotel and watch people they envy go by, to look at mountains—mountains, mind you, and great trees—he with his worried eyes and she thinking how the sun will dry her skin. Going to look at the Pacific Ocean, and I'll bet a hundred thousand dollars to nothing at all, he will say, "It isn't as big as I thought it would be." And

she will envy plump young bodies on the beach. Going to California really to go home again. To say,
"So-and-So was at the table next to us at the Troca-
dero. She's really a mess, but she does wear nice
clothes." And he, "I talked to good sound business
men out there. They don't see a chance till we get rid
of that fellow in the White House." And, "I got it
from a man in the know—she has syphilis, you know.
She was in that Warner picture. Man said she'd slept
her way into pictures. Well, she got what she was
looking for." But the worried eyes are never calm,
and the pouting mouth is never glad. The big car
cruising along at sixty.

I want a cold drink.

Well, there's something up ahead. Want to stop?

Do you think it would be clean?

Clean as you're going to find in this God-forsaken
country.

Well, maybe the bottled soda will be all right.

The great car squeals and pulls to a stop. The fat
worried man helps his wife out.

Mae looks at and past them as they enter. Al looks
up from his griddle, and down again. Mae knows.
They'll drink a five-cent soda and crab that it ain't
cold enough. The woman will use six paper napkins
and drop them on the floor. The man will choke and
try to put the blame on Mae. The woman will sniff as
though she smelled rotting meat and they will go out
again and tell forever afterward that the people in the
West are sullen. And Mae, when she is alone with Al,
has a name for them. She calls them shitheels.

Truck drivers. That's the stuff.

Here's a big transport comin'. Hope they stop; take
away the taste of them shitheels. When I worked in
that hotel in Albuquerque, Al, the way they steal—
ever' darn thing. An' the bigger the car they got, the
more they steal—towels, silver, soap dishes. I can't
figger it.

And Al, morosely, Where ya think they get them big cars and stuff? Born with 'em? You won't never have nothin'.

The transport truck, a driver and relief. How 'bout stoppin' for a cup a Java. I know this dump.

How's the schedule?

Oh, we're ahead!

Pull up, then. They's a ol' war horse in here that's a kick. Good Java, too.

The truck pulls up. Two men in khaki riding trousers, boots, short jackets, and shiny-visored military caps. Screen door—slam.

H'ya, Mae?

Well, if it ain't Big Bill the Rat? When'd you get back on this run?

Week ago.

The other man puts a nickel in the phonograph, watches the disk slip free and the turntable rise up under it. Bing Crosby's voice—golden. "Thanks for the memory, of sunburn at the shore—You might have been a headache, but you never were a bore—" And the truck driver sings for Mae's ears, you might have been a haddock but you never was a whore—

Mae laughs. Who's ya frien', Bill? New on this run, ain't he?

The other puts a nickel in the slot machine, wins four slugs, and puts them back. Walks to the counter.

Well, what's it gonna be?

Oh, cup a Java. Kinda pie ya got?

Banana cream, pineapple cream, chocolate cream— an' apple.

Make it apple. Wait— Kind is that big thick one?

Mae lifts it out and sniffs it. Banana cream.

Cut off a hunk; make it a big hunk.

Man at the slot machine says, Two all around.

Two it is. Seen any new etchin's lately, Bill?

Well, here's one.

Now, you be careful front of a lady.

Oh, this ain't bad. Little kid comes in late ta school. Teacher says, "Why ya late?" Kid says, "Had a take a heifer down—get 'er bred." Teacher says, "Couldn't your ol' man do it?" Kid says, "Sure he could, but not as good as the bull."

Mae squeaks with laughter, harsh screeching laughter. Al, slicing onions carefully on a board, looks up and smiles, and then looks down again. Truck drivers, that's the stuff. Gonna leave a quarter each for Mae. Fifteen cents for pie an' coffee an' a dime for Mae. An' they ain't tryin' to make her, neither.

Sitting together on the stools, spoons sticking out of the coffee mugs. Passing the time of day. And Al, rubbing down his griddle, listening but making no comment. Bing Crosby's voice stops. The turntable drops down and the record swings into its place in the pile. The purple light goes off. The nickel, which has caused all this mechanism to work, has caused Crosby to sing and an orchestra to play—this nickel drops from between the contact points into the box where the profits go. This nickel, unlike most money, has actually done a job of work, has been physically responsible for a reaction.

Steam spurts from the valve of the coffee urn. The compressor of the ice machine chugs softly for a time and then stops. The electric fan in the corner waves its head slowly back and forth, sweeping the room with a warm breeze. On the highway, on 66, the cars whiz by.

They was a Massachusetts car stopped a while ago, said Mae.

Big Bill grasped his cup around the top so that the spoon stuck up between his first and second fingers. He drew in a snort of air with the coffee, to cool it. "You ought to be out on 66. Cars from all over the country. All headin' west. Never seen so many before. Sure some honeys on the road."

"We seen a wreck this mornin'," his companion

said. "Big car. Big Cad', a special job and a honey, low, cream-color, special job. Hit a truck. Folded the radiator right back to the driver. Must a been doin' ninety. Steerin' wheel went right on through the guy an' lef' him a-wigglin' like a frog on a hook. Peach of a car. A honey. You can have her for peanuts now. Drivin' alone, the guy was."

Al looked up from his work. "Hurt the truck?"

"Oh, Jesus Christ! Wasn't a truck. One of them cut-down cars full a stoves an' pans an' mattresses an' kids an' chickens. Goin' west, you know. This guy come by us doin' ninety—r'ared up on two wheels just to pass us, an' a car's comin' so he cuts in an' whangs this here truck. Drove like he's blin' drunk. Jesus, the air was full a bed clothes an' chickens an' kids. Killed one kid. Never seen such a mess. We pulled up. Ol' man that's drivin' the truck, he jus' stan's there lookin' at that dead kid. Can't get a word out of 'im. Jus' rum-dumb. God Almighty, the road is full of them families goin' west. Never seen so many. Gets worse all a time. Wonder where the hell they all come from?"

"Wonder where they all go to," said Mae. "Come here for gas sometimes, but they don't hardly never buy nothin' else. People says they steal. We ain't got nothin' layin' around. They never stole nothin' from us."

Big Bill, munching his pie, looked up the road through the screened window. "Better tie your stuff down. I think you got some of 'em comin' now."

A 1926 Nash sedan pulled wearily off the highway. The back seat was piled nearly to the ceiling with sacks, with pots and pans, and on the very top, right up against the ceiling, two boys rode. On the top of the car, a mattress and a folded tent; tent poles tied along the running board. The car pulled up to the gas pumps. A dark-haired, hatchet-faced man got slowly out. And the two boys slid down from the load and hit the ground.

Mae walked around the counter and stood in the door. The man was dressed in gray wool trousers and a blue shirt, dark blue with sweat on the back and under the arms. The boys in overalls and nothing else, ragged patched overalls. Their hair was light, and it stood up evenly all over their heads, for it had been roached. Their faces were streaked with dust. They went directly to the mud puddle under the hose and dug their toes into the mud.

The man asked, "Can we git some water, ma'am?"

A look of annoyance crossed Mae's face. "Sure, go ahead." She said softly over her shoulder, "I'll keep my eye on the hose." She watched while the man slowly unscrewed the radiator cap and ran the hose in.

A woman in the car, a flaxen-haired woman, said, "See if you can't git it here."

The man turned off the hose and screwed on the cap again. The little boys took the hose from him and they upended it and drank thirstily. The man took off his dark, stained hat and stood with a curious humility in front of the screen. "Could you see your way to sell us a loaf of bread, ma'am?"

Mae said, "This ain't a grocery store. We got bread to make san'widges."

"I know, ma'am." His humility was insistent. "We need bread and there ain't nothin' for quite a piece, they say."

" 'F we sell bread we gonna run out." Mae's tone was faltering.

"We're hungry," the man said.

"Whyn't you buy a san'widge. We got nice san'widges, hamburgs."

"We'd sure admire to do that, ma'am. But we can't. We got to make a dime do all of us." And he said embarrassedly, "We ain't got but a little."

Mae said, "You can't get no loaf of bread for a dime. We only got fifteen-cent loafs."

From behind her, Al growled, "God Almighty, Mae, give 'em bread."

"We'll run out 'fore the bread truck comes."

"Run out, then, goddamn it," said Al. And he looked sullenly down at the potato salad he was mixing.

Mae shrugged her plump shoulders and looked to the truck drivers to show them what she was up against.

She held the screen door open and the man came in, bringing a smell of sweat with him. The boys edged in behind him, and they went immediately to the candy case and stared in—not with craving or with hope or even with desire, but just with a kind of wonder that such things could be. They were alike in size and their faces were alike. One scratched his dusty ankle with the toe nails of his other foot. The other whispered some soft message and then they straightened their arms so that their clenched fists in the overall pockets showed through the thin blue cloth.

Mae opened a drawer and took out a long waxpaper-wrapped loaf. "This here is a fifteen-cent loaf."

The man put his hat back on his head. He answered with inflexible humility, "Won't you—can't you see your way to cut off ten cents' worth?"

Al said snarlingly, "Goddamn it, Mae. Give 'em the loaf."

The man turned toward Al. "No, we want ta buy ten cents' worth of it. We got it figgered awful close, mister, to get to California."

Mae said resignedly, "You can have this for ten cents."

"That'd be robbin' you, ma'am."

"Go ahead—Al says to take it." She pushed the waxpapered loaf across the counter. The man took a deep leather pouch from his rear pocket, untied the strings, and spread it open. It was heavy with silver and with greasy bills.

"May soun' funny to be so tight," he apologized. "We got a thousan' miles to go, an' we don' know if we'll make it." He dug in the pouch with a forefinger, located a dime, and pinched for it. When he put it down on the counter he had a penny with it. He was about to drop the penny back into the pouch when his eye fell on the boys frozen before the candy counter. He moved slowly down to them. He pointed in the case at big long sticks of striped peppermint. "Is them penny candy, ma'am?"

Mae moved down and looked in. "Which ones?"

"There, them stripy ones."

The little boys raised their eyes to her face and they stopped breathing; their mouths were partly opened, their half-naked bodies were rigid.

"Oh—them. Well, no—them's two for a penny."

"Well, gimme two then, ma'am." He placed the copper cent carefully on the counter. The boys expelled their held breath softly. Mae held the big sticks out.

"Take 'em," said the man.

They reached timidly, each took a stick, and they held them down at their sides and did not look at them. But they looked at each other, and their mouth corners smiled rigidly with embarrassment.

"Thank you, ma'am." The man picked up the bread and went out the door, and the little boys marched stiffly behind him, the red-striped sticks held tightly against their legs. They leaped like chipmunks over the front seat and onto the top of the load, and they burrowed back out of sight like chipmunks.

The man got in and started his car, and with a roaring motor and a cloud of blue oily smoke the ancient Nash climbed up on the highway and went on its way to the west.

From inside the restaurant the truck drivers and Mae and Al stared after them.

Big Bill wheeled back. "Them wasn't two-for-a-cent candy," he said.

"What's that to you?" Mae said fiercely.

"Them was nickel apiece candy," said Bill.

"We got to get goin'," said the other man. "We're droppin' time." They reached in their pockets. Bill put a coin on the counter and the other man looked at it and reached again and put down a coin. They swung around and walked to the door.

"So long," said Bill.

Mae called, "Hey! Wait a minute. You got change."

"You go to hell," said Bill, and the screen door slammed.

Mae watched them get into the great truck, watched it lumber off in low gear, and heard the shift up the whining gears to cruising ratio. "Al—" she said softly.

He looked up from the hamburger he was patting thin and stacking between waxed papers. "What ya want?"

"Look there." She pointed at the coins beside the cups—two half-dollars. Al walked near and looked, and then he went back to his work.

"Truck drivers," Mae said reverently, "an' after them shitheels."

Flies struck the screen with little bumps and droned away. The compressor chugged for a time and then stopped. On 66 the traffic whizzed by, trucks and fine streamlined cars and jalopies; and they went by with a vicious whiz. Mae took down the plates and scraped the pie crusts into a bucket. She found her damp cloth and wiped the counter with circular sweeps. And her eyes were on the highway, where life whizzed by.

Al wiped his hands on his apron. He looked at a paper pinned to the wall over the griddle. Three lines of marks in columns on the paper. Al counted the

longest line. He walked along the counter to the cash
register, rang "No Sale," and took out a handful of
nickels.

"What ya doin'?" Mae asked.

"Number three's ready to pay off," said Al. He went
to the third slot machine and played his nickels in,
and on the fifth spin of the wheels the three bars came
up and the jack pot dumped out into the cup. Al
gathered up the big handful of coins and went back of
the counter. He dropped them in the drawer and
slammed the cash register. Then he went back to his
place and crossed out the line of dots. "Number three
gets more play'n the others," he said. "Maybe I ought
to shift 'em around." He lifted a lid and stirred the
slowly simmering stew.

"I wonder what they'll do in California?" said Mae.

"Who?"

"Them folks that was just in."

"Christ knows," said Al.

"S'pose they'll get work?"

"How the hell would I know?" said Al.

She stared eastward along the highway. "Here
comes a transport, double. Wonder if they'll stop?
Hope they do." And as the huge truck came heavily
down from the highway and parked, Mae seized her
cloth and wiped the whole length of the counter. And
she took a few swipes at the gleaming coffee urn too,
and turned up the bottle-gas under the urn. Al brought
out a handful of little turnips and started to peel them.
Mae's face was gay when the door opened and the two
uniformed truck drivers entered.

"Hi, sister."

"I won't be a sister to no man," said Mae. They
laughed and Mae laughed. "What'll it be, boys?"

"Oh, a cup a Java. What kinda pie ya got?"

"Pineapple cream an' banana cream an' chocolate
cream an' apple."

"Give me apple. No, wait—what's that big thick one?"

Mae picked up the pie and smelled it. "Pineapple cream," she said.

"Well, chop out a hunk a that."

The cars whizzed viciously by on 66.

16

Joads and Wilsons crawled westward as a unit: El Reno and Bridgeport, Clinton, Elk City, Sayre, and Texola. There's the border, and Oklahoma was behind. And this day the cars crawled on and on, through the Panhandle of Texas. Shamrock and Alanreed, Groom and Yarnell. They went through Amarillo in the evening, drove too long, and camped when it was dusk. They were tired and dusty and hot. Granma had convulsions from the heat, and she was weak when they stopped.

That night Al stole a fence rail and made a ridge pole on the truck, braced at both ends. That night they ate nothing but pan biscuits, cold and hard, held over from breakfast. They flopped down on the mattresses and slept in their clothes. The Wilsons didn't even put up their tent.

Joads and Wilsons were in flight across the Panhandle, the rolling gray country, lined and cut with old flood scars. They were in flight out of Oklahoma and across Texas. The land turtles crawled through the dust and the sun whipped the earth, and in the evening the heat went out of the sky and the earth sent up a wave of heat from itself.

Two days the families were in flight, but on the

third the land was too huge for them and they settled
into a new technique of living; the highway became
their home and movement their medium of expression.
Little by little they settled into the new way of life.
Ruthie and Winfield first, then Al, then Connie and
Rose of Sharon, and, last, the older ones. The land
rolled like great stationary ground swells. Wildorado
and Vega and Boise and Glenrio. That's the end of
Texas. New Mexico and the mountains. In the far distance, waved up against the sky, the mountains stood.
And the wheels of the cars creaked around, and the
engines were hot, and the steam spurted around the
radiator caps. They crawled to the Pecos River, and
crossed at Santa Rosa. And they went on for twenty
miles.

Al Joad drove the touring car, and his mother sat
beside him, and Rose of Sharon beside her. Ahead the
truck crawled. The hot air folded in waves over the
land, and the mountains shivered in the heat. Al drove
listlessly, hunched back in the seat, his hand hooked
easily over the cross-bar of the steering wheel; his gray
hat, peaked and pulled to an incredibly cocky shape,
was low over one eye; and as he drove, he turned and
spat out the side now and then.

Ma, beside him, had folded her hands in her lap, had
retired into a resistance against weariness. She sat
loosely, letting the movement of the car sway her body
and her head. She squinted her eyes ahead at the mountains. Rose of Sharon was braced against the movement
of the car, her feet pushed tight against the floor, and
her right elbow hooked over the door. And her plump
face was tight against the movement, and her head jiggled sharply because her neck muscles were tight. She
tried to arch her whole body as a rigid container to
preserve her fetus from shock. She turned her head
toward her mother.

"Ma," she said. Ma's eyes lighted up and she drew
her attention toward Rose of Sharon. Her eyes went
over the tight, tired, plump face, and she smiled.
"Ma," the girl said, "when we get there, all you gonna
pick fruit an' kinda live in the country, ain't you?"

Ma smiled a little satirically. "We ain't there yet,"
she said. "We don't know what it's like. We got to
see."

"Me an' Connie don't want to live in the country no
more," the girl said. "We got it all planned up what
we gonna do."

For a moment a little worry came on Ma's face.
"Ain't you gonna stay with us—with the family?" she
asked.

"Well, we talked about it, me an' Connie. Ma, we
wanna live in a town." She went on excitedly, "Connie
gonna get a job in a store or maybe a fact'ry. An' he's
gonna study at home, maybe radio, so he can git to be
a expert an' maybe later have his own store. An' we'll
go to pitchers whenever. An' Connie says I'm gonna
have a *doctor* when the baby's born; an' he says we'll
see how times is, an' maybe I'll go to a hospiddle. An'
we'll have a car, little car. An' after he studies at
night, why—it'll be nice, an' he tore a page outa *Western Love Stories,* an' he's gonna send off for a course,
'cause it don't cost nothin' to send off. Says right on
that clipping. I seen it. An', why—they even get you a
job when you take that course—radios, it is—nice
clean work, and a future. An' we'll live in town an' go
to pitchers whenever, an'—well. I'm gonna have a
'lectric iron, an' the baby'll have all new stuff. Connie
says all new stuff—white an'— Well, you seen in the
catalogue all the stuff they got for a baby. Maybe right
at first while Connie's studyin' at home it won't be so
easy, but—well, when the baby comes, maybe he'll be
all done studyin' an' we'll have a place, little bit of a
place. We don't want nothin' fancy, but we want it
nice for the baby—" Her face glowed with excitement.

"An' I thought—well, I thought maybe we could all go in town, an' when Connie gets his store—maybe Al could work for him."

Ma's eyes had never left the flushing face. Ma watched the structure grow and followed it. "We don' want you to go 'way from us," she said. "It ain't good for folks to break up."

Al snorted, "Me work for Connie? How about Connie comes a-workin' for me? He thinks he's the on'y son-of-a-bitch can study at night?"

Ma suddenly seemed to know it was all a dream. She turned her head forward again and her body relaxed, but the little smile stayed around her eyes. "I wonder how Granma feels today," she said.

Al grew tense over the wheel. A little rattle had developed in the engine. He speeded up and the rattle increased. He retarded his spark and listened, and then he speeded up for a moment and listened. The rattle increased to a metallic pounding. Al blew his horn and pulled the car to the side of the road. Ahead the truck pulled up and then backed slowly. Three cars raced by, westward, and each one blew its horn and the last driver leaned out and yelled, "Where the hell ya think you're stoppin'?"

Tom backed the truck close, and then he got out and walked to the touring car. From the back of the loaded truck heads looked down. Al retarded his spark and listened to his idling motor. Tom asked, "What's a matter, Al?"

Al speeded the motor. "Listen to her." The rattling pound was louder now.

Tom listened. "Put up your spark an' idle," he said. He opened the hood and put his head inside. "Now speed her." He listened for a moment and then closed the hood. "Well, I guess you're right, Al," he said.

"Con-rod bearing, ain't it?"

"Sounds like it," said Tom.

"I kep' plenty oil in," Al complained.

"Well, it jus' didn' get to her. Drier'n a bitch monkey now. Well, there ain't nothin' to do but tear her out. Look, I'll pull ahead an' find a flat place to stop. You come ahead slow. Don't knock the pan out of her."

Wilson asked, "Is it bad?"

"Purty bad," said Tom, and walked back to the truck and moved slowly ahead.

Al explained, "I don' know what made her go out. I give her plenty of oil." Al knew the blame was on him. He felt his failure.

Ma said, "It ain't your fault. You done ever'thing right." And then she asked a little timidly, "Is it terrible bad?"

"Well, it's hard to get at, an' we got to get a new con-rod or else some babbitt in this one." He sighed deeply. "I sure am glad Tom's here. I never fixed no bearing. Hope to Jesus Tom did."

A huge red billboard stood beside the road ahead, and it threw a great oblong shadow. Tom edged the truck off the road and across the shallow roadside ditch, and he pulled up in the shadow. He got out and waited until Al came up.

"Now go easy," he called. "Take her slow or you'll break a spring too."

Al's face went red with anger. He throttled down his motor. "Goddamn it," he yelled, "I didn't burn that bearin' out! What d'ya mean, I'll bust a spring too?"

Tom grinned. "Keep all four feet on the groun'," he said. "I didn' mean nothin'. Jus' take her easy over this ditch."

Al grumbled as he inched the touring car down, and up the other side. "Don't you go givin' nobody no idear I burned out that bearin'." The engine clattered loudly now. Al pulled into the shade and shut down the motor.

Tom lifted the hood and braced it. "Can't even start on her before she cools off," he said. The family piled down from the cars and clustered about the touring car.

Pa asked, "How bad?" And he squatted on his hams.

Tom turned to Al. "Ever fitted one?"

"No," said Al, "I never. 'Course I had pans off."

Tom said, "Well, we got to tear the pan off an' get the rod out, an' we got to get a new part an' hone her an' shim her an' fit her. Good day's job. Got to go back to that las' place for a part, Santa Rosa. Albuquerque's about seventy-five miles on— Oh, Jesus, tomorra's Sunday! We can't get nothin' tomorra." The family stood silently. Ruthie crept close and peered into the open hood, hoping to see the broken part. Tom went on softly, "Tomorra's Sunday. Monday we'll get the thing an' prob'ly won't get her fitted 'fore Tuesday. We ain't got the tools to make it easy. Gonna be a job." The shadow of a buzzard slid across the earth, and the family all looked up at the sailing black bird.

Pa said, "What I'm scairt of is we'll run outa money so we can't git there 't all. Here's all us eatin', an' got to buy gas an' oil. 'F we run outa money, I don't know what we gonna do."

Wilson said, "Seems like it's my fault. This here goddamn wreck's given me trouble right along. You folks been nice to us. Now you jus' pack up an' get along. Me an' Sairy'll stay, an' we'll figger some way. We don't aim to put you folks out none."

Pa said slowly, "We ain't a-gonna do it. We got almost a kin bond. Grampa, he died in your tent."

Sairy said tiredly, "We been nothin' but trouble, nothin' but trouble."

Tom slowly made a cigarette, and inspected it and lighted it. He took off his ruined cap and wiped his forehead. "I got an idear," he said. "Maybe nobody gonna like it, but here she is: The nearer to California our folks get, the quicker they's gonna be money rollin' in. Now this here car'll go twice as fast as that truck. Now here's my idea. You take out some of that stuff in the truck, an' then all you folks but me an' the preacher get in an' move on. Me an' Casy'll stop here an' fix this here car an' then we drive on, day an' night. an' we'll catch up, or if we don't meet on the road, you'll be a-workin' anyways. An' if you break down, why, jus' camp 'longside the road till we come. You can't be no worse off, an' if you get through, why, you'll be a-workin', an' stuff'll be easy. Casy can give me a lif' with this here car, an' we'll come a-sailin'."

The gathered family considered it. Uncle John dropped to his hams beside Pa.

Al said, "Won't ya need me to give ya a han' with that con-rod?"

"You said your own se'f you never fixed one."

"That's right," Al agreed. "All ya got to have is a strong back. Maybe the preacher don' wanta stay."

"Well—whoever—I don' care," said Tom.

Pa scratched the dry earth with his forefinger. "I kind a got a notion Tom's right," he said. "It ain't goin' ta do no good all of us stayin' here. We can get fifty, a hunderd miles on 'fore dark."

Ma said worriedly, "How you gonna find us?"

"We'll be on the same road," said Tom. "Sixty-six right on through. Come to a place name' Bakersfiel'. Seen it on the map I got. You go straight on there."

"Yeah, but when we get to California an' spread out sideways off this road—?"

"Don't you worry," Tom reassured her. "We're gonna find ya. California ain't the whole world."

"Looks like an awful big place on the map," said Ma.

Pa appealed for advice. "John, you see any reason why not?"

"No," said John.

"Mr. Wilson, it's your car. You got any objections if my boy fixes her an' brings her on?"

"I don' see none," said Wilson. "Seems like you folks done ever'thing for us awready. Don' see why I cain't give your boy a han'."

"You can be workin', layin' in a little money, if we don' ketch up with ya," said Tom. "An' suppose we all jus' lay aroun' here. There ain't no water here, an' we can't move this here car. But s'pose you all git out there an' git to work. Why, you'd have money, an' maybe a house to live in. How about it, Casy? Wanna stay with me an' give me a lif'?"

"I wanna do what's bes' for you folks," said Casy. "You took me in, carried me along. I'll do whatever."

"Well, you'll lay on your back an' get grease in your face if you stay here," Tom said.

"Suits me awright."

Pa said, "Well, if that's the way she's gonna go, we better get a-shovin'. We can maybe squeeze in a hunderd miles 'fore we stop."

Ma stepped in front of him. "I ain't a-gonna go."

"What you mean, you ain't gonna go? You got to go. You got to look after the family." Pa was amazed at the revolt.

Ma stepped to the touring car and reached in on the floor of the back seat. She brought out a jack handle and balanced it in her hand easily. "I ain't a-gonna go," she said.

"I tell you, you got to go. We made up our mind."

And now Ma's mouth set hard. She said softly, "On'y way you gonna get me to go is whup me." She moved the jack handle gently again. "An' I'll shame you, Pa. I won't take no whuppin', cryin' an' a-beggin'. I'll light into you. An' you ain't so sure you can whup me anyways. An' if ya do get me, I swear to God I'll wait till you got your back turned, or you're settin' down, an' I'll knock you belly-up with a bucket. I swear to Holy Jesus' sake I will."

Pa looked helplessly about the group. "She sassy," he said. "I never seen her so sassy." Ruthie giggled shrilly.

The jack handle flicked hungrily back and forth in Ma's hand. "Come on," said Ma. "You made up your mind. Come on an' whup me. Jus' try it. But I ain't a-goin'; or if I do, you ain't never gonna get no sleep, 'cause I'll wait an' I'll wait, an' jus' the minute you take sleep in your eyes, I'll slap ya with a stick a stove wood."

"So goddamn sassy," Pa murmured. "An' she ain't young, neither."

The whole group watched the revolt. They watched Pa, waiting for him to break into fury. They watched his lax hands to see the fists form. And Pa's anger did not rise, and his hands hung limply at his sides. And in a moment the group knew that Ma had won. And Ma knew it too.

Tom said, "Ma, what's eatin' on you? What ya wanna do this-a-way for? What's the matter'th you anyways? You gone johnrabbit on us?"

Ma's face softened, but her eyes were still fierce. "You done this 'thout thinkin' much," Ma said. "What we got lef' in the worl'? Nothin' but us. Nothin' but the folks. We come out an' Grampa, he reached for the shovel-shelf right off. An' now, right off, you wanna bust up the folks——"

Tom cried, "Ma, we was gonna catch up with ya. We wasn't gonna be gone long."

Ma waved the jack handle. "S'pose we was camped, and you went on by. S'pose we got on through, how'd we know where to leave the word, an' how'd you know where to ask?" She said, "We got a bitter road. Granma's sick. She's up there on the truck a-pawin' for a shovel herself. She's jus' tar'd out. We got a long bitter road ahead."

Uncle John said, "But we could be makin' some money. We could have a little bit saved up, come time the other folks got there."

The eyes of the whole family shifted back to Ma. She was the power. She had taken control. "The money we'd make wouldn't do no good," she said. "All we got is the family unbroke. Like a bunch a cows, when the lobos are ranging, stick all together. I ain't scared while we're all here, all that's alive, but I ain't gonna see us bust up. The Wilsons here is with us, an' the preacher is with us. I can't say nothin' if they want to go, but I'm a-goin' cat-wild with this here piece of bar-arn if my own folks busts up." Her tone was cold and final.

Tom said soothingly, "Ma, we can't all camp here. Ain't no water here. Ain't even much shade here. Granma, she needs shade."

"All right," said Ma. "We'll go along. We'll stop first place they's water an' shade. An'—the truck'll come back and take you in town to get your part, an' it'll bring you back. You ain't goin' walkin' along in the sun, an' I ain't havin' you out all alone, so if you get picked up there ain't nobody of your folks to he'p ya."

Tom drew his lips over his teeth and then snapped them open. He spread his hands helplessly and let them flop against his sides. "Pa," he said, "if you was to rush her one side an' me the other an' then the res' pile on, an' Granma jump down on top, maybe we can get Ma 'thout more'n two-three of us gets killed with that there jack handle. But if you ain't willin' to get your head smashed, I guess Ma's went an' filled her flush. Jesus Christ, one person with their mind made up can shove a lot of folks aroun'! You win, Ma. Put away that jack handle 'fore you hurt somebody."

Ma looked in astonishment at the bar of iron. Her hand trembled. She dropped her weapon on the ground, and Tom, with elaborate care, picked it up and put it back in the car. He said, "Pa, you jus' got set back on your heels. Al, you drive the folks on an' get 'em camped, an' then you bring the truck back here. Me an' the preacher'll get the pan off. Then, if we can make it, we'll run in Santa Rosa an' try an' get a con-rod. Maybe we can, seein' it's Sat'dy night. Get jumpin' now so we can go. Lemme have the monkey wrench an' pliers outa the truck." He reached under the car and felt the greasy pan. "Oh, yeah, lemme have a can, that ol' bucket, to catch the oil. Got to save that." Al handed over the bucket and Tom set it under the car and loosened the oil cap with a pair of pliers. The black oil flowed down his arm while he unscrewed the cap with his fingers, and then the black stream ran silently into the bucket. Al had loaded the family on the truck by the time the bucket was half full. Tom, his face already smudged with oil, looked out between the wheels. "Get back fast!" he called. And he was loosening the pan bolts as the truck moved gently across the shallow ditch and crawled away. Tom turned each bolt a single turn, loosening them evenly to spare the gasket.

The preacher knelt beside the wheels. "What can I do?"

"Nothin', not right now. Soon's the oil's out an' I get these here bolts loose, you can he'p me drop the pan off." He squirmed away under the car, loosening the bolts with a wrench and turning them out with his fingers. He left the bolts on each end loosely threaded to keep the pan from dropping. "Ground's still hot under here," Tom said. And then, "Say, Casy, you been awful goddamn quiet the las' few days. Why, Jesus! When I first come up with you, you was makin' a speech ever' half-hour or so. An' here you ain't said ten words the las' couple days. What's a matter— gettin' sour?"

Casy was stretched out on his stomach, looking under the car. His chin, bristly with sparse whiskers, rested on the back of one hand. His hat was pushed back so that it covered the back of his neck. "I done enough talkin' when I was a preacher to las' the rest a my life," he said.

"Yeah, but you done some talkin' sence, too."

"I'm all worried up," Casy said. "I didn't even know it when I was a-preachin' aroun', but I was doin' consid'able tom-cattin' aroun'. If I ain't gonna preach no more, I got to get married. Why, Tommy, I'm a-lustin' after the flesh."

"Me too," said Tom. "Say, the day I come outa McAlester I was smokin'. I run me down a girl, a hoor girl, like she was a rabbit. I won't tell ya what happened. I wouldn' tell nobody what happened."

Casy laughed. "I know what happened. I went a-fastin' into the wilderness one time, an' when I come out the same damn thing happened to me."

"Hell it did!" said Tom. "Well, I saved my money anyway, an' I give that girl a run. Thought I was nuts. I should a paid her, but I on'y got five bucks to my name. She said she didn't want no money. Here, roll in under here an' grab a-holt. I'll tap her loose. Then you turn out that bolt an' I turn out my end, an' we let her down easy. Careful that gasket. See, she comes off in one piece. They's on'y four cylinders to these here ol' Dodges. I took one down one time. Got main bearings big as a cantaloupe. Now—let her down—hold it. Reach up an' pull down that gasket where it's stuck— easy now. There!" The greasy pan lay on the ground between them, and a little oil still lay in the wells. Tom reached into one of the front wells and picked out some broken pieces of babbitt. "There she is," he said. He turned the babbitt in his fingers. "Shaft's up. Look in back an' get the crank. Turn her over till I tell you."

Casy got to his feet and found the crank and fitted it. "Ready?"

"Reach—now easy—little more—little more—right there."

Casy kneeled down and looked under again. Tom rattled the connecting-rod bearing against the shaft. "There she is."

"What ya s'pose done it?" Casy asked.

"Oh, hell, I don' know! This buggy been on the road thirteen years. Says sixty thousand miles on the speedometer. That means a hunderd an' sixty, an' God knows how many times they turned the numbers back. Gets hot—maybe somebody let the oil get low—jus' went out." He pulled the cotter pins and put his wrench on a bearing bolt. He strained and the wrench slipped. A long gash appeared on the back of his hand. Tom looked at it—the blood flowed evenly from the wound and met the oil and dripped into the pan.

"That's too bad," Casy said. "Want I should do that an' you wrap up your han'?"

"Hell, no! I never fixed no car in my life 'thout cuttin' myself. Now it's done I don't have to worry no more." He fitted the wrench again. "Wisht I had a crescent wrench," he said, and he hammered the wrench with the butt of his hand until the bolts loosened. He took them out and laid them with the pan bolts in the pan, and the cotter-pins with them. He loosened the bearing bolts and pulled out the piston. He put piston and connecting-rod in the pan. "There, by God!" He squirmed free from under the car and pulled the pan out with him. He wiped his hand on a piece of gunny sacking and inspected the cut. "Bleedin' like a son-of-a-bitch," he said. "Well, I can stop that." He urinated on the ground, picked up a handful of the resulting mud, and plastered it over the wound. Only for a moment did the blood ooze out, and then it stopped. "Bes' damn thing in the worl' to stop bleedin'," he said.

"Han'ful a spider web'll do it too," said Casy.

"I know, but there ain't no spider web, an' you can always get piss." Tom sat on the running board and inspected the broken bearing. "Now if we can only find a '25 Dodge an' get a used con-rod an' some shims, maybe we'll make her all right. Al must a gone a hell of a long ways."

The shadow of the billboard was sixty feet out by now. The afternoon lengthened away. Casy sat down on the running board and looked westward. "We gonna be in high mountains pretty soon," he said, and he was silent for a few moments. Then, "Tom!"

"Yeah?"

"Tom, I been watchin' the cars on the road, them we passed an' them that passed us. I been keepin' track."

"Track a what?"

"Tom, they's hunderds of families like us all a-goin' west. I watched. There ain't none of 'em goin' east— hunderds of 'em. Did you notice that?"

"Yeah, I noticed."

"Why—it's like—it's like they was runnin' away from soldiers. It's like a whole country is movin'."

"Yeah," Tom said. "They is a whole country movin'. We're movin' too."

"Well—s'pose all these here folks an' ever'body— s'pose they can't get no jobs out there?"

"Goddamn it!" Tom cried. "How'd I know? I'm jus' puttin' one foot in front a the other. I done it at Mac for four years, jus' marchin' in cell an' out cell an' in mess an' out mess. Jesus Christ, I though it'd be somepin different when I come out! Couldn't think a nothin' in there, else you go stir happy, an' now can't think a nothin'." He turned on Casy. "This here bearing went out. We didn' know it was goin' so we didn' worry none. Now she's out an' we'll fix her. An' by Christ that goes for the rest of it! I ain't gonna worry. I can't do it. This here little piece of iron an' babbitt. See it? Ya see it? Well, that's the only god- damn thing in the world I got on my mind. I wonder where the hell Al is."

Casy said, "Now look, Tom. Oh, wnat the hell! So goddamn hard to say anything."

Tom lifted the mud pack from his hand and threw it on the ground. The edge of the wound was lined with dirt. He glanced over to the preacher. "You fixin' to make a speech," Tom said. "Well, go ahead. I like speeches. Warden used to make speeches all the time. Didn't do us no harm an' he got a hell of a bang out of it. What you tryin' to roll out?"

Casy picked the backs of his long knotty fingers. "They's stuff goin' on and they's folks doin' things. Them people layin' one foot down in front of the other, like you says, they ain't thinkin' where they're goin', like you says—but they're all layin' 'em down the same direction, jus' the same. An' if ya listen, you'll hear a movin', an' a sneakin', an' a rustlin', an'—an' a res'lessness. They's stuff goin' on that the folks doin' it don't know nothin' about—yet. They's gonna come somepin outa all these folks goin' wes'—outa all their farms lef' lonely. They's gonna come a thing that's gonna change the whole country."

Tom said, "I'm still layin' my dogs down one at a time."

"Yeah, but when a fence comes up at ya, ya gonna climb that fence."

"I climb fences when I got fences to climb," said Tom.

Casy sighed. "It's the bes' way. I gotta agree. But they's different kinda fences. They's folks like me that climbs fences that ain't even strang up yet—an' can't he'p it."

"Ain't that Al a-comin'?" Tom asked.

"Yeah. Looks like."

Tom stood up and wrapped the connecting-rod and both halves of the bearing in the piece of sack. "Wanta make sure I get the same," he said.

The truck pulled alongside the road and Al leaned out the window.

Tom said, "You was a hell of a long time. How far'd you go?"

Al sighed. "Got the rod out?"

"Yeah." Tom held up the sack. "Babbitt's jus' broke down."

"Well, it wasn't no fault of mine," said Al.

"No. Where'd you take the folks?"

"We had a mess," Al said. "Granma got to bel-
lerin', an' that set Rosasharn off an' she bellered
some. Got her head under a mattress an' bellered. But
Granma, she was just layin' back her jaw an' bayin'
like a moonlight houn' dog. Seems like Granma ain't
got no sense no more. Like a little baby. Don' speak to
nobody, don' seem to reco'nize nobody. Jus' talks on
like she's talkin' to Grampa."

"Where'd ya leave 'em?" Tom insisted.

"Well, we come to a camp. Got shade an' got water in
pipes. Costs half a dollar a day to stay there. But
ever'body's so goddamn tired an' wore out an' mis'able,
they stayed there. Ma says they got to 'cause Granma's so
tired an' wore out. Got Wilson's tent up an' got our tarp
for a tent. I think Granma gone nuts."

Tom looked toward the lowering sun. "Casy," he
said, "somebody got to stay with this car or she'll get
stripped. You jus' as soon?"

"Sure, I'll stay."

Al took a paper bag from the seat. "This here's
some bread an' meat Ma sent, an' I got a jug a water
here."

"She don't forget nobody," said Casy.

Tom got in beside Al. "Look," he said. "We'll get
back jus' as soon as we can. But we can't tell how
long."

"I'll be here."

"Awright. Don't make no speeches to yourself. Get
goin', Al." The truck moved off in the late afternoon.
"He's a nice fella," Tom said. "He thinks about stuff
all the time."

"Well, hell—if you been a preacher, I guess you got
to. Pa's all mad about it costs fifty cents jus' to camp
under a tree. He can't see that nowadays. Settin'
a-cussin'. Says nex' thing they'll sell ya a little tank a
air. But Ma says they gotta be near shade an' water
'cause a Granma." The truck rattled along the high-

way, and now that it was unloaded, every part of it
rattled and clashed. The side-board of the bed, the cut
body. It rode hard and light. Al put it up to thirty-
eight miles an hour and the engine clattered heavily
and a blue smoke of burning oil drifted up through the
floor boards.

"Cut her down some," Tom said. "You gonna burn
her right down to the hub caps. What's eatin' on
Granma?"

"I don't know. 'Member the las' couple days she's
been airy-nary, sayin' nothin' to nobody? Well, she's
yellin' an' talkin' plenty now, on'y she's talkin' to
Grampa. Yellin' at him. Kinda scary, too. You can
almos' see 'im a-settin' there grinnin' at her the way he
always done, a-fingering hisself an' grinnin'. Seems
like she sees him a-settin' there, too. She's jus' givin'
him hell. Say, Pa, he give me twenty dollars to hand
you. He don't know how much you gonna need. Ever
see Ma stand up to 'im like she done today?"

"Not I remember. I sure did pick a nice time to get
paroled. I figgered I was gonna lay aroun' an' get up
late an' eat a lot when I come home. I was goin' out an'
dance, an' I was gonna go tom-cattin'—an' here I ain't
had time to do none of them things."

Al said, "I forgot. Ma give me a lot of stuff to tell
you. She says don't drink nothin' an' don' get in no
arguments, an' don't fight nobody. 'Cause she says
she's scairt you'll get sent back."

"She got plenty to get worked up about 'thout me
givin' her no trouble," said Tom.

"Well, we could get a couple beers, can't we? I'm
jus' a-ravin' for a beer."

"I dunno," said Tom. "Pa'd crap a litter of lizards if
we buy beers."

"Well, look, Tom. I got six dollars. You an' me
could get a couple pints an' go down the line. Nobody
don't know I got that six bucks. Christ, we could have
a hell of a time for ourselves."

"Keep ya jack," Tom said. "When we get out to the coast you an' me'll take her an' we'll raise hell. Maybe when we're workin'—" He turned in the seat. "I didn' think you was a fella to go down the line. I figgered you was talkin' 'em out of it."

"Well, hell, I don't know nobody here. If I'm gonna ride aroun' much, I'm gonna get married. I'm gonna have a hell of a time when we get to California."

"Hope so," said Tom.

"You ain't sure a nothin' no more."

"No, I ain't sure a nothin'."

"When ya killed that fella—did—did ya ever dream about it or anything? Did it worry ya?"

"No."

"Well, didn' ya never think about it?"

"Sure. I was sorry 'cause he was dead."

"Ya didn't take no blame to yourself?"

"No. I done my time, an' I done my own time."

"Was it—awful bad—there?"

Tom said nervously, "Look, Al. I done my time, an' now it's done. I don' wanna do it over an' over. There's the river up ahead, an' there's the town. Let's jus' try an' get a con-rod an' the hell with the res' of it."

"Ma's awful partial to you," said Al. "She mourned when you was gone. Done it all to herself. Kinda cryin' down inside of her throat. We could tell what she was thinkin' about, though."

Tom pulled his cap down low over his eyes. "Now look here, Al. S'pose we talk 'bout some other stuff."

"I was jus' tellin' ya what Ma done."

"I know—I know. But—I ruther not. I ruther jus'—lay one foot down in front a the other."

Al relapsed into an insulted silence. "I was jus' tryin' to tell ya," he said, after a moment.

Tom looked at him, and Al kept his eyes straight ahead. The lightened truck bounced noisily along. Tom's long lips drew up from his teeth and he laughed softly. "I know you was, Al. Maybe I'm kinda stir-nuts.

I'll tell ya about it sometime maybe. Ya see, it's jus'
somepin you wanta know. Kinda interestin'. But I got a
kind of funny idear the bes' thing'd be if I forget about it
for a while. Maybe in a little while it won't be that way.
Right now when I think about it my guts gets all droopy
an' nasty feelin'. Look here, Al, I'll tell ya one thing—
the jail house is jus' a kind a way a drivin' a guy slowly
nuts. See? An' they go nuts, an' you see 'em an' hear
'em, an' pretty soon you don' know if you're nuts or not.
When they get to screamin' in the night sometimes you
think it's you doin' the screamin'—an' sometimes it is."

Al said, "Oh! I won't talk about it no more, Tom."

"Thirty days is all right," Tom said. "An' a hunderd
an' eighty days is all right. But over a year—I dunno.
There's somepin about it that ain't like nothin' else in
the worl'. Somepin screwy about it, somepin screwy
about the whole idea a lockin' people up. Oh, the hell
with it! I don' wanna talk about it. Look a the sun
a-flashin' on them windas."

The truck drove to the service-station belt, and
there on the right-hand side of the road was a
wrecking yard—an acre lot surrounded by a high
barbed-wire fence, a corrugated iron shed in front
with used tires piled up by the doors, and price-
marked. Behind the shed there was a little shack
built of scrap, scrap lumber and pieces of tin. The
windows were windshields built into the walls. In
the grassy lot the wrecks lay, cars with twisted,
stove-in noses, wounded cars lying on their sides
with the wheels gone. Engines rusting on the ground
and against the shed. A great pile of junk; fenders
and truck sides, wheels and axles; over the whole
lot a spirit of decay, of mold and rust; twisted iron,
half-gutted engines, a mass of derelicts.

Al drove the truck up on the oily ground in front of
the shed. Tom got out and looked into the dark doorway. "Don't see nobody," he said, and he called,
"Anybody here?"

"Jesus, I hope they got a '25 Dodge."

Behind the shed a door banged. A specter of a man came through the dark shed. Thin, dirty, oily skin tight against stringy muscles. One eye was gone, and the raw, uncovered socket squirmed with eye muscles when his good eye moved. His jeans and shirt were thick and shiny with old grease, and his hands cracked and lined and cut. His heavy, pouting under-lip hung out sullenly.

Tom asked, "You the boss?"

The one eye glared. "I work for the boss," he said sullenly. "Whatcha want?"

"Got a wrecked '25 Dodge? We need a con-rod."

"I don't know. If the boss was here he could tell ya—but he ain't here. He's went home."

"Can we look an' see?"

The man blew his nose into the palm of his hand and wiped his hand on his trousers. "You from hereabouts?"

"Come from east—goin' west."

"Look aroun' then. Burn the goddamn place down, for all I care."

"Looks like you don't love your boss none."

The man shambled close, his one eye flaring. "I hate 'im," he said softly. "I hate the son-of-a-bitch! Gone home now. Gone home to his house." The words fell stumbling out. "He got a way—he got a way a-pickin' a fella an' a-tearin' a fella. He—the son-of-a-bitch. Got a girl nineteen, purty. Says to me, 'How'd ya like ta marry her?' Says that right to me. An' tonight—says, 'They's a dance; how'd ya like to go?' Me, he says it to me!" Tears formed in his eyes and tears dripped from the corner of the red eye socket. "Some day, by God—some day I'm gonna have a pipe wrench in my pocket. When he says them things he looks at my eye. An' I'm gonna, I'm gonna jus' take his head right down off his neck with that wrench, little piece at a time." He panted with his fury. "Little piece at a time, right down off'n his neck."

The sun disappeared behind the mountains. Al looked into the lot at the wrecked cars. "Over there, look, Tom! That there looks like a '25 or '26."

Tom turned to the one-eyed man. "Mind if we look?"

"Hell, no! Take any goddamn thing you want."

They walked, threading their way among the dead automobiles, to a rusting sedan, resting on flat tires.

"Sure, it's a '25," Al cried. "Can we yank off the pan, mister?"

Tom kneeled down and looked under the car. "Pan's off awready. One rod's been took. Looks like one gone." He wriggled under the car. "Get a crank an' turn her over, Al." He worked the rod against the shaft. "Purty much froze with grease." Al turned the crank slowly. "Easy," Tom called. He picked a splinter of wood from the ground and scraped the cake of grease from the bearing and the bearing bolts.

"How is she for tight?" Al asked.

"Well, she's a little loose, but not bad."

"Well, how is she for wore?"

"Got plenty shim. Ain't been all took up. Yeah, she's O.K. Turn her over easy now. Get her down, easy—there! Run over the truck an' get some tools."

The one-eyed man said, "I'll get you a box a tools." He shuffled off among the rusty cars and in a moment he came back with a tin box of tools. Tom dug out a socket wrench and handed it to Al.

"You take her off. Don' lose no shims an' don' let the bolts get away, an' keep track a the cotter pins. Hurry up. The light's gettin' dim."

Al crawled under the car. "We oughta get us a set a socket wrenches," he called. "Can't get in no place with a monkey wrench."

"Yell out if you want a hand," Tom said.

The one-eyed man stood helplessly by. "I'll help ya if ya want," he said. "Know what that son-of-a-bitch done? He come by an' he got on white pants. An' he

says, 'Come on, le's go out to my yacht.' By God, I'll
whang him some day!" He breathed heavily. "I ain't
been out with a woman sence I los' my eye. An he says
stuff like that." And big tears cut channels in the dirt
beside his nose.

Tom said impatiently, "Whyn't you roll on? Got no
guards to keep ya here."

"Yeah, that's easy to say. Ain't so easy to get a
job—not for a one-eye' man."

Tom turned on him. "Now, look-a-here, fella. You
got that eye wide open. An' ya dirty, ya stink. Ya jus'
askin' for it. Ya like it. Lets ya feel sorry for yaself.
'Course ya can't get no woman with that empty eye
flappin' aroun'. Put somepin over it an' wash ya face.
You ain't hittin' nobody with no pipe wrench."

"I tell ya, a one-eye' fella got a hard row," the man
said. "Can't see stuff the way other fellas can. Can't
see how far off a thing is. Ever'thing's jus' flat."

Tom said, "Ya full a crap. Why, I knowed a one-
legged whore one time. Think she was takin' two-bits in
an alley? No, by God! She's gettin' half a dollar extra.
She says, 'How many one-legged women you slep' with?
None!' she says. 'O.K.,' she says. 'You got somepin
pretty special here, an' it's gonna cos' ya half a buck
extry.' An' by God, she was gettin' 'em too, an' the fellas
comin' out thinkin' they're pretty lucky. She says she's
good luck. An' I knowed a hump-back in—in a place I
was. Make his whole livin' lettin' folks rub his hump for
luck. Jesus Christ, an' all you got is one eye gone."

The man said stumblingly, "Well, Jesus, ya see
somebody edge away from ya, an' it gets into ya."

"Cover it up then, goddamn it. Ya stickin' it out
like a cow's ass. Ya like to feel sorry for yaself. There
ain't nothin' the matter with you. Buy yaself some
white pants. Ya gettin' drunk an' cryin' in ya bed, I
bet. Need any help, Al?"

"No," said Al. "I got this here bearin' loose. Jus'
tryin' to work the piston down."

"Don't bang yaself," said Tom.

The one-eyed man said softly, "Think—somebody'd
like—me?"

"Why, sure," said Tom. "Tell 'em ya dong's growed
sence you los' your eye."

"Where at you fellas goin'?"

"California. Whole family. Gonna get work out
there."

"Well, ya think a fella like me could get work?
Black patch on my eye?"

"Why not? You ain't no cripple."

"Well—could I catch a ride with you fellas?"

"Christ, no. We're so goddamn full now we can't
move. You get out some other way. Fix up one a these
here wrecks an' go out by yaself."

"Maybe I will, by God," said the one-eyed man.

There was a clash of metal. "I got her," Al called.

"Well, bring her out, let's look at her." Al handed
him the piston and connecting-rod and the lower half
of the bearing.

Tom wiped the babbitt surface and sighted along it
sideways. "Looks O.K. to me," he said. "Say, by God,
if we had a light we could get this here in tonight."

"Say, Tom," Al said, "I been thinkin'. We got no
ring clamps. Gonna be a job gettin' them rings in,
specially underneath."

Tom said, "Ya know, a fella tol' me one time ya
wrap some fine brass wire aroun' the ring to hol' her."

"Yeah, but how ya gonna get the wire off?"

"Ya don't get her off. She melts off an' don't hurt
nothin'."

"Copper wire'd be better."

"It ain't strong enough," said Tom. He turned to the
one-eyed man. "Got any fine brass wire?"

"I dunno. I think they's a spool somewheres. Where
d'ya think a fella could get one a them patches one-
eye' fellas wear?"

"I don' know," said Tom. "Le's see if you can fin' that wire."

In the iron shed they dug through boxes until they found the spool. Tom set the rod in a vise and carefully wrapped the wire around the piston rings, forcing them deep into their slots, and where the wire was twisted he hammered it flat; and then he turned the piston and tapped the wire all around until it cleared the piston wall. He ran his finger up and down to make sure that the rings and wire were flush with the wall. It was getting dark in the shed. The one-eyed man brought a flashlight and shone its beam on the work.

"There she is!" said Tom. "Say—what'll ya take for that light?"

"Well, it ain't much good. Got fifteen cents' a new batteries. You can have her for—oh, thirty-five cents."

"O.K. An' what we owe ya for this here con-rod an' piston?"

The one-eyed man rubbed his forehead with a knuckle, and a line of dirt peeled off. "Well, sir, I jus' dunno. If the boss was here, he'd go to a parts book an' he'd find out how much is a new one, an' while you was workin', he'd be findin' out how bad you're hung up, an' how much jack ya got, an' then he'd—well, say it's eight bucks in the part book—he'd make a price a five bucks. An' if you put up a squawk, you'd get it for three. You say it's all me, but, by God, he's a son-of-a-bitch. Figgers how bad ya need it. I seen him get more for a ring gear than he gave for the whole car."

"Yeah! But how much am I gonna give you for this here?"

" 'Bout a buck, I guess."

"Awright, an' I'll give ya a quarter for this here socket wrench. Make it twice as easy." He handed

over the silver. "Thank ya. An' cover up that goddamn
eye."

Tom and Al got into the truck. It was deep dark. Al
started the motor and turned on the lights. "So long,"
Tom called. "See ya maybe in California." They
turned across the highway and started back.

The one-eyed man watched them go, and then he
went through the iron shed to his shack behind. It was
dark inside. He felt his way to the mattress on the
floor, and he stretched out and cried in his bed, and
the cars whizzing by on the highway only strengthened
the walls of his loneliness.

Tom said, "If you'd tol' me we'd get this here thing
an' get her in tonight, I'd a said you was nuts."

"We'll get her in awright," said Al. "You got to do
her, though. I'd be scared I'd get her in too tight an'
she'd burn out, or too loose an' she'd hammer out."

"I'll stick her in," said Tom. "If she goes out again,
she goes out. I got nothin' to lose."

Al peered into the dusk. The lights made no impression on the gloom; but ahead, the eyes of a hunting cat
flashed green in reflection of the lights. "You sure give
that fella hell," Al said. "Sure did tell him where to
lay down his dogs."

"Well, goddamn it, he was askin' for it! Jus' a pat-
tin' hisself 'cause he got one eye, puttin' all the blame
on his eye. He's a lazy, dirty son-of-a-bitch. Maybe he
can snap out of it if he knowed people was wise to
him."

Al said, "Tom, it wasn't nothin' I done burned out
that bearin'."

Tom was silent for a moment, then, "I'm gonna take
a fall outa you, Al. You jus' scrabblin' ass over tit,
fear somebody gonna pin some blame on you. I know
what's a matter. Young fella, all full a piss an' vinegar. Wanta be a hell of a guy all the time. But, goddamn it, Al, don' keep ya guard up when nobody ain't
sparrin' with ya. You gonna be all right."

Al did not answer him. He looked straight ahead. The truck rattled and banged over the road. A cat whipped out from the side of the road and Al swerved to hit it, but the wheels missed and the cat leaped into the grass.

"Nearly got him," said Al. "Say, Tom. You heard Connie talkin' how he's gonna study nights? I been thinkin' maybe I'd study nights too. You know, radio or television or Diesel engines. Fella might get started that-a-way."

"Might," said Tom. "Find out how much they gonna sock ya for the lessons, first. An' figger out if you're gonna study 'em. There was fellas takin' them mail lessons in McAlester. I never knowed one of 'em that finished up. Got sick of it an' left 'em slide."

"God Awmighty, we forgot to get somepin to eat."

"Well, Ma sent down plenty; preacher couldn' eat it all. Be some lef'. I wonder how long it'll take us to get to California."

"Christ, I don' know. Jus' plug away at her."

They fell into silence, and the dark came and the stars were sharp and white.

Casy got out of the back seat of the Dodge and strolled to the side of the road when the truck pulled up. "I never expected you so soon," he said.

Tom gathered the parts in the piece of sacking on the floor. "We was lucky," he said. "Got a flashlight, too. Gonna fix her right up."

"You forgot to take your dinner," said Casy.

"I'll get it when I finish. Here, Al, pull off the road a little more an' come hol' the light for me." He went directly to the Dodge and crawled under on his back. Al crawled under on his belly and directed the beam of the flashlight. "Not in my eyes. There, put her up." Tom worked the piston up into the cylinder, twisting and turning. The brass wire caught a little on the cylinder wall. With a quick push he forced it past the rings. "Lucky she's loose or the compression'd stop her. I think she's gonna work all right."

"Hope that wire don't clog the rings," said Al.

"Well, that's why I hammered her flat. She won't roll off. I think she'll jus' melt out an' maybe give the walls a brass plate."

"Think she might score the walls?"

Tom laughed. "Jesus Christ, them walls can take it. She's drinkin' oil like a gopher hole awready. Little more ain't gonna hurt none." He worked the rod down over the shaft and tested the lower half. "She'll take some shim." He said, "Casy!"

"Yeah."

"I'm takin' up this here bearing now. Get out to that crank an' turn her over slow when I tell ya." He tightened the bolts. "Now. Over slow!" And as the angular shaft turned, he worked the bearing against it. "Too much shim," Tom said. "Hold it, Casy." He took out the bolts and removed thin shims from each side and put the bolts back. "Try her again, Casy!" And he worked the rod again. "She's a lit-tle bit loose yet. Wonder if she'd be too tight if I took out more shim. I'll try her." Again he removed the bolts and took out another pair of the thin strips. "Now try her, Casy."

"That looks good," said Al.

Tom called, "She any harder to turn, Casy?"

"No, I don't think so."

"Well, I think she's snug here. I hope to God she is. Can't hone no babbitt without tools. This here socket wrench makes her a hell of a lot easier."

Al said, "Boss a that yard gonna be purty mad when he looks for that size socket an' she ain't there."

"That's his screwin'," said Tom. "We didn' steal her." He tapped the cotter-pins in and bent the ends out. "I think that's good. Look, Casy, you hold the light while me an' Al get this here pan up."

Casy knelt down and took the flashlight. He kept

the beam on the working hands as they patted the gasket gently in place and lined the holes with the pan bolts. The two men strained at the weight of the pan, caught the end bolts, and then set in the others; and when they were all engaged, Tom took them up little by little until the pan settled evenly in against the gasket, and he tightened hard against the nuts.

"I guess that's her," Tom said. He tightened the oil tap, looked carefully up at the pan, and took the light and searched the ground. "There she is. Le's get the oil back in her."

They crawled out and poured the bucket of oil back in the crank case. Tom inspected the gasket for leaks.

"O.K., Al. Turn her over," he said. Al got into the car and stepped on the starter. The motor caught with a roar. Blue smoke poured from the exhaust pipe. "Throttle down!" Tom shouted. "She'll burn oil till that wire goes. Gettin' thinner now." And as the motor tuned over, he listened carefully. "Put up the spark an' let her idle." He listened again. "O.K., Al. Turn her off. I think we done her. Where's that meat now?"

"You make a darn good mechanic," Al said.

"Why not? I worked in the shop a year. We'll take her good an' slow for a couple hunderd miles. Give her a chance to work in."

They wiped their grease-covered hands on bunches of weeds and finally rubbed them on their trousers. They fell hungrily on the boiled pork and swigged the water from the bottle.

"I like to starved," said Al. "What we gonna do now, go on to the camp?"

"I dunno," said Tom. "Maybe they'd charge us an extry half-buck. Le's go on an' talk to the folks—tell 'em we're fixed. Then if they wanta sock us extry— we'll move on. The folks'll wanta know. Jesus, I'm glad Ma stopped us this afternoon. Look around with the light, Al. See we don't leave nothin'. Get that socket wrench in. We may need her again."

Al searched the ground with the flashlight. "Don't see nothin'."

"All right. I'll drive her. You bring the truck, Al." Tom started the engine. The preacher got in the car. Tom moved slowly, keeping the engine at a low speed, and Al followed in the truck. He crossed the shallow ditch, crawling in low gear. Tom said, "These here Dodges can pull a house in low gear. She's sure ratio'd down. Good thing for us—I wanta break that bearin' in easy."

On the highway the Dodge moved along slowly. The 12-volt headlights threw a short blob of yellowish light on the pavement.

Casy turned to Tom. "Funny how you fellas can fix a car. Jus' light right in an' fix her. I couldn't fix no car, not even now when I seen you do it."

"Got to grow into her when you're a little kid," Tom said. "It ain't jus' knowin'. It's more'n that. Kids now can tear down a car 'thout even thinkin' about it."

A jackrabbit got caught in the lights and he bounced along ahead, cruising easily, his great ears flopping with every jump. Now and then he tried to break off the road, but the wall of darkness thrust him back. Far ahead bright headlights appeared and bore down on them. The rabbit hesitated, faltered, then turned and bolted toward the lesser lights of the Dodge. There was a small soft jolt as he went under the wheels. The oncoming car swished by

"We sure squashed him," said Casy.

Tom said, "Some fellas like to hit 'em. Gives me a little shakes ever' time. Car sounds O.K. Them rings musta broke loose by now. She ain't smokin' so bad."

"You done a nice job," said Casy.

A small wooden house dominated the camp ground, and on the porch of the house a gasoline lantern hissed and threw its white glare in a great circle. Half a dozen tents were pitched near the house, and cars stood beside the tents. Cooking for the night was over, but the coals of the campfires still glowed on the ground by the camping places. A group of men had gathered to the porch where the lantern burned, and their faces were strong and muscled under the harsh white light, light that threw black shadows of their hats over their foreheads and eyes and made their chins seem to jut out. They sat on the steps, and some stood on the ground, resting their elbows on the porch floor. The proprietor, a sullen lanky man, sat in a chair on the porch. He leaned back against the wall, and he drummed his fingers on his knee. Inside the house a kerosene lamp burned, but its thin light was blasted by the hissing glare of the gasoline lantern. The gathering of men surrounded the proprietor.

Tom drove the Dodge to the side of the road and parked. Al drove through the gate in the truck. "No need to take her in," Tom said. He got out and walked through the gate to the white glare of the lantern.

The proprietor dropped his front chair legs to the floor and leaned forward. "You men wanta camp here?"

"No," said Tom. "We got folks here. Hi, Pa."

Pa, seated on the bottom step, said, "Thought you was gonna be all week. Get her fixed?"

"We was pig lucky," said Tom. "Got a part 'fore dark. We can get goin' fust thing in the mornin'."

"That's a pretty nice thing," said Pa. "Ma's worried. Ya Granma's off her chump."

"Yeah, Al tol' me. She any better now?"

"Well, anyways she's a-sleepin'."

The proprietor said, "If you wanta pull in here an' camp it'll cost you four bits. Get a place to camp an' water an' wood. An' nobody won't bother you."

"What the hell," said Tom. "We can sleep in the ditch right beside the road, an' it won't cost nothin'."

The owner drummed his knee with his fingers. "Dep-

uty sheriff comes on by in the night. Might make it
tough for ya. Got a law against sleepin' out in this
State. Got a law about vagrants."

"If I pay you a half a dollar I ain't a vagrant, huh?"

"That's right."

Tom's eyes glowed angrily. "Deputy sheriff ain't
your brother-'n-law by any chance?"

The owner leaned forward. "No, he ain't. An' the
time ain't come yet when us local folks got to take no
talk from you goddamn bums, neither."

"It don't trouble you none to take our four bits. An'
when'd we get to be bums? We ain't asked ya for
nothin'. All of us bums, huh? Well, we ain't askin' no
nickels from you for the chance to lay down an' rest."

The men on the porch were rigid, motionless, quiet.
Expresssion was gone from their faces; and their eyes,
in the shadows under their hats, moved secretly up to
the face of the proprietor.

Pa growled, "Come off it, Tom."

"Sure, I'll come off it."

The circle of men were quiet, sitting on the steps,
leaning on the high porch. Their eyes glittered under
the harsh light of the gas lantern. Their faces were
hard in the hard light, and they were very still. Only
their eyes moved from speaker to speaker, and their
faces were expressionless and quiet. A lamp bug
slammed itself into the lantern and broke itself, and
fell into the darkness.

In one of the tents a child wailed in complaint, and
a woman's soft voice soothed it and then broke into a
low song, "Jesus loves you in the night. Sleep good,
sleep good. Jesus watches in the night. Sleep, oh,
sleep, oh."

The lantern hissed on the porch. The owner
scratched in the V of his open shirt, where a tangle of
white chest hair showed. He was watchful and ringed
with trouble. He watched the men in the circle,
watched for some expression. And they made no move.

Tom was silent for a long time. His dark eyes looked slowly up at the proprietor. "I don't wanta make no trouble," he said. "It's a hard thing to be named a bum. I ain't afraid," he said softly. "I'll go for you an' your deputy with my mitts—here now, or jump Jesus. But there ain't no good in it."

The men stirred, changed positions, and their glittering eyes moved slowly upward to the mouth of the proprietor, and their eyes watched for his lips to move. He was reassured. He felt that he had won, but not decisively enough to charge in. "Ain't you got half a buck?" he asked.

"Yeah, I got it. But I'm gonna need it. I can't set it out jus' for sleepin'."

"Well, we all got to make a livin'."

"Yeah," Tom said. "On'y I wisht they was some way to make her 'thout takin' her away from somebody else."

The men shifted again. And Pa said, "We'll get movin' smart early. Look, mister. We paid. This here fella is part a our folks. Can't he stay? We paid."

"Half a dollar a car," said the proprietor.

"Well, he ain't got no car. Car's out in the road."

"He came in a car," said the proprietor. "Ever'body'd leave their car out there an' come in an' use my place for nothin'."

Tom said, "We'll drive along the road. Meet ya in the morning. We'll watch for ya. Al can stay an' Uncle John can come with us—" He looked at the proprietor. "That awright with you?"

He made a quick decision, with a concession in it. "If the same number stays that come an' paid—that's awright."

Tom brought out his bag of tobacco, a limp gray rag by now, with a little damp tobacco dust in the bottom of it. He made a lean cigarette and tossed the bag away. "We'll go along pretty soon," he said.

Pa spoke generally to the circle. "It's dirt hard for

folks to tear up an' go. Folks like us that had our
place. We ain't shif'less. Till we got tractored off, we
was people with a farm."

A young thin man, with eyebrows sunburned yellow,
turned his head slowly. "Croppin'?" he asked.

"Sure we was sharecroppin'. Use' ta own the place."

The young man faced forward again. "Same as us,"
he said.

"Lucky for us it ain't gonna las' long," said Pa.
"We'll get out west an' we'll get work an' we'll get a
piece a growin' land with water."

Near the edge of the porch a ragged man stood. His
black coat dripped torn streamers. The knees were
gone from his dungarees. His face was black with
dust, and lined where sweat had washed through. He
swung his head toward Pa. "You folks must have a
nice little pot a money."

"No, we ain't got no money," Pa said. "But they's
plenty of us to work, an' we're all good men. Get good
wages out there an' we'll put 'em together. We'll make
out."

The ragged man stared while Pa spoke, and then he
laughed, and his laughter turned to a high whinnying
giggle. The circle of faces turned to him. The giggling
got out of control and turned into coughing. His eyes
were red and watering when he finally controlled the
spasms. "You goin' out there—oh, Christ!" The giggling started again. "You goin' out an' get—good
wages—oh, Christ!" He stopped and said slyly,
"Pickin' oranges maybe? Gonna pick peaches?"

Pa's tone was dignified. "We gonna take what they
got. They got lots a stuff to work in." The ragged man
giggled under his breath.

Tom turned irritably. "What's so goddamn funny
about that?"

The ragged man shut his mouth and looked sullenly
at the porch boards. "You folks all goin' to California,
I bet."

"I tol' you that," said Pa. "You didn' guess nothin'."

The ragged man said slowly, "Me—I'm comin' back. I been there."

The faces turned quickly toward him. The men were rigid. The hiss of the lantern dropped to a sigh and the proprietor lowered the front chair legs to the porch, stood up, and pumped the lantern until the hiss was sharp and high again. He went back to his chair, but he did not tilt back again. The ragged man turned toward the faces. "I'm goin' back to starve. I ruther starve all over at oncet."

Pa said, "What the hell you talkin' about? I got a han'bill says they got good wages, an' little while ago I seen a thing in the paper says they need folks to pick fruit."

The ragged man turned to Pa. "You got any place to go, back home?"

"No," said Pa. "We're out. They put a tractor past the house."

"You wouldn' go back then?"

" 'Course not."

"Then I ain't gonna fret you," said the ragged man.

" 'Course you ain't gonna fret me. I got a han'bill says they need men. Don't make no sense if they don't need men. Costs money for them bills. They wouldn' put 'em out if they didn' need men."

"I don' wanna fret you."

Pa said angrily, "You done some jackassin'. You ain't gonna shut up now. My han'bill says they need men. You laugh an' say they don't. Now, which one's a liar?"

The ragged man looked down into Pa's angry eyes. He looked sorry. "Han'bill's right," he said. "They need men."

"Then why the hell you stirrin' us up laughin'?"

" 'Cause you don't know what kind a men they need."

"What you talkin' about?"

The ragged man reached a decision. "Look," he said. "How many men they say they want on your han'bill?"

"Eight hunderd, an' that's in one little place."

"Orange color han'bill?"

"Why—yes."

"Give the name a the fella—says so and so, labor contractor?"

Pa reached in his pocket and brought out the folded handbill. "That's right. How'd you know?"

"Look," said the man. "It don't make no sense. This fella wants eight hunderd men. So he prints up five thousand of them things an' maybe twenty thousan' people sees 'em. An' maybe two-three thousan' folks get movin' account a this here han'bill. Folks that's crazy with worry."

"But it don't make no sense!" Pa cried.

"Not till you see the fella that put out this here bill. You'll see him, or somebody that's workin' for him. You'll be a-campin' by a ditch, you an' fifty other families. An' he'll look in your tent an' see if you got anything lef' to eat. An' if you got nothin', he says, 'Wanna job?' An' you'll say, 'I sure do, mister. I'll sure thank you for a chance to do some work.' An' he'll say, 'I can use you.' An' you'll say, 'When do I start?' An' he'll tell you where to go, an' what time, an' then he'll go on. Maybe he needs two hunderd men, so he talks to five hunderd, an' they tell other folks an' when you get to the place, they's a thousan' men. This here fella says, 'I'm payin' twenty cents an hour.' An' maybe half the men walk off. But they's still five hunderd that's so goddamn hungry they'll work for nothin' but biscuits. Well, this here fella's got a contract to pick them peaches or—chop that cotton. You see now? The more fellas he can get, an' the hungrier, less he's gonna pay. An' he'll get a fella with kids if he can, 'cause—hell, I says I wasn't gonna fret ya." The circle of faces looked coldly at him. The eyes tested his words. The ragged man grew self-conscious. "I says I wasn't gonna fret ya, an' here I'm a-doin' it. You gonna go on. You ain't goin' back." The silence hung on the porch. And the light hissed, and a halo of moths swung around and around the lantern. The ragged man went on nervously, "Lemme tell ya what to do when ya meet the fella says he got work. Lemme tell ya. Ast him what he's gonna pay. Ast him to write down what he's gonna pay. Ast him that. I tell you men you're gonna get fooled if you don't."

The proprietor leaned forward in his chair, the better to see the ragged dirty man. He scratched among the gray hairs on his chest. He said coldly, "You sure you ain't one of these here troublemakers? You sure you ain't a labor faker?"

And the ragged man cried, "I swear to God I ain't!"

"They's plenty of 'em," the proprietor said. "Goin' aroun' stirrin' up trouble. Gettin' folks mad. Chiselin' in. They's plenty of 'em. Time's gonna come when we string 'em all up, all them troublemakers. We gonna run 'em outa the country. Man wants to work, O.K. If he don't—the hell with him. We ain't gonna let him stir up no trouble."

The ragged man drew himself up. "I tried to tell you folks," he said. "Somepin it took me a year to find out. Took two kids dead, took my wife dead to show me. But I can't tell you. I should of knew that. Nobody couldn't tell me, neither. I can't tell ya about them little fellas layin' in the tent with their bellies puffed out an' jus' skin on their bones, an' shiverin' an' whinin' like pups, an' me runnin' aroun' tryin' to get work—not for money, not for wages!" he shouted. "Jesus Christ, jus' for a cup a flour an' a spoon a lard. An' then the coroner come. 'Them children died a heart failure,' he said. Put it on his paper. Shiverin', they was, an' their bellies stuck out like a pig bladder."

The circle was quiet, and mouths were open a little. The men breathed shallowly, and watched.

The ragged man looked around at the circle, and then he turned and walked quickly away into the darkness. The dark swallowed him, but his dragging footsteps could be heard a long time after he had gone, footsteps along the road, and a car came by on the highway, and its lights showed the ragged man shuffling along the road, his head hanging down and his hands in the black coat pockets.

The men were uneasy. One said, "Well—gettin' late. Got to get to sleep."

The proprietor said, "Prob'ly shif'less. They's so goddamn many shif'less fellas on the road now." And then he was quiet. And he tipped his chair back against the wall again and fingered his throat.

Tom said, "Guess I'll go see Ma for a minute, an' then we'll shove along a piece." The Joad men moved away.

Pa said, "S'pose he's tellin' the truth—that fella?"

The preacher answered, "He's tellin' the truth, awright. The truth for him. He wasn't makin' nothin' up."

"How about us?" Tom demanded. "Is that the truth for us?"

"I don' know," said Casy.

"I don' know," said Pa.

They walked to the tent, tarpaulin spread over a rope. And it was dark inside, and quiet. When they came near, a grayish mass stirred near the door and arose to person height. Ma came out to meet them.

"All sleepin'," she said. "Granma finally dozed off." Then she saw it was Tom. "How'd you get here?" she demanded anxiously. "You ain't had no trouble?"

"Got her fixed," said Tom. "We're ready to go when the rest is."

"Thank the dear God for that," Ma said. "I'm just

a-twitterin' to go on. Wanta get where it's rich an' green. Wanta get there quick."

Pa cleared his throat. "Fella was jus' sayin'——"

Tom grabbed his arm and yanked it. "Funny what he says," Tom said. "Says they's lots a folks on the way."

Ma peered through the darkness at them. Inside the tent Ruthie coughed and snorted in her sleep. "I washed 'em up," Ma said. "Fust water we got enough of to give 'em a goin'-over. Lef' the buckets out for you fellas to wash too. Can't keep nothin' clean on the road."

"Ever'body in?" Pa asked.

"All but Connie an' Rosasharn. They went off to sleep in the open. Says it's too warm in under cover."

Pa observed querulously. "That Rosasharn is gettin' awful scary an' nimsy-mimsy."

"It's her first," said Ma. "Her an' Connie sets a lot a store by it. You done the same thing."

"We'll go now," Tom said. "Pull off the road a little piece ahead. Watch out for us ef we don't see you. Be off right-han' side."

"Al's stayin'?"

"Yeah. Leave Uncle John come with us. 'Night, Ma."

They walked away through the sleeping camp. In front of one tent a low fitful fire burned, and a woman watched a kettle that cooked early breakfast. The smell of the cooking beans was strong and fine.

"Like to have a plate a them," Tom said politely as they went by.

The woman smiled. "They ain't done or you'd be welcome," she said. "Come aroun' in the daybreak."

"Thank you, ma'am," Tom said. He and Casy and Uncle John walked by the porch. The proprietor still sat in his chair, and the lantern hissed and flared. He turned his head as the three went by. "Ya runnin' outa gas," Tom said.

"Well, time to close up anyways."

"No more half-bucks rollin' down the road, I guess," Tom said.

The chair legs hit the floor. "Don't you go a-sassin' me. I 'member you. You're one of these here trouble-makers."

"Damn right," said Tom. "I'm bolshevisky."

"They's too damn many of you kinda guys aroun'."

Tom laughed as they went out the gate and climbed into the Dodge. He picked up a clod and threw it at the light. They heard it hit the house and saw the proprietor spring to his feet and peer into the darkness. Tom started the car and pulled into the road. And he listened closely to the motor as it turned over, listened for knocks. The road spread dimly under the weak lights of the car.

17

The cars of the migrant people crawled out of the side roads onto the great cross-country highway, and they took the migrant way to the West. In the daylight they scuttled like bugs to the westward; and as the dark caught them, they clustered like bugs near to shelter and to water. And because they were lonely and perplexed, because they had all come from a place of sadness and worry and defeat, and because they were all going to a new mysterious place, they huddled together; they talked together; they shared their lives, their food, and the things they hoped for in the new country. Thus it might be that one familly camped near a spring, and another camped for the spring and for company, and a third because two families had pioneered the place and found it good. And when the sun went down, perhaps twenty families and twenty cars were there.

In the evening a strange thing happened: the twenty families became one family, the children were the children of all. The loss of home became one loss, and the golden time in the West was one dream. And it might be that a sick child threw despair into the hearts of twenty families, of a hundred people; that a birth

there in a tent kept a hundred people quiet and awestruck through the night and filled a hundred people
with the birth-joy in the morning. A family which the
night before had been lost and fearful might search its
goods to find a present for a new baby. In the evening,
sitting about the fires, the twenty were one. They grew
to be units of the camps, units of the evenings and the
nights. A guitar unwrapped from a blanket and
tuned—and the songs, which were all of the people,
were sung in the nights. Men sang the words, and
women hummed the tunes.

Every night a world created, complete with furniture—friends made and enemies established; a world
complete with braggarts and with cowards, with quiet
men, with humble men, with kindly men. Every night
relationships that make a world, established; and
every morning the world torn down like a circus.

At first the families were timid in the building and
tumbling worlds, but gradually the technique of building worlds became their technique. Then leaders
emerged, then laws were made, then codes came into
being. And as the worlds moved westward they were
more complete and better furnished, for their builders
were more experienced in building them.

The families learned what rights must be observed—the right of privacy in the tent; the right to
keep the past black hidden in the heart; the right to
talk and to listen; the right to refuse help or to accept,
to offer help or to decline it; the right of son to court
and daughter to be courted; the right of the hungry to
be fed; the rights of the pregnant and the sick to
transcend all other rights.

And the families learned, although no one told
them, what rights are monstrous and must be destroyed: the right to intrude upon privacy, the right
to be noisy while the camp slept, the right of seduc-
tion or rape, the right of adultery and theft and
murder. These rights were crushed, because the

little worlds could not exist for even a night with such rights alive.

And as the worlds moved westward, rules became laws, although no one told the families. It is unlawful to foul near the camp; it is unlawful in any way to foul the drinking water; it is unlawful to eat good rich food near one who is hungry, unless he is asked to share.

And with the laws, the punishments—and there were only two—a quick and murderous fight or ostracism; and ostracism was the worst. For if one broke the laws his name and face went with him, and he had no place in any world, no matter where created.

In other worlds, social conduct became fixed and rigid, so that a man must say "Good morning" when asked for it, so that a man might have a willing girl if he stayed with her, if he fathered her children and protected them. But a man might not have one girl one night and another the next, for this would endanger the worlds.

The families moved westward, and the technique of building the worlds improved so that the people could be safe in their worlds; and the form was so fixed that a family acting in the rules knew it was safe in the rules.

There grew up government in the worlds, with leaders, with elders. A man who was wise found that his wisdom was needed in every camp; a man who was a fool could not change his folly with his world. And a kind of insurance developed in these nights. A man with food fed a hungry man, and thus insured himself against hunger. And when a baby died a pile of silver coins grew at the door flap, for a baby must be well buried, since it has had nothing else of life. An old man may be left in a potter's field, but not a baby.

A certain physical pattern is needed for the building of a world—water, a river bank, a stream, a spring, or even a faucet unguarded. And there is needed enough flat land to pitch the tents, a little brush or wood to build the fires. If there is a garbage dump not too far off, all the better; for there can be found equipment—stove tops, a curved fender to shelter the fire, and cans to cook in and to eat from.

And the worlds were built in the evening. The people, moving in from the highways, made them with their tents and their hearts and their brains.

In the morning the tents came down, the canvas was folded, the tent poles tied along the running board, the beds put in place on the cars, the pots in their places. And as the families moved westward, the technique of building up a home in the evening and tearing it down with the morning light became fixed; so that the folded tent was packed in one place, the cooking pots counted in their box. And as the cars moved westward, each member of the family grew into his proper place, grew into his duties; so that each member, old and young, had his place in the car; so that in the weary, hot evenings, when the cars pulled into the camping places, each member had his duty and went to it without instruction: children to gather wood, to carry water; men to pitch the tents and bring down the beds; women to cook the supper and to watch while the family fed. And this was done without command. The families, which had been units of which the boundaries were a house at night, a farm by day, changed their boundaries. In the long hot light, they were silent in the cars moving slowly westward; but at night they integrated with any group they found.

Thus they changed their social life—changed as in the whole universe only man can change. They were not farm men any more, but migrant men. And the thought, the planning, the long staring silence that had gone out to the fields, went now to the roads, to the distance, to the West. That man whose mind had been bound with acres lived with narrow concrete miles. And his thought and his worry were not any more with rainfall, with wind and dust, with the thrust of the crops. Eyes watched the tires, ears listened to the clattering motors, and minds struggled with oil, with gasoline, with the thinning rubber between air and road. Then a broken gear was tragedy. Then water in the evening was the yearning, and food over the fire. Then health to go on was the need and strength to go on, and spirit to go on. The wills thrust westward ahead of them, and fears that had once apprehended drought or flood now lingered with anything that might stop the westward crawling.

The camps became fixed—each a short day's journey from the last.

And on the road the panic overcame some of the families, so that they drove night and day, stopped to sleep in the cars, and drove on to the West, flying from the road, flying from movement. And these lusted so greatly to be settled that they set their faces into the West and drove toward it, forcing the clashing engines over the roads.

But most of the families changed and grew quickly into the new life. And when the sun went down—

Time to look out for a place to stop.

And—there's some tents ahead.

The car pulled off the road and stopped, and because others were there first, certain courtesies were necessary. And the man, the leader of the family, leaned from the car.

Can we pull up here an' sleep?

Why, sure, be proud to have you. What State you from?

Come all the way from Arkansas.

They's Arkansas people down that fourth tent.

That so?

And the great question, How's the water?

Well, she don't taste so good, but they's plenty.

Well, thank ya.

No thanks to me.

But the courtesies had to be. The car lumbered over the ground to the end tent, and stopped. Then down from the car the weary people climbed, and stretched stiff bodies. Then the new tent sprang up; the children went for water and the older boys cut brush or wood. The fires started and supper was put on to boil or to fry. Early comers moved over, and States were exchanged, and friends and sometimes relatives discovered.

Oklahoma, huh? What county?

Cherokee.

Why, I got folks there. Know the Allens? They's Allens all over Cherokee. Know the Willises?

Why, sure.

And a new unit was formed. The dusk came, but before the dark was down the new family was of the camp. A word had been passed with every family. They were known people—good people.

I knowed the Allens all my life. Simon Allen, ol' Simon, had trouble with his first wife. She was part Cherokee. Purty as—as a black colt.

Sure, an' young Simon, he married a Rudolph, didn' he? That's what I thought. They went to live in Enid an' done well—real well.

Only Allen that ever done well. Got a garage.

When the water was carried and the wood cut, the children walked shyly, cautiously among the tents. And they made elaborate acquaintanceship gestures. A boy stopped near another boy and studied a stone, picked it up, examined it closely, spat on it, and rubbed it clean and inspected it until he forced the other to demand, What you got there?

And casually, Nothin'. Jus' a rock.

Well, what you lookin' at it like that for?

Thought I seen gold in it.

How'd you know? Gold ain't gold, it's black in a rock.

Sure, every'body knows that.

I bet it's fool's gold, an' you figgered it was gold.

That ain't so, 'cause Pa, he's foun' lots a gold an' he tol' me how to look.

How'd you like to pick up a big ol' piece a gold?

Sa-a-ay! I'd git the bigges' old son-a-bitchin' piece a candy you ever seen.

I ain't let to swear, but I do, anyways.

Me too. Le's go to the spring.

And young girls found each other and boasted shyly of their popularity and their prospects. The women worked over the fire, hurrying to get food to the stomachs of the family—pork if there was money in plenty, pork and potatoes, and onions. Dutch-oven biscuits or cornbread, and plenty of gravy to go over it. Side-meat or chops and a can of boiled tea, black and bitter. Fried dough in drippings if money was slim, dough fried crisp and brown and the drippings poured over it.

Those families which were very rich or very foolish with their money ate canned beans and canned peaches and packaged bread and bakery cake; but they ate secretly, in their tents, for it would not have been good to eat such fine things openly. Even so, children eating their fried dough smelled the warming beans and were unhappy about it.

When supper was over and the dishes dipped and wiped, the dark had come, and then the men squatted down to talk.

And they talked of the land behind them. I don' know what it's coming to, they said. The country's spoilt.

It'll come back though, on'y we won't be there.

Maybe, they thought, maybe we sinned some way we didn't know about.

Fella says to me, gov'ment fella, an' he says, she's gullied up on ya. Gov'ment fella. He says, if ya plowed 'cross the contour, she won't gully. Never did have no chance to try her. An' the new super' ain't plowin' 'cross the contour. Runnin' a furrow four miles long that ain't stoppin' or goin' aroun' Jesus Christ Hisself.

And they spoke softly of their homes: They was a little cool-house under the win'mill. Use' ta keep milk in there ta cream up, an' watermelons. Go in there midday when she was hotter'n a heifer, an' she'd be jus' as cool, as cool as you'd want. Cut open a melon in there an' she'd hurt your mouth, she was so cool. Water drippin' down from the tank.

They spoke of their tragedies: Had a brother Charley, hair as yella as corn, an' him a growed man. Played the 'cordeen nice too. He was harrowin' one day an' he went up to clear his lines. Well, a rattle-snake buzzed an' them horses bolted an' the harrow went over Charley, an' the points dug into his guts an' his stomach, an' they pulled his face off an'—God Almighty!

They spoke of the future: Wonder what it's like out there?

Well, the pitchers sure do look nice. I seen one where it's hot an' fine, an' walnut trees an' berries; an' right behind, close as a mule's ass to his withers, they's a tall up mountain covered with snow. That was a pretty thing to see.

If we can get work it'll be fine. Won't have no cold in the winter. Kids won't freeze on the way to school. I'm gonna take care my kids don't miss no more school. I can read good, but it ain't no pleasure to me like with a fella that's used to it.

And perhaps a man brought out his guitar to the front of his tent. And he sat on a box to play, and everyone in the camp moved slowly in toward him, drawn in toward him. Many men can chord a guitar, but perhaps this man was a picker. There you have something—the deep chords beating, beating, while the melody runs on the strings like little footsteps. Heavy hard fingers marching on the frets. The man played and the people moved slowly in on him until the circle was closed and tight, and then he sang, "Ten-Cent Cotton and Forty-Cent Meat." And the circle sang softly with him. And he sang "Why Do You Cut Your Hair, Girls?" And the circle sang. He wailed the song, "I'm Leaving Old Texas," that eerie song that was sung before the Spaniards came, only the words were Indian then.

And now the group was welded to one thing, one unit, so that in the dark the eyes of the people were inward, and their minds played in other times, and their sadness was like rest, like sleep. He sang the "McAlester Blues" and then, to make up for it to the older people, he sang "Jesus Calls Me to His Side." The children drowsed with the music and went into the tents to sleep, and the singing came into their dreams.

And after a while the man with the guitar stood up and yawned. Good night, folks, he said.

And they murmured, Good night to you.

And each wished he could pick a guitar, because it is a gracious thing. Then the people went to their beds, and the camp was quiet. And the owls coasted overhead, and the coyotes gabbled in the distance, and into the camp skunks walked, looking for bits of food—waddling, arrogant skunks, afraid of nothing.

The night passed, and with the first streak of dawn the women came out of the tents, built up the fires, and put the coffee to boil. And the men came out and talked softly in the dawn.

When you cross the Colorado River, there's the desert, they say. Look out for the desert. See you don't get hung up. Take plenty water, case you get hung up.

I'm gonna take her at night.

Me too. She'll cut the living Jesus outa you.

The families ate quickly, and the dishes were dipped and wiped. The tents came down. There was a rush to go. And when the sun arose, the camping place was vacant, only a little litter left by the people. And the camping place was ready for a new world in a new night.

But along the highway the cars of the migrant people crawled out like bugs, and the narrow concrete miles stretched ahead.

18

The Joad family moved
slowly westward, up into the mountains of New Mexico, past the pinnacles and pyramids of the upland.
They climbed into the high country of Arizona, and
through a gap they looked down on the Painted Desert.
A border guard stopped them.

"Where you going?"

"To California," said Tom.

"How long you plan to be in Arizona?"

"No longer'n we can get acrost her."

"Got any plants?"

"No plants."

"I ought to look your stuff over."

"I tell you we ain't got no plants."

The guard put a little sticker on the windshield.

"O.K. Go ahead, but you better keep movin'."

"Sure. We aim to."

They crawled up the slopes, and the low twisted
trees covered the slopes. Holbrook, Joseph City, Wins-
low. And then the tall trees began, and the cars
spouted steam and labored up the slopes. And there
was Flagstaff, and that was the top of it all. Down from
Flagstaff over the great plateaus, and the road disappeared in the distance ahead. The water grew scarce,

water was to be bought, five cents, ten cents, fifteen cents a gallon. The sun drained the dry rocky country, and ahead were jagged broken peaks, the western wall of Arizona. And now they were in flight from the sun and the drought. They drove all night, and came to the mountains in the night. And they crawled the jagged ramparts in the night, and their dim lights flickered on the pale stone walls of the road. They passed the summit in the dark and came slowly down in the late night, through the shattered stone debris of Oatman; and when the daylight came they saw the Colorado River below them. They drove to Topock, pulled up at the bridge while a guard washed off the windshield sticker. Then across the bridge and into a broken rock wilderness. And although they were dead weary and the morning heat was growing, they stopped.

Pa called, "We're there—we're in California!" They looked dully at the broken rock glaring under the sun, and across the river the terrible ramparts of Arizona.

"We got the desert," said Tom. "We got to get to the water and rest."

The road runs parallel to the river, and it was well into the morning when the burning motors came to Needles, where the river runs swiftly among the reeds.

The Joads and Wilsons drove to the river, and they sat in the cars looking at the lovely water flowing by, and the green reeds jerking slowly in the current. There was a little encampment by the river, eleven tents near the water, and the swamp grass on the ground. And Tom leaned out of the truck window. "Mind if we stop here a piece?"

A stout woman, scrubbing clothes in a bucket, looked up. "We don't own it, mister. Stop if you want. They'll be a cop down to look you over." And she went back to her scrubbing in the sun.

The two cars pulled to a clear place on the swamp grass. The tents were passed down, the Wilson tent set up, the Joad tarpaulin stretched over its rope.

Winfield and Ruthie walked slowly down through the willows to a reedy place. Ruthie said, with soft vehemence, "California. This here's California an' we're right in it!"

Winfield broke a tule and twisted it free, and he put the white pulp in his mouth and chewed it. They walked into the water and stood quietly, the water about the calves of their legs.

"We got the desert yet," Ruthie said.

"What's the desert like?"

"I don't know. I seen pitchers once says a desert. They was bones ever'place."

"Man bones?"

"Some, I guess, but mos'ly cow bones."

"We gonna get to see them bones?"

"Maybe. I don' know. Gonna go 'crost her at night. That's what Tom said. Tom says we get the livin' Jesus burned outa us if we go in daylight."

"Feels nicet an' cool," said Winfield, and he squidged his toes in the sand of the bottom.

They heard Ma calling, "Ruthie! Winfiel'! You come back." They turned and walked slowly back through the reeds and the willows.

The other tents were quiet. For a moment, when the cars came up, a few heads had stuck out between the flaps, and then were withdrawn. Now the family tents were up and the men gathered together.

Tom said, "I'm gonna go down an' take a bath. That's what I'm gonna do—before I sleep. How's Granma sence we got her in the tent?"

"Don' know," said Pa. "Couldn' seem to wake her up." He cocked his head toward the tent. A whining, babbling voice came from under the canvas. Ma went quickly inside.

"She woke up, awright," said Noah. "Seems like all night she was a-croakin' up on the truck. She's all outa sense."

Tom said, "Hell! She's wore out. If she don't get

some res' pretty soon, she ain' gonna las'. She's jes'
wore out. Anybody comin' with me? I'm gonna wash,
an' I'm gonna sleep in the shade—all day long." He
moved away, and the other men followed him. They
took off their clothes in the willows and then they
walked into the water and sat down. For a long time
they sat, holding themselves with heels dug into the
sand, and only their heads stuck out of the water.

"Jesus, I needed this," Al said. He took a handful
of sand from the bottom and scrubbed himself with it.
They lay in the water and looked across at the sharp
peaks called Needles, and at the white rock mountains
of Arizona.

"We come through them," Pa said in wonder.

Uncle John ducked his head under the water.
"Well, we're here. This here's California, an' she don't
look so prosperous."

"Got the desert yet," said Tom. "An' I hear she's a
son-of-a-bitch."

Noah asked, "Gonna try her tonight?"

"What ya think, Pa?" Tom asked.

"Well, I don't know. Do us good to get a little res',
'specially Granma. But other ways, I'd kinda like to
get acrost her an' get settled into a job. On'y got 'bout
forty dollars left. I'll feel better when we're all workin',
an' a little money comin' in."

Each man sat in the water and felt the tug of the
current. The preacher let his arms and hands float on
the surface. The bodies were white to the neck and
wrists, and burned dark brown on hands and faces,
with V's of brown at the collar bones. They scratched
themselves with sand.

And Noah said lazily, "Like to jus' stay here. Like
to lay here forever. Never get hungry an' never get
sad. Lay in the water all life long, lazy as a brood sow
in the mud."

And Tom, looking at the ragged peaks across the
river and the Needles downstream: "Never seen such

tough mountains. This here's a murder country. This
here's the bones of a country. Wonder if we'll ever get
in a place where folks can live 'thout fightin' hard
scrabble an' rocks. I seen pitchers of a country flat an'
green, an' with little houses like Ma says, white. Ma
got her heart set on a white house. Get to thinkin' they
ain't no such country. I seen pitchers like that."

Pa said, "Wait till we get to California. You'll see
nice country then."

"Jesus Christ, Pa! This here *is* California."

Two men dressed in jeans and sweaty blue shirts
came through the willows and looked toward the naked
men. They called, "How's the swimmin'?"

"Dunno," said Tom, "We ain't tried none. Sure
feels good to set here, though."

"Mind if we come in an' set?"

"She ain't our river. We'll len' you a little piece of
her."

The men shucked off their pants, peeled their
shirts, and waded out. The dust coated their legs to
the knee; their feet were pale and soft with sweat.
They settled lazily into the water and washed listlessly
at their flanks. Sun-bitten, they were, a father and a
boy. They grunted and groaned with the water.

Pa asked politely, "Goin' west?"

"Nope. We come from there. Goin' back home. We
can't make no livin' out there."

"Where's home?" Tom asked.

"Panhandle, come from near Pampa."

Pa asked, "Can you make a livin' there?"

"Nope. But at leas' we can starve to death with folks
we know. Won't have a bunch a fellas that hates us to
starve with."

Pa said, "Ya know, you're the second fella talked
like that. What makes 'em hate you?"

"Dunno," said the man. He cupped his hands full of
water and rubbed his face, snorting and bubbling.
Dusty water ran out of his hair and streaked his neck.

"I like to hear some more 'bout this," said Pa.

"Me too," Tom added. "Why these folks out west hate ya?"

The man looked sharply at Tom. "You jus' goin' wes'?"

"Jus' on our way."

"You ain't never been in California?"

"No, we ain't."

"Well, don' take my word. Go see for yourself."

"Yeah," Tom said, "but a fella kind a likes to know what he's gettin' into."

"Well, if you truly wanta know, I'm a fella that's asked questions an' give her some thought. She's a nice country. But she was stole a long time ago. You git acrost the desert an' come into the country aroun' Bakersfield. An' you never seen such purty country— all orchards an' grapes, purtiest country you ever seen. An' you'll pass lan' flat an' fine with water thirty feet down, and that lan's layin' fallow. But you can't have none of that lan'. That's a Lan' and Cattle Company. An' if they don't want ta work her, she ain't gonna git worked. You go in there an' plant you a little corn, an' you'll go to jail!"

"Good lan', you say? An' they ain't workin' her?"

"Yes, sir. Good lan' an' they ain't! Well, sir, that'll get you a little mad, but you ain't seen nothin'. People gonna have a look in their eye. They gonna look at you an' their face says 'I don't like you, you son-of-a-bitch.' Gonna be deputy sheriffs, an' they'll push you aroun'. You camp on the roadside, an' they'll move you on. You gonna see in people's face how they hate you. An'—I'll tell you somepin. They hate you 'cause they're scairt. They know a hungry fella gonna get food even if he got to take it. They know that fallow lan's a sin an' somebody' gonna take it. What the hell! You never been called 'Okie' yet."

Tom said, "Okie? What's that?"

"Well, Okie use' ta mean you was from Oklahoma.

Now it means you're a dirty son-of-a-bitch. Okie means you're scum. Don't mean nothing itself, it's the way they say it. But I can't tell you nothin'. You got to go there. I hear there's three hunderd thousan' of our people there—an' livin' like hogs, 'cause ever'thing in California is owned. They ain't nothin' left. An' them people that owns it is gonna hang on to it if they got ta kill ever'body in the worl' to do it. An' they're scairt, an' that makes 'em mad. You got to see it. You got to hear it. Purtiest goddamn country you ever seen, but they ain't nice to you, them folks. They're so scairt an' worried they ain't even nice to each other."

Tom looked down into the water, and he dug his heels into the sand. "S'pose a fella got work an' saved, couldn' he get a little lan'?"

The older man laughed and he looked at his boy, and his silent boy grinned almost in triumph. And the man said, "You ain't gonna get no steady work. Gonna scrabble for your dinner ever' day. An' you gonna do her with people lookin' mean at you. Pick cotton, an' you gonna be sure the scales ain't honest. Some of 'em is, an' some of 'em ain't. But you gonna think all the scales is crooked, an' you don' know which ones. Ain't nothin' you can do about her anyways."

Pa asked slowly, "Ain't—ain't it nice out there at all?"

"Sure, nice to look at, but you can't have none of it. They's a grove of yella oranges—an' a guy with a gun that got the right to kill you if you touch one. They's a fella, newspaper fella near the coast, got a million acres—"

Casy looked up quickly. "Million acres? What in the worl' can he do with a million acres?"

"I dunno. He jus' got it. Runs a few cattle. Got guards ever'place to keep folks out. Rides aroun' in a bullet-proof car. I seen pitchers of him. Fat, sof' fella with little mean eyes an' a mouth like a ass-hole. Scairt he's gonna die. Got a million acres an' scairt of dyin'."

Casy demanded, "What in hell can he do with a million acres? What's he want a million acres for?"

The man took his whitening, puckering hands out of the water and spread them, and he tightened his lower lip and he bent his head down to one shoulder. "I dunno," he said. "Guess he's crazy. Mus' be crazy. Seen a pitcher of him. He looks crazy. Crazy an' mean."

"Say he's scairt to die?" Casy asked.

"That's what I heard."

"Scairt God'll get him?"

"I dunno. Jus' scairt."

"What's he care?" Pa said. "Don't seem like he's havin' no fun."

"Grampa wasn't scairt," Tom said. "When Grampa was havin' the most fun, he come clostest to gettin' kil't. Time Grampa an' another fella whanged into a bunch a Navajo in the night. They was havin' the time a their life, an' same time you wouldn' give a gopher for their chance."

Casy said, "Seems like that's the way. Fella havin' fun, he don't give a damn; but a fella mean an' lonely an' old an' disappointd—he's scared of dyin'!"

Pa asked, "What's he disappointed about if he got a million acres?"

The preacher smiled, and he looked puzzled. He splashed a floating water bug away with his hand. "If he needs a million acres to make him feel rich, seems to me he needs it 'cause he feels awful poor inside hisself, and if he's poor in hisself, there ain't no million acres gonna make him feel rich, an' maybe he's disappointed that nothin' he can do'll make him feel rich—not rich like Mis' Wilson was when she give her tent when Grampa died. I ain't tryin' to preach no sermon, but I never seen nobody that's busy as a prairie dog collectin' stuff that wasn't disappointed." He grinned. "Does kinda soun' like a sermon, don't it?"

The sun was flaming fiercely now. Pa said, "Better scrunch down under water. She'll burn the living Jesus outa you." And he reclined and let the gently moving water flow around his neck. "If a fella's willin' to work hard, can't he cut her?" Pa asked.

The man sat up and faced him. "Look, mister. I don' know ever'thing. You might go out there an' fall into a steady job, an' I'd be a liar. An' then, you might never get no work, an' I didn' warn ya. I can tell ya mos' of the folks is purty mis'able." He lay back in the water. "A fella don' know ever'thing," he said.

Pa turned his head and looked at Uncle John. "You never was a fella to say much," Pa said. "But I'll be goddamned if you opened your mouth twicet sence we lef' home. What you think 'bout this here?"

Uncle John scowled, "I don't think nothin' about it. We're a-goin' there, ain't we? None of this here talk gonna keep us from goin' there. When we get there, we'll get there. When we get a job we'll work, an' when we don't get a job we'll set on our tail. This here talk ain't gonna do no good no way."

Tom lay back and filled his mouth with water, and he spurted it into the air and he laughed. "Uncle John don't talk much, but he talks sense. Yes, by God! He talks sense. We goin' on tonight, Pa?"

"Might's well. Might's well get her over."

"Well, I'm goin' up in the brush an' get some sleep then." Tom stood up and waded to the sandy shore. He slipped his clothes on his wet body and winced under the heat of the cloth. The others followed him.

In the water, the man and his boy watched the Joads disappear. And the boy said, "Like to see 'em in six months. Jesus!"

The man wiped his eye corners with his forefinger. "I shouldn' of did that," he said. "Fella always wants to be a wise guy, wants to tell folks stuff."

"Well, Jesus, Pa! They asked for it."

"Yeah, I know. But like that fella says, they're a-goin' anyways. Nothin' won't be changed from what I tol' 'em, 'cept they'll be mis'able 'fore they hafta.''

Tom walked in among the willows, and he crawled into a cave of shade to lie down. And Noah followed him.

"Gonna sleep here," Tom said.

"Tom!"

"Yeah?"

"Tom, I ain't a-goin' on."

Tom sat up. "What you mean?"

"Tom, I ain't a-gonna leave this here water. I'm a-gonna walk on down this here river."

"You're crazy," Tom said.

"Get myself a piece a line. I'll catch fish. Fella can't starve beside a nice river."

Tom said, "How 'bout the fam'ly? How 'bout Ma?"

"I can't he'p it. I can't leave this here water." Noah's wide-set eyes were half closed. "You know how it is, Tom. You know how the folks are nice to me. But they don't really care for me."

"You're crazy."

"No, I ain't. I know how I am. I know they're sorry. But—Well, I ain't a-goin'. You tell Ma—Tom."

"Now you look-a-here," Tom began.

"No. It ain't no use. I was in that there water. An' I ain't a-gonna leave her. I'm a-gonna go now, Tom— down the river. I'll catch fish an' stuff, but I can't leave her. I can't." He crawled back out of the willow cave. "You tell Ma, Tom." He walked away.

Tom followed him to the river bank. "Listen, you goddamn fool——"

"It ain't no use," Noah said. "I'm sad, but I can't he'p it. I got to go." He turned abruptly and walked downstream along the shore. Tom started to follow, and then he stopped. He saw Noah disappear into the brush, and then appear again, following the edge of the river. And he watched Noah growing smaller on the edge of the river, until he disappeared into the willows at last. And Tom took off his cap and scratched his head. He went back to his willow cave and lay down to sleep.

Under the spread tarpaulin Granma lay on a mattress, and Ma sat beside her. The air was stiflingly hot, and the flies buzzed in the shade of the canvas. Granma was naked under a long piece of pink curtain. She turned her old head restlessly from side to side, and she muttered and choked. Ma sat on the ground beside her, and with a piece of cardboard drove the flies away and fanned a stream of moving hot air over the tight old face. Rose of Sharon sat on the other side and watched her mother.

Granma called imperiously, "Will! Will! You come here, Will." And her eyes opened and she looked fiercely about. "Tol' him to come right here," she said. "I'll catch him. I'll take the hair off'n him." She closed her eyes and rolled her head back and forth and muttered thickly. Ma fanned the cardboard.

Rose of Sharon looked helplessly at the old woman. She said softly, "She's awful sick."

Ma raised her eyes to the girl's face. Ma's eyes were patient, but the lines of strain were on her forehead. Ma fanned and fanned the air, and her piece of cardboard warned off the flies. "When you're young, Rosasharn, ever'thing that happens is a thing all by itself. It's a lonely thing. I know, I 'member, Rosasharn." Her mouth loved the name of her daughter. "You're gonna have a baby, Rosasharn, and that's somepin to you lonely and away. That's gonna hurt you, an' the hurt'll be lonely hurt, an' this here tent is alone in the worl', Rosasharn." She whipped the air for a moment to drive a buzzing blow fly on, and the big shining fly circled the tent twice and zoomed out into the blinding sunlight. And Ma went on, "They's a time of change, an' when that comes, dyin' is a piece of all dyin', and bearin' is a piece of all bearin', an' bearin' an' dyin' is two pieces of the same thing. An' then things ain't lonely any more. An' then a hurt don't hurt so bad, 'cause it ain't a lonely hurt no more, Rosasharn. I wisht I could tell you so you'd know, but I can't." And her voice was so soft, so full of love, that tears crowded into Rose of Sharon's eyes, and flowed over her eyes and blinded her.

"Take an' fan Granma," Ma said, and she handed the cardboard to her daughter. "That's a good thing to do. I wisht I could tell you so you'd know."

Granma, scowling her brows down over her closed eyes, bleated, "Will! You're dirty! You ain't never gonna get clean." Her little wrinkled claws moved up and scratched her cheek. A red ant ran up the curtain cloth and scrambled over the folds of loose skin on the old lady's neck. Ma reached quickly and picked it off, crushed it between thumb and forefinger, and brushed her fingers on her dress.

Rose of Sharon waved the cardboard fan. She looked up at Ma. "She—?" And the words parched in her throat.

"Wipe your feet, Will—you dirty pig!" Granma cried.

Ma said, "I dunno. Maybe if we can get her where it ain't so hot, but I dunno. Don't worry yourself, Rosasharn. Take your breath in when you need it, an' let it go when you need to."

A large woman in a torn black dress looked into the tent. Her eyes were bleared and indefinite, and the skin sagged to her jowls and hung down in little flaps. Her lips were loose, so that the upper lip hung like a curtain over her teeth, and her lower lip, by its weight, folded outward, showing her lower gums. "Mornin', ma'am," she said. "Mornin', an' praise God for victory."

Ma looked around. "Mornin'," she said.

The woman stooped into the tent and bent her head over Granma. "We heerd you got a soul here ready to join her Jesus. Praise God!"

Ma's face tightened and her eyes grew sharp. "She's tar'd, tha's all," Ma said. "She's wore out with the road an' the heat. She's jus' wore out. Get a little res', an' she'll be well."

The woman leaned down over Granma's face, and she seemed almost to sniff. Then she turned to Ma and nodded quickly, and her lips jiggled and her jowl quivered. "A dear soul gonna join her Jesus," she said.

Ma cried, "That ain't so!"

The woman nodded, slowly, this time, and put a puffy hand on Granma's forehead. Ma reached to snatch the hand away, and quickly restrained herself. "Yes, it's so, sister," the woman said. "We got six in Holiness in our tent. I'll go git 'em, an' we'll hol' a meetin'—a prayer an' grace. Jehovites, all. Six, countin' me. I'll go git 'em out."

Ma stiffened. "No—no," she said. "No, Granma's tar'd. She couldn't stan' a meetin'."

The woman said, "Couldn't stan' grace? Couldn' stan' the sweet breath of Jesus? What you talkin' about, sister?"

Ma said, "No, not here. She's too tar'd."

The woman looked reproachfully at Ma. "Ain't you believers, ma'am?"

"We always been Holiness," Ma said, "but Granma's tar'd, an' we been a-goin' all night. We won't trouble you."

"It ain't no trouble, an' if it was, we'd want ta do it for a soul a-soarin' to the Lamb."

Ma arose to her knees. "We thank ya," she said coldly. "We ain't gonna have no meetin' in this here tent."

The woman looked at her for a long time. "Well, we

ain't a-gonna let a sister go away 'thout a little praisin'.
We'll git the meetin' goin' in our own tent, ma'am. An'
we'll forgive ya for your hard heart."

Ma settled back again and turned her face to
Granma, and her face was still set and hard. "She's
tar'd," Ma said. "She's on'y tar'd." Granma swung her
head back and forth and muttered under her breath.

The woman walked stiffly out of the tent. Ma continued to look down at the old face.

Rose of Sharon fanned her cardboard and moved the
hot air in a stream. She said, "Ma!"

"Yeah?"

"Whyn't ya let 'em hol' a meetin'?"

"I dunno," said Ma. "Jehovites is good people.
They're howlers an' jumpers. I dunno. Somepin jus'
come over me. I didn' think I could stan' it. I'd jus' fly
all apart."

From some little distance there came the sound of the
beginning meeting, a sing-song chant of exhortation.
The words were not clear, only the tone. The voice rose
and fell, and went higher at each rise. Now a response
filled in the pause, and the exhortation went up with a
tone of triumph, and a growl of power came into the
voice. It swelled and paused, and a growl came into the
response. And now gradually the sentences of exhortation shortened, grew sharper, like commands; and into
the responses came a complaining note. The rhythym
quickened. Male and female voices had been one tone,
but now in the middle of a response one woman's voice
went up and up in a wailing cry, wild and fierce, like
the cry of a beast; and a deeper woman's voice rose up
beside it, a baying voice, and a man's voice traveled up
the scale in the howl of a wolf. The exhortation stopped,
and only the feral howling came from the tent, and with
it a thudding sound on the earth. Ma shivered. Rose of
Sharon's breath was panting and short, and the chorus
of howls went on so long it seemed that lungs must
burst.

THE GRAPES OF WRATH

Ma said, "Makes me nervous. Somepin happened to me."

Now the high voice broke into hysteria, the gabbling screams of a hyena, the thudding became louder. Voices cracked and broke, and then the whole chorus fell to a sobbing, grunting undertone, and the slap of flesh and the thuddings on the earth; and the sobbing changed to a little whining, like that of a litter of puppies at a food dish.

Rose of Sharon cried softly with nervousness. Granma kicked the curtain off her legs, which lay like gray, knotted sticks. And Granma whined with the whining in the distance. Ma pulled the curtain back in place. And then Granma sighed deeply and her breathing grew steady and easy, and her closed eyelids ceased their flicking. She slept deeply, and snored through her half-open mouth. The whining from the distance was softer and softer until it could not be heard at all any more.

Rose of Sharon looked at Ma, and her eyes were blank with tears. "It done good," said Rose of Sharon. "It done Granma good. She's a-sleepin'."

Ma's head was down, and she was ashamed. "Maybe I done them good people wrong. Granma is asleep."

"Whyn't you ast our preacher if you done a sin?" the girl asked.

"I will—but he's a queer man. Maybe it's him made me tell them people they couldn' come here. That preacher, he's gettin' roun' to thinkin' that what people does is right to do." Ma looked at her hands, and then she said, "Rosasharn, we got to sleep. 'F we're gonna go tonight, we got to sleep." She stretched out on the ground beside the mattress.

Rose of Sharon asked, "How about fannin' Granma?"

"She's asleep now. You lay down an' rest."

"I wonder where at Connie is?" the girl complained. "I ain't seen him around for a long time."

Ma said, "Sh! Get some rest."

"Ma, Connie gonna study nights an' get to be some-pin'."

"Y,eah. You tol' me about that. Get some rest."

The girl lay down on the edge of Granma's mattress. "Connie's got a new plan. He's thinkin' all a time. When he gets all up on 'lectricity he gonna have his own store, an' then guess what we gonna have?"

"What?"

"Ice—all the ice you want. Gonna have a ice box. Keep it full. Stuff don't spoil if you got ice."

"Connie's thinkin' all a time," Ma chuckled. "Better get some rest now."

Rose of Sharon closed her eyes. Ma turned over on her back and crossed her hands under her head. She listened to Granma's breathing and to the girl's breathing. She moved a hand to start a fly from her forehead. The camp was quiet in the blinding heat, but the noises of hot grass—of crickets, the hum of flies— were a tone that was close to silence. Ma sighed deeply and then yawned and closed her eyes. In her half-sleep she heard footsteps approaching, but it was a man's voice that started her awake.

"Who's in here?"

Ma sat up quickly. A brown-faced man bent over and looked in. He wore boots and khaki pants and a khaki shirt with epaulets. On a Sam Browne belt a pistol holster hung, and a big silver star was pinned to his shirt at the left breast. A loose-crowned military cap was on the back of his head. He beat on the tarpaulin with his hand, and the tight canvas vibrated like a drum.

"Who's in here?" he demanded again.

Ma asked, "What is it you want, mister?"

"What you think I want? I want to know who's in here."

"Why, they's jus' us three in here. Me an' Granma an' my girl."

"Where's your men?"

"Why, they went down to clean up. We was drivin' all night."

"Where'd you come from?"

"Right near Sallisaw, Oklahoma."

"Well, you can't stay here."

"We aim to get out tonight an' cross the desert, mister."

"Well, you better. If you're here tomorra this time I'll run you in. We don't want none of you settlin' down here."

Ma's face blackened with anger. She got slowly to her feet. She stooped to the utensil box and picked out the iron skillet. "Mister," she said, "you got a tin button an' a gun. Where I come from, you keep your voice down." She advanced on him with the skillet. He loosened the gun in the holster. "Go ahead," said Ma. "Scarin' women. I'm thankful the men folks ain't here. They'd tear ya to pieces. In my country you watch your tongue."

The man took two steps backward. "Well, you ain't in your country now. You're in California, an' we don't want you goddamn Okies settlin' down."

Ma's advance stopped. She looked puzzled. "Okies?" she said softly. "Okies."

"Yeah, Okies! An' if you're here when I come to-morra, I'll run ya in." He turned and walked to the next tent and banged on the canvas with his hand. "Who's in here?" he said.

Ma went slowly back under the tarpaulin. She put the skillet in the utensil box. She sat down slowly. Rose of Sharon watched her secretly. And when she saw Ma fighting with her face, Rose of Sharon closed her eyes and pretended to be asleep.

The sun sank low in the afternoon, but the heat did not seem to decrease. Tom awakened under his wil-

low, and his mouth was parched and his body was wet
with sweat, and his head was dissatisfied with his rest.
He staggered to his feet and walked to the water. He
peeled off his clothes and waded into the stream. And
the moment the water was about him, his thirst was
gone. He lay back in the shallows and his body
floated. He held himself in place with his elbows in
the sand, and looked at his toes, which bobbed above
the surface.

A pale skinny little boy crept like an animal through
the reeds and slipped off his clothes. And he squirmed
into the water like a muskrat, and pulled himself along
like a muskrat, only his eyes and nose above the surface.
Then suddenly he saw Tom's head and saw that Tom was
watching him. He stopped his game and sat up.

Tom said, "Hello."

" 'Lo!"

"Looks like you was playin' mushrat."

"Well, I was." He edged gradually away toward the
bank; he moved casually, and then he leaped out,
gathered his clothes with a sweep of his arms, and was
gone among the willows.

Tom laughed quietly. And then he heard his name
called shrilly. "Tom, oh, Tom!" He sat up in the water
and whistled through his teeth, a piercing whistle with
a loop on the end. The willows shook, and Ruthie
stood looking at him.

"Ma wants you," she said. "Ma wants you right
away."

"Awright." He stood up and strode through the
water to the shore; and Ruthie looked with interest and
amazement at his naked body.

Tom, seeing the direction of her eyes, said, "Run
on now. Git!" And Ruthie ran. Tom heard her calling
excitedly for Winfield as she went. He put the hot
clothes on his cool wet body and he walked slowly up
through the willows toward the tent.

Ma had started a fire of dry willow twigs, and she

had a pan of water heating. She looked relieved when she saw him.

"What's a matter, Ma?" he asked.

"I was scairt," she said. "They was a policeman here. He says we can't stay here. I was scairt he talked to you. I was scairt you'd hit him if he talked to you."

Tom said, "What'd I go an' hit a policeman for?"

Ma smiled. "Well—he talked so bad—I nearly hit him myself."

Tom grabbed her arm and shook her roughly and loosely, and he laughed. He sat down on the ground, still laughing. "My God, Ma. I knowed you when you was gentle. What's come over you?"

She looked serious. "I don' know, Tom."

"Fust you stan' us off with a jack handle, and now you try to hit a cop." He laughed softly, and he reached out and patted her bare foot tenderly. "A ol' hell-cat," he said.

"Tom."

"Yeah?"

She hesitated a long time. "Tom, this here police-man—he called us—Okies. He says, 'We don' want you goddamn Okies settlin' down.'"

Tom studied her, and his hand still rested gently on her bare foot. "Fella tol' about that," he said. "Fella tol' how they say it." He considered. "Ma, would you say I was a bad fella? Oughta be locked up—like that?"

"No," she said. "You been tried— No. What you ast me for?"

"Well, I dunno. I'd a took a sock at that cop."

Ma smiled with amusement. "Maybe I oughta ast you that, 'cause I nearly hit 'im with a skillet."

"Ma, why'd he say we couldn' stop here?"

"Jus' says they don' want no damn Okies settlin' down. Says he's gonna run us in if we're here tomorra."

"But we ain't use' ta gettin' shoved aroun' by no cops."

"I tol' him that," said Ma. "He says we ain't home now. We're in California, and they do what they want."

Tom said uneasily, "Ma, I got somepin to tell ya. Noah—he went on down the river. He ain't a-goin' on."

It took a moment for Ma to understand. "Why?" she asked softly.

"I don' know. Says he got to. Says he got to stay. Says for me to tell you."

"How'll he eat?" she demanded.

"I don' know. Says he'll catch fish."

Ma was silent a long time. "Family's fallin' apart," she said. "I don' know. Seems like I can't think no more. I jus' can't think. They's too much."

Tom said lamely, "He'll be awright, Ma. He's a funny kind a fella."

Ma turned stunned eyes toward the river. "I jus' can't seem to think no more."

Tom looked down the line of tents and he saw Ruthie and Winfield standing in front of a tent in decorous conversation with someone inside. Ruthie was twisting her skirt in her hands, while Winfield dug a hole in the ground with his toe. Tom called, "You, Ruthie!" She looked up and saw him and trotted toward him, with Winfield behind her. When she came up, Tom said, "You go get our folks. They're sleepin' down the willows. Get 'em. An' you, Winfiel'. You tell the Wilsons we're gonna get rollin' soon as we can." The children spun around and charged off.

Tom said, "Ma, how's Granma now?"

"Well, she got a sleep today. Maybe she's better. She's still a-sleepin'."

"Tha's good. How much pork we got?"

"Not very much. Quarter hog."

"Well, we got to fill that other keg with water. Got

to take water along." They could hear Ruthie's shrill cries for the men down in the willows.

Ma shoved willow sticks into the fire and made it crackle up about the black pot. She said, "I pray God we gonna get some res'. I pray Jesus we gonna lay down in a nice place."

The sun sank toward the baked and broken hills to the west. The pot over the fire bubbled furiously. Ma went under the tarpaulin and came out with an apronful of potatoes, and she dropped them into the boiling water. "I pray God we gonna be let to wash some clothes. We ain't never been dirty like this. Don't even wash potatoes 'fore we boil 'em. I wonder why? Seems like the heart's took out of us."

The men came trooping up from the willows, and their eyes were full of sleep, and their faces were red and puffed with daytime sleep.

Pa said, "What's a matter?"

"We're goin'," said Tom. "Cop says we got to go. Might's well get her over. Get a good start an' maybe we'll be through her. Near three hunderd miles where we're goin'."

Pa said, "I thought we was gonna get a rest."

"Well, we ain't. We got to go. Pa," Tom said, "Noah ain't a-goin'. He walked on down the river."

"Ain't goin'? What the hell's the matter with him?" And then Pa caught himself. "My fault," he said miserably. "That boy's all my fault."

"No."

"I don't wanta talk about it no more," said Pa. "I can't—my fault."

"Well, we got to go," said Tom.

Wilson walked near for the last words. "We can't go, folks," he said. "Sairy's done up. She got to res'. She ain't gonna git acrost that desert alive."

They were silent at his words; then Tom said, "Cop says he'll run us in if we're here tomorra."

Wilson shook his head. His eyes were glazed with

worry, and a paleness showed through his dark skin. "Jus' hafta do 'er, then. Sairy can't go. If they jail us, why, they'll hafta jail us. She got to res' an' get strong."

Pa said, "Maybe we better wait an' all go together."

"No," Wilson said. "You been nice to us; you been kin', but you can't stay here. You got to get on an' get jobs and work. We ain't gonna let you stay."

Pa said excitedly, "But you ain't got nothing."

Wilson smiled. "Never had nothin' when you took us up. This ain't none of your business. Don't you make me git mean. You got to go, or I'll get mean an' mad."

Ma beckoned Pa into the cover of the tarpaulin and spoke softly to him.

Wilson turned to Casy. "Sairy wants you should go see her."

"Sure," said the preacher. He walked to the Wilson tent, tiny and gray, and he slipped the flaps aside and entered. It was dusky and hot inside. The mattress lay on the ground, and the equipment was scattered about, as it had been unloaded in the morning. Sairy lay on the mattress, her eyes wide and bright. He stood and looked down at her, his large head bent and the stringy muscles of his neck tight along the sides. And he took off his hat and held it in his hand.

She said, "Did my man tell ya we couldn' go on?"

"Tha's what he said."

Her low, beautiful voice went on, "I wanted us to go. I knowed I wouldn' live to the other side, but he'd be acrost anyways. But he won't go. He don' know. He thinks it's gonna be all right. He don' know."

"He says he won't go."

"I know," she said. "An' he's stubborn. I ast you to come to say a prayer."

"I ain't a preacher," he said softly. "My prayers ain't no good."

She moistened her lips. "I was there when the ol'
man died. You said one then."

"It wasn't no prayer."

"It was a prayer," she said.

"It wasn't no preachers' prayer."

"It was a good prayer. I want you should say one for
me."

"I don' know what to say."

She closed her eyes for a minute and then opened
them again. "Then say one to yourself. Don't use no
words to it. That'd be awright."

"I got no God," he said.

"You got a God. Don't make no difference if you
don' know what he looks like." The preacher bowed
his head. She watched him apprehensively. And when
he raised his head again she looked relieved. "That's
good," she said. "That's what I needed. Somebody
close enough——to pray."

He shook his head as though to awaken himself. "I
don' understan' this here," he said.

And she replied, "Yes——you know, don't you?"

"I know," he said, "I know, but I don't understan'.
Maybe you'll res' a few days an' then come on."

She shook her head slowly from side to side. "I'm
jus' pain covered with skin. I know what it is, but I
won't tell him. He'd be too sad. He wouldn' know
what to do anyways. Maybe in the night, when he's
a-sleepin'——when he waked up, it won't be so bad."

"You want I should stay with you an' not go on?"

"No," she said. "No. When I was a little girl I use'
ta sing. Folks roun' about use' ta say I sung as nice as
Jenny Lind. Folks use' ta come an' listen when I sung.
An'——when they stood——an' me a-singin', why, me an'
them was together more'n you could ever know. I was
thankful. There ain't so many folks can feel so full up,
so close, an' them folks standin' there an' me a-
singin'. Thought maybe I'd sing in theaters, but I

never done it. An' I'm glad. They wasn't nothin' got in
between me an' them. An'—that's why I wanted you to
pray. I wanted to feel that clostness, oncet more. It's
the same thing, singin' an' prayin', jus' the same
thing. I wisht you could a-heerd me sing."

He looked down at her, into her eyes. "Good-by,"
he said.

She shook her head slowly back and forth and
closed her lips tight. And the preacher went out of the
dusky tent into the blinding light.

The men were loading up the truck, Uncle John on
top, while the others passed equipment up to him. He
stowed it carefully, keeping the surface level. Ma
emptied the quarter of a keg of salt pork into a pan,
and Tom and Al took both little barrels to the river and
washed them. They tied them to the running boards
and carried water in buckets to fill them. Then over
the tops they tied canvas to keep them from slopping
the water out. Only the tarpaulin and Granma's mattress were left to be put on.

Tom said, "With the load we'll take, this ol'
wagon'll boil her head off. We got to have plenty
water."

Ma passed the boiled potatoes out and brought the
half sack from the tent and put it with the pan of pork.
The family ate standing, shuffling their feet and toss-
ing the hot potatoes from hand to hand until they
cooled.

Ma went to the Wilson tent and stayed for ten minutes, and then she came out quietly. "It's time to go,"
she said.

The men went under the tarpaulin. Granma still
slept, her mouth wide open. They lifted the whole
mattress gently and passed it up on top of the truck.
Granma drew up her skinny legs and frowned in her
sleep, but she did not awaken.

Uncle John and Pa tied the tarpaulin over the cross-

piece, making a little tight tent on top of the load.
They lashed it down to the side-bars. And then they
were ready. Pa took out his purse and dug two crushed
bills from it. He went to Wilson and held them out.
"We want you should take this, an' "—he pointed to
the pork and potatoes—"an' that."

Wilson hung his head and shook it sharply. "I ain't
a-gonna do it," he said. "You ain't got much."

"Got enough to get there," said Pa. "We ain't left it
all. We'll have work right off."

"I ain't a-gonna do it," Wilson said. "I'll git mean if
you try."

Ma took the two bills from Pa's hand. She folded
them neatly and put them on the ground and placed
the pork pan over them. "That's where they'll be," she
said. "If you don' get 'em, somebody else will." Wilson, his head still down, turned and went to his tent;
he stepped inside and the flaps fell behind him.

For a few moments the family waited, and then,
"We got to go," said Tom. "It's near four, I bet."

The family climbed on the truck, Ma on top, beside
Granma. Tom and Al and Pa in the seat, and Winfield
on Pa's lap. Connie and Rose of Sharon made a nest
against the cab. The preacher and Uncle John and
Ruthie were in a tangle on the load.

Pa called, "Good-by, Mister and Mis' Wilson."
There was no answer from the tent. Tom started the
engine and the truck lumbered away. And as they
crawled up the rough road toward Needles and the
highway, Ma looked back. Wilson stood in front of his
tent, staring after them, and his hat was in his hand.
The sun fell full on his face. Ma waved her hand at
him, but he did not respond.

Tom kept the truck in second gear over the rough
road, to protect the springs. At Needles he drove into
a service station, checked the worn tires for air,
checked the spares tied to the back. He had the gas

tank filled, and he bought two five-gallon cans of gasoline and a two-gallon can of oil. He filled the radiator, begged a map, and studied it.

The service-station boy, in his white uniform, seemed uneasy until the bill was paid. He said, "You people sure have got nerve."

Tom looked up from the map. "What you mean?"

"Well, crossin' in a jalopy like this."

"You been acrost?"

"Sure, plenty, but not in no wreck like this."

Tom said, "If we broke down maybe somebody'd give us a han'."

"Well, maybe. But folks are kind of scared to stop at night. I'd hate to be doing it, Takes more nerve than I've got."

Tom grinned. "It don't take no nerve to do somepin when there ain't nothin' else you can do. Well, thanks. We'll drag on." And he got in the truck and moved away.

The boy in white went into the iron building where his helper labored over a book of bills. "Jesus, what a hard-looking outfit!"

"Them Okies? They're all hard-lookin'."

"Jesus, I'd hate to start out in a jalopy like that."

"Well, you and me got sense. Them goddamn Okies got no sense and no feeling. They ain't human. A human being wouldn't live like they do. A human being couldn't stand it to be so dirty and miserable. They ain't a hell of a lot better than gorillas."

"Just the same I'm glad I ain't crossing the desert in no Hudson Super-Six. She sounds like a threshing machine."

The other boy looked down at his book of bills. And a big drop of sweat rolled down his finger and fell on the pink bills. "You know, they don't have much trouble. They're so goddamn dumb they don't know it's dangerous. And, Christ Almighty, they don't know any better than what they got. Why worry?"

"I'm not worrying. Just thought if it was me, I wouldn't like it."

"That's 'cause you know better. They don't know any better." And he wiped the sweat from the pink bill with his sleeve.

The truck took the road and moved up the long hill, through the broken, rotten rock. The engine boiled very soon and Tom slowed down and took it easy. Up the long slope, winding and twisting through dead country, burned white and gray, and no hint of life in it. Once Tom stopped for a few minutes to let the engine cool, and then he traveled on. They topped the pass while the sun was still up, and looked down on the desert—black cinder mountains in the distance, and the yellow sun reflected on the gray desert. The little starved bushes, sage and greasewood, threw bold shadows on the sand and bits of rock. The glaring sun was straight ahead. Tom held his hand before his eyes to see at all. They passed the crest and coasted down to cool the engine. They coasted down the long sweep to the floor of the desert, and the fan turned over to cool the water in the radiator. In the drivers' seat, Tom and Al and Pa, and Winfield on Pa's knee, looked into the bright descending sun, and their eyes were stony, and their brown faces were damp with perspiration. The burnt land and the black, cindery hills broke the even distance and made it terrible in the reddening light of the setting sun.

Al said, "Jesus, what a place. How'd you like to walk acrost her?"

"People done it," said Tom. "Lots a people done it; an' if they could, we could."

"Lots must a died," said Al.

"Well, we ain't come out exac'ly clean."

Al was silent for a while, and the reddening desert swept past. "Think we'll ever see them Wilsons again?" Al asked.

Tom flicked his eyes down to the oil gauge. "I got a hunch nobody ain't gonna see Mis' Wilson for long. Jus' a hunch I got."

Winfield said, "Pa, I wanta get out."

Tom looked over at him. "Might's well let ever'body out 'fore we settle down to drivin' tonight." He slowed the car and brought it to a stop. Winfield scrambled out and urinated at the side of the road. Tom leaned out. "Anybody else?"

"We're holdin' our water up here," Uncle John called.

Pa said, "Winfiel', you crawl up on top. You put my legs to sleep a-settin' on 'em." The little boy buttoned his overalls and obediently crawled up the back board and on his hands and knees crawled over Granma's mattress and forward to Ruthie.

The truck moved on into the evening, and the edge of the sun struck the rough horizon and turned the desert red.

Ruthie said, "Wouldn' leave you set up there, huh?"

"I didn' want to. It wasn't so nice as here. Couldn' lie down."

"Well, don' you bother me, a-squawkin' an' a-talkin'," Ruthie said, " 'cause I'm goin' to sleep, an' when I wake up, we gonna be there! 'Cause Tom said so! Gonna seem funny to see pretty country."

The sun went down and left a great halo in the sky. And it grew very dark under the tarpaulin, a long cave with light at each end—a flat triangle of light.

Connie and Rose of Sharon leaned back against the cab, and the hot wind tumbling through the tent struck the backs of their heads, and the tarpaulin whipped and drummed above them. They spoke together in low tones, pitched to the drumming canvas, so that no one could hear them. When Connie spoke he turned his head and spoke into her ear, and she did the same to him. She said, "Seems like we wasn't never gonna do nothin' but move. I'm so tar'd."

He turned his head to her ear. "Maybe in the mornin'. How'd you like to be alone now?" In the dusk his hand moved out and stroked her hip.

She said, "Don't. You'll make me crazy as a loon. Don't do that." And she turned her head to hear his response.

"Maybe—when ever'body's asleep."

"Maybe," she said. "But wait till they get to sleep. You'll make me crazy, an' maybe they won't get to sleep."

"I can't hardly stop," he said.

"I know. Me neither. Le's talk about when we get there; an' you move away 'fore I get crazy."

He shifted away a little. "Well, I'll get to studyin' nights right off," he said. She sighed deeply. "Gonna get one of them books that tells about it an' cut the coupon, right off."

"How long, you think?" she asked.

"How long what?"

"How long 'fore you'll be makin' big money an' we got ice?"

"Can't tell," he said importantly. "Can't really rightly tell. Fella oughta be studied up pretty good 'fore Christmus."

"Soon's you get studied up we could get ice an' stuff, I guess."

He chuckled. "It's this here heat," he said. "What you gonna need ice roun' Christmus for?"

She giggled. "Tha's right. But I'd like ice any time. Now don't. You'll get me crazy!"

The dusk passed into dark and the desert stars came out in the soft sky, stars stabbing and sharp, with few points and rays to them, and the sky was velvet. And the heat changed. While the sun was up, it was a beating, flailing heat, but now the heat came from below, from the earth itself, and the heat was thick and muffling. The lights of the truck came on, and they illuminated a little blur of highway ahead, and a strip of desert on either side of the road. And sometimes eyes gleamed in the lights far ahead, but no animal showed in the lights. It was pitch dark under the canvas now. Uncle John and the preacher were curled in the middle of the truck, resting on their elbows, and staring out the back triangle. They could see the two bumps that were Ma and Granma against the outside. They could see Ma move occasionally, and her dark arm moving against the outside.

Uncle John talked to the preacher. "Casy," he said, "you're a fella oughta know what to do."

"What to do about what?"

"I dunno," said Uncle John.

Casy said, "Well, that's gonna make it easy for me!"

"Well, you been a preacher."

"Look, John, ever'body takes a crack at me 'cause I been a preacher. A preacher ain't nothin' but a man."

"Yeah, but—he's—a *kind* of a man, else he wouldn' be a preacher. I wanna ast you—well, you think a fella could bring bad luck to folks?"

"I dunno," said Casy. "I dunno."

"Well—see—I was married—fine, good girl. An' one night she got a pain in her stomach. An' she says, 'You better get a doctor.' An' I says, 'Hell, you jus' et too much.'" Uncle John put his hand on Casy's knee and he peered through the darkness at him. "She give me a *look*. An' she groaned all night, an' she died the next afternoon." The preacher mumbled something. "You see," John went on, "I kil't her. An' sence then I tried to make it up—mos'ly to kids. An' I tried to be good, an' I can't. I get drunk, an' I go wild."

"Ever'body goes wild," said Casy. "I do too."

"Yeah, but you ain't got a sin on your soul like me."

Casy said gently, "Sure I got sins. Ever'body got sins. A sin is somepin you ain't sure about. Them people that's sure about ever'thing an' ain't got no sin—well, with that kind a son-of-a-bitch, if I was God I'd kick their ass right outa heaven! I couldn' stand 'em!"

Uncle John said, "I got a feelin' I'm bringin' bad luck to my own folks. I got a feelin' I oughta go away an' let 'em be. I ain't comf'table bein' like this."

Casy said quickly, "I know this—a man got to do what he got to do. I can't tell you. I can't tell you. I don't think they's luck or bad luck. On'y one thing in this worl' I'm sure of, an' that's I'm sure nobody got a right to mess with a fella's life. He got to do it all hisself. Help him, maybe, but not tell him what to do."

Uncle John said disappointedly, "Then you don' know?"

"I don' know."

"You think it was a sin to let my wife die like that?"

"Well," said Casy, "for anybody else it was a mistake, but if you think it was a sin—then it's a sin. A fella builds his own sins right up from the groun'."

"I got to give that a goin'-over," said Uncle John, and he rolled on his back and lay with his knees pulled up.

The truck moved on over the hot earth, and the hours passed. Ruthie and Winfield went to sleep. Connie loosened a blanket from the load and covered himself and Rose of Sharon with it, and in the heat they struggled together, and held their breaths. And after a time Connie threw off the blanket and the hot tunneling wind felt cool on their wet bodies.

On the back of the truck Ma lay on the mattress beside Granma, and she could not see with her eyes, but she could feel the struggling body and the struggling heart; and the sobbing breath was in her ear. And Ma said over and over, "All right. It's gonna be all right." And she said hoarsely, "You know the family got to get acrost. You know that."

Uncle John called, "You all right?"

It was a moment before she answered. "All right. Guess I dropped off to sleep." And after a time Granma was still, and Ma lay rigid beside her.

The night hours passed, and the dark was in against the truck. Sometimes cars passed them, going west and away; and sometimes great trucks came up out of the west and rumbled eastward. And the stars flowed down in a slow cascade over the western horizon. It was near midnight when they neared Daggett, where the inspection station is. The road was floodlighted there, and a sign illuminated, "KEEP RIGHT AND STOP." The officers loafed in the office, but they came out and stood under the long covered shed when Tom pulled in. One officer put down the license number and raised the hood.

Tom asked, "What's this here?"

"Agricultural inspection. We got to look over your stuff. Got any vegetables or seeds?"

"No," said Tom.

"Well, we got to look over your stuff. You got to unload."

Now Ma climbed heavily down from the truck. Her face was swollen and her eyes were hard. "Look, mister. We got a sick ol' lady. We got to get her to a doctor. We can't wait." She seemed to fight with hysteria. "You can't make us wait."

"Yeah? Well, we got to look you over."

"I swear we ain't got any thing!" Ma cried. "I swear it. An' Granma's awful sick."

"You don't look so good yourself," the officer said.

Ma pulled herself up the back of the truck, hoisted herself with huge strength. "Look," she said.

The officer shot a flashlight beam up on the old shrunken face. "By God, she is," he said. "You swear you got no seeds or fruits or vegetables, no corn, no oranges?"

"No, no. I swear it!"

"Then go ahead. You can get a doctor in Barstow. That's only eight miles. Go on ahead."

Tom climbed in and drove on.

The officer turned to his companion. "I couldn' hold 'em."

"Maybe it was a bluff," said the other.

"Oh, Jesus, no! You should of seen that ol' woman's face. That wasn't no bluff."

Tom increased his speed to Barstow, and in the little town he stopped, got out, and walked around the truck. Ma leaned out. "It's awright," she said. "I didn' wanta stop there, fear we wouldn' get acrost."

"Yeah! But how's Granma?"

"She's awright—awright. Drive on. We got to get acrost." Tom shook his head and walked back.

"Al," he said, "I'm gonna fill her up, an' then you drive some." He pulled to an all-night gas station and filled the tank and the radiator, and filled the crank case. Then Al slipped under the wheel and Tom took the outside, with Pa in the middle. They drove away into the darkness and the little hills near Barstow were behind them.

Tom said, "I don' know what's got into Ma. She's flighty as a dog with a flea in his ear. Wouldn' a took long to look over the stuff. An' she says Granma's sick; an' now she says Granma's awright. I can't figger her out. She ain't right. S'pose she wore her brains out on the trip."

Pa said, "Ma's almost like she was when she was a girl. She was a wild one then. She wasn't scairt of nothin'. I thought havin' all the kids an' workin' took it out a her, but I guess it ain't. Christ! When she got that jack handle back there, I tell you I wouldn' wanna be the fella took it away from her."

"I dunno what's got into her," Tom said. "Maybe she's jus' tar'd out."

Al said, "I won't be doin' no weepin' an' a-moanin' to get through. I got this goddamn car on my soul."

Tom said, "Well, you done a damn good job a pickin'. We ain't had hardly no trouble with her at all."

All night they bored through the hot darkness, and jackrabbits scuttled into the lights and dashed away in long jolting leaps. And the dawn came up behind them when the lights of Mojave were ahead. And the dawn showed high mountains to the west. They filled with water and oil at Mojave and crawled into the mountains, and the dawn was about them.

Tom said, "Jesus, the desert's past! Pa, Al, for Christ sakes! The desert's past!"

"I'm too goddamn tired to care," said Al.

"Want me to drive?"

"No, wait awhile."

They drove through Tehachapi in the morning glow, and the sun came up behind them, and then— suddenly they saw the great valley below them. Al jammed on the brake and stopped in the middle of the road, and, "Jesus Christ! Look!" he said. The vineyards, the orchards, the great flat valley, green and beautiful, the trees set in rows, and the farm houses.

And Pa said, "God Almighty!" The distant cities, the little towns in the orchard land, and the morning sun, golden on the valley. A car honked behind them. Al pulled to the side of the road and parked.

"I want ta look at her." The grain fields golden in the morning, and the willow lines, the eucalyptus trees in rows.

Pa sighed, "I never knowed they was anything like her." The peach trees and the walnut groves, and the dark green patches of oranges. And red roofs among the trees, and barns—rich barns. Al got out and stretched his legs.

He called, "Ma—come look. We're there!"

Ruthie and Winfield scrambled down from the car, and then they stood, silent and awestruck, embarrassed before the great valley. The distance was thinned with haze, and the land grew softer and softer in the distance. A windmill flashed in the sun, and its turning blades were like a little heliograph, far away. Ruthie and Winfield looked at it, and Ruthie whispered, "It's California."

Winfield moved his lips silently over the syllables. "There's fruit," he said aloud.

Casy and Uncle John, Connie and Rose of Sharon climbed down. And they stood silently. Rose of Sharon had started to brush her hair back, when she caught sight of the valley and her hand had dropped slowly to her side.

Tom said, "Where's Ma? I want Ma to see it. Look, Ma! Come here, Ma." Ma was climbing slowly, stiffly, down the back board. Tom looked at her. "My God, Ma, you sick?" Her face was stiff and putty-like, and her eyes seemed to have sunk deep into her head, and the rims were red with weariness. Her feet touched the ground and she braced herself by holding the truck-side.

Her voice was a croak. "Ya say we're acrost?"

Tom pointed to the great valley. "Look!"

She turned her head, and her mouth opened a little. Her fingers went to her throat and gathered a little pinch of skin and twisted gently. "Thank God!" she said. "The fambly's here." Her knees buckled and she sat down on the running board.

"You sick, Ma?"

"No, jus' tar'd."

"Didn' you get no sleep?"

"No."

"Was Granma bad?"

Ma looked down at her hands, lying together like tired lovers in her lap. "I wisht I could wait an' not tell you. I wisht it could be all—nice."

Pa said, "Then Granma's bad."

Ma raised her eyes and looked over the valley. "Granma's dead."

They looked at her, all of them, and Pa asked, "When?"

"Before they stopped us las' night."

"So that's why you didn' want 'em to look."

"I was afraid we wouldn' get acrost," she said. "I tol' Granma we couldn' he'p her. The fambly had ta get acrost. I tol' her, tol' her when she was a-dyin'. We couldn' stop in the desert. There was the young ones—an' Rosasharn's baby. I tol' her." She put up her hands and covered her face for a moment. "She can get buried in a nice green place," Ma said softly. "Trees aroun' an' a nice place. She got to lay her head down in California.

The family looked at Ma with a little terror at her strength.

Tom said, "Jesus Christ! You layin' there with her all night long!"

"The fambly hadda get acrost," Ma said miserably.

Tom moved close to put his hand on her shoulder.

"Don' touch me," she said. "I'll hol' up if you don' touch me. That'd get me."

Pa said, "We got to go on now. We got to go on down."

Ma looked up at him. "Can—can I set up front? I don' wanna go back there no more—I'm tar'd. I'm awful tar'd."

They climbed back on the load, and they avoided the long stiff figure covered and tucked in a comforter, even the head covered and tucked. They moved to their places and tried to keep their eyes from it—from the hump on the comforter that would be the nose, and the steep cliff that would be the jut of the chin. They tried to keep their eyes away, and they could not. Ruthie and Winfield, crowded in a forward corner as far away from the body as they could get, stared at the tucked figure.

And Ruthie whispered, "Tha's Granma, an' she's dead."

Winfield nodded solemnly. "She ain't breathin' at all. She's awful dead."

And Rose of Sharon said softly to Connie, "She was a-dyin' right when we———"

"How'd we know?" he reassured her.

Al climbed on the load to make room for Ma in the seat. And Al swaggered a little because he was sorry. He plumped down beside Casy and Uncle John. "Well, she was ol'. Guess her time was up," Al said. "Ever'body got to die." Casy and Uncle John turned eyes expressionlessly on him and looked at him as though he were a curious talking bush. "Well, ain't they?" he demanded. And the eyes looked away, leaving Al sullen and shaken.

Casy said in wonder, "All night long, an' she was alone." And he said, "John, there's a woman so great with love—she scares me. Makes me afraid an' mean."

John asked, "Was it a sin? Is they any part of it you might call a sin?"

Casy turned on him in astonishment. "A sin? No, there ain't no part of it that's a sin."

"I ain't never done nothin' that wasn't part sin," said John, and he looked at the long wrapped body.

Tom and Ma and Pa got into the front seat. Tom let the truck roll and started on compression. And the heavy truck moved, snorting and jerking and popping down the hill. The sun was behind them, and the valley golden and green before them. Ma shook her head slowly from side to side. "It's purty," she said. "I wisht they could of saw it."

"I wisht so too," said Pa.

Tom patted the steering wheel under his hand. "They was too old," he said. "They wouldn't of saw nothin' that's here. Grampa would a been a-seein' the Injuns an' the prairie country when he was a young fella. An' Granma would a remembered an' seen the first home she lived in. They was too ol'. Who's really seein' it is Ruthie an' Winfiel'."

Pa said, "Here's Tommy talkin' like a growed-up man, talkin' like a preacher almos'."

And Ma smiled sadly. "He is. Tommy's growed way up—way up so I can't get aholt of 'im sometimes."

They popped down the mountain, twisting and looping, losing the valley sometimes, and then finding it again. And the hot breath of the valley came up to them, with hot green smells on it, and with resinous sage and tarweed smells. The crickets crackled along the road. A rattlesnake crawled across the road and Tom hit it and broke it and left it squirming.

Tom said, "I guess we got to go to the coroner, wherever he is. We got to get her buried decent. How much money might be lef', Pa?"

" 'Bout forty dollars," said Pa.

Tom laughed. "Jesus, are we gonna start clean! We sure ain't bringin' nothin' with us." He chuckled a moment, and then his face straightened quickly. He pulled the visor of his cap down low over his eyes. And the truck rolled down the mountain into the great valley.

19

Once California belonged to Mexico and its land to Mexicans; and a horde of tattered feverish Americans poured in. And such was their hunger for land that they took the land—stole Sutter's land, Guerrero's land, took the grants and broke them up and growled and quarreled over them, those frantic hungry men; and they guarded with guns the land they had stolen. They put up houses and barns, they turned the earth and planted crops. And these things were possession, and possession was ownership.

The Mexicans were weak and fed. They could not resist, because they wanted nothing in the world as frantically as the Americans wanted land.

Then, with time, the squatters were no longer squatters, but owners; and their children grew up and had children on the land. And the hunger was gone from them, the feral hunger, the gnawing, tearing hunger for land, for water and earth and the good sky over it, for the green thrusting grass, for the swelling roots. They had these things so completely that they did not know about them any more. They had no more the stomach-tearing lust for a rich acre and a shining blade to plow it, for seed and a windmill beating its wings in the air. They arose in the dark no more to hear the sleepy birds' first chittering, and the morning wind around the house while they waited for the first light to go out to the dear acres. These things were lost, and crops were reckoned in dollars, and land was valued by principal plus interest, and crops were bought and sold before they were planted. Then crop failure, drought, and flood were no longer little deaths within life, but simple losses of money. And all their love was thinned with money, and all their fierceness dribbled away in interest until they were no longer farmers at all, but little shopkeepers of crops, little manufacturers who must sell before they can make. Then those farmers who were not good shopkeepers lost their land to good shopkeepers. No matter how clever, how loving a man might be with earth and growing things, he could not survive if he were not a good shopkeeper. And as time went on, the business men had the farms, and the farms grew larger, but there were fewer of them.

Now farming became industry, and the owners followed Rome, although they did not know it. They imported slaves, although they did not call them slaves: Chinese, Japanese, Mexicans, Filipinos. They live on rice and beans, the business men said. They don't need much. They wouldn't know what to do with good wages. Why, look how they live. Why, look what they eat. And if they get funny—deport them.

And all the time the farms grew larger and the owners fewer. And there were pitifully few farmers on the land any more. And the imported serfs were beaten and frightened and starved until some went home again, and some grew fierce and were killed or driven from the country. And the farms grew larger and the owners fewer.

And the crops changed. Fruit trees took the place of grain fields, and vegetables to feed the world spread out on the bottoms: lettuce, cauliflower, artichokes, potatoes—stoop crops. A man may stand to use a scythe, a plow, a pitchfork; but he must crawl like a bug between the rows of lettuce, he must bend his back and pull his long bag between the cotton rows, he must go on his knees like a penitent across a cauliflower patch.

And it came about that the owners no longer worked on their farms. They farmed on paper; and they forgot the land, the smell, the feel of it, and remembered only that they owned it, remembered only what they gained and lost by it. And some of the farms grew so large that one man could not even conceive of them any more, so large that it took batteries of bookkeepers to keep track of interest and gain and loss; chemists to test the soil, to replenish; straw bosses to see that the stooping men were moving along the rows as swiftly as the material of their bodies could stand. Then such a farmer really became a storekeeper, and kept a store. He paid the men, and sold them food, and took the money back. And after a while he did not pay the men at all, and saved bookkeeping. These farms gave food on credit. A man might work and feed himself; and when the work was done, he might find that he owed money to the company. And the owners not only did not work the farms any more, many of them had never seen the farms they owned.

And then the dispossessed were drawn west—from Kansas, Oklahoma, Texas, New Mexico; from Nevada and Arkansas families, tribes, dusted out, tractored out. Carloads, caravans, homeless and hungry; twenty thousand and fifty thousand and a hundred thousand and two hundred thousand. They streamed over the mountains, hungry and restless—restless as ants, scurrying to find work to do—to lift, to push, to pull, to pick, to cut—anything, any burden to bear, for food. The kids are hungry. We got no place to live. Like ants scurrying for work, for food, and most of all for land.

We ain't foreign. Seven generations back Americans, and beyond that Irish, Scotch, English, German. One of our folks in the Revolution, an' they was lots of our folks in the Civil War—both sides. Americans.

They were hungry, and they were fierce. And they had hoped to find a home, and they found only hatred. Okies—the owners hated them because the owners knew they were soft and the Okies strong, that they were fed and the Okies hungry; and perhaps the owners had heard from their grandfathers how easy it is to steal land from a soft man if you are fierce and hungry and armed. The owners hated them. And in the towns, the storekeepers hated them because they had no money to spend. There is no shorter path to a storekeeper's contempt, and all his admirations are exactly opposite. The town men, little bankers, hated Okies because there was nothing to gain from them. They had nothing. And the laboring people hated Okies because a hungry man must work, and if he must work, if he has to work, the wage payer automatically gives him less for his work; and then no one can get more.

And the dispossessed, the migrants, flowed into California, two hundred and fifty thousand, and three hundred thousand. Behind them new tractors were going on the land and the tenants were being forced off. And new waves were on the way, new waves of the dispossessed and the homeless, hardened, intent, and dangerous.

And while the Californians wanted many things, accumulation, social success, amusement, luxury, and a curious banking security, the new barbarians wanted only two things—land and food; and to them the two were one. And whereas the wants of the Californians were nebulous and undefined, the wants of the Okies were beside the roads, lying there to be seen and coveted: the good fields with water to be dug for, the good green fields, earth to crumble experimentally in the hand, grass to smell, oaten stalks to chew until the sharp sweetness was in the throat. A man might look at a fallow field and know, and see in his mind that his own bending back and his own straining arms would bring the cabbages into the light, and the golden eating corn, the turnips and carrots.

And a homeless hungry man, driving the roads with his wife beside him and his thin children in the back seat, could look at the fallow fields which might produce food but not profit, and that man could know how a fallow field is a sin and the unused land a crime against the thin children. And such a man drove along the roads and knew temptation at every field, and knew the lust to take these fields and make them grow strength for his children and a little comfort for his wife. The temptation was before him always. The fields goaded him, and the company ditches with good water flowing were a goad to him.

And in the south he saw the golden oranges hanging on the trees, the little golden oranges on the dark green trees; and guards with shotguns patrolling the lines so a man might not pick an orange for a thin child, oranges to be dumped if the price was low.

He drove his old car into a town. He scoured the farms for work. Where can we sleep tonight?

Well, there's Hooverville on the edge of the river. There's a whole raft of Okies there.

He drove his old car to Hooverville. He never asked again, for there was a Hooverville on the edge of every town.

The rag town lay close to water; and the houses were tents, and weed-thatched enclosures, paper houses, a

great junk pile. The man drove his family in and became a citizen of Hooverville—always they were
called Hooverville. The man put up his own tent as
near to water as he could get; or if he had no tent, he
went to the city dump and brought back cartons and
built a house of corrugated paper. And when the rains
came the house melted and washed away. He settled
in Hooverville and he scoured the countryside for
work, and the little money he had went for gasoline to
look for work. In the evening the men gathered and
talked together. Squatting on their hams they talked of
the land they had seen.

There's thirty thousan' acres, out west of here.
Layin' there. Jesus, what I could do with that, with
five acres of that! Why, hell, I'd have ever'thing to eat.

Notice one thing? They ain't no vegetables nor
chickens nor pigs at the farms. They raise one thing—
cotton, say, or peaches, or lettuce. 'Nother place'll be
all chickens. They buy the stuff they could raise in the
dooryard.

Jesus, what I could do with a couple pigs!

Well, it ain't yourn, an' it ain't gonna be yourn.

What we gonna do? The kids can't grow up this
way.

In the camps the word would come whispering,
There's work at Shafter. And the cars would be loaded
in the night, the highways crowded—a gold rush for
work. At Shafter the people would pile up, five times
too many to do the work. A gold rush for work. They
stole away in the night, frantic for work. And along the
roads lay the temptations, the fields that could bear
food.

That's owned. That ain't our'n.

Well, maybe we could get a little piece of her.
Maybe—a little piece. Right down there—a patch.
Jimson weed now. Christ, I could git enough potatoes
off'n that little patch to feed my whole family!

It ain't our'n. It got to have Jimson weeds.

Now and then a man tried; crept on the land and cleared a piece, trying like a thief to steal a little richness from the earth. Secret gardens hidden in the weeds. A package of carrot seeds and a few turnips. Planted potato skins, crept out in the evening secretly to hoe in the stolen earth.

Leave the weeds around the edge—then nobody can see what we're a-doin'. Leave some weeds, big tall ones, in the middle.

Secret gardening in the evenings, and water carried in a rusty can.

And then one day a deputy sheriff: Well, what you think you're doin'?

I ain't doin' no harm.

I had my eye on you. This ain't your land. You're trespassing.

The land ain't plowed, an' I ain't hurtin' it none.

You goddamned squatters. Pretty soon you'd think you owned it. You'd be sore as hell. Think you owned it. Get off now.

And the little green carrot tops were kicked off and the turnip greens trampled. And then the Jimson weed moved back in. But the cop was right. A crop raised— why, that makes ownership. Land hoed and the carrots eaten—a man might fight for land he's taken food from. Get him off quick! He'll think he owns it. He might even die fighting for the little plot among the Jimson weeds.

Did you see his face when we kicked them turnips out? Why, he'd kill a fella soon's he'd look at him. We got to keep these here people down or they'll take the country. They'll take the country.

Outlanders, foreigners.

Sure, they talk the same language, but they ain't the same. Look how they live. Think any of us folks'd live like that? Hell, no!

In the evenings, squatting and talking. And an excited man: Whyn't twenty of us take a piece of lan'?

We got guns. Take it an' say, "Put us off if you can."
Whyn't we do that?

They'd jus' shoot us like rats.

Well, which'd you ruther be, dead or here? Under
groun' or in a house all made of gunny sacks? Which'd
you ruther for your kids, dead now or dead in two
years with what they call malnutrition? Know what we
et all week? Biled nettles an' fried dough! Know where
we got the flour for the dough? Swep' the floor of a
boxcar.

Talking in the camps, and the deputies, fat-assed
men with guns slung on fat hips, swaggering through
the camps: Give 'em somepin to think about. Got to
keep 'em in line or Christ only knows what they'll do!
Why, Jesus, they're as dangerous as niggers in the
South! If they ever get together there ain't nothin'
that'll stop 'em.

Quote: In Lawrenceville a deputy sheriff evicted a
squatter, and the squatter resisted, making it necessary for the officer to use force. The eleven-year-old
son of the squatter shot and killed the deputy with a
.22 rifle.

Rattlesnakes! Don't take chances with 'em, an' if
they argue, shoot first. If a kid'll kill a cop, what'll the
men do? Thing is, get tougher'n they are. Treat 'em
rough. Scare 'em.

What if they won't scare? What if they stand up and
take it and shoot back? These men were armed when
they were children. A gun is an extension of themselves. What if they won't scare? What if some time an
army of them marches on the land as the Lombards did
in Italy, as the Germans did on Gaul and the Turks
did on Byzantium? They were land-hungry, ill-armed

hordes too, and the legions could not stop them. Slaughter and terror did not stop them. How can you frighten a man whose hunger is not only in his own cramped stomach but in the wretched bellies of his children? You can't scare him—he has known a fear beyond every other.

In Hooverville the men talking: Grampa took his lan' from the Injuns.

Now, this ain't right. We're a-talkin' here. This here you're talkin' about is stealin'. I ain't no thief.

No? You stole a bottle of milk from a porch night before last. An' you stole some copper wire and sold it for a piece of meat.

Yeah, but the kids was hungry.

It's stealin', though.

Know how the Fairfiel' ranch was got? I'll tell ya. It was all gov'ment lan', an' could be took up. Ol' Fairfiel', he went into San Francisco to the bars, an' he got him three hunderd stew bums. Them bums took up the lan'. Fairfiel' kep' 'em in food an' whisky, an' then when they'd proved the lan', ol' Fairfiel' took it from 'em. He used to say the lan' cost him a pint of rotgut an acre. Would you say that was stealin'?

Well, it wasn't right, but he never went to jail for it.

No, he never went to jail for it. An' the fella that put a boat in a wagon an' made his report like it was all under water 'cause he went in a boat—he never went to jail neither. An' the fellas that bribed congressmen and the legislatures never went to jail neither.

All over the State, jabbering in the Hoovervilles.

And then the raids—the swoop of armed deputies on the squatters' camps. Get out. Department of Health orders. This camp is a menace to health.

Where we gonna go?

That's none of our business. We got orders to get you out of here. In half an hour we set fire to the camp.

They's typhoid down the line. You want ta spread it
all over?

We got orders to get you out of here. Now get! In
half an hour we burn the camp.

In half an hour the smoke of paper houses, of weed-
thatched huts, rising to the sky, and the people in
their cars rolling over the highways, looking for
another Hooverville.

And in Kansas and Arkansas, in Oklahoma and
Texas and New Mexico, the tractors moved in and
pushed the tenants out.

Three hundred thousand in California and more
coming. And in California the roads full of frantic
people running like ants to pull, to push, to lift, to
work. For every manload to lift, five pairs of arms
extended to lift it; for every stomachful of food available, five mouths open.

And the great owners, who must lose their land in
an upheaval, the great owners with access to history,
with eyes to read history and to know the great fact:
when property accumulates in too few hands it is taken
away. And that companion fact: when a majority of the
people are hungry and cold they will take by force
what they need. And the little screaming fact that
sounds through all history: repression works only to
strengthen and knit the repressed. The great owners
ignored the three cries of history. The land fell into
fewer hands, the number of dispossessed increased,
and every effort of the great owners was directed at
repression. The money was spent for arms, for gas to
protect the great holdings, and spies were sent to catch
the murmuring of revolt so that it might be stamped
out. The changing economy was ignored, plans for the
change ignored; and only means to destroy revolt were
considered, while the causes of revolt went on.

The tractors which throw men out of work, the belt
lines which carry loads, the machines which produce,

all were increased; and more and more families scampered on the highways, looking for crumbs from the great holdings, lusting after the land beside the roads. The great owners formed associations for protection and they met to discuss ways to intimidate, to kill, to gas. And always they were in fear of a principal—three hundred thousand—if they ever move under a leader—the end. Three hundred thousand, hungry and miserable; if they ever know themselves, the land will be theirs and all the gas, all the rifles in the world won't stop them. And the great owners, who had become through their holdings both more and less than men, ran to their destruction, and used every means that in the long run would destroy them. Every little means, every violence, every raid on a Hooverville, every deputy swaggering through a ragged camp put off the day a little and cemented the inevitability of the day.

The men squatted on their hams, sharp-faced men, lean from hunger and hard from resisting it, sullen eyes and hard jaws. And the rich land was around them.

D'ja hear about the kid in that fourth tent down?

No, I jus' come in.

Well, that kid's been a-cryin' in his sleep an' a-rollin' in his sleep. Them folks thought he got worms. So they give him a blaster, an' he died. It was what they call black-tongue the kid had. Comes from not gettin' good things to eat.

Poor little fella.

Yeah, but them folks can't bury him. Got to go to the county stone orchard.

Well, hell.

And hands went into pockets and little coins came out. In front of the tent a little heap of silver grew. And the family found it there.

Our people are good people; our people are kind

people. Pray God some day kind people won't all be poor. Pray God some day a kid can eat.

And the associations of owners knew that some day the praying would stop.

And there's the end.

20

The family, on top of the
load, the children and Connie and Rose of Sharon and
the preacher were stiff and cramped. They had sat in
the heat in front of the coroner's office in Bakersfield
while Pa and Ma and Uncle John went in. Then a
basket was brought out and the long bundle lifted
down from the truck. And they sat in the sun while the
examination went on, while the cause of death was
found and the certificate signed.

Al and Tom strolled along the street and looked in
store windows and watched the strange people on the
sidewalks.

And at last Pa and Ma and Uncle John came out,
and they were subdued and quiet. Uncle John climbed
up on the load. Pa and Ma got in the seat. Tom and Al
strolled back and Tom got under the steering wheel.
He sat there silently, waiting for some instruction. Pa
looked straight ahead, his dark hat pulled low. Ma
rubbed the sides of her mouth with her fingers, and
her eyes were far away and lost, dead with weariness.

Pa sighed deeply. "They wasn't nothin' else to do,"
he said.

"I know," said Ma. "She would a liked a nice funeral, though. She always wanted one."

Tom looked sideways at them. "County?" he asked.

"Yeah." Pa shook his head quickly, as though to get back to some reality. "We didn' have enough. We couldn' of done it." He turned to Ma. "You ain't to feel bad. We couldn' no matter how hard we tried, no matter what we done. We jus' didn' have it; embalming, an' a coffin an' a preacher, an' a plot in a graveyard. It would of took ten times what we got. We done the bes' we could."

"I know," Ma said. "I jus' can't get it outa my head what store she set by a nice funeral. Got to forget it." She sighed deeply and rubbed the side of her mouth. "That was a purty nice fella in there. Awful bossy, but he was purty nice."

"Yeah," Pa said. "He give us the straight talk, awright."

Ma brushed her hair back with her hand. Her jaw tightened. "We got to git," she said. "We got to find a place to stay. We got to get work an' settle down. No use a-lettin' the little fellas go hungry. That wasn't never Granma's way. She always et a good meal at a funeral."

"Where we goin'?" Tom asked.

Pa raised his hat and scratched among his hair. "Camp," he said. "We ain't gonna spen' what little's lef' till we get work. Drive out in the country.

Tom started the car and they rolled through the streets and out toward the country. And by a bridge they saw a collection of tents and shacks. Tom said, "Might's well stop here. Find out what's doin', an' where at the work is." He drove down a steep dirt incline and parked on the edge of the encampment.

There was no order in the camp; little gray tents, shacks, cars were scattered about at random. The first house was nondescript. The south wall was made of three sheets of rusy corrugated iron, the east wall a square of moldy carpet tacked between two boards, the north wall a strip of roofing paper and a strip of tattered canvas, and the west wall six pieces of gunny sacking. Over the square frame, on untrimmed willow limbs, grass had been piled, not thatched, but heaped up in a low mound. The entrance, on the gunny sack side, was cluttered with equipment. A five-gallon kerosene can served for a stove. It was laid on its side, with a section of rusty stovepipe thrust in one end. A wash boiler rested on its side against the wall; and a collection of boxes lay about, boxes to sit on, to eat on. A Model T Ford sedan and a two-wheel trailer were parked beside the shack, and about the camp there hung a slovenly despair.

Next to the shack there was a little tent, gray with weathering, but neatly, properly set up; and the boxes in front of it were placed against the tent wall. A stovepipe stuck out of the door flap, and the dirt in front of the tent had been swept and sprinkled. A bucketful of soaking clothes stood on a box. The camp was neat and sturdy. A Model A roadster and a little home-made bed trailer stood beside the tent.

And next there was a huge tent, ragged, torn in strips and the tears mended with pieces of wire. The flaps were up, and inside four wide mattresses lay on the ground. A clothes line strung along the side bore pink cotton dresses and several pairs of overalls. There were forty tents and shacks, and beside each habitation some kind of automobile. Far down the line a few children stood and stared at the newly arrived truck, and they moved toward it, little boys in overalls and bare feet, their hair gray with dust.

Tom stopped the truck and looked at Pa. "She ain't very purty," he said. "Want to go somewheres else?"

"Can't go nowheres else till we know where we're at," Pa said. "We got to ast about work."

Tom opened the door and stepped out. The family climbed down from the load and looked curiously at the camp. Ruthie and Winfield, from the habit of the road, took down the bucket and walked toward the willows, where there would be water; and the line of children parted for them and closed after them.

The flaps of the first shack parted and a woman looked out. Her gray hair was braided, and she wore a dirty, flowered Mother Hubbard. Her face was wizened and dull, deep gray pouches under blank eyes, and a mouth slack and loose.

Pa said, "Can we jus' pull up anywheres an' camp?"

The head was withdrawn inside the shack. For a moment there was quiet and then the flaps were pushed aside and a bearded man in shirt sleeves stepped out. The woman looked out after him, but she did not come into the open.

The bearded man said, "Howdy, folks," and his restless dark eyes jumped to each member of the family, and from them to the truck to the equipment.

Pa said, "I jus' ast your woman if it's all right to set our stuff anywheres."

The bearded man looked at Pa intently, as though he had said something very wise that needed thought. "Set down anywheres, here in this place?" he asked.

"Sure. Anybody own this place, that we got to see 'fore we can camp?"

The bearded man squinted one eye nearly closed and studied Pa. "You wanta camp here?"

Pa's irritation arose. The gray woman peered out of the burlap shack. "What you think I'm a-sayin'?" Pa said.

"Well, if you wanta camp here, why don't ya? I ain't a-stoppin' you."

Tom laughed. "He got it."

Pa gathered his temper. "I jus' wanted to know does anybody own it? Do we got to pay?"

The bearded man thrust out his jaw. "Who owns it?" he demanded.

Pa turned away. "The hell with it," he said. The woman's head popped back in the tent.

The bearded man stepped forward menacingly.

"Who owns it?" he demanded. "Who's gonna kick us outa here? You tell *me*."

Tom stepped in front of Pa. "You better go take a good long sleep," he said. The bearded man dropped his mouth open and put a dirty finger against his lower gums. For a moment he continued to look wisely, speculatively at Tom, and then he turned on his heel and popped into the shack after the gray woman.

Tom turned on Pa. "What the hell was that?" he asked.

Pa shrugged his shoulders. He was looking across the camp. In front of a tent stood an old Buick, and the head was off. A young man was grinding the valves, and as he twisted back and forth, back and forth, on the tool, he looked up at the Joad truck. They could see that he was laughing to himself. When the bearded man had gone, the young man left his work and sauntered over.

"H'are ya?" he said, and his blue eyes were shiny with amusement. "I seen you just met the Mayor."

"What the hell's the matter with 'im?" Tom demanded.

The young man chuckled. "He's jus' nuts like you an' me. Maybe he's a little nutser'n me, I don' know."

Pa said, "I jus' ast him if we could camp here."

The young man wiped his greasy hands on his trousers. "Sure. Why not? You folks jus' come acrost?"

"Yeah," said Tom. "Jus' got in this mornin'."

"Never been in Hooverville before?"

"Where's Hooverville?"

"This here's her."

"Oh!" said Tom. "We jus' got in."

Winfield and Ruthie came back, carrying a bucket of water between them.

Ma said, "Le's get the camp up. I'm tuckered out. Maybe we can all rest." Pa and Uncle John climbed up on the truck to unload the canvas and the beds.

Tom sauntered to the young man, and walked beside him back to the car he had been working on. The valve-grinding brace lay on the exposed block, and a little yellow can of valve-grinding compound was wedged on top of the vacuum tank. Tom asked, "What the hell was the matter'th that ol' fella with the beard?"

The young man picked up his brace and went to work, twisting back and forth, grinding valve against valve seat. "The Mayor? Chris' knows. I guess maybe he's bull-simple."

"What's 'bull-simple'?"

"I guess cops push 'im aroun' so much he's still spinning."

Tom asked, "Why would they push a fella like that aroun'?"

The young man stopped his work and looked in Tom's eyes. "Chris' knows," he said. "You jus' come. Maybe you can figger her out. Some fellas says one thing, an' some says another thing. But you jus' camp in one place a little while, an' you see how quick a deputy sheriff shoves you along." He lifted a valve and smeared compound on the seat.

"But what the hell for?"

"I tell ya I don' know. Some says they don' want us to vote; keep us movin' so we can't vote. An' some says so we can't get on relief. An' some says if we set in one place we'd get organized. I don' know why. I on'y know we got rode all the time. You wait, you'll see."

"We ain't no bums," Tom insisted. "We're lookin' for work. We'll take any kind a work."

The young man paused in fitting the brace to the valve slot. He looked in amazement at Tom. "Lookin' for work?" he said. "So you're lookin' for work. What ya think ever'body else is lookin' for? Di'monds? What you think I wore my ass down to a nub lookin' for?" He twisted the brace back and forth.

Tom looked about at the grimy tents, the junk equipment, at the old cars, the lumpy mattresses out in the sun, at the blackened cans on fire-blackened holes where the people cooked. He asked quietly, "Ain't they no work?"

"I don' know. Mus' be. Ain't no crop right here now. Grapes to pick later, an' cotton to pick later. We're a-movin' on, soon's I get these here valves groun'. Me an' my wife an' my kid. We heard they was work up north. We're shovin' north, up aroun' Salinas."

Tom saw Uncle John and Pa and the preacher hoisting the tarpaulin on the tent poles and Ma on her knees inside, brushing off the mattresses on the ground. A circle of quiet children stood to watch the new family get settled, quiet children with bare feet and dirty faces. Tom said, "Back home some fellas come through with han'bills—orange ones. Says they need lots a people out here to work the crops."

The young man laughed. "They say they's three hunderd thousan' us folks here, an' I bet ever' dam' fam'ly seen them han'bills."

"Yeah, but if they don' need folks, what'd they go to the trouble puttin' them things out for?"

"Use your head, why don'cha?"

"Yeah, but I wanta know."

"Look," the young man said. "S'pose you got a job a work, an' there's jus' one fella wants the job. You got to pay 'im what he asts. But s'pose they's a hunderd men." He put down his tool. His eyes hardened and his voice sharpened. "S'pose they's a hunderd men wants that job. S'pose them men got kids, an' them kids is hungry. S'pose a lousy dime'll buy a box a mush for them kids. S'pose a nickel'll buy at leas' somepin for them kids. An' you got a hunderd men. Jus' offer 'em a nickel— why, they'll kill each other fightin' for that nickel. Know what they was payin', las' job I had? Fifteen cents an hour. Ten hours for a dollar an' a half, an' ya can't

stay on the place. Got to burn gasoline gettin' there."
He was panting with anger, and his eyes blazed with
hate. "That's why them han'bills was out. You can print
a hell of a lot of han'bills with what ya save payin'
fifteen cents an hour for fiel' work."

Tom said, "That's stinkin'."

The young man laughed harshly. "You stay out here
a little while, an' if you smell any roses, you come let
me smell, too."

"But they is work," Tom insisted. "Christ Almighty,
with all this stuff a-growin': orchards, grapes, vegetables—I seen it. They got to have men. I seen all that
stuff."

A child cried in the tent beside the car. The young
man went into the tent and his voice came softly
through the canvas. Tom picked up the brace, fitted it
in the slot of the valve, and ground away, his hand
whipping back and forth. The child's crying stopped.
The young man came out and watched Tom. "You can
do her," he said. "Damn good thing. You'll need to."

"How 'bout what I said?" Tom resumed. "I seen all
the stuff growin'."

The young man squatted on his heels. "I'll tell ya,"
he said quietly. "They's a big son-of-a-bitch of a peach
orchard I worked in. Takes nine men all the year
roun'." He paused impressively. "Takes three thousan'
men for two weeks when them peaches is ripe. Got to
have 'em or them peaches'll rot. So what do they do?
They send out han'bills all over hell. They need three
thousan', an' they get six thousan'. They get them men
for what they wanta pay. If ya don' wanta take what
they pay, goddamn it, they's a thousan' men waitin' for
your job. So ya pick, an' ya pick, an' then she's done.
Whole part a the country's peaches. All ripe together.
When ya get 'em picked, ever' goddamn one is picked.
There ain't another damn thing in that part a the country to do. An' then them owners don' want you there no
more. Three thousan' of you. The work's done. You

might steal, you might get drunk, you might jus' raise hell. An' besides, you don' look nice, livin' in ol' tents; an' it's a pretty country, but you stink it up. They don' want you aroun'. So they kick you out, they move you along. That's how it is."

Tom, looking down toward the Joad tent, saw his mother heavy and slow with weariness, build a little trash fire and put the cooking pots over the flame. The circle of children drew closer, and the calm wide eyes of the children watched every move of Ma's hands. An old, old man with a bent back came like a badger out of a tent and snooped near, sniffing the air as he came. He laced his arms behind him and joined the children to watch Ma. Ruthie and Winfield stood near to Ma and eyed the strangers belligerently.

Tom said angrily, "Them peaches got to be picked right now, don't they? Jus' when they're ripe?"

" 'Course they do."

"Well, s'pose them people got together an' says, 'Let 'em rot.' Wouldn' be long 'fore the price went up, by God!"

The young man looked up from the valves, looked sardonically at Tom. "Well, you figgered out somepin, didn' you. Come right outa your own head."

"I'm tar'd," said Tom. "Drove all night. I don' wanta start no argument. An' I'm so goddamn tar'd I'd argue easy. Don' be smart with me. I'm askin' you."

The young man grinned. "I didn' mean it. You ain't been here. Folks figgered that out. An' the folks with the peach orchard figgered her out too. Look, if the folks gets together, they's a leader—got to be—fella that does the talkin'. Well, first time this fella opens his mouth they grab 'im an' stick 'im in jail. An' if they's another leader pops up, why, they stick *im* in jail."

Tom said, "Well, a fella eats in jail anyways."

"His kids don't. How'd you like to be in an' your kids starvin' to death?"

"Yeah," said Tom slowly. "Yeah."

"An' here's another thing. Ever hear a the black-list?"

"What's that?"

"Well, you jus' open your trap about us folks gettin' together, an' you'll see. They take your pitcher an' send it all over. Then you can't get work nowhere. An' if you got kids——"

Tom took off his cap and twisted it in his hands. "So we take what we can get, huh, or we starve; an' if we yelp we starve."

The young man made a sweeping circle with his hand, and his hand took in the ragged tents and rusty cars.

Tom looked down at his mother again, where she sat scraping potatoes. And the children had drawn closer. He said, "I ain't gonna take it. Goddamn it, I an' my folks ain't no sheep. I'll kick the hell outa somebody."

"Like a cop?"

"Like anybody."

"You're nuts," said the young man. "They'll pick you right off. You got no name, no property. They'll find you in a ditch, with the blood dried on your mouth an' your nose. Be one little line in the paper—know what it'll say? 'Vagrant foun' dead.' An' that's all. You'll see a lot of them little lines, 'Vagrant foun' dead.'"

Tom said, "They'll be somebody else foun' dead right 'longside of this here vagrant."

"You're nuts," said the young man. "Won't be no good in that."

"Well, what you doin' about it?" He looked into the grease-streaked face. And a veil drew down over the eyes of the young man.

"Nothin'. Where you from?"

"Us? Right near Sallisaw, Oklahoma."

"Jus' get in?"

"Jus' today."

"Gonna be aroun' here long?"

"Don't know. We'll stay wherever we can get work. Why?"

"Nothin'." And the veil came down again.

"Got to sleep up," said Tom. "Tomorra we'll go out lookin' for work."

"You kin try."

Tom turned away and moved toward the Joad tent. The young man took up the can of valve compound and dug his finger into it. "Hi!" he called.

Tom turned. "What you want?"

"I want ta tell ya." He motioned with his finger, on which a blob of compound stuck. "I jus' want ta tell ya. Don' go lookin' for no trouble. 'Member how that bull-simple guy looked?"

"Fella in the tent up there?"

"Yeah—looked dumb—no sense?"

"What about him?"

"Well, when the cops come in, an' they come in all a time, that's how you want ta be. Dumb—don't know nothin'. Don't understan' nothin'. That's how the cops like us. Don't hit no cops. That's jus' suicide. Be bull-simple."

"Let them goddamn cops run over me, an' me do nothin'?"

"No, looka here. I'll come for ya tonight. Maybe I'm wrong. There's stools aroun' all a time. I'm takin' a chancet, an' I got a kid, too. But I'll come for ya. An' if ya see a cop, why, you're a goddamn dumb Okie, see?"

"Tha's awright if we're doin' anythin'," said Tom.

"Don' you worry. We're doin' somepin, on'y we ain't stickin' our necks out. A kid starves quick. Two-three days for a kid." He went back to his job, spread the compound on a valve seat, and his hand jerked rapidly back and forth on the brace, and his face was dull and dumb.

Tom strolled slowly back to his camp. "Bull-simple," he said under his breath.

Pa and Uncle John came toward the camp, their arms loaded with dry willow sticks, and they threw them down by the fire and squatted on their hams. "Got her picked over pretty good," said Pa. "Had ta go a long ways for wood." He looked up at the circle of staring children. "Lord God Almighty!" he said. "Where'd you come from?" All of the children looked self-consciously at their feet.

"Guess they smelled the cookin'," said Ma. "Winfiel', get out from under foot." She pushed him out of her way. "Got ta make us up a little stew," she said. "We ain't et nothin' cooked right sence we come from home. Pa, you go up to the store there an' get me some neck meat. Make a nice stew here." Pa stood up and sauntered away.

Al had the hood of the car up, and he looked down at the greasy engine. He looked up when Tom approached. "You sure look happy as a buzzard," Al said.

"I'm jus' gay as a toad in spring rain," said Tom.

"Looka the engine," Al pointed. "Purty good, huh?" Tom peered in. "Looks awright to me."

"Awright? Jesus, she's wonderful. She ain't shot no oil nor nothin'." He unscrewed a spark plug and stuck his forefinger in the hole. "Crusted up some, but she's dry."

Tom said, "You done a nice job a pickin'. That what ya want me to say?"

"Well, I sure was scairt the whole way, figgerin' she'd bust down an' it'd be my fault."

"No, you done good. Better get her in shape, 'cause tomorra we're goin' out lookin' for work."

"She'll roll," said Al. "Don't you worry none about that." He took out a pocket knife and scraped the points of the spark plug.

Tom walked around the side of the tent, and he found Casy sitting on the earth, wisely regarding one bare foot. Tom sat down heavily beside him. "Think she's gonna work?"

"What?" asked Casy.

"Them toes of yourn."

"Oh! Jus' settin' here a-thinkin'."

"You always get good an' comf'table for it," said Tom.

Casy waggled his big toe up and his second toe down, and he smiled quietly. "Hard enough for a fella to think 'thout kinkin' hisself up to do it."

"Ain't heard a peep outa you for days," said Tom. "Thinkin' all the time?"

"Yeah, thinkin' all the time."

Tom took off his cloth cap, dirty now, and ruinous, the visor pointed as a bird's beak. He turned the sweat band out and removed a long strip of folded newspaper. "Sweat so much she's shrank," he said. He looked at Casy's waving toes. "Could ya come down from your thinkin' an' listen a minute?"

Casy turned his head on the stalk-like neck. "Listen all the time. That's why I been thinkin'. Listen to people a-talkin', an' purty soon I hear the way folks are feelin'. Goin' on all the time. I hear 'em an' feel 'em; an' they're beating their wings like a bird in a attic. Gonna bust their wings on a dusty winda tryin' ta get out."

Tom regarded him with widened eyes, and then he turned and looked at a gray tent twenty feet away. Washed jeans and shirts and a dress hung to dry on the tent guys. He said softly, "That was about what I was gonna tell ya. An' you seen awready."

"I seen," Casy agreed. "They's a army of us without no harness." He bowed his head and ran his extended hand slowly up his forehead and into his hair. "All along I seen it," he said. "Ever' place we stopped I seen it. Folks hungry for side-meat, an' when they get it, they ain't fed. An' when they'd get so hungry they couldn' stan' it no more, why, they'd ast me to pray for 'em, an' sometimes I done it." He clasped his hands around drawn-up knees and pulled his legs in. "I use ta think that'd cut 'er," he said. "Use ta rip off a prayer an' all the troubles'd stick to that prayer like flies on fly paper, an' the prayer'd go a-sailin' off, a-takin' them troubles along. But it don' work no more."

Tom said, "Prayer never brought in no side-meat. Takes a shoat to bring in pork."

"Yeah," Casy said. "An' Almighty God never raised no wages. These here folks want to live decent and bring up their kids decent. An' when they're old they wanta set in the door an' watch the downing sun. An' when they're young they wanta dance an' sing an' lay together. They wanta eat an' get drunk and work. An' that's it—they wanta jus' fling their goddamn muscles aroun' an' get tired. Christ! What'm I talkin' about?"

"I dunno," said Tom. "Sounds kinda nice. When ya think you can get ta work an' quit thinkin' a spell? We got to get work. Money's 'bout gone. Pa give five dollars to get a painted piece of board stuck up over Granma. We ain't got much lef'."

A lean brown mongrel dog came sniffing around the side of the tent. He was nervous and flexed to run. He sniffed close before he was aware of the two men, and then looking up he saw them, leaped sideways, and fled, ears back, bony tail clamped protectively. Casy watched him go, dodging around a tent to get out of sight. Casy sighed. "I ain't doin' nobody no good," he said. "Me or nobody else. I was thinkin' I'd go off alone by myself. I'm a-eatin' your food an' a-takin' up room. An' I ain't give you nothin'. Maybe I could get a steady job an' maybe pay back some a the stuff you've give me."

Tom opened his mouth and thrust his lower jaw forward, and he tapped his lower teeth with a dried piece of mustard stalk. His eyes stared over the camp,

over the gray tents and the shacks of weed and tin and
paper. "Wisht I had a sack of Durham," he said. "I
ain't had a smoke in a hell of a time. Use ta get
tobacco in McAlester. Almost wisht I was back." He
tapped his teeth again and suddenly he turned on the
preacher. "Ever been in a jail house?"

"No," said Casy. "Never been."

"Don't go away right yet," said Tom. "Not right
yet."

"Quicker I get lookin' for work—quicker I'm gonna
find some."

Tom studied him with half-shut eyes and he put on
his cap again. "Look," he said, "this ain't no lan' of
milk an' honey like the preachers say. They's a mean
thing here. The folks here is scared of us people
comin' west; an' so they got cops out tryin' to scare us
back."

"Yeah," said Casy. "I know. What you ask about
me bein' in jail for?"

Tom said slowly, "When you're in jail—you get to
kinda—sensin' stuff. Guys ain't let to talk a hell of a
lot together—two maybe, but not a crowd. An' so you
get kinda sensy. If somepin's gonna bust—if say a
fella's goin' stir-bugs an' takes a crack at a guard with
a mop handle—why, you know it 'fore it happens. An'
if they's gonna be a break or a riot, nobody don't have
to tell ya. You're sensy about it. You know."

"Yeah?"

"Stick aroun'," said Tom. "Stick aroun' till tomorra
anyways. Somepin's gonna come up. I was talkin' to a
kid up the road. An' he's bein' jus' as sneaky an'
wise as a dog coyote, but he's too wise. Dog coyote
a-mindin' his own business an' innocent an' sweet,
jus' havin' fun an' no harm—well, they's a hen roost
clost by."

Casy watched him intently, started to ask a question, and then shut his mouth tightly. He waggled his
toes slowly and, releasing his knees, pushed out his

foot so he could see it. "Yeah," he said, "I won't go right yet."

Tom said, "When a bunch a folks, nice quiet folks, don't know nothin' about nothin'—somepin's goin' on."

"I'll stay," said Casy.

"An' tomorra we'll go out in the truck an' look for work."

"Yeah!" said Casy, and he waved his toes up and down and studied them gravely. Tom settled back on his elbow and closed his eyes. Inside the tent he could hear the murmur of Rose of Sharon's voice and Connie's answering.

The tarpaulin made a dark shadow and the wedge-shaped light at each end was hard and sharp. Rose of Sharon lay on a mattress and Connie squatted beside her. "I oughta help Ma," Rose of Sharon said. "I tried, but ever' time I stirred about I throwed up."

Connie's eyes were sullen. "If I'd of knowed it would be like this I wouldn' of came. I'd a studied nights 'bout tractors back home an' got me a three-dollar job. Fella can live awful nice on three dollars a day, an' go to the pitcher show ever' night, too."

Rose of Sharon looked apprehensive. "You're gonna study nights 'bout radios," she said. He was long in answering. "Ain't you?" she demanded.

"Yeah, sure. Soon's I get on my feet. Get a little money."

She rolled up on her elbow. "You ain't givin' it up!"

"No—no—'course not. But—I didn' know they was places like this we got to live in."

The girl's eyes hardened. "You got to," she said quietly.

"Sure. Sure, I know. Got to get on my feet. Get a little money. Would a been better to stay home an' study 'bout tractors. Three dollars a day they get, an' pick up extra money, too." Rose of Sharon's eyes were calculating. When he looked down at her he saw in her eyes a measuring of him, a calculation of him. "But I'm gonna study," he said. "Soon's I get on my feet."

She said fiercely, "We got to have a house 'fore the baby comes. We ain't gonna have this baby in no tent."

"Sure," he said. "Soon's I get on my feet." He went out of the tent and looked down at Ma, crouched over the brush fire. Rose of Sharon rolled on her back and stared at the top of the tent. And then she put her thumb in her mouth for a gag and she cried silently.

Ma knelt beside the fire, breaking twigs to keep the flame up under the stew kettle. The fire flared and dropped and flared and dropped. The children, fifteen of them, stood silently and watched. And when the smell of the cooking stew came to their noses, their noses crinkled slightly. The sunlight glistened on hair tawny with dust. The children were embarrassed to be there, but they did not go. Ma talked quietly to a little girl who stood inside the lusting circle. She was older than the rest. She stood on one foot, caressing the back of her leg with a bare instep. Her arms were clasped behind her. She watched Ma with steady small gray eyes. She suggested, "I could break up some bresh if you want me, ma'am."

Ma looked up from her work. "You want ta get ast to eat, huh?"

"Yes, ma'am," the girl said steadily.

Ma slipped the twigs under the pot and the flame made a puttering sound. "Didn' you have no breakfast?"

"No, ma'am. They ain't no work hereabouts. Pa's in tryin' to sell some stuff to git gas so's we can git 'long."

Ma looked up. "Didn' none of these here have no breakfast?"

The circle of children shifted nervously and looked away from the boiling kettle. One small boy said boastfully, "I did—me an' my brother did—an' them two did, 'cause I seen 'em. We et good. We're a-goin' south tonight."

Ma smiled. "Then you ain't hungry. They ain't enough here to go around."

The small boy's lip stuck out. "We et good," he said, and he turned and ran and dived into a tent. Ma looked after him so long that the oldest girl reminded her.

"The fire's down, ma'am. I can keep it up if you want."

Ruthie and Winfield stood inside the circle, comporting themselves with proper frigidity and dignity. They were aloof, and at the same time possessive. Ruthie turned cold and angry eyes on the little girl. Ruthie squatted down to break up the twigs for Ma.

Ma lifted the kettle lid and stirred the stew with a stick. "I'm sure glad some of you ain't hungry. That little fella ain't, anyways."

The girl sneered. "Oh, him! He was a-braggin'. High an' mighty. If he don't have no supper—know what he done? Las' night, come out an' say they got chicken to eat. Well, sir, I looked whilst they was a-eatin' an' it was fried dough jus' like ever'body else."

"Oh!" And Ma looked down toward the tent where the small boy had gone. She looked back at the little girl. "How long you been in California?" she asked.

"Oh, 'bout six months. We lived in a gov'ment camp a while, an' then we went north, an' when we come back it was full up. That's a nice place to live, you bet."

"Where's that?" Ma asked. And she took the sticks from Ruthie's hand and fed the fire. Ruthie glared with hatred at the older girl.

"Over by Weedpatch. Got nice toilets an' baths, an' you kin wash clothes in a tub, an' they's water right handy, good drinkin' water; an' nights the folks plays music an' Sat'dy night they give a dance. Oh, you never seen anything so nice. Got a place for kids to play, an' them toilets with paper. Pull down a little jigger an' the water comes right in the toilet; an' they ain't no cops let to come look in your tent any time they want, an' the fella runs the camp is so polite, come a-visitin' an' talks an' ain't high an' mighty. I wisht we could go live there again."

Ma said, "I never heard about it. I sure could use a wash tub, I tell you."

The girl went on excitedly, "Why, God Awmighty, they got hot water right in pipes, an' you get in under a shower bath an' it's warm. You never seen such a place."

Ma said, "All full now, ya say?"

"Yeah. Las' time we ast it was."

"Mus' cost a lot," said Ma.

"Well, it costs, but if you ain't got the money, they let you work it out—couple hours a week, cleanin' up, an' garbage cans. Stuff like that. An' nights they's music an' folks talks together an' hot water right in the pipes. You never seen nothin' so nice."

Ma said, "I sure wisht we could go there."

Ruthie had stood all she could. She blurted fiercely, "Granma died right on top a the truck." The girl looked questioningly at her. "Well, she did," Ruthie said. "An' the cor'ner got her." She closed her lips tightly and broke up a little pile of sticks.

Winfield blinked at the boldness of the attack. "Right on the truck," he echoed. "Cor'ner stuck her in a big basket."

Ma said, "You shush now, both of you, or you got to go away." And she fed twigs into the fire.

Down the line Al had strolled to watch the valve-grinding job. "Looks like you're 'bout through," he said.

"Two more."

"Is they any girls in this here camp?"

"I got a wife," said the young man. "I got no time for girls."

"I always got time for girls," said Al. "I got no time for nothin' else."

"You get a little hungry an' you'll change."

Al laughed. "Maybe. But I ain't never changed that notion yet."

"Fella I talked to while ago, he's with you, ain't he?"

"Yeah! My brother Tom. Better not fool with him. He killed a fella."

"Did? What for?"

"Fight. Fella got a knife in Tom. Tom busted 'im with a shovel."

"Did, huh? What'd the law do?"

"Let 'im off 'cause it was a fight," said Al.

"He don't look like a quarreler."

"Oh, he ain't. But Tom don't take nothin' from no-body." Al's voice was very proud. "Tom, he's quiet. But—look out!"

"Well—I talked to 'im. He didn' soun' mean."

"He ain't. Jus' as nice as pie till he's roused, an' then—look out." The young man ground at the last valve. "Like me to he'p you get them valves set an' the head on?"

"Sure, if you got nothin' else to do."

"Oughta get some sleep," said Al. "But, hell, I can't keep my han's out of a tore-down car. Jus' got to git in."

"Well, I'd admire to git a hand," said the young man. "My name's Floyd Knowles."

"I'm Al Joad."

"Proud to meet ya."

"Me too," said Al. "Gonna use the same gasket?"

"Got to," said Floyd.

Al took out his pocket knife and scraped at the block. "Jesus!" he said. "They ain't nothin' I love like the guts of a engine."

"How 'bout girls?"

"Yeah, girls too! Wisht I could tear down a Rolls an' put her back. I looked under the hood of a Cad' 16 one time an', God Awmighty, you never seen nothin' so sweet in your life! In Sallisaw—an' here's this 16 a-standin' in front of a restaurant, so I lifts the hood. An' a guy comes out an' says, 'What the hell you doin'?' I says, 'Jus' lookin'. Ain't she swell?' An' he jus' stands there. I don't think he ever looked in her before. Jus' stands there. Rich fella in a straw hat. Got a stripe' shirt on, an' eye glasses. We don' say nothin'. Jus' look. An' purty soon he says, 'How'd you like to drive her?'"

Floyd said, "The hell!"

"Sure—'How'd you like to drive her?' Well, hell, I got on jeans—all dirty. I says, 'I'd get her dirty.' 'Come on!' he says. 'Jus' take her roun' the block.' Well, sir, I set in that seat an' I took her roun' the block eight times, an', oh, my God Almighty!"

"Nice?" Floyd asked.

"Oh, Jesus!" said Al. "If I could of tore her down why—I'd a give—anythin'."

Floyd slowed his jerking arm. He lifted the last valve from its seat and looked at it. "You better git use' ta a jalopy," he said, " 'cause you ain't goin' a drive no 16." He put his brace down on the running board and took up a chisel to scrape the crust from the block. Two stocky women, bare-headed and bare-footed, went by carrying a bucket of milky water between them. They limped against the weight of the bucket, and neither one looked up from the ground. The sun was half down in afternoon.

Al said, "You don't like nothin' much."

Floyd scraped harder with the chisel. "I been here six months," he said. "I been scrabblin' over this here State tryin' to work hard enough and move fast enough to get meat an' potatoes for me an' my wife an' my kid. I've run myself like a jackrabbit an'—I can't quite make her. There just ain't quite enough to eat no matter what I do. I'm gettin' tired, that's all. I'm gettin' tired way past where sleep rests me. An' I jus' don' know what to do."

"Ain't there no steady work for a fella?" Al asked.

"No, they ain't no steady work." With his chisel he pushed the crust off the block, and he wiped the dull metal with a greasy rag.

A rusty touring car drove down into the camp and there were four men in it, men with brown hard faces. The car drove slowly through the camp. Floyd called to them, "Any luck?"

The car stopped. The driver said, "We covered a hell of a lot a ground. They ain't a hand's work in this here country. We gotta move."

"Where to?" Al called.

"God knows. We worked this here place over." He let in his clutch and moved slowly down the camp.

Al looked after them. "Wouldn't it be better if one fella went alone? Then if they was a piece a work, a fella'd get it."

Floyd put down the chisel and smiled sourly. "You ain't learned," he said. "Takes gas to get roun' the country. Gas costs fifteen cents a gallon. Them four fellas can't take four cars. So each of 'em puts in a dime an' they get gas. You got to learn."

"Al!"

Al looked down at Winfield standing importantly beside him. "Al, Ma's dishin' up stew. She says come git it."

Al wiped his hands on his trousers. "We ain't et today," he said to Floyd. "I'll come give you a han' when I eat."

"No need 'less you want ta."

"Sure, I'll do it." He followed Winfield toward the Joad camp.

It was crowded now. The strange children stood close to the stew pot, so close that Ma brushed them with her elbows as she worked. Tom and Uncle John stood beside her.

Ma said helplessly, "I dunno what to do. I got to feed the fambly. What'm I gonna do with these here?" The children stood stiffly and looked at her. Their faces were blank, rigid, and their eyes went mechanically from the pot to the tin plate she held. Their eyes followed the spoon from pot to plate, and when she passed the steaming plate up to Uncle John, their eyes followed it up. Uncle John dug his spoon into the stew, and the banked eyes rose up with the spoon. A piece of potato went into John's mouth and the banked eyes were on his face, watching to see how he would react. Would it be good? Would he like it?

And then Uncle John seemed to see them for the first time. He chewed slowly. "You take this here," he said to Tom. "I ain't hungry."

"You ain't et today," Tom said.

"I know, but I got a stomickache. I ain't hungry."

Tom said quietly, "You take that plate inside the tent an' you eat it."

"I ain't hungry," John insisted. "I'd still see 'em inside the tent."

Tom turned on the children. "You git," he said. "Go on now, git." The bank of eyes left the stew and rested wondering on his face. "Go on now, git. You ain't doin' no good. There ain't enough for you."

Ma ladled stew into the tin plates, very little stew, and she laid the plates on the ground. "I can't send 'em away," she said. "I don' know what to do. Take your plates an' go inside. I'll let 'em have what's lef'. Here, take a plate in to Rosasharn." She smiled up at the children. "Look," she said, "you little fellas go an' get you each a flat stick an' I'll put what's lef' for you. But they ain't to be no fightin'." The group broke up with a deadly, silent swiftness. Children ran to find sticks, they ran to their own tents and brought spoons. Before Ma had finished with the plates they were

back, silent and wolfish. Ma shook her head. "I
dunno what to do. I can't rob the fambly. I got to
feed the fambly. Ruthie, Winfiel', Al," she cried
fiercely. "Take your plates. Hurry up. Git in the tent
quick." She looked apologetically at the waiting children. "There ain't enough," she said humbly. "I'm
a-gonna set this here kettle out, an' you'll all get a
little tas', but it ain't gonna do you no good." She
faltered, "I can't he'p it. Can't keep it from you." She
lifted the pot and set it down on the ground. "Now
wait. It's too hot," she said, and she went into the
tent quickly so she would not see. Her family sat on
the ground, each with his plate; and outside they
could hear the children digging into the pot with their
sticks and their spoons and their pieces of rusty tin.
A mound of children smothered the pot from sight.
They did not talk, did not fight or argue; but there
was a quiet intentness in all of them, a wooden
fierceness. Ma turned her back so she couldn't see.
"We can't do that no more," she said. "We got to eat
alone." There was the sound of scraping at the kettle,
and then the mound of children broke and the children walked away and left the scraped kettle on the
ground. Ma looked at the empty plates. "Didn' none
of you get nowhere near enough."

Pa got up and left the tent without answering. The
preacher smiled to himself and lay back on the
ground, hands clasped behind his head. Al got to his
feet. "Got to help a fella with a car."

Ma gathered the plates and took them outside to
wash. "Ruthie," she called, "Winfiel'. Go get me a
bucket a water right off." She handed them the bucket
and they trudged off toward the river.

A strong broad woman walked near. Her dress was
streaked with dust and splotched with car oil. Her
chin was held high with pride. She stood a short distance away and regarded Ma belligerently. At last she
approached. "Afternoon," she said coldly.

"Afternoon," said Ma, and she got up from her knees and pushed a box forward. "Won't you set down?"

The woman walked near. "No, I won't set down."

Ma looked questioningly at her. "Can I he'p you in any way?"

The woman set her hands on her hips. "You kin he'p me by mindin' your own childern an' lettin' mine alone."

Ma's eyes opened wide. "I ain't done nothin'—" she began.

The woman scowled at her. "My little fella come back smellin' of stew. You give it to 'im. He tol' me. Don' you go a-boastin' an' a-braggin' 'bout havin' stew. Don' you do it. I got 'nuf troubles 'thout that. Come in ta me, he did, an' says, 'Whyn't we have stew?' " Her voice shook with fury.

Ma moved close. "Set down," she said. "Set down an' talk a piece."

"No, I ain't gonna set down. I'm tryin' to feed my folks, an' you come along with your stew."

"Set down," Ma said. "That was 'bout the las' stew we're gonna have till we get work. S'pose you was cookin' a stew an' a bunch of little fellas stood aroun' moonin', what'd you do? We didn't have enough, but you can't keep it when they look at ya like that."

The woman's hands dropped from her hips. For a moment her eyes questioned Ma, and then she turned and walked quickly away, and she went into a tent and pulled the flaps down behind her. Ma stared after her, and then she dropped to her knees again beside the stack of tin dishes.

Al hurried near. "Tom," he called. "Ma, is Tom inside?"

Tom stuck his head out. "What you want?"

"Come on with me," Al said excitedly.

They walked away together. "What's a matter with you?" Tom asked.

"You'll find out. Jus' wait." He led Tom to the torn-down car. "This here's Floyd Knowles," he said.

"Yeah, I talked to him. How ya?"

"Jus' gettin' her in shape," Floyd said.

Tom ran his finger over the top of the block. "What kinda bugs is crawlin' on you, Al?"

"Floyd jus' tol' me. Tell 'em, Floyd."

Floyd said, "Maybe I shouldn' but—yeah, I'll tell ya. Fella come through an' he says they's gonna be work up north."

"Up north?"

"Yeah—place called Santa Clara Valley, way to hell an' gone up north."

"Yeah? Kinda work?"

"Prune pickin', an' pears an' cannery work. Says it's purty near ready."

"How far?" Tom demanded.

"Oh, Christ knows. Maybe two hundred miles."

"That's a hell of a long ways," said Tom. "How we know they's gonna be work when we get there?"

"Well, we don' know," said Floyd. "But they ain't nothin' here, an' this fella says he got a letter from his brother, an' he's on his way. He says not to tell nobody, they'll be too many. We oughta get out in the night. Oughta get there an' get some work lined up."

Tom studied him. "Why we gotta sneak away?"

"Well, if ever'body gets there, ain't gonna be work for nobody."

"It's a hell of a long ways," Tom said.

Floyd sounded hurt. "I'm jus' givin' you the tip. You don' have to take it. Your brother here he'ped me, an' I'm givin' you the tip."

"You sure there ain't no work here?"

"Look, I been scourin' aroun' for three weeks all over hell, an' I ain't had a bit a work, not a single han'-holt. 'F you wanta look aroun' an' burn up gas lookin', why, go ahead. I ain't beggin' you. More that goes, the less chance I got."

Tom said, "I ain't findin' fault. It's jus' such a hell of a long ways. An' we kinda hoped we could get work here an' rent a house to live in."

Floyd said patiently, "I know ya jus' got here. They's stuff ya got to learn. If you'd let me tell ya, it'd save ya somepin. If ya don' let me tell ya, then ya got to learn the hard way. You ain't gonna settle down 'cause they ain't no work to settle ya. An' your belly ain't gonna let ya settle down. Now—that's straight."

"Wisht I could look aroun' first," Tom said uneasily.

A sedan drove through the camp and pulled up at the next tent. A man in overalls and a blue shirt climbed out. Floyd called to him, "Any luck?"

"There ain't a han'-turn of work in the whole darn county, not till cotton pickin'." And he went into the ragged tent.

"See?" said Floyd.

"Yeah, I see. But two hunderd miles, Jesus!"

"Well, you ain't settlin' down no place for a while. Might's well make up your mind to that."

"We better go," Al said.

Tom asked, "When is they gonna be work aroun' here?"

"Well, in a month the cotton'll start. If you got plenty money you can wait for the cotton."

Tom said, "Ma ain't a-gonna wanta move. She's all tar'd out."

Floyd shrugged his shoulders. "I ain't a-tryin' to push ya north. Suit yaself. I jus' tol' ya what I heard." He picked the oily gasket from the running board and fitted it carefully on the block and pressed it down. "Now," he said to Al, " 'f you want to give me a han' with that engine head."

Tom watched while they set the heavy head gently down over the head bolts and dropped it evenly. "Have to talk about it," he said.

Floyd said, "I don't want nobody but your folks to

know about it. Jus' you. An' I wouldn' of tol' you if ya brother didn' he'p me out here."

Tom said, "Well, I sure thank ya for tellin' us. We got to figger it out. Maybe we'll go."

Al said, "By God, I think I'll go if the res' goes or not. I'll hitch there."

"An' leave the fambly?" Tom asked.

"Sure. I'd come back with my jeans plumb fulla jack. Why not?"

"Ma ain't gonna like no such thing," Tom said. "An' Pa, he ain't gonna like it neither."

Floyd set the nuts and screwed them down as far as he could with his fingers. "Me an' my wife come out with our folks," he said. "Back home we wouldn' of thought of goin' away. Wouldn' of thought of it. But, hell, we was all up north a piece and I come down here, an' they moved on, an' now God knows where they are. Been lookin' an' askin' about 'em ever since." He fitted his wrench to the engine bolts and turned them down evenly, one turn on each nut, around and around the series.

Tom squatted down beside the car and squinted his eyes up the line of tents. A little stubble was beaten into the earth between the tents. "No, sir," he said, "Ma ain't gonna like you goin' off."

"Well, seems to me a lone fella got more chance of work."

"Maybe, but Ma ain't gonna like it at all."

Two cars loaded with disconsolate men drove down into the camp. Floyd lifted his eyes, but he didn't ask them about their luck. Their dusty faces were sad and resistant. The sun was sinking now, and the yellow sunlight fell on the Hooverville, and on the willows behind it. The children began to come out of the tents, to wander about the camp. And from the tents the women came and built their little fires. The men gathered in squatting groups and talked together.

A new Chevrolet coupé turned off the highway and headed down into the camp. It pulled to the center of the camp. Tom said, "Who's this? They don't belong here."

Floyd said, "I dunno—cops, maybe."

The car door opened and a man got out and stood beside the car. His companion remained seated. Now all the squatting men looked at the newcomers and the conversation was still. And the women building their fires looked secretly at the shiny car. The children moved closer with elaborate circuitousness, edging inward in long curves.

Floyd put down his wrench. Tom stood up. Al wiped his hands on his trousers. The three strolled toward the Chevrolet. The man who had got out of the car was dressed in khaki trousers and a flannel shirt. He wore a flat-brimmed Stetson hat. A sheaf of papers was held in his shirt pocket by a little fence of fountain pens and yellow pencils; and from his hip pocket protruded a notebook with metal covers. He moved to one of the groups of squatting men, and they looked up at him, suspicious and quiet. They watched him and did not move; the whites of their eyes showed beneath the irises, for they did not raise their heads to look. Tom and Al and Floyd strolled casually near.

The man said, "You men want to work?" Still they looked quietly, suspiciously. And men from all over the camp moved near.

One of the squatting men spoke at last. "Sure we wanta work. Where's at's work?"

"Tulare County. Fruit's opening up. Need a lot of pickers."

Floyd spoke up. "You doin' the hiring?"

"Well, I'm contracting the land."

The men were in a compact group now. An overalled man took off his black hat and combed back his long black hair with his fingers. "What you payin'?" he asked.

"Well, can't tell exactly, yet. 'Bout thirty cents, I guess."

"Why can't you tell? You took the contract, didn' you?"

"That's true," the khaki man said. "But it's keyed to the price. Might be a little more, might be a little less."

Floyd stepped out ahead. He said quietly, "I'll go, mister. You're a contractor, an' you got a license. You jus' show your license, an' then you give us an order to go to work, an' where, an' when, an' how much we'll get, an' you sign that, an' we'll all go."

The contractor turned, scowling. "You telling me how to run my own business?"

Floyd said, " 'F we're workin' for you, it's our business too."

"Well, you ain't telling me what to do. I told you I need men."

Floyd said angrily, "You didn' say how many men, an' you didn' say what you'd pay."

"Goddamn it, I don't know yet."

"If you don' know, you got no right to hire men."

"I got a right to run my business my own way. If you men want to sit here on your ass, O.K. I'm out getting men for Tulare County. Going to need a lot of men."

Floyd turned to the crowd of men. They were standing up now, looking quietly from one speaker to the other. Floyd said, "Twicet now I've fell for that. Maybe he needs a thousan' men. He'll get five thousan' there, an' he'll pay fifteen cents an hour. An' you poor bastards'll have to take it 'cause you'll be hungry. 'F he wants to hire men, let him hire 'em an' write it out an' say what he's gonna pay. Ast ta see his license. He ain't allowed to contract men without a license."

The contractor turned to the Chevrolet and called, "Joe!" His companion looked out and then swung the car door open and stepped out. He wore riding breeches and laced boots. A heavy pistol holster hung on a cartridge belt around his waist. On his brown shirt a deputy sheriff's star was pinned. He walked heavily over. His face was set to a thin smile. "What you want?" The holster slid back and forth on his hip.

"Ever see this guy before, Joe?"

The deputy asked "Which one?"

"This fella." The contractor pointed to Floyd.

"What'd he do?" The deputy smiled at Floyd.

"He's talkin' red, agitating trouble."

"Hm-m-m." The deputy moved slowly around to see Floyd's profile, and the color slowly flowed up Floyd's face.

"You see?" Floyd cried. "If this guy's on the level, would he bring a cop along?"

"Ever see 'im before?" the contractor insisted.

"Hmmm, seems like I have. Las' week when that used-car lot was busted into. Seems like I seen this fella hangin' aroun'. Yep! I'd swear it's the same fella." Suddenly the smile left his face. "Get in that car," he said, and he unhooked the strap that covered the butt of his automatic.

Tom said, "You got nothin' on him."

The deputy swung around. " 'F you'd like to go in too, you jus' open your trap once more. They was two fellas hangin' around that lot."

"I wasn't even in the State las' week," Tom said.

"Well, maybe you're wanted someplace else. You keep your trap shut."

The contractor turned back to the men. "You fellas don't want ta listen to these goddamn reds. Trouble-makers—they'll get you in trouble. Now I can use all of you in Tulare County."

The men didn't answer.

The deputy turned back to them. "Might be a good idear to go," he said. The thin smile was back on his face. "Board of Health says we got to clean out this camp. An' if it gets around that you got reds out here—why, somebody might git hurt. Be a good idear

if all you fellas moved on to Tulare. They isn't a thing
to do aroun' here. That's jus' a friendly way a telling
you. Be a bunch a guys down here, maybe with pick
handles, if you ain't gone."

The contractor said, "I told you I need men. If you
don't want to work—well, that's your business."

The deputy smiled. "If they don't want to work, they
ain't a place for 'em in this county. We'll float 'em
quick."

Floyd stood stiffly beside the deputy, and Floyd's
thumbs were hooked over his belt. Tom stole a look at
him, and then stared at the ground.

"That's all," the contractor said. "There's men
needed in Tulare County; plenty of work."

Tom looked slowly at Floyd's hands, and he saw the
strings at the wrists standing out under the skin. Tom's
own hands came up, and his thumbs hooked over his
belt.

"Yeah, that's all. I don't want one of you here by
tomorra morning."

The contractor stepped into the Chevrolet.

"Now, you," the deputy said to Floyd, "you get in
that car." He reached a large hand up and took
hold of Floyd's left arm. Floyd spun and swung with
one movement. His fist splashed into the large face,
and in the same motion he was away, dodging down
the line of tents. The deputy staggered and Tom put
out his foot for him to trip over. The deputy fell
heavily and rolled, reaching for his gun. Floyd
dodged in and out of sight down the line. The deputy fired from the ground. A woman in front of a
tent screamed and then looked at a hand with no
knuckles. The fingers hung on strings against her
palm, and the torn flesh was white and bloodless.
Far down the line Floyd came in sight, sprinting for
the willows. The deputy, sitting on the ground,
raised his gun again and then, suddenly, from the
group of men, the Reverend Casy stepped. He

kicked the deputy in the neck and then stood back as the heavy man crumpled into unconsciousness.

The motor of the Chevrolet roared and it streaked away, churning the dust. It mounted to the highway and shot away. In front of her tent, the woman still looked at her shattered hand. Little droplets of blood began to ooze from the wound. And a chuckling hysteria began in her throat, a whining laugh that grew louder and higher with each breath.

The deputy lay on his side, his mouth open against the dust.

Tom picked up his automatic, pulled out the magazine and threw it into the brush, and he ejected the live shell from the chamber. "Fella like that ain't got no right to a gun," he said; and he dropped the automatic to the ground.

A crowd had collected around the woman with the broken hand, and her hysteria increased, a screaming quality came into her laughter.

Casy moved close to Tom. "You got to git out," he said. "You go down in the willas an' wait. He didn' see me kick 'im, but he seen you stick out your foot."

"I don' want ta go," Tom said.

Casy put his head close. He whispered, "They'll fingerprint you. You broke parole. They'll send you back."

Tom drew in his breath quietly. "Jesus! I forgot."

"Go quick," Casy said. " 'Fore he comes to."

"Like to have his gun," Tom said.

"No. Leave it. If it's awright to come back, I'll give ya four high whistles."

Tom strolled away casually, but as soon as he was away from the group he hurried his steps and he disappeared among the willows that lined the river.

Al stepped over to the fallen deputy. "Jesus," he said admiringly, "you sure flagged 'im down!"

The crowd of men had continued to stare at the unconscious man. And now in the great distance a siren screamed up the scale and dropped, and it screamed again, nearer this time. Instantly the men were nervous. They shifted their feet for a moment and then they moved away, each one to his own tent. Only Al and the preacher remained.

Casy turned to Al. "Get out," he said. "Go on, get out—to the tent. You don't know nothin'."

"Yeah? How 'bout you?"

Casy grinned at him. "Somebody got to take the blame. I got no kids. They'll jus' put me in jail, an' I ain't doin' nothin' but set aroun'."

Al said, "Ain't no reason for——"

"Go on now," Casy said sharply. "You get outa this."

Al bristled. "I ain't takin' orders."

Casy said softly, "If you mess in this your whole fambly, all your folks, gonna get in trouble. I don' care about you. But your ma and your pa, they'll get in trouble. Maybe they'll send Tom back to McAlester."

Al considered it for a moment. "O.K.," he said. "I think you're a damn fool, though."

Sure," said Casy. "Why not?"

The siren screamed again and again, and always it came closer. Casy knelt beside the deputy and turned him over. The man groaned and fluttered his eyes, and tried to see. Casy wiped the dust off his lips. The families were in the tents now, and the flaps were down, and the setting sun made the air red and the gray tents bronze.

Tires squealed on the highway and an open car came swiftly into the camp. Four men, armed with rifles, piled out. Casy stood up and walked to them.

"What the hell's goin' on here?"

Casy said, "I knocked out your man there."

One of the armed men went to the deputy. He was conscious now, trying weakly to sit up.

"Now what happened here?"

"Well," Casy said, "he got tough an' I hit 'im, and

he started shootin'—hit a woman down the line. So I hit 'im again."

"Well, what'd you do in the first place?"

"I talked back," said Casy.

"Get in that car."

"Sure," said Casy, and he climbed into the back seat and sat down. Two men helped the hurt deputy to his feet. He felt his neck gingerly. Casy said, "They's a woman down the row like to bleed to death from his bad shootin'."

"We'll see about that later. Mike, is this the fella that hit you?"

The dazed man stared sickly at Casy. "Don't look like him."

"It was me, all right," Casy said. "You got smart with the wrong fella."

Mike shook his head slowly. "You don't look like the right fella to me. By God, I'm gonna be sick!"

Casy said, "I'll go 'thout no trouble. You better see how bad that woman's hurt."

"Where's she?"

"That tent over there."

The leader of the deputies walked to the tent, rifle in hand. He spoke through the tent walls, and then went inside. In a moment he came out and walked back. And he said, a little proudly, "Jesus, what a mess a .45 does make! They got a tourniquet on. We'll send a doctor out."

Two deputies sat on either side of Casy. The leader sounded his horn. There was no movement in the camp. The flaps were down tight, and the people in their tents. The engine started and the car swung around and pulled out of the camp. Between his guards Casy sat proudly, his head up and the stringy muscles of his neck prominent. On his lips there was a faint smile and on his face a curious look of conquest.

When the deputies had gone, the people came out of the tents. The sun was down now, and the gentle blue evening light was in the camp. To the east the mountains were still yellow with sunlight. The women went back to the fires that had died. The men collected to squat together and to talk softly.

Al crawled from under the Joad tarpaulin and walked toward the willows to whistle for Tom. Ma came out and built her little fire of twigs.

"Pa," she said, "we ain't goin' to have much. We et so late."

Pa and Uncle John stuck close to the camp, watching Ma peeling potatoes and slicing them raw into a frying pan of deep grease. Pa said, "Now what the hell made the preacher do that?"

Ruthie and Winfield crept close and crouched down to hear the talk.

Uncl John scratched the earth deeply with a long rusty nail. "He knowed about sin. I ast him about sin, an' he tol' me; but I don't know if he's right. He says a fella's sinned if he thinks he's sinned." Uncle John's eyes were tired and sad. "I been secret all my days," he said. "I done things I never tol' about."

Ma turned from the fire. "Don' go tellin', John," she said. "Tell 'em to God. Don' go burdenin' other people with your sins. That ain't decent."

"They're a-eatin' on me," said John.

"Well, don' tell 'em. Go down the river an' stick your head under an' whisper 'em in the stream."

Pa nodded his head slowly at Ma's words. "She's right," he said. "It gives a fella relief to tell, but it jus' spreads out his sin."

Uncle John looked up to the sun-gold mountains, and the mountains were reflected in his eyes. "I wisht I could run it down," he said. "But I can't. She's a-bitin' in my guts."

Behind him Rose of Sharon moved dizzily out of the tent. "Where's Connie?" she asked irritably. "I ain't seen Connie for a long time. Where'd he go?"

"I ain't seen him," said Ma. "If I see 'im, I'll tell 'im you want 'im."

"I ain't feelin' good," said Rose of Sharon. "Connie shouldn' of left me."

Ma looked up to the girl's swollen face. "You been a-cryin'," she said.

The tears started freshly in Rose of Sharon's eyes.

Ma went on firmly, "You git aholt on yaself. They's a lot of us here. You git aholt on yaself. Come here now an' peel some potatoes. You're feelin' sorry for yaself."

The girl started to go back in the tent. She tried to avoid Ma's stern eyes, but they compelled her and she came slowly toward the fire. "He shouldn' of went away," she said, but the tears were gone.

"You got to work," Ma said. "Set in the tent an' you'll get feelin' sorry about yaself. I ain't had time to take you in han'. I will now. You take this here knife an' get to them potatoes."

The girl knelt down and obeyed. She said fiercely, "Wait'll I see 'im. I'll tell 'im."

Ma smiled slowly. "He might smack you. You got it comin' with whinin' aroun' an' candyin' yaself. If he smacks some sense in you I'll bless 'im." The girl's eyes blazed with resentment, but she was silent.

Uncle John pushed his rusty nail deep into the ground with his broad thumb. "I got to tell," he said.

Pa said, "Well, then, goddamn it! Who'd ya kill?"

Uncle John dug with his thumb into the watch pocket of his blue jeans and scooped out a folded dirty bill. He spread it out and showed it. "Fi' dollars," he said.

"Steal her?" Pa asked.

"No, I had her. Kept her out."

"She was yourn, wasn't she?"

"Yeah, but I didn't have no right to keep her out."

"I don't see much sin in that," Ma said. "It's yourn."

Uncle John said slowly, "It ain't only the keepin' her out. I kep' her out to get drunk. I knowed they was gonna come a time when I got to get drunk, when I'd get to hurtin' inside so I got to get drunk. Figgered time wasn't yet, an' then—the preacher went an' give 'imself up to save Tom."

Pa nodded his head up and down and cocked his head to hear. Ruthie moved closer, like a puppy, crawling on her elbows, and Winfield followed her. Rose of Sharon dug at a deep eye in a potato with the point of her knife. The evening light deepened and became more blue.

Ma said, in a sharp matter-of-fact tone, "I don' see why him savin' Tom got to get you drunk."

John said sadly, "Can't say her. I feel awful. He done her so easy. Jus' stepped up there an' says, 'I done her.' An' they took 'im away. An' I'm a-gonna get drunk."

Pa still nodded his head. "I don't see why you got to tell," he said. "If it was me, I'd jus' go off an' get drunk if I had to."

"Come a time when I could a did somepin' an' took the big sin off my soul," Uncle John said sadly. "An' I slipped up. I didn' jump on her, an'—an' she got away. Lookie!" he said. "You got the money. Gimme two dollars."

Pa reached reluctantly into his pocket and brought out the leather pouch. "You ain't gonna need no seven dollars to get drunk. You don't need to drink champagny water."

Uncle John held out his bill. "You take this here an' gimme two dollars. I can get good an' drunk for two dollars. I don' want no sin of waste on me. I'll spend whatever I got. Always do."

Pa took the dirty bill and gave Uncle John two silver dollars. "There ya are," he said. "A fella got to do what he got to do. Nobody don' know enough to tell 'im."

Uncle John took the coins. "You ain't gonna be mad? You know I got to?"

"Christ, yes," said Pa. "You know what you got to do."

"I wouldn' be able to get through this night no other way," he said. He turned to Ma. "You ain't gonna hold her over me?"

Ma didn't look up. "No," she said softly. "No—you go 'long."

He stood up and walked forlornly away in the evening. He walked up to the concrete highway and across the pavement to the grocery store. In front of the screen door he took off his hat, dropped it into the dust, and ground it with his heel in self-abasement. And he left his black hat there, broken and dirty. He entered the store and walked to the shelves where the whisky bottles stood behind wire netting.

Pa and Ma and the children watched Uncle John move away. Rose of Sharon kept her eyes resentfully on the potatoes.

"Poor John," Ma said. "I wondered if it would a done any good if—no—I guess not. I never seen a man so drove."

Ruthie turned on her side in the dust. She put her head close to Winfield's head and pulled his ear against her mouth. She whispered, "I'm gonna get drunk." Winfield snorted and pinched his mouth tight. The two children crawled away, holding their breath, their faces purple with the pressure of their giggles. They crawled around the tent and leaped up and ran squealing away from the tent. They ran to the willows, and once concealed, they shrieked with laughter. Ruthie crossed her eyes and loosened her joints; she staggered about, tripping loosely, with her tongue hanging out. "I'm drunk," she said.

"Look," Winfield cried. "Looka me, here's me, an' I'm Uncle John." He flapped his arms and puffed, he whirled until he was dizzy.

"No," said Ruthie. "Here's the way. Here's the way. *I'm* Uncle John. I'm awful drunk."

Al and Tom walked quietly through the willows, and they came on the children staggering crazily about. The dusk was thick now. Tom stopped and peered. "Ain't that Ruthie an' Winfiel'? What the hell's the matter with 'em?" They walked nearer. "You crazy?" Tom asked.

The children stopped, embarrassed. "We was—jus' playin'," Ruthie said.

"It's a crazy way to play," said Al.

Ruthie said pertly, "It ain't no crazier'n a lot of things."

Al walked on. He said to Tom, "Ruthie's workin' up a kick in the pants. She been workin' it up a long time. 'Bout due for it."

Ruthie mushed her face at his back, pulled out her mouth with her forefingers, slobbered her tongue at him, outraged him in every way she knew, but Al did not turn back to look at her. She looked at Winfield again to start the game, but it had been spoiled. They both knew it.

"Le's go down the water an' duck our heads," Winfield suggested. They walked down through the willows, and they were angry at Al.

Al and Tom went quickly in the dusk. Tom said, "Casy shouldn' of did it. I might of knew, though. He was talkin' how he ain't done nothin' for us. He's a funny fella, Al. All the time thinkin'."

"Comes from bein' a preacher," Al said. "They get all messed up with stuff."

"Where ya s'pose Connie was a-goin'?"

"Goin' to take a crap, I guess."

"Well, he was goin' a hell of a long way."

They walked among the tents, keeping close to the walls. At Floyd's tent a soft hail stopped them. They came near to the tent flap and squatted down. Floyd raised the canvas a little. "You gettin' out?"

Tom said, "I don' know. Think we better?"

Floyd laughed sourly. "You heard what that bull said. They'll burn ya out if ya don't. 'F you think that guy's gonna take a beatin' 'thout gettin' back, you're nuts. The pool-room boys'll be down here tonight to burn us out."

"Guess we better git, then," Tom said. "Where you a-goin'?"

"Why, up north, like I said."

Al said, "Look, a fella tol' me 'bout a gov'ment camp near here. Where's it at?"

"Oh, I think that's full up."

"Well, where's it at?"

"Go south on 99 'bout twelve-fourteen miles, an' turn east to Weedpatch. It's right near there. But I think she's full up."

"Fella says it's nice," Al said.

"Sure, she's nice. Treat ya like a man 'stead of a dog. Ain't no cops there. But she's full up."

Tom said, "What I can't understan's why that cop was so mean. Seemed like he was aimin' for trouble; seemed like he's pokin' a fella to make trouble."

Floyd said, "I don' know about here, but up north I knowed one a them fellas, an' he was a nice fella. He tol' me up there the deputies got to take guys in. Sheriff gets seventy-five cents a day for each prisoner, an' he feeds 'em for a quarter. If he ain't got prisoners, he don't make no profit. This fella says he didn' pick up nobody for a week, an' the sheriff tol' 'im he better bring in guys or give up his button. This fella today sure looks like he's out to make a pinch one way or another."

"We got to get on," said Tom. "So long, Floyd."

"So long. Prob'ly see you. Hope so."

"Good-by," said Al. They walked through the dark gray camp to the Joad tent.

The frying pan of potatoes was hissing and spitting over the fire. Ma moved the thick slices about with a spoon. Pa sat near by, hugging his knees. Rose of Sharon was sitting under the tarpaulin.

"It's Tom!" Ma cried. "Thank God."

"We got to get outa here," said Tom.

"What's the matter now?"

"Well, Floyd says they'll burn the camp tonight."

"What the hell for?" Pa asked. "We ain't done nothin'."

"Nothin' 'cept beat up a cop," said Tom.

"Well, we never done it."

"From what that cop said, they wanta push us along."

Rose of Sharon demanded, "You seen Connie?"

"Yeah," said Al. "Way to hell an' gone up the river. He's goin' south."

"Was—was he goin' away?"

"I don' know."

Ma turned on the girl. "Rosasharn, you been talkin' an' actin' funny. What'd Connie say to you?"

Rose of Sharon said sullenly, "Said it would a been a good thing if he stayed home an' studied up tractors."

They were quiet. Rose of Sharon looked at the fire and her eyes glistened in the firelight. The potatoes hissed sharply in the frying pan. The girl sniffled and wiped her nose with the back of her hand.

Pa said, "Connie wasn' no good. I seen that a long time. Didn' have no guts, jus' too big for his overhalls."

Rose of Sharon got up and went into the tent. She lay down on the mattress and rolled over on her stomach and buried her head in her crossed arms.

"Wouldn' do no good to catch 'im, I guess," Al said.

Pa replied, "No. If he ain't no good, we don' want him."

Ma looked into the tent, where Rose of Sharon lay on her mattress. Ma said, "Sh. Don' say that."

"Well, he ain't no good," Pa insisted. "All the time

a-sayin' what he's a-gonna do. Never doin' nothin'. I didn' want ta say nothin' while he's here. But now he's run out——"

"Sh!" Ma said softly.

"Why, for Christ's sake? Why do I got to sh? He run out, didn' he?"

Ma turned over the potatoes with her spoon, and the grease boiled and spat. She fed twigs to the fire, and the flames laced up and lighted the tent. Ma said, "Rosasharn gonna have a little fella an' that baby is half Connie. It ain't good for a baby to grow up with folks a-sayin' his pa ain't no good."

"Better'n lyin' about it," said Pa.

"No, it ain't," Ma interrupted. "Make out like he's dead. You wouldn' say no bad things about Connie if he's dead."

Tom broke in, "Hey, what is this? We ain't sure Connie's gone for good. We got no time for talkin'. We got to eat an' get on our way."

"On our way? We jus' come here." Ma peered at him through the firelighted darkness.

He explained carefully, "They gonna burn the camp tonight, Ma. Now you know I ain't got it in me to stan' by an' see our stuff burn up, nor Pa ain't got it in him, nor Uncle John. We'd come up a-fightin', an' I jus' can't afford to be took in an' mugged. I nearly got it today, if the preacher hadn' jumped in."

Ma had been turning the frying potatoes in the hot grease. Now she took her decision. "Come on!" she cried. "Le's eat this stuff. We got to be quick." She set out the tin plates.

Pa said, "How 'bout John?"

"Where is Uncle John?" Tom asked.

Pa and Ma were silent for a moment, and then Pa said, "He went to get drunk."

"Jesus!" Tom said. "What a time he picked out! Where'd he go?"

"I don' know," said Pa.

Tom stood up. "Look," he said, "you all eat an' get
the stuff loaded. I'll go look for Uncle John. He'd of
went to the store 'crost the road."

Tom walked quickly away. The little cooking fires
burned in front of the tents and the shacks, and the
light fell on the faces of ragged men and women, on
crouched children. In a few tents the light of kerosene
lamps shone through the canvas and placed shadows of
people hugely on the cloth.

Tom walked up the dusty road and crossed the concrete highway to the little grocery store. He stood in
front of the screen door and looked in. The proprietor,
a little gray man with an unkempt mustache and watery eyes, leaned on the counter reading a newspaper.
His thin arms were bare and he wore a long white
apron. Heaped around and in back of him were
mounds, pyramids, walls of canned goods. He looked
up when Tom came in, and his eyes narrowed as
though he aimed a shotgun.

"Good evening," he said. "Run out of something?"

"Run out of my uncle," said Tom, "Or he run out,
or something."

The gray man looked puzzled and worried at the
same time. He touched the tip of his nose tenderly and
waggled it around to stop an itch. "Seems like you
people always lost somebody," he said. "Ten times a
day or more somebody comes in here an' says, 'If you
see a man named so an' so, an' looks like so an' so,
will you tell 'im we went up north?' Somepin like that
all the time."

Tom laughed. "Well, if you see a young snot-nose
name' Connie, looks a little bit like a coyote, tell 'im
to go to hell. We've went south. But he ain't the fella
I'm lookin' for. Did a fella 'bout sixty years ol', black
pants, sort of grayish hair, come in here an' get some
whisky?"

The eyes of the gray man brightened. "Now he sure
did. I never seen anything like it. He stood out front

an' he dropped his hat an' stepped on it. Here, I got his hat here." He brought the dusty broken hat from under the counter.

Tom took it from him. "That's him, all right."

"Well, sir, he got a couple pints of whisky an' he didn' say a thing. He pulled the cork an' tipped up the bottle. I ain't got a license to drink here. I says, 'Look, you can't drink here. You got to go outside.' Well, sir! He jus' stepped outside the door, an' I bet he didn't tilt up that pint more'n four times till it was empty. He throwed it away an' he leaned in the door. Eyes kinda dull. He says, 'Thank you, sir,' an' he went on. I never seen no drinkin' like that in my life."

"Went on? Which way? I got to get him."

"Well, it so happens I can tell you. I never seen such drinkin', so I looked out after him. He went north; an' then a car come along an' lighted him up, an' he went down the bank. Legs was beginnin' to buckle a little. He got the other pint open awready. He won't be far—not the way he was goin'."

Tom said, "Thank ya. I got to find him."

"You want ta take his hat?"

"Yeah! Yeah! He'll need it. Well, thank ya."

"What's the matter with him?" the gray man asked. "He wasn't takin' pleasure in his drink."

"Oh, he's kinda—moody. Well, good night. An' if you see that squirt Connie, tell 'im we've went south."

"I got so many people to look out for an' tell stuff to, I can't ever remember 'em all."

"Don't put yourself out too much," Tom said. He went out the screen door carrying Uncle John's dusty black hat. He crossed the concrete road and walked along the edge of it. Below him in the sunken field, the Hooverville lay; and the little fires flickered and the lanterns shone through the tents. Somewhere in the camp a guitar sounded, slow chords, struck without any sequence, practice chords. Tom stopped and listened, and then he moved slowly along the side of the

road, and every few steps he stopped to listen again.
He had gone a quarter of a mile before he heard what
he listened for. Down below the embankment the
sound of a thick, tuneless voice, singing drably. Tom
cocked his head, the better to hear.

And the dull voice sang, "I've give my heart to
Jesus, so Jesus take me home. I've give my soul to
Jesus, so Jesus is my home." The song trailed off to a
murmur, and then stopped. Tom hurried down from
the embankment, toward the song. After a while he
stopped and listened again. And the voice was close
this time, the same slow, tuneless singing, "Oh, the
night that Maggie died, she called me to her side, an'
give to me them ol' red flannel drawers that Maggie
wore. They was baggy at the knees———"

Tom moved cautiously forward. He saw the black
form sitting on the ground, and he stole near and sat
down. Uncle John tilted the pint and the liquor gurgled out of the neck of the bottle.

Tom said quietly, "Hey, wait! Where do I come in?"

Uncle John turned his head, "Who you?"

"You forgot me awready? You had four drinks to my
one."

"No, Tom. Don' try fool me. I'm all alone here. You
ain't been here."

"Well, I'm sure here now. How 'bout givin' me a
snort?"

Uncle John raised the pint again and the whisky
gurgled. He shook the bottle. It was empty. "No
more," he said. "Wanta die so bad. Wanta die awful.
Die a little bit. Got to. Like sleepin'. Die a little bit.
So tar'd. Tar'd. Maybe—don' wake up no more." His
voice crooned off. "Gonna wear a crown—a golden
crown."

Tom said, "Listen here to me, Uncle John. We're
gonna move on. You come along, an' you can go right
to sleep up on the load."

John shook his head. "No. Go on. Ain't goin'.

Gonna res' here. No good goin' back. No good to no-body—jus' a-draggin' my sins like dirty drawers 'mongst nice folks. No. Ain't goin'."

"Come on. We can't go 'less you go."

"Go ri' 'long. I ain't no good. I ain't no good. Jus' a-draggin' my sins, a-dirtyin' ever'body."

"You got no more sin'n anybody else."

John put his head close, and he winked one eye wisely. Tom could see his face dimly in the starlight. "Nobody don' know my sins, nobody but Jesus. He knows."

Tom got down on his knees. He put his hand on Uncle John's forehead, and it was hot and dry. John brushed his hand away clumsily.

"Come on," Tom pleaded. "Come on now, Uncle John."

"Ain't goin' go. Jus' tar'd. Gon' res' ri' here. Ri' here."

Tom was very close. He put his fist against the point of Uncle John's chin. He made a small practice arc twice, for distance; and then, with his shoulder in the swing, he hit the chin a delicate perfect blow. John's chin snapped up and he fell backwards and tried to sit up again. But Tom was kneeling over him and as John got one elbow up Tom hit him again. Uncle John lay still on the ground.

Tom stood up and, bending, he lifted the loose sagging body and boosted it over his shoulder. He staggered under the loose weight. John's hanging hands tapped him on the back as he went, slowly, puffing up the bank to the highway. Once a car came by and lighted him with the limp man over his shoulder. The car slowed for a moment and then roared away.

Tom was panting when he came back to Hooverville, down from the road and to the Joad truck. John was coming to; he struggled weakly. Tom set him gently down on the ground.

Camp had been broken while he was gone. Al

passed bundles up on the truck. The tarpaulin lay ready to bind over the load.

Al said, "He sure got a quick start."

Tom apologized. "I had to hit 'im a little to make 'im come. Poor fella."

"Didn' hurt 'im?" Ma asked.

"Don' think so. He's a-comin' out of it."

Uncle John was weakly sick on the ground. His spasms of vomiting came in little gasps.

Ma said, "I lef' a plate a potatoes for you, Tom."

Tom chuckled. "I ain't just in the mood right now."

Pa called, "Awright, Al. Sling up the tarp."

The truck was loaded and ready. Uncle John had gone to sleep. Tom and Al boosted and pulled him up on the load while Winfield made a vomiting noise behind the truck and Ruthie plugged her mouth with her hand to keep from squealing.

"Awready," Pa said.

Tom asked, "Where's Rosasharn?"

"Over there," said Ma. "Come on, Rosasharn. We're a-goin'."

The girl sat still, her chin sunk on her breast. Tom walked over to her. "Come on," he said.

"I ain't a-goin'." She did not raise her head.

"You got to go."

"I want Connie. I ain't a-goin' till he comes back."

Three cars pulled out of the camp, up the road to the highway, old cars loaded with the camps and the people. They clanked up to the highway and rolled away, their dim lights glancing along the road.

Tom said, "Connie'll find us. I lef' word up at the store where we'd be. He'll find us."

Ma came up and stood beside him. "Come on, Rosasharn. Come on, honey," she said gently.

"I wanta wait."

"We can't wait." Ma leaned down and took the girl by the arm and helped her to her feet.

"He'll find us," Tom said. "Don' you worry. He'll find us." They walked on either side of the girl.

"Maybe he went to get them books to study up," said Rose of Sharon. "Maybe he was a-gonna surprise us."

Ma said, "Maybe that's jus' what he done." They led her to the truck and helped her up on top of the load, and she crawled under the tarpaulin and disappeared into the dark cave.

Now the bearded man from the weed shack came timidly to the truck. He waited about, his hands clutched behind his back. "You gonna leave any stuff a fella could use?" he asked at last.

Pa said, "Can't think of nothin'. We ain't got nothin' to leave."

Tom asked, "Ain't ya gettin' out?"

For a long time the bearded man stared at him. "No," he said at last.

"But they'll burn ya out."

The unsteady eyes dropped to the ground. "I know. They done it before."

"Well, why the hell don't ya get out?"

The bewildered eyes looked up for a moment, and then down again, and the dying firelight was reflected redly. "I don't know. Takes so long to git stuff together."

"You won't have nothin' if they burn ya out."

"I know. You ain't leavin' nothin' a fella could use?"

"Cleaned out, slick," said Pa. The bearded man vaguely wandered away. "What's a matter with him?" Pa demanded.

"Cop-happy," said Tom. "Fella was sayin'—he's bull-simple. Been beat over the head too much."

A second little caravan drove past the camp and climbed to the road and moved away.

"Come on, Pa. Let's go. Look here, Pa. You an' me an' Al ride in the seat. Ma can get on the load. No.

Ma, you ride in the middle. Al"—Tom reached under
the seat and brought out a big monkey wrench—"Al,
you get up behind. Take this here. Jus' in case. If
anybody tries to climb up—let 'im have it."

Al took the wrench and climbed up the back board,
and he settled himself cross-legged, the wrench in his
hand. Tom pulled the iron jack handle from under the
seat and laid it on the floor, under the brake pedal.
"Awright," he said. "Get in the middle, Ma."

Pa said, "I ain't got nothin' in my han'."

"You can reach over an' get the jack handle," said
Tom. "I hope to Jesus you don' need it." He stepped
on the starter and the clanking flywheel turned over,
the engine caught and died, and caught again. Tom
turned on the lights and moved out of the camp in low
gear. The dim lights fingered the road nervously. They
climbed up to the highway and turned south. Tom
said, "They comes a time when a man gets mad."

Ma broke in, "Tom—you tol' me—you promised me
you wasn't like that. You promised."

"I know, Ma. I'm a-tryin'. But them deputies— Did
you ever see a deputy that didn' have a fat ass? An'
they waggle their ass an' flop their gun aroun'. Ma,"
he said, "if it was the law they was workin' with, why,
we could take it. But it *ain't* the law. They're a-workin'
away at our spirits. They're a-tryin' to make us cringe
an' crawl like a whipped bitch. They tryin' to break
us. Why, Jesus Christ, Ma, they comes a time when
the on'y way a fella can keep his decency is by takin' a
sock at a cop. They're workin' on our decency."

Ma said, "You promised, Tom. That's how Pretty
Boy Floyd done. I knowed his ma. They hurt him."

"I'm a-tryin', Ma. Honest to God, I am. You don'
want me to crawl like a beat bitch, with my belly on
the groun', do you?"

"I'm a-prayin'. You got to keep clear, Tom. The
fambly's breakin' up. You got to keep clear."

"I'll try, Ma. But when one a them fat asses gets to

workin' me over, I got a big job tryin'. If it was the law, it'd be different. But burnin' the camp ain't the law."

The car jolted along. Ahead, a little row of red lanterns stretched across the highway.

"Detour, I guess," Tom said. He slowed the car and stopped it, and immediately a crowd of men swarmed about the truck. They were armed with pick handles and shotguns. They wore trench helmets and some American Legion caps. One man leaned in the window, and the warm smell of whisky preceded him.

"Where you think you're goin'?" He thrust a red face near to Tom's face.

Tom stiffened. His hand crept down to the floor and felt for the jack handle. Ma caught his arm and held it powerfully. Tom said, "Well—" and then his voice took on a servile whine. "We're strangers here," he said. "We heard about they's work in a place called Tulare."

"Well, goddamn it, you're goin' the wrong way. We ain't gonnna have no goddamn Okies in this town."

Tom's shoulders and arms were rigid, and a shiver went through him. Ma clung to his arm. The front of the truck was surrounded by the armed men. Some of them, to make a military appearance, wore tunics and Sam Browne belts.

Tom whined, "Which way is it at, mister?"

"You turn right around an' head north. An' don't come back till the cotton's ready."

Tom shivered all over. "Yes, sir," he said. He put the car in reverse, backed around and turned. He headed back the way he had come. Ma released his arm and patted him softly. And Tom tried to restrain his hard smothered sobbing.

"Don' you mind," Ma said. "Don' you mind."

Tom blew his nose out the window and wiped his eyes on his sleeve. "The sons-of-bitches——"

"You done good," Ma said tenderly. "You done jus' good."

Tom swerved into a side dirt road, ran a hundred
yards, and turned off his light and motor. He got out of
the car, carrying the jack handle.

"Where you goin'?" Ma demanded.

"Jus' gonna look. We ain't goin' north." The red
lanterns moved up the highway. Tom watched them
cross the entrance of the dirt road and continue on. In
a few moments there came the sounds of shouts and
screams, and then a flaring light arose from the direction of the Hooverville. The light grew and spread, and
from the distance came a crackling sound. Tom got in
the truck again. He turned around and ran up the dirt
road without lights. At the highway he turned south
again, and he turned on his lights.

Ma asked timidly, "Where we goin', Tom?"

"Goin' south," he said. "We couldn' let them bastards push us aroun'. We couldn'. Try to get aroun' the
town 'thout goin' through it."

"Yeah, but where we goin'?" Pa spoke for the first
time. "That's what I want ta know."

"Gonna look for that gov'ment camp," Tom said. "A
fella said they don' let no deputies in there. Ma—I got
to get away from 'em. I'm scairt I'll kill one."

"Easy, Tom." Ma soothed him. "Easy, Tommy. You
done good once. You can do it again."

"Yeah, an' after a while I won't have no decency
lef'."

"Easy," she said. "You got to have patience. Why,
Tom—us people will go on livin' when all them
people is gone. Why, Tom, we're the people that live.
They ain't gonna wipe us out. Why, we're the people—we go on."

"We take a beatin' all the time."

"I know." Ma chuckled. "Maybe that makes us
tough. Rich fellas come up an' they die, an' their kids
ain't no good, an' they die out. But, Tom, we keep
a-comin'. Don' you fret none, Tom. A different time's
comin'."

"How do you know?"

"I don' know how."

They entered the town and Tom turned down a side street to avoid the center. By the street lights he looked at his mother. Her face was quiet and a curious look was in her eyes, eyes like the timeless eyes of a statue. Tom put out his right hand and touched her on the shoulder. He had to. And then he withdrew his hand. "Never heard you talk so much in my life," he said.

"Wasn't never so much reason," she said.

He drove through the side streets and cleared the town, and then he crossed back. At an intersection the sign said "99." He turned south on it.

"Well, anyways they never shoved us north," he said. "We still go where we want, even if we got to crawl for the right."

The dim lights felt along the broad black highway ahead.

21

The moving, questing people were migrants now. Those families which had lived on a little piece of land, who had lived and died on forty acres, had eaten or starved on the produce of forty acres, had now the whole West to rove in. And they scampered about, looking for work; and the highways were streams of people, and the ditch banks were lines of people. Behind them more were coming. The great highways streamed with moving people. There in the Middle- and Southwest had lived a simple agrarian folk who had not changed with industry, who had not farmed with machines or known the power and danger of machines in private hands. They had not grown up in the paradoxes of industry. Their senses were still sharp to the ridiculousness of the industrial life.

And then suddenly the machines pushed them out and they swarmed on the highways. The movement changed them; the highways, the camps along the road, the fear of hunger and the hunger itself, changed them. The children without dinner changed them, the endless moving changed them. They were migrants. And the hostility changed them, welded them, united them—hostility that made the little towns group and arm as though to repel an invader, squads with pick handles, clerks and storekeepers with shotguns, guarding the world against their own people.

In the West there was panic when the migrants multiplied on the highways. Men of property were terrified for their property. Men who had never been hungry saw the eyes of the hungry. Men who had never wanted anything very much saw the flare of want in the eyes of the migrants. And the men of the towns and of the soft suburban country gathered to defend themselves; and they reassured themselves that they were good and the invaders bad, as a man must do before he fights. They said, These goddamned Okies are dirty and ignorant. They're degenerate, sexual maniacs. These goddamned Okies are thieves. They'll steal anything. They've got no sense of property rights.

And the latter was true, for how can a man without property know the ache of ownership? And the defending people said, They bring disease, they're filthy. We can't have them in the schools. They're strangers. How'd you like to have your sister go out with one of 'em?

The local people whipped themselves into a mold of cruelty. Then they formed units, squads, and armed them—armed them with clubs, with gas, with guns. We own the country. We can't let these Okies get out of hand. And the men who were armed did not own the land, but they thought they did. And the clerks who drilled at night owned nothing, and the little storekeepers possessed only a drawerful of debts. But even a debt is something, even a job is something. The clerk thought, I get fifteen dollars a week. S'pose a goddamn Okie would work for twelve? And the little storekeeper thought, How could I compete with a debtless man?

And the migrants streamed in on the highways and their hunger was in their eyes, and their need was in their eyes. They had no argument, no system, nothing but their numbers and their needs. When there was work for a man, ten men fought for it—fought with a low wage. If that fella'll work for thirty cents, I'll work for twenty-five.

If he'll take twenty-five, I'll do it for twenty.

No, me, I'm hungry. I'll work for fifteen. I'll work for food. The kids. You ought to see them. Little boils, like, comin' out, an' they can't run aroun'. Give 'em some windfall fruit, an' they bloated up. Me. I'll work for a little piece of meat.

And this was good, for wages went down and prices stayed up. The great owners were glad and they sent out more handbills to bring more people in. And wages went down and prices stayed up. And pretty soon now we'll have serfs again.

And now the great owners and the companies invented a new method. A great owner bought a cannery. And when the peaches and the pears were ripe he cut the price of fruit below the cost of raising it. And as cannery owner he paid himself a low price for the fruit and kept the price of canned goods up and took his profit. And the little farmers who owned no canneries lost their farms, and they were taken by the great owners, the banks, and the companies who also owned the canneries. As time went on, there were fewer farms. The little farmers moved into town for a while and exhausted their credit, exhausted their friends, their relatives. And then they too went on the highways. And the roads were crowded with men ravenous for work, murderous for work.

And the companies, the banks worked at their own doom and they did not know it. The fields were fruitful, and starving men moved on the roads. The granaries were full and the children of the poor grew up rachitic, and the pustules of pellagra swelled on their sides. The great companies did not know that the line between hunger and anger is a thin line. And money that might have gone to wages went for gas, for guns, for agents and spies, for blacklists, for drilling. On the highways the people moved like ants and searched for work, for food. And the anger began to ferment.

22

It was late when Tom Joad drove along a country road looking for the Weedpatch camp. There were few lights in the countryside. Only a sky glare behind showed the direction of Bakersfield. The truck jiggled slowly along and hunting cats left the road ahead of it. At a crossroad there was a little cluster of white wooden buildings.

Ma was sleeping in the seat and Pa had been silent and withdrawn for a long time.

Tom said, "I don't know where she is. Maybe we'll wait till daylight an' ast somebody." He stopped at a boulevard signal and another car stopped at the crossing. Tom leaned out. "Hey, mister. Know where the big camp is at?"

"Straight ahead."

Tom pulled across into the opposite road. A few hundred yards, and then he stopped. A high wire fence faced the road, and a wide-gated driveway turned in. A little way inside the gate there was a small house with a light in the window. Tom turned in. The whole truck leaped into the air and crashed down again.

"Jesus!" Tom said. "I didn' even see that hump."

A watchman stood up from the porch and walked to the car. He leaned on the side. "You hit her too fast," he said. "Next time you'll take it easy."

"What is it, for God's sake?"

The watchman laughed. "Well, a lot of kids play in here. You tell folks to go slow and they're liable to forget. But let 'em hit that hump once and they don't forget."

"Oh! Yeah. Hope I didn' break nothin'. Say—you got any room here for us?"

"Got one camp. How many of you?"

Tom counted on his fingers. "Me an' Pa an' Ma, Al an' Rosasharn an' Uncle John an' Ruthie an' Winfiel'. Them last is kids."

"Well, I guess we can fix you. Got any camping stuff?"

"Got a big tarp an' beds."

The watchman stepped up on the running board. "Drive down the end of that line an' turn right. You'll be in Number Four Sanitary Unit."

"What's that?"

"Toilets and showers and wash tubs."

Ma demanded, "You got wash tubs—running water?"

"Sure."

"Oh! Praise God," said Ma.

Tom drove down the long dark row of tents. In the sanitary building a low light burned. "Pull in here," the watchman said. "It's a nice place. Folks that had it just moved out."

Tom stopped the car. "Right there?"

"Yeah. Now you let the others unload while I sign you up. Get to sleep. The camp committee'll call on you in the morning and get you fixed up."

Tom's eyes drew down. "Cops?" he asked.

The watchman laughed. "No cops. We got our own cops. Folks here elect their own cops. Come along."

Al dropped off the truck and walked around. "Gonna stay here?"

"Yeah," said Tom. "You an' Pa unload while I go to the office."

"Be kinda quiet," the watchman said. "They's a lot of folks sleeping."

Tom followed through the dark and climbed the office steps and entered a tiny room containing an old desk and a chair. The guard sat down at the desk and took out a form.

"Name?"

"Tom Joad."

"That your father?"

"Yeah."

"His name?"

"Tom Joad, too."

The questions went on. Where from, how long in the State, what work done. The watchman looked up. "I'm not nosy. We got to have this stuff."

"Sure," said Tom.

"Now—got any money?"

"Little bit."

"You ain't destitute?"

"Got a little. Why?"

"Well, the camp site costs a dollar a week, but you can work it out, carrying garbage, keeping the camp clean—stuff like that."

"We'll work it out," said Tom.

"You'll see the committee tomorrow. They'll show you how to use the camp and tell you the rules."

Tom said, "Say—what is this? What committee is this, anyways?"

The watchman settled himself back. "Works pretty nice. There's five sanitary units. Each one elects a Central Committee man. Now that committee makes the laws. What they say goes."

"S'pose they get tough," Tom said.

THE GRAPES OF WRATH 369

"Well, you can vote 'em out jus' as quick as you vote 'em in. They've done a fine job. Tell you what they did—you know the Holy Roller preachers all the time follow the people around, preachin' an' takin' up collections? Well, they wanted to preach in this camp. And a lot of the older folks wanted them. So it was up to the Central Committee. They went into meeting and here's how they fixed it. They say, 'Any preacher can preach in this camp. Nobody can take up a collection in this camp.' And it was kinda sad for the old folks, 'cause there hasn't been a preacher in since."

Tom laughed and then he asked, "You mean to say the fellas that runs the camp is jus' fellas—camping here?"

"Sure. And it works."

"You said about cops———"

"Central Committee keeps order an' makes rules. Then there's the ladies. They'll call on your ma. They keep care of kids an' look after the sanitary units. If your ma isn't working, she'll look after kids for the ones that is working, an' when she gets a job—why, there'll be others. They sew, and a nurse comes out an' teaches 'em. All kinds of things like that."

"You mean to say they ain't no cops?"

"No, sir. No cop can come in here without a warrant."

"Well, s'pose a fella is jus' mean, or drunk an' quarrelsome. What then?"

The watchman stabbed the blotter with a pencil. "Well, the first time the Central Committee warns him. And the second time they really warn him. The third time they kick him out of the camp."

"God Almighty, I can't hardly believe it! Tonight the deputies an' them fellas with the little caps, they burned the camp out by the river."

"They don't get in here," the watchman said. "Some

nights the boys patrol the fences, 'specially dance nights."

"Dance nights? Jesus Christ!"

"We got the best dances in the county every Saturday night."

"Well, for Christ's sake! Why ain't they more places like this?"

The watchman looked sullen. "You'll have to find that out yourself. Go get some sleep."

"Good night," said Tom. "Ma's gonna like this place. She ain't been treated decent for a long time."

"Good night," the watchman said. "Get some sleep. This camp wakes up early."

Tom walked down the street between the rows of tents. His eyes grew used to the starlight. He saw that the rows were straight and that there was no litter about the tents. The ground of the street had been swept and sprinkled. From the tents came the snores of sleeping people. The whole camp buzzed and snorted. Tom walked slowly. He neared Number Four Sanitary Unit and he looked at it curiously, an unpainted building, low and rough. Under a roof, but open at the sides, the rows of wash trays. He saw the Joad truck standing near by, and went quietly toward it. The tarpaulin was pitched and the camp was quiet. As he drew near a figure moved from the shadow of the truck and came toward him.

Ma said softly, "That you, Tom?"

"Yeah."

"Sh!" she said. "They're all asleep. They was tar'd out."

"You ought to be asleep too," Tom said.

"Well, I wanted to see ya. Is it awright?"

"It's nice," Tom said. "I ain't gonna tell ya. They'll tell ya in the mornin'. Ya gonna like it."

She whispered, "I heard they got hot water."

"Yeah. Now you get to sleep. I don't know when you slep' las'."

She begged, "What ain't you a-gonna tell me?"

"I ain't. You get to sleep."

Suddenly she seemed girlish. "How can I sleep if I got to think about what you ain't gonna tell me?"

"No, you don't," Tom said. "First thing in the mornin' you get on your other dress an' then—you'll find out."

"I can't sleep with nothin' like that hangin' over me."

"You got to," Tom chuckled happily. "You jus' got to."

"Good night," she said softly; and she bent down and slipped under the dark tarpaulin.

Tom climbed up over the tail-board of the truck. He lay down on his back on the wooden floor and he pillowed his head on his crossed hands, and his forearms pressed against his ears. The night grew cooler. Tom buttoned his coat over his chest and settled back again. The stars were clear and sharp over his head.

It was still dark when he awakened. A small clashing noise brought him up from sleep. Tom listened and heard again the squeak of iron on iron. He moved stiffly and shivered in the morning air. The camp still slept. Tom stood up and looked over the side of the truck. The eastern mountains were blue-black, and as he watched, the light stood up faintly behind them, colored at the mountain rims with a washed red, then growing colder, grayer, darker, as it went up overhead, until at a place near the western horizon it merged with pure night. Down in the valley the earth was the lavender-gray of dawn.

The clash of iron sounded again. Tom looked down the line of tents, only a little lighter gray than the ground. Beside a tent he saw a flash of orange fire seeping from the cracks in an old iron stove. Gray smoke spurted up from a stubby smoke-pipe.

Tom climbed over the truck side and dropped to the ground. He moved slowly toward the stove. He saw a girl working about the stove, saw that she carried a baby on her crooked arm, and that the baby was nursing, its head up under the girl's shirtwaist. And the girl moved about, poking the fire, shifting the rusty stove lids to make a better draft, opening the oven door; and all the time the baby sucked, and the mother shifted it deftly from arm to arm. The baby didn't interfere with her work or with the quick gracefulness of her movements. And the orange fire licked out of the stove cracks and threw flickering reflections on the tent.

Tom moved closer. He smelled frying bacon and baking bread. From the east the light grew swiftly. Tom came near to the stove and stretched out his hands to it. The girl looked at him and nodded, so that her two braids jerked.

"Good mornin'," she said, and she turned the bacon in the pan.

The tent flap jerked up and a young man came out and an older man followed him. They were dressed in new blue dungarees and in dungaree coats, stiff with filler, the brass buttons shining. They were sharp-faced men, and they looked much alike. The younger man had a dark stubble beard and the older man a white stubble beard. Their heads and faces were wet, their hair dripped, water stood in drops on their stiff beards. Their cheeks shone with dampness. Together they stood looking quietly into the lightening east. They yawned together and watched the light on the hill rims. And then they turned and saw Tom.

"Mornin'," the older man said, and his face was neither friendly nor unfriendly.

"Mornin'," said Tom.

And, "Mornin'," said the younger man.

The water slowly dried on their faces. They came to the stove and warmed their hands at it.

The girl kept to her work. Once she set the baby down and tied her braids together in back with a string, and the two braids jerked and swung as she worked. She set tin cups on a big packing box, set tin plates and knives and forks out. Then she scooped bacon from the deep grease and laid it on a tin platter, and the bacon cricked and rustled as it grew crisp. She opened the rusty oven door and took out a square pan full of big high biscuits.

When the smell of the biscuits struck the air both of the men inhaled deeply. The younger said, "Kee-rist!" softly.

Now the older man said to Tom, "Had your breakfast?"

"Well, no, I ain't. But my folks is over there. They ain't up. Need the sleep."

"Well, set down with us, then. We got plenty— thank God!"

"Why, thank ya," Tom said. "Smells so darn good I couldn't say no."

"Don't she?" the younger man asked. "Ever smell anything so good in ya life?" They marched to the packing box and squatted around it.

"Workin' around here?" the young man asked.

"Aim to," said Tom. "We jus' got in las' night. Ain't had no chance to look aroun'."

"We had twelve days' work," the young man said.

The girl, working by the stove, said, "They even got new clothes." Both men looked down at their stiff blue clothes, and they smiled a little shyly. The girl set out the platter of bacon and the brown, high biscuits and a bowl of bacon gravy and a pot of coffee, and then she squatted down by the box too. The baby still nursed, its head up under the girl's shirtwaist.

They filled their plates, poured bacon gravy over the biscuits, and sugared their coffee.

The older man filled his mouth full, and he chewed and chewed and gulped and swallowed. "God Almighty, it's good!" he said, and he filled his mouth again.

The younger man said, "We been eatin' good for twelve days now. Never missed a meal in twelve days—none of us. Workin' an' gettin' our pay an' eatin'." He fell to again, almost frantically, and re-filled his plate. They drank the scalding coffee and threw the grounds to the earth and filled their cups again.

There was color in the light now, a reddish gleam. The father and son stopped eating. They were facing to the east and their faces were lighted by the dawn. The image of the mountain and the light coming over it were reflected in their eyes. And then they threw the grounds from their cups to the earth, and they stood up together.

"Got to git goin'," the older man said.

The younger turned to Tom. "Lookie," he said. "We're layin' some pipe. 'F you want to walk over with us, maybe we could get you on."

Tom said, "Well, that's mighty nice of you. An' I sure thank ya for the breakfast."

"Glad to have you," the older man said. "We'll try to git you workin' if you want."

"Ya goddamn right I want," Tom said. "Jus' wait a minute. I'll tell my folks." He hurried to the Joad tent and bent over and looked inside. In the gloom under the tarpaulin he saw the lumps of sleeping figures. But a little movement started among the bed-clothes. Ruthie came wriggling out like a snake, her hair down over her eyes and her dress wrinkled and twisted. She crawled carefully out and stood up. Her gray eyes were clear and calm from sleep, and mis-chief was not in them. Tom moved off from the tent and beckoned her to follow, and when he turned, she looked up at him.

"Lord God, you're growin' up," he said.

She looked away in sudden embarrassment. "Listen here," Tom said. "Don't you wake nobody up, but when they get up, you tell 'em I got a chancet at a job, an' I'm a-goin' for it. Tell Ma I et breakfas' with some neighbors. You hear that?"

Ruthie nodded and turned her head away, and her eyes were little girl's eyes. "Don't you wake 'em up," Tom cautioned. He hurried back to his new friends. And Ruthie cautiously approached the sanitary unit and peeked in the open doorway.

The two men were waiting when Tom came back. The young woman had dragged a mattress out and put the baby on it while she cleaned up the dishes.

Tom said, "I wanted to tell my folks where-at I was. They wasn't awake." The three walked down the street between the tents.

The camp had begun to come to life. At the new fires the women worked, slicing meat, kneading the dough for the morning's bread. And the men were stirring about the tents and about the automobiles. The sky was rosy now. In front of the office a lean old man raked the ground carefully. He so dragged his rake that the tine marks were straight and deep.

"You're out early, Pa," the young man said as they went by.

"Yep, yep. Got to make up my rent."

"Rent, hell!" the young man said. "He was drunk last Sat'dy night. Sung in his tent all night. Committee give him work for it." They walked along the edge of the oiled road; a row of walnut trees grew beside the way. The sun shoved its edge over the mountains.

Tom said, "Seems funny. I've et your food, an' I aint tol' you my name—nor you ain't mentioned yours. I'm Tom Joad."

The older man looked at him, and then he smiled a little. "You ain't been out here long?"

"Hell, no! Jus' a couple days."

"I knowed it. Funny, you git outa the habit a mentionin' your name. They's so goddamn many. Jist fellas. Well, sir—I'm Timothy Wallace, an' this here's my boy Wilkie."

"Proud to know ya," Tom said. "You been out here long?"

"Ten months," Wilkie said. "Got here right on the tail a the floods las' year. Jesus! We had *a* time, *a* time! Goddamn near starve' to death." Their feet rattled on the oiled road. A truckload of men went by, and each man was sunk into himself. Each man braced himself in the truck bed and scowled down.

"Goin' out for the Gas Company," Timothy said. "They got a nice job of it."

"I could of took our truck," Tom suggested.

"No." Timothy leaned down and picked up a green walnut. He tested it with his thumb and then shied it at a blackbird sitting on a fence wire. The bird flew up, let the nut sail under it, and then settled back on the wire and smoothed its shining feathers with its beak.

Tom asked, "Ain't you got no car?"

Both Wallaces were silent, and Tom, looking at their faces, saw that they were ashamed.

Wilkie said, "Place we work at is on'y a mile up the road."

Timothy said angrily, "No, we ain't got no car. We sol' our car. Had to. Run outa food, run outa ever'thing. Couldn' git no job. Fellas come aroun' ever' week, buying cars. Come aroun', an' if you're hungry, why, they'll buy your car. An' if you're hungry enough, they don't hafta pay nothin' for it. An'— we was hungry enough. Give us ten dollars for her." He spat into the road.

Wilkie said quietly, "I was in Bakersfiel' las' week. I seen her—a-settin' in a use'-car lot—settin' right there, an' seventy-five dollars was the sign on her."

"We had to," Timothy said. "It was either us let 'em

steal our car or us steal somepin from them. We ain't had to steal yet, but, goddamn it, we been close!"

Tom said, "You know, 'fore we lef' home, we heard they was plenty work out here. Seen han'bills askin' folks to come out."

"Yeah," Timothy said. "We seen 'em too. An' they ain't much work. An' wages is comin' down all a time. I git so goddamn tired jus' figgerin' how to eat."

"You got work now," Tom suggested.

"Yeah, but it ain't gonna las' long. Workin' for a nice fella. Got a little place. Works 'longside of us. But, hell—it ain't gonna las' no time."

Tom said, "Why in hell you gonna git me on? I'll make it shorter. What you cuttin' your own throat for?"

Timothy shook his head slowly. "I dunno. Got no sense, I guess. We figgered to get us each a hat. Can't do it, I guess. There's the place, off to the right there. Nice job, too. Gettin' thirty cents an hour. Nice frien'ly fella to work for."

They turned off the highway and walked down a graveled road, through a small kitchen orchard; and behind the trees they came to a small white farm house, a few shade trees, and a barn; behind the barn a vineyard and a field of cotton. As the three men walked past the house a screen door banged, and a stocky sunburned man came down the back steps. He wore a paper sun helmet, and he rolled up his sleeves as he came across the yard. His heavy sunburned eyebrows were drawn down in a scowl. His cheeks were sunburned a beef red.

"Mornin', Mr. Thomas," Timothy said.

"Morning." The man spoke irritably.

Timothy said, "This here's Tom Joad. We wondered if you could see your way to put him on?"

Thomas scowled at Tom. And then he laughed shortly, and his brows still scowled. "Oh, sure! I'll put him on. I'll put everybody on. Maybe I'll get a hundred men on."

"We jus' thought—" Timothy began apologetically.

Thomas interrupted him. "Yes, I been thinkin' too." He swung around and faced them. "I've got some things to tell you. I been paying you thirty cents an hour—that right?"

"Why, sure, Mr. Thomas—but——"

"And I been getting thirty cents' worth of work." His heavy hard hands clasped each other.

"We try to give a good day of work."

"Well, goddamn it, this morning you're getting twenty-five cents an hour, and you take it or leave it." The redness of his face deepened with anger.

Timothy said, "We've give you good work. You said so yourself."

"I know it. But it seems like I ain't hiring my own men any more." He swallowed. "Look," he said. "I got sixty-five acres here. Did you ever hear of the Farmers' Association?"

"Why, sure."

"Well, I belong to it. We had a meeting last night. Now, do you know who runs the Farmers' Association? I'll tell you. The Bank of the West. That bank owns most of this valley, and it's got paper on everything it don't own. So last night the member from the bank told me, he said, 'You're paying thirty cents an hour. You'd better cut it down to twenty-five.' I said, 'I've got good men. They're worth thirty.' And he says, 'It isn't that,' he says. 'The wage is twenty-five now. If you pay thirty, it'll only cause unrest. And by the way,' he says, 'you going to need the usual amount for a crop loan next year?' " Thomas stopped. His breath was panting through his lips. "You see? The rate is twenty-five cents—and like it."

"We done good work," Timothy said helplessly.

"Ain't you got it yet? Mr. Bank hires two thousand men an' I hire three. I've got paper to meet. Now if you can figure some way out, by Christ, I'll take it! They got me."

Timothy shook his head. "I don't know what to say."

"You wait here." Thomas walked quickly to the house. The door slammed after him. In a moment he was back, and he carried a newspaper in his hand. "Did you see this? Here, I'll read it: 'Citizens, angered at red agitators, burn squatters' camp. Last night a band of citizens, infuriated at the agitation going on in a local squatters' camp, burned the tents to the ground and warned agitators to get out of the county.'"

Tom began, "Why, I——" and then he closed his mouth and was silent.

Thomas folded the paper carefully and put it in his pocket. He had himself in control again. He said quietly, "Those men were sent out by the Association. Now I'm giving 'em away. And if they ever find out I told, I won't have a farm next year."

"I jus' don't know what to say," Timothy said. "If they was agitators, I can see why they was mad."

Thomas said, "I watched it a long time. There's always red agitators just before a pay cut. Always. Goddamn it, they got me trapped. Now, what are you going to do? Twenty-five cents?"

Timothy looked at the ground. "I'll work," he said.

"Me too," said Wilkie.

Tom said, "Seems like I walked into somepin. Sure, I'll work. I got to work.

Thomas pulled a bandanna out of his hip pocket and wiped his mouth and chin. "I don't know how long it can go on. I don't know how you men can feed a family on what you get now."

"We can while we work," Wilkie said. "It's when we don't git work."

Thomas looked at his watch. "Well, let's go out and dig some ditch. By God," he said, "I'm a-gonna tell you. You fellas live in that government camp, don't you?"

Timothy stiffened. "Yes, sir."

"And you have dances every Saturday night?"

Wilkie smiled. "We sure do."

"Well, look out next Saturday night."

Suddenly Timothy straightened. He stepped close. "What you mean? I belong to the Central Committee. I got to know."

Thomas looked apprehensive. "Don't you ever tell I told."

"What is it?" Timothy demanded.

"Well, the Association don't like the government camps. Can't get a deputy in there. The people make their own laws, I hear, and you can't arrest a man without a warrant. Now if there was a big fight and maybe shooting—a bunch of deputies could go in and clean out the camp."

Timothy had changed. His shoulders were straight and his eyes cold. "What you mean?"

"Don't you ever tell where you heard," Thomas said uneasily. "There's going to be a fight in the camp Saturday night. And there's going to be deputies ready to go in."

Tom demanded, "Why for God's sake? Those folks ain't bothering nobody "

"I'll tell you why," Thomas said. "Those folks in the camp are getting used to being treated like humans. When they go back to the squatters' camps they'll be hard to handle." He wiped his face again. "Go on out to work now. Jesus, I hope I haven't talked myself out of my farm. But I like you people."

Timothy stepped in front of him and put out a hard lean hand, and Thomas took it. "Nobody won't know who tol'. We thank you. They won't be no fight."

"Go on to work," Thomas said. "And it's twenty-five cents an hour."

"We'll take it," Wilkie said, "from you."

Thomas walked away toward the house. "I'll be out in a piece," he said. "You men get to work." The screen door slammed behind him.

The three men walked out past the little white-washed barn, and along a field edge. They came to a long narrow ditch with sections of concrete pipe lying beside it.

"Here's where we're a-workin'," Wilkie said.

His father opened the barn and passed out two picks and three shovels. And he said to Tom, "Here's your beauty."

Tom hefted the pick. "Jumping Jesus! If she don't feel good!"

"Wait'll about 'leven o'clock," Wilkie suggested. "See how good she feels then."

They walked to the end of the ditch. Tom took off his coat and dropped it on the dirt pile. He pushed up his cap and stepped into the ditch. Then he spat on his hands. The pick arose into the air and flashed down. Tom grunted softly. The pick rose and fell, and the grunt came at the moment it sank into the ground and loosened the soil.

Wilkie said, "Yes, sir, Pa, we got here a first-grade muck-stick man. This here boy been married to that there little digger."

Tom said, "I put in time (*umph*). Yes, sir, I sure did (*umph*). Put in my years (*umph!*). Kinda like the feel (*umph!*)." The soil loosened ahead of him. The sun cleared the fruit trees now and the grape leaves were golden green on the vines. Six feet along and Tom stepped aside and wiped his forehead. Wilkie came behind him. The shovel rose and fell and the dirt flew out to the pile beside the lengthening ditch.

"I heard about this here Central Committee," said Tom. "So you're one of 'em."

"Yes, sir," Timothy replied. "And it's a responsibility. All them people. We're doin' our best. An' the people in the camp a-doin' their best. I wisht them big farmers wouldn' plague us so. I wisht they wouldn'."

Tom climbed back into the ditch and Wilkie stood

aside. Tom said, "How 'bout this fight (*umph!*) at the dance, he tol' about (*umph*)? What they wanta do that for?"

Timothy followed behind Wilkie, and Timothy's shovel beveled the bottom of the ditch and smoothed it ready for the pipe. "Seems like they got to drive us," Timothy said. "They're scairt we'll organize, I guess. An' maybe they're right. This here camp is a organization. People there look out for theirselves. Got the nicest strang band in these parts. Got a little charge account in the store for folks that's hungry. Fi' dollars—you can git that much food an' the camp'll stan' good. We ain't never had no trouble with the law. I guess the big farmers is scairt of that. Can't throw us in jail—why, it scares 'em. Figger maybe if we can gove'n ourselves, maybe we'll do other things."

Tom stepped clear of the ditch and wiped the sweat out of his eyes. "You hear what the paper said 'bout agitators up north a Bakersfiel'?"

"Sure," said Wilkie. "They do that all a time."

"Well, I was there. They wasn't no agitators. What they call reds. What the hell is these reds anyways?"

Timothy scraped a little hill level in the bottom of the ditch. The sun made his white bristle beard shine. "They's a lot a fellas wanta know what reds is." He laughed. "One of our boys foun' out." He patted the piled earth gently with his shovel. "Fella named Hines—got 'bout thirty thousan' acres, peaches, and grapes—got a cannery an' a winery. Well, he's all a time talkin' about 'them goddamn reds.' 'Goddamn reds is drivin' the country to ruin,' he says, an' 'We got to drive these here red bastards out.' Well, they were a young fella jus' come out west here, an' he's listenin' one day. He kinda scratched his head an' he says, 'Mr. Hines, I ain't been here long. What is these goddamn reds?' Well, sir, Hines says, 'A red is any son-of-a-bitch that wants thirty cents an hour when we're payin' twenty-five!' Well, this young fella he thinks about her, an' he scratches his head, an' he says, 'Well, Jesus, Mr. Hines. I ain't a son-of-a-bitch, but if that's what a red is—why, I want thirty cents an hour. Ever'body does. Hell, Mr. Hines, we're all reds.' " Timothy drove his shovel along the ditch bottom, and the solid earth shone where the shovel cut it.

Tom laughed. "Me too, I guess." His pick arced up and drove down, and the earth cracked under it. The sweat rolled down his forehead and down the sides of his nose, and it glistened on his neck. "Damn it," he said, "a pick is a nice tool (*umph*), if you don't fight it (*umph*). You an' the pick (*umph*) workin' together (*umph*)."

In line, the three men worked, and the ditch inched along, and the sun shone hotly down on them in the growing morning.

When Tom left her, Ruthie gazed in at the door of the sanitary unit for a while. Her courage was not strong without Winfield to boast for. She put a bare foot in on the concrete floor, and then withdrew it. Down the line a woman came out of a tent and started a fire in a tin camp stove. Ruthie took a few steps in that direction, but she could not leave. She crept to the entrance of the Joad tent and looked in. On one side, lying on the ground, lay Uncle John, his mouth open and his snores bubbling spittily in his throat. Ma and Pa were covered with a comfort, their heads in, away from the light. Al was on the far side from Uncle John, and his arm was flung over his eyes. Near the front of the tent Rose of Sharon and Winfield lay, and there was the space where Ruthie had been, beside Winfield. She squatted down and peered in. Her eyes remained on Winfield's tow head; and as she looked, the little boy opened his eyes and stared out at her, and his eyes were solemn. Ruthie put her finger to her lips and beckoned with her other hand. Winfield rolled his eyes over to Rose of Sharon. Her pink flushed face was near to him, and her mouth was open a little. Winfield carefully loosened the blanket and slipped out. He crept out of the tent cautiously and joined Ruthie. "How long you been up?" he whispered.

She led him away with elaborate caution, and when they were safe, she said, "I never been to bed. I was up all night."

"You was not," Winfield said. "You're a dirty liar."

"Awright," she said. "If I'm a liar I ain't gonna tell you nothin' that happened. I ain't gonna tell you how the fella got killed with a stab knife an' how they was a bear come in an' took off a little chile."

"They wasn't no bear," Winfield said uneasily. He brushed up his hair with his fingers and he pulled down his overalls at the crotch.

"All right—they wasn't no bear," she said sarcastically. "An' they ain't no white things made outa dish-stuff, like in the catalogues."

Winfield regarded her gravely. He pointed to the sanitary unit. "In there?" he asked.

"I'm a dirty liar," Ruthie said. "It ain't gonna do me no good to tell stuff to you."

"Le's go look," Winfield said.

"I already been," Ruthie said. "I already set on 'em. I even pee'd in one."

"You never neither," said Winfield.

They went to the unit building, and that time Ruthie was not afraid. Boldly she led the way into the building. The toilets lined one side of the large room, and each toilet had its compartment with a door in front of it. The porcelain was gleaming white. Hand basins lined another wall, while on the third wall were four shower compartments.

"There," said Ruthie. "Them's the toilets. I seen 'em in the catalogue." The children drew near to one of the toilets. Ruthie, in a burst of bravado, boosted her skirt and sat down. "I tol' you I been here," she said. And to prove it, there was a tinkle of water in the bowl.

Winfield was embarrassed. His hand twisted the flushing lever. There was a roar of water. Ruthie leaped into the air and jumped away. She and Winfield stood in the middle of the room and looked at the toilet. The hiss of water continued in it.

"You done it," Ruthie said. "You went an' broke it. I seen you."

"I never. Honest I never."

"I seen you," Ruthie said. "You jus' ain't to be trusted with no nice stuff."

Winfield sunk his chin. He looked up at Ruthie and his eyes filled with tears. His chin quivered. And Ruthie was instantly contrite.

"Never you mind," she said. "I won't tell on you. We'll pretend like she was already broke. We'll pretend we ain't even been in here." She led him out of the building.

The sun lipped over the mountain by now, shone on the corrugated-iron roofs of the five sanitary units, shone on the gray tents and on the swept ground of the streets between the tents. And the camp was waking up. The fires were burning in camp stoves, in the stoves made of kerosene cans and of sheets of metal. The smell of smoke was in the air. Tent flaps were thrown back and people moved about in the streets. In front of the Joad tent Ma stood looking up and down the street. She saw the children and came over to them.

"I was worryin'," Ma said. "I didn' know where you was."

"We was jus' lookin'," Ruthie said.

"Well, where's Tom? You seen him?"

Ruthie became important. "Yes, ma'am. Tom, he got me up an' he tol' me what to tell you." She paused to let her importance be apparent.

"Well—what?" Ma demanded.

"He said tell you—" She paused again and looked to see that Winfield appreciated her position.

Ma raised her hand, the back of it toward Ruthie. "What?"

"He got work," said Ruthie quickly. "Went out to work." She looked apprehensively at Ma's raised hand. The hand sank down again, and then it reached out for Ruthie. Ma embraced Ruthie's shoulders in a quick convulsive hug, and then released her.

Ruthie stared at the ground in embarrassment, and changed the subject. "They got toilets over there," she said. "White ones."

"You been in there?" Ma demanded.

"Me an' Winfiel'," she said; and then, treacherously, "Winfiel', he bust a toilet."

Winfield turned red. He glared at Ruthie. "She pee'd in one," he said viciously.

Ma was apprehensive. "Now what did you do? You show me." She forced them to the door and inside. "Now what'd you do?"

Ruthie pointed. "It was a-hissin' and a-swishin'. Stopped now."

"Show me what you done," Ma demanded.

Winfield went reluctantly to the toilet. "I didn't push it hard," he said. "I jus' had aholt of this here, an'—" The swish of water came again. He leaped away.

Ma threw back her head and laughed, while Ruthie and Winfield regarded her resentfully. "Tha's the way she works," Ma said. "I seen them before. When you finish, you push that."

The shame of their ignorance was too great for the children. They went out the door, and they walked down the street to stare at a large family eating breakfast.

Ma watched them out of the door. And then she looked about the room. She went to the shower closets and looked in. She walked to the wash basins and ran her finger over the white porcelain. She turned the water on a little and held her finger in the stream, and jerked her hand away when the water came hot. For a moment she regarded the basin, and then, setting the plug, she filled the bowl a little from the hot faucet, a little from the cold. And then she washed her hands in the warm water, and she washed her face. She was brushing water through her hair with her fingers when a step sounded on the concrete floor behind her. Ma swung around. An elderly man stood looking at her with an expression of righteous shock.

He said harshly, "How you come in here?"

Ma gulped, and she felt the water dripping from her chin and soaking through her dress. "I didn' know," she said apologetically. "I thought this here was for folks to use."

The elderly man frowned on her. "For men folks," he said sternly. He walked to the door and pointed to a sign on it: MEN. "There," he said. "That proves it. Didn' you see that?"

"No," Ma said in shame, "I never seen it. Ain't they a place where I can go?"

The man's anger departed. "You jus' come?" he asked more kindly.

"Middle of the night," said Ma.

"Then you ain't talked to the Committee?"

"What committee?"

"Why, the Ladies' Committee."

"No, I ain't."

He said proudly, "The Committee'll call on you purty soon an' fix you up. We take care of folks that jus' come in. Now, if you want a ladies' toilet, you jus' go on the other side of the building. That side's yourn."

Ma said uneasily, "Ya say a ladies' committee— comin' to my tent?"

He nodded his head. "Purty soon, I guess."

"Thank ya," said Ma. She hurried out, and half ran to the tent.

"Pa," she called. "John, git up! You, Al. Git up an' git washed." Startled sleepy eyes looked out at her. "All of you," Ma cried. "You git up an' git your face washed. An' comb your hair."

Uncle John looked pale and sick. There was a red bruised place on his chin.

Pa demanded, "What's the matter?"

"The Committee," Ma cried. "They's a committee— a ladies' committee a-comin' to visit. Git up now, an' git washed. An' while we was a-sleepin' an' a-snorin', Tom's went out an' got work. Git up, now."

They came sleepily out of the tent. Uncle John staggered a little, and his face was pained.

"Git over to that house and wash up," Ma ordered. "We got to get breakfus' an' be ready for the Committee." She went to a little pile of split wood in the camp lot. She started a fire and put up her cooking irons. "Pone," she said to herself. "Pone an' gravy. That's quick. Got to be quick." She talked on to herself, and Ruthie and Winfield stood by, wondering.

The smoke of the morning fires arose all over the camp, and the mutter of talk came from all sides.

Rose of Sharon, unkempt and sleepy-eyed, crawled out of the tent. Ma turned from the cornmeal she was measuring in fistfuls. She looked at the girl's wrinkled dirty dress, at her frizzled uncombed hair. "You got to clean up," she said briskly. "Go right over and clean up. You got a clean dress. I washed it. Git your hair combed. Git the seeds out a your eyes." Ma was excited.

Rose of Sharon said sullenly, "I don' feel good. I

wisht Connie would come. I don't feel like doin' nothin' 'thout Connie."

Ma turned full around on her. The yellow cornmeal clung to her hands and wrists. "Rosasharn," she said sternly, "you git upright. You jus' been mopin' enough. They's a ladies' committee a-comin', an' the fambly ain't gonna be frawny when they get here."

"But I don' feel good."

Ma advanced on her, mealy hands held out. "Git," Ma said. "They's times when how you feel got to be kep' to yourself."

"I'm a-goin' to vomit," Rose of Sharon whined.

"Well, go an' vomit. 'Course you're gonna vomit. Ever'body does. Git it over an' then you clean up, an' you wash your legs an' out on them shoes of yourn." She turned back to her work. "An' braid your hair," she said.

A frying pan of grease sputtered over the fire, and it splashed and hissed when Ma dropped the pone in with a spoon. She mixed flour with grease in a kettle and added water and salt and stirred the gravy. The coffee began to turn over in the gallon can, and the smell of coffee rose from it.

Pa wandered back from the sanitary unit, and Ma looked critically up. Pa said, "Ya say Tom's got work?"

"Yes, sir. Went out 'fore we was awake. Now look in that box an' get you some clean overhalls an' a shirt. An', Pa, I'm awful busy. You git in Ruthie an' Winfiel's ears. They's hot water. Will you do that? Scrounge aroun' in their ears good, an' their necks. Get 'em red an' shinin'."

"Never seen you so bubbly," Pa said.

Ma cried, "This here's the time the fambly got to get decent. Comin' acrost they wasn't no chancet. But now we can. Th'ow your dirty overhalls in the tent an' I'll wash 'em out."

Pa went inside the tent, and in a moment he came

out with pale blue, washed overalls and shirt on. And he led the sad and startled children toward the sanitary unit.

Ma called after him, "Scrounge aroun' good in their ears."

Uncle John came to the door of the men's side and looked out, and then he went back and sat on the toilet a long time and held his aching head in his hands.

Ma had taken up a panload of brown pone and was dropping spoons of dough in the grease for a second pan when a shadow fell on the ground beside her. She looked over her shoulder. A little man dressed all in white stood behind her—a man with a thin, brown, lined face and merry eyes. He was lean as a picket. His white clean clothes were frayed at the seams. He smiled at Ma. "Good morning," he said.

Ma looked at his white clothes and her face hardened with suspicion. "Mornin'," she said.

"Are you Mrs. Joad?"

"Yes."

"Well, I'm Jim Rawley. I'm camp manager. Just dropped by to see if everything's all right. Got everything you need?"

Ma studied him suspiciously. "Yes," she said.

Rawley said, "I was asleep when you came last night. Lucky we had a place for you." His voice was warm.

Ma said simply, "It's nice. 'Specially them wash tubs."

"You wait till the women get to washing. Pretty soon now. You never heard such a fuss. Like a meeting. Know what they did yesterday, Mrs. Joad? They had a chorus. Singing a hymn tune and rubbing the clothes all in time. That was something to hear, I tell you."

The suspicion was going out of Ma's face. "Must a been nice. You're the boss?"

"No," he said. "The people here worked me out of a job. They keep the camp clean, they keep order, they do everything. I never saw such people. They're making clothes in the meeting hall. And they're making toys. Never saw such people."

Ma looked down at her dirty dress. "We ain't clean yet," she said. "You jus' can't keep a clean a-travelin'."

"Don't I know it," he said. He sniffed the air. "Say—is that your coffee smells so good?"

Ma smiled. "Does smell nice, don't it? Outside it always smells nice." And she said proudly, "We'd take it in honor 'f you'd have some breakfus' with us."

He came to the fire and squatted on his hams, and the last of Ma's resistance went down. "We'd be proud to have ya," she said. "We ain't got much that's nice, but you're welcome."

The little man grinned at her. "I had my breakfast. But I'd sure like a cup of that coffee. Smells so good."

"Why—why, sure."

"Don't hurry yourself."

Ma poured a tin cup of coffee from the gallon can. She said, "We ain't got sugar yet. Maybe we'll get some today. If you need sugar, it won't taste good."

"Never use sugar," he said. "Spoils the taste of good coffee."

"Well, I like a little sugar," said Ma. She looked at him suddenly and closely, to see how he had come so close so quickly. She looked for motive on his face, and found nothing but friendliness. Then she looked at the frayed seams on his white coat, and she was reassured.

He sipped the coffee. "I guess the ladies'll be here to see you this morning."

"We ain't clean," Ma said. "They shouldn't be comin' till we get cleaned up a little."

"But they know how it is," the manager said. "They came in the same way. No, sir. The committees are good in this camp because they do know." He finished his coffee and stood up. "Well, I got to go on. Anything you want, why, come over to the office. I'm there all the time. Grand coffee. Thank you." He put the cup on the box with the others, waved his hand, and walked down the line of tents. And Ma heard him speaking to the people as he went.

Ma put down her head and she fought with a desire to cry.

Pa came back leading the children, their eyes still wet with pain at the ear-scrounging. They were subdued and shining. The sunburned skin on Winfield's nose was scrubbed off. "There," Pa said. "Got dirt an' two layers a skin. Had to almost lick 'em to make 'em stan' still."

Ma appraised them. "They look nice," she said. "He'p yaself to pone an' gravy. We got to get stuff outta the way an' the tent in order."

Pa served plates for the children and for himself. "Wonder where Tom got work?"

"I dunno."

"Well, if he can, we can."

Al came excitedly to the tent. "What a place!" he said. He helped himself and poured coffee. "Know what a fella's doin'? He's buildin' a house trailer. Right over there, back a them tents. Got beds an' a stove— ever'thing. Jus' live in her. By God, that's the way to live! Right where you stop—tha's where you live."

Ma said, "I ruther have a little house. Soon's we can, I want a little house."

Pa said, "Al—after we've et, you an' me an' Uncle John'll take the truck an' go out lookin' for work."

"Sure," said Al. "I like to get a job in a garage if they's any jobs. Tha's what I really like. An' get me a little ol' cut-down Ford. Paint her yella an' go a-kyoodlin' aroun'. Seen a purty girl down the road. Give her a big wink, too. Purty as hell, too."

Pa said sternly, "You better get some work 'fore you go a-tom-cattin'."

Uncle John came out of the toilet and moved slowly near. Ma frowned at him.

"You ain't washed—" she began, and then she saw how sick and weak and sad he looked. "You go on in the tent an' lay down," she said. "You ain't well."

He shook his head. "No," he said. "I sinned, an' I got to take my punishment." He squatted down disconsolately and poured himself a cup of coffee.

Ma took the last pones from the pan. She said casually, "The manager of the camp come an' set an' had a cup a coffee."

Pa looked over slowly. "Yeah? What's he want awready?"

"Jus' come to pass the time," Ma said daintily. "Jus' set down an' had coffee. Said he didn' get good coffee so often, an' smelt our'n."

"What'd he want?" Pa demanded again.

"Didn' want nothin'. Come to see how we was gettin' on."

"I don' believe it," Pa said. "He's probably a-snootin' an' a-smellin' aroun'."

"He was not!" Ma cried angrily. "I can tell a fella that's snootin' aroun' quick as the nex' person."

Pa tossed his coffee grounds out of his cup.

"You got to quit that," Ma said. "This here's a clean place."

"You see she don't get so goddamn clean a fella can't live in her," Pa said jealously. "Hurry up, Al. We're goin' out lookin' for a job."

Al wiped his mouth with his hand. "I'm ready," he said.

Pa turned to Uncle John. "You a-comin'?"

"Yes, I'm a-comin'."

"You don't look so good."

"I ain't so good, but I'm comin'."

Al got in the truck. "Have to get gas," he said. He started the engine. Pa and Uncle John climbed in beside him and the truck moved away down the street.

Ma watched them go. And then she took a bucket

and went to the wash trays under the open part of the sanitary unit. She filled her bucket with hot water and carried it back to her camp. And she was washing the dishes in the bucket when Rose of Sharon came back.

"I put your stuff on a plate," Ma said. And then she looked closely at the girl. Her hair was dripping and combed, and her skin was bright and pink. She had put on the blue dress printed with little white flowers. On her feet she wore the heeled slippers of her wedding. She blushed under Ma's gaze. "You had a bath," Ma said.

Rose of Sharon spoke huskily. "I was in there when a lady come in an' done it. Know what you do? You get in a little stall-like, an' you turn handles, an' water comes a-floodin' down on you—hot water or col' water, jus' like you want it—an' I done it!"

"I'm a-goin' to myself," Ma cried. "Jus' soon as I get finish' here. You show me how."

"I'm a-gonna do it ever'day," the girl said. "An' that lady—she seen me, an' she seen about the baby, an'—know what she said? Said they's a nurse comes ever' week. An' I'm to go see that nurse an' she'll tell me jus' what to do so's the baby'll be strong. Says all the ladies here do that. An' I'm a-gonna do it." The words bubbled out. "An'—know what—? Las' week they was a baby borned an' the whole camp give a party, an' they give clothes, an' they give stuff for the baby—even give a baby buggy—wicker one. Wasn't new, but they give it a coat a paint, an' it was jus' like new. An' they give the baby a name, an' had a cake. Oh, Lord!" She subsided, breathing heavily.

Ma said, "Praise God, we come home to our own people. I'm a-gonna have a bath."

"Oh, it's nice," the girl said.

Ma wiped the tin dishes and stacked them. She said, "We're Joads. We don't look up to nobody. Grampa's grampa, he fit in the Revolution. We was farm people till the debt. And then—them people. They done somepin to us. Ever' time they come seemed like they was a-whippin' me—all of us. An' in Needles, that police. He done somepin to me, made me feel mean. Made me feel ashamed. An' now I ain't ashamed. These folks is our folks—is our folks. An' that manager, he come an' set an' drank coffee, an' he says, 'Mrs. Joad' this, an' 'Mrs. Joad' that—an' 'How you gettin' on, Mrs. Joad?' " She stopped and sighed. "Why, I feel like people again." She stacked the last dish. She went into the tent and dug through the clothes box for her shoes and a clean dress. And she found a little paper package with her earrings in it. As she went past Rose of Sharon, she said, "If them ladies comes, you tell 'em I'll be right back." She disappeared around the side of the sanitary unit.

Rose of Sharon sat down heavily on a box and regarded her wedding shoes, black patent leather and tailored black bows. She wiped the toes with her finger and wiped her finger on the inside of her skirt. Leaning down put a pressure on her growing abdomen. She sat up straight and touched herself with exploring fingers, and she smiled a little as she did it.

Along the road a stocky woman walked, carrying an apple box of dirty clothes toward the wash tubs. Her face was brown with sun, and her eyes were black and intense. She wore a great apron, made from a cotton bag, over her gingham dress, and men's brown oxfords were on her feet. She saw that Rose of Sharon caressed herself, and she saw the little smile on the girl's face.

"So!" she cried and she laughed with pleasure. "What you think it's gonna be?"

Rose of Sharon blushed and looked down at the ground, and then peeked up, and the little shiny black eyes of the woman took her in. "I don' know," she mumbled.

The woman plopped the apple box on the ground. "Got a live tumor," she said, and she cackled like a happy hen. "Which'd you ruther?" she demanded.

"I dunno—boy, I guess. Sure—boy."

"You jus' come in, didn' ya?"

"Las' night—late."

"Gonna stay?"

"I don' know. 'F we can get work, guess we will."

A shadow crossed the woman's face, and the little black eyes grew fierce. " 'F you can git work. That's what we all say."

"My brother got a job already this mornin'."

"Did, huh? Maybe you're lucky. Look out for luck. You can't trus' luck." She stepped close. "You can only git one kind a luck. Cain't have more. You be a good girl," she said fiercely. "You be good. If you got sin on you—you better watch out for that there baby." She squatted down in front of Rose of Sharon. "They's scandalous things goes on in this here camp," she said darkly. "Ever' Sat'dy night they's dancin', an' not only squar' dancin', neither. They's some does clutch-an'-hug dancin'! I seen 'em."

Rose of Sharon said guardedly, "I like dancin', squar' dancin'." And she added virtuously, "I never done that other kind."

The brown woman nodded her head dismally. "Well, some does. An' the Lord ain't lettin' it get by, neither; an' don' you think He is."

"No, ma'am," the girl said softly.

The woman put one brown wrinkled hand on Rose of Sharon's knee, and the girl flinched under the touch. "You let me warn you now. They ain't but a few deep down Jesus-lovers lef'. Every' Sat'dy night when that there strang ban' starts up an' should be a-playin' hymnody, they're a-reelin'—yes, sir, a-reelin'. I seen 'em. Won' go near, myself, nor I don' let my kin go near. They's clutch-an'-hug, I tell ya." She paused for emphasis and then said, in a hoarse whisper, "They do more. They give a stage play." She backed away and cocked her head to see how Rose of Sharon would take such a revelation.

"Actors?" the girl said in awe.

"No, sir!" the woman exploded. "Not *actors*, not them already damn' people. Our own kinda folks. Our own people. An' they was little children didn' know no better, in it, an' they was pertendin' to be stuff they wasn't. I didn' go near. But I hearn 'em talkin' what they was a-doin'. The devil was jus' a-struttin' through this here camp."

Rose of Sharon listened, her eyes and mouth open. "Oncet in school we give a Chris' chile play—Christmus."

"Well—I ain' sayin' tha's bad or good. They's good folks thinks a Chris' chile is awright. But—well, I wouldn' care to come right out flat an' say so. But this here wasn' no Chris' chile. This here was sin an' delusion an' devil stuff. Struttin' an' paradin' an' speakin' like they're somebody they ain't. An' dancin' an' clutchin' an' a-huggin'."

Rose of Sharon sighed.

"An' not jus' a few, neither," the brown woman went on. "Gettin' so's you can almos' count the deep-down lamb-blood folks on your toes. An' don' you think them sinners is puttin' nothin' over on God, neither. No, sir, He's a-chalkin' 'em up sin by sin, an' He's drawin' His line an' addin' 'em up sin by sin. God's a-watchin', an' I'm a-watchin'. He's awready smoked two of 'em out."

Rose of Sharon panted, "Has?"

The brown woman's voice was rising in intensity. "I seen it. Girl a-carryin' a little one, jes' like you. An' she play-acted, an' she hug-danced. And"—the voice grew bleak and ominous—"she thinned out and she skinnied out, an'—she dropped that baby, dead."

"Oh, my!" The girl was pale.

"Dead and bloody. 'Course nobody wouldn't speak to her no more. She had a go away. Can't tech sin 'thout catchin' it. No, sir. An' they was another, done the same thing. An' she skinnied out, an'—know what? One night she was gone. An' two days, she's back. Says she was visitin'. But—she ain't got no baby. Know what I think? I think the manager, he took her away to drop her baby. He don' believe in sin. Tol' me hisself. Says the sin is bein' hungry. Says the sin is bein' cold. Says—I tell ya, he tol' me hisself—can't see God in them things. Says them girls skinnied out 'cause they didn' git 'nough food. Well, I fixed him up." She rose to her feet and stepped back. Her eyes were sharp. She pointed a rigid forefinger in Rose of Sharon's face. "I says, 'Git back!' I says. I says, 'I knowed the devil was rampagin' in this here camp. Now I know who the devil is. Git back, Satan,' I says. An', by Chris', he got back! Tremblin' he was, an' sneaky. Says, 'Please!' Says, 'Please don' make the folks unhappy.' I says, 'Unhappy? How 'bout their soul? How 'bout them dead babies an' them poor sinners ruint 'count of play-actin'?' He jes' looked, an' he give a sick grin an' went away. He knowed when he met a real testifier to the Lord. I says, 'I'm a-helpin' Jesus watch the goin's-on. An' you an' them other sinners ain't gittin' away with it.'" She picked up her box of dirty clothes. "You take heed. I warned you. You take heed a that pore chile in your belly an' keep outa sin." And she strode away titanically, and her eyes shone with virtue.

Rose of Sharon watched her go, and then she put her head down on her hands and whimpered into her palms. A soft voice sounded beside her. She looked up, ashamed. It was the little white-clad manager. "Don't worry," he said. "Don't you worry."

Her eyes blinded with tears. "But I done it," she cried. "I hug-danced. I didn' tell her. I done it in Sallisaw. Me an' Connie."

"Don't worry," he said.

"She says I'll drop the baby."

"I know she does. I kind of keep my eye on her. She's a good woman, but she makes people unhappy."

Rose of Sharon sniffled wetly. "She knowed two girls los' their baby right in this here camp."

The manager squatted down in front of her. "Look!" he said. "Listen to me. I know them too. They were too hungry and too tired. And they worked too hard. And they rode on a truck over bumps. They were sick. It wasn't their fault."

"But she said———"

"Don't worry. That woman likes to make trouble."

"But she says you was the devil."

"I know she does. That's because I won't let her make people miserable." He patted her shoulder. "Don't you worry. She doesn't know." And he walked quickly away.

Rose of Sharon looked after him; his lean shoulders jerked as he walked. She was still watching his slight figure when Ma came back, clean and pink, her hair combed and wet, and gathered in a knot. She wore her figured dress and the old cracked shoes; and the little earrings hung in her ears.

"I done it," she said. "I stood in there an' let warm water come a-floodin' an' a-flowin' down over me. An' they was a lady says you can do it ever' day if you want. An'—them ladies' committee come yet?"

"Uh-uh!" said the girl.

"An' you jus' set there an' didn' redd up the camp none!" Ma gathered up the tin dishes as she spoke. "We got to get in shape," she said. "Come on, stir! Get that sack and kinda sweep along the groun'." She picked up the equipment, put the pans in their box and the box in the tent. "Get them beds neat," she ordered. "I tell ya I ain't never felt nothin' so nice as that water."

Rose of Sharon listlessly followed orders. "Ya think Connie'll be back today?"

"Maybe—maybe not. Can't tell."

"You sure he knows where-at to come?"

"Sure."

"Ma—ya don' think—they could a killed him when they burned——?"

"Not him," Ma said confidently. "He can travel when he wants—jackrabbit-quick an' fox-sneaky."

"I wisht he'd come."

"He'll come when he comes."

"Ma——"

"I wisht you'd get to work."

"Well, do you think dancin' an' play-actin' is sins an'll make me drop the baby?"

Ma stopped her work and put her hands on her hips. "Now what you talkin' about? You ain't done no play-actin'."

"Well, some folks here done it, an' one girl, she dropped her baby—dead—an' bloody, like it was a judgment."

Ma stared at her. "Who tol' you?"

"Lady that come by. An' that little fella in white clothes, he come by an' he says that ain't what done it."

Ma frowned. "Rosasharn," she said, "you stop pickin' at yourself. You're jest a-teasin' yourself up to cry. I don' know what's come at you. Our folks ain't never did that. They took what come to 'em dry-eyed. I bet it's that Connie give you all them notions. He was jes' too big for his overhalls." And she said sternly, "Rosasharn, you're jest one person, an' they's a lot of other folks. You git to your proper place. I knowed people built theirself up with sin till they figgered they was big mean shucks in the sight a the Lord."

"But, Ma——"

"No. Jes' shut up an' git to work. You ain't big enough or mean enough to worry God much. An' I'm gonna give you the back a my han' if you don' stop this pickin' at your-self." She swept the ashes into the fire hole and brushed the stones on its edge. She saw the committee coming along the road. "Git workin'," she said. "Here's the ladies comin'. Git a-workin' now, so's I can be proud." She didn't look again, but she was conscious of the approach of the committee.

There could be no doubt that it was the committee; three ladies, washed, dressed in their best clothes: a lean woman with stringy hair and steel-rimmed glasses, a small stout lady with curly gray hair and a small sweet mouth, and a mammoth lady, big of hock and buttock, big of breast, muscled like a dray-horse, powerful and sure. And the committee walked down the road with dignity.

Ma managed to have her back turned when they arrived. They stopped, wheeled, stood in a line. And the great woman boomed, "Mornin', Mis' Joad, ain't it?"

Ma whirled around as though she had been caught off guard. "Why, yes—yes. How'd you know my name?"

"We're the committee," the big woman said. "Ladies' Committee of Sanitary Unit Number Four. We got your name in the office."

Ma flustered, "We ain't in very good shape yet. I'd be proud to have you ladies come an' set while I make up some coffee."

The plump committee woman said, "Give our names, Jessie. Mention our names to Mis' Joad. Jessie's the Chair," she explained.

Jessie said formally, "Mis' Joad, this here's Annie Littlefield an' Ella Summers, an' I'm Jessie Bullitt."

"I'm proud to make your acquaintance," Ma said. "Won't you set down? They ain't nothin' to set on yet," she added. "But I'll make up some coffee."

"Oh, no," said Annie formally. "Don't put yaself out. We jes' come to call an' see how you was, an' try to make you feel at home."

Jessie Bullitt said sternly, "Annie, I'll thank you to remember I'm Chair."

"Oh! Sure, sure. But next week I am."

"Well, you wait'll next week then. We change ever' week," she explained to Ma.

"Sure you wouldn' like a little coffee?" Ma asked helplessly.

"No, thank you." Jessie took charge. "We gonna show you 'bout the sanitary unit fust, an' then if you wanta, we'll sign you up in the Ladies' Club an' give you duty. 'Course you don' have to join."

"Does—does it cost much?"

"Don't cost nothing but work. An' when you're knowed, maybe you can be 'lected to this committee," Annie interupted. "Jessie, here, is on the committee for the whole camp. She's a big committee lady."

Jessie smiled with pride. " 'Lected unanimous," she said. "Well, Mis' Joad, I guess it's time we tol' you 'bout how the camp runs."

Ma said, "This here's my girl, Rosasharn."

"How do," they said.

"Better come 'long too."

The huge Jessie spoke, and her manner was full of dignity and kindness, and her speech was rehearsed.

"You shouldn' think we're a-buttin' into your business, Mis' Joad. This here camp got a lot of stuff ever'body uses. An' we got rules we made ourself. Now we're a-goin to the unit. That there, ever'body uses, an' ever'body got to take care of it." They strolled to the unroofed section where the wash trays were, twenty of them. Eight were in use, the women bending over, scrubbing the clothes, and the piles of wrung-out clothes were heaped on the clean concrete floor. "Now you can use these here any time you want," Jessie said. "The on'y thing is, you got to leave 'em clean."

The women who were washing looked up with interest. Jessie said loudly, "This here's Mis' Joad an' Rosasharn, come to live." They greeted Ma in a chorus, and Ma made a dumpy little bow at them and said, "Proud to meet ya." Jessie led the committee into the toilet and shower room.

"I been here awready," Ma said. "I even took a bath."

"That's what they're for," Jessie said. "An' they's the same rule. You got to leave 'em clean. Ever' week they's a new committee to swab out oncet a day. Maybe you'll git on that committee. You got to bring your own soap."

"We got to get some soap," Ma said. "We're all out."

Jessie's voice became almost reverential. "You ever used this here kind?" she asked, and pointed to the toilets.

"Yes, ma'am. Right this mornin'."

Jessie sighed. "Tha's good."

Ella Summers said, "Jes' las' week——"

Jessie interrupted sternly, "Mis' Summers—I'll tell."

Ella gave ground. "Oh, awright."

Jessie said, "Las' week, when you was Chair, you done it all. I'll thank you to keep out this week."

"Well, tell what that lady done," Ella said.

"Well," said Jessie, "it ain't this committee's business to go a-blabbin', but I won't pass no names. Lady comes in las' week, an' she got in here 'fore the committee got to her, an' she had her ol' man's pants in the toilet, an' she says, 'It's too low, an' it ain't big enough. Bust your back over her,' she says. 'Why couldn' they stick her higher?' " The committee smiled superior smiles.

Ella broke in, "Says, 'Can't put 'nough in at on-cet.'" And Ella weathered Jessie's stern glance.

Jessie said, "We got our troubles with toilet paper. Rule says you can't take none away from here." She clicked her tongue sharply. "Whole camp chips in for toilet paper." For a moment she was silent, and then she confessed. "Number Four is usin' more than any other. Somebody's a-stealin' it. Come up in general ladies' meetin'. 'Ladies' side, Unit Number Four is usin' too much.' Come right up in meetin'!"

Ma was following the conversation breathlessly. "Stealin' it—what for?"

"Well," said Jessie, "we had trouble before. Las' time they was three little girls cuttin' paper dolls out of it. Well, we caught them. But this time we don't know. Hardly put a roll out 'fore it's gone. Come right up in meetin'. One lady says we oughta have a little bell that rings ever' time the roll turns oncet. Then we could count how many ever'body takes." She shook her head. "I jes' don' know," she said. "I been worried all week. Somebody's a-stealin' toilet paper from Unit Four."

From the doorway came a whining voice, "Mis' Bul-litt." The committee turned. "Mis' Bullitt, I hearn what you says." A flushed perspiring woman stood in the doorway. "I couldn' git up in meetin', Mis' Bullitt. I jes' couldn'. They'd a-laughed or somepin."

"What you talkin' about?" Jessie advanced.

"Well, we-all—maybe—it's us. But we ain't a-stealin', Mis' Bullitt."

Jessie advanced on her, and the perspiration beaded out on the flustery confessor. "We can't he'p it, Mis' Bullitt."

"Now you tell what you're tellin'," Jessie said. "This here unit's suffered a shame 'bout that toilet paper."

"All week, Mis' Bullitt. We couldn' he'p it. You know I got five girls."

"What they been a-doin' with it?" Jessie demanded ominously.

"Jes' usin' it. Hones', jes' usin' it."

"They ain't got the right! Four-five sheets is enough. What's the matter'th 'em?"

The confessor bleated, "Skitters. All five of 'em. We been low on money. They et green grapes. They all five got the howlin' skitters. Run out ever' ten minutes." She defended them, "But they ain't stealin' it."

Jessie sighed. "You should a tol'," she said. "You got to tell. Here's Unit Four sufferin' shame 'cause you never tol'. Anybody can git the skitters."

The meek voice whined, "I jes' can't keep 'em from eatin' them green grapes. An' they're a-gettin' worse all a time."

Ella Summers burst out, "The Aid. She oughta git the Aid."

"Ella Summers," Jessie said, "I'm a-tellin' you for the las' time, you ain't the Chair." She turned back to the raddled little woman. "Ain't you got no money, Mis' Joyce?"

She looked ashamedly down. "No, but we might git work any time."

"Now you hol' up your head," Jessie said. "That ain't no crime. You jes' waltz right over t' the Weedpatch store an' git you some groceries. The camp got twenty dollars' credit there. You git yourself fi' dollars' worth. An' you kin pay it back to the Central Committee when you git work. Mis' Joyce, you knowed that," she said sternly. "How come you let your girls git hungry?"

"We ain't never took no charity," Mrs. Joyce said.

"This ain't charity, an' you know it," Jessie raged. "We had all that out. They ain't no charity in this here camp. We won't have no charity. Now you waltz right over an' git you some groceries, an' you bring the slip to me."

Mrs. Joyce said timidly, "S'pose we can't never pay? We ain't had work for a long time."

"You'll pay if you can. If you can't, that ain't none of our business, an' it ain't your business. One fella went away, an' two months later he sent back the money. You ain't got the right to let your girls git hungry in this here camp."

Mrs. Joyce was cowed. "Yes, ma'am," she said.

"Git you some cheese for them girls," Jessie ordered. "That'll take care a them skitters."

"Yes, ma'am." And Mrs. Joyce scuttled out of the door.

Jessie turned in anger on the committee. "She got no right to be stiff-necked. She got no right, not with our own people."

Annie Littlefield said, "She ain't been here long. Maybe she don't know. Maybe she's took charity one time-another. Nor," Annie said, "don't you try to shut me up, Jessie. I got a right to pass speech." She turned half to Ma. "If a body's ever took charity, it makes a burn that don't come out. This ain't charity, but if you ever took it, you don't forget it. I bet Jessie ain't ever done it."

"No, I ain't," said Jessie.

"Well, I did," Annie said. "Las' winter; an' we was a-starvin'—me an' Pa an' the little fellas. An' it was a-rainin'. Fella tol' us to go to the Salvation Army." Her eyes grew fierce. "We was hungry—they made us crawl for our dinner. They took our dignity. They—I hate 'em! An'—maybe Mis' Joyce took charity. Maybe she didn' know this ain't charity. Mis' Joad, we don't allow nobody in this camp to build theirself up that-a-way. We don't allow nobody to give nothing to another person. They can give it to the camp, an' the camp can pass it out. We won't have no charity!" Her voice was fierce and hoarse. "I hate 'em," she said. "I ain't never seen my man beat before, but them—them Salvation Army done it to 'im."

Jessie nodded. "I heard," she said softly, "I heard. We got to take Mis' Joad aroun'."

Ma said, "It sure is nice."

"Let's go to the sewin' room," Annie suggested. "Got two machines. They's a-quiltin', an' they're makin' dresses. You might like ta work over there."

When the committee called on Ma, Ruthie and Winfield faded imperceptibly back out of reach.

"Whyn't we go along an' listen?" Winfield asked.

Ruthie gripped his arm. "No," she said. "We got washed for them sons-a-bitches. I ain't goin' with 'em."

Winfield said, "You tol' on me 'bout the toilet. I'm a-gonna tell what you called them ladies."

A shadow of fear crossed Ruthie's face. "Don' do it. I tol' 'cause I knowed you didn't really break it."

"You did not," said Winfield.

Ruthie said, "Le's look aroun'." They strolled down the line of tents, peering into each one, gawking self-consciously. At the end of the unit there was a level place on which a croquet court had been set up. Half a dozen children played seriously. In front of a tent an elderly lady sat on a bench and watched. Ruthie and Winfield broke into a trot. "Leave us play," Ruthie cried. "Leave us get in."

The children looked up. A pig-tailed little girl said, "Nex' game you kin."

"I wanta play now," Ruthie cried.

"Well, you can't. Not till nex' game."

Ruthie moved menacingly out on the court. "I'm a-gonna play." The pig-tails gripped her mallet tightly. Ruthie sprang at her, slapped her, pushed her, and wrested the mallet from her hands. "I says I was gonna play," she said triumphantly.

The elderly lady stood up and walked onto the court. Ruthie scowled fiercely and her hands tightened on the mallet. The lady said, "Let her play—like you done with Ralph las' week."

The children laid their mallets on the ground and trooped silently off the court. They stood at a distance and looked on with expressionless eyes. Ruthie watched them go. Then she hit a ball and ran after it. "Come on, Winfiel'. Get a stick," she called. And then she looked in amazement. Winfield had joined the watching children, and he too looked at her with expressionless eyes. Defiantly she hit the ball again. She kicked up a great dust. She pretended to have a good time. And the children stood and watched. Ruthie lined up two balls and hit both of them, and she turned her back on the watching eyes, and then turned back. Suddenly she advanced on them, mallet in hand. "You come an' play," she demanded. They moved silently back at her approach. For a moment she stared at them, and then she flung down the mallet and ran crying for home. The children walked back on the court.

Pigtails said to Winfield, "You can git in the nex' game."

The watching lady warned them, "When she comes back an' wants to be decent, you let her. You was mean yourself, Amy." The game went on, while in the Joad tent Ruthie wept miserably.

The truck moved along the beautiful roads, past orchards where the peaches were beginning to color, past vineyards with the clusters pale and green, under lines of walnut trees whose branches spread half across the road. At each entrance-gate Al slowed; and at each gate there was a sign: "No help wanted. No trespassing."

Al said, "Pa, they's boun' to be work when them fruits gets ready. Funny place—they tell ya they ain't no work 'fore you ask 'em." He drove slowly on.

Pa said, "Maybe we could go in anyways an' ask if they know where they's any work. Might do that."

A man in blue overalls and a blue shirt walked along the edge of the road. Al pulled up beside him. "Hey, mister," Al said. "Know where they's any work?"

The man stopped and grinned, and his mouth was vacant of front teeth. "No," he said. "Do you? I been walkin' all week, an' I can't tree none."

"Live in that gov'ment camp?" Al asked.

"Yeah!"

"Come on, then. Git up back, an' we'll all look." The man climbed over the side-boards and dropped in the bed.

Pa said, "I ain't got no hunch we'll find work. Guess we got to look, though. We don't even know where-at to look."

"Shoulda talked to the fellas in the camp," Al said. "How you feelin', Uncle John?"

"I ache," said Uncle John. "I ache all over, an' I got it comin'. I oughta go away where I won't bring down punishment on my own folks."

Pa put his hand on John's knee. "Look here," he said, "don' you go away. We're droppin' folks all the time—Grampa an' Granma dead, Noah an' Connie—run out, an' the preacher—in jail."

"I got a hunch we'll see that preacher ag'in," John said.

Al fingered the ball on the gear-shift lever. "You don' feel good enough to have no hunches," he said. "The hell with it. Le's go back an' talk, an' find out where they's some work. We're jus' huntin' skunks under water." He stopped the truck and leaned out the window and called back, "Hey! Lookie! We're a-goin' back to the camp an' try an' see where they's work. They ain't no use burnin' gas like this."

The man leaned over the truck side. "Suits me," he said. "My dogs is wore clean up to the ankle. An' I ain't even got a nibble."

Al turned around in the middle of the road and headed back.

Pa said, "Ma's gonna be purty hurt, 'specially when Tom got work so easy."

"Maybe he never got none," Al said. "Maybe he jus' went lookin', too. I wisht I could get work in a garage. I'd learn that stuff quick, an' I'd like it."

Pa grunted, and they drove back toward the camp in silence.

When the committee left, Ma sat down on a box in front of the Joad tent, and she looked helplessly at Rose of Sharon. "Well—" she said, "well—I ain't been so perked up in years. *Wasn't* them ladies nice?"

"I get to work in the nursery," Rose of Sharon said. "They tol' me. I can find out all how to do for babies, an' then I'll know."

Ma nodded in wonder. "Wouldn' it be nice if the menfolks all got work?" she asked. "Them a-workin', an' a little money comin' in?" Her eyes wandered into space. "Them a-workin', an' us a-workin' here, an' all them nice people. Fust thing we get a little ahead I'd get me a little stove—nice one. They don' cost much. An' then we'd get a tent, big enough, an' maybe secon'-han' springs for the beds. An' we'd use this here tent jus' to eat under. An' Sat'dy night we'll go to the dancin'. They says you can invite folks if you want. I wisht we had some frien's to invite. Maybe the men'll know somebody to invite."

Rose of Sharon peered down the road. "That lady that says I'll lose the baby—" she began.

"Now you stop that," Ma warned her.

Rose of Sharon said softly, "I seen her. She's a-comin' here, I think. Yeah! Here she comes. Ma, don' let her——"

Ma turned and looked at the approaching figure.

"Howdy," the woman said. "I'm Mis' Sandry—Lisbeth Sandry. I seen your girl this mornin'."

"Howdy do," said Ma.

"Are you happy in the Lord?"

"Pretty happy," said Ma.

"Are you saved?"

"I been saved." Ma's face was closed and waiting.

"Well, I'm glad," Lisbeth said. "The sinners is awful strong aroun' here. You come to a awful place. They's wicketness all around about. Wicket people, wicket goin's-on that lamb'-blood Christians jes' can't hardly stan'. They's sinners all around us."

Ma colored a little, and shut her mouth tightly. "Seems to me they's nice people here," she said shortly.

Mrs. Sandry's eyes stared. "Nice!" she cried. "You think they're nice when they's dancin' an' huggin'? I tell ya, ya eternal soul ain't got a chance in this here camp. Went out to a meetin' in Weedpatch las' night. Know what the preacher says? He says, 'They's wicketness in that camp.' He says, 'The poor is tryin' to be rich.' He says, 'They's dancin' an' huggin' when they should be wailin' an' moanin' in sin.' That's what he says. 'Ever'body that ain't here is a black sinner,' he says. I tell you it made a person feel purty good to hear 'im. An' we knowed we was safe. We ain't danced."

Ma's face was red. She stood up slowly and faced Mrs. Sandry. "Git!" she said. "Git out now, 'fore I git to be a sinner a-tellin' you where to go. Git to your wailin' an' moanin'."

Mrs. Sandry's mouth dropped open. She stepped back. And then she became fierce. "I thought you was Christians."

"So we are," Ma said.

"No, you ain't. You're hell-burnin' sinners, all of you! An' I'll mention it in meetin', too. I can see your

black soul a-burnin'. I can see that innocent child in
that there girl's belly a-burnin'.' "

A low wailing cry escaped from Rose of Sharon's
lips. Ma stooped down and picked up a stick of wood.

"Git!" she said coldly. "Don' you never come back.
I seen your kind before. You'd take the little pleasure,
wouldn' you?" Ma advanced on Mrs. Sandry.

For a moment the woman backed away and then
suddenly she threw back her head and howled. Her
eyes rolled up, her shoulders and arms flopped loosely
at her side, and a string of thick ropy saliva ran from
the corner of her mouth. She howled again and again,
long deep animal howls. Men and women ran up from
the other tents, and they stood near—frightened and
quiet. Slowly the woman sank to her knees and the
howls sank to a shuddering, bubbling moan. She fell
sideways and her arms and legs twitched. The white
eyeballs showed under the open eyelids.

A man said softly, "The sperit. She got the sperit."
Ma stood looking down at the twitching form.

The little manager strolled up casually. "Trouble?"
he asked. The crowd parted to let him through. He
looked down at the woman. "Too bad," he said. "Will
some of you help get her back to her tent?" The silent
people shuffled their feet. Two men bent over and
lifted the woman, one held her under the arms and the
other took her feet. They carried her away, and the
people moved slowly after them. Rose of Sharon went
under the tarpaulin and lay down and covered her face
with a blanket.

The manager looked at Ma, looked down at the stick
in her hand. He smiled tiredly. "Did you clout her?"
he asked.

Ma continued to stare after the retreating people.
She shook her head slowly. "No—but I would a.
Twicet today she worked my girl up."

The manager said, "Try not to hit her. She isn't

well. She just isn't well." And he added softly, "I wish she'd go away, and all her family. She brings more trouble on the camp than all the rest together."

Ma got herself in hand again. "If she comes back, I might hit her. I ain't sure. I won't let her worry my girl no more."

"Don't worry about it, Mrs. Joad," he said. "You won't ever see her again. She works over the new-comers. She won't ever come back. She thinks you're a sinner."

"Well, I am," said Ma.

"Sure. Everybody is, but not the way she means. She isn't well, Mrs. Joad."

Ma looked at him gratefully, and she called, "You hear that, Rosasharn? She ain't well. She's crazy." But the girl did not raise her head. Ma said, "I'm warnin' you, mister. If she comes back, I ain't to be trusted. I'll hit her."

He smiled wryly. "I know how you feel," he said. "But just try not to. That's all I ask—just try not to." He walked slowly away toward the tent where Mrs. Sandry had been carried.

Ma went into the tent and sat down beside Rose of Sharon. "Look up," she said. The girl lay still. Ma gently lifted the blanket from her daughter's face. "That woman's kinda crazy," she said. "Don't you believe none of them things."

Rose of Sharon whispered in terror, "When she said about burnin', I—felt burnin'."

"That ain't true," said Ma.

"I'm tar'd out," the girl whispered. "I'm tar'd a things happenin'. I wanta sleep. I wanta sleep."

"Well, you sleep, then. This here's a nice place. You can sleep."

"But she might come back."

"She won't," said Ma. "I'm a-gonna set right outside, an' I won't let her come back. Res' up now,

'cause you got to get to work in the nu'sery purty
soon."

Ma struggled to her feet and went to sit in the entrance to the tent. She sat on a box and put her elbows
on her knees and her chin in her cupped hands. She
saw the movement in the camp, heard the voices of the
children, the hammering of an iron rim; but her eyes
were staring ahead of her.

Pa, coming back along the road, found her there,
and he squatted near her. She looked slowly over at
him. "Git work?" she asked.

"No," he said, ashamed. "We looked."

"Where's Al and John and the truck?"

"Al's fixin' somepin. Had ta borry some tools. Fella
says Al got to fix her there."

Ma said sadly, "This here's a nice place. We could
be happy here awhile."

"If we could get work."

"Yeah! If you could get work."

He felt her sadness, and studied her face. "What
you a-mopin' about? If it's sech a nice place why have
you got to mope?"

She gazed at him, and she closed her eyes slowly.
"Funny, ain't it. All the time we was a-movin' an'
shovin', I never thought none. An' now these here
folks been nice to me, been awful nice; an' what's the
first thing I do? I go right back over the sad things—
that night Grampa died an' we buried him. I was all
full up of the road, and bumpin' and movin', an' it
wasn't so bad. But now I come out here, an' it's worse
now. An' Granma—an' Noah walkin' away like that!
Walkin' away jus' down the river. Them things was
part of all, an' now they come a-flockin' back. Granma
a pauper, an' buried a pauper. That's sharp now.
That's awful sharp. An' Noah walkin' away down the
river. He don' know what's there. He jus' don' know.
An' we don' know. We ain't never gonna know if he's

alive or dead. Never gonna know. An' Connie sneakin' away. I didn' give 'em brain room before, but now they're a-flockin' back. An' I oughta be glad 'cause we're in a nice place." Pa watched her mouth while she talked. Her eyes were closed. "I can remember how them mountains was, sharp as ol' teeth beside the river where Noah walked. I can remember how the stubble was on the groun' where Grampa lies. I can remember the choppin' block back home with a feather caught on it, all criss-crossed with cuts, an' black with chicken blood."

Pa's voice took on her tone. "I seen the ducks to-day," he said. "Wedgin' south—high up. Seems like they're awful dinky. An' I seen the blackbirds a-settin' on the wires, an' the doves was on the fences." Ma opened her eyes and looked at him. He went on, "I seen a little whirlwin,' like a man a-spinnin' acrost a fiel'. An' the ducks drivin' on down, wedgin' on down to the southward."

Ma smiled. "Remember?" she said. "Remember what we'd always say at home? 'Winter's a-comin' early,' we said, when the ducks flew. Always said that, an' winter come when it was ready to come. But we always said, 'She's a-comin' early.' I wonder what we meant."

"I seen the blackbirds on the wires," said Pa. "Set-tin' so close together. An' the doves. Nothin' sets so still as a dove—on the fence wires—maybe two, side by side. An' this little whirlwin'—big as a man, an' dancin' off acrost a fiel'. Always did like the little fellas, big as a man."

"Wisht I wouldn't think how it is home," said Ma. "It ain't our home no more. Wisht I'd forget it. An' Noah."

"He wasn't ever right—I mean—well, it was my fault."

"I tol' you never to say that. Woudn' a lived at all, maybe."

"But I should a knowed more."

"Now stop," said Ma. "Noah was strange. Maybe he'll have a nice time by the river. Maybe it's better so. We can't do no worryin'. This here is a nice place, an' maybe you'll get work right off."

Pa pointed at the sky. "Look—more ducks. Big bunch. An' Ma, 'Winter's a-comin' early.' "

She chuckled. "They's things you do, an' you don' know why."

"Here's John," said Pa. "Come on an' set, John."

Uncle John joined them. He squatted down in front of Ma. "We didn' get nowheres," he said. "Jus' run aroun'. Say, Al wants to see ya. Says he got to git a tire. Only one layer a cloth lef', he says."

Pa stood up. "I hope he can git her cheap. We ain't got much lef'. Where is Al?"

"Down there, to the nex' cross-street an' turn right. Says gonna blow out an' spoil a tube if we don' get a new one." Pa strolled away, and his eyes followed the giant V of ducks down the sky.

Uncle John picked a stone from the ground and dropped it from his palm and picked it up again. He did not look at Ma. "They ain't no work," he said.

"You didn' look all over," Ma said.

"No, but they's signs out."

"Well, Tom musta got work. He ain't been back."

Uncle John suggested, "Maybe he went away—like Connie, or like Noah."

Ma glanced sharply at him, and then her eyes softened. "They's things you know," she said. "They's stuff you're sure of. Tom's got work, an' he'll come in this evenin'. That's true." She smiled in satisfaction. "Ain't he a fine boy!" she said. "Ain't he a good boy!"

The cars and trucks began to come into the camp, and the men trooped by toward the sanitary unit. And each man carried clean overalls and shirt in his hand.

Ma pulled herself together. "John, you go find Pa.

Get to the store. I want beans an' sugar an'—a piece of fryin' meat an' carrots an'—tell Pa to get somepin nice—anything—but nice—for tonight. Tonight— we'll have—somepin nice."

23

The migrant people, scuttling for work, scrabbling to live, looked always for pleasure, dug for pleasure, manufactured pleasure, and they were hungry for amusement. Sometimes amusement lay in speech, and they climbed up their lives with jokes. And it came about in the camps along the roads, on the ditch banks beside the streams, under the sycamores, that the story teller grew into being, so that the people gathered in the low firelight to hear the gifted ones. And they listened while the tales were told, and their participation made the stories great.

I was a recruit against Geronimo——

And the people listened, and their quiet eyes reflected the dying fire.

Them Injuns was cute—slick as snakes, an' quiet when they wanted. Could go through dry leaves, an' make no rustle. Try to do that sometime.

And the people listened and remembered the crash of dry leaves under their feet.

Come the change of season an' the clouds up. Wrong time. Ever hear of the army doing anything right? Give the army ten chances, an' they'll stumble along. Took three regiments to kill a hundred braves—always.

And the people listened, and their faces were quiet with listening. The story tellers, gathering attention into their tales, spoke in great rhythms, spoke in great words because the tales were great, and the listeners became great through them.

They was a brave on a ridge, against the sun. Knowed he stood out. Spread his arms an' stood. Naked as morning, an' against the sun. Maybe he was crazy. I don' know. Stood there, arms spread out; like a cross he looked. Four hundred yards. An' the men—well, they raised their sights an' they felt the wind with their fingers; an' then they jus' lay there an' couldn' shoot. Maybe that Injun knowed somepin. Knowed we couldn' shoot. Jes' laid there with the rifles cocked, an' didn' even put 'em to our shoulders. Lookin' at him. Head-band, one feather. Could see it, an' naked as the sun. Long time we laid there an' looked, an' he never moved. An' then the captain got mad. "Shoot, you crazy bastards, shoot!" he yells. An' we jus' laid there. "I'll give you to a five-count, an' then mark you down," the captain says. Well, sir—we put up our rifles slow, an' ever' man hoped some-body'd shoot first. I ain't never been so sad in my life. An' I laid my sights on his belly, 'cause you can't stop a Injun no other place—an'—then. Well, he jest plunkered down an' rolled. An' we went up. An' he wasn' big—he'd looked so grand—up there. All tore to pieces an' little. Ever see a cock pheasant, stiff and beautiful, ever' feather drawed an' painted, an' even his eyes drawed in pretty? An' bang! You pick him up—bloody an' twisted, an' you spoiled somepin better'n you; an' eatin' him don't never make it up to you, 'cause you spoiled somepin in yaself, an' you can't never fix it up.

And the people nodded, and perhaps the fire

spurted a little light and showed their eyes looking in on themselves.

Against the sun, with his arms out. An' he looked big—as God.

And perhaps a man balanced twenty cents between food and pleasure, and he went to a movie in Marysville or Tulare, in Ceres or Mountain View. And he came back to the ditch camp with his memory crowded. And he told how it was:

They was this rich fella, an' he makes like he's poor an' they's this rich girl, an' she purtends like she's poor too, an' they meet in a hamburg' stan'.

Why?

I don't know why—that's how it was.

Why'd they purtend like they's poor?

Well, they're tired of bein' rich.

Horseshit!

You want to hear this, or not?

Well, go on then, Sure, I wanta hear it, but if I was rich, if I was rich I'd git so many pork chops—I'd cord 'em up aroun' me like wood, an' I'd eat my way out. Go on.

Well, they each think the other one's poor. An' they git arrested an' they git in jail, an' they don' git out 'cause the other one'd find out the first is rich. An' the jail keeper, he's mean to 'em 'cause he thinks they're poor. Oughta see how he looks when he finds out. Jes' nearly faints, that's all.

What they git in jail for?

Well, they git caught at some kind a radical meetin' but they ain't radicals. They jes' happen to be there. An' they don't each one wanta marry fur money, ya see.

So the sons-of-bitches start lyin' to each other right off.

Well, in the pitcher it was like they was doin' good. They're nice to people, you see.

I was to a show oncet that was me, an' more'n me; an'

my life, an' more'n my life, so ever'thing was bigger.

Well, I git enough sorrow. I like to git away from it.

Sure—if you can believe it.

So they got married, an' then they foun' out, an' all them people that's treated 'em mean. They was a fella had been uppity, an' he nearly fainted when this fella come in with a plug hat on. Jes' nearly fainted. An' they was a newsreel with them German soldiers kickin' up their feet—funny as hell.

And always, if he had a little money, a man could get drunk. The hard edges gone, and the warmth. Then there was no loneliness, for a man could people his brain with friends, and he could find his enemies and destroy them. Sitting in a ditch, the earth grew soft under him. Failures dulled and the future was no threat. And hunger did not skulk about, but the world was soft and easy, and a man could reach the place he started for. The stars came down wonderfully close and the sky was soft. Death was a friend, and sleep was death's brother. The old times came back—a girl with pretty feet, who danced one time at home—a horse—a long time ago. A horse and a saddle. And the leather was carved. When was that? Ought to find a girl to talk to. That's nice. Might lay with her too. But warm here. And the stars down so close, and sadness and pleasure so close together, really the same thing. Like to stay drunk all the time. Who says it's bad? Who dares to say it's bad? Preachers—but they got their own kinda drunkenness. Thin, barren women, but they're too miserable to know. Reformers—but they don't bite deep enough into living to know. No—the stars are close and dear and I have joined the brotherhood of the worlds. And everything's holy—everything, even me.

*

A harmonica is easy to carry. Take it out of your hip pocket, knock it against your palm to shake out the dirt and pocket fuzz and bits of tobacco. Now it's ready. You can do anything with a harmonica: thin reedy single tone, or chords, or melody with rhythm chords. You can mold the music with curved hands, making it wail and cry like bagpipes, making it full and round like an organ, making it as sharp and bitter as the reed pipes of the hills. And you can play and put it back in your pocket. It is always with you, always in your pocket. And as you play, you learn new tricks, new ways to mold the tone with your hands, to pinch the tone with your lips, and no one teaches you. You feel around—sometimes alone in the shade at noon, sometimes in the tent door after supper when the women are washing up. Your foot taps gently on the ground. Your eyebrows rise and fall in rhythm. And if you lose it or break it, why, it's no great loss. You can buy another for a quarter.

A guitar is more precious. Must learn this thing. Fingers of the left hand must have callus caps. Thumb of the right hand a horn of callus. Stretch the left-hand fingers, stretch them like a spider's legs to get the hard pads on the frets.

This was my father's box. Wasn't no bigger'n a bug first time he give me C chord. An' when I learned as good as him, he hardly never played no more. Used to set in the door, an' listen an' tap his foot. I'm tryin' for a break, an' he'd scowl mean till I get her, an' then he'd settle back easy, an' he'd nod. "Play," he'd say. "Play nice." It's a good box. See how the head is wore. They's many a million songs wore down that wood an' scooped her out. Some day she'll cave in like a egg. But you can't patch her nor worry her no way or she'll lose tone. Play her in the evening, an' they's a harmonica player in the nex' tent. Makes it pretty nice together.

The fiddle is rare, hard to learn. No frets, no teacher.

Jes' listen to a ol' man an' try to pick it up. Won't tell how to double. Says it's a secret. But I watched. Here's how he done it.

Shrill as a wind, the fiddle, quick and nervous and shrill.

She ain't much of a fiddle. Give two dollars for her. Fella says they's fiddles four hunderd years old, and they git mellow like whisky. Says they'll cost fifty-sixty thousan' dollars. I don't know. Soun's like a lie. Harsh ol' bastard, ain't she? Wanta dance? I'll rub up the bow with plenty rosin. Man! Then she'll squawk. Hear her a mile.

These three in the evening, harmonica and fiddle and guitar. Playing a reel and tapping out the tune, and the big deep strings of the guitar beating like a heart, and the harmonica's sharp chords and the skirl and squeal of the fiddle. People have to move close. They can't help it. "Chicken Reel" now, and the feet tap and a young lean buck takes three quick steps, and his arms hang limp. The square closes up and the dancing starts, feet on the bare ground, beating dull, strike with your heels. Hands 'round and swing. Hair falls down, and panting breaths. Lean to the side now.

Look at that Texas boy, long legs loose, taps four times for ever' damn step. Never seen a boy swing aroun' like that. Look at him swing that Cherokee girl, red in her cheeks an' her toe points out. Look at her pant, look at her heave. Think she's tired? Think she's winded? Well, she ain't. Texas boy got his hair in his eyes, mouth's wide open, can't get air, but he pats four times for ever' darn step, an' he'll keep a-goin' with the Cherokee girl.

The fiddle squeaks and the guitar bongs. Mouth-organ man is red in the face. Texas boy and the Cherokee girl, pantin' like dogs an' a-beatin' the groun'. Ol' folks stan' a-pattin' their han's. Smilin' a little, tappin' their feet.

Back home—in the schoolhouse, it was. The big

moon sailed off to the westward. An' we walked, him an' me—a little ways. Didn' talk 'cause our throats was choked up. Didn' talk none at all. An' purty soon they was a haycock. Went right to it and laid down there. Seein' the Texas boy an' that girl a-steppin' away into the dark—think nobody seen 'em go. Oh, God! I wisht I was a-goin' with that Texas boy. Moon'll be up 'fore long. I seen that girl's ol' man move out to stop 'em, an' then he didn'. He knowed. Might as well stop the fall from comin', and might as well stop the sap from movin' in the trees. An' the moon'll be up 'fore long.

Play more—play the story songs—"As I Walked through the Streets of Laredo."

The fire's gone down. Be a shame to build her up. Little ol' moon'll be up 'fore long.

Beside an irrigation ditch a preacher labored and the people cried. And the preacher paced like a tiger, whipping the people with his voice, and they groveled and whined on the ground. He calculated them, gauged them, played on them, and when they were all squirming on the ground he stooped down and of his great strength he picked each one up in his arms and shouted, Take 'em, Christ! and threw each one in the water. And when they were all in, waist deep in the water, and looking with frightened eyes at the master, he knelt down on the bank and he prayed for them; and he prayed that all men and women might grovel and whine on the ground. Men and women, dripping, clothes sticking tight, watched; then gurgling and sloshing in their shoes they walked back to the camp, to the tents, and they talked softly in wonder:

We been saved, they said. We're washed white as snow. We won't never sin again.

And the children, frightened and wet, whispered together:

We been saved. We won't sin no more.

Wisht I knowed what all the sins was, so I could do 'em.

The migrant people looked humbly for pleasure on the roads.

24

On Saturday morning the wash tubs were crowded. The women washed dresses, pink ginghams and flowered cottons, and they hung them in the sun and stretched the cloth to smooth it. When afternoon came the whole camp quickened and the people grew excited. The children caught the fever and were more noisy than usual. About mid-afternoon child bathing began and as each child was caught, subdued, and washed, the noise on the playground gradually subsided. Before five, the children were scrubbed and warned about getting dirty again; and they walked about, stiff in clean clothes, miserable with carefulness.

At the big open-air dance platform a committee was busy. Every bit of electric wire had been requisitioned. The city dump had been visited for wire, every tool box had contributed friction tape. And now the patched, spliced wire was strung out to the dance floor, with bottle necks as insulators. This night the floor would be lighted for the first time. By six o'clock the men were back from work or from looking for work, and a new wave of bathing started. By seven, dinners were over, men had on their best clothes: freshly washed overalls, clean blue shirts, sometimes the decent blacks. The girls were ready in their print dresses, stretched and clean, their hair braided and ribboned. The worried women watched the families and cleaned up the evening dishes. On the platform the string band practiced, surrounded by a double wall of children. The people were intent and excited.

In the tent of Ezra Huston, chairman, the Central Committee of five men went into meeting. Huston, a tall spare man, wind-blackened, with eyes like little blades, spoke to his committee, one man from each sanitary unit.

"It's goddamn lucky we got the word they was gonna try to bust up the dance!" he said.

The tubby little representative from Unit Three spoke up. "I think we oughta squash the hell out of 'em, an' show 'em."

"No," said Huston. "That's what they want. No, sir. If they can git a fight goin', they can run in the cops an' say we ain't orderly. They tried it before—other places." He turned to the sad dark boy from Unit Two. "Got the fellas together to go roun' the fences an' see nobody sneaks in?"

The sad boy nodded. "Yeah! Twelve. Tol' 'em not to hit nobody. Jes' push 'em out ag'in."

Huston said, "Will you go out an' find Willie Eaton? He's chairman a the entertainment, ain't he?"

"Yeah."

"Well, tell 'im we wanta see 'im."

The boy went out, and he returned in a moment with a stringy Texas man. Willie Eaton had a long fragile jaw and dust-colored hair. His arms and legs were long and loose, and he had the gray sunburned eyes of the Panhandle. He stood in the tent, grinning, and his hands pivoted restlessly on his wrists.

Huston said, "You heard about tonight?"

Willie grinned. "Yeah!"

"Did anything 'bout it?"

"Yeah!"

"Tell what you done."

Willie Eaton grinned happily. "Well, sir, ordinary ent'tainment committee is five. I got twenty more—all good strong boys. They're a-gonna be a-dancin' an' a-keepin' their eyes open an' their ears open. First sign—any talk or argament, they close in tight. Worked her out purty nice. Can't even see nothing. Kinda move out, an' the fella will go out with 'em."

"Tell 'em they ain't to hurt the fellas."

Willie laughed gleefully. "I tol' 'em," he said.

"Well, tell 'em so they know."

"They know. Got five men out to the gate lookin' over the folks that comes in. Try to spot 'em 'fore they git started."

Huston stood up. His steel-colored eyes were stern. "Now you look here, Willie. We don't want them fellas hurt. They's gonna be deputies out by the front gate. If you blood 'em up, why—them deputies'll git you."

"Got that there figgered out," said Willie. "Take 'em out the back way, into the fiel'. Some a the boys'll see they git on their way."

"Well, it soun's awright," Huston said worriedly. "But don't you let nothing happen, Willie. You're responsible. Don' you hurt them fellas. Don' you use no stick nor no knife or arn, or nothing like that."

"No, sir," said Willie. "We won't mark 'em."

Huston was suspicious. "I wisht I knowed I could trus' you, Willie. If you got to sock 'em, sock 'em where they won't bleed."

"Yes, sir!" said Willie.

"You sure of the fellas you picked?"

"Yes, sir."

"Awright. An' if she gits outa han', I'll be in the right-han' corner, this way on the dance floor."

Willie saluted in mockery and went out.

Huston said, "I dunno. I jes' hope Willie's boys don't kill nobody. What the hell the deputies want to hurt the camp for? Why can't they let us be?"

The sad boy from Unit Two said, "I lived out at Sunlan' Lan' an' Cattle Company's place. Honest to God, they got a cop for ever' ten people. Got one water faucet for 'bout two hundred people."

The tubby man said, "Jesus, God, Jeremy. You ain't got to tell me. I was there. They got a block of shacks—thirty-five of 'em in a row, an' fifteen deep. An' they got ten crappers for the whole shebang. An', Christ, you could smell 'em a mile. One of them deputies give me the lowdown. We was settin' aroun', an' he says, 'Them goddamn gov'ment camps,' he says. 'Give 'em flush toilets, an' they gonna want 'em.' He says, 'You give these goddamn Okies stuff like that an' they'll want 'em. An' he says, 'They hol' red meetin's in them gov'ment camps. All figgerin' how to git on relief,' he says."

Huston asked, "Didn' nobody sock him?"

"No. They was a little fella, an' he says, 'What you mean, relief?'

" 'I mean relief—what us taxpayers puts in an' you goddamn Okies takes out.'

" 'We pay sales tax an' gas tax an' tobacco tax,' this little guy says. An' he says, 'Farmers get four cents a cotton poun' from the gov'ment—ain't that relief?' An' he says, 'Railroads an' shippin' companies draws subsidies—ain't that relief?'

" 'They're doin' stuff got to be done,' this deputy says.

" 'Well,' the little guy says, 'how'd your goddamn crops get picked if it wasn't for us?' " The tubby man looked around.

"What'd the deputy say?" Huston asked.

"Well, the deputy got mad. An' he says, 'You goddamn reds is all the time stirrin' up trouble,' he says. 'You better come along with me.' So he takes this little guy in, an' they give him sixty days in jail for vagrancy."

"How'd they do that if he had a job?" asked Timothy Wallace.

The tubby man laughed. "You know better'n that," he said. "You know a vagrant is anybody a cop don't like. An' that's why they hate this here camp. No cops can get in. This here's United States, not California."

Huston sighed. "Wisht we could stay here. Got to be goin' 'fore long. I like this here. Folks git along nice; an', God Awmighty, why can't they let us do it 'stead of keepin' us miserable an' puttin' us in jail? I swear to God they gonna push us into fightin' if they don't quit a-worryin' us." Then he calmed his voice. "We jes' got to keep peaceful," he reminded himself. "The committee got no right to fly off'n the handle."

The tubby man from Unit Three said, "Anybody that thinks this committee got all cheese an' crackers ought to jes' try her. They was a fight in my unit today— women. Got to callin' names, an' then got to throwin' garbage. Ladies' Committee couldn' handle it, an' they come to me. Want me to bring the fight in this here committee. I tol' 'em they got to handle women trouble theirselves. This here committee ain't gonna mess with no garbage fights."

Huston nodded. "You done good," he said.

And now the dusk was falling, and as the darkness deepened the practicing of the string band seemed to grow louder. The lights flashed on and two men inspected the patched wire to the dance floor. The children crowded thickly about the musicians. A boy with a guitar sang the "Down Home Blues," chording delicately for himself, and on his second chorus three harmonicas and a fiddle joined him. From the tents the people streamed toward the platform, men in their clean blue denim and women in their ginghams. They came near to the platform and then stood quietly waiting, their faces bright and intent under the light.

Around the reservation there was a high wire fence, and along the fence, at intervals of fifty feet, the guards sat in the grass and waited.

Now the cars of the guests began to arrive, small farmers and their families, migrants from other camps. And as each guest came through the gate he mentioned the name of the camper who had invited him.

The string band took a reel tune up and played loudly, for they were not practicing any more. In front of their tents the Jesus-lovers sat and watched, their faces hard and contemptuous. They did not speak to one another, they watched for sin, and their faces condemned the whole proceeding.

At the Joad tent Ruthie and Winfield had bolted what little dinner they had, and then they started for the platform. Ma called them back, held up their faces with a hand under each chin, and looked into their nostrils, pulled their ears and looked inside, and sent them to the sanitary unit to wash their hands once more. They dodged around the back of the building and bolted for the platform, to stand among the children, close-packed about the band.

Al finished his dinner and spent half an hour shaving with Tom's razor. Al had a tight-fitting wool suit and a striped shirt, and he bathed and washed and combed his straight hair back. And when the washroom was vacant for a moment, he smiled engagingly at himself in the mirror, and he turned and tried to see himself in profile when he smiled. He slipped his purple arm-bands on and put on his tight coat. And he rubbed up his yellow shoes with a piece of toilet paper. A late bather came in, and Al hurried out and walked recklessly toward the platform, his eye peeled for girls. Near the dance floor he saw a pretty blond girl sitting in front of a tent. He sidled near and threw open his coat to show his shirt.

"Gonna dance tonight?" he asked.

The girl looked away and did not answer.

"Can't a fella pass a word with you? How 'bout you an' me dancin'?" And he said nonchalantly, "I can waltz."

The girl raised her eyes shyly, and she said, "That ain't nothin'—anybody can waltz."

"Not like me," said Al. The music surged, and he tapped one foot in time. "Come on," he said.

A very fat woman poked her head out of the tent and scowled at him. "You git along," she said fiercely. "This here girl's spoke for. She's a-gonna be married, an' her man's a-comin' for her."

Al winked rakishly at the girl, and he tripped on, striking his feet to the music and swaying his shoulders and swinging his arms. And the girl looked after him intently.

Pa put down his plate and stood up. "Come on, John," he said; and he explained to Ma, "We're a-gonna talk to some fellas about gettin' work." And Pa and Uncle John walked toward the manager's house.

Tom worked a piece of store bread into the stew gravy on his plate and ate the bread. He handed his plate to Ma, and she put it in the bucket of hot water and washed it and handed it to Rose of Sharon to wipe. "Ain't you goin' to the dance?" Ma asked.

"Sure," said Tom. "I'm on a committee. We're gonna entertain some fellas."

"Already on a committee?" Ma said. "I guess it's 'cause you got work."

Rose of Sharon turned to put the dish away. Tom pointed at her. "My God, she's a-gettin' big," he said.

Rose of Sharon blushed and took another dish from Ma. "Sure she is," Ma said.

"An' she's gettin' prettier," said Tom.

The girl blushed more deeply and hung her head. "You stop it," she said, softly.

" 'Course she is," said Ma. "Girl with a baby always gets prettier."

Tom laughed. "If she keeps a-swellin' like this, she gonna need a wheelbarra to carry it."

"Now you stop," Rose of Sharon said, and she went inside the tent, out of sight.

Ma chuckled. "You shouldn' ought to worry her."

"She likes it," said Tom.

"I know she likes it, but it worries her, too. And she's a-mournin' for Connie."

"Well, she might's well give him up. He's prob'ly studyin' to be President of the United States by now."

"Don't worry her," Ma said. "She ain't got no easy row to hoe."

Willie Eaton moved near, and he grinned and said, "You Tom Joad?"

"Yeah."

"Well, I'm Chairman the Entertainment Committee. We gonna need you. Fella tol' me 'bout you."

"Sure, I'll play with you," said Tom. "This here's Ma."

"Howdy," said Willie.

"Glad to meet ya."

Willie said, "Gonna put you on the gate to start, an' then on the floor. Want ya to look over the guys when they come in, an' try to spot 'em. You'll be with another fella. Then later I want ya to dance an' watch."

"Yeah! I can do that awright," said Tom.

Ma said apprehensively, "They ain't no trouble?"

"No, ma'am," Willie said. "They ain't gonna be no trouble."

"None at all," said Tom. "Well, I'll come 'long. See you at the dance, Ma." The two young men walked quickly away toward the main gate.

Ma piled the washed dishes on a box. "Come on out," she called, and when there was no answer, "Rosasharn, you come out."

The girl stepped from the tent, and she went on with the dish-wiping.

"Tom was on'y jollyin' ya."

"I know. I didn't mind; on'y I hate to have folks look at me."

"Ain't no way to he'p that. Folks gonna look. But it

makes folks happy to see a girl in a fambly way—
makes folks sort of giggly an' happy. Ain't you a-goin'
to the dance?"

"I was—but I don' know. I wisht Connie was here."
Her voice rose. "Ma, I wisht he was here. I can't
hardly stan' it."

Ma looked closely at her. "I know," she said. "But,
Rosasharn—don' shame your folks."

"I don' aim to, Ma."

"Well, don't you shame us. We got too much on us
now, without no shame."

The girl's lip quivered. "I—I ain' goin' to the
dance. I couldn'—Ma—he'p me!" She sat down and
buried her head in her arms.

Ma wiped her hands on the dish towel and she
squatted down in front of her daughter, and she put
her two hands on Rose of Sharon's hair. "You're a
good girl," she said. "You always was a good girl. I'll
take care a you. Don't you fret." She put an interest in
her tone. "Know what you an' me's gonna do? We're
a-goin' to that dance, an' we're a-gonna set there an'
watch. If anybody says to come dance—why, I'll say
you ain't strong enough. I'll say you're poorly. An' you
can hear the music an' all like that."

Rose of Sharon raised her head. "You won't let me
dance?"

"No, I won't."

"An' don' let nobody touch me."

"No, I won't."

The girl sighed. She said desperately, "I don' know
what I'm a-gonna do, Ma. I jus' don' know. I don'
know."

Ma patted her knee. "Look," she said. "Look here
at me. I'm a-gonna tell ya. In a little while it ain't
gonna be so bad. In a little while. An' that's true. Now
come on. We'll go get washed up, an' we'll put on our
nice dress an' we'll set by the dance." She led Rose of
Sharon toward the sanitary unit.

Pa and Uncle John squatted with a group of men by the porch of the office. "We nearly got work today," Pa said. "We was jus' a few minutes late. They awready got two fellas. An', well, sir, it was a funny thing. They's a straw boss there, an' he says, 'We jus' got some two-bit men. 'Course we could use twenty-cent men. We can use a lot a twenty-cent men. You go to your camp an' say we'll put a lot a fellas on for twenty cents.' "

The squatting men moved nervously. A broad-shouldered man, his face completely in the shadow of a black hat, spatted his knee with his palm. "I know it, goddamn it!" he cried. "An' they'll git men. They'll git hungry men. You can't feed your fam'ly on twenty cents an hour, but you'll take anything. They got you goin' an' comin'. They jes' auction a job off. Jesus Christ, pretty soon they're gonna make us pay to work."

"We would of took her," Pa said. "We ain't had no job. We sure would a took her, but they was them guys in there, an' the way they looked, we was scairt to take her."

Black Hat said, "Get crazy thinkin'! I been workin' for a fella, an' he can't pick his crop. Cost more jes' to pick her than he can git for her, an' he don' know what to do."

"Seems to me—" Pa stopped. The circle was silent for him. "Well—I jus' thought, if a fella had a acre. Well, my woman she could raise a little truck an' a couple pigs an' some chickens. An' us men could get out an' find work, an' then go back. Kids could maybe go to school. Never seen sech schools as out here."

"Our kids ain't happy in them schools," Black Hat said.

"Why not? They're pretty nice, them schools."

"Well, a raggedy kid with no shoes, an' them other kids with socks on, an' nice pants, an' them a-yellin' 'Okie.' My boy went to school. Had a fight ever' day.

Done good, too. Tough little bastard. Ever' day he got
to fight. Come home with his clothes tore an' his nose
bloody. An' his ma'd whale him. Made her stop that.
No need ever'body beatin' the hell outa him, poor little
fella. Jesus! He give some a them kids a goin'-over,
though—them nice-pants sons-a-bitches. I dunno. I
dunno."

Pa demanded, "Well, what the hell am I gonna do?
We're outa money. One of my boys got a short job, but
that won't feed us. I'm a-gonna go an' take twenty
cents. I got to."

Black Hat raised his head, and his bristled chin
showed in the light, and his stringy neck where the
whiskers lay flat like fur. "Yeah!" he said bitterly.
"You'll do that. An' I'm a two-bit man. You'll take my
job for twenty cents. An' then I'll git hungry an' I'll
take my job back for fifteen. Yeah! You go right on an'
do her."

"Well, what the hell can I do?" Pa demanded. "I
can't starve so's you can get two bits."

Black Hat dipped his head again, and his chin went
into the shadow. "I dunno," he said. "I jes' dunno. It's
bad enough to work twelve hours a day an' come out
jes' a little bit hungry, but we got to figure all a time,
too. My kid ain't gettin' enough to eat. I can't think all
the time, goddamn it! It drives a man crazy." The
circle of men shifted their feet nervously.

Tom stood at the gate and watched the people coming in to the dance. A floodlight shone down into their
faces. Willie Eaton said, "Jes' keep your eyes open.
I'm sendin' Jule Vitela over. He's half Cherokee. Nice
fella. Keep your eyes open. An' see if you can pick out
the ones."

"O.K.," said Tom. He watched the farm families
come in, the girls with braided hair and the boys polished for the dance. Jule came and stood beside him.

"I'm with you," he said.

Tom looked at the hawk nose and the high brown cheek bones and the slender receding chin. "They says you're half Injun. You look all Injun to me."

"No," said Jule. "Jes' half. Wisht I was a full-blood. I'd have my lan' on the reservation. Them full-bloods got it pretty nice, some of 'em."

"Look a them people," Tom said.

The guests were moving in through the gateway, families from the farms, migrants from the ditch camps. Children straining to be free and quiet parents holding them back.

Jule said, "These here dances done funny things. Our people got nothing, but jes' because they can ast their frien's to come here to the dance, sets 'em up an' makes 'em proud. An' the folks respects 'em 'count of these here dances. Fella got a little place where I was a-workin'. He come to a dance here. I ast him myself, an' he come. Says we got the only decent dance in the county, where a man can take his girls an' his wife. Hey! Look."

Three young men were coming through the gate—young working men in jeans. They walked close together. The guard at the gate questioned them, and they answered and passed through.

"Look at 'em careful," Jule said. He moved to the guard. "Who ast them three?" he asked.

"Fella named Jackson, Unit Four."

Jule came back to Tom. "I think them's our fellas."

"How ya know?"

"I dunno how. Jes' got a feelin'. They're kinda scared. Foller 'em an' tell Willie to look 'em over, an' tell Willie to check with Jackson, Unit Four. Get him to see if they're all right. I'll stay here."

Tom strolled after the three young men. They moved toward the dance floor and took their positions quietly on the edge of the crowd. Tom saw Willie near the band and signaled him.

"What cha want?" Willie asked.

"Them three—see—there?"

"Yeah."

"They say a fella name' Jackson, Unit Four, ast 'em."

Willie craned his neck and saw Huston and called him over. "Them three fellas," he said. "We better get Jackson, Unit Four, an' see if he ast 'em."

Huston turned on his heel and walked away; and in a few moments he was back with a lean and bony Kansan. "This here's Jackson," Huston said. "Look, Jackson, see them three young fellas—?"

"Yeah."

"Well, did you ast 'em?"

"No."

"Ever see 'em before?"

Jackson peered at them. "Sure. Worked at Gregorio's with 'em."

"So they knowed your name."

"Sure. I worked right beside 'em."

"Awright," Huston said. "Don't you go near 'em. We ain't gonna tho'w 'em out if they're nice. Thanks, Mr. Jackson."

"Good work," he said to Tom. "I guess them's the fellas."

"Jule picked 'em out," said Tom.

"Hell, no wonder," said Willie. "His Injun blood smelled 'em. Well, I'll point 'em out to the boys."

A sixteen-year-old boy came running through the crowd. He stopped, panting, in front of Huston. "Mista Huston," he said. "I been like you said. They's a car with six men parked down by the euc'lyptus trees, an' they's one with four men up that north-side road. I ast 'em for a match. They got guns. I seen 'em."

Huston's eyes grew hard and cruel. "Willie," he said, "you sure you got ever'thing ready?"

Willie grinned happily. "Sure have, Mr. Huston. Ain't gonna be no trouble."

"Well, don't hurt 'em. 'Member now. If you kin, quiet an' nice, I kinda like to see 'em. Be in my tent."

"I'll see what we kin do," said Willie.

Dancing had not formally started, but now Willie climbed onto the platform. "Choose up your squares," he called. The music stopped. Boys and girls, young men and women, ran about until eight squares were ready on the big floor, ready and waiting. The girls held their hands in front of them and squirmed their fingers. The boys tapped their feet restlessly. Around the floor the old folks sat, smiling slightly, holding the children back from the floor. And in the distance the Jesus-lovers sat with hard condemning faces and watched the sin.

Ma and Rose of Sharon sat on a bench and watched. And as each boy asked Rose of Sharon as partner, Ma said, "No, she ain't well." And Rose of Sharon blushed and her eyes were bright.

The caller stepped to the middle of the floor and held up his hands. "All ready? Then let her go!"

The music snarled out "Chicken Reel," shrill and clear, fiddle skirling, harmonicas nasal and sharp, and the guitars booming on the bass strings. The caller named the turns, the squares moved. And they danced forward and back, hands 'round, swing your lady. The caller, in a frenzy, tapped his feet, strutted back and forth, went through the figures as he called them.

"Swing your ladies an' a dol ce do. Join han's roun' an' away we go." The music rose and fell, and the moving shoes beating in time on the platform sounded like drums. "Swing to the right an' a swing to the lef'; break, now—break—back to—back," the caller sang the high vibrant monotone. Now the girls' hair lost the careful combing. Now perspiration stood out on the foreheads of the boys. Now the experts showed the tricky inter-steps. And the old people on the edge of the floor took up the rhythm, patted their hands softly, and tapped their feet; and they smiled gently and then caught one another's eyes and nodded.

Ma leaned her head close to Rose of Sharon's ear. "Maybe you wouldn' think it, but your Pa was as nice a dancer as I ever seen, when he was young." And Ma smiled. "Makes me think of ol' times," she said. And on the faces of the watchers the smiles were of old times.

"Up near Muskogee twenty years ago, they was a blin' man with a fiddle——"

"I seen a fella oncet could slap his heels four times in one jump."

"Swedes up in Dakota—know what they do sometimes? Put pepper on the floor. Gits up the ladies' skirts an' makes 'em purty lively—lively as a filly in season. Swedes do that sometimes."

In the distance, the Jesus-lovers watched their restive children. "Look on sin," they said. "Them folks is ridin' to hell on a poker. It's a shame the godly got to see it." And their children were silent and nervous.

"One more roun' an' then a little res'," the caller chanted. "Hit her hard, 'cause we're gonna stop soon." And the girls were damp and flushed, and they danced with open mouths and serious reverent faces, and the boys flung back their long hair and pranced, pointed their toes, and clicked their heels. In and out the squares moved, crossing, backing, whirling, and the music shrilled.

Then suddenly it stopped. The dancers stood still, panting with fatigue. And the children broke from restraint, dashed on the floor, chased one another madly, ran, slid, stole caps, and pulled hair. The dancers sat down, fanning themselves with their hands. The members of the band got up and stretched themselves and sat down again. And the guitar players worked softly over their strings.

Now Willie called, "Choose again for another square, if you can." The dancers scrambled to their feet and new dancers plunged forward for partners. Tom stood near the three young men. He saw them force their way through, out on the floor, toward one of the forming squares. He waved his hand at Willie, and Willie spoke to the fiddler. The fiddler squawked his bow across the strings. Twenty young men lounged slowly across the floor. The three reached the square. And one of them said, "I'll dance with this here."

A blond boy looked up in astonishment. "She's my partner."

"Listen, you little son-of-a-bitch——"

Off in the darkness a shrill whistle sounded. The three were walled in now. And each one felt the grip of hands. And then the wall of men moved slowly off the platform.

Willie yelped, "Le's go!" The music shrilled out, the caller intoned the figures, the feet thudded on the platform.

A touring car drove to the entrance. The driver called, "Open up. We hear you got a riot."

The guard kept his position. "We got no riot. Listen to that music. Who are you?"

"Deputy sheriffs."

"Got a warrant?"

"We don't need a warrant if there's a riot."

"Well, we got no riots here," said the gate guard.

The men in the car listened to the music and the sound of the caller, and then the car pulled slowly away and parked in a crossroad and waited.

In the moving squad each of the three young men was pinioned, and a hand was over each mouth. When they reached the darkness the group opened up.

Tom said, "That sure was did nice." He held both arms of his victim from behind.

Willie ran over to them from the dance floor. "Nice work," he said. "On'y need six now. Huston wants to see these here fellers."

Huston himself emerged from the darkness. "These the ones?"

"Sure," said Jule. "Went right up an' started it. But they didn' even swing once."

"Let's look at 'em." The prisoners were swung around to face him. Their heads were down. Huston put a flashlight beam in each sullen face. "What did you wanta do it for?" he asked. There was no answer. "Who the hell tol' you to do it?"

"Goddarn it, we didn' do nothing. We was jes' gonna dance."

"No, you wasn't," Jule said. "You was gonna sock that kid."

Tom said, "Mr. Huston, jus' when these here fellas moved in, somebody give a whistle."

"Yeah, I know! The cops come right to the gate." He turned back. "We ain't gonna hurt you. Now who tol' you to come bus' up our dance?" He waited for a reply. "You're our own folks," Huston said sadly. "You belong with us. How'd you happen to come? We know all about it," he added.

"Well, goddamn it, a fella got to eat."

"Well, who sent you? Who paid you to come?"

"We ain't been paid."

"An' you ain't gonna be. No fight, no pay. Ain't that right?"

One of the pinioned men said, "Do what you want. We ain't gonna tell nothing."

Huston's head sank down for a moment, and then he said softly, "O.K. Don't tell. But looka here. Don't knife your own folks. We're trying to get along, havin' fun an' keepin' order. Don't tear all that down. Jes' think about it. You're jes' harmin' yourself."

"Awright, boys, put 'em over the back fence. An' don't hurt 'em. They don't know what they're doin'."

The squad moved slowly toward the rear of the camp, and Huston looked after them.

Jule said, "Le's jes' take one good kick at 'em."

"No, you don't!" Willie cried. "I said we wouldn'."

"Jes' one nice little kick," Jule pleaded. "Jes' loft 'em over the fence."

"No, sir," Willie insisted.

"Listen you," he said, "we're lettin' you off this time. But you take back the word. If'n ever this here happens again, we'll jes' natcherally kick the hell outa whoever comes; we'll bust ever' bone in their body. Now you tell your boys that. Huston says you're our kinda folks—maybe. I'd hate to think it."

They neared the fence. Two of the seated guards stood up and moved over. "Got some fellas goin' home early," said Willie. The three men climbed over the fence and disappeared into the darkness.

And the squad moved quickly back toward the dance floor. And the music of "Ol' Dan Tucker" skirled and whined from the string band.

Over near the office the men still squatted and talked, and the shrill music came to them.

Pa said, "They's change a-comin'. I don' know what. Maybe we won't live to see her. But she's a-comin'. They's a res'less feelin'. Fella can't figger nothin' out, he's so nervous."

And Black Hat lifted his head up again, and the light fell on his bristly whiskers. He gathered some little rocks from the ground and shot them like marbles, with his thumb. "I don' know. She's a-comin' awright, like you say. Fella tol' me what happened in Akron, Ohio. Rubber companies. They got mountain people in 'cause they'd work cheap. An' these here mountain people up an' joined the union. Well, sir, hell jes' popped. All them storekeepers and legioners an' people like that, they get drillin' an' yellin', 'Red!' An' they're gonna run the union right outa Akron. Preachers git a-preachin' about it, an' papers a-yowlin', an' they's pick handles put out by the rubber companies, an' they're a-buyin' gas. Jesus, you'd think them mountain boys was reg'lar devils!" He stopped and found some more rocks to shoot. "Well, sir—it was las' March, an' one Sunday five thousan' of them mountain men had a turkey shoot outside a town. Five thousan' of 'em jes' marched through town with their rifles. An' they had their turkey shoot, an' then they marched back. An' that's all they done. Well, sir, they ain't been no trouble sence then. These here citizens committees give back the pick handles, an' the store-keepers keep their stores, an' nobody been clubbed or tarred an' feathered, an' nobody been killed." There was a long silence, and then Black Hat said, "They're gettin' purty mean out here. Burned that camp an' beat up folks. I been thinkin'. All our folks got guns. I been thinkin' maybe we ought to git up a turkey shoo-tin' club an' have meetin's ever' Sunday."

The men looked up at him, and then down at the ground, and their feet moved restlessly and they shifted their weight from one leg to the other.

25

The spring is beautiful in California. Valleys in which the fruit blossoms are fragrant pink and white waters in a shallow sea. Then the first tendrils of the grapes, swelling from the old gnarled vines, cascade down to cover the trunks. The full green hills are round and soft as breasts. And on the level vegetable lands are the mile-long rows of pale green lettuce and the spindly little cauliflowers, the gray-green unearthly artichoke plants.

And then the leaves break out on the trees, and the petals drop from the fruit trees and carpet the earth with pink and white. The centers of the blossoms swell and grow and color: cherries and apples, peaches and pears, figs which close the flower in the fruit. All California quickens with produce, and the fruit grows heavy, and the limbs bend gradually under the fruit so that little crutches must be placed under them to support the weight.

Behind the fruitfulness are men of understanding and knowledge and skill, men who experiment with seed, endlessly developing the techniques for greater crops of plants whose roots will resist the million enemies of the earth: the molds, the insects, the rusts, the blights. These men work carefully and endlessly to perfect the seed, the roots. And there are the men of chemistry who spray the trees against pests, who sulphur the grapes, who cut out disease and rots, mildews and sicknesses. Doctors of preventive medicine, men at the borders who look for fruit flies, for Japanese beetle, men who quarantine the sick trees and root them out and burn them, men of knowledge. The men who graft the young trees, the little vines, are the cleverest of all, for theirs is a surgeon's job, as tender and delicate; and these men must have surgeons' hands and surgeons' hearts to slit the bark, to place the grafts, to bind the wounds and cover them from the air. These are great men.

Along the rows, the cultivators move, tearing the spring grass and turning it under to make a fertile earth, breaking the ground to hold the water up near the surface, ridging the ground in little pools for the irrigation, destroying the weed roots that may drink the water away from the trees.

And all the time the fruit swells and the flowers break out in long clusters on the vines. And in the growing year the warmth grows and the leaves turn dark green. The prunes lengthen like little green bird's eggs, and the limbs sag down against the crutches under the weight. And the hard little pears take shape, and the beginning of the fuzz comes out on the peaches. Grape blossoms shed their tiny petals and the hard little beads become green buttons, and the buttons grow heavy. The men who work in the fields, the owners of the little orchards, watch and calculate. The year is heavy with produce. And men are proud, for of their knowledge they can make the year heavy. They have transformed the world with their knowledge. The short, lean wheat has been made big and productive. Little sour apples have grown large and sweet, and that old grape that grew among the trees and fed the birds its tiny fruit has mothered a thousand varieties, red and black, green and pale pink, purple and yellow; and each variety with its own flavor. The men who work in the experimental farms have made new fruits: nectarines and forty kinds of plums, walnuts with paper shells. And always they work, selecting, grafting, changing, driving themselves, driving the earth to produce.

And first the cherries ripen. Cent and a half a pound. Hell, we can't pick 'em for that. Black cherries and red cherries, full and sweet, and the birds eat half of each cherry and the yellowjackets buzz into the holes the birds made. And on the ground the seeds drop and dry with black shreds hanging from them.

The purple prunes soften and sweeten. My God, we can't pick them and dry and sulphur them. We can't pay wages, no matter what wages. And the purple prunes carpet the ground. And first the skins wrinkle a little and swarms of flies come to feast, and the valley is filled with the odor of sweet decay. The meat turns dark and the crop shrivels on the ground.

And the pears grow yellow and soft. Five dollars a ton. Five dollars for forty fifty-pound boxes; trees pruned and sprayed, orchards cultivated—pick the fruit, put it in boxes, load the trucks, deliver the fruit to the cannery—forty boxes for five dollars. We can't do it. And the yellow fruit falls heavily to the ground and splashes on the ground. The yellowjackets dig into the soft meat, and there is a smell of ferment and rot.

Then the grapes—we can't make good wine. People can't buy good wine. Rip the grapes from the vines, good grapes, rotten grapes, wasp-stung grapes. Press stems, press dirt and rot.

But there's mildew and formic acid in the vats.

Add sulphur and tannic acid.

The smell from the ferment is not the rich odor of wine, but the smell of decay and chemicals.

Oh, well. It has alcohol in it, anyway. They can get drunk.

The little farmers watched debt creep up on them

like the tide. They sprayed the trees and sold no crop, they pruned and grafted and could not pick the crop. And the men of knowledge have worked, have considered, and the fruit is rotting on the ground, and the decaying mash in the wine vats is poisoning the air. And taste the wine—no grape flavor at all, just sulphur and tannic acid and alcohol.

This little orchard will be a part of a great holding next year, for the debt will have choked the owner.

This vineyard will belong to the bank. Only the great owners can survive, for they own the canneries too. And four pears peeled and cut in half, cooked and canned, still cost fifteen cents. And the canned pears do not spoil. They will last for years.

The decay spreads over the State, and the sweet smell is a great sorrow on the land. Men who can graft the trees and make the seed fertile and big can find no way to let the hungry people eat their produce. Men who have created new fruits in the world cannot create a system whereby their fruits may be eaten. And the failure hangs over the State like a great sorrow.

The works of the roots of the vines, of the trees, must be destroyed to keep up the price, and this is the saddest, bitterest thing of all. Carloads of oranges dumped on the ground. The people came for miles to take the fruit, but this could not be. How would they buy oranges at twenty cents a dozen if they could drive out and pick them up? And men with hoses squirt kerosene on the oranges, and they are angry at the crime, angry at the people who have come to take the fruit. A million people hungry, needing the fruit—and kerosene sprayed over the golden mountains.

And the smell of rot fills the country.

Burn coffee for fuel in the ships. Burn corn to keep warm, it makes a hot fire. Dump potatoes in the rivers and place guards along the banks to keep the hungry people from fishing them out. Slaughter the pigs and bury them, and let the putrescence drip down into the earth.

There is a crime here that goes beyond denunciation. There is a sorrow here that weeping cannot symbolize. There is a failure here that topples all our success. The fertile earth, the straight tree rows, the sturdy trunks, and the ripe fruit. And children dying of pellagra must die because a profit cannot be taken from an orange. And coroners must fill in the certificates—died of malnutrition—because the food must rot, must be forced to rot.

The people come with nets to fish for potatoes in the river, and the guards hold them back; they come in rattling cars to get the dumped oranges, but the kerosene is sprayed. And they stand still and watch the potatoes float by, listen to the screaming pigs being killed in a ditch and covered with quicklime, watch the mountains of oranges slop down to a putrefying ooze; and in the eyes of the people there is the failure; and in the eyes of the hungry there is a growing wrath. In the souls of the people the grapes of wrath are filling and growing heavy, growing heavy for the vintage.

26

In the Weedpatch camp, on an evening when the long, barred clouds hung over the set sun and inflamed their edges, the Joad family lingered after their supper. Ma hesitated before she started to do the dishes.

"We got to do somepin," she said. And she pointed at Winfield. "Look at 'im," she said. And when they stared at the little boy, "He's a-jerkin' an' a-twistin' in his sleep. Lookut his color." The members of the family looked at the earth again in shame. "Fried dough," Ma said. "One month we been here. An' Tom had five days' work. An' the rest of you scrabblin' out ever' day, an' no work. An' scairt to talk. An' the money gone. You're scairt to talk it out. Ever' night you jus' eat, an' then you get wanderin' away. Can't bear to talk it out. Well, you got to. Rosasharn ain't far from due, an' lookut her color. You got to talk it out. Now don't none of you get up till we figger somepin out. One day' more grease an' two days' flour, an' ten potatoes. You set here an' get busy!"

They looked at the ground. Pa cleaned his thick nails with his pocket knife. Uncle John picked at a splinter on the box he sat on. Tom pinched his lower lip and pulled it away from his teeth.

He released his lip and said softly, "We been a-lookin', Ma. Been walkin' out sence we can't use the gas no more. Been goin' in ever' gate, walkin' up to ever' house, even when we knowed they wasn't gonna be nothin'. Puts a weight on ya. Goin' out lookin' for somepin you know you ain't gonna find."

Ma said fiercely, "You ain't got the right to get discouraged. This here fambly's goin' under. You jus' ain't got the right."

Pa inspected his scraped nail. "We gotta go," he said. "We didn' wanta go. It's nice here, an' folks is nice here. We're feared we'll have to go live in one a them Hoovervilles."

"Well, if we got to, we got to. First thing is, we got to eat."

Al broke in. "I got a tankful a gas in the truck. I didn' let nobody get into that."

Tom smiled. "This here Al got a lot of sense along with he's randy-pandy."

"Now you figger," Ma said. "I ain't watchin' this here fambly starve no more. One day' more grease. That's what we got. Come time for Rosasharn to lay in, she got to be fed up. You figger!"

"This here hot water an' toilets—" Pa began.

"Well, we can't eat no toilets."

Tom said, "They was a fella come by today lookin' for men to go to Marysville. Pickin' fruit."

"Well, why don' we go to Marysville?" Ma demanded.

"I dunno," said Tom. "Didn' seem right, somehow. He was so anxious. Wouldn' say how much the pay was. Said he didn' know exactly."

Ma said, "We're a-goin' to Marysville. I don' care what the pay is. We're a-goin'."

"It's too far," said Tom. "We ain't got the money for gasoline. We couldn' get there. Ma, you say we got to figger. I ain't done nothin' but figger the whole time."

Uncle John said, "Feller says they's cotton a-comin'

in up north, near a place called Tulare. That ain't very far, the feller says."

"Well, we got to git goin', an' goin' quick. I ain't a-settin' here no longer, no matter how nice." Ma took up her bucket and walked toward the sanitary unit for hot water.

"Ma gets tough," Tom said. "I seen her a-gettin' mad quite a piece now. She jus' boils up."

Pa said with relief, "Well, she brang it into the open, anyways. I been layin' at night a-burnin' my brains up. Now we can talk her out, anyways."

Ma came back with her bucket of steaming water. "Well," she demanded, "figger anything out?"

"Jus' workin' her over," said Tom. "Now s'pose we jus' move up north where that cotton's at. We been over this here country. We know they ain't nothin' here. S'pose we pack up an' shove north. Then when the cotton's ready, we'll be there. I kinda like to get my han's aroun' some cotton. You got a full tank, Al?"

"Almos'——'bout two inches down."

"Should get us up to that place."

Ma poised a dish over the bucket. "Well?" she demanded.

Tom said, "You win. We'll move on, I guess. Huh, Pa?"

"Guess we got to," Pa said.

Ma glanced at him. "When?"

"Well——no need waitin'. Might's well go in the mornin'."

"We got to go in the mornin'. I tol' you what's lef'."

"Now, Ma, don' think I don' wanta go. I ain't had a good gutful to eat in two weeks. 'Course I filled up, but I didn' take no good from it."

Ma plunged the dish into the bucket. "We'll go in the mornin'," she said.

Pa sniffled. "Seems like times is changed," he said

sarcastically. "Time was when a man said what we'd do. Seems like women is tellin' now. Seems like it's purty near time to get out a stick."

Ma put the clean dripping tin dish out on a box. She smiled down at her work. "You get your stick, Pa," she said. "Times when they's food an' a place to set, then maybe you can use your stick an' keep your skin whole. But you ain't a-doin' your job, either a-thinkin' or a-workin'. If you was, why, you could use your stick, an' women folks'd sniffle their nose an creep-mouse aroun'. But you jus' get you a stick now an' you ain't lickin' no woman; you're a-fightin', 'cause I got a stick all laid out too."

Pa grinned with embarrassment. "Now it ain't good to have the little fellas hear you talkin' like that," he said.

"You get some bacon inside the little fellas 'fore you come tellin' what else is good for 'em," said Ma.

Pa got up in disgust and moved away, and Uncle John followed him.

Ma's hands were busy in the water, but she watched them go, and she said proudly to Tom, "He's all right. He ain't beat. He's like as not to take a smack at me."

Tom laughed. "You jus' a-treadin' him on?"

"Sure," said Ma. "Take a man, he can get worried an' worried, an' it eats out his liver, an' purty soon he'll jus' lay down and die with his heart et out. But if you can take an' make 'im mad, why, he'll be awright. Pa, he didn' say nothin', but he's mad now. He'll show me now. He's awright."

Al got up. "I'm gonna walk down the row," he said.

"Better see the truck's ready to go," Tom warned him.

"She's ready."

"If she ain't, I'll turn Ma on ya."

"She's ready." Al strolled jauntily along the row of tents.

Tom sighed. "I'm a-gettin' tired, Ma. How 'bout makin' me mad?"

"You got more sense, Tom. I don' need to make you mad. I got to lean on you. Them others—they're kinda strangers, all but you. You won't give up, Tom."

The job fell on him. "I don' like it," he said. "I wanta go out like Al. An' I wanta get mad like Pa, an' I wanta get drunk like Uncle John."

Ma shook her head. "You can't, Tom. I know. I knowed from the time you was a little fella. You can't. They's some folks that's just theirself an' nothin' more. There's Al—he's jus' a young fella after a girl. You wasn't never like that, Tom."

"Sure I was," said Tom. "Still am."

"No you ain't. Ever'thing you do is more'n you. When they sent you up to prison I knowed it. You're spoke for."

"Now, Ma—cut it out. It ain't true. It's all in your head."

She stacked the knives and forks on top of the plates. "Maybe. Maybe it's in my head. Rosasharn, you wipe up these here an' put 'em away."

The girl got breathlessly to her feet and her swollen middle hung out in front of her. She moved sluggishly to the box and picked up a washed dish.

Tom said, "Gettin' so tightful it's a-pullin' her eyes wide."

"Don't you go a-jollyin'," said Ma. "She's doin' good. You go 'long an' say goo'-by to anybody you wan'."

"O.K.," he said. "I'm gonna see how far it is up there."

Ma said to the girl, "He ain't sayin' stuff like that to make you feel bad. Where's Ruthie an' Winfiel'?"

"They snuck off after Pa. I seen 'em."

"Well, leave 'em go."

Rose of Sharon moved sluggishly about her work.

Ma inspected her cautiously. "You feelin' pretty good? Your cheeks is kinda saggy."

"I ain't had milk like they said I ought."

"I know. We jus' didn' have no milk."

Rose of Sharon said dully, "Ef Connie hadn' went away, we'd a had a little house by now, with him studyin' an' all. Would a got milk like I need. Would a had a nice baby. This here baby ain't gonna be no good. I ought a had milk." She reached in her apron pocket and put something into her mouth.

Ma said, "I seen you nibblin' on somepin. What you eatin'?"

"Nothin'."

"Come on, what you nibblin' on?"

"Jus' a piece a slack lime. Foun' a big hunk."

"Why, tha's jus' like eatin' dirt."

"I kinda feel like I wan' it."

Ma was silent. She spread her knees and tightened her skirt. "I know," she said at last. "I et coal oncet when I was in a fambly way. Et a big piece a coal. Granma says I shouldn'. Don' you say that about the baby. You got no right even to think it."

"Got no husban'! Got no milk!"

Ma said, "If you was a well girl, I'd take a whang at you. Right in the face." She got up and went inside the tent. She came out and stood in front of Rose of Sharon, and she held out her hand. "Look!" The small gold earrings were in her hand. "These is for you."

The girl's eyes brightened for a moment, and then she looked aside. "I ain't pierced."

"Well, I'm a-gonna pierce ya." Ma hurried back into the tent. She came back with a cardboard box. Hurriedly she threaded a needle, doubled the thread and tied a series of knots in it. She threaded a second needle and knotted the thread. In the box she found a piece of cork.

"It'll hurt. It'll hurt."

Ma stepped to her, put the cork in back of the ear lobe and pushed the needle through the ear, into the cork.

The girl twitched. "It sticks. It'll hurt."

"No more'n that."

"Yes, it will."

"Well, then. Le's see the other ear first." She placed the cork and pierced the other ear.

"It'll hurt."

"Hush!" said Ma. "It's all done."

Rose of Sharon looked at her in wonder. Ma clipped the needles off and pulled one knot of each thread through the lobes.

"Now," she said. "Ever' day we'll pull one knot, and in a couple weeks it'll be all well an' you can wear 'em. Here—they're your'n now. You can keep 'em."

Rose of Sharon touched her ears tenderly and looked at the tiny spots of blood on her fingers. "It didn' hurt. Jus' stuck a little."

"You oughta been pierced long ago," said Ma. She looked at the girl's face, and she smiled in triumph. "Now get them dishes all done up. Your baby gonna be a good baby. Very near let you have a baby without your ears was pierced. But you're safe now."

"Does it mean somepin?"

"Why, 'course it does," said Ma. " 'Course it does."

Al strolled down the street toward the dancing platform. Outside a neat little tent he whistled softly, and then moved along the street. He walked to the edge of the grounds and sat down in the grass.

The clouds over the west had lost the red edging now, and the cores were black. Al scratched his legs and looked toward the evening sky.

In a few moments a blond girl walked near; she was pretty and sharp-featured. She sat down in the grass beside him and did not speak. Al put his hand on her waist and walked his fingers around.

"Don't," she said. "You tickle."

"We're goin' away tomorra," said Al.

She looked at him, startled. "Tomorra? Where?"

"Up north," he said lightly.

"Well, we're gonna git married, ain't we?"

"Sure, sometime."

"You said purty soon!" she cried angrily.

"Well, soon is when soon comes."

"You promised." He walked his fingers around farther. "Git away," she cried. "You said we was."

"Well, sure we are."

"An' now you're goin' away."

Al demanded, "What's the matter with you? You in a fambly way?"

"No, I ain't."

Al laughed. "I jus' been wastin' my time, huh?"

Her chin shot out. She jumped to her feet. "You git away from me, Al Joad. I don' wanta see you no more."

"Aw, come on. What's the matter?"

"You think you're jus'—hell on wheels."

"Now wait a minute."

"You think I got to go out with you. Well, I don't! I got lots a chances."

"Now wait a minute."

"No, sir—you git away."

Al lunged suddenly, caught her by the ankle, and tripped her. He grabbed her when she fell and held her and put his hand over her angry mouth. She tried to bite his palm, but he cupped it out over her mouth, and he held her down with his other arm. And in a moment she lay still, and in another moment they were giggling together in the dry grass.

"Why, we'll be a-comin' back purty soon," said Al. "An' I'll have a pocketful a jack. We'll go down to Hollywood an' see the pitchers."

She was lying on her back. Al bent over her. And he saw the bright evening star reflected in her eyes, and he saw the black cloud reflected in her eyes. "We'll go on the train," he said.

"How long ya think it'll be?" she asked.

"Oh, maybe a month," he said.

The evening dark came down and Pa and Uncle John squatted with the heads of families out by the office. They studied the night and the future. The little manager, in his white clothes, frayed and clean, rested his elbows on the porch rail. His face was drawn and tired.

Huston looked up at him. "You better get some sleep, mister."

"I guess I ought. Baby born last night in Unit Three. I'm getting to be a good midwife."

"Fella oughta know," said Huston. "Married fella got to know."

Pa said, "We're a-gittin' out in the mornin'."

"Yeah? Which way you goin'?"

"Thought we'd go up north a little. Try to get in the first cotton. We ain't had work. We're outa food."

"Know if they's any work?" Huston asked.

"No, but we're sure they ain't none here."

"They will be, a little later," Huston said. "We'll hold on."

"We hate to go," said Pa. "Folks been so nice here—an' the toilets an' all. But we got to eat. Got a tank of gas. That'll get us a little piece up the road. We had a bath ever' day here. Never was so clean in my life. Funny thing—use ta be I on'y got a bath ever' week an' I never seemed to stink. But now if I don't get one ever' day I stink. Wonder if takin' a bath so often makes that?"

"Maybe you couldn't smell yourself before," the manager said.

"Maybe. I wisht we could stay."

The little manager held his temples between his

palms. "I think there's going to be another baby to-night," he said.

"We gonna have one in our fambly 'fore long," said Pa. "I wisht we could have it here. I sure wisht we could."

Tom and Willie and Jule the half-breed sat on the edge of the dance floor and swung their feet.

"I got a sack of Durham," Jule said. "Like a smoke?"

"I sure would," said Tom. "Ain't had a smoke for a hell of a time." He rolled the brown cigarette carefully, to keep down the loss of tobacco.

"Well, sir, we'll be sorry to see you go," said Willy. "You folks is good folks."

Tom lighted his cigarette. "I been thinkin' about it a lot. Jesus Christ, I wisht we could settle down."

Jule took back his Durham. "It ain't nice," he said. "I got a little girl. Thought when I come out here she'd get some schoolin'. But hell, we ain't in one place hardly long enough. Jes' gits goin' an' we got to drag on."

"I hope we don't get in no more Hoovervilles," said Tom. "I was really scairt, there."

"Deputies push you aroun'?"

"I was scairt I'd kill somebody," said Tom. "Was on'y there a little while, but I was a-stewin' aroun' the whole time. Depity come in an' picked up a frien', jus' because he talked outa turn. I was jus' stewin' all the time."

"Ever been in a strike?" Willie asked.

"No."

"Well, I been a-thinkin' a lot. Why don' them depities get in here an' raise hell like ever' place else? Think that little guy in the office is a-stoppin' 'em? No, sir."

"Well, what is?" Jule asked.

"I'll tell ya. It's 'cause we're all a-workin' together.

Depity can't pick on one fella in this camp. He's
pickin' on the whole darn camp. An' he don't dare. All
we got to do is give a yell an' they's two hunderd men
out. Fella organizin' for the union was a-talkin' out on
the road. He says we could do that any place. Jus'
stick together. They ain't raisin' hell with no two hunderd men. They're pickin' on one man."

"Yeah," said Jule, "an' suppose you got a union?
You got to have leaders. They'll jus' pick up your
leaders, an' where's your union?"

"Well," said Willie, "we got to figure her out some
time. I been out here a year, an' wages is goin' right
on down. Fella can't feed his fam'ly on his work now,
an' it's gettin' worse all the time. It ain't gonna do no
good to set aroun' an' starve. I don' know what to do. If
a fella owns a team a horses, he don't raise no hell if
he got to feed 'em when they ain't workin'. But if a
fella got men workin' for him, he jus' don't give a
damn. Horses is a hell of a lot more worth than men. I
don' understan' it."

"Gets so I don' wanta think about it," said Jule.
"An' I got to think about it. I got this here little girl.
You know how purty she is. One week they give her a
prize in this camp 'cause she's so purty. Well, what's
gonna happen to her? She's gettin' spindly. I ain't
gonna stan' it. She's so purty. I'm gonna bust out."

"How?" Willie asked. "What you gonna do—steal
some stuff an' git in jail? Kill somebody an' git hung?"

"I don' know," said Jule. "Gits me nuts thinkin'
about it. Gits me clear nuts."

"I'm a-gonna miss them dances," Tom said. "Them
was some of the nicest dances I ever seen. Well, I'm
gonna turn in. So long. I'll be seein' you someplace."
He shook hands.

"Sure will," said Jule.

"Well, so long." Tom moved away into the darkness.

*

In the darkness of the Joad tent Ruthie and Winfield lay on their mattress, and Ma lay beside them. Ruthie whispered, "Ma!"

"Yeah? Ain't you asleep yet?"

"Ma—they gonna have croquet where we're goin'?"

"I don' know. Get some sleep. We want to get an early start."

"Well, I wisht we'd stay here where we're sure we got croquet."

"Sh!" said Ma.

"Ma, Winfiel' hit a kid tonight."

"He shouldn' of."

"I know. I tol' 'im, but he hit the kid right in the nose an', Jesus, how the blood run down!"

"Don' talk like that. It ain't a nice way to talk."

Winfield turned over. "That kid says we was Okies," he said in an outraged voice. "He says he wasn't no Okie 'cause he come from Oregon. Says we was goddamn Okies. I socked him."

"Sh! You shouldn'. He can't hurt you callin' names."

"Well, I won't let 'im," Winfield said fiercely.

"Sh! Get some sleep."

Ruthie said, "You oughta seen the blood run down—all over his clothes."

Ma reached a hand from under the blanket and snapped Ruthie on the cheek with her finger. The little girl went rigid for a moment, and then dissolved into sniffling, quiet crying.

In the sanitary unit Pa and Uncle John sat in adjoining compartments. "Might's well get in a good las' one," said Pa. "It's sure nice. 'Member how the little fellas was so scairt when they flushed 'em the first time?"

"I wasn't so easy myself," said Uncle John. He pulled his overalls neatly up around his knees. "I'm gettin' bad," he said. "I feel sin."

"You can't sin none," said Pa. "You ain't got no money. Jus' sit tight. Cos' you at leas' two bucks to sin, an' we ain't got two bucks amongst us."

"Yeah! But I'm a-thinkin' sin."

"Awright. You can think sin for nothin'."

"It's jus' as bad," said Uncle John.

"It's a whole hell of a lot cheaper," said Pa.

"Don't you go makin' light of sin."

"I ain't. You jus' go ahead. You always gets sinful jus' when hell's a-poppin'."

"I know it," said Uncle John. "Always was that way. I never tol' half the stuff I done."

"Well, keep it to yaself."

"These here nice toilets gets me sinful."

"Go out in the bushes then. Come on, pull up ya pants an' le's get some sleep." Pa pulled his overall straps in place and snapped the buckle. He flushed the toilet and watched thoughtfully while the water whirled in the bowl.

It was still dark when Ma roused her camp. The low night lights shone through the open doors of the sanitary units. From the tents along the road came the assorted snores of the campers.

Ma said, "Come on, roll out. We got to be on our way. Day's not far off." She raised the screechy shade of the lantern and lighted the wick. "Come on, all of you."

The floor of the tent squirmed into slow action. Blankets and comforts were thrown back and sleepy eyes squinted blindly at the light. Ma slipped on her dress over the underclothes she wore to bed. "We got no coffee," she said. "I got a few biscuits. We can eat 'em on the road. Jus' get up now, an' we'll load the truck. Come on now. Don't make no noise. Don' wanta wake the neighbors."

It was a few moments before they were fully aroused. "Now don' you get away," Ma warned the

children. The family dressed. The men pulled down
the tarpaulin and loaded up the truck. "Make it nice
an' flat," Ma warned them. They piled the mattress on
top of the load and bound the tarpaulin in place over
its ridge pole.

"Awright, Ma," said Tom. "She's ready."

Ma held a plate of cold biscuits in her hand.
"Awright. Here. Each take one. It's all we got."

Ruthie and Winfield grabbed their biscuits and
climbed up on the load. They covered themselves with
a blanket and went back to sleep, still holding the cold
hard biscuits in their hands. Tom got into the driver's
seat and stepped on the starter. It buzzed a little, and
then stopped.

"Goddamn you, Al!" Tom cried. "You let the battery run down."

Al blustered, "How the hell was I gonna keep her
up if I ain't got gas to run her?"

Tom chuckled suddenly. "Well, I don' know how,
but it's your fault. You got to crank her."

"I tell you it ain't my fault."

Tom got out and found the crank under the seat.
"It's my fault," he said.

"Gimme that crank." Al seized it. "Pull down the
spark so she don't take my arm off."

"O.K. Twist her tail."

Al labored at the crank, around and around. The
engine caught, spluttered, and roared as Tom choked
the car delicately. He raised the spark and reduced
the throttle.

Ma climbed in beside him. "We woke up ever'body
in the camp," she said.

"They'll go to sleep again."

Al climbed in on the other side. "Pa 'n' Uncle John
got up top," he said. "Goin' to sleep again."

Tom drove toward the main gate. The watchman
came out of the office and played his flashlight on the
truck. "Wait a minute."

"What ya want?"

"You checkin' out?"

"Sure."

"Well, I got to cross you off."

"O.K."

"Know which way you're goin'?"

"Well, we're gonna try up north."

"Well, good luck," said the watchman.

"Same to you. So long."

The truck edged slowly over the big hump and into the road. Tom retraced the road he had driven before, past Weedpatch and west until he came to 99, then north on the great paved road, toward Bakersfield. It was growing light when he came into the outskirts of the city.

Tom said, "Ever' place you look is restaurants. An' them places all got coffee. Lookit that all-nighter there. Bet they got ten gallons a coffee in there, all hot!"

"Aw, shut up," said Al.

Tom grinned over at him. "Well, I see you got yaself a girl right off."

"Well, what of it?"

"He's mean this mornin', Ma. He ain't good company."

Al said irritably, "I'm goin' out on my own purty soon. Fella can make his way lot easier if he ain't got a fambly."

Tom said, "You have yaself a fambly in nine months. I seen you playin' aroun'."

"Ya crazy," said Al. "I'd get myself a job in a garage an' I'd eat in restaurants——"

"An' you'd have a wife an' kid in nine months."

"I tell ya I wouldn'."

Tom said, "You're a wise guy, Al. You gonna take some beatin' over the head."

"Who's gonna do it?"

"They'll always be guys to do it," said Tom.

"You think jus' because you——"

"Now you jus' stop that," Ma broke in.

"I done it," said Tom. "I was a-badgerin' him. I didn' mean no harm, Al. I didn' know you liked that girl so much."

"I don't like no girls much."

"Awright, then, you don't. You ain't gonna get no argument out of me."

The truck came to the edge of the city. "Look a them hotdog stan's—hunderds of 'em," said Tom.

Ma said, "Tom! I got a dollar put away. You wan' coffee bad enough to spen' it?"

"No, Ma. I'm jus' foolin'."

"You can have it if you wan' it bad enough."

"I wouldn' take it."

Al said, "Then shut up about coffee."

Tom was silent for a time. "Seems like I got my foot in it all the time," he said. "There's the road we run up that night."

"I hope we don't never have nothin' like that again," said Ma. "That was a bad night."

"I didn' like it none either."

The sun rose on their right, and the great shadow of the truck ran beside them, flicking over the fence posts beside the road. They ran on past the rebuilt Hooverville.

"Look," said Tom. "They got new people there. Looks like the same place."

Al came slowly out of his sullenness. "Fella tol' me some a them people been burned out fifteen-twenty times. Says they jus' go hide down the willows an' then they come out an' build 'em another weed shack. Jus' like gophers. Got so use' to it they don't even get mad no more, this fella says. They jus' figger it's like bad weather."

"Sure was bad weather for me that night," said Tom. They moved up the wide highway. And the sun's warmth made them shiver. "Gettin' snappy in the mornin'," said Tom. "Winter's on the way. I jus' hope we can get some money 'fore it comes. Tent ain't gonna be nice in the winter."

Ma sighed, and then she straightened her head. "Tom," she said, "we gotta have a house in the winter. I tell ya we got to. Ruthie's awright, but Winfiel' ain't so strong. We got to have a house when the rains come. I heard it jus' rains cats aroun' here."

"We'll get a house, Ma. You res' easy. You gonna have a house."

"Jus' so's it's got a roof an' a floor. Jus' to keep the little fellas off'n the groun'.'"

"We'll try, Ma."

"I don' wanna worry ya now."

"We'll try, Ma."

"I jus' get panicky sometimes," she said. "I jus' lose my spunk."

"I never seen you when you lost it."

"Nights I do, sometimes."

There came a harsh hissing from the front of the truck. Tom grabbed the wheel tight and he thrust the brake down to the floor. The truck bumped to a stop. Tom sighed. "Well, there she is." He leaned back in the seat. Al leaped out and ran to the right front tire.

"Great big nail," he called.

"We got any tire patch?"

"No," said Al. "Used it all up. Got patch, but no glue stuff."

Tom turned and smiled sadly at Ma. "You shouldn' a tol' about that dollar," he said. "We'd a fixed her some way." He got out of the car and went to the flat tire.

Al pointed to a big nail protruding from the flat casing. "There she is!"

"If they's one nail in the county, we run over it."

"Is it bad?" Ma called.

"No, not bad, but we got to fix her."

The family piled down from the top of the truck.

"Puncture?" Pa asked, and then he saw the tire and was silent.

Tom moved Ma from the seat and got the can of tire patch from underneath the cushion. He unrolled the rubber patch and took out the tube of cement, squeezed it gently. "She's almos' dry," he said. "Maybe they's enough. Awright, Al. Block the back wheels. Le's get her jacked up."

Tom and Al worked well together. They put stones behind the wheels, put the jack under the front axle, and lifted the weight off the limp casing. They ripped off the casing. They found the hole, dipped a rag in the gas tank and washed the tube around the hole. And then, while Al held the tube tight over his knee, Tom tore the cement tube in two and spread the little fluid thinly on the rubber with his pocket knife. He scraped the gum delicately. "Now let her dry while I cut a patch." He trimmed and beveled the edge of the blue patch. Al held the tube tight while Tom put the patch tenderly in place. "There! Now bring her to the running board while I tap her with a hammer." He pounded the patch carefully, then stretched the tube and watched the edges of the patch. "There she is! She's gonna hold. Stick her on the rim an' we'll pump her up. Looks like you keep your buck, Ma."

Al said, "I wisht we had a spare. We got to get us a spare, Tom, on a rim an' all pumped up. Then we can fix a puncture at night."

"When we get money for a spare we'll get us some coffee an' side-meat instead," Tom said.

The light morning traffic buzzed by on the highway, and the sun grew warm and bright. A wind, gentle and sighing, blew in puffs from the southwest, and the mountains on both sides of the great valley were indistinct in a pearly mist.

Tom was pumping at the tire when a roadster, coming from the north, stopped on the other side of the road. A brown-faced man dressed in a light gray business suit got out and walked across to the truck. He was bareheaded. He smiled, and his teeth were very white against his brown skin. He wore a massive gold wedding ring on the third finger of his left hand. A little gold football hung on a slender chain across his vest.

"Morning," he said pleasantly.

Tom stopped pumping and looked up. "Mornin'."

The man ran his fingers through his coarse, short, graying hair. "You people looking for work?"

"We sure are, mister. Lookin' even under boards."

"Can you pick peaches?"

"We never done it," Pa said.

"We can do anything," Tom said hurriedly. "We can pick anything there is."

The man fingered his gold football. "Well, there's plenty of work for you about forty miles north."

"We'd sure admire to get it," said Tom. "You tell us how to get there, an' we'll go a-lopin'."

"Well, you go north to Pixley, that's thirty-five or -six miles, and you turn east. Go about six miles. Ask anybody where the Hooper ranch is. You'll find plenty of work there."

"We sure will."

"Know where there's other people looking for work?"

"Sure," said Tom. "Down at the Weedpatch camp they's plenty lookin' for work."

"I'll take a run down there. We can use quite a few. Remember now, turn east at Pixley and keep straight east to the Hooper ranch."

"Sure," said Tom. "An' we thank ya, mister. We need work awful bad."

"All right. Get along as soon as you can." He walked back across the road, climbed into his open roadster, and drove away south.

Tom threw his weight on the pump. "Twenty apiece," he called. "One—two—three—four—" At twenty Al took the pump, and then Pa and then Uncle John. The tire filled out and grew plump and smooth. Three times around, the pump went. "Let 'er down an' le's see," said Tom.

Al released the jack and lowered the car. "Got plenty," he said. "Maybe a little too much."

They threw the tools into the car. "Come on, le's go," Tom called. "We're gonna get some work at last."

Ma got in the middle again. Al drove this time.

"Now take her easy. Don't burn her up, Al."

They drove on through the sunny morning fields. The mist lifted from the hilltops and they were clear and brown, with black-purple creases. The wild doves flew up from the fences as the truck passed. Al unconsciously increased his speed.

"Easy," Tom warned him. "She'll blow up if you crowd her. We got to get there. Might even get in some work today."

Ma said excitedly, "With four men a-workin' maybe I can get some credit right off. Fust thing I'll get is coffee, 'cause you been wanting that, an' then some flour an' bakin' powder an' some meat. Better not get no side-meat right off. Save that for later. Maybe Sat'd'y. An' soap. Got to get soap. Wonder where we'll stay." She babbled on. "An' milk. I'll get some milk 'cause Rosasharn, she ought to have milk. The lady nurse says that."

A snake wriggled across the warm highway. Al zipped over and ran it down and came back to his own lane.

"Gopher snake," said Tom. "You oughtn't to done that."

"I hate 'em," said Al gaily. "Hate all kinds. Give me the stomach-quake."

The forenoon traffic on the highway increased, salesmen in shiny coupés with the insignia of their companies painted on the doors, red and white gasoline trucks dragging clinking chains behind them,

great square-doored vans from wholesale grocery
houses, delivering produce. The country was rich
along the roadside. There were orchards, heavy leafed
in their prime, and vineyards with the long green
crawlers carpeting the ground between the rows. There
were melon patches and grain fields. White houses
stood in the greenery, roses growing over them. And
the sun was gold and warm.

In the front seat of the truck Ma and Tom and Al
were overcome with happiness. "I ain't really felt so
good for a long time," Ma said. " 'F we pick plenty
peaches we might get a house, pay rent even, for a
couple months. We got to have a house."

Al said, "I'm a-gonna save up. I'll save up an' then
I'm a-goin' in a town an' get me a job in a garage. Live
in a room an' eat in restaurants. Go to the movin'
pitchers ever' damn night. Don' cost much. Cowboy
pitchers." His hands tightened on the wheel.

The radiator bubbled and hissed steam. "Did you
fill her up?" Tom asked.

"Yeah. Wind's kinda behind us. That's what makes
her boil."

"It's a awful nice day," Tom said. "Use' ta work
there in McAlester an' think all the things I'd do. I'd
go in a straight line way to hell an' gone an' never stop
nowheres. Seems like a long time ago. Seems like it's
years ago I was in. They was a guard made it tough. I
was gonna lay for 'im. Guess that's what makes me
mad at cops. Seems like ever' cop got his face. He
use' ta get red in the face. Looked like a pig. Had a
brother out west, they said. Use' ta get fellas paroled
to his brother, an' then they had to work for nothin'. If
they raised a stink, they'd get sent back for breakin'
parole. That's what the fellers said."

"Don' think about it," Ma begged him. "I'm a-gonna
lay in a lot a stuff to eat. Lot a flour an' lard."

"Might's well think about it," said Tom. "Try to
shut it out, an' it'll whang back at me. They was a

screwball. Never tol' you 'bout him. Looked like Happy Hooligan. Harmless kinda fella. Always was gonna make a break. Fellas all called him Hooligan." Tom laughed to himself.

"Don' think about it," Ma begged.

"Go on," said Al. "Tell about the fella."

"It don't hurt nothin', Ma," Tom said. "This fella was always gonna break out. Make a plan, he would; but he couldn' keep it to hisself an' purty soon ever'body knowed it, even the warden. He'd make his break an' they'd take 'im by the han' an' lead 'im back. Well, one time he drawed a plan where he's goin' over. 'Course he showed it aroun', an' ever'body kep' still. An' he hid out, an' ever'body kep' still. So he's got himself a rope somewheres, an' he goes over the wall. They's six guards outside with a great big sack, an' Hooligan comes quiet down the rope an' they jus' hol' the sack out an' he goes right inside. They tie up the mouth an' take 'im back inside. Fellas laughed so hard they like to died. But it busted Hooligan's spirit. He jus' cried an' cried, an' moped aroun' an' got sick. Hurt his feelin's so bad. Cut his wrists with a pin an' bled to death 'cause his feelin's was hurt. No harm in 'im at all. They's all kinds a screwballs in stir."

"Don't talk about it," Ma said. "I knowed Purty Boy Floyd's ma. He wan't a bad boy. Jus' got drove in a corner."

The sun moved up toward noon and the shadow of the truck grew lean and moved in under the wheels.

"Mus' be Pixley up the road," Al said. "Seen a sign a little back." They drove into the little town and turned eastward on a narrower road. And the orchards lined the way and made an aisle.

"Hope we can find her easy," Tom said.

Ma said, "That fella said the Hooper ranch. Said anybody'd tell us. Hope they's a store near by. Might get some credit, with four men workin'. I could get a

real nice supper if they'd gimme some credit. Make up
a big stew maybe."

"An' coffee," said Tom. "Might even get me a sack
a Durham. I ain't had no tobacca of my own for a long
time."

Far ahead the road was blocked with cars, and a
line of white motorcycles was drawn up along the roadside. "Mus' be a wreck," Tom said.

As they drew near a State policeman, in boots and
Sam Browne belt, stepped around the last parked car.
He held up his hand and Al pulled to a stop. The
policeman leaned confidentially on the side of the car.
"Where you going?"

Al said, "Fella said they was work pickin' peaches
up this way."

"Want to work, do you?"

"Damn right," said Tom.

"O.K. Wait here a minute." He moved to the side of
the road and called ahead. "One more. That's six cars
ready. Better take this batch through."

Tom called, "Hey! What's the matter?"

The patrol man lounged back. "Got a little trouble
up ahead. Don't you worry. You'll get through. Just
follow the line."

There came the splattering blast of motorcycles
starting. The line of cars moved on, with the Joad
truck last. Two motorcycles led the way, and two
followed.

Tom said uneasily, "I wonder what's a matter."

"Maybe the road's out," Al suggested.

"Don' need four cops to lead us. I don' like it."

The motorcycles ahead speeded up. The line of old
cars speeded up. Al hurried to keep in back of the last
car.

"These here is our own people, all of 'em," Tom
said. "I don' like this."

Suddenly the leading policemen turned off the road
into a wide graveled entrance. The old cars whipped

after them. The motorcycles roared their motors. Tom saw a line of men standing in the ditch beside the road, saw their mouths open as though they were yelling, saw their shaking fists and their furious faces. A stout woman ran toward the cars, but a roaring motorcycle stood in her way. A high wire gate swung open. The six old cars moved through and the gate closed behind them. The four motorcycles turned and sped back in the direction from which they had come. And now that the motors were gone, the distant yelling of the men in the ditch could be heard. Two men stood beside the graveled road. Each one carried a shotgun.

One called, "Go on, go on. What the hell are you waiting for?" The six cars moved ahead, turned a bend and came suddenly on the peach camp.

There were fifty little square, flat-roofed boxes, each with a door and a window, and the whole group in a square. A water tank stood high on one edge of the camp. And a little grocery store stood on the other side. At the end of each row of square houses stood two men armed with shotguns and wearing big silver stars pinned to their shirts.

The six cars stopped. Two bookkeepers moved from car to car. "Want to work?"

Tom answered, "Sure, but what is this?"

"That's not your affair. Want to work?"

"Sure we do."

"Name?"

"Joad."

"How many men?"

"Four."

"Women?"

"Two."

"Kids?"

"Two."

"Can all of you work?"

"Why—I guess so."

"O.K. Find house sixty-three. Wages five cents a

box. No bruised fruit. All right, move along now. Go to work right away."

The cars moved on. On the door of each square red house a number was painted. "Sixty," Tom said. "There's sixty. Must be down that way. There, sixty-one, sixty-two—There she is."

Al parked the truck close 'to the door of the little house. The family came down from the top of the truck and looked about in bewilderment. Two deputies approached. They looked closely into each face.

"Name?"

"Joad," Tom said impatiently. "Say, what is this here?"

One of the deputies took out a long list. "Not here. Ever see these here? Look at the license. Nope. Ain't got it. Guess they're O.K."

"Now you look here. We don't want no trouble with you. Jes' do your work and mind your own business and you'll be all right." The two turned abruptly and walked away. At the end of the dusty street they sat down on two boxes and their position commanded the length of the street.

Tom stared after them. "They sure do wanta make us feel at home."

Ma opened the door of the house and stepped inside. The floor was splashed with grease. In the one room stood a rusty tin stove and nothing more. The tin stove rested on four bricks and its rusty stovepipe went up through the roof. The room smelled of sweat and grease. Rose of Sharon stood beside Ma. "We gonna live here?"

Ma was silent for a moment. "Why, sure," she said at last. "It ain't so bad once we wash it out. Get her mopped."

"I like the tent better," the girl said.

"This got a floor," Ma suggested. "This here wouldn' leak when it rains." She turned to the door. "Might as well unload," she said.

The men unloaded the truck silently. A fear had fallen on them. The great square of boxes was silent. A woman went by in the street, but she did not look at them. Her head was sunk and her dirty gingham dress was frayed at the bottom in little flags.

The pall had fallen on Ruthie and Winfield. They did not dash away to inspect the place. They stayed close to the truck, close to the family. They looked forlornly up and down the dusty street. Winfield found a piece of baling wire and he bent it back and forth until it broke. He made a little crank of the shortest piece and turned it around and around in his hands.

Tom and Pa were carrying the mattresses into the house when a clerk appeared. He wore khaki trousers and a blue shirt and a black necktie. He wore silver-bound eyeglasses, and his eyes, through the thick lenses, were weak and red, and the pupils were staring little bull's eyes. He leaned forward to look at Tom.

"I want to get you checked down," he said. "How many of you going to work?"

Tom said, "They's four men. Is this here hard work?"

"Picking peaches," the clerk said. "Piece work. Give five cents a box."

"Ain't no reason why the little fellas can't help?"

"Sure not, if they're careful."

Ma stood in the doorway. "Soon's I get settled down I'll come out an' help. We got nothin' to eat, mister. Do we get paid right off?"

"Well, no, not money right off. But you can get credit at the store for what you got coming."

"Come on, let's hurry," Tom said. "I want ta get some meat an' bread in me tonight. Where do we go, mister?"

"I'm going out there now. Come with me."

Tom and Pa and Al and Uncle John walked with him down the dusty street and into the orchard, in among the peach trees. The narrow leaves were beginning to turn a pale yellow. The peaches were little globes of gold and red on the branches. Among the trees were piles of empty boxes. The pickers scurried about, filling their buckets from the branches, putting the peaches in the boxes, carrying the boxes to the checking station; and at the stations, where the piles of filled boxes waited for the trucks, clerks waited to check against the names of the pickers.

"Here's four more," the guide said to a clerk.

"O.K. Ever picked before?"

"Never did," said Tom.

"Well, pick careful. No bruised fruit, no windfalls. Bruise your fruit an' we won't check 'em. There's some buckets."

Tom picked up a three-gallon bucket and looked at it. "Full a holes on the bottom."

"Sure," said the near-sighted clerk. "That keeps people from stealing them. All right—down in that section. Get going."

The four Joads took their buckets and went into the orchard. "They don't waste no time," Tom said.

"Christ Awmighty," Al said. "I ruther work in a garage."

Pa had followed docilely into the field. He turned suddenly on Al. "Now you jus' quit it," he said. "You been a-hankerin' an' a-complainin' an' a-bullblowin'. You get to work. You ain't so big I can't lick you yet."

Al's face turned red with anger. He started to bluster.

Tom moved near to him. "Come on, Al," he said quietly. "Bread an' meat. We got to get 'em."

They reached for the fruit and dropped them in the buckets. Tom ran at his work. One bucket full, two buckets. He dumped them in a box. Three buckets. The box was full. "I jus' made a nickel," he called. He picked up the box and walked hurriedly to the station. "Here's a nickel's worth," he said to the checker.

The man looked into the box, turned over a peach or two. "Put it over there. That's out," he said. "I told you not to bruise them. Dumped 'em outa the bucket, didn't you? Well, every damn peach is bruised. Can't check that one. Put 'em in easy or you're working for nothing."

"Why—goddamn it——"

"Now go easy. I warned you before you started."

Tom's eyes drooped sullenly. "O.K." he said. "O.K." He went quickly back to the others. "Might's well dump what you got," he said. "Yours is the same as mine. Won't take 'em."

"Now, what the hell!" Al began.

"Got to pick easier. Can't drop 'em in the bucket. Got to lay 'em in."

They started again, and this time they handled the fruit gently. The boxes filled more slowly. "We could figger somepin out, I bet," Tom said. "If Ruthie an' Winfiel' or Rosasharn jus' put 'em in the boxes, we could work out a system." He carried his newest box to the station. "Is this here worth a nickel?"

The checker looked them over, dug down several layers. "That's better," he said. He checked the box in. "Just take it easy."

Tom hurried back. "I got a nickel," he called. "I got a nickel. On'y got to do that there twenty times for a dollar."

They worked on steadily through the afternoon. Ruthie and Winfield found them after a while. "You got to work," Pa told them. "You got to put the peaches careful in the box. Here, now, one at a time."

The children squatted down and picked the peaches out of the extra bucket, and a line of buckets stood ready for them. Tom carried the full boxes to the station. "That's seven," he said. "That's eight. Forty cents we got. Get a nice piece of meat for forty cents."

The afternoon passed. Ruthie tried to go away. "I'm tar'd," she whined. "I got to rest."

"You got to stay right where you're at," said Pa.

Uncle John picked slowly. He filled one bucket to two of Tom's. His pace didn't change.

In mid-afternoon Ma came trudging out. "I would a come before, but Rosasharn fainted," she said. "Jes' fainted away."

"You been eatin' peaches," she said to the children. "Well, they'll blast you out." Ma's stubby body moved quickly. She abandoned her bucket quickly and picked into her apron. When the sun went down they had picked twenty boxes.

Tom set the twentieth box down. "A buck," he said. "How long do we work?"

"Work till dark, long as you can see."

"Well, can we get credit now? Ma oughta go in an' buy some stuff to eat."

"Sure. I'll give you a slip for a dollar now." He wrote on a strip of paper and handed it to Tom.

He took it to Ma. "Here you are. You can get a dollar's worth of stuff at the store."

Ma put down her bucket and straightened her shoulders. "Gets you, the first time, don't it?"

"Sure. We'll all get used to it right off. Roll on in an' get some food."

Ma said, "What'll you like to eat?"

"Meat," said Tom. "Meat an' bread an' a big pot a coffee with sugar in. Great big piece a meat."

Ruthie wailed, "Ma, we're tar'd."

"Better come along in, then."

"They was tar'd when they started," Pa said. "Wild as rabbits they're a-gettin'. Ain't gonna be no good at all 'less we can pin 'em down."

"Soon's we get set down, they'll go to school," said Ma. She trudged away, and Ruthie and Winfield timidly followed her.

"We got to work ever' day?" Winfield asked.

Ma stopped and waited. She took his hand and walked along holding it. "It ain't hard work," she said.

"Be good for you. An' you're helpin' us. If we all work, purty soon we'll live in a nice house. We all got to help."

"But I got so tar'd."

"I know. I got tar'd too. Ever'body gets wore out. Got to think about stuff. Think about when you'll go to school."

"I don't wanta go to no school. Ruthie don't, neither. Them kids that goes to school, we seen 'em, Ma. Snots! Calls us Okies. We seen 'em. I ain't a-goin'."

Ma looked pityingly down on his straw hair. "Don' give us no trouble right now," she begged. "Soon's we get on our feet, you can be bad. But not now. We got too much, now."

"I et six of them peaches," Ruthie said.

"Well, you'll have the skitters. An' it ain't close to no toilet where we are."

The company's store was a large shed of corrugated iron. It had no display window. Ma opened the screen door and went in. A tiny man stood behind the counter. He was completely bald, and his head was blue-white. Large, brown eyebrows covered his eyes in such a high arch that his face seemed surprised and a little frightened. His nose was long and thin, and curved like a bird's beak, and his nostrils were blocked with light brown hair. Over the sleeves of his blue shirt he wore black sateen sleeve protectors. He was leaning on his elbows on the counter when Ma entered.

"Afternoon," she said.

He inspected her with interest. The arch over his eyes became higher. "Howdy."

"I got a slip here for a dollar."

"You can get a dollar's worth," he said, and he giggled shrilly. "Yes, sir. A dollar's worth. One dollar's worth." He moved his hand at the stock. "Any of it." He pulled his sleeve protectors up neatly.

"Thought I'd get a piece of meat."

"Got all kinds," he said. "Hamburg, like to have some hamburg? Twenty cents a pound, hamburg."

"Ain't that awful high? Seems to me hamburg was fifteen las' time I got some."

"Well," he giggled softly, "yes, it's high, an' same time it ain't high. Time you go on in town for a couple poun's of hamburg, it'll cos' you 'bout a gallon gas. So you see it ain't really high here, 'cause you got no gallon a gas."

Ma said sternly, "It didn' cos' you no gallon a gas to get it out here."

He laughed delightedly. "You're lookin' at it bass-ackwards," he said. "We ain't a-buyin' it, we're a-sellin' it. If we was buyin' it, why, that'd be different."

Ma put two fingers to her mouth and frowned with thought. "It looks all full a fat an' gristle."

"I ain't guaranteein' she won't cook down," the storekeeper said. "I ain't guaranteein' I'd eat her myself; but they's lots of stuff I wouldn' do."

Ma looked up at him fiercely for a moment. She controlled her voice. "Ain't you got some cheaper kind a meat?"

"Soup bones," he said. "Ten cents a pound."

"But them's jus' bones."

"Them's jes' bones," he said. "Make nice soup. Jes' bones."

"Got any boilin' beef?"

"Oh, yeah! Sure. That's two bits a poun'."

"Maybe I can't get no meat," Ma said. "But they want meat. They said they wanted meat."

"Ever'body wants meat—needs meat. That hamburg is purty nice stuff. Use the grease that comes out a her for gravy. Purty nice. No waste. Don't throw no bone away."

"How—how much is side-meat?"

"Well, now you're gettin' into fancy stuff. Christmas

stuff. Thanksgivin' stuff. Thirty-five cents a poun'. I could sell you turkey cheaper, if I had some turkey."

Ma sighed. "Give me two pounds hamburg."

"Yes, ma'am." He scooped the pale meat on a piece of waxed paper. "An' what else?"

"Well, some bread."

"Right here. Fine big loaf, fifteen cents."

"That there's a twelve-cent loaf."

"Sure, it is. Go right in town an' get her for twelve cents. Gallon a gas. What else can I sell you, potatoes?"

"Yes, potatoes."

"Five pounds for a quarter."

Ma moved menacingly toward him. "I heard enough from you. I know what they cost in town."

The little man clamped his mouth tight. "Then go git 'em in town."

Ma looked at her knuckles. "What is this?" she asked softly. "You own this here store?"

"No. I jus' work here."

"Any reason you got to make fun? That help you any?" She regarded her shiny wrinkled hands. The little man was silent. "Who owns this here store?"

"Hooper Ranches, Incorporated, ma'am."

"An' they set the prices?"

"Yes, ma'am."

She looked up, smiling a little. "Ever'body comes in talks like me, is mad?"

He hesitated for a moment. "Yes, ma'am."

"An' that's why you make fun?"

"What cha mean?"

"Doin' a dirty thing like this. Shames ya, don't it? Got to act flip, huh?" Her voice was gentle. The clerk watched her, fascinated. He didn't answer. "That's how it is," Ma said finally. "Forty cents for meat, fifteen for bread, quarter for potatoes. That's eighty cents. Coffee?"

"Twenty cents the cheapest, ma'am."

"An' that's the dollar. Seven of us workin', an' that's supper." She studied her hand. "Wrap 'em up," she said quickly.

"Yes, ma'am," he said. "Thanks." He put the potatoes in a bag and folded the top carefully down. His eyes slipped to Ma, and then hid in his work again. She watched him, and she smiled a little.

"How'd you get a job like this?" she asked.

"A fella got to eat," he began; and then, belligerently, "A fella got a right to eat."

"What fella?" Ma asked.

He placed the four packages on the counter. "Meat," he said. "Potatoes, bread, coffee. One dollar, even." She handed him her slip of paper and watched while he entered the name and the amount in a ledger. "There," he said. "Now we're all even."

Ma picked up her bags. "Say," she said. "We got no sugar for the coffee. My boy Tom, he wants sugar. Look!" she said. "They're a-workin' out there. You let me have some sugar an' I'll bring the slip in later."

The little man looked away—took his eyes as far from Ma as he could. "I can't do it," he said softly. "That's the rule. I can't. I'd get in trouble. I'd get canned."

"But they're a-workin' out in the field now. They got more'n a dime comin'. Gimme ten cents' of sugar. Tom, he wanted sugar in his coffee. Spoke about it."

"I can't do it, ma'am. That's the rule. No slip, no groceries. The manager, he talks about that all the time. No, I can't do it. No, I can't. They'd catch me. They always catch fellas. Always. I can't."

"For a dime?"

"For anything, ma'am." He looked pleadingly at her. And then his face lost its fear. He took ten cents from his pocket and rang it up in the cash register. "There," he said with relief. He pulled a little bag from under the counter, whipped it open and scooped some sugar into it, weighed the bag, and added a little more sugar. "There you are," he said. "Now it's all right. You bring in your slip an' I'll get my dime back."

Ma studied him. Her hand went blindly out and put the little bag of sugar on the pile in her arm. "Thanks to you," she said quietly. She started for the door, and when she reached it, she turned about. "I'm learnin' one thing good," she said. "Learnin' it all a time, ever' day. If you're in trouble or hurt or need—go to poor people. They're the only ones that'll help—the only ones." The screen door slammed behind her.

The little man leaned his elbows on the counter and looked after her with his surprised eyes. A plump tortoise-shell cat leaped up on the counter and stalked lazily near to him. It rubbed sideways against his arms, and he reached out with his hand and pulled it against his cheek. The cat purred loudly, and the tip of its tail jerked back and forth.

Tom and Al and Pa and Uncle John walked in from the orchard when the dusk was deep. Their feet were a little heavy against the road.

"You wouldn' think jus' reachin' up an' pickin'd get you in the back," Pa said.

"Be awright in a couple days," said Tom. "Say, Pa, after we eat I'm a-gonna walk out an' see what all that fuss is outside the gate. It's been a-workin' on me. Wanta come?"

"No," said Pa. "I like to have a little while to jus' work an' not think about nothin'. Seems like I jus' been beatin' my brains to death for a hell of a long time. No, I'm gonna set awhile, an' then go to bed."

"How 'bout you, Al?"

Al looked away. "Guess I'll look aroun' in here, first," he said.

"Well, I know Uncle John won't come. Guess I'll go her alone. Got me all curious."

Pa said, "I'll get a hell of a lot curiouser 'fore I'll do anything about it—with all them cops out there."

"Maybe they ain't there at night," Tom suggested.

"Well, I ain't gonna find out. An' you better not tell Ma where you're a-goin'. She'll jus' squirt her head off worryin'."

Tom turned to Al. "Ain't you curious?"

"Guess I'll jes' look aroun' this here camp," Al said.

"Lookin' for girls, huh?"

"Mindin' my own business," Al said acidly.

"I'm still a-goin'," said Tom.

They emerged from the orchard into the dusty street between the red shacks. The low yellow light of kerosene lanterns shone from some of the doorways, and inside, in the half-gloom, the black shapes of people moved about. At the end of the street a guard still sat, his shotgun resting against his knee.

Tom paused as he passed the guard. "Got a place where a fella can get a bath, mister?"

The guard studied him in the half-light. At last he said, "See that water tank?"

"Yeah."

"Well, there's a hose over there."

"Any warm water?"

"Say, who in hell you think you are, J. P. Morgan?"

"No," said Tom. "No, I sure don't. Good night, mister."

The guard grunted contemptuously. "Hot water, for Christ's sake. Be wantin' tubs next." He stared glumly after the four Joads.

A second guard came around the end house. " 'S'matter, Mack?"

"Why, them goddamn Okies. 'Is they warm water?' he says."

The second guard rested his gun butt on the ground. "It's them gov'ment camps," he said. "I bet that fella been in a gov'ment camp. We ain't gonna have no peace till we wipe them camps out. They'll be wantin' clean sheets, first thing we know."

Mack asked, "How is it out at the main gate—hear anything?"

"Well, they was out there yellin' all day. State police got it in hand. They're runnin' the hell outa them smart guys. I heard they's a long lean son-of-bitch spark-pluggin' the thing. Fella says they'll get him tonight, an' then she'll go to pieces."

"We won't have no job if it comes too easy," Mack said.

"We'll have a job, all right. These goddamn Okies! You got to watch 'em all the time. Things get a little quiet, we can always stir 'em up a little."

"Have trouble when they cut the rate here, I guess."

"We sure will. No, you needn' worry about us havin' work—not while Hooper's snubbin' close."

The fire roared in the Joad house. Hamburger patties splashed and hissed in the grease, and the potatoes bubbled. The house was full of smoke, and the yellow lantern light threw heavy black shadows on the walls. Ma worked quickly about the fire while Rose of Sharon sat on a box resting her heavy abdomen on her knees.

"Feelin' better now?" Ma asked.

"Smell a cookin' gets me. I'm hungry, too."

"Go set in the door," Ma said. "I got to have that box to break up anyways."

The men trooped in. "Meat, by God!" said Tom. "And coffee. I smell her. Jesus, I'm hungry! I et a lot of peaches, but they didn' do no good. Where can we wash, Ma?"

"Go down to the water tank. Wash down there. I jus' sent Ruthie an' Winfiel' to wash." The men went out again.

"Go on now, Rosasharn," Ma ordered. "Either you set in the door or else on the bed. I got to break that box up."

The girl helped herself up with her hands. She moved heavily to one of the mattresses and sat down on it. Ruthie and Winfield came in quietly, trying by silence and by keeping close to the wall to remain obscure.

Ma looked over at them. "I got a feelin' you little fellas is lucky they ain't much light," she said. She pounced at Winfield and felt his hair. "Well, you got wet, anyway, but I bet you ain't clean."

"They wasn't no soap," Winfield complained.

"No, that's right. I couldn' buy no soap. Not today. Maybe we can get soap tomorra." She went back to the stove, laid out the plates, and began to serve the supper. Two patties apiece and a big potato. She placed three slices of bread on each plate. When the meat was all out of the frying pan she poured a little of the grease on each plate. The men came in again, their faces dripping and their hair shining with water.

"Leave me at her," Tom cried.

They took the plates. They ate silently, wolfishly, and wiped up the grease with the bread. The children retired into the corner of the room, put their plates on the floor, and knelt in front of the food like little animals.

Tom swallowed the last of his bread. "Got any more, Ma?"

"No," she said. "That's all. You made a dollar, an' that's a dollar's worth."

"That?"

"They charge extry out here. We got to go in town when we can."

"I ain't full," said Tom.

"Well, tomorra you'll get in a full day. Tomorra night—we'll have plenty."

Al wiped his mouth on his sleeve. "Guess I'll take a look around," he said.

"Wait, I'll go with you." Tom followed him outside.

In the darkness Tom went close to his brother. "Sure you don' wanta come with me?"

"No. I'm gonna look aroun' like I said."

"O.K.," said Tom. He turned away and strolled down the street. The smoke from the houses hung low to the ground, and the lanterns threw their pictures of doorways and windows into the street. On the doorsteps people sat and looked out into the darkness. Tom could see their heads turn as their eyes followed him down the street. At the street end the dirt road continued across a stubble field, and the black lumps of haycocks were visible in the starlight. A thin blade of moon was low in the sky toward the west, and the long cloud of the Milky Way trailed clearly overhead. Tom's feet sounded softly on the dusty road, a dark patch against the yellow stubble. He put his hands in his pockets and trudged along toward the main gate. An embankment came close to the road. Tom could hear the whisper of water against the grasses in the irrigation ditch. He climbed up the bank and looked down on the dark water, and saw the stretched reflections of the stars. The State road was ahead. Car lights swooping past showed where it was. Tom set out again toward it. He could see the high wire gate in the starlight.

A figure stirred beside the road. A voice said, "Hello—who is it?"

Tom stopped and stood still. "Who are you?"

A man stood up and walked near. Tom could see the gun in his hand. Then a flashlight played on his face. "Where you think you're going?"

"Well, I thought I'd take a walk. Any law against it?"

"You better walk some other way."

Tom asked, "Can't I even get out of here?"

"Not tonight you can't. Want to walk back, or shall I whistle some help an' take you?"

"Hell," said Tom, "it ain't nothin' to me. If it's

gonna cause a mess, I don't give a darn. Sure, I'll go back."

The dark figure relaxed. The flash went off. "Ya see, it's for your own good. Them crazy pickets might get you."

"What pickets?"

"Them goddamn reds."

"Oh," said Tom. "I didn' know 'bout them."

"You seen 'em when you come, didn' you?"

"Well, I seen a bunch a guys, but they was so many cops I didn' know. Thought it was a accident."

"Well, you better git along back."

"That's O.K. with me, mister." He swung about and started back. He walked quietly along the road a hundred yards, and then he stopped and listened. The twittering call of a raccoon sounded near the irrigation ditch and, very far away, the angry howl of a tied dog. Tom sat down beside the road and listened. He heard the high soft laughter of a night hawk and the stealthy movement of a creeping animal in the stubble. He inspected the skyline in both directions, dark frames both ways, nothing to show against. Now he stood up and walked slowly to the right of the road, off into the stubble field, and he walked bent down, nearly as low as the haycocks. He moved slowly and stopped occasionally to listen. At last he came to the wire fence, five strands of taut barbed wire. Beside the fence he lay on his back, moved his head under the lowest strand, held the wire up with his hands and slid himself under, pushing against the ground with his feet.

He was about to get up when a group of men walked by on the edge of the highway. Tom waited until they were far ahead before he stood up and followed them. He watched the side of the road for tents. A few automobiles went by. A stream cut across the fields, and the highway crossed it on a small concrete bridge. Tom looked over the side of the bridge. In the bottom of the deep ravine he saw a tent and a lantern was burning inside. He watched it for a moment, saw the shadows of people against the canvas walls. Tom climbed a fence and moved down into the ravine through brush and dwarf willows; and in the bottom, beside a tiny stream, he found a trail. A man sat on a box in front of the tent.

"Evenin'," Tom said.

"Who are you?"

"Well—I guess, well—I'm jus' goin' past."

"Know anybody here?"

"No. I tell you I was jus' goin' past."

A head stuck out of the tent. A voice said, "What's the matter?"

"Casy!" Tom cried. "Casy! For Chris' sake, what you doin' here?"

"Why, my God, it's Tom Joad! Come on in, Tommy. Come on in."

"Know him, do ya?" the man in front asked.

"Know him? Christ, yes. Knowed him for years. I come west with him. Come on in, Tom." He clutched Tom's elbow and pulled him into the tent.

Three other men sat on the ground, and in the center of the tent a lantern burned. The men looked up suspiciously. A dark-faced, scowling man held out his hand. "Glad to meet ya," he said. "I heard what Casy said. This the fella you was tellin' about?"

"Sure. This is him. Well, for God's sake! Where's your folks? What you doin' here?"

"Well," said Tom, "we heard they was work this-a-way. An' we come, an' a bunch a State cops run us into this here ranch an' we been a-pickin' peaches all afternoon. I seen a bunch a fellas yellin'. They wouldn' tell me nothin', so I come out here to see what's goin' on. How'n hell'd you get here, Casy?"

The preacher leaned forward and the yellow lantern light fell on his high pale forehead. "Jail house is a kinda funny place," he said. "Here's me, been a-goin' into the wilderness like Jesus to try find out somepin.

Almost got her sometimes, too. But it's in the jail house I really got her." His eyes were sharp and merry. "Great big ol' cell, an' she's full all a time. New guys come in, and guys go out. An' 'course I talked to all of 'em."

"'Course you did," said Tom. "Always talk. If you was up on the gallows you'd be passin' the time a day with the hangman. Never seen sech a talker."

The men in the tent chuckled. A wizened little man with a wrinkled face slapped his knee. "Talks all the time," he said. "Folks kinda likes to hear 'im, though."

"Use' ta be a preacher," said Tom. "Did he tell that?"

"Sure, he told."

Casy grinned. "Well, sir," he went on, "I begin gettin' at things. Some a them fellas in the tank was drunks, but mostly they was there 'cause they stole stuff; an' mostly it was stuff they needed an' couldn' get no other way. Ya see?" he asked.

"No," said Tom.

"Well, they was nice fellas, ya see. What made 'em bad was they needed stuff. An' I begin to see, then. It's need that makes all the trouble. I ain't got it worked out. Well, one day they give us some beans that was sour. One fella started yellin', an' nothin' happened. He yelled his head off. Trusty come along an' looked in an' went on. Then another fella yelled. Well, sir, then we all got yellin'. And we all got on the same tone, an' I tell ya, it jus' seemed like that tank bulged an' give and swelled up. By God! Then somepin happened! They come a-runnin', and they give us some other stuff to eat—give it to us. Ya see?"

"No," said Tom.

Casy put his chin down on his hands. "Maybe I can't tell you," he said. "Maybe you got to find out. Where's your cap?"

"I come out without it."

"How's your sister?"

"Hell, she's big as a cow. I bet she got twins. Gonna need wheels under her stomach. Got to holdin' it with her han's, now. You ain' tol' me what's goin' on."

The wizened man said, "We struck. This here's a strike."

"Well, fi' cents a box ain't much, but a fella can eat."

"Fi' cents?" the wizened man cried. "Fi' cents! They payin' you fi' cents?"

"Sure. We made a buck an' a half."

A heavy silence fell in the tent. Casy stared out the entrance, into the dark night. "Lookie, Tom," he said at last. "We come to work there. They says it's gonna be fi' cents. They was a hell of a lot of us. We got there an' they says they're payin' two an' a half cents. A fella can't even eat on that, an' if he got kids—So we says we won't take it. So they druv us off. An' all the cops in the worl' come down on us. Now they're payin' you five. When they bust this here strike—ya think they'll pay five?"

"I dunno," Tom said. "Payin' five now."

"Lookie," said Casy. "We tried to camp together, an' they druv us like pigs. Scattered us. Beat the hell outa fellas. Druv us like pigs. They run you in like pigs, too. We can't las' much longer. Some people ain't et for two days. You goin' back tonight?"

"Aim to," said Tom.

"Well—tell the folks in there how it is, Tom. Tell 'em they're starvin' us an' stabbin' theirself in the back. 'Cause sure as cowflops she'll drop to two an' a half jus' as soon as they clear us out."

"I'll tell 'em," said Tom. "I don' know how. Never seen so many guys with guns. Don' know if they'll even let a fella talk. An' folks don' pass no time of day. They jus' hang down their heads an' won't even give a fella a howdy."

"Try an' tell 'em, Tom. They'll get two an' a half, jus' the minute we're gone. You know what two an' a half is—that's one ton of peaches picked an' carried for a dollar." He dropped his head. "No—you can't do it. You can't get your food for that. Can't eat for that."

"I'll try to get to tell the folks."

"How's your ma?"

"Purty good. She liked that gov'ment camp. Baths an' hot water."

"Yeah—I heard."

"It was pretty nice there. Couldn' find no work, though. Had a leave."

"I'd like to go to one," said Casy. "Like to see it. Fella says they ain't no cops."

"Folks is their own cops."

Casy looked up excitedly. "An' was they any trouble? Fightin', stealin', drinkin'?"

"No," said Tom.

"Well, if a fella went bad—what then? What'd they do?"

"Put 'im outa the camp."

"But they wasn' many?"

"Hell, no," said Tom. "We was there a month, an' on'y one."

Casy's eyes shone with excitement. He turned to the other men. "Ya see?" he cried. "I tol' you. Cops cause more trouble than they stop. Look, Tom. Try an' get the folks in there to come on out. They can do it in a couple days. Them peaches is ripe. Tell 'em."

"They won't," said Tom. "They're a-gettin' five, an' they don' give a damn about nothin' else."

"But jus' the minute they ain't strikebreakin' they won't get no five."

"I don' think they'll swalla that. Five they're a-gettin'. Tha's all they care about."

"Well, tell 'em anyways."

"Pa wouldn' do it," Tom said. "I know 'im. He'd say it wasn't none of his business."

"Yes," Casy said disconsolately. "I guess that's right. Have to take a beatin' 'fore he'll know."

"We was outa food," Tom said. "Tonight we had meat. Not much, but we had it. Think Pa's gonna give up his meat on account a other fellas? An' Rosasharn oughta get milk. Think Ma's gonna wanta starve that baby jus' 'cause a bunch a fellas is yellin' outside a gate?"

Casy said sadly, "I wisht they could see it. I wisht they could see the on'y way they can depen' on their meat—Oh, the hell! Get tar'd sometimes. God-awful tar'd. I knowed a fella. Brang 'im in while I was in the jail house. Been tryin' to start a union. Got one started. An' then them vigilantes bust it up. An' know what? Them very folks he been tryin' to help tossed him out. Wouldn' have nothin' to do with 'im. Scared they'd get saw in his comp'ny. Says, 'Git out. You're a danger on us.' Well, sir, it hurt his feelin's purty bad. But then he says, 'It ain't so bad if you know.' He says, 'French Revolution—all them fellas that figgered her out got their heads chopped off. Always that way,' he says. 'Jus' as natural as rain. You didn' do it for fun no way. Doin' it 'cause you have to. 'Cause it's you. Look a Washington,' he says. 'Fit the Revolution, an' after, them sons-a-bitches turned on him. An' Lincoln' the same. Same folks yellin' to kill 'em. Natural as rain.' "

"Don't soun' like no fun," said Tom.

"No, it don't. This fella in jail, he says, 'Anyways, you do what you can. An',' he says, 'the on'y thing you got to look at is that ever' time they's a little step fo'ward, she may slip back a little, but she never slips clear back. You can prove that,' he says, 'an' that makes the whole thing right. An' that means they wasn't no waste even if it seemed like they was.' "

"Talkin'," said Tom. "Always talkin'. Take my brother Al. He's out lookin' for a girl. He don't care 'bout nothin' else. Couple days he'll get him a girl. Think about it all day an' do it all night. He don't give a damn 'bout steps up or down or sideways."

"Sure," said Casy. "Sure. He's jus' doin' what he's got to do. All of us like that."

The man seated outside pulled the tent flap wide. "Goddamn it, I don' like it," he said.

Casy looked out at him. "What's the matter?"

"I don' know. I jus' itch all over. Nervous as a cat."

"Well, what's the matter?"

"I don' know. Seems like I hear somepin, an' then I listen an' they ain't nothin' to hear."

"You're jus' jumpy," the wizened man said. He got up and went outside. And in a second he looked into the tent. "They's a great big ol' black cloud a-sailin' over. Bet she's got thunder. That's what's itchin' him—'lectricity." He ducked out again. The other two men stood up from the ground and went outside.

Casy said softly, "All of 'em's itchy. Them cops been sayin' how they're gonna beat the hell outa us an' run us outa the county. They figger I'm a leader 'cause I talk so much."

The wizened face looked in again. "Casy, turn out that lantern an' come outside. They's somepin."

Casy turned the screw. The flame drew down into the slots and popped and went out. Casy groped outside and Tom followed him. "What is it?" Casy asked softly.

"I dunno. Listen!"

There was a wall of frog sounds that merged with silence. A high, shrill whistle of crickets. But through this background came other sounds—faint footsteps from the road, a crunch of clods up on the bank, a little swish of brush down the stream.

"Can't really tell if you hear it. Fools you. Get nervous," Casy reassured them. "We're all nervous. Can't really tell. You hear it, Tom?"

"I hear it," said Tom. "Yeah, I hear it. I think they's guys comin' from ever' which way. We better get outa here."

The wizened man whispered, "Under the bridge span—out that way. Hate to leave my tent."

"Le's go," said Casy.

They moved quietly along the edge of the stream. The black span was a cave before them. Casy bent over and moved through, Tom behind. Their feet slipped into the water. Thirty feet they moved, and their breathing echoed from the curved ceiling. Then they came out on the other side and straightened up.

A sharp call, "There they are!" Two flashlight beams fell on the men, caught them, blinded them. "Stand where you are." The voices came out of the darkness. "That's him. That shiny bastard. That's him."

Casy stared blindly at the light. He breathed heavily. "Listen," he said. "You fellas don' know what you're doin'. You're helpin' to starve kids."

"Shut up, you red son-of-a-bitch."

A short heavy man stepped into the light. He carried a new white pick handle.

Casy went on, "You don' know what you're a-doin'."

The heavy man swung with the pick handle. Casy dodged down into the swing. The heavy club crashed into the side of his head with a dull crunch of bone, and Casy fell sideways out of the light.

"Jesus, George. I think you killed him."

"Put the light on him," said George. "Serve the son-of-a-bitch right." The flashlight beam dropped, searched and found Casy's crushed head.

Tom looked down at the preacher. The light crossed the heavy man's legs and the white new pick handle. Tom leaped silently. He wrenched the club free. The first time he knew he had missed and struck a shoulder, but the second time his crushing blow found the head, and as the heavy man sank down, three more blows found his head. The lights danced about. There were shouts, the sound of running feet, crashing through brush. Tom stood over the prostrate man. And then a club reached his head, a glancing blow. He felt the stroke like an electric shock. And then he was running along the stream, bending low. He heard the splash of footsteps following him. Suddenly he turned and squirmed up into the brush, deep into a poison-oak thicket. And he lay still. The footsteps came near, the light beams glanced along the stream bottom. Tom wriggled up through the thicket to the top. He emerged in an orchard. And still he could hear the calls, the pursuit in the stream bottom. He bent low and ran over the cultivated earth; the clods slipped and rolled under his feet. Ahead he saw the bushes that bounded the field, bushes along the edges of an irrigation ditch. He slipped through the fence, edged in among vines and blackberry bushes. And then he lay still, panting hoarsely. He felt his numb face and nose. The nose was crushed, and a trickle of blood dripped from his chin. He lay still on his stomach until his mind came back. And then he crawled slowly over the edge of the ditch. He bathed his face in the cool water, tore off the tail of his blue shirt and dipped it and held it against his torn cheek and nose. The water stung and burned.

The black cloud had crossed the sky, a blob of dark against the stars. The night was quiet again.

Tom stepped into the water and felt the bottom drop from under his feet. He threshed the two strokes across the ditch and pulled himself heavily up the other bank. His clothes clung to him. He moved and made a slopping noise; his shoes squished. Then he sat down, took off his shoes and emptied them. He wrung the bottoms of his trousers, took off his coat and squeezed the water from it.

Along the highway he saw the dancing beams of the flashlights, searching the ditches. Tom put on his shoes and moved cautiously across the stubble field. The squishing noise no longer came from his shoes. He went by instinct toward the other side of the stubble field, and at last he came to the road. Very cautiously he approached the square of houses.

Once a guard, thinking he heard a noise, called, "Who's there?"

Tom dropped and froze to the ground, and the flashlight beam passed over him. He crept silently to the door of the Joad house. The door squalled on its hinges. And Ma's voice, calm and steady and wide awake:

"What's that?"

"Me. Tom."

"Well, you better get some sleep. Al ain't in yet."

"He must a foun' a girl."

"Go on to sleep," she said softly. "Over under the window."

He found his place and took off his clothes to the skin. He lay shivering under his blanket. And his torn face awakened from its numbness, and his whole head throbbed.

It was an hour more before Al came in. He moved cautiously near and stepped on Tom's wet clothes.

"Sh!" said Tom.

Al whispered, "You awake? How'd you get wet?"

"Sh," said Tom. "Tell you in the mornin'."

Pa turned on his back, and his snoring filled the room with gasps and snorts.

"You're col'," Al said.

"Sh. Go to sleep." The little square of the window showed gray against the black of the room.

Tom did not sleep. The nerves of his wounded face came back to life and throbbed, and his cheek bone ached, and his broken nose bulged and pulsed with pain that seemed to toss him about, to shake him. He watched the little square window, saw the stars slide down over it and drop from sight. At intervals he heard the footsteps of the watchmen.

At last the roosters crowed, far away, and gradually the window lightened. Tom touched his swollen face with his fingertips, and at his movement Al groaned and murmured in his sleep.

The dawn came finally. In the houses, packed together, there was a sound of movement, a crash of breaking sticks, a little clatter of pans. In the graying gloom Ma sat up suddenly. Tom could see her face, swollen with sleep. She looked at the window, for a long moment. And then she threw the blanket off and found her dress. Still sitting down, she put it over her head and held her arms up and let the dress slide down to her waist. She stood up and pulled the dress down around her ankles. Then, in bare feet, she stepped carefully to the window and looked out, and while she stared at the growing light, her quick fingers unbraided her hair and smoothed the strands and braided them up again. Then she clasped her hands in front of her and stood motionless for a moment. Her face was lighted sharply by the window. She turned, stepped carefully among the mattresses, and found the lantern. The shade screeched up, and she lighted the wick.

Pa rolled over and blinked at her. She said, "Pa, you got more money?"

"Huh? Yeah. Paper wrote for sixty cents."

"Well, git up an' go buy some flour an' lard. Quick, now." Pa yawned. "Maybe the store ain't open."

"Make 'em open it. Got to get somepin in you fellas. You got to get out to work."

Pa struggled into his overalls and put on his rusty coat. He went sluggishly out the door, yawning and stretching.

The children awakened and watched from under their blanket, like mice. Pale light filled the room now, but colorless light, before the sun. Ma glanced at the mattresses. Uncle John was awake, Al slept heavily. Her eyes moved to Tom. For a moment she peered at him, and then she moved quickly to him. His face was puffed and blue, and the blood was dried black on his lips and chin. The edges of the torn cheek were gathered and tight.

"Tom," she whispered, "what's the matter?"

"Sh!" he said. "Don't talk loud. I got in a fight."

"Tom!"

"I couldn' help it, Ma."

She knelt down beside him. "You in trouble?"

He was a long time answering. "Yeah," he said. "In trouble. I can't go out to work. I got to hide."

The children crawled near on their hands and knees, staring greedily. "What's the matter'th him, Ma?"

"Hush!" Ma said. "Go wash up."

"We got no soap."

"Well, use water."

"What's the matter'th Tom?"

"Now you hush. An' don't you tell nobody."

They backed away and squatted down against the far wall, knowing they would not be inspected.

Ma asked, "Is it bad?"

"Nose busted."

"I mean the trouble?"

"Yeah. Bad!"

Al opened his eyes and looked at Tom. "Well, for Chris' sake! What was you in?"

"What's a matter?" Uncle John asked.

Pa clumped in. "They was open all right." He put a tiny bag of flour and his package of lard on the floor beside the stove. " 'S'a matter?" he asked.

Tom braced himself on one elbow for a moment, and then he lay back. "Jesus, I'm weak. I'm gonna tell ya once. So I'll tell all of ya. How 'bout the kids?"

Ma looked at them, huddled against the wall. "Go wash ya face."

"No," Tom said. "They got to hear. They got to know. They might blab if they don' know."

"What the hell is this?" Pa demanded.

"I'm a-gonna tell. Las' night I went out to see what all the yellin' was about. An' I come on Casy."

"The preacher?"

"Yeah, Pa. The preacher, on'y he was a-leadin' the strike. They come for him."

Pa demanded, "Who come for him?"

"I dunno. Same kinda guys that turned us back on the road that night. Had pick handles." He paused. "They killed 'im. Busted his head. I was standin' there. I went nuts. Grabbed the pick handle." He looked bleakly back at the night, the darkness, the flashlights, as he spoke. "I—I clubbed a guy."

Ma's breath caught in her throat. Pa stiffened. "Kill 'im?" he asked softly.

"I—don't know. I was nuts. Tried to."

Ma asked, "Was you saw?"

"I dunno. I dunno. I guess so. They had the lights on us."

For a moment Ma stared into his eyes. "Pa," she said, "break up some boxes. We got to get breakfas'. You got to go to work. Ruthie, Winfiel'. If anybody asts you—Tom is sick—you hear? If you tell—he'll—get sent to jail. You hear?"

"Yes, ma'am."

"Keep your eye on 'em, John. Don' let 'em talk to nobody." She built the fire as Pa broke the boxes that had held the goods. She made her dough, put a pot of coffee to boil. The light wood caught and roared its flame in the chimney.

Pa finished breaking the boxes. He came near to Tom. "Casy—he was a good man. What'd he wanta mess with that stuff for?"

Tom said dully, "They come to work for fi' cents a box."

"That's what we're a-gettin'."

"Yeah. What we was a-doin' was breakin' strike. They give them fellas two an' a half cents."

"You can't eat on that."

"I know," Tom said wearily. "That's why they

struck. Well, I think they bust that strike las' night. We'll maybe be gettin' two an' a half cents today."

"Why, the sons-a-bitches——"

"Yeah! Pa. You see? Casy was still a—good man. Goddamn it, I can't get that pitcher outa my head. Him layin' there—head jus' crushed flat an' oozin'. Jesus!" He covered his eyes with his hand.

"Well, what we gonna do?" Uncle John asked.

Al was standing up now. "Well, by God, I know what I'm gonna do. I'm gonna get out of it."

"No, you ain't, Al," Tom said. "We need you now. I'm the one. I'm a danger now. Soon's I get on my feet I got to go."

Ma worked at the stove. Her head was half turned to hear. She put grease in the frying pan, and when it whispered with heat, she spooned the dough into it.

Tom went on, "You got to stay, Al. You got to take care a the truck."

"Well, I don' like it."

"Can't help it, Al. It's your folks. You can help 'em. I'm a danger to 'em."

Al grumbled angrily. "I don' know why I ain't let to get me a job in a garage."

"Later, maybe." Tom looked past him, and he saw Rose of Sharon lying on the mattress. Her eyes were huge—opened wide. "Don't worry," he called to her. "Don't you worry. Gonna get you some milk today." She blinked slowly, and didn't answer him.

Pa said, "We got to know, Tom. Think ya killed this fella?"

"I don' know. It was dark. An' somebody smacked me. I don' know. I hope so. I hope I killed the bastard."

"Tom!" Ma called. "Don't talk like that."

From the street came the sound of many cars moving slowly. Pa stepped to the window and looked out. "They's a whole slew a new people comin' in," he said.

"I guess they bust the strike, awright," said Tom. "I guess you'll start at two an' a half cents."

"But a fella could work at a run, an' still he couldn' eat."

"I know," said Tom. "Eat win'fall peaches. That'll keep ya up."

Ma turned the dough and stirred the coffee. "Listen to me," she said. "I'm gettin' cornmeal today. We're a-gonna eat cornmeal mush. An' soon's we get enough for gas, we're movin' away. This ain't a good place. An' I ain't gonna have Tom out alone. No, sir."

"Ya can't do that, Ma. I tell you I'm jus' a danger to ya."

Her chin was set. "That's what we'll do. Here, come eat this here, an' then get out to work. I'll come out soon's I get washed up. We got to make some money."

They ate the fried dough so hot that it sizzled in their mouths. And they tossed the coffee down and filled their cups and drank more coffee.

Uncle John shook his head over his plate. "Don't look like we're a-gonna get shet of this here. I bet it's my sin."

"Oh, shut up!" Pa cried. "We ain't got the time for your sin now. Come on now. Le's get out to her. Kids, you come he'p. Ma's right. We got to go outa here."

When they were gone, Ma took a plate and a cup to Tom. "Better eat a little somepin."

"I can't, Ma. I'm so darn sore I couldn' chew."

"You better try."

"No, I can't, Ma."

She sat down on the edge of his mattress. "You got to tell me," she said. "I got to figger how it was. I got to keep straight. What was Casy a-doin'? Why'd they kill 'im?"

"He was jus' standin' there with the lights on' 'im."

"What'd he say? Can ya 'member what he says?"

Tom said, "Sure. Casy said, 'You got no right to starve people.' An' then this heavy fella called him a red son-of-a-bitch. An' Casy says, 'You don' know what you're a-doin'.' An' then this guy smashed 'im."

Ma looked down. She twisted her hands together. "Tha's what he said—'You don' know what you're doin' '?"

"Yeah!"

Ma said, "I wisht Granma could a heard."

"Ma—I didn' know what I was a-doin', no more'n when you take a breath. I didn' even know I was gonna do it."

"It's awright. I wisht you didn' do it. I wisht you wasn' there. But you done what you had to do. I can't read no fault on you." She went to the stove and dipped a cloth in the heating dishwater. "Here," she said. "Put that there on your face."

He laid the warm cloth over his nose and cheek, and winced at the heat. "Ma, I'm a-gonna go away tonight. I can't go puttin' this on you folks."

Ma said angrily, "Tom! They's a whole lot I don' un'erstan'. But goin' away ain't gonna ease us. It's gonna bear us down." And she went on, "They was the time when we was on the lan'. They was a boundary to us then. Ol' folks died off, an' little fellas come, an' we was always one thing—we was the fambly—kinda whole and clear. An' now we ain't clear no more. I can't get straight. They ain't nothin' keeps us clear. Al—he's a-hankerin' an' a-jibbitin' to go off on his own. An' Uncle John is jus' a-draggin' along. Pa's lost his place. He ain't the head no more. We're crackin' up, Tom. There ain't no fambly now. An' Rosasharn—" She looked around and found the girl's wide eyes. "She gonna have her baby an' they won't be no fambly. I don' know. I been a-tryin' to keep her goin'. Winfiel'— what's he gonna be, this-a-way? Gettin' wild, an' Ruthie too—like animals. Got nothin' to trus'. Don' go, Tom. Stay an' help."

"O.K.," he said tiredly. "O.K. I shouldn', though. I know it."

Ma went to her dishpan and washed the tin plates and dried them. "You didn' sleep."

"No."

"Well, you sleep. I seen your clothes was wet. I'll hang 'em by the stove to dry." She finished her work. "I'm goin' now. I'll pick. Rosasharn, if anybody comes, Tom's sick, you hear? Don' let nobody in. You hear?" Rose of Sharon nodded. "We'll come back at noon. Get some sleep, Tom. Maybe we can get outa here tonight." She moved swiftly to him. "Tom, you ain't gonna slip out?"

"No, Ma."

"You sure? You won't go?"

"No, Ma. I'll be here."

"Awright. 'Member, Rosasharn." She went out and closed the door firmly behind her.

Tom lay still—and then a wave of sleep lifted him to the edge of unconsciousness and dropped him slowly back and lifted him again.

"You—Tom!"

"Huh? Yeah!" He started awake. He looked over at Rose of Sharon. Her eyes were blazing with resentment. "What you want?"

"You killed a fella!"

"Yeah. Not so loud! You wanta rouse somebody?"

"What da I care?" she cried. "That lady tol' me. She says what sin's gonna do. She tol' me. What chance I got to have a nice baby? Connie's gone, an' I ain't gettin' good food. I ain't gettin' milk." Her voice rose hysterically. "An' now you kill a fella. What chance that baby got to get bore right? I know—gonna be a freak—a freak! I never done no dancin'."

Tom got up. "Sh!" he said. "You're gonna get folks in here."

"I don' care. I'll have a freak! I didn' dance no hug-dance."

He went near to her. "Be quiet."

"You get away from me. It ain't the first fella you

killed, neither." Her face was growing red with hysteria. Her words blurred. "I don' wanta look at you." She covered her head with her blanket.

Tom heard the choked, smothered cries. He bit his lower lip and studied the floor. And then he went to Pa's bed. Under the edge of the mattress the rifle lay, a lever-action Winchester .38, long and heavy. Tom picked it up and dropped the lever to see that a cartridge was in the chamber. He tested the hammer on half-cock. And then he went back to his mattress. He laid the rifle on the floor beside him, stock up and barrel pointing down. Rose of Sharon's voice thinned to a whimper. Tom lay down again and covered himself, covered his bruised cheek with the blanket and made a little tunnel to breathe through. He sighed, "Jesus, oh, Jesus!"

Outside, a group of cars went by, and voices sounded.

"How many men?"

"Jes' us—three. Whatcha payin'?"

"You go to house twenty-five. Number's right on the door."

"O.K., mister. Whatcha payin'?"

"Two and a half cents."

"Why, goddamn it, a man can't make his dinner!"

"That's what we're payin'. There's two hundred men coming from the South that'll be glad to get it."

"But, Jesus, mister!"

"Go on now. Either take it or go on along. I got no time to argue."

"But——"

"Look. I didn' set the price. I'm just checking you in. If you want it, take it. If you don't, turn right around and go along."

"Twenty-five, you say?"

"Yes, twenty-five."

*

Tom dozed on his mattress. A stealthy sound in the room awakened him. His hand crept to the rifle and tightened on the grip. He drew back the covers from his face. Rose of Sharon was standing beside his mattress.

"What you want?" Tom demanded.

"You sleep," she said. "You jus' sleep off. I'll watch the door. They won't nobody get in."

He studied her face for a moment. "O.K.," he said, and he covered his face with the blanket again.

In the beginning dusk Ma came back to the house. She paused on the doorstep and knocked and said, "It's me," so that Tom would not be worried. She opened the door and entered, carrying a bag. Tom awakened and sat up on his mattress. His wound had dried and tightened so that the unbroken skin was shiny. His left eye was drawn nearly shut. "Anybody come while we was gone?" Ma asked.

"No," he said. "Nobody. I see they dropped the price."

"How'd you know?"

"I heard folks talkin' outside."

Rose of Sharon looked dully up at Ma.

Tom pointed at her with his thumb. "She raised hell, Ma. Thinks all the trouble is aimed right smack at her. If I'm gonna get her upset like that I oughta go 'long."

Ma turned on Rose of Sharon. "What you doin'?"

The girl said resentfully, "How'm I gonna have a nice baby with stuff like this?"

Ma said, "Hush! You hush now. I know how you're a-feelin', an' I know you can't he'p it, but you jus' keep your mouth shut."

She turned back to Tom. "Don't pay her no mind, Tom. It's awful hard, an' I 'member how it is. Ever'thing is a-shootin' right at you when you're gonna have a baby, an' ever'thing anybody says is a insult, an' ever'thing's against you. Don't pay no mind. She can't he'p it. It's jus' the way she feels."

"I don' wanta hurt her."

"Hush! Jus' don' talk." She set her bag down on the cold stove. "Didn' hardly make nothin'," she said. "I tol' you, we're gonna get outa here. Tom, try an' wrassle me some wood. No—you can't. Here, we got on'y this one box lef'. Break it up. I tol' the other fellas to pick up some sticks on the way back. Gonna have mush an' a little sugar on."

Tom got up and stamped the last box to small pieces. Ma carefully built her fire in one end of the stove, conserving the flame under one stove hole. She filled a kettle with water and put it over the flame. The kettle rattled over the direct fire, rattled and wheezed.

"How was it pickin' today?" Tom asked.

Ma dipped a cup into her bag of cornmeal. "I don' wanta talk about it. I was thinkin' today how they use' to be jokes. I don' like it, Tom. We don't joke no more. When they's a joke, it's a mean bitter joke, an' they ain't no fun in it. Fella says today, 'Depression is over. I seen a jackrabbit, an' they wasn't nobody after him.' An' another fella says, 'That ain't the reason. Can't afford to kill jackrabbits no more. Catch 'em and milk 'em an' turn 'em loose. One you seen prob'ly gone dry.' That's how I mean. Ain't really funny, not funny like that time Uncle John converted an Injun an' brang him home, an' that Injun et his way clean to the bottom of the bean bin, an' then backslid with Uncle John's whisky. Tom, put a rag with col' water on your face."

The dusk deepened. Ma lighted the lantern and hung it on a nail. She fed the fire and poured cornmeal gradually into the hot water. "Rosasharn," she said, "can you stir the mush?"

Outside there was a patter of running feet. The door burst open and banged against the wall. Ruthie rushed in. "Ma!" she cried. "Ma, Winfiel' got a fit!"

"Where? Tell me!"

Ruthie panted, "Got white an' fell down. Et so many peaches he skittered hisself all day. Jus' fell down. White!"

"Take me!" Ma demanded. "Rosasharn, you watch that mush."

She went out with Ruthie. She ran heavily up the street behind the little girl. Three men walked toward her in the dusk, and the center man carried Winfield in his arms. Ma ran up to them. "He's mine," she cried. "Give 'im to me."

"I'll carry 'im for you, ma'am."

"No, here, give 'im to me." She hoisted the little boy and turned back; and then she remembered herself. "I sure thank ya," she said to the men.

"Welcome, ma'am. The little fella's purty weak. Looks like he got worms."

Ma hurried back, and Winfield was limp and relaxed in her arms. Ma carried him into the house and knelt down and laid him on a mattress. "Tell me. What's the matter?" she demanded. He opened his eyes dizzily and shook his head and closed his eyes again.

Ruthie said, "I tol' ya, Ma. He skittered all day. Ever' little while. Et too many peaches."

Ma felt his head. "He ain't fevered. But he's white and drawed out."

Tom came near and held the lantern down. "I know," he said. "He's hungered. Got no strength. Get him a can a milk an' make him drink it. Make 'im take milk on his mush."

"Winfiel'," Ma said. "Tell how ya feel."

"Dizzy," said Winfield, "jus' a-whirlin' dizzy."

"You never seen sech skitters," Ruthie said importantly.

Pa and Uncle John and Al came into the house. Their arms were full of sticks and bits and brush. They dropped their loads by the stove. "Now what?" Pa demanded.

"It's Winfiel'. He needs some milk."

"Christ Awmighty! We all need stuff!"

Ma said, "How much'd we make today?"

"Dollar forty-two."

"Well, you go right over'n get a can a milk for Winfiel'."

"Now why'd he have to get sick?"

"I don't know why, but he is. Now you git!" Pa went grumbling out the door. "You stirrin' that mush?"

"Yeah." Rose of Sharon speeded up the stirring to prove it.

Al complained, "God Awmighty, Ma! Is mush all we get after workin' till dark?"

"Al, you know we got to git. Take all we got for gas. You know."

"But, God Awmighty, Ma! A fella needs meat if he's gonna work."

"Jus' you sit quiet," she said. "We got to take the bigges' thing an' whup it fust. An' you know what that thing is."

Tom asked, "Is it about me?"

"We'll talk when we've et," said Ma. "Al, we got enough gas to go a ways, ain't we?"

" 'Bout a quarter tank," said Al.

"I wisht you'd tell me," Tom said.

"After. Jus' wait."

"Keep a-stirrin' that mush, you. Here, lemme put on some coffee. You can have sugar on your mush or in your coffee. They ain't enough for both."

Pa came back with one tall can of milk. " 'Leven cents," he said disgustedly.

"Here!" Ma took the can and stabbed it open. She let the thick stream out into a cup, and handed it to Tom. "Give that to Winfiel'."

Tom knelt beside the mattress. "Here, drink this."

"I can't. I'd sick it all up. Leave me be."

Tom stood up. "He can't take it now, Ma. Wait a little."

Ma took the cup and set it on the window ledge. "Don't none of you touch that," she warned. "That's for Winfiel'."

"I ain't had no milk," Rose of Sharon said sullenly. "I oughta have some."

"I know, but you're still on your feet. This here little fella's down. Is that mush good an' thick?"

"Yeah. Can't hardly stir it no more."

"Awright, le's eat. Now here's the sugar. They's about one spoon each. Have it on ya mush or in ya coffee."

Tom said, "I kinda like salt an' pepper on mush."

"Salt her if you like," Ma said. "The pepper's out."

The boxes were all gone. The family sat on the mattresses to eat their mush. They served themselves again and again, until the pot was nearly empty. "Save some for Winfiel'," Ma said.

Winfield sat up and drank his milk, and instantly he was ravenous. He put the mush pot between his legs and ate what was left and scraped at the crust on the sides. Ma poured the rest of the canned milk in a cup and sneaked it to Rose of Sharon to drink secretly in a corner. She poured the hot black coffee into the cups and passed them around.

"Now will you tell what's goin' on?" Tom asked. "I wanta hear."

Pa said uneasily, "I wisht Ruthie an' Winfiel' didn' hafta hear. Can't they go outside?"

Ma said, "No. They got to act growed up, even if they ain't. They's no help for it. Ruthie—you an' Winfiel' ain't ever to say what you hear, else you'll jus' break us to pieces."

"We won't," Ruthie said. "We're growed up."

"Well, jus' be quiet, then." The cups of coffee were on the floor. The short thick flame of the lantern, like a stubby butterfly's wing, cast a yellow gloom on the walls.

"Now tell," said Tom.

Ma said, "Pa, you tell."

Uncle John slupped his coffee. Pa said, "Well, they dropped the price like you said. An' they was a whole slew a new pickers so goddamn hungry they'd pick for a loaf a bread. Go for a peach, an' somebody'd get it first. Gonna get the whole crop picked right off. Fellas runnin' to a new tree. I seen fights—one fella claims it's his tree, 'nother fella wants to pick off'n it. Brang these here folks from as far's El Centro. Hungrier'n hell. Work all day for a piece a bread. I says to the checker, 'We can't work for two an' a half cents a box,' an' he says, 'Go on, then, quit. These fellas can.' I says, 'Soon's they get fed up they won't.' An' he says, 'Hell, we'll have these here peaches in 'fore they get fed up.' " Pa stopped.

"She was a devil," said Uncle John. "They say they's two hunderd more men comin' in tonight."

Tom said, "Yeah! But how about the other?"

Pa was silent for a while. "Tom," he said, "looks like you done it."

"I kinda thought so. Couldn' see. Felt like it."

"Seems like the people ain't talkin' 'bout much else," said Uncle John. "They got posses out, an' they's fellas talkin' up a lynchin'—'course when they catch the fella."

Tom looked over at the wide-eyed children. They seldom blinked their eyes. It was as though they were afraid something might happen in the split second of darkness. Tom said, "Well—this fella that done it, he on'y done it after they killed Casy."

Pa interrupted. "That ain't the way they're tellin' it now. They're sayin' he done it fust."

Tom's breath sighed out, "Ah-h!"

"They're workin' up a feelin' against us folks. That's what I heard. All them drum-corpse fellas an' lodges an' all that. Say they're gonna get this here fella."

"They know what he looks like?" Tom asked.

"Well—not exactly—but the way I heard it, they think he got hit. They think—he'll have——"

Tom put his hand up slowly and touched his bruised cheek.

Ma cried, "It ain't so, what they say!"

"Easy, Ma," Tom said. "They got it cold. Anything them drum-corpse fellas say is right if it's against us."

Ma peered through the ill light, and she watched Tom's face, and particularly his lips. "You promised," she said.

"Ma, I—maybe this fella oughta go away. If—this fella done somepin wrong, maybe he'd think, 'O.K. Le's get the hangin' over. I done wrong an' I got to take it.' But this fella didn' do nothin' wrong. He don' feel no worse'n if he killed a skunk."

Ruthie broke in. "Ma, me an' Winfiel' knows. He don' have to go this-fella'in' for us."

Tom chuckled. "Well, this fella don' want no hangin', 'cause he'd do it again. An' same time, he don't aim to bring trouble down on his folks. Ma—I got to go."

Ma covered her mouth with her fingers and coughed to clear her throat. "You can't," she said. "They wouldn' be no way to hide out. You couldn' trus' nobody. But you can trus' us. We can hide you, an' we can see you get to eat while your face gets well."

"But, Ma——"

She got to her feet. "You ain't goin'. We're a-takin' you. Al, you back the truck against the door. Now, I got it figgered out. We'll put one mattress on the bottom, an' then Tom gets quick there, an' we take another mattress an' sort of fold it so it makes a cave, an' he's in the cave; and then we sort of wall it in. He can breathe out the end, ya see. Don't argue. That's what we'll do."

Pa complained, "Seems like the man ain't got no say no more. She's jus' a heller. Come time we get settled down, I'm a-gonna smack her."

"Come that time, you can," said Ma. "Roust up, Al. It's dark enough."

Al went outside to the truck. He studied the matter and backed up near the steps.

Ma said, "Quick now. Git that mattress in!"

Pa and Uncle John flung it over the end gate. "Now that one." They tossed the second mattress up. "Now—Tom, you jump up there an' git under. Hurry up."

Tom climbed quickly, and dropped. He straightened one mattress and pulled the second on top of him. Pa bent it upwards, stood it sides up, so that the arch covered Tom. He could see out between the sideboards of the truck. Pa and Al and Uncle John loaded quickly, piled the blankets on top of Tom's cave, stood the buckets against the sides, spread the last mattress behind. Pots and pans, extra clothes, went in loose, for their boxes had been burned. They were nearly finished loading when a guard moved near, carrying his shotgun across his crooked arm.

"What's goin' on here?" he asked.

"We're goin' out," said Pa.

"What for?"

"Well—we got a job offered—good job."

"Yeah? Where's it at?"

"Why—down by Weedpatch."

"Let's have a look at you." He turned a flashlight in Pa's face, in Uncle John's, and in Al's. "Wasn't there another fella with you?"

Al said, "You mean that hitch-hiker? Little short fella with a pale face?"

"Yeah. I guess that's what he looked like."

"We jus' picked him up on the way in. He went away this mornin' when the rate dropped."

"What did he look like again?"

"Short fella. Pale face."

"Was he bruised up this mornin'?"

"I didn' see nothin'," said Al. "Is the gas pump open?"

"Yeah, till eight."

"Git in," Al cried. "If we're gonna get to Weedpatch 'fore mornin' we gotta ram on. Gettin' in front, Ma?"

"No, I'll set in back," she said. "Pa, you set back here too. Let Rosasharn set in front with Al an' Uncle John."

"Give me the work slip, Pa," said Al. "I'll get gas an' change if I can."

The guard watched them pull along the street and turn left to the gasoline pumps.

"Put in two," said Al.

"You ain't goin' far."

"No, not far. Can I get change on this here work slip?"

"Well—I ain't supposed to."

"Look, mister," Al said. "We got a good job offered if we get there tonight. If we don't, we miss out. Be a good fella."

"Well, O.K. You sign her over to me."

Al got out and walked around the nose of the Hudson. "Sure I will," he said. He unscrewed the water cap and filled the radiator.

"Two, you say?"

"Yeah, two."

"Which way you goin'?"

"South. We got a job."

"Yeah? Jobs is scarce—reg'lar jobs."

"We got a frien'," Al said. "Job's all waitin' for us. Well, so long." The truck swung around and bumped over the dirt street into the road. The feeble headlight jiggled over the way, and the right headlight blinked on and off from a bad connection. At every jolt the loose pots and pans in the truck-bed jangled and crashed.

Rose of Sharon moaned softly.

"Feel bad?" Uncle John asked.

"Yeah! Feel bad all a time. Wisht I could set still in a nice place. Wisht we was home an' never come. Connie wouldn' a went away if we was home. He would a studied up an' got someplace." Neither Al nor Uncle John answered her. They were embarrassed about Connie.

At the white painted gate to the ranch a guard came to the side of the truck. "Goin' out for good?"

"Yeah," said Al. "Goin' north. Got a job."

The guard turned his flashlight on the truck, turned it up into the tent. Ma and Pa looked stonily down into the glare. "O.K." The guard swung the gate open. The truck turned left and moved toward 101, the great north-south highway.

"Know where we're a-goin'?" Uncle John asked.

"No," said Al. "Jus' goin', an' gettin' goddamn sick of it."

"I ain't so tur'ble far from my time," Rose of Sharon said threateningly. "They better be a nice place for me."

The night air was cold with the first sting of frost. Beside the road the leaves were beginning to drop from the fruit trees. On the load, Ma sat with her back against the truck side, and Pa sat opposite, facing her.

Ma called, "You all right, Tom?"

His muffled voice came back. "Kinda tight in here. We all through the ranch?"

"You be careful," said Ma. "Might git stopped."

Tom lifted up one side of his cave. In the dimness of the truck the pots jangled. "I can pull her down quick," he said. " 'Sides, I don' like gettin' trapped in here." He rested up on his elbow. "By God, she's gettin' cold, ain't she?"

"They's clouds up," said Pa. "Fellas says it's gonna be an early winter."

"Squirrels a-buildin' high, or grass seeds?" Tom asked. "By God, you can tell weather from anythin'. I bet you could find a fella could tell weather from a old pair of underdrawers."

"I dunno," Pa said. "Seems like it's gittin' on winter to me. Fella'd have to live here a long time to know."

"Which way we a-goin'?" Tom asked.

"I dunno. Al, he turned off lef'. Seems like he's goin' back the way we come."

Tom said, "I can't figger what's best. Seems like if we get on the main highway they'll be more cops. With my face this-a-way, they'd pick me right up. Maybe we oughta keep to back roads."

Ma said, "Hammer on the back. Get Al to stop."

Tom pounded the front board with his fist; the truck pulled to a stop on the side of the road. Al got out and walked to the back. Ruthie and Winfield peeked out from under their blanket.

"What ya want?" Al demanded.

Ma said, "We got to figger what to do. Maybe we better keep on the back roads. Tom says so."

"It's my face," Tom added. "Anybody'd know. Any cop'd know me."

"Well, which way you wanta go? I figgered north. We been south."

"Yeah," said Tom, "but keep on back roads."

Al asked, "How 'bout pullin' off an' catchin' some sleep, goin' on tomorra?"

Ma said quickly, "Not yet. Le's get some distance fust."

"O.K." Al got back in his seat and drove on.

Ruthie and Winfield covered up their heads again. Ma called, "Is Winfiel' all right?"

"Sure, he's awright," Ruthie said. "He been sleep-in'."

Ma leaned back against the truck side. "Gives ya a funny feelin' to be hunted like. I'm gittin' mean."

"Ever'body's gittin' mean," said Pa. "Ever'body. You seen that fight today. Fella changes. Down that gov'ment camp we wasn' mean."

Al turned right on a graveled road, and the yellow lights shuddered over the ground. The fruit trees were gone now, and cotton plants took their place. They drove on for twenty miles through the cotton, turning,

angling on the country roads. The road paralleled a
bushy creek and turned over a concrete bridge and
followed the stream on the other side. And then, on
the edge of the creek, the lights showed a long line of
red boxcars, wheelless; and a big sign on the edge of
the road said, "Cotton Pickers Wanted." Al slowed
down. Tom peered between the side-bars of the truck.
A quarter of a mile past the boxcars Tom hammered on
the car again. Al stopped beside the road and got out
again.

"Now what ya want?"

"Shut off the engine an' climb up here," Tom said.

Al got into the seat, drove off into the ditch, cut
lights and engine. He climbed over the tail gate.
"Awright," he said.

Tom crawled over the pots and knelt in front of Ma.
"Look," he said. "It says they want cotton pickers. I
seen that sign. Now I been tryin' to figger how I'm
gonna stay with you, an' not make no trouble. When
my face gets well, maybe it'll be awright, but not now.
Ya see them cars back there. Well, the pickers live in
them. Now maybe they's work there. How about if you
get work there an' live in one of them cars?"

"How 'bout you?" Ma demanded.

"Well, you seen that crick, all full a brush. Well, I
could hide in that brush an' keep outa sight. An' at
night you could bring me out somepin to eat. I seen a
culvert, little ways back. I could maybe sleep in
there."

Pa said, "By God, I'd like to get my hands on some
cotton! There's work I un'erstan'."

"Them cars might be a purty place to stay," said
Ma. "Nice an' dry. You think they's enough brush to
hide in, Tom?"

"Sure. I been watchin'. I could fix up a little place,
hide away. Soon's my face gets well, why, I'd come
out."

"You gonna scar purty bad," said Ma.

"Hell! Ever'body got scars."

"I picked four hunderd poun's oncet," Pa said. " 'Course it was a good heavy crop. If we all pick, we could get some money."

"Could get some meat," said Al. "What'll we do right now?"

"Go back there, an' sleep in the truck till mornin'," Pa said. "Git work in the mornin'. I can see them bolls even in the dark."

"How 'bout Tom?" Ma asked.

"Now you jus' forget me, Ma. I'll take me a blanket. You look out on the way back. They's a nice culvert. You can bring me some bread or potatoes, or mush, an' just leave it there. I'll come get it."

"Well!"

"Seems like good sense to me," said Pa.

"It is good sense," Tom insisted. "Soon's my face gets a little better, why, I'll come out an' go to pickin'."

"Well, awright," Ma agreed. "But don' you take no chancet. Don' let nobody see you for a while."

Tom crawled to the back of the truck. "I'll jus' take this here blanket. You look for that culvert on the way back, Ma."

"Take care," she begged. "You take care."

"Sure," said Tom. "Sure I will." He climbed the tail board, stepped down the bank. "Good night," he said.

Ma watched his figure blur with the night and disappear into the bushes beside the stream. "Dear Jesus, I hope it's awright," she said.

Al asked, "You want I should go back now?"

"Yeah," said Pa.

"Go slow," said Ma. "I wanta be sure an' see that culvert he said about. I got to see that."

Al backed and filled on the narrow road, until he had reversed his direction. He drove slowly back to the line of boxcars. The truck lights showed the cat-walks up to the wide car doors. The doors were dark. No one moved in the night. Al shut off his lights.

"You and Uncle John climb up back," he said to Rose of Sharon. "I'll sleep in the seat here."

Uncle John helped the heavy girl to climb up over the tail board. Ma piled the pots in a small space. The family lay wedged close together in the back of the truck.

A baby cried, in long jerking cackles, in one of the boxcars. A dog trotted out, sniffing and snorting, and moved slowly around the Joad truck. The tinkle of moving water came from the streambed.

27

Cotton Pickers Wanted—
placards on the road, handbills out, orange-colored
handbills—Cotton Pickers Wanted.

Here, up this road, it says.

The dark green plants stringy now, and the heavy
bolls clutched in the pod. White cotton spilling out
like popcorn.

Like to get our hands on the bolls. Tenderly, with
the fingertips.

I'm a good picker.

Here's the man, right here.

I aim to pick some cotton.

Got a bag?

Well, no, I ain't.

Cost ya a dollar, the bag. Take it out o' your first
hunderd and fifty. Eighty cents a hunderd first time
over the field. Ninety cents second time over. Get your
bag there. One dollar. 'F you ain't got the buck, we'll
take it out of your first hunderd and fifty. That's fair,
and you know it.

Sure it's fair. Good cotton bag, last all season. An'
when she's wore out, draggin', turn 'er aroun', use the
other end. Sew up the open end. Open up the wore
end. And when both ends is gone, why, that's nice

cloth! Makes a nice pair a summer drawers. Makes nightshirts. And well, hell—a cotton bag's a nice thing.

Hang it around your waist. Straddle it, drag it between your legs. She drags light at first. And your fingertips pick out the fluff, and the hands go twisting into the sack between your legs. Kids come along behind; got no bags for the kids—use a gunny sack or put it in your ol' man's bag. She hangs heavy, some, now. Lean forward, hoist 'er along. I'm a good hand with cotton. Finger-wise, boll-wise. Jes' move along talkin', an' maybe singin' till the bag gets heavy. Fingers go right to it. Fingers know. Eyes see the work—and don't see it.

Talkin' across the rows——

They was a lady back home, won't mention no names—had a nigger kid all of a sudden. Nobody knowed before. Never did hunt out the nigger. Couldn' never hold up her head no more. But I started to tell—she was a good picker.

Now the bag is heavy, boost it along. Set your hips and tow it along, like a work horse. And the kids pickin' into the old man's sack. Good crop here. Gets thin in the low places, thin and stringy. Never seen no cotton like this here California cotton. Long fiber, bes' damn cotton I ever seen. Spoil the lan' pretty soon. Like a fella wants to buy some cotton lan'—Don' buy her, rent her. Then when she's cottoned on down, move someplace new.

Lines of people moving across the fields. Finger-wise. Inquisitive fingers snick in and out and find the bolls. Hardly have to look.

Bet I could pick cotton if I was blind. Got a feelin' for a cotton boll. Pick clean, clean as a whistle.

Sack's full now. Take her to the scales. Argue. Scale man says you got rocks to make weight. How 'bout him? His scales is fixed. Sometimes he's right, you got rocks in the sack. Sometimes you're right, the

scales is crooked. Sometimes both; rocks an' crooked
scales. Always argue, always fight. Keeps your head
up. An' his head up. What's a few rocks? Jus' one,
maybe. Quarter pound? Always argue.

Back with the empty sack. Got our own book. Mark
in the weight. Got to. If they know you're markin',
then they don't cheat. But God he'p ya if ya don' keep
your own weight.

This is good work. Kids runnin' aroun'. Heard 'bout
the cotton-pickin' machine?

Yeah, I heard.

Think it'll ever come?

Well, if it comes—fella says it'll put han' pickin'
out.

Come night. All tired. Good pickin', though. Got
three dollars, me an' the ol' woman an' the kids.

The cars move to the cotton fields. The cotton
camps set up. The screened high trucks and trailers
are piled high with white fluff. Cotton clings to the
fence wires, and cotton rolls in little balls along the
road when the wind blows. And clean white cotton,
going to the gin. And the big, lumpy bales standing,
going to the compress. And cotton clinging to your
clothes and stuck to your whiskers. Blow your nose,
there's cotton in your nose.

Hunch along now, fill up the bag 'fore dark. Wise
fingers seeking in the bolls. Hips hunching along,
dragging the bag. Kids are tired, now in the evening.
They trip over their feet in the cultivated earth. And
the sun is going down.

Wisht it would last. It ain't much money, God
knows, but I wisht it would last.

On the highway the old cars piling in, drawn by the
handbills.

Got a cotton bag?

No.

Cost ya a dollar, then.

If they was on'y fifty of us, we could stay awhile,

but they's five hunderd. She won't last hardly at all. I knowed a fella never did git his bag paid out. Ever' job he got a new bag, an' ever' fiel' was done 'fore he got his weight.

Try for God's sake ta save a little money! Winter's comin' fast. They ain't no work at all in California in the winter. Fill up the bag 'fore it's dark. I seen that fella put two clods in.

Well, hell. Why not? I'm jus' balancin' the crooked scales.

Now here's my book, three hunderd an' twelve poun's.

Right!

Jesus, he never argued! His scales mus' be crooked. Well, that's a nice day anyways.

They say a thousan' men are on their way to this field. We'll be fightin' for a row tomorra. We'll be snatchin' cotton, quick.

Cotton Pickers Wanted. More men picking, quicker to the gin.

Now into the cotton camp.

Side-meat tonight, by God! We got money for side-meat! Stick out a han' to the little fella, he's wore out. Run in ahead an' git us four poun' of side-meat. The ol' woman'll make some nice biscuits tonight, ef she ain't too tired.

28

The boxcars, twelve of them, stood end to end on a little flat beside the stream. There were two rows of six each, the wheels removed. Up the big sliding doors slatted planks ran for cat-walks. They made good houses, water-tight and draftless, room for twenty-four families, one family in each end of each car. No windows, but the wide doors stood open. In some of the cars a canvas hung down in the center of the car, while in others only the position of the door made the boundary.

The Joads had one end of an end car. Some previous occupant had fitted up an oil can with a stovepipe, had made a hole in the wall for the stovepipe. Even with the wide door open, it was dark in the ends of the car. Ma hung the tarpaulin across the middle of the car.

"It's nice," she said. "It's almost nicer than anything we had 'cept the gov'ment camp."

Each night she unrolled the mattresses on the floor, and each morning rolled them up again. And every day they went into the fields and picked the cotton, and every night they had meat. On a Saturday they drove into Tulare, and they bought a tin stove and new overalls for Al and Pa and Winfield and Uncle John, and they bought a dress for Ma and gave Ma's best dress to Rose of Sharon.

"She's so big," Ma said. "Jus' a waste of good money to get her a new dress now."

The Joads had been lucky. They got in early enough to have a place in the boxcars. Now the tents of the late-comers filled the little flat, and those who had the boxcars were old-timers, and in a way aristocrats.

The narrow stream slipped by, out of the willows, and back into the willows again. From each car a hard-beaten path went down to the stream. Between the cars the clothes lines hung, and every day the lines were covered with drying clothes.

In the evening they walked back from the fields, carrying their folded cotton bags under their arms. They went into the store at the crossroads, and there were many pickers in the store, buying their supplies.

"How much today?"

"We're doin' fine. We made three and a half today. Wisht she'd keep up. Them kids is gettin' to be good pickers. Ma's worked 'em up a little bag for each. They couldn' tow a growed-up bag. Dump into ours. Made bags outa a couple old shirts. Work fine."

And Ma went to the meat counter, her forefinger pressed her lips, blowing on her finger, thinking deeply. "Might get some pork chops," she said. "How much?"

"Thirty cents a pound, ma'am."

"Well, lemme have three poun's. An' a nice piece a boilin' beef. My girl can cook it tomorra. An' a bottle a milk for my girl. She dotes on milk. Gonna have a baby. Nurse-lady tol' her to eat lots a milk. Now, le's see, we got potatoes."

Pa came close, carrying a can of sirup in his hands. "Might get this here," he said. "Might have some hotcakes."

Ma frowned. "Well—well, yes. Here, we'll take this here. Now—we got plenty lard."

Ruthie came near, in her hands two large boxes of Cracker Jack, in her eyes a brooding question, which on a nod or a shake of Ma's head might become tragedy or joyous excitement. "Ma?" She held up the boxes, jerked them up and down to make them attractive.

"Now you put them back——"

The tragedy began to form in Ruthie's eyes. Pa said, "They're on'y a nickel apiece. Them little fellas worked good today."

"Well——" The excitement began to steal into Ruthie's eyes. "Awright."

Ruthie turned and fled. Halfway to the door she caught Winfield and rushed him out the door, into the evening.

Uncle John fingered a pair of canvas gloves with yellow leather palms, tried them on and took them off and laid them down. He moved gradually to the liquor shelves, and he stood studying the labels on the bottles. Ma saw him. "Pa," she said, and motioned with her head toward Uncle John.

Pa lounged over to him. "Gettin' thirsty, John?"

"No, I ain't."

"Jus' wait till cotton's done," said Pa. "Then you can go on a hell of a drunk."

" 'Tain't sweatin' me none," Uncle John said. "I'm workin' hard an' sleepin' good. No dreams nor nothin'."

"Jus' seen you sort of droolin' out at them bottles."

"I didn' hardly see 'em. Funny thing. I wanta buy stuff. Stuff I don't need. Like to git one a them safety razors. Thought I'd like to have some a them gloves over there. Awful cheap."

"Can't pick no cotton with gloves," said Pa.

"I know that. An' I don't need no safety razor, neither. Stuff settin' out there, you jus' feel like buyin' it whether you need it or not."

Ma called, "Come on. We got ever'thing." She carried a bag. Uncle John and Pa each took a package.

Outside Ruthie and Winfield were waiting, their eyes strained, their cheeks puffed and full of Cracker Jack.

"Won't eat no supper, I·bet," Ma said.

People streamed toward the boxcar camp. The tents were lighted. Smoke poured from the stovepipes. The Joads climbed up their cat-walk and into their end of the boxcar. Rose of Sharon sat on a box beside the stove. She had a fire started, and the tin stove was wine-colored with heat. "Did ya get milk?" she demanded.

"Yeah. Right here."

"Give it to me. I ain't had any sence noon."

"She thinks it's like medicine."

"That nurse-lady says so."

"You got potatoes ready?"

"Right there—peeled."

"We'll fry 'em," said Ma. "Got pork chops. Cut up them potatoes in the new fry pan. And th'ow in a onion. You fellas go out an' wash, an' bring in a bucket a water. Where's Ruthie an' Winfiel'? They oughta wash. They each got Cracker Jack," Ma told Rose of Sharon. "Each got a whole box."

The men went out to wash in the stream. Rose of Sharon sliced the potatoes into the frying pan and stirred them about with the knife point.

Suddenly the tarpaulin was thrust aside. A stout perspiring face looked in from the other end of the car. "How'd you all make out, Mis' Joad?"

Ma swung around. "Why, evenin', Mis' Wainwright. We done good. Three an' a half. Three fifty-seven, exact."

"We done four dollars."

"Well," said Ma. " 'Course they's more of you."

"Yeah. Jonas is growin' up. Havin' pork chops, I see."

Winfield crept in through the door. "Ma!"

"Hush a minute. Yes, my men jus' loves pork chops."

"I'm cookin' bacon," said Mrs. Wainwright. "Can you smell it cookin'?"

"No—can't smell it over these here onions in the potatoes."

"She's burnin'!" Mrs. Wainwright cried, and her head jerked back.

"Ma," Winfield said.

"What? You sick from Cracker Jack?"

"Ma—Ruthie tol'."

"Tol' what?"

" 'Bout Tom."

Ma stared. "Tol'?" Then she knelt in front of him. "Winfiel', who'd she tell?"

Embarrassment seized Winfield. He backed away. "Well, she on'y tol' a little bit."

"Winfiel'! Now you tell what she said."

"She—she didn' eat all her Cracker Jack. She kep' some, an' she et jus' one piece at a time, slow, like she always done, an' she says, 'Bet you wisht you had some lef'.'"

"Winfiel'!" Ma demanded. "You tell now." She looked back nervously at the curtain. "Rosasharn, you go over talk to Mis' Wainwright so she don' listen."

"How 'bout these here potatoes?"

"I'll watch 'em. Now you go. I don' want her listenin' at that curtain." The girl shuffled heavily down the car and went around the side of the hung tarpaulin.

Ma said, "Now, Winfiel', you tell."

"Like I said, she et jus' one little piece at a time, an' she bust some in two so it'd las' longer."

"Go on, hurry up."

"Well, some kids come aroun', an' 'course they tried to get some, but Ruthie, she jus' nibbled an' nibbled, an' wouldn' give 'em none. So they got mad. An' one kid grabbed her Cracker Jack box."

"Winfiel', you tell quick about the other."

"I am," he said. "So Ruthie got mad an' chased 'em, an' she fit one, an' then she fit another, an' then one big girl up an' licked her. Hit 'er a good one. So then Ruthie cried, an' she said she'd git her big brother, an' he'd kill that big girl. An' that big girl said, Oh, yeah? Well, she got a big brother too." Winfield was breathless in his telling. "So then they fit, an' that big girl hit Ruthie a good one, an' Ruthie said her brother'd kill that big girl's brother. An' that big girl said how about if her brother kil't our brother. An' then—an' then, Ruthie said our brother already kil't two fellas. An'—an'—that big girl said, 'Oh, yeah! You're jus' a little smarty liar.' An' Ruthie said, Oh, yeah? Well, our brother's a-hidin' right now from killin' a fella, an' he can kill that big girl's brother too. An' then they called names an' Ruthie throwed a rock, an' that big girl chased her, an' I come home."

"Oh, my!" Ma said wearily. "Oh! My dear sweet Lord Jesus asleep in a manger! What we goin' to do now?" She put her forehead in her hand and rubbed her eyes. "What we gonna do now?" A smell of burning potatoes came from the roaring stove. Ma moved automatically and turned them.

"Rosasharn!" Ma called. The girl appeared around the curtain. "Come watch this here supper. Winfiel', you go out an' you fin' Ruthie an' bring her back here."

"Gonna whup her, Ma?" he asked hopefully.

"No. This here you couldn' do nothin' about. Why, I wonder, did she haf' to do it? No. It won't do no good to whup her. Run now, an' find her an' bring her back."

Winfield ran for the car door, and he met the three men tramping up the cat-walk, and he stood aside while they came in.

Ma said softly, "Pa, I got to talk to you. Ruthie tol' some kids how Tom's a-hidin'."

"What?"

"She tol'. Got in a fight an' tol'."

"Why, the little bitch!"

"No, she didn' know what she was a-doin'. Now
look, Pa. I want you to stay here. I'm goin' out an' try
to fin' Tom an' tell him. I got to tell 'im to be careful.
You stick here, Pa, an' kinda watch out for things. I'll
take 'im some dinner."

"Awright," Pa agreed.

"Don' you even mention to Ruthie what she done.
I'll tell her."

At that moment Ruthie came in, with Winfield behind her. The little girl was dirtied. Her mouth was
sticky, and her nose still dripped a little blood from
her fight. She looked shamed and frightened. Winfield
triumphantly followed her. Ruthie looked fiercely
about, but she went to a corner of the car and put her
back in the corner. Her shame and fierceness were
blended.

"I tol' her what she done," Winfield said.

Ma was putting two chops and some fried potatoes
on a tin plate. "Hush, Winfiel'," she said. "They ain't
no need to hurt her feelings no more'n what they're
hurt."

Ruthie's body hurtled across the car. She grabbed
Ma around the middle and buried her head in Ma's
stomach, and her strangled sobs shook her whole
body. Ma tried to loosen her, but the grubby fingers
clung tight. Ma brushed the hair on the back of her
head gently, and she patted her shoulders. "Hush,"
she said. "You didn' know."

Ruthie raised her dirty, tear-stained, bloody face.
"They stoled my Cracker Jack!" she cried. "That big
son-of-a-bitch of a girl, she belted me—" She went off
into hard crying again.

"Hush!" Ma said. "Don' talk like that. Here. Let
go. I'm a-goin' now."

"Whyn't ya whup her, Ma? If she didn't git snotty
with her Cracker Jack 'twouldn' a happened. Go on,
give her a whup."

"You jus' min' your business, mister," Ma said

fiercely. "You'll git a whup yourself. Now leggo, Ruthie."

Winfield retired to a rolled mattress, and he regarded the family cynically and dully. And he put himself in a good position of defense, for Ruthie would attack him at the first opportunity, and he knew it. Ruthie went quietly, heartbrokenly to the other side of the car.

Ma put a sheet of newspaper over the tin plate. "I'm a-goin' now," she said.

"Ain't you gonna eat nothin' yourself?" Uncle John demanded.

"Later. When I come back. I wouldn' want nothin' now." Ma walked to the open door; she steadied herself down the steep, cleated cat-walk.

On the stream side of the boxcars, the tents were pitched close together, their guy ropes crossing one another, and the pegs of one at the canvas line of the next. The lights shone through the cloth, and all the chimneys belched smoke. Men and women stood in the doorways talking. Children ran feverishly about. Ma moved majestically down the line of tents. Here and there she was recognized as she went by. "Evenin', Mis' Joad."

"Evenin'."

"Takin' somepin out, Mis' Joad?"

"They's a frien'. I'm takin' back some bread."

She came at last to the end of the line of tents. She stopped and looked back. A glow of light was on the camp, and the soft overtone of a multitude of speakers. Now and then a harsher voice cut through. The smell of smoke filled the air. Someone played a harmonica softly, trying for an effect, one phrase over and over.

Ma stepped in among the willows beside the stream. She moved off the trail and waited, silently, listening to hear any possible follower. A man walked down the trail toward the camp, boosting his suspenders and buttoning his jeans as he went. Ma sat very still, and he passed on without seeing her. She waited five minutes and then she stood up and crept on up the trail beside the stream. She moved quietly, so quietly that she could hear the murmur of the water above her soft steps on the willow leaves. Trail and stream swung to the left and then to the right again until they neared the highway. In the gray starlight she could see the embankment and the black round hole of the culvert where she always left Tom's food. She moved forward cautiously, thrust her package into the hole, and took back the empty tin plate which was left there. She crept back among the willows, forced her way into a thicket, and sat down to wait. Through the tangle she could see the black hole of the culvert. She clasped her knees and sat silently. In a few moments the thicket crept to life again. The field mice moved cautiously over the leaves. A skunk padded heavily and unself-consciously down the trail, carrying a faint effluvium with him. And then a wind stirred the willows delicately, as though it tested them, and a shower of golden leaves coasted down to the ground. Suddenly a gust boiled in and racked the trees, and a cricking downpour of leaves fell. Ma could feel them on her hair and on her shoulders. Over the sky a plump black cloud moved, erasing the stars. The fat drops of rain scattered down, splashing loudly on the fallen leaves, and the cloud moved on and unveiled the stars again. Ma shivered. The wind blew past and left the thicket quiet, but the rushing of the trees went on down the stream. From back at the camp came the thin penetrating tone of a violin feeling about for a tune.

Ma heard a stealthy step among the leaves far to her left, and she grew tense. She released her knees and straightened her head, the better to hear. The movement stopped, and after a long moment began again. A vine rasped harshly on the dry leaves. Ma saw a dark figure creep into the open and draw to the culvert. The black round hole was obscured for a moment, and then the figure moved back. She called softly, "Tom!" The figure stood still, so still, so low to the ground that it might have been a stump. She called again, "Tom, oh, Tom!" Then the figure moved.

"That you, Ma?"

"Right over here." She stood up and went to meet him.

"You shouldn' of came," he said.

"I got to see you, Tom. I got to talk to you."

"It's near the trail," he said. "Somebody might come by."

"Ain't you got a place, Tom?"

"Yeah—but if—well, s'pose somebody seen you with me—whole fambly'd be in a jam."

"I got to, Tom."

"Then come along. Come quiet." He crossed the little stream, wading carelessly through the water, and Ma followed him. He moved through the brush, out into a field on the other side of the thicket, and along the plowed ground. The blackening stems of the cotton were harsh against the ground, and a few fluffs of cotton clung to the stems. A quarter of a mile they went along the edge of the field, and then he turned into the brush again. He approached a great mound of wild blackberry bushes, leaned over and pulled a mat of vines aside. "You got to crawl in," he said.

Ma went down on her hands and knees. She felt sand under her, and then the black inside of the mound no longer touched her, and she felt Tom's blanket on the ground. He arranged the vines in place again. It was lightless in the cave.

"Where are you, Ma?"

"Here. Right here. Talk soft, Tom."

"Don't worry. I been livin' like a rabbit some time."

She heard him unwrap his tin plate.

"Pork chops," she said. "And fry potatoes."

"God Awmighty, an' still warm."

Ma could not see him at all in the blackness, but

she could hear him chewing, tearing at the meat and swallowing.

"It's a pretty good hide-out," he said.

Ma said uneasily, "Tom—Ruthie tol' about you." She heard him gulp.

"Ruthie? What for?"

"Well, it wasn' her fault. Got in a fight, an' says her brother'll lick that other girl's brother. You know how they do. An' she tol' that her brother killed a man an' was hidin'."

Tom was chuckling. "With me I was always gonna get Uncle John after 'em, but he never would do it. That's jus' kid talk, Ma. That's awright."

"No, it ain't," Ma said. "Them kids'll tell it aroun' an' then the folks'll hear, an' they'll tell aroun', an' pretty soon, well, they liable to get men out to look, jus' in case. Tom, you got to go away."

"That's what I said right along. I was always scared somebody'd see you put stuff in that culvert, an' then they'd watch."

"I know. But I wanted you near. I was scared for you. I ain't seen you. Can't see you now. How's your face?"

"Gettin' well quick."

"Come clost, Tom. Let me feel it. Come clost." He crawled near. Her reaching hand found his head in the blackness and her fingers moved down to his nose, and then over his left cheek. "You got a bad scar, Tom. An' your nose is all crooked."

"Maybe tha's a good thing. Nobody wouldn't know me, maybe. If my prints wasn't on record, I'd be glad." He went back to his eating.

"Hush," she said. "Listen!"

"It's the wind, Ma. Jus' the wind." The gust poured down the stream, and the trees rustled under its passing.

She crawled close to his voice. "I wanta touch ya again, Tom. It's like I'm blin', it's so dark. I wanta remember, even if it's on'y my fingers that remember. You got to go away, Tom."

"Yeah! I knowed it from the start."

"We made purty good," she said. "I been squirrelin' money away. Hol' out your han', Tom. I got seven dollars here."

"I ain't gonna take ya money," he said. "I'll get 'long all right."

"Hol' out ya han', Tom. I ain't gonna sleep none if you got no money. Maybe you got to take a bus, or somepin. I want you should go a long ways off, three-four hunderd miles."

"I ain't gonna take it."

"Tom," she said sternly. "You take this money. You hear me? You got no right to cause me pain."

"You ain't playin' fair," he said.

"I thought maybe you could go to a big city. Los Angeles, maybe. They wouldn' never look for you there."

"Hm-m," he said. "Lookie, Ma. I been all day an' all night hidin' alone. Guess who I been thinkin' about? Casy! He talked a lot. Use' ta bother me. But now I been thinkin' what he said, an' I can remember—all of it. Says one time he went out in the wilderness to find his own soul, an' he foun' he didn' have no soul that was his'n. Says he foun' he jus' got a little piece of a great big soul. Says a wilderness ain't no good, 'cause his little piece of a soul wasn't no good 'less it was with the rest, an' was whole. Funny how I remember. Didn' think I was even listenin'. But I know now a fella ain't no good alone."

"He was a good man," Ma said.

Tom went on, "He spouted out some Scripture once, an' it didn' soun' like no hell-fire Scripture. He tol' it twicet, an' I remember it. Says it's from the Preacher."

"How's it go, Tom?"

"Goes, 'Two are better than one, because they have a good reward for their labor. For if they fall, the one will lif' up his fellow, but woe to him that is alone when he falleth, for he hath not another to help him up.' That's part of her."

"Go on," Ma said. "Go on, Tom."

"Jus' a little bit more. 'Again, if two lie together, then they have heat: but how can one be warm alone? And if one prevail against him, two shall withstand him, and a three-fold cord is not quickly broken.'"

"An' that's Scripture?"

"Casy said it was. Called it the Preacher."

"Hush—listen."

"On'y the wind, Ma. I know the wind. An' I got to thinkin', Ma—most of the preachin' is about the poor we shall have always with us, an' if you got nothin', why, jus' fol' your hands an' to hell with it, you gonna git ice cream on gol' plates when you're dead. An' then this here Preacher says two get a better reward for their work."

"Tom," she said. "What you aimin' to do?"

He was quiet for a long time. "I been thinkin' how it was in that gov'ment camp, how our folks took care a theirselves, an' if they was a fight they fixed it theirself; an' they wasn't no cops wagglin' their guns, but they was better order than them cops ever give. I been a-wonderin' why we can't do that all over. Throw out the cops that ain't our people. All work together for our own thing—all farm our own lan'."

"Tom," Ma repeated, "what you gonna do?"

"What Casy done," he said.

"But they killed him."

"Yeah," said Tom. "He didn' duck quick enough. He wasn' doing nothin' against the law, Ma. I been thinkin' a hell of a lot, thinkin' about our people livin' like pigs, an' the good rich lan' layin' fallow, or maybe one fella with a million acres, while a hunderd thousan' good farmers is starvin'. An' I been wonderin' if all our folks got together an' yelled, like them fellas yelled, only a few of 'em at the Hooper ranch——"

Ma said, "Tom, they'll drive you, an' cut you down like they done to young Floyd."

"They gonna drive me anyways. They drivin' all our people."

"You don't aim to kill nobody, Tom?"

"No. I been thinkin', long as I'm a outlaw anyways, maybe I could— Hell, I ain't thought it out clear, Ma. Don' worry me now. Don' worry me."

They sat silent in the coal-black cave of vines. Ma said, "How'm I gonna know 'bout you? They might kill ya an' I wouldn' know. They might hurt ya. How'm I gonna know?"

Tom laughed uneasily. "Well, maybe like Casy says, a fella ain't got a soul of his own, but on'y a piece of a big one—an' then——"

"Then what, Tom?"

"Then it don' matter. Then I'll be all aroun' in the dark. I'll be ever'where—wherever you look. Wherever they's a fight so hungry people can eat, I'll be there. Wherever they's a cop beatin' up a guy, I'll be there. If Casy knowed, why, I'll be in the way guys yell when they're mad an'—I'll be in the way kids laugh when they're hungry an' they know supper's ready. An' when our folks eat the stuff they raise an' live in the houses they build—why, I'll be there. See? God, I'm talkin' like Casy. Comes of thinkin' about him so much. Seems like I can see him sometimes."

"I don' un'erstan'," Ma said. "I don' really know."

"Me neither," said Tom. "It's jus' stuff I been thinkin' about. Get thinkin' a lot when you ain't movin' aroun'. You got to get back, Ma."

"You take the money then."

He was silent for a moment. "Awright," he said.

"An', Tom, later—when it's blowed over, you'll come back. You'll find us?"

"Sure," he said. "Now you better go. Here, gimme your han'." He guided her toward the entrance. Her fingers clutched his wrist. He swept the vines aside and followed her out. "Go up to the field till you come to a sycamore on the edge, an' then cut acrost the stream. Good-by."

"Good-by," she said, and she walked quickly away. Her eyes were wet and burning, but she did not cry. Her footsteps were loud and careless on the leaves as she went through the brush. And as she went, out of the dim sky the rain began to fall, big drops and few, splashing on the dry leaves heavily. Ma stopped and stood still in the dripping thicket. She turned about— took three steps back toward the mound of vines; and then she turned quickly and went back toward the boxcar camp. She went straight out to the culvert and climbed up on the road. The rain had passed now, but the sky was overcast. Behind her on the road she heard footsteps, and she turned nervously. The blinking of a dim flashlight played on the road. Ma turned back and started for home. In a moment a man caught up with her. Politely, he kept his light on the ground and did not play it in her face.

"Evenin'," he said.

Ma said, "Howdy."

"Looks like we might have a little rain."

"I hope not. Stop the pickin'. We need the pickin'."

"I need the pickin' too. You live at the camp there?"

"Yes, sir." Their footsteps beat on the road together.

"I got twenty acres of cotton. Little late, but it's ready now. Thought I'd go down and try to get some pickers."

"You'll get 'em awright. Season's near over."

"Hope so. My place is only a mile up that way."

"Six of us," said Ma. "Three men an' me an' two little fellas."

"I'll put out a sign. Two miles—this road."

"We'll be there in the mornin'."

"I hope it don't rain."

"Me too," said Ma. "Twenty acres won' las' long."

"The less it lasts the gladder I'll be. My cotton's late. Didn' get it in till late."

"What you payin', mister?"

"Ninety cents."

"We'll pick. I hear fellas say nex' year it'll be seventy-five or even sixty."

"That's what I hear."

"They'll be trouble," said Ma.

"Sure. I know. Little fella like me can't do anything. The Association sets the rate, and we got to mind. If we don't—we ain't got a farm. Little fella gets crowded all the time."

They came to the camp. "We'll be there," Ma said. "Not much pickin' lef'." She went to the end boxcar and climbed the cleated walk. The low light of the lantern made gloomy shadows in the car. Pa and Uncle John and an elderly man squatted against the car wall.

"Hello," Ma said. "Evenin', Mr. Wainwright."

He raised a delicately chiseled face. His eyes were deep under the ridges of his brows. His hair was blue-white and fine. A patina of silver beard covered his jaws and chin. "Evenin', Ma'am," he said.

"We got pickin' tomorra," Ma observed. "Mile north. Twenty acres."

"Better take the truck, I guess," Pa said. "Get in more pickin'."

Wainwright raised his head eagerly. "S'pose we can pick?"

"Why, sure. I walked a piece with the fella. He was comin' to get pickers."

"Cotton's nearly gone. Purty thin, these here seconds. Gonna be hard to make a wage on the seconds. Got her pretty clean the fust time."

"Your folks could maybe ride with us," Ma said. "Split the gas."

"Well—that's frien'ly of you, ma'am."

"Saves us both," said Ma.

Pa said, "Mr. Wainwright—he's got a worry he come to us about. We was a-talkin' her over."

"What's the matter?"

Wainwright looked down at the floor. "Our Aggie," he said. "She's a big girl—near sixteen, an' growed up."

"Aggie's a pretty girl," said Ma.

"Listen 'im out," Pa said.

"Well, her an' your boy Al, they're a-walkin' out ever' night. An' Aggie's a good healthy girl that oughta have a husban', else she might git in trouble. We never had no trouble in our family. But what with us bein' so poor off, now, Mis' Wainwright an' me, we got to worryin'. S'pose she got in trouble?"

Ma rolled down a mattress and sat on it. "They out now?" she asked.

"Always out," said Wainwright. "Ever' night."

"Hm. Well, Al's a good boy. Kinda figgers he's a dung-hill rooster these days, but he's a good steady boy. I couldn' want for a better boy."

"Oh, we ain't complainin' about Al as a fella! We like him. But what scares Mis' Wainwright an' me— well, she's a growed-up woman-girl. An' what if we go away, or you go away, an' we find out Aggie's in trouble? We ain't had no shame in our family."

Ma said softly, "We'll try an' see that we don't put no shame on you."

He stood up quickly. "Thank you, ma'am. Aggie's a growed-up woman-girl. She's a good girl—jes' as nice an' good. We'll sure thank you, Ma'am, if you'll keep shame from us. It ain't Aggie's fault. She's growed up."

"Pa'll talk to Al," said Ma. "Or if Pa won't, I will."

Wainwright said, "Good night, then, an' we sure thank ya." He went around the end of the curtain. They could hear him talking softly in the other end of the car, explaining the result of his embassy.

Ma listened a moment, and then, "You fellas," she said. "Come over an' set here."

Pa and Uncle John got heavily up from their squats. They sat on the mattress beside Ma.

"Where's the little fellas?"

Pa pointed to a mattress in the corner. "Ruthie, she jumped Winfiel' an' bit 'im. Made 'em both lay down. Guess they're asleep. Rosasharn, she went to set with a lady she knows."

Ma sighed. "I foun' Tom," she said softly. "I—sent 'im away. Far off."

Pa nodded slowly. Uncle John dropped his chin on his chest. "Couldn' do nothin' else," Pa said. "Think he could, John?"

Uncle John looked up. "I can't think nothin' out," he said. "Don't seem like I'm hardly awake no more."

"Tom's a good boy," Ma said; and then she apologized. "I didn' mean no harm a-sayin' I'd talk to Al."

"I know," Pa said quietly. "I ain't no good any more. Spen' all my time a-thinkin' how it use' ta be. Spen' all my time thinkin' of home, an' I ain't never gonna see it no more."

"This here's purtier—better lan'," said Ma.

"I know. I never even see it, thinkin' how the willow's los' its leaves now. Sometimes figgerin' to mend that hole in the south fence. Funny! Woman takin' over the fambly. Woman sayin' we'll do this here, an' we'll go there. An' I don' even care."

"Woman can change better'n a man," Ma said soothingly. "Woman got all her life in her arms. Man got it all in his head. Don' you mind. Maybe—well, maybe nex' year we can get a place."

"We got nothin', now," Pa said. "Comin' a long time—no work, no crops. What we gonna do then? How we gonna git stuff to eat? An' I tell you Rosasharn ain't so far from due. Git so I hate to think. Go diggin' back to a ol' time to keep from thinkin'. Seems like our life's over an' done."

"No, it ain't," Ma smiled. "It ain't, Pa. An' that's one more thing a woman knows. I noticed that. Man, he lives in jerk—baby born an' a man dies, an' that's a jerk—gets a farm an' loses his farm, an' that's a jerk. Woman, it's all one flow, like a stream, little eddies, little waterfalls, but the river, it goes right on. Woman looks at it like that. We ain't gonna die out. People is goin' on—changin' a little, maybe, but goin' right on."

"How can you tell?" Uncle John demanded. "What's to keep ever'thing from stoppin'; all the folks from jus' gittin' tired an' layin' down?"

Ma considered. She rubbed the shiny back of one hand with the other, pushed the fingers of her right hand between the fingers of her left. "Hard to say," she said. "Ever'thing we do—seems to me is aimed right at goin' on. Seems that way to me. Even gettin' hungry—even bein' sick; some die, but the rest is tougher. Jus' try to live the day, jus' the day."

Uncle John said, "If on'y she didn' die that time——"

"Jus' live the day," Ma said. "Don' worry yaself."

"They might be a good year nex' year, back home," said Pa.

Ma said, "Listen!"

There were creeping steps on the cat-walk, and then Al came in past the curtain. "Hullo," he said. "I thought you'd be sleepin' by now."

"Al," Ma said. "We're a-talkin'. Come set here."

"Sure—O.K. I wanta talk too. I'll hafta be goin' away pretty soon now."

"You can't. We need you here. Why you got to go away?"

"Well, me an' Aggie Wainwright, we figgers to get married, an' I'm gonna git a job in a garage, an' we'll have a rent' house for a while, an'—" He looked up fiercely. "Well, we are, an' they ain't nobody can stop us!"

They were staring at him. "Al," Ma said at last, "we're glad. We're awful glad."

"You are?"

"Why, 'course we are. You're a growed man. You need a wife. But don' go right now, Al."

"I promised Aggie," he said. "We got to go. We can't stan' this no more."

"Jus' stay till spring," Ma begged. "Jus' till spring. Won't you stay till spring? Who'd drive the truck?"

"Well——"

Mrs. Wainwright put her head around the curtain. "You heard yet?" she demanded.

"Yeah! Jus' heard."

"Oh, my! I wisht—I wisht we had a cake. I wisht we had—a cake or somepin."

"I'll set on some coffee an' make up some pancakes," Ma said. "We got sirup."

"Oh, my!" Mrs. Wainwright said. "Why—well. Look, I'll bring some sugar. We'll put sugar in them pancakes."

Ma broke twigs into the stove, and the coals from the dinner cooking started them blazing. Ruthie and Winfield came out of their bed like hermit crabs from shells. For a moment they were careful; they watched to see whether they were still criminals. When no one noticed them, they grew bold. Ruthie hopped all the way to the door and back on one foot, without touching the wall.

Ma was pouring flour into a bowl when Rose of Sharon climbed the cat-walk. She steadied herself and advanced cautiously. "What's a matter?" she asked.

"Why, it's news!" Ma cried. "We're gonna have a little party 'count a Al an' Aggie Wainwright is gonna get married."

Rose of Sharon stood perfectly still. She looked slowly at Al, who stood there flustered and embarrassed.

Mrs. Wainwright shouted from the other end of the car, "I'm puttin' a fresh dress on Aggie. I'll be right over."

Rose of Sharon turned slowly. She went back to the wide door, and she crept down the cat-walk. Once on the ground, she moved slowly toward the stream and the trail that went beside it. She took the way Ma had gone earlier—into the willows. The wind blew more steadily now, and the bushes whished steadily. Rose of Sharon went down on her knees and crawled deep into the brush. The berry vines cut her face and pulled at her hair, but she didn't mind. Only when she felt the bushes touching her all over did she stop. She stretched out on her back. And she felt the weight of the baby inside of her.

In the lightless car, Ma stirred, and then she pushed the blanket back and got up. At the open door of the car the gray starlight penetrated a little. Ma walked to the door and stood looking out. The stars were paling in the east. The wind blew softly over the willow thickets, and from the little stream came the quiet talking of the water. Most of the camp was still asleep, but in front of one tent a little fire burned, and people were standing about it, warming themselves. Ma could see them in the light of the new dancing fire as they stood facing the flames, rubbing their hands; and then they turned their backs and held their hands behind them. For a moment Ma looked out, and she held her hands clasped in front of her. The uneven wind whisked up and passed, and a bite of frost was in the air. Ma shivered and rubbed her hands together. She crept back and fumbled for the matches, beside the lantern. The shade screeched up. She lighted the wick, watched it burn blue for a moment and then put up its yellow, delicately curved ring of light. She carried the lantern to the stove and set it down while she broke the brittle dry willow twigs into the fire box. In a moment the fire was roaring up the chimney.

Rose of Sharon rolled heavily over and sat up. "I'll git right up," she said.

"Whyn't you lay a minute till it warms?" Ma asked.

"No, I'll git."

Ma filled the coffee pot from the bucket and set it on the stove, and she put on the frying pan, deep with fat, to get hot for the pones. "What's over you?" she said softly.

"I'm a goin' out," Rose of Sharon said.

"Out where?"

"Goin' out to pick cotton."

"You can't," Ma said. "You're too far along."

"No, I ain't. An' I'm a-goin'."

Ma measured coffee into the water. "Rosasharn, you wasn't to the pancakes las' night." The girl didn't answer. "What you wanta pick cotton for?" Still no answer. "Is it 'cause of Al an' Aggie?" This time Ma looked closely at her daughter. "Oh. Well, you don' need to pick."

"I'm goin'."

"Awright, but don' you strain yourself."

"Git up, Pa! Wake up, git up!"

Pa blinked and yawned. "Ain't slep' out," he moaned. "Musta been on to eleven o'clock when we went down."

"Come on, git up, all a you, an' wash."

The inhabitants of the car came slowly to life, squirmed up out of the blankets, writhed into their clothes. Ma sliced salt pork into her second frying pan. "Git out an' wash," she commanded.

A light sprang up in the other end of the car. And there came the sound of the breaking of twigs from the Wainwright end. "Mis' Joad," came the call. "We're gettin' ready. We'll be ready."

Al grumbled, "What we got to be up so early for?"

"It's on'y twenty acres," Ma said. "Got to get there. Ain't much cotton lef'. Got to be there 'fore she's picked." Ma rushed them dressed, rushed the breakfast into them. "Come on, drink your coffee," she said. "Got to start."

"We can't pick no cotton in the dark, Ma."

"We can *be* there when it gets light."

"Maybe it's wet."

"Didn' rain enough. Come on now, drink your coffee. Al, soon's you're through, better get the engine runnin'."

She called, "You near ready, Mis' Wainwright?"

"Jus' eatin'. Be ready in a minute."

Outside, the camp had come to life. Fires burned in front of the tents. The stovepipes from the boxcars spurted smoke.

Al tipped up his coffee and got a mouthful of grounds. He went down the cat-walk spitting them out.

"We're awready, Mis' Wainwright," Ma called. She turned to Rose of Sharon. She said, "You got to stay."

The girl set her jaw. "I'm a-goin'," she said. "Ma, I got to go."

"Well, you got no cotton sack. You can't pull no sack."

"I'll pick into your sack."

"I wisht you wouldn'."

"I'm a-goin'."

Ma sighed. "I'll keep my eye on you. Wisht we could have a doctor." Rose of Sharon moved nervously about the car. She put on a light coat and took it off. "Take a blanket," Ma said. "Then if you wanta res', you can keep warm." They heard the truck motor roar up behind the boxcar. "We gonna be first out," Ma said exultantly. "Awright, get your sacks. Ruthie, don' you forget them shirts I fixed for you to pick in."

Wainwrights and Joads climbed into the truck in the dark. The dawn was coming, but it was slow and pale.

"Turn lef'," Ma told Al. "They'll be a sign out where we're goin'." They drove along the dark road. And other cars followed them, and behind, in the camp, the cars were being started, the families piling in; and the cars pulled out on the highway and turned left.

A piece of cardboard was tied to a mailbox on the righthand side of the road, and on it, printed with blue crayon, "Cotton Pickers Wanted." Al turned into the entrance and drove out to the barnyard. And the barnyard was full of cars already. An electric globe on the end of the white barn lighted a group of men and women standing near the scales, their bags rolled under their arms. Some of the women wore the bags over their shoulders and crossed in front.

"We ain't so early as we thought," said Al. He pulled the truck against a fence and parked. The families climbed down and went to join the waiting group, and more cars came in from the road and parked, and more families joined the group. Under the light on the barn end, the owner signed them in.

"Hawley?" he said. "H-a-w-l-e-y? How many?"

"Four. Will——"

"Will."

"Benton——"

"Benton."

"Amelia——"

"Amelia."

"Claire——"

"Claire. Who's next? Carpenter? How many?"

"Six."

He wrote them in the book, with a space left for the weights. "Got your bags? I got a few. Cost you a dollar." And the cars poured into the yard. The owner pulled his sheep-lined leather jacket up around his throat. He looked at the driveway apprehensively. "This twenty isn't gonna take long to pick with all these people," he said.

Children were climbing into the big cotton trailer, digging their toes into the chicken-wire sides. "Git off there," the owner cried. "Come on down. You'll tear that wire loose." And the children climbed slowly down, embarrassed and silent. The gray dawn came. "I'll have to take a tare for dew," the owner said. "Change it when the sun comes out. All right, go out when you want. Light enough to see."

The people moved quickly out into the cotton field and took their rows. They tied the bags to their waists and they slapped their hands together to warm stiff fingers that had to be nimble. The dawn colored over the eastern hills, and the wide line moved over the rows. And from the highway the cars still moved in and parked in the barnyard until it was full, and they parked along the road on both sides. The wind blew briskly across the field. "I don't know how you all found out," the owner said. "There must be a hell of a grapevine. The twenty won't last till noon. What name? Hume? How many?"

The line of people moved out across the field, and the strong steady west wind blew their clothes. Their fingers flew to the spilling bolls, and flew to the long sacks growing heavy behind them.

Pa spoke to the man in the row to his right. "Back home we might get rain out of a wind like this. Seems a little mite frosty for rain. How long you been out here?" He kept his eyes down on his work as he spoke.

His neighbor didn't look up. "I been here nearly a year."

"Would you say it was gonna rain?"

"Can't tell, an' that ain't no insult, neither. Folks that lived here all their life can't tell. If the rain can git in the way of a crop, it'll rain. Tha's what they say out here."

Pa looked quickly at the western hills. Big gray clouds were coasting over the ridge, riding the wind swiftly. "Them looks like rain-heads," he said.

His neighbor stole a squinting look. "Can't tell," he

said. And all down the line of rows the people looked back at the clouds. And then they bent lower to their work, and their hands flew to the cotton. They raced at the picking, raced against time and cotton weight, raced against the rain and against each other—only so much cotton to pick, only so much money to be made. They came to the other side of the field and ran to get a new row. And now they faced into the wind, and they could see the high gray clouds moving over the sky toward the rising sun. And more cars parked along the roadside, and new pickers came to be checked in. The line of people moved frantically across the field, weighed at the end, marked their cotton, checked the weights into their own books, and ran for new rows.

At eleven o'clock the field was picked and the work was done. The wire-sided trailers were hooked on behind wire-sided trucks, and they moved out to the highway and drove away to the gin. The cotton fluffed out through the chicken wire and little clouds of cotton blew through the air, and rags of cotton caught and waved on the weeds beside the road. The pickers clustered disconsolately back to the barnyard and stood in line to be paid off.

"Hume, James. Twenty-two cents. Ralph, thirty cents. Joad, Thomas, ninety ·cents. Winfield, fifteen cents." The money lay in rolls, silver and nickels and pennies. And each man looked in his own book as he was being paid. "Wainwright, Agnes, thirty-four cents. Tobin, sixty-three cents." The line moved past slowly. The families went back to their cars, silently. And they drove slowly away.

Joads and Wainwrights waited in the truck for the driveway to clear. And as they waited, the first drops of rain began to fall. Al put his hand out of the cab to feel them. Rose of Sharon sat in the middle, and Ma on the outside. The girl's eyes were lusterless again.

"You shouldn' of came," Ma said. "You didn' pick more'n ten-fifteen pounds." Rose of Sharon looked down at her great bulging belly, and she didn't reply. She shivered suddenly and held her head high. Ma, watching her closely, unrolled her cotton bag, spread it over Rose of Sharon's shoulders, and drew her close.

At last the way was clear. Al started his motor and drove out into the highway. The big infrequent drops of rain lanced down and splashed on the road, and as the truck moved along, the drops became smaller and closer. Rain pounded on the cab of the truck so loudly that it could be heard over the pounding of the old worn motor. On the truck bed the Wainwrights and Joads spread their cotton bags over their heads and shoulders.

Rose of Sharon shivered violently against Ma's arm, and Ma cried, "Go faster, Al. Rosasharn got a chill. Gotta get her feet in hot water."

Al speeded the pounding motor, and when he came to the boxcar camp, he drove close to the red cars. Ma was spouting orders before they were well stopped. "Al," she commanded, "you an' John an' Pa go into the willows an' c'lect all the dead stuff you can. We got to keep warm."

"Wonder if the roof leaks."

"No, I don' think so. Be nice an' dry, but we got to have wood. Got to keep warm. Take Ruthie an' Winfiel' too. They can get twigs. This here girl ain't well." Ma got out, and Rose of Sharon tried to follow, but her knees buckled and she sat down heavily on the running board.

Fat Mrs. Wainwright saw her. "What's a matter? Her time come?"

"No, I don' think so," said Ma. "Got a chill. Maybe took col'. Gimme a han', will you?" The two women supported Rose of Sharon. After a few steps her strength came back—her legs took her weight.

"I'm awright, Ma," she said. "It was jus' a minute there."

The older women kept hands on her elbows. "Feet in hot water," Ma said wisely. They helped her up the cat-walk and into the boxcar.

"You rub her," Mrs. Wainwright said. "I'll get a far' goin'." She used the last of the twigs and built up a blaze in the stove. The rain poured now, scoured at the roof of the car.

Ma looked up at it. "Thank God we got a tight roof," she said. "Them tents leaks, no matter how good. Jus' put on a little water, Mis' Wainwright."

Rose of Sharon lay still on a mattress. She let them take off her shoes and rub her feet. Mrs. Wainwright bent over her. "You got pain?" she demanded.

"No. Jus' don' feel good. Jus' feel bad."

"I got pain killer an' salts," Mrs. Wainwright said. "You're welcome to 'em if you want 'em. Perfec'ly welcome."

The girl shivered violently. "Cover me up, Ma. I'm col'." Ma brought all the blankets and piled them on top of her. The rain roared down on the roof.

Now the wood-gatherers returned, their arms piled high with sticks and their hats and coats dripping. "Jesus, she's wet," Pa said. "Soaks you in a minute."

Ma said, "Better go back an' get more. Burns up awful quick. Be dark purty soon." Ruthie and Winfield dripped in and threw their sticks on the pile. They turned to go again. "You stay," Ma ordered. "Stan' up close to the fire an' get dry."

The afternoon was silver with rain, the roads glittered with water. Hour by hour the cotton plants seemed to blacken and shrivel. Pa and Al and Uncle John made trip after trip into the thickets and brought back loads of dead wood. They piled it near the door, until the heap of it nearly reached the ceiling, and at last they stopped and walked toward the stove. Streams of water ran from their hats to their shoulders. The edges of their coats dripped and their shoes squished as they walked.

"Awright, now, get off them clothes," Ma said. "I got some nice coffee for you fellas. An' you got dry overhalls to put on. Don' stan' there."

The evening came early. In the boxcars the families huddled together, listening to the pouring water on the roofs.

29

Over the high coast mountains and over the valleys the gray clouds marched in from the ocean. The wind blew fiercely and silently, high in the air, and it swished in the brush, and it roared in the forests. The clouds came in brokenly, in puffs, in folds, in gray crags; and they piled in together and settled low over the west. And then the wind stopped and left the clouds deep and solid. The rain began with gusty showers, pauses and downpours; and then gradually it settled to a single tempo, small drops and a steady beat, rain that was gray to see through, rain that cut midday light to evening. And at first the dry earth sucked the moisture down and blackened. For two days the earth drank the rain, until the earth was full. Then puddles formed, and in the low places little lakes formed in the fields. The muddy lakes rose higher, and the steady rain whipped the shining water. At last the mountains were full, and the hillsides spilled into the streams, built them to freshets, and sent them roaring down the canyons into the valleys. The rain beat on steadily. And the streams and the little rivers edged up to the bank sides and worked at willows and tree roots, bent the willows deep in the current, cut out the roots of cottonwoods and brought down the trees. The

muddy water whirled along the bank sides and crept up
the banks until at last it spilled over, into the fields,
into the orchards, into the cotton patches where the
black stems stood. Level fields became lakes, broad
and gray, and the rain whipped up the surfaces. Then
the water poured over the highways, and cars moved
slowly, cutting the water ahead, and leaving a boiling
muddy wake behind. The earth whispered under the
beat of the rain, and the streams thundered under the
churning freshets.

When the first rain started, the migrant people huddled in their tents, saying, It'll soon be over, and
asking, How long's it likely to go on?

And when the puddles formed, the men went out in
the rain with shovels and built little dikes around the
tents. The beating rain worked at the canvas until it
penetrated and sent streams down. And then the little
dikes washed out and the water came inside, and the
streams wet the beds and the blankets. The people sat
in wet clothes. They set up boxes and put planks on
the boxes. Then, day and night, they sat on the
planks.

Beside the tents the old cars stood, and water fouled
the ignition wires and water fouled the carburetors. The
little gray tents stood in lakes. And at last the people
had to move. Then the cars wouldn't start because the
wires were shorted; and if the engines would run, deep
mud engulfed the wheels. And the people waded away,
carrying their wet blankets in their arms. They splashed
along, carrying the children, carrying the very old, in
their arms. And if a barn stood on high ground, it was
filled with people, shivering and hopeless.

Then some went to the relief offices, and they came
sadly back to their own people.

They's rules—you got to be here a year before you
can git relief. They say the gov'ment is gonna help.
They don' know when.

And gradually the greatest terror of all came along.

They ain't gonna be no kinda work for three months.

In the barns, the people sat huddled together; and the terror came over them, and their faces were gray with terror. The children cried with hunger, and there was no food.

Then the sickness came, pneumonia, and measles that went to the eyes and to the mastoids.

And the rain fell steadily, and the water flowed over the highways, for the culverts could not carry the water.

Then from the tents, from the crowded barns, groups of sodden men went out, their clothes slopping rags, their shoes muddy pulp. They splashed out through the water, to the towns, to the country stores, to the relief offices, to beg for food, to cringe and beg for food, to beg for relief, to try to steal, to lie. And under the begging, and under the cringing, a hopeless anger began to smolder. And in the little towns pity for the sodden men changed to anger, and anger at the hungry people changed to fear of them. Then sheriffs swore in deputies in droves, and orders were rushed for rifles, for tear gas, for ammunition. Then the hungry men crowded the alleys behind the stores to beg for bread, to beg for rotting vegetables, to steal when they could.

Frantic men pounded on the doors of the doctors; and the doctors were busy. And sad men left word at country stores for the coroner to send a car. The coroners were not too busy. The coroners' wagons backed up through the mud and took out the dead.

And the rain pattered relentlessly down, and the streams broke their banks and spread out over the country.

Huddled under sheds, lying in wet hay, the hunger and the fear bred anger. Then boys went out, not to beg, but to steal; and men went out weakly, to try to steal.

The sheriffs swore in new deputies and ordered new

rifles; and the comfortable people in tight houses felt pity at first, and then distaste, and finally hatred for the migrant people.

In the wet hay of leaking barns babies were born to women who panted with pneumonia. And old people curled up in corners and died that way, so that the coroners could not straighten them. At night the frantic men walked boldly to hen roosts and carried off the squawking chickens. If they were shot at, they did not run, but splashed sullenly away; and if they were hit, they sank tiredly in the mud.

The rain stopped. On the fields the water stood, reflecting the gray sky, and the land whispered with moving water. And the men came out of the barns, out of the sheds. They squatted on their hams and looked out over the flooded land. And they were silent. And sometimes they talked very quietly.

No work till spring. No work.

And if no work—no money, no food.

Fella had a team of horses, had to use 'em to plow an' cultivate an' mow, wouldn' think a turnin' 'em out to starve when they wasn't workin'.

Them's horses—we're men.

The women watched the men, watched to see whether the break had come at last. The women stood silently and watched. And where a number of men gathered together, the fear went from their faces, and anger took its place. And the women sighed with relief, for they knew it was all right—the break had not come; and the break would never come as long as fear could turn to wrath.

Tiny points of grass came through the earth, and in a few days the hills were pale green with the beginning year.

30

In the boxcar camp the water stood in puddles, and the rain splashed in the mud. Gradually the little stream crept up the bank toward the low flat where the boxcars stood.

On the second day of the rain Al took the tarpaulin down from the middle of the car. He carried it out and spread it on the nose of the truck, and he came back into the car and sat down on his mattress. Now, without the separation, the two families in the car were one. The men sat together, and their spirits were damp. Ma kept a little fire going in the stove, kept a few twigs burning, and she conserved her wood. The rain poured down on the nearly flat roof of the boxcar.

On the third day the Wainwrights grew restless. "Maybe we better go 'long," Mrs. Wainwright said.

And Ma tried to keep them. "Where'd you go an' be sure of a tight roof?"

"I dunno, but I got a feelin' we oughta go along." They argued together, and Ma watched Al.

Ruthie and Winfield tried to play for a while, and then they too relapsed into sullen inactivity, and the rain drummed down on the roof.

On the third day the sound of the stream could be heard above the drumming rain. Pa and Uncle John stood in the open door and looked out on the rising stream. At both ends of the camp the water ran near to the highway, but at the camp it looped away so that the highway embankment surrounded the camp at the back and the stream closed it in on the front. And Pa said, "How's it look to you, John? Seems to me if that crick comes up, she'll flood us."

Uncle John opened his mouth and rubbed his bristling chin. "Yeah," he said. "Might at that."

Rose of Sharon was down with a heavy cold, her face flushed and her eyes shining with fever. Ma sat beside her with a cup of hot milk. "Here," she said. "Take this here. Got bacon grease in it for strength. Here, drink it!"

Rose of Sharon shook her head weakly. "I ain't hungry."

Pa drew a curved line in the air with his finger. "If we was all to get our shovels an' throw up a bank, I bet we could keep her out. On'y have to go from up there down to there."

"Yeah," Uncle John agreed. "Might. Dunno if them other fellas'd wanta. They'd maybe ruther move somewheres else."

"But these here cars is dry," Pa insisted. "Couldn' find no dry place as good as this. You wait." From the pile of brush in the car he picked a twig. He ran down the cat-walk, splashed through the mud to the stream and he set his twig upright on the edge of the swirling water. In a moment he was back in the car. "Jesus, ya get wet through," he said.

Both men kept their eyes on the little twig on the water's edge. They saw the water move slowly up around it and creep up the bank. Pa squatted down in the doorway. "Comin' up fast," he said. "I think we oughta go talk to the other fellas. See if they'll help ditch up. Got to git outa here if they won't." Pa looked down the long car to the Wainwright end. Al was with them, sitting beside Aggie. Pa walked into their pre-

cinct. "Water's risin'," he said. "How about if we
throwed up a bank? We could do her if ever'body
helped."

Wainwright said, "We was jes' talkin'. Seems like
we oughta be gettin' outa here."

Pa said, "You been aroun'. You know what chancet
we got a gettin' a dry place to stay."

"I know. But jes' the same——"

Al said, "Pa, if they go, I'm a-goin' too."

Pa looked startled. "You can't, Al. The truck— We
ain't fit to drive that truck."

"I don' care. Me an' Aggie got to stick together."

"Now you wait," Pa said. "Come on over here."
Wainwright and Al got to their feet and approached
the door. "See?" Pa said, pointing. "Jus' a bank from
there an' down to there." He looked at his stick. The
water swirled about it now, and crept up the bank.

"Be a lot a work, an' then she might come over
anyways," Wainwright protested.

"Well, we ain't doin' nothin', might's well be
workin'. We ain't gonna find us no nice place to live
like this. Come on, now. Le's go talk to the other
fellas. We can do her if ever'body helps."

Al said, "If Aggie goes, I'm a-goin' too."

Pa said, "Look, Al, if them fellas won't dig, then
we'll all hafta go. Come on, le's go talk to 'em." They
hunched their shoulders and ran down the cat-walk to
the next car and up the walk into its open door.

Ma was at the stove, feeding a few sticks to the
feeble flame. Ruthie crowded close beside her. "I'm
hungry," Ruthie whined.

"No, you ain't," Ma said. "You had good mush."

"Wisht I had a box a Cracker Jack. There ain't
nothin' to do. Ain't no fun."

"They'll be fun," Ma said. "You jus' wait. Be fun
purty soon. Git a house an' a place, purty soon."

"Wisht we had a dog," Ruthie said.

"We'll have a dog; have a cat, too."

"Yella cat?"

"Don't bother me," Ma begged. "Don't go plaguin' me now, Ruthie. Rosasharn's sick. Jus' you be a good girl a little while. They'll be fun." Ruthie wandered, complaining, away.

From the mattress where Rose of Sharon lay covered up there came a quick sharp cry, cut off in the middle. Ma whirled and went to her. Rose of Sharon was holding her breath and her eyes were filled with terror.

"What is it?" Ma cried. The girl expelled her breath and caught it again. Suddenly Ma put her hand under the covers. Then she stood up. "Mis' Wainwright," she called. "Oh, Mis' Wainwright!"

The fat little woman came down the car. "Want me?"

"Look!" Ma pointed at Rose of Sharon's face. Her teeth were clamped on her lower lip and her forehead was wet with perspiration, and the shining terror was in her eyes.

"I think it's come," Ma said. "It's early."

The girl heaved a great sigh and relaxed. She released her lip and closed her eyes. Mrs. Wainwright bent over her.

"Did it kinda grab you all over—quick? Open up an' answer me." Rose of Sharon nodded weakly. Mrs. Wainwright turned to Ma. "Yep," she said. "It's come. Early, ya say?"

"Maybe the fever brang it."

"Well, she oughta be up on her feet. Oughta be walkin' aroun'."

"She can't," Ma said. "She ain't got the strength."

"Well, she oughta." Mrs. Wainwright grew quiet and stern with efficiency. "I he'ped with lots," she said. "Come on, le's close that door, nearly. Keep out the draf'." The two women pushed on the heavy sliding door, boosted it along until only a foot was open. "I'll git our lamp, too," Mrs. Wainwright said. Her face was purple with excitement. "Aggie," she called. "You take care of these here little fellas."

Ma nodded, "Tha's right. Ruthie! You an' Winfiel' go down with Aggie. Go on now."

"Why?" they demanded.

" 'Cause you got to. Rosasharn gonna have her baby."

"I wanta watch, Ma. Please let me."

"Ruthie! You git now. You git quick." There was no argument against such a tone. Ruthie and Winfield went reluctantly down the car. Ma lighted the lantern. Mrs. Wainwright brought her Rochester lamp down and set it on the floor, and its big circular flame lighted the boxcar brightly.

Ruthie and Winfield stood behind the brush pile and peered over. "Gonna have a baby, an' we're a-gonna see," Ruthie said softly. "Don't you make no noise now. Ma won't let us watch. If she looks this-a-way, you scrunch down behin' the brush. Then we'll see."

"There ain't many kids seen it," Winfield said.

"There ain't no kids seen it," Ruthie insisted proudly. "On'y us."

Down by the mattress, in the bright light of the lamp, Ma and Mrs. Wainwright held conference. Their voices were raised a little over the hollow beating of the rain. Mrs. Wainwright took a paring knife from her apron pocket and slipped it under the mattress. "Maybe it don't do no good," she said apologetically. "Our folks always done it. Don't do no harm, anyways."

Ma nodded. "We used a plow point. I guess anything sharp'll work, long as it can cut birth pains. 'I hope it ain't gonna be a long one."

"You feelin' awright now?"

Rose of Sharon nodded nervously. "Is it a-comin'?"

"Sure," Ma said. "Gonna have a nice baby. You jus' got to help us. Feel like you could get up an' walk?"

"I can try."

"That's a good girl," Mrs. Wainwright said. "That *is* a good girl. We'll he'p you, honey. We'll walk with ya." They helped her to her feet and pinned a blanket over her shoulders. Then Ma held her arm from one side, and Mrs. Wainwright from the other. They walked her to the brush pile and turned slowly and walked her back, over and over; and the rain drummed deeply on the roof.

Ruthie and Winfield watched anxiously. "When's she goin' to have it?" he demanded.

"Sh! Don't draw 'em. We won't be let to look."

Aggie joined them behind the brush pile. Aggie's lean face and yellow hair showed in the lamplight, and her nose was long and sharp in the shadow of her head on the wall.

Ruthie whispered, "You ever saw a baby bore?"

"Sure," said Aggie.

"Well, when's she gonna have it?"

"Oh, not for a long, long time."

"Well, how long?"

"Maybe not 'fore tomorrow mornin'."

"Shucks!" said Ruthie. "Ain't no good watchin' now, then. Oh! Look!"

The walking women had stopped. Rose of Sharon had stiffened, and she whined with pain. They laid her down on the mattress and wiped her forehead while she grunted and clenched her fists. And Ma talked softly to her. "Easy," Ma said. "Gonna be all right— all right. Jus' grip ya han's. Now, then, take your lip inta your teeth. Tha's good—tha's good." The pain passed on. They let her rest awhile, and then helped her up again, and the three walked back and forth, back and forth between the pains.

Pa stuck his head in through the narrow opening. His hat dripped with water. "What ya shut the door for?" he asked. And then he saw the walking women. Ma said, "Her time's come."

"Then—then we couldn' go 'f we wanted to."

"No."

"Then we got to buil' that bank."

"You got to."

Pa sloshed through the mud to the stream. His marking stick was four inches down. Twenty men stood in the rain. Pa cried, "We got to build her. My girl got her pains." The men gathered about him.

"Baby?"

"Yeah. We can't go now."

A tall man said, "It ain't our baby. We kin go."

"Sure," Pa said. "You can go. Go on. Nobody's stoppin' you. They's only eight shovels." He hurried to the lowest part of the bank and drove his shovel into the mud. The shovelful lifted with a sucking sound. He drove it again, and threw the mud into the low place on the stream bank. And beside him the other men ranged themselves. They heaped the mud up in a long embankment, and those who had no shovels cut live willow whips and wove them in a mat and kicked them into the bank. Over the men came a fury of work, a fury of battle. When one man dropped his shovel, another took it up. They had shed their coats and hats. Their shirts and trousers clung tightly to their bodies, their shoes were shapeless blobs of mud. A shrill scream came from the Joad car. The men stopped, listened uneasily, and then plunged to work again. And the little levee of earth extended until it connected with the highway embankment on either end. They were tired now, and the shovels moved more slowly. And the stream rose slowly. It edged above the place where the first dirt had been thrown.

Pa laughed in triumph. "She'd come over if we hadn' a built up!" he cried.

The stream rose slowly up the side of the new wall, and tore at the willow mat. "Higher!" Pa cried. "We got to git her higher!"

The evening came, and the work went on. And now

the men were beyond weariness. Their faces were set and dead. They worked jerkily, like machines. When it was dark the women set lanterns in the car doors, and kept pots of coffee handy. And the women ran one by one to the Joad car and wedged themselves inside.

The pains were coming close now, twenty minutes apart. And Rose of Sharon had lost her restraint. She screamed fiercely under the fierce pains. And the neighbor women looked at her and patted her gently and went back to their own cars.

Ma had a good fire going now, and all her utensils, filled with water, sat on the stove to heat. Every little while Pa looked in the car door. "All right?" he asked.

"Yeah! I think so," Ma assured him.

As it grew dark, someone brought out a flashlight to work by. Uncle John plunged on, throwing mud on top of the wall.

"You take it easy," Pa said. "You'll kill yaself."

"I can't he'p it. I can't stan' that yellin'. It's like—— it's like when——"

"I know," Pa said. "But jus' take it easy."

Uncle John blubbered, "I'll run away. By God, I got to work or I'll run away."

Pa turned from him. "How's she stan' on the last marker?"

The man with the flashlight threw the beam on the stick. The rain cut whitely through the light. "Comin' up."

"She'll come up slower now," Pa said. "Got to flood purty far on the other side."

"She's comin' up, though."

The women filled the coffee pots and set them out again. And as the night went on, the men moved slower and slower, and they lifted their heavy feet like draft horses. More mud on the levee, more willows interlaced. The rain fell steadily. When the flashlight turned on faces, the eyes showed staring, and the muscles on the cheeks were welted out.

For a long time the screams continued from the car, and at last they were still.

Pa said, "Ma'd call me if it was bore." He went on shoveling the mud sullenly.

The stream eddied and boiled against the bank. Then, from up the stream there came a ripping crash. The beam of the flashlight showed a great cottonwood toppling. The men stopped to watch. The branches of the tree sank into the water and edged around with the current while the stream dug out the little roots. Slowly the tree was freed, and slowly it edged down the stream. The weary men watched, their mouths hanging open. The tree moved slowly down. Then a branch caught on a stump, snagged and held. And very slowly the roots swung around and hooked themselves on the new embankment. The water piled up behind. The tree moved and tore the bank. A little stream slipped through. Pa threw himself forward and jammed mud in the break. The water piled against the tree. And then the bank washed quickly down, washed around ankles, around knees. The men broke and ran, and the current worked smoothly into the flat, under the cars, under the automobiles.

Uncle John saw the water break through. In the murk he could see it. Uncontrollably his weight pulled him down. He went to his knees, and the tugging water swirled about his chest.

Pa saw him go. "Hey! What's the matter?" He lifted him to his feet. "You sick? Come on, the cars is high."

Uncle John gathered his strength. "I dunno," he said apologetically. "Legs give out. Jus' give out." Pa helped him along toward the cars.

When the dike swept out, Al turned and ran. His feet moved heavily. The water was about his calves when he reached the truck. He flung the tarpaulin off the nose and jumped into the car. He stepped on the starter. The engine turned over and over, and there was no bark of the motor. He choked the engine deeply. The battery turned the sodden motor more and more slowly, and there was no cough. Over and over, slower and slower. Al set the spark high. He felt under the seat for the crank and jumped out. The water was higher than the running board. He ran to the front end. Crank case was under water now. Frantically he fitted the crank and twisted around and around, and his clenched hand on the crank splashed in the slowly flowing water at each turn. At last his frenzy gave out. The motor was full of water, the battery fouled by now. On slightly higher ground two cars were started and their lights on. They floundered in the mud and dug their wheels down until finally the drivers cut off the motors and sat still, looking into the headlight beams. And the rain whipped white streaks through the lights. Al went slowly around the truck, reached in, and turned off the ignition.

When Pa reached the cat-walk, he found the lower end floating. He stepped it down into the mud, under water. "Think ya can make it awright, John?" he asked.

"I'll be awright. Jus' go on."

Pa cautiously climbed the cat-walk and squeezed himself in the narrow opening. The two lamps were turned low. Ma sat on the mattress beside Rose of Sharon, and Ma fanned her still face with a piece of cardboard. Mrs. Wainwright poled dry brush into the stove, and a dank smoke edged out around the lids and filled the car with a smell of burning tissue. Ma looked up at Pa when he entered, and then quickly down.

"How—is she?" Pa asked.

Ma did not look up at him again. "Awright, I think. Sleepin'."

The air was fetid and close with the smell of the birth. Uncle John clambered in and held himself upright against the side of the car. Mrs. Wainwright left her work and came to Pa. She pulled him by the elbow toward the corner of the car. She picked up a lantern and held it over an apple box in the corner. On a newspaper lay a blue shriveled little mummy.

"Never breathed," said Mrs. Wainwright softly. "Never was alive."

Uncle John turned and shuffled tiredly down the car to the dark end. The rain whished softly on the roof now, so softly that they could hear Uncle John's tired sniffling from the dark.

Pa looked up at Mrs. Wainwright. He took the lantern from her hand and put it on the floor. Ruthie and Winfield were asleep on their own mattress, their arms over their eyes to cut out the light.

Pa walked slowly to Rose of Sharon's mattress. He tried to squat down, but his legs were too tired. He knelt instead. Ma fanned her square of cardboard back and forth. She looked at Pa for a moment, and her eyes were wide and staring, like a sleepwalker's eyes.

Pa said, "We—done—what we could."

"I know."

"We worked all night. An' a tree cut out the bank."

"I know."

"You can hear it under the car."

"I know. I heard it."

"Think she's gonna be all right?"

"I dunno."

"Well—couldn' we—of did nothin'?"

Ma's lips were stiff and white. "No. They was on'y one thing to do—ever—an' we done it."

"We worked till we dropped, an' a tree— Rain's lettin' up some." Ma looked at the ceiling, and then down again. Pa went on, compelled to talk. "I dunno how high she'll rise. Might flood the car."

"I know."

"You know ever'thing."

She was silent, and the cardboard moved slowly back and forth.

"Did we slip up?" he pleaded. "Is they anything we could of did?"

Ma looked at him strangely. Her white lips smiled in a dreaming compassion. "Don't take no blame. Hush! It'll be awright. They's changes—all over."

"Maybe the water—maybe we'll have to go."

"When it's time to go—we'll go. We'll do what we got to do. Now hush. You might wake her."

Mrs. Wainwright broke twigs and poked them in the sodden, smoking fire.

From outside came the sound of an angry voice. "I'm goin' in an' see the son-of-a-bitch myself."

And then, just outside the door, Al's voice, "Where you think you're goin'?"

"Goin' in to see that bastard Joad."

"No, you ain't. What's the matter'th you?"

"If he didn't have that fool idear about the bank, we'd a got out. Now our car is dead."

"You think ours is burnin' up the road?"

"I'm a-goin' in."

Al's voice was cold. "You're gonna fight your way in."

Pa got slowly to his feet and went to the door. "Awright, Al. I'm comin' out. It's awright, Al." Pa slid down the cat-walk. Ma heard him say, "We got sickness. Come on down here."

The rain scattered lightly on the roof now, and a new-risen breeze blew it along in sweeps. Mrs. Wainwright came from the stove and looked down at Rose of Sharon. "Dawn's a-comin' soon, ma'am. Whyn't you git some sleep? I'll set with her."

"No," Ma said. "I ain't tar'd."

"In a pig's eye," said Mrs. Wainwright. "Come on, you lay down awhile."

Ma fanned the air slowly with her cardboard. "You been frien'ly," she said. "We thank you."

The stout woman smiled. "No need to thank. Ever'body's in the same wagon. S'pose we was down. You'd a give us a han'."

"Yes," Ma said, "we would."

"Or anybody."

"Or anybody. Use' ta be the fambly was fust. It ain't so now. It's anybody. Worse off we get, the more we got to do."

"We couldn' a saved it."

"I know," said Ma.

Ruthie sighed deeply and took her arm from over her eyes. She looked blindly at the lamp for a moment, and then turned her head and looked at Ma. "Is it bore?" she demanded. "Is the baby out?"

Mrs. Wainwright picked up a sack and spread it over the apple box in the corner.

"Where's the baby?" Ruthie demanded.

Ma wet her lips. "They ain't no baby. They never was no baby. We was wrong."

"Shucks!" Ruthie yawned. "I wisht it had a been a baby."

Mrs. Wainwright sat down beside Ma and took the cardboard from her and fanned the air. Ma folded her hands in her lap, and her tired eyes never left the face of Rose of Sharon, sleeping in exhaustion. "Come on," Mrs. Wainwright said. "Jus' lay down. You'll be right beside her. Why, you'd wake up if she took a deep breath, even."

"Awright, I will." Ma stretched out on the mattress beside the sleeping girl. And Mrs. Wainwright sat on the floor and kept watch.

Pa and Al and Uncle John sat in the car doorway and watched the steely dawn come. The rain had stopped, but the sky was deep and solid with cloud. As the light came, it was reflected on the water. The men could see the current of the stream, slipping swiftly down, bearing black branches of trees, boxes, boards. The water swirled into the flat where the box-cars stood. There was no sign of the embankment left. On the flat the current stopped. The edges of the flood were lined with yellow foam. Pa leaned out the door and placed a twig on the cat-walk, just above the water line. The men watched the water slowly climb to it, lift it gently and float it away. Pa placed another twig an inch above the water and settled back to watch.

"Think it'll come inside the car?" Al asked.

"Can't tell. They's a hell of a lot of water got to come down from the hills yet. Can't tell. Might start up to rain again."

Al said, "I been a-thinkin'. If she come in, ever'-thing'll get soaked."

"Yeah."

"Well, she won't come up more'n three-four feet in the car 'cause she'll go over the highway an' spread out first."

"How you know?" Pa asked.

"I took a sight on her, off the end of the car." He held his hand. " 'Bout this far up she'll come."

"Awright," Pa said. "What about it? We won't be here."

"We got to be here. Truck's here. Take a week to get the water out of her when the flood goes down."

"Well—what's your idear?"

"We can tear out the side-boards of the truck an' build a kinda platform in here to pile our stuff an' to set up on."

"Yeah? How'll we cook—how'll we eat?"

"Well, it'll keep our stuff dry."

The light grew stronger outside, a gray metallic light. The second little stick floated away from the cat-walk. Pa placed another one higher up. "Sure climbin'," he said. "I guess we better do that."

Ma turned restlessly in her sleep. Her eyes started wide open. She cried sharply in warning, "Tom! Oh, Tom! Tom!"

Mrs. Wainwright spoke soothingly. The eyes flicked closed again and Ma squirmed under her dream. Mrs. Wainwright got up and walked to the doorway. "Hey!" she said softly. "We ain't gonna git out soon." She pointed to the corner of the car where the apple box

was. "That ain't doin' no good. Jus' cause trouble an'
sorra. Couldn' you fellas kinda—take it out an' bury
it?"

The men were silent. Pa said at last, "Guess you're
right. Jus' cause sorra. 'Gainst the law to bury it."

"They's lots a things 'gainst the law that we can't
he'p doin'."

"Yeah."

Al said, "We oughta git them truck sides tore off
'fore the water comes up much more."

Pa turned to Uncle John. "Will you take an' bury it
while Al an' me git that lumber in?"

Uncle John said sullenly, "Why do I got to do it?
Why don't you fellas? I don' like it." And then, "Sure.
I'll do it. Sure, I will. Come on, give it to me." His
voice began to rise. "Come on! Give it to me."

"Don' wake 'em up," Mrs. Wainwright said. She
brought the apple box to the doorway and straightened
the sack decently over it.

"Shovel's standin' right behin' you," Pa said.

Uncle John took the shovel in one hand. He slipped
out the doorway into the slowly moving water, and it
rose nearly to his waist before he struck bottom. He
turned and settled the apple box under his other arm.

Pa said, "Come on, Al. Le's git that lumber in."

In the gray dawn light Uncle John waded around
the end of the car, past the Joad truck; and he climbed
the slippery bank to the highway. He walked down the
highway, past the boxcar flat, until he came to a place
where the boiling stream ran close to the road, where
the willows grew along the road side. He put his
shovel down, and holding the box in front of him, he
edged through the brush until he came to the edge of
the swift stream. For a time he stood watching it swirl
by, leaving its yellow foam among the willow stems.
He held the apple box against his chest. And then he
leaned over and set the box in the stream and steadied
it with his hand. He said fiercely, "Go down an' tell

'em. Go down in the street an' rot an' tell 'em that way. That's the way you can talk. Don' even know if you was a boy or a girl. Ain't gonna find out. Go on down now, an' lay in the street. Maybe they'll know then." He guided the box gently out into the current and let it go. It settled low in the water, edged sideways, whirled around, and turned slowly over. The sack floated away, and the box, caught in the swift water, floated quickly away, out of sight, behind the brush. Uncle John grabbed the shovel and went rapidly back to the boxcars. He sloshed down into the water and waded to the truck, where Pa and Al were working, taking down the one-by-six planks.

Pa looked over at him. "Get it done?"

"Yeah."

"Well, look," Pa said. "If you'll he'p Al, I'll go down the store an' get some stuff to eat."

"Get some bacon," Al said. "I need some meat."

"I will," Pa said. He jumped down from the truck and Uncle John took his place.

When they pushed the planks into the car door, Ma awakened and sat up. "What you doin'?"

"Gonna build up a place to keep outa the wet."

"Why?" Ma asked. "It's dry in here."

"Ain't gonna be. Water's comin' up."

Ma struggled up to her feet and went to the door. "We got to git outa here."

"Can't," Al said. "All our stuff's here. Truck's here. Ever'thing we got."

"Where's Pa?"

"Gone to get stuff for breakfas'."

Ma looked down at the water. It was only six inches down from the floor by now. She went back to the mattress and looked at Rose of Sharon. The girl stared back at her.

"How you feel?" Ma asked.

"Tar'd. Jus' tar'd out."

"Gonna get some breakfas' into you."

"I ain't hungry."

Mrs. Wainwright moved beside Ma. "She looks all right. Come through it fine."

Rose of Sharon's eyes questioned Ma, and Ma tried to avoid the question. Mrs. Wainwright walked to the stove.

"Ma."

"Yeah? What you want?"

"Is—it—all right?"

Ma gave up the attempt. She kneeled down on the mattress. "You can have more," she said. "We done ever'thing we knowed."

Rose of Sharon struggled and pushed herself up. "Ma!"

"You couldn' he'p it."

The girl lay back again, and covered her eyes with her arms. Ruthie crept close and looked down in awe. She whispered harshly, "She sick, Ma? She gonna die?"

" 'Course not. She's gonna be awright. Awright."

Pa came in with his armload of packages. "How is she?"

"Awright," Ma said. "She's gonna be awright."

Ruthie reported to Winfield. "She ain't gonna die. Ma says so."

And Winfield, picking his teeth with a splinter in a very adult manner, said, "I knowed it all the time."

"How'd you know?"

"I won't tell," said Winfield, and he spat out a piece of the splinter.

Ma built the fire up with the last twigs and cooked the bacon and made gravy. Pa had brought store bread. Ma scowled when she saw it. "We got any money lef'?"

"Nope," said Pa. "But we was so hungry."

"An' you got store bread," Ma said accusingly.

"Well, we was awful hungry. Worked all night long."

Ma sighed. "Now what we gonna do?"

As they ate, the water crept up and up. Al gulped his food and he and Pa built the platform. Five feet wide, six feet long, four feet above the floor. And the water crept to the edge of the doorway, seemed to hesitate a long time, and then moved slowly inward over the floor. And outside, the rain began again, as it had before, big heavy drops splashing on the water, pounding hollowly on the roof.

Al said, "Come on now, let's get the mattresses up. Let's put the blankets up, so they don't git wet." They piled their possessions up on the platform, and the water crept over the floor. Pa and Ma, Al and Uncle John, each at a corner, lifted Rose of Sharon's mattress, with the girl on it, and put it on top of the pile.

And the girl protested, "I can walk. I'm awright." And the water crept over the floor, a thin film of it. Rose of Sharon whispered to Ma, and Ma put her hand under the blanket and felt her breast and nodded.

In the other end of the boxcar, the Wainwrights were pounding, building a platform for themselves. The rain thickened, and then passed away.

Ma looked down at her feet. The water was half an inch deep on the car floor by now. "You, Ruthie—Winfield!" she called distractedly. "Come get on top of the pile. You'll get cold." She saw them safely up, sitting awkwardly beside Rose of Sharon. Ma said suddenly, "We got to git out."

"We can't," Pa said. "Like Al says, all our stuff's here. We'll pull off the boxcar door an' make more room to set on."

The family huddled on the platforms, silent and fretful. The water was six inches deep in the car before the flood spread evenly over the embankment and moved into the cotton field on the other side. During that day and night the men slept soddenly, side by side on the boxcar door. And Ma lay close to Rose of Sharon. Sometimes Ma whispered to her and sometimes sat up quietly, her face brooding. Under the blanket she hoarded the remains of the store bread.

The rain had become intermittent now—little wet squalls and quiet times. On the morning of the second day Pa splashed through the camp and came back with ten potatoes in his pockets. Ma watched him sullenly while he chopped out part of the inner wall of the car, built a fire, and scooped water into a pan. The family ate the steaming boiled potatoes with their fingers. And when this last food was gone, they stared at the gray water; and in the night they did not lie down for a long time.

When the morning came they awakened nervously. Rose of Sharon whispered to Ma.

Ma nodded her head. "Yes," she said. "It's time for it." And then she turned to the car door, where the men lay. "We're a-gettin' outa here," she said savagely, "gettin' to higher groun'. An' you're comin' or you ain't comin', but I'm takin' Rosasharn an' the little fellas outa here."

"We can't!" Pa said weakly.

"Awright, then. Maybe you'll pack Rosasharn to the highway, anyways, an' then come back. It ain't rainin' now, an' we're a-goin'."

"Awright, we'll go," Pa said.

Al said, "Ma, I ain't goin'."

"Why not?"

"Well—Aggie—why, her an' me——"

Ma smiled. " 'Course," she said. "You stay here, Al. Take care of the stuff. When the water goes down—why, we'll come back. Come quick, 'fore it rains again," she told Pa. "Come on, Rosasharn. We're goin' to a dry place."

"I can walk."

"Maybe a little, on the road. Git your back bent, Pa."

Pa slipped into the water and stood waiting. Ma helped Rose of Sharon down from the platform and steadied her across the car. Pa took her in his arms, held her as high as he could, and pushed his way carefully through the deep water, around the car, and the highway. He set her down on her feet and held onto her. Uncle John carried Ruthie and followed. Ma slid down into the water, and for a moment her skirts billowed out around her.

"Winfiel', set on my shoulder. Al—we'll come back soon's the water's down. Al—" She paused. "If—if Tom comes—tell him we'll be back. Tell him be careful. Winfiel'! Climb on my shoulder—there! Now, keep your feet still." She staggered off through the breast-high water. At the highway embankment they helped her up and lifted Winfield from her shoulder.

They stood on the highway and looked back over the sheet of water, the dark red blocks of the cars, the trucks and automobiles deep in the slowly moving water. And as they stood, a little misting rain began to fall.

"We got to git along," Ma said. "Rosasharn, you feel like you could walk?"

"Kinda dizzy," the girl said. "Feel like I been beat."

Pa complained, "Now we're a-goin', where' we goin'?"

"I dunno. Come on, give your han' to Rosasharn." Ma took the girl's right arm to steady her, and Pa her left. "Goin' someplace where it's dry. Got to. You fellas ain't had dry clothes on for two days." They moved slowly along the highway. They could hear the rushing of the water in the stream beside the road. Ruthie and Winfield marched together, splashing their feet against the road. They went slowly along the road. The sky grew darker and the rain thickened. No traffic moved along the highway.

"We got to hurry," Ma said. "If this here girl gits good an' wet—I don't know what'll happen to her."

"You ain't said where-at we're a-hurryin' to," Pa reminded her sarcastically.

The road curved along beside the stream. Ma searched the land and the flooded fields. Far off the road, on the left, on a slight rolling hill a rain-blackened barn stood. "Look!" Ma said. "Look there! I bet it's dry in that barn. Le's go there till the rain stops."

Pa sighed. "Prob'ly get run out by the fella owns it."

Ahead, beside the road, Ruthie saw a spot of red. She raced to it. A scraggly geranium gone wild, and there was one rain-beaten blossom on it. She picked the flower. She took a petal carefully off and stuck it on her nose. Winfield ran up to see.

"Lemme have one?" he said.

"No, sir! It's all mine. I foun' it." She stuck another red petal on her forehead, a little bright-red heart.

"Come on, Ruthie! Lemme have one. Come on, now." He grabbed at the flower in her hand and missed it, and Ruthie banged him in the face with her open hand. He stood for a moment, surprised, and then his lips shook and his eyes welled.

The others caught up. "Now what you done?" Ma asked. "Now what you done?"

"He tried to grab my fl'ar."

Winfield sobbed, "I—on'y wanted one—to—stick on my nose."

"Give him one, Ruthie."

"Leave him find his own. This here's mine."

"Ruthie! You give him one."

Ruthie heard the threat in Ma's tone, and changed her tactics. "Here," she said with elaborate kindness.

"I'll stick on one for you." The older people walked
on. Winfield held his nose to her. She wet a petal with
her tongue and jabbed it cruelly on his nose. "You
little son-of-a-bitch," she said softly. Winfield felt for
the petal with his fingers, and pressed it down on his
nose. They walked quickly after the others. Ruthie felt
how the fun was gone. "Here," she said. "Here's some
more. Stick some on your forehead."

From the right of the road there came a sharp swish-
ing. Ma cried, "Hurry up. They's a big rain. Le's go
through the fence here. It's shorter. Come on, now!
Bear on, Rosasharn." They half dragged the girl across
the ditch, helped her through the fence. And then the
storm struck them. Sheets of rain fell on them. They
plowed through the mud and up the little incline. The
black barn was nearly obscured by the rain. It hissed
and splashed, and the growing wind drove it along.
Rose of Sharon's feet slipped and she dragged between
her supporters.

"Pa! Can you carry her?"

Pa leaned over and picked her up. "We're wet
through anyways," he said. "Hurry up. Winfiel'—
Ruthie! Run on ahead."

They came panting up to the rain-soaked barn and
staggered into the open end. There was no door in this
end. A few rusty farm tools lay about, a disk plow and
a broken cultivator, an iron wheel. The rain hammered
on the roof and curtained the entrance. Pa gently set
Rose of Sharon down on an oily box. "God Awmighty!"
he said.

Ma said, "Maybe they's hay inside. Look, there's a
door." She swung the door on its rusty hinges. "They
is hay," she cried. "Come on in, you."

It was dark inside. A little light came in through the
cracks between the boards.

"Lay down, Rosasharn," Ma said. "Lay down an'
res'. I'll try to figger some way to dry you off."

Winfield said, "Ma!" and the rain roaring on the roof drowned his voice. "Ma!"

"What is it? What you want?"

"Look! In the corner."

Ma looked. There were two figures in the gloom; a man who lay on his back, and a boy sitting beside him, his eyes wide, staring at the newcomers. As she looked, the boy got slowly up to his feet and came toward her. His voice croaked. "You own this here?"

"No," Ma said. "Jus' come in outa the wet. We got a sick girl. You got a dry blanket we could use an' get her wet clothes off?"

The boy went back to the corner and brought a dirty comfort and held it out to Ma.

"Thank ya," she said. "What's the matter'th that fella?"

The boy spoke in a croaking monotone. "Fust he was sick—but now he's starvin'."

"What?"

"Starvin'. Got sick in the cotton. He ain't et for six days."

Ma walked to the corner and looked down at the man. He was about fifty, his whiskery face gaunt, and his open eyes were vague and staring. The boy stood beside her. "Your pa?" Ma asked.

"Yeah! Says he wasn' hungry, or he jus' et. Give me the food. Now he's too weak. Can't hardly move."

The pounding of the rain decreased to a soothing swish on the roof. The gaunt man moved his lips. Ma knelt beside him and put her ear close. His lips moved again.

"Sure," Ma said. "You jus' be easy. He'll be awright. You jus' wait'll I get them wet clo'es off'n my girl."

Ma went back to the girl. "Now slip 'em off," she said. She held the comfort up to screen her from view.

And when she was naked, Ma folded the comfort about her.

The boy was at her side again explaining, "I didn' know. He said he et, or he wasn' hungry. Las' night I went an' bust a winda an' stoled some bread. Made 'im chew 'er down. But he puked it all up, an' then he was weaker. Got to have soup or milk. You folks got money to git milk?"

Ma said, "Hush. Don' worry. We'll figger somepin out."

Suddenly the boy cried, "He's dyin', I tell you! He's starvin' to death, I tell you."

"Hush," said Ma. She looked at Pa and Uncle John standing helplessly gazing at the sick man. She looked at Rose of Sharon huddled in the comfort. Ma's eyes passed Rose of Sharon's eyes, and then came back to them. And the two women looked deep into each other. The girl's breath came short and gasping.

She said, "Yes."

Ma smiled. "I knowed you would. I knowed!" She looked down at her hands, tight-locked in her lap.

Rose of Sharon whispered, "Will—will you all—go out?" The rain whisked lightly on the roof.

Ma leaned forward and with her palm she brushed the tousled hair back from her daughter's forehead, and she kissed her on the forehead. Ma got up quickly. "Come on, you fellas," she called. "You come out in the tool shed."

Ruthie opened her mouth to speak. "Hush," Ma said. "Hush and git." She herded them through the door, drew the boy with her; and she closed the squeaking door.

For a minute Rose of Sharon sat still in the whispering barn. Then she hoisted her tired body up and drew the comfort about her. She moved slowly to the corner and stood looking down at the wasted face, into the wide, frightened eyes. Then slowly she lay down beside him. He shook his head slowly from side to side. Rose of Sharon loosened one side of the blanket and bared her breast. "You got to," she said. She squirmed closer and pulled his head close. "There!" she said. "There." Her hand moved behind his head and supported it. Her fingers moved gently in his hair. She looked up and across the barn, and her lips came together and smiled mysteriously.

CANNERY
ROW

For
ED RICKETTS
who knows why or should

CANNERY ROW

Cannery Row in Monterey in California is a poem, a stink, a grating noise, a quality of light, a tone, a habit, a nostalgia, a dream. Cannery Row is the gathered and scattered, tin and iron and rust and splintered wood, chipped pavement and weedy lots and junk heaps, sardine canneries of corrugated iron, honky tonks, restaurants and whore houses, and little crowded groceries, and laboratories and flophouses. Its inhabitants are, as the man once said, "whores, pimps, gamblers, and sons of bitches," by which he meant Everybody. Had the man looked through another peephole he might have said, "Saints and angels and martyrs and holy men," and he would have meant the same thing.

In the morning when the sardine fleet has made a catch, the purse-seiners waddle heavily into the bay blowing their whistles. The deep-laden boats pull in against the coast where the canneries dip their tails into the bay. The figure is advisedly chosen, for if the canneries dipped their mouths into the bay the canned sardines which emerge from the other end would be metaphorically, at least, even more horrifying. Then cannery whistles scream and all over the town men and women scramble into their clothes and come running down to the Row to go to work. Then shining cars bring the upper classes down: superintendents, accountants, owners who disappear into offices. Then from the town pour Wops and Chinamen and Polaks, men and women in trousers and rubber coats and oilcloth aprons. They come running to clean and cut and pack and cook and can the fish. The whole street rumbles and groans and screams and rattles while the silver rivers of fish pour in out of the boats and the boats rise higher and higher in the water until they are empty. The canneries rumble and rattle and squeak until the last fish is cleaned and cut and cooked and canned and then the whistles scream again and the dripping, smelly, tired Wops and Chinamen and Polaks, men and women, straggle out and droop their ways up the hill into the town and Cannery Row becomes itself again—quiet and magical. Its normal life returns. The bums who retired in disgust under the black cypress tree come out to sit on the rusty pipes in the vacant lot. The girls from Dora's emerge for a bit of sun if there is any. Doc strolls from the Western Biological Laboratory and crosses the street to Lee Chong's grocery for two quarts of beer. Henri the painter noses like an Airedale through the junk in the grass-grown lot for some part or piece of wood or metal he needs for the boat he is building. Then the darkness edges in and the street light comes on in front of Dora's—the lamp which makes perpetual moonlight in Cannery Row. Callers arrive at Western Biological to see Doc, and he crosses the street to Lee Chong's for five quarts of beer.

How can the poem and the stink and the grating noise—the quality of light, the tone, the habit and the dream—be set down alive? When you collect marine animals there are certain flat worms so delicate that they are almost impossible to capture whole, for they break and tatter under the touch. You must let them ooze and crawl of their own will onto a knife blade and then lift them gently into your bottle of sea water. And perhaps that might be the way to write this book—to open the page and to let the stories crawl in by themselves.

1

Lee Chong's grocery, while not a model of neatness, was a miracle of supply. It was small and crowded but within its single room a man could find everything he needed or wanted to live and to be happy—clothes, food, both fresh and canned, liquor, tobacco, fishing equipment, machinery, boats, cordage, caps, pork chops. You could buy at Lee Chong's a pair of slippers, a silk kimono, a quarter pint of whiskey and a cigar. You could work out combinations to fit almost any mood. The one commodity Lee Chong did not keep could be had across the lot at Dora's.

The grocery opened at dawn and did not close until the last wandering vagrant dime had been spent or retired for the night. Not that Lee Chong was avaricious. He wasn't, but if one wanted to spend money, he was available. Lee's position in the community surprised him as much as he could be surprised. Over the course of the years everyone in Cannery Row owed him money. He never pressed his clients, but when the bill became too large, Lee cut off credit. Rather

than walk into the town up the hill, the client usually
paid or tried to.

Lee was round-faced and courteous. He spoke a
stately English without ever using the letter R. When
the tong wars were going on in California, it happened
now and then that Lee found a price on his head. Then
he would go secretly to San Francisco and enter a
hospital until the trouble blew over. What he did with
his money, no one ever knew. Perhaps he didn't get it.
Maybe his wealth was entirely in unpaid bills. But he
lived well and he had the respect of all his neighbors.
He trusted his clients until further trust became ri-
diculous. Sometimes he made business errors, but
even these he turned to advantage in good will if in no
other way. It was that way with the Palace Flophouse
and Grill. Anyone but Lee Chong would have considered the transaction a total loss.

Lee Chong's station in the grocery was behind the
cigar counter. The cash register was then on his left and
the abacus on his right. Inside the glass case were the
brown cigars, the cigarettes, the Bull Durham, the
Duke's mixture, the Five Brothers, while behind him in
racks on the wall were the pints, half pints and quarters
of Old Green River, Old Town House, Old Colonel, and
the favorite—Old Tennessee, a blended whiskey guaranteed four months old, very cheap and known in the
neighborhood as Old Tennis Shoes. Lee Chong did not
stand between the whiskey and the customer without
reason. Some very practical minds had on occasion
tried to divert his attention to another part of the store.
Cousins, nephews, sons and daughters-in-law waited on
the rest of the store, but Lee never left the cigar
counter. The top of the glass was his desk. His fat

delicate hands rested on the glass, the fingers moving like small restless sausages. A broad golden wedding ring on the middle finger of his left hand was his only jewelry and with it he silently tapped on the rubber change mat from which the little rubber tits had long been worn. Lee's mouth was full and benevolent and the flash of gold when he smiled was rich and warm. He wore half-glasses and since he looked at everything through them, he had to tilt his head back to see in the distance. Interest and discounts, addition, subtraction he worked out on the abacus with his little restless sausage fingers, and his brown friendly eyes roved over the grocery and his teeth flashed at the customers.

On an evening when he stood in his place on a pad of newspaper to keep his feet warm, he contemplated with humor and sadness a business deal that had been consummated that afternoon and reconsummated later that same afternoon. When you leave the grocery, if you walk catty-cornered across the grass-grown lot, threading your way among the great rusty pipes thrown out of the canneries, you will see a path worn in the weeds. Follow it past the cypress tree, across the railroad track, up a chicken walk with cleats, and you will come to a long low building which for a long time was used as a storage place for fish meal. It was just a great big roofed room and it belonged to a worried gentleman named Horace Abbeville. Horace had two wives and six children and over a period of years he had managed through pleading and persuasion to build a grocery debt second to none in Monterey. That afternoon he had come into the grocery and his sensitive tired face had flinched at the shadow of sternness that crossed Lee's face. Lee's fat finger tapped the rubber mat. Horace laid his hands palm up on the cigar counter. "I guess I owe you plenty dough," he said simply.

Lee's teeth flashed up in appreciation of an approach so different from any he had ever heard. He nodded gravely, but he waited for the trick to develop.

Horace wet his lips with his tongue, a good job from corner to corner. "I hate to have my kids with that hanging over them," he said. "Why, I bet you wouldn't let them have a pack of spearmint now."

Lee Chong's face agreed with this conclusion. "Plenty dough," he said.

Horace continued, "You know that place of mine across the track up there where the fish meal is."

Lee Chong nodded. It was his fish meal.

Horace said earnestly, "If I was to give you that place—would it clear me up with you?"

Lee Chong tilted his head back and stared at Horace through his half-glasses while his mind flicked among accounts and his right hand moved restlessly to the abacus. He considered the construction which was flimsy and the lot which might be valuable if a cannery ever wanted to expand. "Shu," said Lee Chong.

"Well, get out the accounts and I'll make you a bill of sale on that place." Horace seemed in a hurry.

"No need papers," said Lee. "I make paid-in-full paper."

They finished the deal with dignity and Lee Chong threw in a quarter pint of Old Tennis Shoes. And then Horace Abbeville walking very straight went across the lot and past the cypress tree and across the track and up the chicken walk and into the building that had been his, and he shot himself on a heap of fish meal. And although it has nothing to do with this story, no Abbeville child, no matter who its mother was, knew the lack of a stick of spearmint ever afterward.

But to get back to the evening. Horace was on the trestles with the embalming needles in him, and his two wives were sitting on the steps of his house with their arms about each other (they were good friends until after the funeral, and then they divided up the children and never spoke to each other again). Lee Chong stood in back of the cigar counter and his nice brown eyes were turned inward on a calm and eternal Chinese sorrow. He knew he could not have helped it, but he wished he might have known and perhaps tried to help. It was deeply a part of Lee's kindness and understanding that man's right to kill himself is inviolable, but sometimes a friend can make it unnecessary. Lee had already underwritten the funeral and sent a wash basket of groceries to the stricken families.

Now Lee Chong owned the Abbeville building—a good roof, a good floor, two windows and a door. True it was piled high with fish meal and the smell of it was delicate and penetrating. Lee Chong considered it as a storehouse for groceries, as a kind of warehouse, but he gave that up on second thought. It was too far away and anyone can go in through a window. He was tapping the rubber mat with his gold ring and considering the problem when the door opened and Mack came in. Mack was the elder, leader, mentor, and to a small extent the exploiter of a little group of men who had in common no families, no money, and no ambitions beyond food, drink, and contentment. But whereas most

men in their search for contentment destroy themselves and fall wearily short of their targets, Mack and
his friends approached contentment casually, quietly,
and absorbed it gently. Mack and Hazel, a young man
of great strength, Eddie who filled in as a bartender at
La Ida, Hughie and Jones who occasionally collected
frogs and cats for Western Biological, were currently
living in those large rusty pipes in the lot next to Lee
Chong's. That is, they lived in the pipes when it was
damp but in fine weather they lived in the shadow of
the black cypress tree at the top of the lot. The limbs
folded down and made a canopy under which a man
could lie and look out at the flow and vitality of Cannery Row.

Lee Chong stiffened ever so slightly when Mack
came in and his eyes glanced quickly about the store
to make sure that Eddie or Hazel or Hughie or Jones
had not come in too and drifted away among the
groceries.

Mack laid out his cards with a winning honesty.
"Lee," he said, "I and Eddie and the rest heard you
own the Abbeville place."

Lee Chong nodded and waited.

"I and my friends thought we'd ast you if we could
move in there. We'll keep up the property," he added
quickly. "Wouldn't let anybody break in or hurt anything. Kids might knock out the windows, you know—"
Mack suggested. "Place might burn down if somebody
don't keep an eye on it."

Lee tilted his head back and looked into Mack's
eyes through the half-glasses and Lee's tapping finger
slowed its tempo as he thought deeply. In Mack's eyes

there was good will and good fellowship and a desire to make everyone happy. Why then did Lee Chong feel slightly surrounded? Why did his mind pick its way as delicately as a cat through cactus? It had been sweetly done, almost in a spirit of philanthropy. Lee's mind leaped ahead at the possibilities—no, they were probabilities, and his finger tapping slowed still further. He saw himself refusing Mack's request and he saw the broken glass from the windows. Then Mack would offer a second time to watch over and preserve Lee's property—and at the second refusal, Lee could smell the smoke, could see the little flames creeping up the walls. Mack and his friends would try to help to put it out. Lee's finger came to a gentle rest on the change mat. He was beaten. He knew that. There was left to him only the possibility of saving face and Mack was likely to be very generous about that. Lee said, "You like pay lent my place? You like live there same hotel?"

Mack smiled broadly and he was generous. "Say—" he cried. "That's an idear. Sure. How much?"

Lee considered. He knew it didn't matter what he charged. He wasn't going to get it anyway. He might just as well make it a really sturdy face-saving sum. "Fi' dolla' week," said Lee.

Mack played it through to the end. "I'll have to talk to the boys about it," he said dubiously. "Couldn't you make that four dollars a week?"

"Fi' dolla'," said Lee firmly.

"Well, I'll see what the boys say," said Mack.

And that was the way it was. Everyone was happy about it. And if it be thought that Lee Chong suffered

a total loss, at least his mind did not work that way.
The windows were not broken. Fire did not break out,
and while no rent was ever paid, if the tenants ever
had any money, and quite often they did have, it never
occurred to them to spend it any place except at Lee
Chong's grocery. What he had was a little group of
active and potential customers under wraps. But it
went further than that. If a drunk caused trouble in the
grocery, if the kids swarmed down from New Monterey
intent on plunder, Lee Chong had only to call and his
tenants rushed to his aid. One further bond it established—you cannot steal from your benefactor. The
saving to Lee Chong in cans of beans and tomatoes
and milk and watermelons more than paid the rent.
And if there was a sudden and increased leakage
among the groceries in New Monterey that was none of
Lee Chong's affair.

The boys moved in and the fish meal moved out. No
one knows who named the house that has been known
ever after as the Palace Flophouse and Grill. In the
pipes and under the cypress tree there had been no
room for furniture and the little niceties which are not
only the diagnoses but the boundaries of our civiliza-
tion. Once in the Palace Flophouse, the boys set about
furnishing it. A chair appeared and a cot and another
chair. A hardware store supplied a can of red paint not
reluctantly because it never knew about it, and as a
new table or footstool appeared it was painted, which
not only made it very pretty but also disguised it to a
certain extent in case a former owner looked in. And
the Palace Flophouse and Grill began to function. The
boys could sit in front of their door and look down

across the track and across the lot and across the
street right into the front windows of Western Biological. They could hear the music from the laboratory at
night. And their eyes followed Doc across the street
when he went to Lee Chong's for beer. And Mack said,
"That Doc is a fine fellow. We ought to do something
for him."

2

The word is a symbol and a
delight which sucks up men and scenes, trees, plants,
factories, and Pekinese. Then the Thing becomes the
Word and back to Thing again, but warped and woven
into a fantastic pattern. The Word sucks up Cannery
Row, digests it and spews it out, and the Row has
taken the shimmer of the green world and the sky-
reflecting seas. Lee Chong is more than a Chinese
grocer. He must be. Perhaps he is evil balanced and
held suspended by good—an Asiatic planet held to its
orbit by the pull of Lao Tze and held away from Lao
Tze by the centrifugality of abacus and cash register—
Lee Chong suspended, spinning, whirling among groceries and ghosts. A hard man with a can of beans—a
soft man with the bones of his grandfather. For Lee
Chong dug into the grave on China Point and found the
yellow bones, the skull with gray ropy hair still sticking to it. And Lee carefully packed the bones, femurs,
and tibias really straight, skull in the middle, with
pelvis and clavicle surrounding it and ribs curving on
either side. Then Lee Chong sent his boxed and brittle

grandfather over the western sea to lie at last in ground made holy by his ancestors.

Mack and the boys, too, spinning in their orbits. They are the Virtues, the Graces, the Beauties of the hurried mangled craziness of Monterey and the cosmic Monterey where men in fear and hunger destroy their stomachs in the fight to secure certain food, where men hungering for love destroy everything lovable about them. Mack and the boys are the Beauties, the Virtues, the Graces. In the world ruled by tigers with ulcers, rutted by strictured bulls, scavenged by blind jackals, Mack and the boys dine delicately with the tigers, fondle the frantic heifers, and wrap up the crumbs to feed the sea gulls of Cannery Row. What can it profit a man to gain the whole world and to come to his property with a gastric ulcer, a blown prostate, and bifocals? Mack and the boys avoid the trap, walk around the poison, step over the noose while a generation of trapped, poisoned, and trussed-up men scream at them and call them no-goods, come-to-bad-ends, blots-on-the-town, thieves, rascals, bums. Our Father who art in nature, who has given the gift of survival to the coyote, the common brown rat, the English sparrow, the house fly and the moth, must have a great and overwhelming love for no-goods and blots-on-the-town and bums, and Mack and the boys. Virtues and graces and laziness and zest. Our Father who art in nature.

3

Lee Chong's is to the right of the vacant lot (although why it is called vacant when it is piled high with old boilers, with rusting pipes, with great square timbers, and stacks of five-gallon cans, no one can say). Up in back of the vacant lot is the railroad track and the Palace Flophouse. But on the left-hand boundary of the lot is the stern and stately whore house of Dora Flood; a decent, clean, honest, old-fashioned sporting house where a man can take a glass of beer among friends. This is no fly-by-night cheap clip-joint but a sturdy, virtuous club, built, maintained, and disciplined by Dora who, madam and girl for fifty years, has through the exercise of special gifts of tact and honesty, charity and a certain realism, made herself respected by the intelligent, the learned, and the kind. And by the same token she is hated by the twisted and lascivious sisterhood of married spinsters whose husbands respect the home but don't like it very much.

Dora is a great woman, a great big woman with flaming orange hair and a taste for Nile green evening dresses. She keeps an honest, one price house, sells no hard liquor, and permits no loud or vulgar talk in her house. Of her girls some are fairly inactive due to age and infirmities, but Dora never puts them aside although, as she says, some of them don't turn three tricks a month but they go right on eating three meals a day. In a moment of local love Dora named her place the Bear Flag Restaurant and the stories are many of people who have gone in for a sandwich. There are normally twelve girls in the house, counting the old ones, a Greek cook, and a man who is known as a watchman but who undertakes all manner of delicate and dangerous tasks. He stops fights, ejects drunks, soothes hysteria, cures headaches, and tends bar. He bandages cuts and bruises, passes the time of day with cops, and since a good half of the girls are Christian Scientists, reads aloud his share of *Science and Health* on a Sunday morning. His predecessor, being a less well-balanced man, came to an evil end as shall be reported, but Alfred has triumphed over his environment and has brought his environment up with him. He knows what men should be there and what men shouldn't be there. He knows more about the home life of Monterey citizens than anyone in town.

As for Dora—she leads a ticklish existence. Being against the law, at least against its letter, she must be twice as law abiding as anyone else. There must be no drunks, no fighting, no vulgarity, or they close Dora up. Also being illegal Dora must be especially philanthropic. Everyone puts the bite on her. If the police give a dance for their pension fund and everyone else gives a dollar, Dora has to give fifty dollars. When the Chamber of Commerce improved its gardens, the merchants each gave five dollars but Dora was asked for and gave a hundred. With everything else it is the same, Red Cross, Community Chest, Boy Scouts, Dora's unsung, unpublicized, shameless dirty wages of sin lead the list of donations. But during the depression she was hardest hit. In addition to the usual charities, Dora saw the hungry children of Cannery Row and the jobless fathers and the worried women and Dora paid grocery bills right and left for two years and very nearly went broke in the process. Dora's girls are well trained and pleasant. They never speak to a man on the street although he may have been in the night before.

Before Alfy the present watchman took over, there was a tragedy in the Bear Flag Restaurant which saddened everyone. The previous watchman was named William and he was a dark and lonesome-looking man. In the daytime when his duties were few he would grow tired of female company. Through the windows he could see Mack and the boys sitting on the pipes in the vacant lot, dangling their feet in the mallow weeds and taking the sun while they discoursed slowly and philosophically of matters of interest but of no importance. Now and then as he watched them he saw them take out a pint of Old Tennis Shoes and wiping the neck of the bottle on a sleeve, raise the pint one after another. And William began to wish he could join that good group. He walked out one day and sat on the pipe. Conversation stopped and an uneasy and hostile silence fell on the group. After a while William went disconsolately back to the Bear Flag and through the window he saw the conversation spring up again and it saddened him. He had a dark and ugly face and a mouth twisted with brooding.

The next day he went again and this time he took a pint of whiskey. Mack and the boys drank the whiskey, after all they weren't crazy, but all the talking they did was "Good luck," and "Lookin' at you."

After a while William went back to the Bear Flag and he watched them through the window and he heard Mack raise his voice saying, "But God damn it, I hate a pimp!" Now this was obviously untrue although William didn't know that. Mack and the boys just didn't like William.

Now William's heart broke. The bums would not receive him socially. They felt that he was too far beneath them. William had always been introspective and self-accusing. He put on his hat and walked out along the sea, clear out to the Lighthouse. And he stood in the pretty little cemetery where you can hear the waves drumming always. William thought dark and broody thoughts. No one loved him. No one cared about him. They might call him a watchman but he was a pimp—a dirty pimp, the lowest thing in the world. And then he thought how he had a right to live and be happy just like anyone else, by God he had. He walked back angrily but his anger went away when he came to the Bear Flag and climbed the steps. It was evening and the juke box was playing *Harvest Moon* and William remembered that the first hooker who ever gaffed for him used to like that song before she ran away and got married and disappeared. The song made him awfully sad. Dora was in the back parlor having a cup of tea when William came in. She said, "What's the matter, you sick?"

"No," said William. "But what's the percentage? I feel lousy. I think I'll bump myself off."

Dora had handled plenty of neurotics in her time. Kid 'em out of it was her motto. "Well, do it on your own time and don't mess up the rugs," she said.

A gray damp cloud folded over William's heart and he walked slowly out and down the hall and knocked on Eva Flanegan's door. She had red hair and went to confession every week. Eva was quite a spiritual girl with a big family of brothers and sisters but she was an unpredictable drunk. She was painting her nails and messing them pretty badly when William went in and he knew she was bagged and Dora wouldn't let a bagged girl work. Her fingers were nail polish to the first joint and she was angry. "What's eating you?" she said. William grew angry too. "I'm going to bump myself off," he said fiercely.

Eva screeched at him. "That's a dirty, lousy, stinking sin," she cried, and then, "Wouldn't it be like you to get the joint pinched just when I got almost enough kick to take a trip to East St. Louis. You're a no-good bastard." She was still screaming at him when William shut her door after him and went to the kitchen. He was very tired of women. The Greek would be restful after women.

The Greek, big apron, sleeves rolled up, was frying pork chops in two big skillets, turning them over with an ice pick. "Hello, Kits. How is going things?" The pork chops hissed and swished in the pan.

"I don't know, Lou," said William. "Sometimes I think the best thing to do would be—kluck!" He drew his finger across his throat.

The Greek laid the ice pick on the stove and rolled his sleeves higher. "I tell you what I hear, Kits," he said. "I hear like the fella talks about it don't never do it." William's hand went out for the ice pick and he held it easily in his hand. His eyes looked deeply into the Greek's dark eyes and he saw disbelief and amusement and then as he stared the Greek's eyes grew troubled and then worried. And William saw the change, saw first how the Greek knew he could do it and then the Greek knew he would do it. As soon as he saw that in the Greek's eyes William knew he had to do it. He was sad because now it seemed silly. His hand rose and the ice pick snapped into his heart. It was amazing how easily it went in. William was the watchman before Alfred came. Everyone liked Alfred. He could sit on the pipes with Mack and the boys any time. He could even visit up at the Palace Flophouse.

4

In the evening just at dusk, a curious thing happened on Cannery Row. It happened in the time between sunset and the lighting of the street light. There is a small quiet gray period then. Down the hill, past the Palace Flophouse, down the chicken walk and through the vacant lot came an old Chinaman. He wore an ancient flat straw hat, blue jeans, both coat and trousers, and heavy shoes of which one sole was loose so that it slapped the ground when he walked. In his hand he carried a covered wicker basket. His face was lean and brown and corded as jerky and his old eyes were brown, even the whites were brown and deep set so that they looked out of holes. He came by just at dusk and crossed the street and went through the opening between Western Biological and the Hediondo Cannery. Then he crossed the little beach and disappeared among the piles and steel posts which support the piers. No one saw him again until dawn.

But in the dawn, during that time when the street light has been turned off and the daylight has not come, the old Chinaman crept out from among the piles, crossed the beach and the street. His wicker basket was heavy and wet and dripping now. His loose sole flap-flapped on the street. He went up the hill to the second street, went through a gate in a high board fence and was not seen again until evening. People, sleeping, heard his flapping shoe go by and they awakened for a moment. It had been happening for years but no one ever got used to him. Some people thought he was God and very old people thought he was Death and children thought he was a very funny old Chinaman, as children always think anything old and strange is funny. But the children did not taunt him or shout at him as they should for he carried a little cloud of fear about with him.

Only one brave and beautiful boy of ten named Andy from Salinas ever crossed the old Chinaman. Andy was visiting in Monterey and he saw the old man and knew he must shout at him if only to keep his self-respect, but even Andy, brave as he was, felt the little cloud of fear. Andy watched him go by evening after evening while his duty and his terror wrestled. And then one evening Andy braced himself and marched behind the old man singing in a shrill falsetto, "Ching-Chong Chinaman sitting on a rail—'Long came a white man an' chopped off his tail."

The old man stopped and turned. Andy stopped. The deep-brown eyes looked at Andy and the thin corded lips moved. What happened then Andy was never able either to explain or to forget. For the eyes spread out until there was no Chinaman. And then it was one eye—one huge brown eye as big as a church door. Andy looked through the shiny transparent brown door and through it he saw a lonely countryside, flat for miles but ending against a row of fantastic mountains shaped like cows' and dogs' heads and tents and mushrooms. There was low coarse grass on the plain and here and there a little mound. And a small animal like a woodchuck sat on each mound. And the loneliness—the desolate cold aloneness of the landscape made Andy whimper because there wasn't anybody at all in the world and he was left. Andy shut his eyes so he wouldn't have to see it any more and when he opened them, he was in Cannery Row and the old Chinaman was just flap-flapping between Western Biological and the Hediondo Cannery. Andy was the only boy who ever did that and he never did it again.

5

Western Biological was
right across the street and facing the vacant lot. Lee
Chong's grocery was on its catty-corner right and
Dora's Bear Flag Restaurant was on its catty-corner
left. Western Biological deals in strange and beautiful
wares. It sells the lovely animals of the sea, the
sponges, tunicates, anemones, the stars and buttle-
stars, and sun stars, the bivalves, barnacles, the
worms and shells, the fabulous and multiform little
brothers, the living moving flowers of the sea, nudibranchs and tectibranchs, the spiked and nobbed and
needly urchins, the crabs and demi-crabs, the little
dragons, the snapping shrimps, and ghost shrimps so
transparent that they hardly throw a shadow. And
Western Biological sells bugs and snails and spiders,
and rattlesnakes, and rats, and honey bees and gila
monsters. These are all for sale. Then there are little
unborn humans, some whole and others sliced thin
and mounted on slides. And for students there are
sharks with the blood drained out and yellow and blue

color substituted in veins and arteries, so that you may
follow the systems with a scapel. And there are cats
with colored veins and arteries, and frogs the same.
You can order anything living from Western Biological
and sooner or later you will get it.

It is a low building facing the street. The basement
is the storeroom with shelves, shelves clear to the
ceiling loaded with jars of preserved animals. And in
the basement is a sink and instruments for embalming
and for injecting. Then you go through the backyard to
a covered shed on piles over the ocean and here are
the tanks for the larger animals, the sharks and rays
and octopi, each in their concrete tanks. There is a
stairway up the front of the building and a door that
opens into an office where there is a desk piled h:gh
with unopened mail, filing cabinets, and a safe with
the door propped open. Once the safe got locked by
mistake and no one knew the combination. And in the
safe was an open can of sardines and a piece of Roque-
fort cheese. Before the combination could be sent by
the maker of the lock, there was trouble in the safe. It
was then that Doc devised a method for getting revenge on a bank if anyone should ever want to. "Rent
a safety deposit box," he said, "then deposit in it one
whole fresh salmon and go away for six months." After
the trouble with the safe, it was not permitted to keep
food there any more. It is kept in the filing cabinets.
Behind the office is a room where in aquaria are many
living animals; there also are the microscopes and the
slides and the drug cabinets, the cases of laboratory
glass, the work benches and little motors, the chemicals. From this room come smells—formaline, and dry

starfish, and sea water and menthol, carbolic acid and acetic acid, smell of brown wrapping paper and straw and rope, smell of chloroform and ether, smell of ozone from the motors, smell of fine steel and thin lubricant from the microscopes, smell of banana oil and rubber tubing, smell of drying wool socks and boots, sharp pungent smell of rattlesnakes, and musty frightening smell of rats. And through the back door comes the smell of kelp and barnacles when the tide is out and the smell of salt and spray when the tide is in.

To the left the office opens into a library. The walls are bookcases to the ceiling, boxes of pamphlets and separates, books of all kinds, dictionaries, encyclopedias, poetry, plays. A great phonograph stands against the wall with hundreds of records lined up beside it. Under the window is a redwood bed and on the walls and to the bookcases are pinned reproductions of Daumiers, and Graham, Titian, and Leonardo and Picasso, Dali and George Grosz, pinned here and there at eye level so that you can look at them if you want to. There are chairs and benches in this little room and of course the bed. As many as forty people have been here at one time.

Behind this library or music room, or whatever you want to call it, is the kitchen, a narrow chamber with a gas stove, a water heater, and a sink. But whereas some food is kept in the filing cabinets in the office, dishes and cooking fat and vegetables are kept in glass-fronted sectional bookcases in the kitchen. No whimsy dictated this. It just happened. From the ceiling of the kitchen hang pieces of bacon, and salami, and black bêche-de-mer. Behind the kitchen is a toilet and a shower. The toilet leaked for five years until a clever and handsome guest fixed it with a piece of chewing gum.

Doc is the owner and operator of the Western Biological Laboratory. Doc is rather small, deceptively small, for he is wiry and very strong and when passionate anger comes on him he can be very fierce. He wears a beard and his face is half Christ and half satyr and his face tells the truth. It is said that he has helped many a girl out of one trouble and into another. Doc has the hands of a brain surgeon, and a cool warm mind. Doc tips his hat to dogs as he drives by and the dogs look up and smile at him. He can kill anything for need but he could not even hurt a feeling for pleasure. He has one great fear—that of getting his head wet, so that summer or winter he ordinarily wears a rain hat. He will wade in a tide pool up to the chest without feeling damp, but a drop of rain water on his head makes him panicky.

Over a period of years Doc dug himself into Cannery Row to an extent not even he suspected. He became the fountain of philosophy and science and art. In the laboratory the girls from Dora's heard the Plain Songs and Gregorian music for the first time. Lee Chong listened while Li Po was read to him in English. Henri the painter heard for the first time the Book of the Dead and was so moved that he changed his medium. Henri had been painting with glue, iron rust, and colored chicken feathers but he changed and his next four paintings were done entirely with different kinds of nutshells. Doc would listen to any kind of nonsense and change it for you to a kind of wisdom. His mind had no horizon—and his sympathy had no warp. He could talk to children, telling them very profound things so that they understood. He lived in a world of wonders, of excitement. He was concupiscent as a rabbit and gentle as hell. Everyone who knew him was indebted to him. And everyone who thought of him thought next, "I really must do something nice for Doc."

6

Doc was collecting marine animals in the Great Tide Pool on the tip of the Peninsula. It is a fabulous place: when the tide is in, a wave-churned basin, creamy with foam, whipped by the combers that roll in from the whistling buoy on the reef. But when the tide goes out the little water world becomes quiet and lovely. The sea is very clear and the bottom becomes fantastic with hurrying, fighting, feeding, breeding animals. Crabs rush from frond to frond of the waving algae. Starfish squat over mussels and limpets, attach their million little suckers and then slowly lift with incredible power until the prey is broken from the rock. And then the starfish stomach comes out and envelops its food. Orange and speckled and fluted nudibranchs slide gracefully over the rocks, their skirts waving like the dresses of Spanish dancers. And black eels poke their heads out of crevices and wait for prey. The snapping shrimps with their trigger claws pop loudly. The lovely, colored world is glassed over. Hermit crabs like frantic children scamper on the bottom sand. And now one, finding an empty snail shell he likes better than his own, creeps out, exposing his soft body to the enemy for a moment, and then pops into the new shell. A wave breaks over the barrier, and churns the glassy water for a moment and mixes bubbles into the pool, and then it clears and is tranquil and lovely and murderous again. Here a crab tears a leg from his brother. The anemones expand like soft and brilliant flowers, inviting any tired and perplexed animal to lie for a moment in their arms, and when some small crab or little tide-pool Johnnie accepts the green and purple invitation, the petals whip in, the stinging cells shoot tiny narcotic needles into the prey and it grows weak and perhaps sleepy while the searing caustic digestive acids melt its body down.

Then the creeping murderer, the octopus, steals out, slowly, softly, moving like a gray mist, pretending now to be a bit of weed, now a rock, now a lump of decaying meat while its evil goat eyes watch coldly. It oozes and flows toward a feeding crab, and as it comes close its yellow eyes burn and its body turns rosy with the pulsing color of anticipation and rage. Then suddenly it runs lightly on the tips of its arms, as ferociously as a charging cat. It leaps savagely on the crab, there is a puff of black fluid, and the struggling mass is obscured in the sepia cloud while the octopus murders the crab. On the exposed rocks out of water, the barnacles bubble behind their closed doors and the limpets dry out. And down to the rocks come the black flies to eat anything they can find. The sharp smell of iodine from the algae, and the lime smell of calcareous bodies and the smell of powerful protean, smell of sperm and ova fill the air. On the exposed rocks the starfish emit semen and eggs from between their rays. The smells of life and richness, of death and digestion, of decay and birth, burden the air. And salt spray blows in from the barrier where the ocean waits for its rising-tide strength to permit it back into the Great Tide Pool again. And on the reef the whistling buoy bellows like a sad and patient bull.

In the pool Doc and Hazel worked together. Hazel lived in the Palace Flophouse with Mack and the boys. Hazel got his name in as haphazard a way as his life was ever afterward. His worried mother had had seven children in eight years. Hazel was the eighth, and his mother became confused about his sex when he was born. She was tired and run down anyway from trying to feed and clothe seven children and their father. She had tried every possible way of making money—paper flowers, mushrooms at home, rabbits for meat and fur—while her husband from a canvas chair gave her every help his advice and reasoning and criticism could offer. She had a great aunt named Hazel who was reputed to carry life insurance. The eighth child was named Hazel before the mother got it through her head that Hazel was a boy and by that time she was used to the name and never bothered to change it. Hazel grew up—did four years in grammar school, four years in reform school, and didn't learn anything in either place. Reform schools are supposed to teach viciousness and criminality but Hazel didn't pay enough attention. He came out of reform school as innocent of viciousness as he was of fractions and long division. Hazel loved to hear conversation but he didn't listen to words—just to the tone of conversation. He asked questions, not to hear the answers but simply to continue the flow. He was twenty-six—dark-haired and pleasant, strong, willing, and loyal. Quite often he went collecting with Doc and he was very good at it once he knew what was wanted. His fingers could creep like an octopus, could grab and hold like an anemone. He was sure-footed on the slippery rocks and he loved the hunt. Doc wore his rain hat and high rubber boots as he worked but Hazel sloshed about in tennis shoes and blue jeans. They were collecting starfish. Doc had an order for three hundred.

Hazel picked a nobby purplish starfish from the bottom of the pool and popped it into his nearly full gunny sack. "I wonder what they do with them," he said.

"Do with what?" Doc asked.

"The starfish," said Hazel. "You sell 'em. You'll send out a barrel of 'em. What do the guys do with 'em? You can't eat 'em."

"They study them," said Doc patiently and he remembered that he had answered this question for Hazel dozens of times before. But Doc had one mental habit he could not get over. When anyone asked a question, Doc thought he wanted to know the answer. That was the way with Doc. *He* never asked unless he wanted to know and he could not conceive of the brain that would ask without wanting to know. But Hazel, who simply wanted to hear talk, had developed a system of making the answer to one question the basis of another. It kept conversation going.

"What do they find to study?" Hazel continued. "They're just starfish. There's millions of 'em around. I could get you a million of 'em."

"They're complicated and interesting animals," Doc

said a little defensively. "Besides, these are going to the Middle West to Northwestern University."

Hazel used his trick. "They got no starfish there?"

"They got no ocean there," said Doc.

"Oh!" said Hazel and he cast frantically about for a peg to hang a new question on. He hated to have a conversation die out like this. He wasn't quick enough. While he was looking for a question Doc asked one. Hazel hated that, it meant casting about in his mind for an answer and casting about in Hazel's mind was like wandering alone in a deserted museum. Hazel's mind was choked with uncatalogued exhibits. He never forgot anything but he never bothered to arrange his memories. Everything was thrown together like fishing tackle in the bottom of a rowboat, hooks and sinkers and line and lures and gaffs all snarled up.

Doc asked, "How are things going up at the Palace?"

Hazel ran his fingers through his dark hair and he peered into the clutter of his mind. "Pretty good," he said. "That fellow Gay is moving in with us I guess. His wife hits him pretty bad. He don't mind that when he's awake but she waits 'til he gets to sleep and then hits him. He hates that. He has to wake up and beat her up and then when he goes back to sleep she hits him again. He don't get any rest so he's moving in with us."

"That's a new one," said Doc. "She used to swear out a warrant and put him in jail."

"Yeah!" said Hazel. "But that was before they built the new jail in Salinas. Used to be thirty days and Gay was pretty hot to get out, but this new jail—radio in the tank and good bunks and the sheriff's a nice fellow. Gay gets in there and he don't want to come out. He likes it so much his wife won't get him arrested any more. So she figured out this hitting him while he's asleep. It's nerve racking, he says. And you know as good as me—Gay never did take any pleasure beating her up. He only done it to keep his self-respect. But he gets tired of it. I guess he'll be with us now."

Doc straightened up. The waves were beginning to break over the barrier of the Great Tide Pool. The tide was coming in and little rivers from the sea had begun to flow over the rocks. The wind blew freshly in from the whistling buoy and the barking of sea lions came from around the point. Doc pushed his rain hat on the back of his head. "We've got enough starfish," he said and then went on, "Look, Hazel, I know you've got six or seven undersized abalones in the bottom of your sack. If we get stopped by a game warden, you're going to say they're mine, on my permit—aren't you?"

"Well—hell," said Hazel.

"Look," Doc said kindly. "Suppose I get an order for abalones and maybe the game warden thinks I'm using my collecting permit too often. Suppose he thinks I'm eating them."

"Well—hell," said Hazel.

"It's like the industrial alcohol board. They've got suspicious minds. They always think I'm drinking the alcohol. They think that about everyone."

"Well, ain't you?"

"Not much of it," said Doc. "That stuff they put in it tastes terrible and it's a big job to redistill it."

"That stuff ain't so bad," said Hazel. "Me and Mack had a snort of it the other day. What is it they put in?"

Doc was about to answer when he saw it was Hazel's trick again. "Let's get moving," he said. He hoisted his sack of starfish on his shoulder. And he had forgotten the illegal abalones in the bottom of Hazel's sack.

Hazel followed him up out of the tide pool and up the slippery trail to solid ground. The little crabs scampered and skittered out of their way. Hazel felt that he had better cement the grave over the topic of the abalones.

"That painter guy came back to the Palace," he offered.

"Yes?" said Doc.

"Yeah! You see, he done all our pictures in chicken feathers and now he says he got to do them all over again with nutshells. He says he changed his—his med—medium."

Doc chuckled. "He still building his boat?"

"Sure," said Hazel. "He's got it all changed around. New kind of a boat. I guess he'll take it apart and change it. Doc—is he nuts?"

Doc swung his heavy sack of starfish to the ground and stood panting a little. "Nuts?" he asked. "Oh, yes, I guess so. Nuts about the same amount we are, only in a different way."

Such a thing had never occurred to Hazel. He looked upon himself as a crystal pool of clarity and on his life as a troubled glass of misunderstood virtue. Doc's last statement had outraged him a little. "But that boat—" he cried. "He's been building that boat for seven years that I know of. The blocks rotted out and he made concrete blocks. Every time he gets it nearly finished he changes it and starts over again. I think he's nuts. Seven years on a boat."

Doc was sitting on the ground pulling off his rubber boots. "You don't understand," he said gently. "Henri loves boats but he's afraid of the ocean."

"What's he want a boat for then?" Hazel demanded.

"He likes boats," said Doc. "But suppose he finishes his boat. Once it's finished people will say, 'Why don't you put it in the water?' Then if he puts it in the water, he'll have to go out in it, and he hates the water. So you see, he never finishes the boat—so he doesn't ever have to launch it."

Hazel had followed this reasoning to a certain point but he abandoned it before it was resolved, not only abandoned it but searched for some way to change the subject. "I think he's nuts," he said lamely.

On the black earth on which the ice plants bloomed, hundreds of black stink bugs crawled. And many of them stuck their tails up in the air. "Look at all them stink bugs," Hazel remarked, grateful to the bugs for being there.

"They're interesting," said Doc.

"Well, what they got their asses up in the air for?"

Doc rolled up his wool socks and put them in the rubber boots and from his pocket he brought out dry socks and a pair of thin moccasins. "I don't know why," he said. "I looked them up recently—they're very common animals and one of the commonest things they do is put their tails up in the air. And in all the books there isn't one mention of the fact that they put their tails up in the air or why."

Hazel turned one of the stink bugs over with the toe of his wet tennis shoe and the shining black beetle strove madly with floundering legs to get upright again. "Well, why do *you* think they do it?"

"I think they're praying," said Doc.

"What!" Hazel was shocked.

"The remarkable thing," said Doc, "isn't that they put their tails up in the air—the really incredibly remarkable thing is that we find it remarkable. We can only use ourselves as yardsticks. If we did something as inexplicable and strange we'd probably be praying—so maybe they're praying."

"Let's get the hell out of here," said Hazel.

7

The Palace Flophouse was no sudden development. Indeed when Mack and Hazel and Eddie and Hughie and Jones moved into it, they looked upon it as little more than shelter from the wind and the rain, as a place to go when everything else had closed or when their welcome was thin and sere with overuse. Then the Palace was only a long bare room, lit dimly by two small windows, walled with unpainted wood smelling strongly of fish meal. They had not loved it then. But Mack knew that some kind of organization was necessary particularly among such a group of ravening individualists.

A training army which has not been equipped with guns and artillery and tanks uses artificial guns and masquerading trucks to simulate its destructive panoply—and its toughening soldiers get used to field guns by handling logs on wheels.

Mack, with a piece of chalk, drew five oblongs on the floor, each seven feet long and four feet wide, and in each square he wrote a name. These were the simulated beds. Each man had property rights inviolable in

his space. He could legally fight a man who encroached on his square. The rest of the room was
property common to all. That was in the first days
when Mack and the boys sat on the floor, played cards
hunkered down, and slept on the hard boards. Perhaps, save for an accident of weather, they might always have lived that way. However, an unprecedented
rainfall which went on for over a month changed all
that. House-ridden, the boys grew tired of squatting on
the floor. Their eyes became outraged by the bare
board walls. Because it sheltered them the house grew
dear to them. And it had the charm of never knowing
the entrance of an outraged landlord. For Lee Chong
never came near it. Then one afternoon Hughie came
in with an army cot which had a torn canvas. He spent
two hours sewing up the rip with fishing line. And that
night the others lying on the floor in their squares
watched Hughie ooze gracefully into his cot—they
heard him sigh with abysmal comfort and he was
asleep and snoring before anyone else.

The next day Mack puffed up the hill carrying a
rusty set of springs he had found on a scrap-iron
dump. The apathy was broken then. The boys outdid
one another in beautifying the Palace Flophouse until
after a few months it was, if anything, overfurnished.
There were old carpets on the floor, chairs with and
without seats. Mack had a wicker chaise longue
painted bright red. There were tables, a grandfather
clock without dial face or works. The walls were whitewashed which made it almost light and airy. Pictures
began to appear—mostly calendars showing improbable luscious blondes holding bottles of Coca-Cola.
Henri had contributed two pieces from his chicken-

feather period. A bundle of gilded cattails stood in one corner and a sheaf of peacock feathers was nailed to the wall beside the grandfather clock.

They were some time acquiring a stove and when they did find what they wanted, a silver-scrolled monster with floriated warming ovens and a front like a nickel-plated tulip garden, they had trouble getting it. It was too big to steal and its owner refused to part with it to the sick widow with eight children whom Mack invented and patronized in the same moment. The owner wanted a dollar and a half and didn't come down to eighty cents for three days. The boys closed at eighty cents and gave him an I.O.U. which he probably still has. This transaction took place in Seaside and the stove weighed three hundred pounds. Mack and Hughie exhausted every possibility of haulage for ten days and only when they realized that no one was going to take this stove home for them did they begin to carry it. It took them three days to carry it to Cannery Row, a distance of five miles, and they camped beside it at night. But once installed in the Palace Flophouse it was the glory and the hearth and the center. Its nickel flowers and foliage shone with a cheery light. It was the gold tooth of the Palace. Fired up, it warmed the big room. Its oven was wonderful and you could fry an egg on its shiny black lids.

With the great stove came pride, and with pride, the Palace became home. Eddie planted morning glories to run over the door and Hazel acquired some rather rare fuchsia bushes planted in five-gallon cans which made the entrance formal and a little cluttered. Mack and the boys loved the Palace and they even cleaned it a little sometimes. In their minds they sneered at un-

settled people who had no house to go to and occasionally in their pride they brought a guest home for a day
or two.

Eddie was understudy bartender at La Ida. He filled
in when Whitey the regular bartender was sick, which
was as often as Whitey could get away with it. Every
time Eddie filled in, a few bottles disappeared, so he
couldn't fill in too often. But Whitey liked to have
Eddie take his place because he was convinced, and
correctly, that Eddie was one man who wouldn't try to
keep his job permanently. Almost anyone could have
trusted Eddie to this extent. Eddie didn't have to remove much liquor. He kept a gallon jug under the bar
and in the mouth of the jug there was a funnel. Anything left in the glasses Eddie poured into the funnel
before he washed the glasses. If an argument or a song
were going on at La Ida, or late at night when good
fellowship had reached its logical conclusion, Eddie
poured glasses half or two-thirds full into the funnel.
The resulting punch which he took back to the Palace
was always interesting and sometimes surprising. The
mixture of rye, beer, bourbon, scotch, wine, rum and
gin was fairly constant, but now and then some effete
customer would order a stinger or an anisette or a
curaçao and these little touches gave a distinct character to the punch. It was Eddie's habit always to
shake a little angostura into the jug just before he left.
On a good night Eddie got three-quarters of a gallon. It
was a source of satisfaction to him that nobody was out
anything. He had observed that a man got just as
drunk on half a glass as on a whole one, that is, if he
was in the mood to get drunk at all.

Eddie was a very desirable inhabitant of the Palace

Flophouse. The others never asked him to help with the housecleaning and once Hazel washed four pairs of Eddie's socks.

Now on the afternoon when Hazel was out collecting with Doc in the Great Tide Pool, the boys were sitting around in the Palace sipping the result of Eddie's latest contribution. Gay was there too, the latest member of the group. Eddie sipped speculatively from his glass and smacked his lips. "It's funny how you get a run," he said. "Take last night. There was at least ten guys ordered Manhattans. Sometimes maybe you don't get two calls for a Manhattan in a month. It's the grenadine gives the stuff that taste."

Mack tasted his—a big taste—and refilled his glass. "Yes," he said somberly, "it's little things make the difference." He looked about to see how this gem had set with the others.

Only Gay got the full impact. "Sure is," he said. "Does—"

"Where's Hazel today?" Mack asked.

Jones said, "Hazel went out with Doc to get some starfish."

Mack nodded his head soberly. "That Doc is a hell of a nice fella," he said. "He'll give you a quarter any time. When I cut myself he put on a new bandage every day. A hell of a nice fella."

The others nodded in profound agreement.

"I been wondering for a long time," Mack continued, "what we could do for him—something nice. Something he'd like."

"He'd like a dame," said Hughie.

"He's got three four dames," said Jones. "You can always tell—when he pulls them front curtains closed and when he plays that kind of church music on the phonograph."

Mack said reprovingly to Hughie, "Just because he doesn't run no dame naked through the streets in the daytime, you think Doc's celebrate."

"What's celebrate?" Eddie asked.

"That's when you can't get no dame," said Mack.

"I thought it was a kind of a party," said Jones.

A silence fell on the room. Mack shifted in his chaise longue. Hughie let the front legs of his chair down on the floor. They looked into space and then they all looked at Mack. Mack said, "Hum!"

Eddie said, "What kind of a party you think Doc'd like?"

"What other kind is there?" said Jones.

Mack mused, "Doc wouldn't like this stuff from the winin' jug."

"How do you know?" Hughie demanded. "You never offered him none."

"Oh, I know," said Mack. "He's been to college. Once I seen a dame in a fur coat go in there. Never did see her come out. It was two o'clock the last I looked—and that church music goin'. No—you couldn't offer him none of this." He filled his glass again.

"This tastes pretty nice after the third glass," Hughie said loyally.

"No," said Mack. "Not for Doc. Have to be whiskey—the real thing."

"He likes beer," said Jones. "He's all the time going over to Lee's for beer—sometimes in the middle of the night."

Mack said, "I figure when you buy beer, you're

buying too much tare. Take 8 percent beer—why you're spending your dough for 92 percent water and color and hops and stuff like that. Eddie," he added, "you think you could get four five bottles of whiskey at La Ida next time Whitey's sick?"

"Sure," said Eddie. "Sure I could get it but that'd be the end—no more golden eggs. I think Johnnie's suspicious anyways. Other day he says, 'I smell a mouse named Eddie.' I was gonna lay low and only bring the jug for a while."

"Yeah!" said Jones. "Don't you lose that job. If something happened to Whitey, you could fall right in there for a week or so 'til they got somebody else. I guess if we're goin' to give a party for Doc, we got to buy the whiskey. How much is whiskey a gallon?"

"I don't know," said Hughie. "I never get more than a half pint at a time myself—at one time that is. I figure you get a quart and right away you got friends. But you get a half pint and you can drink it in the lot before—well before you got a lot of folks around."

"It's going to take dough to give Doc a party," said Mack. "If we're going to give him a party at all it ought to be a good one. Should have a big cake. I wonder when is his birthday?"

"Don't need a birthday for a party," said Jones.

"No—but it's nice," said Mack. "I figure it would take ten or twelve bucks to give Doc a party you wouldn't be ashamed of."

They looked at one another speculatively. Hughie suggested, "The Hediondo Cannery is hiring guys."

"No," said Mack quickly. "We got good reputations and we don't want to spoil them. Every one of us keeps a job for a month or more when we take one. That's why we can always get a job when we need one. S'pose we take a job for a day or so—why we'll lose our reputation for sticking. Then if we needed a job there wouldn't nobody have us." The rest nodded quick agreement.

"I figure I'm gonna work a couple of months—November and part of December," said Jones. "Makes it nice to have money around Christmas. We could cook a turkey this year."

"By God, we could," said Mack. "I know a place up Carmel Valley where there's fifteen hundred in one flock."

"Valley," said Hughie. "You know I used to collect stuff up the Valley for Doc, turtles and crayfish and frogs. Got a nickel apiece for frogs."

"Me, too," said Gay. "I got five hundred frogs one time."

"If Doc needs frogs it's a setup," said Mack. "We could go up the Carmel River and have a little outing and we wouldn't tell Doc what it was for and then we'd give him one hell of a party."

A quiet excitement grew in the Palace Flophouse. "Gay," said Mack, "take a look out the door and see if Doc's car is in front of his place."

Gat set down his glass and looked out. "Not yet," he said.

"Well, he ought to be back any minute," said Mack. "Now here's how we'll go about it. . . ."

8

In April 1932 the boiler at the Hediondo Cannery blew a tube for the third time in two weeks and the board of directors consisting of Mr. Randolph and a stenographer decided that it would be cheaper to buy a new boiler than to have to shut down so often. In time the new boiler arrived and the old one was moved into the vacant lot between Lee Chong's and the Bear Flag Restaurant where it was set on blocks to await an inspiration on Mr. Randolph's part on how to make some money out of it. Gradually the plant engineer removed the tubing to use to patch other outworn equipment at the Hediondo. The boiler looked like an old-fashioned locomotive without wheels. It had a big door in the center of its nose and a low fire door. Gradually it became red and soft with rust and gradually the mallow weeds grew up around it and the flaking rust fed the weeds. Flowering myrtle crept up its sides and the wild anise perfumed the air about it. Then someone threw out a datura root and the thick fleshy tree grew up and the great white bells hung down over the boiler door and at night the flowers smelled of love and excitement, an incredibly sweet and moving odor.

In 1935 Mr. and Mrs. Sam Malloy moved into the boiler. The tubing was all gone now and it was a roomy, dry, and safe apartment. True, if you came in through the fire door you had to get down on your hands and knees, but once in there was head room in the middle and you couldn't want a dryer, warmer place to stay. They shagged a mattress through the fire door and settled down. Mr. Malloy was happy and contented there and for quite a long time so was Mrs. Malloy.

Below the boiler on the hill there were numbers of large pipes also abandoned by the Hediondo. Toward the end of 1937 there was a great catch of fish and the canneries were working full time and a housing shortage occurred. Then it was that Mr. Malloy took to renting the larger pipes as sleeping quarters for single men at a very nominal fee. With a piece of tar paper over one end and a square of carpet over the other, they made comfortable bedrooms, although men used to sleeping curled up had to change their habits or move out. There were those too who claimed that their snores echoing back from the pipes woke them up. But on the whole Mr. Malloy did a steady small business and was happy.

Mrs. Malloy had been contented until her husband became a landlord and then she began to change. First it was a rug, then a washtub, then a lamp with a colored silk shade. Finally she came into the boiler on her hands and knees one day and she stood up and said a little breathlessly, "Holman's are having a sale of curtains. Real lace curtains and edges of blue and pink—$1.98 a set with curtain rods thrown in."

Mr. Malloy sat up on the mattress. "Curtains?" he demanded. "What in God's name do you want curtains for?"

"I like things nice," said Mrs. Malloy. "I always did like to have things nice for you," and her lower lip began to tremble.

"But, darling," Sam Malloy cried, "I got nothing against curtains. I like curtains."

"Only $1.98," Mrs. Malloy quavered, "and you begrutch me $1.98," and she sniffed and her chest heaved.

"I don't begrutch you," said Mr. Malloy. "But, darling—for Christ's sake what are we going to do with curtains? We got no windows."

Mrs. Malloy cried and cried and Sam held her in his arms and comforted her.

"Men just don't understand how a woman feels," she sobbed. "Men just never try to put themselves in a woman's place."

And Sam lay beside her and rubbed her back for a long time before she went to sleep.

9

When Doc's car came back to the laboratory, Mack and the boys secretly watched Hazel help to carry in the sacks of starfish. In a few minutes Hazel came damply up the chicken walk to the Palace. His jeans were wet with sea water to the thighs and where it was drying the white salt rings were forming. He sat heavily in the patent rocker that was his and shucked off his wet tennis shoes.

Mack asked, "How is Doc feeling?"

"Fine," said Hazel. "You can't understand a word he says. Know what he said about stink bugs? No—I better not tell you."

"He seem in a nice friendly mood?" Mack asked.

"Sure," said Hazel. "We got two three hundred starfish. He's all right."

"I wonder if we better all go over?" Mack asked himself and he answered himself, "No I guess it would be better if one went alone. It might get him mixed up if we all went."

"What is this?" Hazel asked.

"We got plans," said Mack. "I'll go myself so as not to startle him. You guys stay here and wait. I'll come back in a few minutes."

Mack went out and he teetered down the chicken walk and across the track. Mr. Malloy was sitting on a brick in front of his boiler.

"How are you, Sam?" Mack asked.

"Pretty good."

"How's the missus?"

"Pretty good," said Mr. Malloy. "You know any kind of glue that you can stick cloth to iron?"

Ordinarily Mack would have thrown himself headlong into this problem but now he was not to be deflected. "No," he said.

He went across the vacant lot, crossed the street and entered the basement of the laboratory.

Doc had his hat off now since there was practically no chance of getting his head wet unless a pipe broke. He was busy removing the starfish from the wet sacks and arranging them on the cool concrete floor. The starfish were twisted and knotted up for a starfish loves to hang onto something and for an hour these had found only each other. Doc arranged them in long lines and very slowly they straightened out until they lay in symmetrical stars on the concrete floor. Doc's pointed brown beard was damp with perspiration as he worked. He looked up a little nervously as Mack entered. It was not that trouble always came in with Mack but something always entered with him.

"Hiya, Doc?" said Mack.

"All right," said Doc uneasily.

"Hear about Phyllis Mae over at the Bear Flag? She

hit a drunk and got his tooth in her fist and it's infected clear to the elbow. She showed me the tooth. It was out of a plate. Is a false tooth poison, Doc?"

"I guess everything that comes out of the human mouth is poison," said Doc warningfully. "Has she got a doctor?"

"The bouncer fixed her up," said Mack.

"I'll take her some sulfa," said Doc, and he waited for the storm to break. He knew Mack had come for something and Mack knew he knew it.

Mack said, "Doc, you got any need for any kind of animals now?"

Doc sighed with relief. "Why?" he asked guardedly.

Mack became open and confidential. "I'll tell you, Doc. I and the boys got to get some dough—we simply got to. It's for a good purpose, you might say a worthy cause."

"Phyllis Mae's arm?"

Mack saw the chance, weighed it and gave it up. "Well—no," he said. "It's more important than that. You can't kill a whore. No—this is different. I and the boys thought if you needed something why we'd get it for you and that way we could make a little piece of change."

It seemed simple and innocent. Doc laid down four more starfish in lines. "I could use three or four hundred frogs," he said. "I'd get them myself but I've got to go down to La Jolla tonight. There's a good tide tomorrow and I have to get some octopi."

"Same price for frogs?" Mack asked. "Five cents apiece?"

"Same price," said Doc.

Mack was jovial. "Don't you worry about frogs, Doc," he said. "We'll get you all the frogs you want. You just rest easy about frogs. Why we can get them right up Carmel River. I know a place."

"Good," said Doc. "I'll take all you get but I need about three hundred."

"Just you rest easy, Doc. Don't you lose no sleep about it. You'll get your frogs, maybe seven eight hundred." He put the Doc at his ease about frogs and then a little cloud crossed Mack's face. "Doc," he said, "any chance of using your car to go up the Valley?"

"No," said Doc. "I told you. I have to drive to La Jolla tonight to make tomorrow's tide."

"Oh," said Mack dispiritedly. "Oh. Well, don't you worry about it, Doc. Maybe we can get Lee Chong's old truck." And then his face fell a little further. "Doc," he said, "on a business deal like this, would you advance two or three bucks for gasoline? I know Lee Chong won't give us gas."

"No," said Doc. He had fallen into this before. Once he had financed Gay to go for turtles. He financed him for two weeks and at the end of that time Gay was in jail on his wife's charge and he never did go for turtles.

"Well, maybe we can't go then," said Mack sadly.

Now Doc really needed the frogs. He tried to work out some method which was business and not philanthropy. "I'll tell you what I'll do," he said. "I'll give you a note to my gas station so you can get ten gallons of gas. How will that be?"

Mack smiled. "Fine," he said. "That will work out just fine. I and the boys will get an early start tomorrow. Time you get back from the south, we'll have more damn frogs than you ever seen in your life."

Doc went to the labeling desk and wrote a note to Red Williams at the gas station, authorizing the issue of ten gallons of gasoline to Mack. "Here you are," he said.

Mack was smiling broadly. "Doc," he said, "you can get to sleep tonight and not even give frogs a thought. We'll have piss pots full of them by the time you get back."

Doc watched him go a little uneasily. Doc's dealings with Mack and the boys had always been interesting but rarely had they been profitable to Doc. He remembered ruefully the time Mack sold him fifteen tom cats and by night the owners came and got every one. "Mack," he had asked, "why all tom cats?"

Mack said, "Doc, it's my own invention but I'll tell you because you're a good friend. You make a big wire trap and then you don't use bait. You use—well—you use a lady cat. Catch every God damn tom cat in the country that way."

From the laboratory Mack crossed the street and went through the swinging screen doors into Lee Chong's grocery. Mrs. Lee was cutting bacon on the big butcher's block. A Lee cousin primped up slightly wilted heads of lettuce the way a girl primps a loose finger wave. A cat lay asleep on a big pile of oranges. Lee Chong stood in his usual place back of the cigar counter and in front of the liquor shelves. His tapping finger on the change mat speeded up a little when Mack came in.

Mack wasted no time in sparring. "Lee," he said,

"Doc over there's got a problem. He's got a big order for frogs from the New York Museum. Means a lot to Doc. Besides the dough there's a lot of credit getting an order like that. Doc's got to go south and I and the boys said we'd help him out. I think a guy's friends ought to help him out of a hole when they can, especially a nice guy like Doc. Why I bet he spends sixty seventy dollars a month with you."

Lee Chong remained silent and watchful. His fat finger barely moved on the change mat but it flicked slightly like a tense cat's tail.

Mack plunged into his thesis. "Will you let us take your old truck to go up Carmel Valley for frogs for Doc—for good old Doc?"

Lee Chong smiled in triumph. "Tluck no good," he said. "Bloke down."

This staggered Mack for a moment but he recovered. He spread the order for gasoline on the cigar counter. "Look!" he said. "Doc needs them frogs. He give me this order for gas to get them. I can't let Doc down. Now Gay is a good mechanic. If he fixes your truck and puts it in good shape, will you let us take it?"

Lee put back his head so that he could see Mack through his half-glasses. There didn't seem to be anything wrong with the proposition. The truck really wouldn't run. Gay really was a good mechanic and the order for gasoline was definite evidence of good faith.

"How long you be gone?" Lee asked.

"Maybe half a day, maybe a whole day. Just 'til we get the frogs."

Lee was worried but he couldn't see any way out.

The dangers were all there and Lee knew all of them. "Okay," said Lee.

"Good," said Mack. "I knew Doc could depend on you. I'll get Gay right to work on that truck." He turned about to leave. "By the way," he said. "Doc's paying us five cents apiece for those frogs. We're going to get seven or eight hundred. How about taking a pint of Old Tennis Shoes just 'til we can get back with the frogs?"

"No!" said Lee Chong.

10

Frankie began coming to Western Biological when he was eleven years old. For a week or so he just stood outside the basement door and looked in. Then one day he stood inside the door. Ten days later he was in the basement. He had very large eyes and his hair was a dark wiry dirty shock. His hands were filthy. He picked up a piece of excelsior and put it in a garbage can and then he looked at Doc where he worked labeling specimen bottles containing purple Velella. Finally Frankie got to the work bench and he put his dirty fingers on the bench. It took Frankie three weeks to get that far and he was ready to bolt every instant of the time.

Finally one day Doc spoke to him. "What's your name, son?"

"Frankie."

"Where do you live?"

"Up there," a gesture up the hill.

"Why aren't you in school?"

"I don't go to school."

"Why not?"

"They don't want me there."

"Your hands are dirty. Don't you ever wash?"

Frankie looked stricken and then he went to the sink and scrubbed his hands and always afterwards he scrubbed his hands almost raw every day.

And he came to the laboratory every day. It was an association without much talk. Doc by a telephone call established that what Frankie said was true. They didn't want him in school. He couldn't learn and there was something a little wrong with his coordination. There was no place for him. He wasn't an idiot, he wasn't dangerous, his parents, or parent, would not pay for his keep in an institution. Frankie didn't often sleep at the laboratory but he spent his days there. And sometimes he crawled in the excelsior crate and slept. That was probably when there was a crisis at home.

Doc asked, "Why do you come here?"

"You don't hit me or give me a nickel," said Frankie.

"Do they hit you at home?"

"There's uncles around all the time at home. Some of them hit me and tell me to get out and some of them give me a nickel and tell me to get out."

"Where's your father?"

"Dead," said Frankie vaguely.

"Where's your mother?"

"With the uncles."

Doc clipped Frankie's hair and got rid of the lice. At Lee Chong's he got him a new pair of overalls and a striped sweater and Frankie became his slave.

"I love you," he said one afternoon. "Oh, I love you."

He wanted to work in the laboratory. He swept out every day, but there was something a little wrong. He couldn't get a floor quite clean. He tried to help with grading crayfish for size. There they were in a bucket, all sizes. They were to be grouped in the big pans— laid out—all the three-inch ones together and all the four-inch ones and so forth. Frankie tried and the perspiration stood on his forehead but he couldn't do it. Size relationships just didn't get through to him.

"No," Doc would say. "Look, Frankie. Put them beside your finger like this so you'll know which ones are this long. See? This one goes from the tip of your finger to the base of your thumb. Now you just pick out another one that goes from the tip of your finger down to the same place and it will be right." Frankie tried and he couldn't do it. When Doc went upstairs Frankie crawled in the excelsior box and didn't come out all afternoon.

But Frankie was a nice, good, kind boy. He learned to light Doc's cigars and he wanted Doc to smoke all the time so he could light the cigars.

Better than anything else Frankie loved it when there were parties upstairs in the laboratory. When girls and men gathered to sit and talk, when the great phonograph played music that throbbed in his stomach and made beautiful and huge pictures form vaguely in his head, Frankie loved it. Then he crouched down in a corner behind a chair where he was hidden and could watch and listen. When there was laughter at a joke he didn't understand Frankie laughed delightedly behind his chair and when the conversation dealt with abstractions his brow furrowed and he became intent and serious.

One afternoon he did a desperate thing. There was a small party in the laboratory. Doc was in the kitchen pouring beer when Frankie appeared beside him. Frankie grabbed a glass of beer and rushed it through the door and gave it to a girl sitting in a big chair.

She took the glass and said, "Why, thank you," and she smiled at him.

And Doc coming through the door said, "Yes, Frankie is a great help to me."

Frankie couldn't forget that. He did the thing in his mind over and over, just how he had taken the glass and just how the girl sat and then her voice—"Why, thank you," and Doc—"a great help to me—Frankie is a great help to me—sure Frankie is a great help— Frankie," and Oh my God!

He knew a big party was coming because Doc bought steaks and a great deal of beer and Doc let him help clean out all the upstairs. But that was nothing, for a great plan had formed in Frankie's mind and he could see just how it would be. He went over it again and again. It was beautiful. It was perfect.

Then the party started and people came and sat in the front room, girls and young women and men.

Frankie had to wait until he had the kitchen to himself and the door closed. And it was some time before he had it so. But at last he was alone and the door was shut. He could hear the chatter of conversation and the music from the great phonograph. He worked very quietly—first the tray—then get out the glasses without breaking any. Now fill them with beer and let the foam settle a little and then fill again.

Now he was ready. He took a great breath and opened the door. The music and the talk roared around him. Frankie picked up the tray of beer and walked through the door. He knew how. He went straight toward the same young woman who had thanked him before. And then right in front of her, the thing happened, the coordination failed, the hands fumbled, the muscles panicked, the nerves telegraphed to a dead operator, the responses did not come back. Tray and beer collapsed forward into the young woman's lap. For a moment Frankie stood still. And then he turned and ran.

The room was quiet. They could hear him run downstairs, and go into the cellar. They heard a hollow scrabbling sound—and then silence.

Doc walked quietly down the stairs and into the cellar. Frankie was in the excelsior box burrowed down clear to the bottom, with the pile of excelsior on top of him. Doc could hear him whimpering there. Doc waited for a moment and then he went quietly back upstairs.

There wasn't a thing in the world he could do.

11

The Model T Ford truck of Lee Chong had a dignified history. In 1923 it had been a passenger car belonging to Dr. W. T. Waters. He used it for five years and sold it to an insurance man named Rattle. Mr. Rattle was not a careful man. The car he got in clean nice condition he drove like fury. Mr. Rattle drank on Saturday nights and the car suffered. The fenders were broken and bent. He was a pedal rider too and the bands had to be changed often. When Mr. Rattle embezzled a client's money and ran away to San José, he was caught with a high-hair blonde and sent up within ten days.

The body of the car was so battered that its next owner cut it in two and added a little truck bed.

The next owner took off the front of the cab and the windshield. He used it to haul squids and he liked a fresh breeze to blow in his face. His name was Francis Almones and he had a sad life, for he always made just a fraction less than he needed to live. His father had left him a little money but year by year and month by month, no matter how hard Francis worked or how careful he was, his money grew less until he just dried up and blew away.

Lee Chong got the truck in payment of a grocery bill.

By this time the truck was little more than four wheels and an engine and the engine was so crotchety and sullen and senile that it required expert care and consideration. Lee Chong did not give it these things, with the result that the truck stood in the tall grass back of the grocery most of the time with the mallows growing between its spokes. It had solid tires on its back wheels and blocks held its front wheels off the ground.

Probably any one of the boys from the Palace Flophouse could have made the truck run, for they were all competent practical mechanics, but Gay was an inspired mechanic. There is no term comparable to green thumbs to apply to such a mechanic, but there should be. For there are men who can look, listen, tap, make an adjustment, and a machine works. Indeed there are men near whom a car runs better. And such a one was Gay. His fingers on a timer or a carburetor adjustment screw were gentle and wise and sure. He could fix the delicate electric motors in the laboratory. He could have worked in the canneries all the time had he wished, for in that industry, which complains bitterly when it does not make back its total investment every year in profits, the machinery is much less important than the fiscal statement. Indeed, if you could can sardines with ledgers, the owners would have been very happy. As it was they used decrepit, struggling old horrors of machines that needed the constant attention of a man like Gay.

Mack got the boys up early. They had their coffee and immediately moved over to the truck where it lay among the weeds. Gay was in charge. He kicked the blocked-up front wheels. "Go borrow a pump and get those pumped up," he said. Then he put a stick in the gasoline tank under the board which served as a seat. By some miracle there was a half inch of gasoline in the tank. Now Gay went over the most probable difficulties. He took out the coil boxes, scraped the points, adjusted the gap, and put them back. He opened the carburetor to see that gas came through. He pushed on the crank to see that the whole shaft wasn't frozen and the pistons rusted in their cylinders.

Meanwhile the pump arrived and Eddie and Jones spelled each other on the tires.

Gay hummed, "Dum tiddy—dum tiddy," as he worked. He removed the spark plugs and scraped the points and bored the carbon out. Then Gay drained a little gasoline into a can and poured some into each cylinder before he put the spark plugs back. He straightened up. "We're going to need a couple of dry cells," he said. "See if Lee Chong will let us have a couple."

Mack departed and returned almost immediately with a universal No which was designed by Lee Chong to cover all future requests.

Gay thought deeply. "I know where's a couple— pretty good ones too, but I won't go get them."

"Where?" asked Mack.

"Down cellar at my house," said Gay. "They run the front doorbell. If one of you fellas wants to kind of edge into my cellar without my wife seeing you, they're on top of the side stringer on the lefthand side as you go in. But for God's sake, don't let my wife catch you."

A conference elected Eddie to go and he departed.

"If you get caught don't mention me," Gay called out after him. Meanwhile Gay tested the bands. The low-high pedal didn't quite touch the floor so he knew there was a little band left. The brake pedal did touch the floor so there was no brake, but the reverse pedal had lots of band left. On a Model T Ford the reverse is your margin of safety. When your brake is gone, you can use reverse as a brake. And when the low gear band is worn too thin to pull up a steep hill, why you can turn around and back up it. Gay found there was plenty of reverse and he knew everything was all right.

It was a good omen that Eddie came back with the dry cells without trouble. Mrs. Gay had been in the kitchen. Eddie could hear her walking about but she didn't hear Eddie. He was very good at such things.

Gay connected the dry cells and he advanced the gas and retarded the spark lever. "Twist her tail," he said.

He was such a wonder, Gay was—the little mechanic of God, the St. Francis of all things that turn and twist and explode, the St. Francis of coils and armatures and gears. And if at some time all the heaps of jalopies, cut-down Dusenbergs, Buicks, De Sotos and Plymouths, American Austins and Isotta-Fraschinis praise God in a great chorus—it will be largely due to Gay and his brotherhood.

One twist—one little twist and the engine caught and labored and faltered and caught again. Gay advanced the spark and reduced the gas. He switched

over to the magneto and the Ford of Lee Chong chuckled and jiggled and clattered happily as though it knew
it was working for a man who loved and understood it.

There were two small technical legal difficulties with
the truck—it had no recent license plates and it had no
lights. But the boys hung a rag permanently and acci-
dentally on the rear plate to conceal its vintage and they
dabbed the front plate with good thick mud. The equipment of the expedition was slight: some long-handled
frog nets and some gunny sacks. City hunters going out
for sport load themselves with food and liquor, but not
Mack. He presumed rightly that the country was where
food came from. Two loaves of bread and what was left
of Eddie's wining jug was all the supply. The party
clambered on the truck—Gay drove and Mack sat beside him; they bumped around the corner of Lee
Chong's and down through the lot, threading among the
pipes. Mr. Malloy waved at them from his seat by the
boiler. Gay eased across the sidewalk and down off the
curb gently because the front tires showed fabric all the
way around. With all their alacrity, it was afternoon
when they got started.

The truck eased into Red Williams' service station.
Mack got out and gave his paper to Red. He said,
"Doc was a little short of change. So if you'll put five
gallons in and just give us a buck instead of the other
five gallons, why that's what Doc wants. He had to go
south, you know. Had a big deal down there."

Red smiled good-naturedly. "You know, Mack," he
said, "Doc got to figuring if there was some kind of
loophole, and he put his finger on the same one you
did. Doc's a pretty bright fellow. So he phoned me last
night."

"Put in the whole ten gallons," said Mack. "No—wait. It'll slop around and spill. Put in five and give us five in a can—one of them sealed cans."

Red smiled happily. "Doc kind of figured that one too," he said.

"Put in ten gallons," said Mack. "And don't go leaving none in the hose."

The little expedition did not go through the center of Monterey. A delicacy about the license plates and the lights made Gay choose back streets. There would be the time when they would go up Carmel Hill and down into the Valley, a good four miles on a main highway, exposed to any passing cop until they turned up the fairly unfrequented Carmel Valley road. Gay chose a back street that brought them out on the main highway at Peter's Gate just before the steep Carmel Hill starts. Gay took a good noisy clattering run at the hill and in fifty yards he put the pedal down to low. He knew it wouldn't work, the band was worn too thin. On the level it was all right but not on a hill. He stopped, let the truck back around and aimed it down the hill. Then he gave it the gas and the reverse pedal. And the reverse was not worn. The truck crawled steadily and slowly but backward up Carmel Hill.

And they very nearly made it. The radiator boiled, of course, but most Model T experts believed that it wasn't working well if it wasn't boiling.

Someone should write an erudite essay on the moral, physical, and esthetic effect of the Model T Ford on the American nation. Two generations of Americans knew more about the Ford coil than the clitoris, about the planetary system of gears than the solar system of stars. With the Model T, part of the concept of private property disappeared. Pliers ceased to be privately owned and a tire pump belonged to the last man who had picked it up. Most of the babies of the period were conceived in Model T Fords and not a few were born in them. The theory of the Anglo Saxon home became so warped that it never quite recovered.

The truck backed sturdily up Carmel Hill and it got past the Jack's Peak road and was just going into the last and steepest pull when the motor's breathing thickened, gulped, and strangled. It seemed very quiet when the motor was still. Gay, who was heading downhill anyway, ran down the hill fifty feet and turned into the Jack's Peak road entrance.

"What is it?" Mack asked.

"Carburetor, I think," said Gay. The engine sizzled and creaked with heat and the jet of steam that blew down the overflow pipe sounded like the hiss of an alligator.

The carburetor of a Model T is not complicated but it needs all of its parts to function. There is a needle valve, and the point must be on the needle and must sit in its hole or the carburetor does not work.

Gay held the needle in his hand and the point was broken off. "How in hell you s'pose that happened?" he asked.

"Magic," said Mack, "just pure magic. Can you fix it?"

"Hell, no," said Gay. "Got to get another one."

"How much they cost?"

"About a buck if you buy one new—quarter at a wrecker's."

"You got a buck?" Mack asked.

"Yeah, but I won't need it."

"Well, get back as soon as you can, will you? We'll just stay right here."

"Anyways you won't go running off without a needle valve," said Gay. He stepped out to the road. He thumbed three cars before one stopped for him. The boys watched him climb in and start down the hill. They didn't see him again for one hundred and eighty days.

Oh, the infinity of possibility! How could it happen that the car that picked up Gay broke down before it got into Monterey? If Gay had not been a mechanic, he would not have fixed the car. If he had not fixed it the owner wouldn't have taken him to Jimmy Brucia's for a drink. And why was it Jimmy's birthday? Out of all the possibilities in the world—the millions of them—only events occurred that lead to the Salinas jail. Sparky Enea and Tiny Colletti had made up a quarrel and were helping Jimmy to celebrate his birthday. The blonde came in. The musical argument in front of the juke box. Gay's new friend who knew a judo hold and tried to show it to Sparky and got his wrist broken when the hold went wrong. The policeman with a bad stomach—all unrelated, irrelevant details and yet all running in one direction. Fate just didn't intend Gay to go on that frog hunt and Fate took a hell of a lot of trouble and people and accidents to keep him from it. When the final climax came with the front of Holman's bootery broken out and the party trying on the shoes in the display window only Gay didn't hear the fire whistle. Only Gay didn't go to the fire and when the police came they found him sitting all alone in Holman's window wearing one brown oxford and one patent leather dress shoe with a gray cloth top.

Back at the truck the boys built a little fire when it got dark and the chill crept up from the ocean. The pines above them soughed in the fresh sea wind. The boys lay in the pine needles and looked at the lonely sky through the pine branches. For a while they spoke of the difficulties Gay must be having getting a needle valve and then gradually as the time passed they didn't mention him any more.

"Somebody should of gone with him," said Mack.

About ten o'clock Eddie got up. "There's a construction camp a piece up the hill," he said. "I think I'll go up and see if they got any Model T's."

12

Monterey is a city with a long and brilliant literary tradition. It remembers with pleasure and some glory that Robert Louis Stevenson lived there. Treasure Island certainly has the topography and the coastal plan of Pt. Lobos. More recently in Carmel there have been a great number of literary men about, but there is not the old flavor, the old dignity of the true belles-lettres. Once the town was greatly outraged over what the citizens considered a slight to an author. It had to do with the death of Josh Billings, the great humorist.

Where the new postoffice is, there used to be a deep gulch with water flowing in it and a little foot bridge over it. On one side of the gulch was a fine old adobe and on the other the house of the doctor who handled all the sickness, birth, and death in the town. He worked with animals too and, having studied in France, he even dabbled in the new practice of embalming bodies before they were buried. Some of the old-timers considered this sentimental and some thought it wasteful and to some it was sacrilegious since there was no provision for it in any sacred volume. But the better and richer families were coming to it and it looked to become a fad.

One morning elderly Mr. Carriaga was walking from his house on the hill down toward Alvarado Street. He was just crossing the foot bridge when his attention was drawn to a small boy and a dog struggling up out of the gulch. The boy carried a liver while the dog dragged yards of intestine at the end of which a stomach dangled. Mr. Carriaga paused and addressed the little boy politely: "Good morning."

In those days little boys were courteous. "Good morning, sir."

"Where are you going with the liver?"

"I'm going to make some chum and catch some mackerel."

Mr. Carriaga smiled. "And the dog, will he catch mackerel too?"

"The dog found that. It's his, sir. We found them in the gulch."

Mr. Carriaga smiled and strolled on and then his mind began to work. That isn't a beef liver, it's too small. And it isn't a calf's liver, it's too red. It isn't a sheep's liver— Now his mind was alert. At the corner he met Mr. Ryan.

"Anyone die in Monterey last night?" he asked.

"Not that I know of," said Mr. Ryan.

"Anyone killed?"

"No."

They walked on together and Mr. Carriaga told about the little boy and the dog.

At the Adobe Bar a number of citizens were gathered for their morning conversation. There Mr. Carri-

aga told his story again and he had just finished when
the constable came into the Adobe. He should know if
anyone had died. "No one died in Monterey," he said.
"But Josh Billings died out at the Hotel del Monte."

The men in the bar were silent. And the same
thought went through all their minds. Josh Billings was
a great man, a great writer. He had honored Monterey
by dying there and he had been degraded. Without
much discussion a committee formed made up of
everyone there. The stern men walked quickly to the
gulch and across the foot bridge and they hammered
on the door of the doctor who had studied in France.

He had worked late. The knocking got him out of
bed and brought him tousled of hair and beard to the
door in his nightgown. Mr. Carriaga addressed him
sternly: "Did you embalm Josh Billings?"

"Why—yes."

"What did you do with his tripas?"

"Why—I threw them in the gulch where I always
do."

They made him dress quickly then and they hurried
down to the beach. If the little boy had gone quickly
about his business, it would have been too late. He
was just getting into a boat when the committee arrived. The intestine was in the sand where the dog had
abandoned it.

Then the French doctor was made to collect the
parts. He was forced to wash them reverently and pick
out as much sand as possible. The doctor himself had
to stand the expense of the leaden box which went into
the coffin of Josh Billings. For Monterey was not a
town to let dishonor come to a literary man.

13

Mack and the boys slept peacefully on the pine needles. Some time before dawn Eddie came back. He had gone a long way before he found a Model T. And then when he did, he wondered whether or not it would be a good idea to take the needle out of its seat. It might not fit. So he took the whole carburetor. The boys didn't wake up when he got back. He lay down beside them and slept under the pine trees. There was one nice thing about Model T's. The parts were not only interchangeable, they were unidentifiable.

There is a beautiful view from the Carmel grade, the curving bay with the waves creaming on the sand, the dune country around Seaside and right at the bottom of the hill, the warm intimacy of the town.

Mack got up in the dawn and hustled his pants where they bound him and he stood looking down on the bay. He could see some of the purse-seiners coming in. A tanker stood over against Seaside, taking on oil. Behind him the rabbits stirred in the bush. Then the sun came up and shook the night chill out of the air the way you'd shake a rug. When he felt the first sun warmth, Mack shivered.

The boys ate a little bread while Eddie installed the new carburetor. And when it was ready, they didn't bother to crank it. They pushed it out to the highway and coasted in gear until it started. And then Eddie driving, they backed up over the rise, over the top and turned and headed forward and down past Hatton Fields. In Carmel Valley the artichoke plants stood gray green, and the willows were lush along the river. They turned left up the valley. Luck blossomed from the first. A dusty Rhode Island red rooster who had wandered too far from his own farmyard crossed the road and Eddie hit him without running too far off the road. Sitting in the back of the truck, Hazel picked him as they went and let the feathers fly from his hand, the most widely distributed evidence on record, for there was a little breeze in the morning blowing down from Jamesburg and some of the red chicken feathers were deposited on Pt. Lobos and some even blew out to sea.

The Carmel is a lovely little river. It isn't very long but in its course it has everything a river should have. It rises in the mountains, and tumbles down a while, runs through shallows, is dammed to make a lake, spills over the dam, crackles among round boulders, wanders lazily under sycamores, spills into pools where trout live, drops in against banks where crayfish live. In the winter it becomes a torrent, a mean little fierce river, and in the summer it is a place for children to wade in and for fishermen to wander in. Frogs blink from its banks and the deep ferns grow beside it. Deer and foxes come to drink from it, secretly in the morning and evening, and now and then a mountain lion crouched flat laps its water. The farms of the rich little valley back up to the river and take its water for the orchards and the vegetables. The quail call beside it and the wild doves come whistling in at dusk. Raccoons pace its edges looking for frogs. It's everything a river should be.

A few miles up the valley the river cuts in under a high cliff from which vines and ferns hang down. At the base of this cliff there is a pool, green and deep, and on the other side of the pool there is a little sandy place where it is good to sit and to cook your dinner.

Mack and the boys came down to this place happily. It was perfect. If frogs were available, they would be here. It was a place to relax, a place to be happy. On the way out they had thriven. In addition to the big red chicken there was a sack of carrots which had fallen from a vegetable truck, half a dozen onions which had not. Mack had a bag of coffee in his pocket. In the truck there was a five-gallon can with the top cut off. The wining jug was nearly half full. Such things as salt and pepper had been brought. Mack and the boys would have thought anyone who traveled without salt, pepper, and coffee very silly indeed.

Without effort, confusion, or much thought, four round stones were rolled together on the little beach. The rooster who had challenged the sunrise of this very day lay dismembered and clean in water in the five-gallon can with peeled onions about him, while a little fire of dead willow sticks sputtered between the stones, a very little fire. Only fools build big fires. It would take a long time to cook this rooster, for it had taken him a long time to achieve his size and muscularity. But as the water began to boil gently about him, he smelled good from the beginning.

Mack gave them a pep talk. "The best time for frogs is at night," he said, "so I guess we'll just lay around 'til it gets dark." They sat in the shade and gradually one by one they stretched out and slept.

Mack was right. Frogs do not move around much in the daytime; they hide under ferns and they look secretly out of holes under rocks. The way to catch frogs is with a flashlight at night. The men slept knowing they might have a very active night. Only Hazel stayed awake to replenish the little fire under the cooking chicken.

There is no golden afternoon next to the cliff. When the sun went over it at about two o'clock a whispering shade came to the beach. The sycamores rustled in the afternoon breeze. Little water snakes slipped down to the rocks and then gently entered the water and swam along through the pool, their heads held up like little periscopes and a tiny wake spreading behind them. A big trout jumped in the pool. The gnats and mosquitoes which avoid the sun came out and buzzed over the water. All of the sun bugs, the flies, the dragonflies, the wasps, the hornets, went home. And as the shadow came to the beach, as the first quail began to call, Mack and the boys awakened. The smell of the chicken stew was heartbreaking. Hazel had picked a fresh bay leaf from a tree by the river and he had dropped it in. The carrots were in now. Coffee in its own can was simmering on its own rock, far enough from the flame so that it did not boil too hard. Mack awakened, started up, stretched, staggered to the pool, washed his face with cupped hands, hacked, spat, washed out his mouth, broke wind, tightened his belt, scratched his legs, combed his wet hair with his fingers, drank from the jug, belched and sat down by the fire. "By God that smells good," he said.

Men all do about the same things when they wake up. Mack's process was loosely the one all of them followed. And soon they had all come to the fire and complimented Hazel. Hazel stuck his pocket knife into the muscles of the chicken.

"He ain't going to be what you'd call tender," said Hazel. "You'd have to cook him about two weeks to get him tender. How old about do you judge he was, Mack?"

"I'm forty-eight and I ain't as tough as he is," said Mack.

Eddie said, "How old can a chicken get, do you think—that's if nobody pushes him around or he don't get sick?"

"That's something nobody isn't ever going to find out," said Jones.

It was a pleasant time. The jug went around and warmed them.

Jones said, "Eddie, I don't mean to complain none. I was just thinkin'. S'pose you had two or three jugs back of the bar. S'pose you put all the whiskey in one and all the wine in another and all the beer in another—"

A slightly shocked silence followed the suggestion. "I didn't mean nothing," said Jones quickly. "I like it this way—" Jones talked too much then because he knew he had made a social blunder and he wasn't able to stop. "What I like about it this way is you never know what kind of a drunk you're going to get out of it," he said. "You take whiskey," he said hurriedly. "You more or less knows what you'll do. A fightin' guy fights and a cryin' guy cries, but this——" he said magnanimously—"why you don't know whether it'll run you up a pine tree or start you swimming to Santa Cruz. It's more fun that way," he said weakly.

"Speaking of swimming," said Mack to fill in the indelicate place in the conversation and to shut Jones up. "I wonder whatever happened to that guy McKinley Moran. Remember that deep sea diver?"

"I remember him," said Hughie. "I and him used to hang around together. He just didn't get much work and then he got to drinking. It's kind of tough on you divin' and drinkin'. Got to worryin' too. Finally he sold his suit and helmet and pump and went on a hell of a drunk and then he left town. I don't know where he went. He wasn't no good after he went down after that Wop that got took down with the anchor from the Twelve Brothers. McKinley just dove down. Bust his eardrums, and he wasn't no good after that. Didn't hurt the Wop a bit."

Mack sampled the jug again. "He used to make a lot of dough during Prohibition," Mack said. "Used to get twenty-five bucks a day from the government to dive lookin' for liquor on the bottom and he got three dollars a case from Louie for not findin' it. Had it worked out so he brought up one case a day to keep the government happy. Louie didn't mind that none. Made it so they didn't get in no new divers. McKinley made a lot of dough."

"Yeah," said Hughie. "But he's like everybody else—gets some dough and he wants to get married. He got married three times before his dough run out. I could always tell. He'd buy a white fox fur piece and bang!—next thing you'd know, he's married."

"I wonder what happened to Gay," Eddie asked. It was the first time they had spoken of him.

"Same thing, I guess," said Mack. "You just can't trust a married guy. No matter how much he hates his old lady why he'll go back to her. Get to thinkin' and broodin' and back he'll go. You can't trust him no more. Take Gay," said Mack. "His old lady hits him. But I bet you when Gay's away from her three days, he gets it figured out that it's his fault and he goes back to make it up to her."

They ate long and daintily, spearing out pieces of chicken, holding the dripping pieces until they cooled and then gnawing the muscled meat from the bone. They speared the carrots on pointed willow switches and finally they passed the can and drank the juice. And around them the evening crept in as delicately as music. The quail called each other down to the water. The trout jumped in the pool. And the moths came down and fluttered about the pool as the daylight mixed into the darkness. They passed the coffee can about and they were warm and fed and silent. At last Mack said, "God damn it. I hate a liar."

"Who's been lyin' to you?" Eddie asked.

"Oh, I don't mind a guy that tells a little one to get along or to hop up a conversation, but I hate a guy that lies to himself."

"Who done that?" Eddie asked.

"Me," said Mack. "And maybe you guys. Here we are," he said earnestly, "the whole God damned shabby lot of us. We worked it out that we wanted to give Doc a party. So we come out here and have a hell of a lot of fun. Then we'll go back and get the dough from Doc. There's five of us, so we'll drink five times as much liquor as he will. And I ain't sure we're doin' it for Doc. I ain't sure we ain't doin' it for ourselves. And Doc's too nice a fella to do that to. Doc is the nicest fella I ever knew. I don't want to be the kind of guy that would take advantage of him. You know one time I put the bee on him for a buck. I give him a hell of a story. Right in the middle I seen he knew God damn well the story was so much malarky. So right in the middle I says, 'Doc, that's a fuggin' lie!' And he put his hand in his pocket and brought out a buck. 'Mack,' he says, 'I figure a guy that needs it bad enough to make up a lie to get it, really needs it,' and he give me the buck. I paid him that buck back the next day. I never did spend it. Just kept it overnight and then give it back to him."

Hazel said, "There ain't nobody likes a party better than Doc. We're givin' him the party. What the hell is the beef?"

"I don't know," said Mack, "I'd just like to give him something when I didn't get most of it back."

"How about a present?" Hughie suggested. "S'pose we just bought the whiskey and give it to him and let him do what he wants."

"Now you're talkin'," said Mack. "That's just what we'll do. We'll just give him the whiskey and fade out."

"You know what'll happen," said Eddie. "Henri and them people from Carmel will smell that whiskey out and then instead of only five of us there'll be twenty. Doc told me one time himself they can smell him fryin' a steak from Cannery Row clear down to Point Sur. I don't see the percentage. He'd come out better if we give him the party ourselves."

Mack considered this reasoning. "Maybe you're right," he said at last. "But s'pose we give him something except whiskey, maybe cuff links with his initials."

"Oh, horse shit," said Hazel. "Doc don't want stuff like that."

The night was in by now and the stars were white in the sky. Hazel fed the fire and it put a little room of light on the beach. Over the hill a fox was barking sharply. And now in the night the smell of sage came down from the hills. The water chuckled on the stones where it went out of the deep pool.

Mack was mulling over the last piece of reasoning when the sound of footsteps on the ground made them turn. A man dark and large stalked near and he had a shotgun over his arm and a pointer walked shyly and delicately at his heel.

"What the hell are you doing here?" he asked.

"Nothing," said Mack.

"The land's posted. No fishing, hunting, fires, camping. Now you just pack up and put that fire out and get off this land."

Mack stood up humbly. "I didn't know, Captain," he said. "Honest we never seen the sign, Captain."

"There's signs all over. You couldn't have missed them."

"Look, Captain, we made a mistake and we're sorry," said Mack. He paused and looked closely at the slouching figure. "You are a military man, aren't you, sir? I can always tell. Military man don't carry his shoulders the same as ordinary people. I was in the army so long, I can always tell."

Imperceptibly the shoulders of the man straightened, nothing obvious, but he held himself differently.

"I don't allow fires on my place," he said.

"Well, we're sorry," said Mack. "We'll get right out, Captain. You see, we're workin' for some scientists. We're tryin' to get some frogs. They're workin' on cancer and we're helpin' out getting some frogs."

The man hesitated for a moment. "What do they do with the frogs?" he asked.

"Well, sir," said Mack, "they give cancer to the frogs and then they can study and experiment and they got it nearly licked if they can just get some frogs. But if you don't want us on your land, Captain, we'll get right out. Never would of come in if we knew." Suddenly Mack seemed to see the pointer for the first time. "By God that's a fine-lookin' bitch," he said enthusiastically. "She looks like Nola that win the field trials in Virginia last year. She a Virginia dog, Captain?"

The captain hesitated and then he lied. "Yes," he said shortly. "She's lame. Tick got her right on her shoulder."

Mack was instantly solicitous. "Mind if I look, Captain? Come, girl. Come on, girl." The pointer looked up at her master and then sidled up to Mack. "Pile on some twigs so I can see," he said to Hazel.

"It's up where she can't lick it," said the captain and he leaned over Mack's shoulder to look.

Mack pressed some pus out of the evil-looking crater on the dog's shoulder. "I had a dog once had a thing like this and it went right in and killed him. She just had pups, didn't she?"

"Yes," said the captain, "six. I put iodine on that place."

"No," said Mack, "that won't draw. You got any epsom salts up at your place?"

"Yes—there's a big bottle."

"Well you make a hot poultice of epsom salts and put it on there. She's weak, you know, from the pups. Be a shame if she got sick now. You'd lose the pups too." The pointer looked deep into Mack's eyes and then she licked his hand.

"Tell you what I'll do, Captain. I'll look after her myself. Epsom salt'll do the trick. That's the best thing."

The captain stroked the dog's head. "You know, I've got a pond up by the house that's so full of frogs I can't sleep nights. Why don't you look up there? They bellow all night. I'd be glad to get rid of them."

"That's mighty nice of you," said Mack. "I'll bet those docs would thank you for that. But I'd like to get a poultice on this dog." He turned to the others. "You put out this fire," he said. "Make sure there ain't a spark left and clean up around. You don't want to leave no mess. I and the captain will go and take care of Nola here. You fellows follow along when you get cleared up." Mack and the captain walked away together.

Hazel kicked sand on the fire. "I bet Mack could of been president of the U.S. if he wanted," he said.

"What could he do with it if he had it?" Jones asked. "There wouldn't be no fun in that."

14

Early morning is a time of magic in Cannery Row. In the gray time after the light has come and before the sun has risen, the Row seems to hang suspended out of time in a silvery light. The street lights go out, and the weeds are a brilliant green. The corrugated iron of the canneries glows with the pearly lucence of platinum or old pewter. No automobiles are running then. The street is silent of progress and business. And the rush and drag of the waves can be heard as they splash in among the piles of the canneries. It is a time of great peace, a deserted time, a little era of rest. Cats drip over the fences and slither like syrup over the ground to look for fish heads. Silent early morning dogs parade majestically picking and choosing judiciously whereon to pee. The sea gulls come flapping in to sit on the cannery roofs to await the day of refuse. They sit on the roof peaks shoulder to shoulder. From the rocks near the Hopkins Marine Station comes the barking of sea lions like the baying of hounds. The air is cool and fresh. In the back gardens the gophers push up the morning mounds of fresh damp earth and they creep out and drag flowers into their holes. Very few people are about, just enough to make it seem more deserted than it is. One of Dora's girls comes home from a call on a patron too wealthy or too sick to visit the Bear Flag. Her makeup is a little sticky and her feet are tired. Lee Chong brings the garbage cans out and stands them on the curb. The old Chinaman comes out of the sea and flap-flaps across the street and up past the Palace. The cannery watchmen look out and blink at the morning light. The bouncer at the Bear Flag steps out on the porch in his shirtsleeves and stretches and yawns and scratches his stomach. The snores of Mr. Malloy's tenants in the pipes have a deep tunnelly quality. It is the hour of the pearl—the interval between day and night when time stops and examines itself.

On such a morning and in such a light two soldiers and two girls strolled easily along the street. They had come out of La Ida and they were very tired and very happy. The girls were hefty, big breasted and strong and their blonde hair was in slight disarray. They wore printed rayon party dresses, wrinkled now and clinging to their convexities. And each girl wore a soldier's cap, one far back on her head and the other with the visor down almost on her nose. They were full-lipped, broad-nosed, hippy girls and they were very tired.

The soldiers' tunics were unbuttoned and their belts were threaded through their epaulets. The ties were pulled down a little so the shirt collars could be unbuttoned. And the soldiers wore the girls' hats, one a tiny yellow straw boater with a bunch of daisies on the crown, the other a white knitted half-hat to which medallions of blue cellophane adhered. They walked holding hands, swinging their hands rhythmically. The soldier on the outside had a large brown paper bag filled with cold canned beer. They strolled softly in the pearly light. They had had a hell of a time and they felt good. They smiled delicately like weary children remembering a party. They looked at one another and smiled and they swung their hands. Past the Bear Flag they went and said "Hiya," to the bouncer who was scratching his stomach. They listened to the snores from the pipes and laughed a little. At Lee Chong's they stopped and looked into the messy display window where tools and clothes and food crowded for attention. Swinging their hands and scuffling their feet, they came to the end of Cannery Row and turned up to the railroad track. The girls climbed up on the rails and walked along on them and the soldiers put their arms around the plump waists to keep them from falling. Then they went past the boat works and turned down into the park-like property of the Hopkins Marine Station. There is a tiny curved beach in front of the station, a miniature beach between little reefs. The gentle morning waves licked up the beach and whispered softly. The fine smell of seaweed came from the exposed rocks. As the four came to the beach a sliver of the sun broke over Tom Work's land across the head of the bay and it gilded the water and made the rocks yellow. The girls sat formally down in the sand and straightened their skirts over their knees. One of the soldiers punched holes in four cans of beer and handed them around. And then the men lay down and put their heads in the girls' laps and looked up into their faces. And they smiled at each other, a tired and peaceful and wonderful secret.

From up near the station came the barking of a dog—the watchman, a dark and surly man, had seen them and his black and surly cocker spaniel had seen them. He shouted at them and when they did not move he came down on the beach and his dog barked monotonously. "Don't you know you can't lay around here? You got to get off. This is private property!"

The soldiers did not even seem to hear him. They smiled on and the girls were stroking their hair over the temples. At last in slow motion one of the soldiers turned his head so that his cheek was cradled between the girl's legs. He smiled benevolently at the caretaker. "Why don't you take a flying fuggut the moon?" he said kindly and he turned back to look at the girl.

The sun lighted her blonde hair and she scratched him over one ear. They didn't even see the caretaker go back to his house.

15

By the time the boys got up to the farmhouse Mack was in the kitchen. The pointer bitch lay on her side, and Mack held a cloth saturated with epsom salts against her tick bite. Among her legs the big fat wiener pups nuzzled and bumped for milk and the bitch looked patiently up into Mack's face saying, "You see how it is? I try to tell him but he doesn't understand."

The captain held a lamp and looked down on Mack.

"I'm glad to know about that," he said.

Mack said, "I don't want to tell you about your business, sir, but these pups ought to be weaned. She ain't got a hell of a lot of milk left and them pups are chewin' her to pieces."

"I know," said the captain. "I s'pose I should have drowned them all but one. I've been so busy trying to keep the place going. People don't take the interest in bird dogs they used to. It's all poodles and boxers and Dobermans."

"I know," said Mack. "And there ain't no dog like a pointer for a man. I don't know what's come over people. But you wouldn't of drowned them, would you, sir?"

"Well," said the captain, "since my wife went into politics, I'm just running crazy. She got elected to the Assembly for this district and when the Legislature isn't in session, she's off making speeches. And when she's home she's studying all the time and writing bills."

"Must be lousy in—I mean it must be pretty lonely," said Mack. "Now if I had a pup like this—" he picked up a squirming fuzz-faced pup—"why I bet I'd have a real bird dog in three years. I'd take a bitch every time."

"Would you like to have one?" the captain asked.

Mack looked up. "You mean you'd let me have one? Oh! Jesus Christ yes."

"Take your pick," said the captain. "Nobody seems to understand bird dogs any more."

The boys stood in the kitchen and gathered quick impressions. It was obvious that the wife was away— the opened cans, the frying pan with lace from fried eggs still sticking to it, the crumbs on the kitchen table, the open box of shotgun shells on the bread box all shrieked of the lack of a woman, while the white curtains and the papers on the dish shelves and the too small towels on the rack told them a woman had been there. And they were unconsciously glad she wasn't there. The kind of women who put papers on shelves and had little towels like that instinctively distrusted and disliked Mack and the boys. Such women knew that they were the worst threats to a home, for they offered ease and thought and companionship as opposed to neatness, order, and properness. They were very glad she was away.

Now the captain seemed to feel that they were doing him a favor. He didn't want them to leave. He said hesitantly, "S'pose you boys would like a little something to warm you up before you go out for the frogs?"

The others looked at Mack. Mack was frowning as though he was thinking it through. "When we're out doin' scientific stuff, we make it a kind of rule not to touch nothin'," he said, and then quickly as though he might have gone too far, "But seein' as how you been so nice to us—well I wouldn't mind a short one myself. I don't know about the boys."

The boys agreed that they wouldn't mind a short one either. The captain got a flashlight and went down in the cellar. They could hear him moving lumber and boxes about and he came back upstairs with a five-gallon oak keg in his arms. He set it on the table. "During Prohibition I got some corn whiskey and laid it away. I just got to thinking I'd like to see how it is. It's pretty old now. I'd almost forgot it. You see—my wife—" he let it go at that because it was apparent that they understood. The captain knocked out the oak plug from the end of the keg and got glasses down from the shelf that had scallop-edged paper laid on it. It is a hard job to pour a small drink from a five-gallon keg. Each of them got half a water glass of the clear brown liquor. They waited ceremoniously for the captain and then they said, "Over the river," and tossed it back. They swallowed, tasted their tongues, sucked their lips, and there was a far-away look in their eyes.

Mack peered into his empty glass as though some holy message were written in the bottom. And then he raised his eyes. "You can't say nothin' about that," he said. "They don't put that in bottles." He breathed in deeply and sucked his breath as it came out. "I don't think I ever tasted nothin' as good as that," he said.

The captain looked pleased. His glance wandered back to the keg. "It is good," he said. "You think we might have another little one?"

Mack stared into his glass again. "Maybe a short one," he agreed. "Wouldn't it be easier to pour out some in a pitcher? You're liable to spill it that way."

Two hours later they recalled what they had come for.

The frog pool was square—fifty feet wide and seventy feet long and four feet deep. Lush soft grass grew about its edge and a little ditch brought the water from the river to it and from it little ditches went out to the orchards. There were frogs there all right, thousands of them. Their voices beat the night, they boomed and barked and croaked and rattled. They sang to the stars, to the waning moon, to the waving grasses. They bellowed love songs and challenges. The men crept through the darkness toward the pool. The captain carried a nearly filled pitcher of whiskey and every man had his own glass. The captain had found them flashlights that worked. Hughie and Jones carried gunny sacks. As they drew quietly near, the frogs heard them coming. The night had been roaring with frog song and then suddenly it was silent. Mack and the boys and the captain sat down on the ground to have one last short one and to map their campaign. And the plan was bold.

During the millennia that frogs and men have lived in the same world, it is probable that men have hunted frogs. And during that time a pattern of hunt and parry has developed. The man with net or bow or lance or gun creeps noiselessly, as he thinks, toward the frog. The pattern requires that the frog sit still, sit very still and wait. The rules of the game require the frog to wait until the final flicker of a second, when the net is descending, when the lance is in the air, when the finger squeezes the trigger, then the frog jumps, plops into the water, swims to the bottom and waits until the man goes away. That is the way it is done, the way it has always been done. Frogs have every right to expect it will always be done that way. Now and then the net is too quick, the lance pierces, the gun flicks and that frog is gone, but it is all fair and in the framework. Frogs don't resent that. But how could they have anticipated Mack's new method? How could they have foreseen the horror that followed? The sudden flashing of lights, the shouting and squealing of men, the rush of feet. Every frog leaped, plopped into the pool, and swam frantically to the bottom. Then into the pool plunged the line of men, stamping, churning, moving in a crazy line up the pool, flinging their feet about. Hysterically the frogs displaced from their placid spots swam ahead of the crazy thrashing feet and the feet came on. Frogs are good swimmers but they haven't much endurance. Down the pool they went until finally they were bunched and crowded against the end. And the feet and wildly plunging bodies followed them. A few frogs lost their heads and floundered among the feet and got through and these were saved. But the majority decided to leave this pool forever, to find a new home in a new country where this kind of thing didn't happen. A wave of frantic, frustrated frogs, big ones, little ones, brown ones, green ones, men frogs and women frogs, a wave of them broke over the bank, crawled, leaped, scrambled. They clambered up the grass, they clutched at each other, little ones rode on big ones. And then—horror on horror—the flashlights found them. Two men gathered them like berries. The line came out of the water and closed in on their rear and gathered them like potatoes. Tens and fifties of them were flung into the gunny sacks, and the sacks filled with tired, frightened, and disillusioned frogs, with dripping, whimpering frogs. Some got away, of course, and some had been saved in the pool. But never in frog history had such an execution taken place. Frogs by the pound, by the fifty pounds. They weren't counted but there must have been six or seven hundred. Then happily Mack tied up the necks of the sacks. They were soaking, dripping wet and the air was cool. They had a short one in the grass before they went back to the house so they wouldn't catch cold.

It is doubtful whether the captain had ever had so much fun. He was indebted to Mack and the boys. Later when the curtains caught fire and were put out with the little towels, the captain told the boys not to mind it. He felt it was an honor to have them burn his house clear down, if they wanted to. "My wife is a wonderful woman," he said in a kind of peroration. "Most wonderful woman. Ought to of been a man. If she was a man I wouldn' of married her." He laughed a long time over that and repeated it three or four times and resolved to remember it so he could tell it to a lot of other people. He filled a jug with whiskey and gave it to Mack. He wanted to go to live with them in the Palace Flophouse. He decided that his wife would like Mack and the boys if she only knew them. Finally he went to sleep on the floor with his head among the puppies. Mack and the boys poured themselves a short one and regarded him seriously.

Mack said, "He give me that jug of whiskey, didn't he? You heard him?"

"Sure he did," said Eddie. "I heard him."

"And he give me a pup?"

"Sure, pick of the litter. We all heard him. Why?"

"I never did roll a drunk and I ain't gonna start now," said Mack. "We got to get out of here. He's gonna wake up feelin' lousy and it's goin' to be all our fault. I just don't want to be here." Mack glanced at the burned curtains, at the floor glistening with whiskey and puppy dirt, at the bacon grease that was coagulating on the stove front. He went to the pups, looked them over carefully, felt bone and frame, looked in eyes and regarded jaws, and he picked out a beautifully spotted bitch with a liver-colored nose and a fine dark yellow eye. "Come on, darling," he said.

They blew out the lamp because of the danger of fire. It was just turning dawn as they left the house.

"I don't think I ever had such a fine trip," said Mack. "But I got to thinkin' about his wife comin' back and it gave me the shivers." The pup whined in his arms and he put it under his coat. "He's a real nice fella," said Mack. "After you get him feelin' easy, that is." He strode on toward the place where they had parked the Ford. "We shouldn't go forgettin' we're doin' all this for Doc," he said. "From the way things are pannin' out, it looks like Doc is a pretty lucky guy."

16

Probably the busiest time the girls of the Bear Flag ever had was the March of the big sardine catch. It wasn't only that the fish ran in silvery billions and money ran almost as freely. A new regiment moved into the Presidio and a new bunch of soldiers always shop around a good deal before they settle down. Dora was short handed just at that time too, for Eva Flanegan had gone to East St. Louis on a vacation, Phyllis Mae had broken her leg getting out of the roller coaster in Santa Cruz, and Elsie Doublebottom had made a novena and wasn't much good for anything else. The men from the sardine fleet, loaded with dough, were in and out all afternoon. They sail at dark and fish all night so they must play in the afternoon. In the evening the soldiers of the new regiment came down and stood around playing the juke box and drinking Coca-Cola and sizing up the girls for the time when they would be paid. Dora was having trouble with her income tax, for she was entangled in that curious enigma which said the business was illegal and then taxed her for it. In addition to everything else there were the regulars—the steady customers who had been coming down for years, the laborers from the gravel pits, the riders from the ranches, the railroad men who came in the front door, and the city officials and prominent business men who came in the rear entrance back by the tracks and who had little chintz sitting rooms assigned to them.

All in all it was a terrific month and right in the middle of it the influenza epidemic had to break out. It came to the whole town. Mrs. Talbot and her daughter of the San Carlos Hotel had it. Tom Work had it. Benjamin Peabody and his wife had it. Excelentísima Maria Antonia Field had it. The whole Gross family came down with it.

The doctors of Monterey—and there were enough of them to take care of the ordinary diseases, accidents and neuroses—were running crazy. They had more business than they could do among clients who if they didn't pay their bills, at least had the money to pay them. Cannery Row which produces a tougher breed than the rest of the town was late in contracting it, but finally it got them too. The schools were closed. There wasn't a house that hadn't feverish children and sick parents. It was not a deadly disease as it was in 1917 but with children it had a tendency to go into the mastoids. The medical profession was very busy, and besides, Cannery Row was not considered a very good financial risk.

Now Doc of the Western Biological Laboratory had no right to practice medicine. It was not his fault that everyone in the Row came to him for medical advice. Before he knew it he found himself running from shanty to shanty taking temperatures, giving physics, borrowing and delivering blankets and even taking food from house to house where mothers looked at him with inflamed eyes from their beds, and thanked him and put the full responsibility for their children's recovery on him. When a case got really out of hand he phoned a local doctor and sometimes one came if it seemed to be an emergency. But to the families it was all emergency. Doc didn't get much sleep. He lived on beer and canned sardines. In Lee Chong's where he went to get beer he met Dora who was there to buy a pair of nail clippers.

"You look done in," Dora said.

"I am," Doc admitted. "I haven't had any sleep for about a week."

"I know," said Dora. "I hear it's bad. Comes at a bad time too."

"Well, we haven't lost anybody yet," said Doc. "But there are some awful sick kids. The Ransel kids have all developed mastoiditis."

"Is there anything I can do?" Dora asked.

Doc said, "You know there is. People get so scared and helpless. Take the Ransels—they're scared to death and they're scared to be alone. If you, or some of the girls, could just sit with them."

Dora, who was soft as a mouse's belly, could be as hard as carborundum. She went back to the Bear Flag and organized it for service. It was a bad time for her but she did it. The Greek cook made a ten-gallon cauldron of strong soup and kept it full and kept it strong. The girls tried to keep up their business but they went in shifts to sit with the families, and they carried pots of soup when they went. Doc was in almost constant demand. Dora consulted him and detailed the girls where he suggested. And all the time the business at the Bear Flag was booming. The juke box never stopped playing. The men of the fishing fleet and the soldiers stood in line. And the girls did their work and then they took their pots of soup and went to sit with the Ransels, with the McCarthys, with the Ferrias. The girls slipped out the back door, and sometimes staying with the sleeping children the girls dropped to sleep in their chairs. They didn't use makeup for work any more. They didn't have to. Dora herself said she could have used the total membership of the old ladies' home. It was the busiest time the girls at the Bear Flag could remember. Everyone was glad when it was over.

17

In spite of his friendliness and his friends Doc was a lonely and a set-apart man. Mack probably noticed it more than anybody. In a group, Doc seemed always alone. When the lights were on and the curtains drawn, and the Gregorian music played on the great phonograph, Mack used to look down on the laboratory from the Palace Flophouse. He knew Doc had a girl in there, but Mack used to get a dreadful feeling of loneliness out of it. Even in the dear close contact with a girl Mack felt that Doc would be lonely. Doc was a night crawler. The lights were on in the lab all night and yet he seemed to be up in the daytime too. And the great shrouds of music came out of the lab at any time of the day or night. Sometimes when it was all dark and when it seemed that sleep had come at last, the diamond-true child voices of the Sistine Choir would come from the windows of the laboratory.

Doc had to keep up his collecting. He tried to get to the good tides along the coast. The sea rocks and the beaches were his stock pile. He knew where everything was when he wanted it. All the articles of his trade were filed away on the coast, sea cradles here, octopi here, tube worms in another place, sea pansies in another. He knew where to get them but he could not go for them exactly when he wanted. For Nature locked up the items and only released them occasionally. Doc had to know not only the tides but when a particular low tide was good in a particular place. When such a low tide occurred, he packed his collecting tools in his car, he packed his jars, his bottles, his plates and preservatives and he went to the beach or reef or rock ledge where the animals he needed were stored.

Now he had an order for small octopi and the nearest place to get them was the boulder-strewn inter-tidal zone at La Jolla between Los Angeles and San Diego. It meant a five-hundred-mile drive each way and his arrival had to coincide with the retreating waters.

The little octopi live among the boulders imbedded in sand. Being timid and young, they prefer a bottom on which there are many caves and little crevices and lumps of mud where they may hide from predators and protect themselves from the waves. But on the same flat there are millions of sea cradles. While filling a definite order for octopi, Doc could replenish his stock of the cradles.

Low tide was 5:17 A.M. on a Thursday. If Doc left Monterey on Wednesday morning he could be there easily in time for the tide on Thursday. He would have taken someone with him for company but quite by accident everyone was away or was busy. Mack and the boys were up Carmel Valley collecting frogs. Three young women he knew and would have enjoyed as companions had jobs and couldn't get away in the middle of the week. Henri the painter was occupied, for Holman's Department Store had employed not a flag-pole sitter but a flag-pole skater. On a tall mast on top of the store he had a little round platform and there he was on skates going around and around. He had been there three days and three nights. He was out to set a new record for being on skates on a platform. The previous record was 127 hours so he had some time to go. Henri had taken up his post across the street at Red Williams' gas station. Henri was fascinated. He thought of doing a huge abstraction called Substratum Dream of a Flag-pole Skater. Henri couldn't leave town while the skater was up there. He protested that there were philosophic implications in flag-pole skating that no one had touched. Henri sat in a chair, leaned back against the lattice which concealed the door of the men's toilet at Red Williams'. He kept his eye on the eyrie skating platform and obviously he couldn't go with Doc to La Jolla. Doc had to go alone because the tide would not wait.

Early in the morning he got his things together. Personal things went in a small satchel. Another satchel held instruments and syringes. Having packed, he combed and trimmed his brown beard, saw that his pencils were in his shirt pocket and his magnifying glass attached to his lapel. He packed the trays, bottles, glass plates, preservatives, rubber boots and a blanket into the back of his car. He worked through the pearly time, washed three days' dishes, put the garbage into the surf. He closed the doors but did not lock them and by nine o'clock was on his way.

It took Doc longer to go places than other people.

He didn't drive fast and he stopped and ate hamburgers very often. Driving up to Lighthouse Avenue he waved at a dog that looked around and smiled at him. In Monterey before he even started, he felt hungry and stopped at Herman's for a hamburger and beer. While he ate his sandwich and sipped his beer, a bit of conversation came back to him. Blaisedell, the poet, had said to him, "You love beer so much. I'll bet some day you'll go in and order a beer milk shake." It was a simple piece of foolery but it had bothered Doc ever since. He wondered what a beer milk shake would taste like. The idea gagged him but he couldn't let it alone. It cropped up every time he had a glass of beer. Would it curdle the milk? Would you add sugar? It was like a shrimp ice cream. Once the thing got into your head you couldn't forget it. He finished his sandwich and paid Herman. He purposely didn't look at the milk shake machines lined up so shiny against the back wall. If a man ordered a beer milk shake, he thought, he'd better do it in a town where he wasn't known. But then, a man with a beard, ordering a beer milk shake in a town where he wasn't known—they might call the police. A man with a beard was always a little suspect anyway. You couldn't say you wore a beard because you liked a beard. People didn't like you for telling the truth. You had to say you had a scar so you couldn't shave. Once when Doc was at the University of Chicago he had love trouble and he had worked too hard. He thought it would be nice to take a very long walk. He put on a little knapsack and he walked through Indiana and Kentucky and North Carolina and Georgia clear to Florida. He walked among farmers and mountain people, among the swamp people and fishermen. And everywhere people asked him why he was walking through the country.

Because he loved true things, he tried to explain. He said he was nervous and besides he wanted to see the country, smell the ground and look at grass and birds and trees, to savor the country, and there was no other way to do it save on foot. And people didn't like him for telling the truth. They scowled, or shook and tapped their heads, they laughed as though they knew it was a lie and they appreciated a liar. And some, afraid for their daughters or their pigs, told him to move on, to get going, just not to stop near their place if he knew what was good for him.

And so he stopped trying to tell the truth. He said he was doing it on a bet—that he stood to win a hundred dollars. Everyone liked him then and believed him. They asked him in to dinner and gave him a bed and they put lunches up for him and wished him good luck and thought he was a hell of a fine fellow. Doc still loved true things but he knew it was not a general love and it could be a very dangerous mistress.

Doc didn't stop in Salinas for a hamburger. But he stopped in Gonzales, in King City, and in Paso Robles. He had hamburger and beer at Santa Maria—two in Santa Maria because it was a long pull from there to Santa Barbara. In Santa Barbara he had soup, lettuce and string bean salad, pot roast and mashed potatoes, pineapple pie and blue cheese and coffee, and after that he filled the gas tank and went to the toilet. While the service station checked his oil and tires, Doc washed his face and combed his beard and when he came back to the car a number of potential hitchhikers were waiting.

"Going south, Mister?"

Doc traveled on the highways a good deal. He was an old hand. You have to pick your hitchhikers very carefully. It's best to get an experienced one, for he relapses into silence. But the new ones try to pay for their ride by being interesting. Doc had had a leg talked off by some of these. Then after you have made up your mind about the one you want to take, you protect yourself by saying you aren't going far. If your man turns out too much for you, you can drop him. On the other hand, you may be just lucky and get a man very much worth knowing. Doc made a quick survey of the line and chose his company, a thin-faced salesman-like man in a blue suit. He had deep lines beside his mouth and dark brooding eyes.

He looked at Doc with dislike. "Going south, Mister?"

"Yes," said Doc, "a little way."

"Mind taking me along?"

"Get in!" said Doc.

When they got to Ventura it was pretty soon after the heavy dinner so Doc only stopped for beer. The hitchhiker hadn't spoken once. Doc pulled up at a roadside stand.

"Want some beer?"

"No," said the hitchhiker. "And I don't mind saying I think it's not a very good idea to drive under the influence of alcohol. It's none of my business what you do with your own life but in this case you've got an automobile and that can be a murderous weapon in the hands of a drunken driver."

At the beginning Doc had been slightly startled. "Get out of the car," he said softly.

"What?"

"I'm going to punch you in the nose," said Doc. "If you aren't out of this car before I count ten— One— two—three—"

The man fumbled at the door catch and backed hurriedly out of the car. But once outside he howled, "I'm going to find an officer. I'm going to have you arrested."

Doc opened the box on the dashboard and took out a monkey wrench. His guest saw the gesture and walked hurriedly away.

Doc walked angrily to the counter of the stand.

The waitress, a blonde beauty with just a hint of a goiter, smiled at him. "What'll it be?"

"Beer milk shake," said Doc.

"What?"

Well here it was and what the hell. Might just as well get it over with now as some time later.

The blonde asked, "Are you kidding?"

Doc knew wearily that he couldn't explain, couldn't tell the truth. "I've got a bladder complaint," he said. "Bipalychaetorsonectomy the doctors call it. I'm supposed to drink a *beer milk shake*. Doctor's orders."

The blonde smiled reassuringly. "Oh! I thought you was kidding," she said archly. "You tell me how to make it. I didn't know you was sick."

"Very sick," said Doc, "and due to be sicker. Put in some milk, and add half a bottle of beer. Give me the other half in a glass—no sugar in the milk shake." When she served it, he tasted it wryly. And it wasn't so bad—it just tasted like stale beer and milk.

"It sounds awful," said the blonde.

"It's not so bad when you get used to it," said Doc. "I've been drinking it for seventeen years."

18

Doc had driven slowly. It was late afternoon when he stopped in Ventura, so late in fact that when he stopped in Carpenteria he only had a cheese sandwich and went to the toilet. Besides he intended to get a good dinner in Los Angeles and it was dark when he got there. He drove on through and stopped at a big Chicken-in-the-Rough place he knew about. And there he had fried chicken, julienne potatoes, hot biscuits and honey, and a piece of pineapple pie and blue cheese. And here he filled his thermos bottle with hot coffee, had them make up six ham sandwiches and bought two quarts of beer for breakfast.

It was not so interesting driving at night. No dogs to see, only the highway lighted with his headlights. Doc speeded up to finish the trip. It was about two o'clock when he got to La Jolla. He drove through the town and down to the cliff below which his tidal flat lay. There he stopped the car, ate a sandwich, drank some beer, turned out the lights and curled up in the seat to sleep.

He didn't need a clock. He had been working in a

tidal pattern so long that he could feel a tide change in his sleep. In the dawn he awakened, looked out through the windshield and saw that the water was already retreating down the bouldery flat. He drank some hot coffee, ate three sandwiches and had a quart of beer.

The tide goes out imperceptibly. The boulders show and seem to rise up and the ocean recedes leaving little pools, leaving wet weed and moss and sponge, iridescence and brown and blue and China red. On the bottoms lie the incredible refuse of the sea, shells broken and chipped and bits of skeleton, claws, the whole sea bottom a fantastic cemetery on which the living scamper and scramble.

Doc pulled on his rubber boots and set his rain hat fussily. He took his buckets and jars and his crowbar and put his sandwiches in one pocket and his thermos bottle in another pocket and he went down the cliff to the tidal flat. Then he worked down the flat after the retreating sea. He turned over the boulders with his crowbar and now and then his hand darted quickly into the standing water and brought out a little angry squirming octopus which blushed with rage and spat ink on his hand. Then he dropped it into a jar of sea water with the others and usually the newcomer was so angry that it attacked its fellows.

It was good hunting that day. He got twenty-two little octopi. And he picked off several hundred sea cradles and put them in his wooden bucket. As the tide moved out he followed it while the morning came and the sun arose. The flat extended out two hundred yards and then there was a line of heavy weed-crusted rocks before it dropped off to deep water. Doc worked out to the barrier edge. He had about what he wanted now and the rest of the time he looked under stones, leaned down and peered into the tide pools with their brilliant mosaics and their scuttling, bubbling life. And he came at last to the outer barrier where the long leathery brown algae hung down into the water. Red starfish clustered on the rocks and the sea pulsed up and down against the barrier waiting to get in again. Between two weeded rocks on the barrier Doc saw a flash of white under water and then the floating weed covered it. He climbed to the place over the slippery rocks, held himself firmly, and gently reached down and parted the brown algae. Then he grew rigid. A girl's face looked up at him, a pretty, pale girl with dark hair. The eyes were open and clear and the face was firm and the hair washed gently about her head. The body was out of sight, caught in the crevice. The lips were slightly parted and the teeth showed and on the face was only comfort and rest. Just under water it was and the clear water made it very beautiful. It seemed to Doc that he looked at it for many minutes, and the face burned into his picture memory.

Very slowly he raised his hand and let the brown weed float back and cover the face. Doc's heart pounded deeply and his throat felt tight. He picked up his bucket and his jars and his crowbar and went slowly over the slippery rocks back toward the beach.

And the girl's face went ahead of him. He sat down on the beach in the coarse dry sand and pulled off his boots. In the jar the little octopi were huddled up, each keeping as far as possible from the others. Music sounded in Doc's ears, a high thin piercingly sweet flute carrying a melody he could never remember, and

against this, a pounding surf-like wood-wind section.
The flute went up into regions beyond the hearing
range and even there it carried its unbelievable melody. Goose pimples came out on Doc's arms. He
shivered and his eyes were wet the way they get in the
focus of great beauty. The girl's eyes had been gray
and clear and the dark hair floated, drifted lightly over
the face. The picture was set for all time. He sat there
while the first little spout of water came over the reef
bringing the returning tide. He sat there hearing the
music while the sea crept in again over the bouldery
flat. His hand tapped out the rhythm, and the terrify-
ing flute played in his brain. The eyes were gray and
the mouth smiled a little or seemed to catch its breath
in ecstasy.

A voice seemed to awaken him. A man stood over
him. "Been fishing?"

"No, collecting."

"Well—what are them things?"

"Baby octopi."

"You mean devilfish? I didn't know there was any
there. I've lived here all my life."

"You've got to look for them," said Doc listlessly.

"Say," said the man, "aren't you feeling well? You
look sick."

The flute climbed again and plucked cellos sounded
below and the sea crept in and in toward the beach.
Doc shook off the music, shook off the face, shook the
chill out of his body. "Is there a police station near?"

"Up in town. Why, what's wrong?"

"There's a body out on the reef."

"Where?"

"Right out there—wedged between two rocks. A girl."

"Say—" said the man. "You get a bounty for finding a body. I forget how much."

Doc stood up and gathered his equipment. "Will you report it? I'm not feelng well."

"Give you a shock, did it? Is it—bad? Rotten or eat up?"

Doc turned away. "You take the bounty," he said. "I don't want it." He started toward the car. Only the tiniest piping of the flute sounded in his head.

19

Probably nothing in the way of promotion Holman's Department Store ever did attracted so much favorable comment as the engagement of the flag-pole skater. Day after day, there he was up on his little round platform skating around and around and at night he could be seen up there too, dark against the sky so that everybody knew he didn't come down. It was generally agreed, however, that a steel rod came up through the center of the platform at night and he strapped himself to it. But he didn't sit down and no one minded the steel rod. People came from Jamesburg to see him and from down the coast as far as Grimes Point. Salinas people came over in droves and the Farmers Mercantile of that town put in a bid for the next appearance when the skater could attempt to break his own record and thus give the new world's record to Salinas. Since there weren't many flag-pole skaters and since this one was by far the best, he had for the last year gone about breaking his own world's record.

Holman's was delighted about the venture. They

had a white sale, a remnant sale, an aluminum sale, and a crockery sale all going at the same time. Crowds of people stood in the street watching the lone man on his platform.

His second day up, he sent down word that someone was shooting at him with an air gun. The display department used its head. It figured the angles and located the offender. It was old Doctor Merrivale hiding behind the curtains of his office, plugging away with a Daisy air rifle. They didn't denounce him and he promised to stop. He was very prominent in the Masonic Lodge.

Henri the painter kept his chair at Red Williams' service station. He worked out every possible philosophic approach to the situation and came to the conclusion that he would have to build a platform at home and try it himself. Everyone in the town was more or less affected by the skater. Trade fell off out of sight of him and got better the nearer you came to Holman's. Mack and the boys went up and looked for a moment and then went back to the Palace. They couldn't see that it made much sense.

Holman's set up a double bed in their window. When the skater broke the world's record he was going to come down and sleep right in the window without taking off his skates. The trade name of the mattress was on a little card at the foot of the bed.

Now in the whole town there was interest and discussion about this sporting event, but the most interesting question of all and the one that bothered the whole town was never spoken of. No one mentioned it and yet it was there haunting everyone. Mrs. Trolat wondered about it as she came out of the Scotch bakery with a bag of sweet buns. Mr. Hall in men's furnishings wondered about it. The three Willoughby girls giggled whenever they thought of it. But no one had the courage to bring it into the open.

Richard Frost, a high-strung and brilliant young man, worried about it more than anyone else. It haunted him. Wednesday night he worried and Thursday night he fidgeted. Friday night he got drunk and had a fight with his wife. She cried for a while and then pretended to be asleep. She heard him slip from bed and go into the kitchen. He was getting another drink. And then she heard him dress quietly and go out. She cried some more then. It was very late. Mrs. Frost was sure he was going down to Dora's Bear Flag.

Richard walked sturdily down the hill through the pines until he came to Lighthouse Avenue. He turned left and went up toward Holman's. He had the bottle in his pocket and just before he came to the store he took one more slug of it. The street lights were turned down low. The town was deserted. Not a soul moved. Richard stood in the middle of the street and looked up.

Dimly on top of the high mast he could see the lonely figure of the skater. He took another drink. He cupped his hand and called huskily, "Hey!" There was no answer. "Hey!" he called louder and looked around to see if the cops had come out of their place beside the bank.

Down from the sky came a surly reply: "What do you want?"

Richard cupped his hands again. "How—how do you—go to the toilet?"

"I've got a can up here," said the voice.

Richard turned and walked back the way he had

come. He walked along Lighthouse and up through the pines and he came to his house and let himself in. As he undressed he knew his wife was awake. She bubbled a little when she was asleep. He got into bed and she made room for him.

"He's got a can up there," Richard said.

20

In mid-morning the Model T truck rolled triumphantly home to Cannery Row and hopped the gutter and creaked up through the weeds to its place behind Lee Chong's. The boys blocked up the front wheels, drained what gasoline was left into a five-gallon can, took their frogs and went wearily home to the Palace Flophouse. Then Mack made a ceremonious visit to Lee Chong while the boys got a fire going in the big stove. Mack thanked Lee with dignity for lending the truck. He spoke of the great success of the trip, of the hundreds of frogs taken. Lee smiled shyly and waited for the inevitable.

"We're in the chips," Mack said enthusiastically. "Doc pays us a nickel a frog and we got about a thousand."

Lee nodded. The price was standard. Everybody knew that.

"Doc's away," said Mack. "Jesus, is he gonna be happy when he sees all them frogs."

Lee nodded again. He knew Doc was away and he also knew where the conversation was going.

"Say, by the way," said Mack as though he had just thought of it. "We're a little bit short right now—" He managed to make it sound like a very unusual situation.

"No whiskey," said Lee Chong and he smiled.

Mack was outraged. "What would we want whiskey for? Why we got a gallon of the finest whiskey you ever laid a lip over—a whole full God damned running over gallon. By the way," he continued, "I and the boys would like to have you just step up for a snort with us. They told me to ask you."

In spite of himself Lee smiled with pleasure. They wouldn't offer it if they didn't have it.

"No," said Mack, "I'll lay it on the line. I and the boys are pretty short and we're pretty hungry. You know the price of frogs is twenty for a buck. Now Doc is away and we're hungry. So what we thought is this. We don't want to see you lose nothing so we'll make over to you twenty-five frogs for a buck. You got a five-frog profit there and nobody loses his shirt."

"No," said Lee. "No money."

"Well, hell, Lee, all we need is a little groceries. I'll tell you what—we want to give Doc a little party when he gets back. We got plenty of liquor but we'd like to get maybe some steaks, and stuff like that. He's such a nice guy. Hell, when your wife had that bad tooth, who gave her the laudanum?"

Mack had him. Lee was indebted to Doc—deeply indebted. What Lee was having trouble comprehending was how his indebtedness to Doc made it necessary that he give credit to Mack.

"We don't want you to have like a mortgage on frogs," Mack went on. "We will actually deliver right

into your hands twenty-five frogs for every buck of
groceries you let us have and you can come to the
party too."

Lee's mind nosed over the proposition like a mouse
in a cheese cupboard. He could find nothing wrong with
it. The whole thing was legitimate. Frogs *were* cash as
far as Doc was concerned, the price was standard and
Lee had a double profit. He had his five-frog margin
and also he had the grocery mark-up. The whole thing
hinged on whether they actually had any frogs.

"We go see flog," Lee said at last.

In front of the Palace he had a drink of the whiskey,
inspected the damp sacks of frogs, and agreed to the
transaction. He stipulated, however, that he would
take no dead frogs. Now Mack counted fifty frogs into
a can and walked back to the grocery with Lee and got
two dollars' worth of bacon and eggs and bread.

Lee, anticipating a brisk business, brought a big
packing case out and put it into the vegetable department. He emptied the fifty frogs into it and covered it
with a wet gunny sack to keep his charges happy.

And business was brisk. Eddie sauntered down and
bought two frogs' worth of Bull Durham. Jones was outraged a little later when the price of Coca-Cola went up
from one to two frogs. In fact bitterness arose as the day
wore on and prices went up. Steak, for instance—the
very best steak shouldn't have been more than ten frogs
a pound but Lee set it at twelve and a half. Canned
peaches were sky high, eight frogs for a No. 2 can. Lee
had a stranglehold on the consumers. He was pretty
sure that the Thrift Market or Holman's would not ap-
prove of this new monetary system. If the boys wanted
steak, they knew they had to pay Lee's prices. Feeling

ran high when Hazel, who had coveted a pair of yellow silk arm bands for a long time, was told that if he didn't want to pay thirty-five frogs for them he could go somewhere else. The poison of greed was already creeping into the innocent and laudable merchandising agreement. Bitterness was piling up. But in Lee's packing case the frogs were piling up too.

Financial bitterness could not eat too deeply into Mack and the boys, for they were not mercantile men. They did not measure their joy in goods sold, their egos in bank balances, nor their loves in what they cost. While they were mildly irritated that Lee was taking them for an economic ride or perhaps hop, two dollars' worth of bacon and eggs was in their stomachs lying right on top of a fine slug of whiskey and right on top of the breakfast was another slug of whiskey. And they sat in their own chairs in their own house and watched Darling learning to drink canned milk out of a sardine can. Darling was and was destined to remain a very happy dog, for in the group of five men there were five distinct theories of dog training, theories which clashed so that Darling never got any training at all. From the first she was a precocious bitch. She slept on the bed of the man who had given her the last bribe. They really stole for her sometimes. They wooed her away from one another. Occasionally all five agreed that things had to change and that Darling must be disciplined, but in the discussion of method the intention invariably drifted away. They were in love with her. They found the little puddles she left on the floor charming. They bored all their acquaintances with her cuteness and they would have killed her with food if in the end she hadn't had better sense than they.

Jones made her a bed in the grandfather clock but Darling never used it. She slept with one or another of them as the fancy moved her. She chewed the blankets, tore the mattresses, sprayed the feathers out of the pillows. She coquetted and played her owners against one another. They thought she was wonderful. Mack intended to teach her tricks and go in vaudeville and he didn't even housebreak her.

They sat in the afternoon, smoking, digesting, considering, and now and then having a delicate drink from the jug. And each time they warned that they must not take too much, for it was to be for Doc. They must not forget that for a minute.

"What time you figure he'll be back?" Eddie asked.

"Usually gets in about eight or nine o'clock," said Mack. "Now we got to figure when we're going to give it. I think we ought to give it tonight."

"Sure," the others agreed.

"Maybe he might be tired," Hazel suggested. "That's a long drive."

"Hell," said Jones, "nothing rests you like a good party. I've been so dog tired my pants was draggin' and then I've went to a party and felt fine."

"We got to do some real thinkin'," said Mack. "Where we going to give it—here?"

"Well, Doc, he likes his music. He's always got his phonograph going at a party. Maybe he'd be more happy if we give it over at his place."

"You got something there," said Mack. "But I figure it ought to be like a surprise party. And how we going to make like it's a party and not just us bringin' over a jug of whiskey?"

"How about decorations?" Hughie suggested. "Like Fourth of July or Halloween."

Mack's eyes looked off into space and his lips were parted. He could see it all. "Hughie," he said, "I think you got something there. I never would of thought you could do it, but by God you really rang a duck that time." His voice grew mellow and his eyes looked into the future. "I can just see it," he said. "Doc comes home. He's tired. He drives up. The place is all lit up. He thinks somebody's broke in. He goes up the stairs and by God the place has got the hell decorated out of it. There's crepe paper and there's favors and a big cake. Jesus, he'd know it was a party then. And it wouldn't be no little mouse fart party neither. And we're kind of hiding so for a minute he don't know who done it. And then we come out yelling. Can't you see his face? By God, Hughie, I don't know how you thought of it."

Hughie blushed. His conception had been much more conservative, based in fact on the New Year's party at La Ida, but if it was going to be like that why Hughie was willing to take credit. "I just thought it would be nice," he said.

"Well, it's a pretty nice thing," said Mack, "and I don't mind saying when the surprise kind of wears off, I'm going to tell Doc who thought it up." They leaned back and considered the thing. And in their minds the decorated laboratory looked like the conservatory at the Hotel del Monte. They had a couple more drinks, just to savor the plan.

Lee Chong kept a very remarkable store. For instance, most stores buy yellow and black crepe paper

and black paper cats, masks and papier-mâché pumpkins in October. There is a brisk business for Halloween and then these items disappear. Maybe they are
sold or thrown out, but you can't buy them say in
June. The same is true of Fourth of July equipment,
flags and bunting and skyrockets. Where are they in
January? Gone—no one knows where. This was not
Lee Chong's way. You could buy Valentines in November at Lee Chong's, shamrocks, hatchets and
paper cherry trees in August. He had firecrackers he
had laid up in 1920. One of the mysteries was where
he kept his stock since his was not a very large store.
He had bathing suits he had bought when long skirts
and black stockings and head bandanas were in style.
He had bicycle clips and tatting shuttles and Mah Jong
sets. He had badges that said "Remember the Maine"
and felt pennants commemorating "Fighting Bob." He
had mementos of the Panama Pacific International Ex-
position of 1915—little towers of jewels. And there
was one other unorthodoxy in Lee's way of doing business. He never had a sale, never reduced a price and
never remaindered. An article that cost thirty cents in
1912 still was thirty cents although mice and moths
might seem to some to have reduced its value. But
there was no question about it. If you wanted to deco-
rate a laboratory in a general way, not being specific
about the season but giving the impression of a cross
between Saturnalia and a pageant of the Flags of all
Nations, Lee Chong's was the place to go for your
stuff.

Mack and the boys knew that, but Mack said,
"Where we going to get a big cake? Lee hasn't got
nothing but them little bakery cakes."

Hughie had been so successful before he tried again. "Why'n't Eddie bake a cake?" he suggested. "Eddie used to be fry cook at the San Carlos for a while."

The instant enthusiasm for the idea drove from Eddie's brain the admission that he had never baked a cake.

Mack put it on a sentimental basis besides. "It would mean more to Doc," he said. "It wouldn't be like no God damned old soggy bought cake. It would have some heart in it."

As the afternoon and the whiskey went down the enthusiasm rose. There were endless trips to Lee Chong's. The frogs were gone from one sack and Lee's packing case was getting crowded. By six o'clock they had finished the gallon of whiskey and were buying half pints of Old Tennis Shoes at fifteen frogs a crack, but the pile of decorating materials was heaped on the floor of the Palace Flophouse—miles of crepe paper commemorating every holiday in vogue and some that had been abandoned.

Eddie watched his stove like a mother hen. He was baking a cake in the wash basin. The recipe was guaranteed not to fail by the company which made the shortening. But from the first the cake had acted strangely. When the batter was completed it writhed and panted as though animals were squirming and crawling inside it. Once in the oven it put up a bubble like a baseball which grew tight and shiny and then collapsed with a hissing sound. This left such a crater that Eddie made a new batch of batter and filled in the hole. And now the cake was behaving very curiously for while the bottom was burning and sending out a black smoke the top was rising and falling gluely with a series of little explosions.

When Eddie finally put it out to cool, it looked like one of Bel Geddes' miniatures of a battlefield on a lava bed.

This cake was not fortunate, for while the boys were decorating the laboratory Darling ate what she could of it, was sick in it, and finally curled up in its still warm dough and went to sleep.

But Mack and the boys had taken the crepe paper, the masks, the broomsticks and paper pumpkins, the red, white, and blue bunting, and moved over the lot and across the street to the laboratory. They disposed of the last of the frogs for a quart of Old Tennis Shoes and two gallons of 49-cent wine.

"Doc is very fond of wine," said Mack. "I think he likes it even better than whiskey."

Doc never locked the laboratory. He went on the theory that anyone who really wanted to break in could easily do it, that people were essentially honest and that, finally, there wasn't much the average person would want to steal there anyway. The valuable things were books and records, surgical instruments and optical glass and such things that a practical working burglar wouldn't look at twice. His theory had been sound as far as burglars, snatch thieves, and kleptomaniacs were concerned, but it had been completely ineffective regarding his friends. Books were often "borrowed." No can of beans ever survived his absence and on several occasions, returning late, he had found guests in his bed.

The boys piled the decorations in the anteroom and then Mack stopped them. "What's going to make Doc happiest?" he asked.

"The party!" said Hazel.

"No," said Mack.

"The decorations?" Hughie suggested. He felt responsible for the decorations.

"No," said Mack, "the frogs. That's going to make him feel best of all. Any maybe by the time he gets here, Lee Chong might be closed and he can't even see his frogs until tomorrow. No, sir," Mack cried. "Them frogs ought to be right here, right in the middle of the room with a piece of bunting on it and a sign that says, 'Welcome Home, Doc.' "

The committee which visited Lee met with stern opposition. All sorts of possibilities suggested themselves to his suspicious brain. It was explained that he was going to be at the party so he could watch his property, that no one questioned that they were his. Mack wrote out a paper transferring the frogs to Lee in case there should be any question.

When his protests weakened a little they carried the packing case over to the laboratory, tacked red, white, and blue bunting over it, lettered the big sign with iodine on a card, and they started the decorating from there. They had finished the whiskey by now and they really felt in a party mood. They criss-crossed the crepe paper, and put the pumpkins up. Passers-by in the street joined the party and rushed over to Lee's to get more to drink. Lee Chong joined the party for a while but his stomach was notoriously weak and he got sick and had to go home. At eleven o'clock they fried the steaks and ate them. Someone digging through the records found an album of Count Basie and the great phonograph roared out. The noise could be heard from the boat works to La Ida. A group of customers from

the Bear Flag mistook Western Biological for a rival
house and charged up the stairs whooping with joy.
They were evicted by the outraged hosts but only after
a long, happy, and bloody battle that took out the front
door and broke two windows. The crashing of jars was
unpleasant. Hazel going through the kitchen to the
toilet tipped the frying pan of hot grease on himself
and the floor and was badly burned.

At one-thirty a drunk wandered in and passed a
remark which was considered insulting to Doc. Mack
hit him a clip which is still remembered and discussed. The man rose off his feet, described a small
arc, and crashed through the packing case in among
the frogs. Someone trying to change a record dropped
the tone arm down and broke the crystal.

No one has studied the psychology of a dying party.
It may be raging, howling, boiling, and then a fever
sets in and a little silence and then quickly quickly it
is gone, the guests go home or go to sleep or wander
away to some other affair and they leave a dead body.

The lights blazed in the laboratory. The front door
hung sideways by one hinge. The floor was littered
with broken glass. Phonograph records, some broken,
some only nicked, were strewn about. The plates with
pieces of steak ends and coagulating grease were on
the floor, on top of the bookcases, under the bed.
Whiskey glasses lay sadly on their sides. Someone
trying to climb the bookcases had pulled out a whole
section of books and spilled them in broken-backed
confusion on the floor. And it was empty, it was over.

Through the broken end of the packing case a frog
hopped and sat feeling the air for danger and then
another joined him. They could smell the fine damp

cool air coming in the door and in through the broken windows. One of them sat on the fallen card which said "Welcome Home, Doc." And then the two hopped timidly toward the door.

For quite a while a little river of frogs hopped down the steps, a swirling, moving river. For quite a while Cannery Row crawled with frogs—was overrun with frogs. A taxi which brought a very late customer to the Bear Flag squashed five frogs in the street. But well before dawn they had all gone. Some found the sewer and some worked their way up the hill to the reservoir and some went into culverts and some only hid among the weeds in the vacant lot.

And the lights blazed in the quiet empty laboratory.

21

In the back room of the laboratory the white rats in their cages ran and skittered and squeaked. In the corner of a separate cage a mother rat lay over her litter of blind naked children and let them suckle and the mother stared about nervously and fiercely.

In the rattlesnake cage the snakes lay with their chins resting on their own coils and they stared straight ahead out of their scowling dusty black eyes. In another cage a Gila monster with a skin like a beaded bag reared slowly up and clawed heavily and sluggishly at the wire. The anemones in the aquaria blossomed open, with green and purple tentacles and pale green stomachs. The little sea water pump whirred softly and the needles of driven water hissed into the tanks forcing lines of bubbles under the surface.

It was the hour of the pearl. Lee Chong brought his garbage cans out to the curb. The bouncer stood on the porch of the Bear Flag and scratched his stomach. Sam Malloy crawled out of the boiler and sat on his wood block and looked at the lightening east. Over on the rocks near Hopkins Marine Station the sea lions barked monotonously. The old Chinaman came up out of the sea with his dripping basket and flip-flapped up the hill.

Then a car turned into Cannery Row and Doc drove up to the front of the laboratory. His eyes were red rimmed with fatigue. He moved slowly with tiredness. When the car had stopped, he sat still for a moment to let the road jumps get out of his nerves. Then he climbed out of the car. At his step on the stairs, the rattlesnakes ran out their tongues and listened with their waving forked tongues. The rats scampered madly about the cages. Doc climbed the stairs. He looked in wonder at the sagging door and at the broken window. The weariness seemed to go out of him. He stepped quickly inside. Then he went quickly from room to room, stepping around the broken glass. He bent down quickly and picked up a smashed phonograph record and looked at its title.

In the kitchen the spilled grease had turned white on the floor. Doc's eyes flamed red with anger. He sat down on his couch and his head settled between his shoulders and his body weaved a little in his rage. Suddenly he jumped up and turned on the power in his great phonograph. He put on a record and put down the arm. Only a hissing roar came from the loud-speaker. He lifted the arm, stopped the turntable, and sat down on the couch again.

On the stairs there were bumbling uncertain footsteps and through the door came Mack. His face was red. He stood uncertainly in the middle of the room. "Doc—" he said— "I and the boys—"

For the moment Doc hadn't seemed to see him. Now

he leaped to his feet. Mack shuffled backward. "Did you do this?"

"Well, I and the boys—" Doc's small hard fist whipped out and splashed against Mack's mouth. Doc's eyes shone with a red animal rage. Mack sat down heavily on the floor. Doc's fist was hard and sharp. Mack's lips were split against his teeth and one front tooth bent sharply inward. "Get up!" said Doc.

Mack lumbered to his feet. His hands were at his sides. Doc hit him again, a cold calculated punishing punch in the mouth. The blood spurted from Mack's lips and ran down his chin. He tried to lick his lips.

"Put up your hands. Fight, you son of a bitch," Doc cried, and he hit him again and heard the crunch of breaking teeth.

Mack's head jolted but he was braced now so he wouldn't fall. And his hands stayed at his sides. "Go ahead, Doc," he said thickly through his broken lips. "I got it coming."

Doc's shoulders sagged with defeat. "You son of a bitch," he said bitterly. "Oh you dirty son of a bitch." He sat down on the couch and looked at his cut knuckles.

Mack sat down in a chair and looked at him. Mack's eyes were wide and full of pain. He didn't even wipe away the blood that flowed down his chin. In Doc's head the monotonal opening of Monteverdi's *Hor ch' el Ciel e la Terra* began to form, the infinitely sad and resigned mourning of Petrarch for Laura. Doc saw Mack's broken mouth through the music, the music that was in his head and in the air. Mack sat perfectly still, almost as though he could hear the music too. Doc glanced at the place where the Monteverdi album was and then he remembered that the phonograph was broken.

He got to his feet. "Go wash your face," he said and he went out and down the stairs and across the street to Lee Chong's. Lee wouldn't look at him as he got two quarts of beer out of the icebox. He took the money without saying anything. Doc walked back across the street.

Mack was in the toilet cleaning his bloody face with wet paper towels. Doc opened a bottle and poured gently into a glass, holding it at an angle so that very little collar rose to the top. He filled a second tall glass and carried the two into the front room. Mack came back dabbing at his mouth with wet towelling. Doc indicated the beer with his head. Now Mack opened his throat and poured down half the glass without swallowing. He sighed explosively and stared into the beer. Doc had already finished his glass. He brought the bottle in and filled both glasses again. He sat down on his couch.

"What happened?" he asked.

Mack looked at the floor and a drop of blood fell from his lips into his beer. He mopped his split lips again. "I and the boys wanted to give you a party. We thought you'd be home last night."

Doc nodded his head. "I see."

"She got out of hand," said Mack. "It don't do no good to say I'm sorry. I been sorry all my life. This ain't no new thing. It's always like this." He swallowed deeply from his glass. "I had a wife," Mack said. "Same thing. Ever'thing I done turned sour. She couldn't stand it any more. If I done a good thing it got poisoned up some way. If I give her a present they was

something wrong with it. She only got hurt from me.
She couldn't stand it no more. Same thing ever' place
'til I just got to clowning. I don't do nothin' but clown
no more. Try to make the boys laugh."

Doc nodded again. The music was sounding in his
head again, complaint and resignation all in one. "I
know," he said.

"I was glad when you hit me," Mack went on. "I
thought to myself—'Maybe this will teach me. Maybe
I'll remember this.' But, hell, I won't remember
nothin'. I won't learn nothin'. Doc," Mack cried, "the
way I seen it, we was all happy and havin' a good
time. You was glad because we was givin' you a party.
And we was glad. The way I seen it, it was a good
party." He waved his hand at the wreckage on the
floor. "Same thing when I was married. I'd think her
out and then—but it never come off that way."

"I know," said Doc. He opened the second quart of
beer and poured the glasses full.

"Doc," said Mack, "I and the boys will clean up
here—and we'll pay for the stuff that's broke. If it
takes us five years we'll pay for it."

Doc shook his head slowly and wiped the beer foam
from his mustache. "No," he said, "I'll clean it up. I
know where everything goes."

"We'll pay for it, Doc."

"No you won't, Mack," said Doc. "You'll think
about it and it'll worry you for quite a long time, but
you won't pay for it. There's maybe three hundred
dollars in broken museum glass. Don't say you'll pay
for it. That will just keep you uneasy. It might be two
or three years before you forgot about it and felt entirely easy again. And you wouldn't pay it anyway."

"I guess you're right," said Mack. "God damn it, I _know_ you're right. What can we do?"

"I'm over it," said Doc. "Those socks in the mouth got it out of my system. Let's forget it."

Mack finished his beer and stood up. "So long, Doc," he said.

"So long. Say, Mack—what happened to your wife?"

"I don't know," said Mack. "She went away." He walked clumsily down the stairs and crossed over and walked up the lot and up the chicken walk to the Palace Flophouse. Doc watched his progress through the window. And then wearily he got a broom from behind the water heater. It took him all day to clean up the mess.

22

Henri the painter was not French and his name was not Henri. Also he was not really a painter. Henri had so steeped himself in stories of the Left Bank in Paris that he lived there although he had never been there. Feverishly he followed in periodicals the Dadaist movements and schisms, the strangely feminine jealousies and religiousness, the obscurantisms of the forming and breaking schools. Regularly he revolted against outworn techniques and materials. One season he threw out perspective. Another year he abandoned red, even as the mother of purple. Finally he gave up paint entirely. It is not known whether Henri was a good painter or not for he threw himself so violently into movements that he had very little time left for painting of any kind.

About his painting there is some question. You couldn't judge very much from his productions in different colored chicken feathers and nutshells. But as a boat builder he was superb. Henri was a wonderful craftsman. He had lived in a tent years ago when he started his boat and until galley and cabin were complete enough to move into. But once he was housed and dry he had taken his time on the boat. The boat was sculptured rather than built. It was thirty-five feet long and its lines were in a constant state of flux. For a while it had a clipper bow and a fantail like a destroyer. Another time it had looked vaguely like a caravel. Since Henri had no money, it sometimes took him months to find a plank or a piece of iron or a dozen brass screws. That was the way he wanted it, for Henri never wanted to finish his boat.

It sat among the pine trees on a lot Henri rented for five dollars a year. This paid the taxes and satisfied the owner. The boat rested in a cradle on concrete foundations. A rope ladder hung over the side except when Henri was at home. Then he pulled up the rope ladder and only put it down when guests arrived. His little cabin had a wide padded seat that ran around three sides of the room. On this he slept and on this his guests sat. A table folded down when it was needed and a brass lamp hung from the ceiling. His galley was a marvel of compactness but every item in it had been the result of months of thought and work.

Henri was swarthy and morose. He wore a beret long after other people abandoned them, he smoked a calabash pipe and his dark hair fell about his face. Henri had many friends whom he loosely classified as those who could feed him and those whom he had to feed. His boat had no name. Henri said he would name it when it was finished.

Henri had been living in and building his boat for ten years. During that time he had been married twice and had promoted a number of semi-permanent liai-

sons. And all of these young women had left him for
the same reason. The seven-foot cabin was too small
for two people. They resented bumping their heads
when they stood up and they definitely felt the need
for a toilet. Marine toilets obviously would not work in
a shore-bound boat and Henri refused to compromise
with a spurious landsman's toilet. He and his friend of
the moment had to stroll away among the pines. And
one after another his loves left him.

Just after the girl he had called Alice left him, a
very curious thing happened to Henri. Each time he
was left alone, he mourned formally for a while but
actually he felt a sense of relief. He could stretch out
in his little cabin. He could eat what he wanted. He
was glad to be free of the endless female biologic
functions for a while.

It had become his custom, each time he was deserted, to buy a gallon of wine, to stretch out on the
comfortably hard bunk and get drunk. Sometimes he
cried a little all by himself but it was luxurious stuff
and he usually had a wonderful feeling of well-being
from it. He would read Rimbaud aloud with a very bad
accent, marveling the while at his fluid speech.

It was during one of his ritualistic mournings for the
lost Alice that the strange thing began to happen. It
was night and his lamp was burning and he had just
barely begun to get drunk when suddenly he knew he
was no longer alone. He let his eye wander cautiously
up and across the cabin and there on the other side sat
a devilish young man, a dark handsome young man.
His eyes gleamed with cleverness and spirit and energy and his teeth flashed. There was something very
dear and yet very terrible in his face. And beside him

sat a golden-haired little boy, hardly more than a baby. The man looked down at the baby and the baby looked back and laughed delightedly as though something wonderful were about to happen. Then the man looked over at Henri and smiled and he glanced back at the baby. From his upper left vest pocket he took an old-fashioned straight-edged razor. He opened it and indicated the child with a gesture of his head. He put a hand among the curls and the baby laughed gleefully and then the man tilted the chin and cut the baby's throat and the baby went right on laughing. But Henri was howling with terror. It took him a long time to realize that neither the man nor the baby was still there.

Henri, when his shaking had subsided a little, rushed out of his cabin, leaped over the side of the boat and hurried away down the hill through the pines. He walked for several hours and at last he walked down to Cannery Row.

Doc was in the basement working on cats when Henri burst in. Doc went on working while Henri told about it and when it was over Doc looked closely at him to see how much actual fear and how much theater was there. And it was mostly fear.

"Is it a ghost do you think?" Henri demanded. "Is it some reflection of something that has happened or is it some Freudian horror out of me or am I completely nuts? I saw it, I tell you. It happened right in front of me as plainly as I see you."

"I don't know," said Doc.

"Well, will you come up with me, and see if it comes back?"

"No," said Doc. "If I saw it, it might be a ghost and

it would scare me badly because I don't believe in ghosts. And if you saw it again and I didn't it would be a hallucination and you would be frightened."

"But what am I going to do?" Henri asked. "If I see it again I'll know what's going to happen and I'm sure I'll die. You see he doesn't look like a murderer. He looks nice and the kid looks nice and neither of them give a damn. But he cut that baby's throat. I saw it."

"I don't know," said Doc. "I'm not a psychiatrist or a witch hunter and I'm not going to start now."

A girl's voice called into the basement. "Hi, Doc, can I come in?"

"Come along," said Doc.

She was a rather pretty and a very alert girl.

Doc introduced her to Henri.

"He's got a problem," said Doc. "He either has a ghost or a terrible conscience and he doesn't know which. Tell her about it, Henri."

Henri went over the story again and the girl's eyes sparkled.

"But that's horrible," she said when he finished. "I've never in my life even caught the smell of a ghost. Let's go back up and see if he comes again."

Doc watched them go a little sourly. After all it had been his date.

The girl never did see the ghost but she was fond of Henri and it was five months before the cramped cabin and the lack of a toilet drove her out.

23

A black gloom settled over the Palace Flophouse. All the joy went out of it. Mack came back from the laboratory with his mouth torn and his teeth broken. As a kind of penance, he did not wash his face. He went to his bed and pulled his blanket over his head and he didn't get up all day. His heart was as bruised as his mouth. He went over all the bad things he had done in his life and everything he had ever done seemed bad. He was very sad.

Hughie and Jones sat for a while staring into space and then morosely they went over to the Hediondo Cannery and applied for jobs and got them.

Hazel felt so bad that he walked to Monterey and picked a fight with a soldier and lost it on purpose. That made him feel a little better to be utterly beaten by a man Hazel could have licked without half trying.

Darling was the only happy one of the whole club. She spent the day under Mack's bed happily eating up his shoes. She was a clever dog and her teeth were very sharp. Twice in his black despair, Mack reached under the bed and caught her and put her in bed with

him for company but she squirmed out and went back
to eating his shoes.

Eddie mooned on down to La Ida and talked to his
friend the bartender. He got a few drinks and borrowed some nickels with which he played *Melancholy
Baby* five times on the juke box.

Mack and the boys were under a cloud and they knew
it and they knew they deserved it. They had become
social outcasts. All of their good intentions were forgotten now. The fact that the party was given for Doc, if it
was known, was never mentioned or taken into consideration. The story ran through the Bear Flag. It was told
in the canneries. At La Ida drunks discussed it virtuously. Lee Chong refused to comment. He was feeling
financially bruised. And the story as it grew went this
way: They had stolen liquor and money. They had mali-
ciously broken into the laboratory and systematically
destroyed it out of pure malice and evil. People who
really knew better took this view. Some of the drunks at
La Ida considered going over and beating the hell out of
the whole lot of them to show them they couldn't do a
thing like that to Doc.

Only a sense of the solidarity and fighting ability of
Mack and the boys saved them from some kind of
reprisal. There were people who felt virtuous about the
affair who hadn't had the material of virtue for a long
time. The fiercest of the whole lot was Tom Sheligan
who would have been at the party if he had known
about it.

Socially Mack and the boys were beyond the pale.
Sam Malloy didn't speak to them as they went by the
boiler. They drew into themselves and no one could
foresee how they would come out of the cloud. For

there are two possible reactions to social ostracism—
either a man emerges determined to be better, purer,
and kindlier or he goes bad, challenges the world and
does even worse things. This last is by far the commonest reaction to stigma.

Mack and the boys balanced on the scales of good
and evil. They were kind and sweet to Darling; they
were forbearing and patient with one another. When
the first reaction was over they gave the Palace Flophouse a cleaning such as it had never had. They polished the bright work on the stove and they washed all
their clothes and blankets. Financially they had become dull and solvent. Hughie and Jones were working and bringing home their pay. They bought groceries up the hill at the Thrift Market because they could
not stand the reproving eyes of Lee Chong.

It was during this time that Doc made an observation which may have been true, but since there was
one factor missing in his reasoning it is not known
whether he was correct. It was the Fourth of July. Doc
was sitting in the laboratory with Richard Frost. They
drank beer and listened to a new album of Scarlatti
and looked out the window. In front of the Palace
Flophouse there was a large log of wood where Mack
and the boys were sitting in the mid-morning sun.
They faced down the hill toward the laboratory.

Doc said, "Look at them. There are your true phi-
losophers. I think," he went on, "that Mack and the
boys know everything that has ever happened in the
world and possibly everything that will happen. I think
they survive in this particular world better than other
people. In a time when people tear themselves to
pieces with ambition and nervousness and covetous-

ness, they are relaxed. All of our so-called successful men are sick men, with bad stomachs, and bad souls, but Mack and the boys are healthy and curiously clean. They can do what they want. They can satisfy their appetites without calling them something else." This speech so dried out Doc's throat that he drained his beer glass. He waved two fingers in the air and smiled. "There's nothing like that first taste of beer," he said.

Richard Frost said, "I think they're just like anyone else. They just haven't any money."

"They could get it," Doc said. "They could ruin their lives and get money. Mack has qualities of genius. They're all very clever if they want something. They just know the nature of things too well to be caught in that wanting."

If Doc had known of the sadness of Mack and the boys he would not have made the next statement, but no one had told him about the social pressure that was exerted against the inmates of the Palace.

He poured beer slowly into his glass. "I think I can show you proof," he said. "You see how they are sitting facing this way? Well—in about half an hour the Fourth of July Parade is going to pass on Lighthouse Avenue. By just turning their heads they can see it, by standing up they can watch it, and by walking two short blocks they can be right beside it. Now I'll bet you a quart of beer they won't even turn their heads."

"Suppose they don't?" said Richard Frost. "What will that prove?"

"What will it prove?" cried Doc. "Why just that they know what will be in the parade. They will know that the Mayor will ride first in an automobile with bunting streaming back from the hood. Next will come Long Bob on his white horse with the flag. Then the city council, then two companies of soldiers from the Presidio, next the Elks with purple umbrellas, then the Knights Templar in white ostrich feathers and carrying swords. Next the Knights of Columbus with red ostrich feathers and carrying swords. Mack and the boys know that. The band will play. They've seen it all. They don't have to look again."

"The man doesn't live who doesn't have to look at a parade," said Richard Frost.

"Is it a bet then?"

"It's a bet."

"It has always seemed strange to me," said Doc. "The things we admire in men, kindness and generosity, openness, honesty, understanding and feeling are the concomitants of failure in our system. And those traits we detest, sharpness, greed, acquisitiveness, meanness, egotism and self-interest are the traits of success. And while men admire the quality of the first they love the produce of the second."

"Who wants to be good if he has to be hungry too?" said Richard Frost.

"Oh, it isn't a matter of hunger. It's something quite different. The sale of souls to gain the whole world is completely voluntary and almost unanimous—but not quite. Everywhere in the world there are Mack and the boys. I've seen them in an ice-cream seller in Mexico and in an Aleut in Alaska. You know how they tried to give me a party and something went wrong. But they wanted to give me a party. That was their impulse.

Listen," said Doc. "Isn't that the band I hear?" Quickly he filled two glasses with beer and the two of them stepped close to the window.

Mack and the boys sat dejectedly on their log and faced the laboratory. The sound of the band came from Lighthouse Avenue, the drums echoing back from the buildings. And suddenly the Mayor's car crossed and it sprayed bunting from the radiator—then Long Bob on his white horse carrying the flag, then the band, then the soldiers, the Elks, the Knights Templar, the Knights of Columbus. Richard and the Doc leaned forward tensely but they were watching the line of men sitting on the log.

And not a head turned, not a neck straightened up. The parade filed past and they did not move. And the parade was gone. Doc drained his glass and waved two fingers gently in the air and he said, "Hah! There's nothing in the world like that first taste of beer."

Richard started for the door. "What kind of beer do you want?"

"The same kind," said Doc gently. He was smiling up the hill at Mack and the boys.

It's all fine to say, "Time will heal everything, this too shall pass away. People will forget"—and things like that when you are not involved, but when you are there is no passage of time, people do not forget and you are in the middle of something that does not change. Doc didn't know the pain and self-destructive criticism in the Palace Flophouse or he might have tried to do something about it. And Mack and the boys did not know how he felt or they would have held up their heads again.

It was a bad time. Evil stalked darkly in the vacant

lot. Sam Malloy had a number of fights with his wife and she cried all the time. The echoes inside the boiler made it sound as though she were crying under water. Mack and the boys seemed to be the node of trouble. The nice bouncer at the Bear Flag threw out a drunk, but threw him too hard and too far and broke his back. Alfred had to go over to Salinas three times before it was cleared up and that didn't make Alfred feel very well. Ordinarily he was too good a bouncer to hurt anyone. His A and C was a miracle of rhythm and grace.

On top of that a group of high-minded ladies in the town demanded that dens of vice must close to protect young American manhood. This happened about once a year in the dead period between the Fourth of July and the County Fair. Dora usually closed the Bear Flag for a week when it happened. It wasn't so bad. Everyone got a vacation and little repairs to the plumbing and the walls could be made. But this year the ladies went on a real crusade. They wanted somebody's scalp. It had been a dull summer and they were restless. It got so bad that they had to be told who actually owned the property where vice was practiced, what the rents were and what little hardships might be the result of their closing. That was how close they were to being a serious menace.

Dora was closed a full two weeks and there were three conventions in Monterey while the Bear Flag was closed. Word got around and Monterey lost five conventions for the following year. Things were bad all over. Doc had to get a loan at the bank to pay for the glass that was broken at the party. Elmer Rechati went to sleep on the Southern Pacific track and lost both legs. A sudden and completely unexpected storm tore a purse-seiner and three lampara boats loose from their moorings and tossed them broken and sad on Del Monte beach.

There is no explaining a series of misfortunes like that. Every man blames himself. People in their black minds remember sins committed secretly and wonder whether they have caused the evil sequence. One man may put it down to sun spots while another invoking the law of probabilities doesn't believe it. Not even the doctors had a good time of it, for while many people were sick none of it was good-paying sickness. It was nothing a good physic or a patent medicine wouldn't take care of.

And to cap it all, Darling got sick. She was a very fat and lively puppy when she was struck down, but five days of fever reduced her to a little skin-covered skeleton. Her liver-colored nose was pink and her gums were white. Her eyes glazed with illness and her whole body was hot although she trembled sometimes with cold. She wouldn't eat and she wouldn't drink and her fat little belly shriveled up against her spine, and even her tail showed the articulations through the skin. It was obviously distemper.

Now a genuine panic came over the Palace Flophouse. Darling had come to be vastly important to them. Hughie and Jones instantly quit their jobs so they could be near to help. They sat up in shifts. They kept a cool damp cloth on her forehead and she got weaker and sicker. Finally, although they didn't want to, Hazel and Jones were chosen to call on Doc. They found him working over a tide chart while he ate a chicken stew of which the principal ingredient was not chicken but sea cucumber. They thought he looked at them a little coldly.

"It's Darling," they said. "She's sick."

"What's the matter with her?"

"Mack says it's distemper."

"I'm no veterinarian," said Doc. "I don't know how to treat these things."

Hazel said, "Well, couldn't you just take a look at her? She's sick as hell."

They stood in a circle while Doc examined Darling. He looked at her eyeballs and her gums and felt in her ear for fever. He ran his finger over the ribs that stuck out like spokes and at the poor spine. "She won't eat?" he asked.

"Not a thing," said Mack.

"You'll have to force feed her—strong soup and eggs and cod liver oil."

They thought he was cold and professional. He went back to his tide charts and his stew.

But Mack and the boys had something to do now. They boiled meat until it was as strong as whiskey. They put cod liver oil far back on her tongue so that some of it got down her. They held up her head and made a little funnel of her chops and poured the cool soup in. She had to swallow or drown. Every two hours they fed her and gave her water. Before they had slept in shifts—now no one slept. They sat silently and waited for Darling's crisis.

It came early in the morning. The boys sat in their chairs half asleep but Mack was awake and his eyes were on the puppy. He saw her ears flip twice, and her chest heave. With infinite weakness she climbed slowly to her spindly legs, dragged herself to the door, took four laps of water and collapsed on the floor.

Mack shouted the others awake. He danced heavily. All the boys shouted at one another. Lee Chong heard them and snorted to himself as he carried out the garbage cans. Alfred the bouncer heard them and thought they were having a party.

By nine o'clock Darling had eaten a raw egg and half a pint of whipped cream by herself. By noon she was visibly putting on weight. In a day she romped a little and by the end of the week she was a well dog.

At last a crack had developed in the wall of evil. There were evidences of it everywhere. The purse-seiner was hauled back into the water and floated. Word came down to Dora that it was all right to open up the Bear Flag. Earl Wakefield caught a sculpin with two heads and sold it to the museum for eight dollars. The wall of evil and of waiting was broken. It broke away in chunks. The curtains were drawn at the laboratory that night and Gregorian music played until two o'clock and then the music stopped and no one came out. Some force wrought with Lee Chong's heart and all in an Oriental moment he forgave Mack and the boys and wrote off the frog debt which had been a monetary headache from the beginning. And to prove to the boys that he had forgiven them he took a pint of Old Tennis Shoes up and presented it to them. Their trading at the Thrift Market had hurt his feelings but it was all over now. Lee's visit coincided with the first destructive healthy impulse Darling had since her illness. She was completely spoiled now and no one thought of housebreaking her. When Lee Chong came in with his gift, Darling was deliberately and happily destroying Hazel's only pair of rubber boots while her happy masters applauded her.

Mack never visited the Bear Flag professionally. It would have seemed a little like incest to him. There was a house out by the baseball park he patronized. Thus, when he went into the front bar, everyone thought he wanted a beer. He stepped up to Alfred. "Dora around?" he asked.

"What do you want with her?" Alfred asked.

"I got something I want to ask her."

"What about?"

"That's none of your God damn business," said Mack.

"Okay. Have it your way. I'll see if she wants to talk to you."

A moment later he led Mack into the sanctum. Dora sat at a rolltop desk. Her orange hair was piled in ringlets on her head and she wore a green eyeshade. With a stub pen she was bringing her books up to date, a fine old double entry ledger. She was dressed in a magnificent pink silk wrapper with lace at the wrists and throat. When Mack came in she whirled her pivot chair about and faced him. Alfred stood in the door and waited. Mack stood until Alfred closed the door and left.

Dora scrutinized him suspiciously. "Well—what can I do for you?" she demanded at last.

"You see, ma'am," said Mack— "Well I guess you heard what we done over at Doc's some time back."

Dora pushed the eyeshade back up on her head and she put the pen in an old-fashioned coil-spring holder. "Yeah!" she said. "I heard."

"Well, ma'am, we did it for Doc. You may not believe it but we wanted to give him a party. Only he didn't get home in time and—well she got out of hand."

"So I heard," said Dora. "Well, what you want me to do?"

"Well," said Mack, "I and the boys thought we'd ask you. You know what we think of Doc. We wanted to ask you what you thought we could do for him that would kind of show him."

Dora said, "Hum," and she flopped back in her pivot chair and crossed her legs and smoothed her wrapper over her knees. She shook out a cigarette, lighted it and studied. "You gave him a party he didn't get to. Why don't you give him a party he does get to?" she said.

"Jesus," said Mack afterwards talking to the boys. "It was just as simple as that. Now there is one hell of a woman. No wonder she got to be a madam. There is one hell of a woman."

24

Mary Talbot, Mrs. Tom Talbot, that is, was lovely. She had red hair with green lights in it. Her skin was golden with a green undercast and her eyes were green with little golden spots. Her face was triangular, with wide cheekbones, wide-set eyes, and her chin was pointed. She had long dancer's legs and dancer's feet and she seemed never to touch the ground when she walked. When she was excited, and she was excited a good deal of the time, her face flushed with gold. Her great-great-great-great-great grandmother had been burned as a witch.

More than anything in the world Mary Talbot loved parties. She loved to give parties and she loved to go to parties. Since Tom Talbot didn't make much money Mary couldn't give parties all the time so she tricked people into giving them. Sometimes she telephoned a friend and said bluntly, "Isn't it about time you gave a party?"

Regularly Mary had six birthdays a year, and she organized costume parties, surprise parties, holiday parties. Christmas Eve at her house was a very exciting thing. For Mary glowed with parties. She carried her husband Tom along on the wave of her excitement.

In the afternoons when Tom was at work Mary sometimes gave tea parties for the neighborhood cats. She set a footstool with doll cups and saucers. She gathered the cats, and there were plenty of them, and then she held long and detailed conversations with them. It was a kind of play she enjoyed very much—a kind of satiric game and it covered and concealed from Mary the fact that she didn't have very nice clothes and the Talbots didn't have any money. They were pretty near absolute bottom most of the time, and when they really scraped, Mary managed to give some kind of a party.

She could do that. She could infect a whole house with gaiety and she used her gift as a weapon against the despondency that lurked always around outside the house waiting to get in at Tom. That was Mary's job as she saw it—to keep the despondency away from Tom because everyone knew he was going to be a great success some time. Mostly she was successful in keeping the dark things out of the house but sometimes they got in at Tom and laid him out. Then he would sit and brood for hours while Mary frantically built up a backfire of gaiety.

One time when it was the first of the month and there were curt notes from the water company and the rent wasn't paid and a manuscript had come back from *Collier's* and the cartoons had come back from *The New Yorker* and pleurisy was hurting Tom pretty badly, he went into the bedroom and lay down on the bed.

Mary came softly in, for the blue-gray color of his gloom had seeped out under the door and through the keyhole. She had a little bouquet of candy tuft in a collar of paper lace.

"Smell," she said and held the bouquet to his nose. He smelled the flowers and said nothing. "Do you know what day this is?" she asked and thought wildly for something to make it a bright day.

Tom said, "Why don't we face it for once? We're down. We're going under. What's the good of kidding ourselves?"

"No we're not," said Mary. "We're magic people. We always have been. Remember that ten dollars you found in a book—remember when your cousin sent you five dollars? Nothing can happen to us."

"Well, it has happened," said Tom. "I'm sorry," he said. "I just can't talk myself out of it this time. I'm sick of pretending everything. For once I'd like to have it real—just for once."

"I thought of giving a little party tonight," said Mary.

"On what? You're not going to cut out the baked ham picture from a magazine again and serve it on a platter, are you? I'm sick of that kind of kidding. It isn't funny any more. It's sad."

"I could give a little party," she insisted. "Just a small affair. Nobody will dress. It's the anniversary of the founding of the Bloomer League—you didn't even remember that."

"It's no use," said Tom. "I know it's mean but I just can't rise to it. Why don't you just go out and shut the door and leave me alone? I'll get you down if you don't."

She looked at him closely and saw that he meant it.

Mary walked quietly out and shut the door, and Tom turned over on the bed and put his face down between his arms. He could hear her rustling about in the other room.

She decorated the door with old Christmas things, glass balls, and tinsel, and she made a placard that said "Welcome Tom, our Hero." She listened at the door and couldn't hear anything. A little disconsolately she got out the footstool and spread a napkin over it. She put her bouquet in a glass in the middle of the footstool and set out four little cups and saucers. She went into the kitchen, put the tea in the teapot and set the kettle to boil. Then she went out into the yard.

Kitty Randolph was sunning herself by the front fence. Mary said, "Miss Randolph—I'm having a few friends in to tea if you would care to come." Kitty Randolph rolled over languorously on her back and stretched in the warm sun. "Don't be later than four o'clock," said Mary. "My husband and I are going to the Bloomer League Centennial Reception at the Hotel."

She strolled around the house to the backyard where the blackberry vines clambered over the fence. Kitty Casini was squatting was squatting on the ground growling to herself and flicking her tail fiercely. "Mrs. Casini," Mary began and then she stopped for she saw what the cat was doing. Kitty Casini had a mouse. She patted it gently with her unarmed paw and the mouse squirmed horribly away dragging its paralyzed hind legs behind it. The cat let it get nearly to the cover of the blackberry vines and then she reached delicately out and white thorns had sprouted on her paw. Daintily she stabbed the mouse through the back and drew it wriggling to her and her tail flicked with tense delight.

Tom must have been at least half asleep when he heard his name called over and over. He jumped up shouting, "What is it? Where are you?" He could hear Mary crying. He ran out into the yard and saw what was happening. "Turn your head," he shouted and he killed the mouse. Kitty Casini had leaped to the top of the fence where she watched him angrily. Tom picked up a rock and hit her in the stomach and knocked her off the fence.

In the house Mary was still crying a little. She poured the water into the teapot and brought it to the table. "Sit there," she told Tom and he squatted down on the floor in front of the footstool.

"Can't I have a big cup?" he asked.

"I can't blame Kitty Casini," said Mary. "I know how cats are. It isn't her fault. But—Oh, Tom! I'm going to have trouble inviting her again. I'm just not going to like her for a while no matter how much I want to." She looked closely at Tom and saw that the lines were gone from his forehead and that he was not blinking badly. "But then I'm so busy with the Bloomer League these days," she said, "I just don't know how I'm going to get everything done."

Mary Talbot gave a pregnancy party that year. And everyone said, "God! A kid of hers is going to have fun."

25

Certainly all of Cannery Row and probably all of Monterey felt that a change had come. It's all right not to believe in luck and omens. Nobody believes in them. But it doesn't do any good to take chances with them and no one takes chances. Cannery Row, like every place else, is not superstitious but will not walk under a ladder or open an umbrella in the house. Doc was a pure scientist and incapable of superstition and yet when he came in late one night and found a line of white flowers across the doorsill he had a bad time of it. But most people in Cannery Row simply do not believe in such things and then live by them.

There was no doubt in Mack's mind that a dark cloud had hung on the Palace Flophouse. He had analyzed the abortive party and found that a misfortune had crept into every crevice, that bad luck had come up like hives on the evening. And once you got into a routine like that the best thing to do was just to go to bed until it was over. You couldn't buck it. Not that Mack was superstitious.

Now a kind of gladness began to penetrate into the Row and to spread out from there. Doc was almost supernaturally successful with a series of lady visitors. He didn't half try. The puppy at the Palace was growing like a pole bean, and having a thousand generations of training behind her, she began to train herself. She got disgusted with wetting on the floor and took to going outside. It was obvious that Darling was going to grow up a good and charming dog. And she had developed no chorea from her distemper.

The benignant influence crept like gas through the Row. It got as far as Herman's hamburger stand, it spread to the San Carlos Hotel. Jimmy Brucia felt it and Johnny his singing bartender. Sparky Evea felt it and joyously joined battle with three new out of town cops. It even got as far as the County Jail in Salinas where Gay, who had lived a good life by letting the sheriff beat him at checkers, suddenly grew cocky and never lost another game. He lost his privileges that way but he felt a whole man again.

The sea lions felt it and their barking took on a tone and a cadence that would have gladdened the heart of St. Francis. Little girls studying their catechism suddenly looked up and giggled for no reason at all. Perhaps some electrical finder could have been developed so delicate that it could have located the source of all this spreading joy and fortune. And triangulation might possibly have located it in the Palace Flophouse and Grill. Certainly the Palace was lousy with it. Mack and the boys were charged. Jones was seen to leap from his chair only to do a quick tap dance and sit down again. Hazel smiled vaguely at nothing at all. The joy was so general and so suffused that Mack had a hard time keeping it centered and aimed at its objective. Eddie who had worked at La Ida pretty regularly was accumulating a cellar of some promise. He no longer added beer to the wining jug. It gave a flat taste to the mixture, he said.

Sam Malloy had planted morning glories to grow over the boiler. He had put out a little awning and under it he and his wife often sat in the evening. She was crocheting a bedspread.

The joy even got into the Bear Flag. Business was good. Phyllis Mae's leg was knitting nicely and she was nearly ready to go to work again. Eva Flanegan got back from East St. Louis very glad to be back. It had been hot in East St. Louis and it hadn't been as fine as she remembered it. But then she had been younger when she had had so much fun there.

The knowledge or conviction about the party for Doc was no sudden thing. It did not burst out full blown. People knew about it but let it grow gradually like a pupa in the cocoons of their imaginations.

Mack was realistic about it. "Last time we forced her," he told the boys. "You can't never give a good party that way. You got to let her creep up on you."

"Well when's it going to be?" Jones asked impatiently.

"I don't know," said Mack.

"Is it gonna be a surprise party?" Hazel asked.

"It ought to, that's the best kind," said Mack.

Darling brought him a tennis ball she had found and he threw it out the door into the weeds. She bounced away after it.

Hazel said, "If we knew when was Doc's birthday, we could give him a birthday party."

Mack's mouth was open. Hazel constantly surprised him. "By God, Hazel, you got something," he cried. "Yes, sir, if it was his birthday there'd be presents. That's just the thing. All we got to find out is when it is."

"That ought to be easy," said Hughie. "Why don't we ask him?"

"Hell," said Mack. "Then he'd catch on. You ask a guy when is his birthday and especially if you've already give him a party like we done, and he'll know what you want to know for. Maybe I'll just go over and smell around a little and not let on."

"I'll go with you," said Hazel.

"No—if two of us went, he might figure we were up to something."

"Well, hell, it was my idear," said Hazel.

"I know," said Mack. "And when it comes off why I'll tell Doc it was your idear. But I think I better go over alone."

"How is he—friendly?" Eddie asked.

"Sure, he's all right."

Mack found Doc way back in the downstairs part of the laboratory. He was dressed in a long rubber apron and he wore rubber gloves to protect his hands from the formaldehyde. He was injecting the veins and arteries of small dogfish with color mass. His little ball mill rolled over and over, mixing the blue mass. The red fluid was already in the pressure gun. Doc's fine hands worked precisely, slipping the needle into place and pressing the compressed air trigger that forced the color into the veins. He laid the finished fish in a neat pile. He would have to go over these again to put blue mass in the arteries. The dogfish made good dissection specimens.

"Hi, Doc," said Mack. "Keepin' pretty busy?"

"Busy as I want," said Doc. "How's the pup?"

"Doin' just fine. She would of died if it hadn't been for you."

For a moment a wave of caution went over Doc and then slipped off. Ordinarily a compliment made him wary. He had been dealing with Mack for a long time. But the tone had nothing but gratefulness in it. He knew how Mack felt about the pup. "How are things going up at the Palace?"

"Fine, Doc, just fine. We got two new chairs. I wish you'd come up and see us. It's pretty nice up there now."

"I will," said Doc. "Eddie still bring back the jug?"

"Sure," said Mack. "He ain't putting' beer in it no more and I think the stuff is better. It's got more zip."

"It had plenty of zip before," said Doc.

Mack waited patiently. Sooner or later Doc was going to wade into it and he was waiting. If Doc seemed to open the subject himself it would be less suspicious. This was always Mack's method.

"Haven't seen Hazel for some time. He isn't sick, is he?"

"No," said Mack and he opened the campaign. "Hazel is all right. Him and Hughie are havin' one hell of a battle. Been goin' on for a week," he chuckled. "An' the funny thing is it's about somethin' they don't neither of them know nothin' about. I stayed out of it because I don't know nothin' about it neither, but not them. They've even got a little mad at each other."

"What's it about?" Doc asked.

"Well, sir," said Mack, "Hazel's all the time buyin' these here charts and lookin' up lucky days and stars and stuff like that. And Hughie says it's all a bunch of malarkey. Hughie, he says if you know when a guy is born you can tell about him and Hughie says they're just sellin' Hazel them charts for two bits apiece. Me, I don't know nothin' about it. What do you think, Doc?"

"I'd kind of side with Hughie," said Doc. He stopped the ball mill, washed out the color gun and filled it with blue mass.

"They got goin' hot the other night," said Mack. "They ask me when I'm born so I tell 'em April 12 and Hazel he goes and buys one of them charts and read all about me. Well it did seem to hit in some places. But it was nearly all good stuff and a guy will believe good stuff about himself. It said I'm brave and smart and kind to my friends. But Hazel says it's all true. When's your birthday, Doc?" At the end of the long discussion it sounded perfectly casual. You couldn't put your finger on it. But it must be remembered that Doc had known Mack a very long time. If he had not he would have said December 18 which was his birthday instead of October 27 which was not. "October 27," said Doc. "Ask Hazel what that makes me."

"It's probably so much malarkey," said Mack, "but Hazel he takes it serious. I'll ask him to look you up, Doc."

When Mack left, Doc wondered casually what the build-up was. For he had recognized it as a lead. He knew Mack's technique, his method. He recognized his style. And he wondered to what purpose Mack could put the information. It was only later when rumors began to creep in that Doc added the whole thing up. Now he felt slightly relieved, for he had expected Mack to put the bite on him.

26

The two boys played in the boat works yard until a cat climbed the fence. Instantly they gave chase, drove it across the tracks and there filled their pockets with granite stones from the roadbed. The cat got away from them in the tall weeds but they kept the stones because they were perfect in weight, shape, and size for throwing. You can't ever tell when you're going to need a stone like that. They turned down Cannery Row and whanged a stone at the corrugated iron front of Morden's Cannery. A startled man looked out the office window and then rushed for the door, but the boys were too quick for him. They were lying behind a wooden stringer in the lot before he even got near the door. He couldn't have found them in a hundred years.

"I bet he could look all his life and he couldn't find us," said Joey.

They got tired of hiding after a while with no one looking for them. They got up and strolled on down Cannery Row. They looked a long time in Lee's window coveting the pliers, the hack saws, the engineers' caps and the bananas. Then they crossed the street and sat down on the lower step of the stairs that went to the second story of the laboratory.

Joey said, "You know, this guy in here got babies in bottles."

"What kind of babies?" Willard asked.

"Regular babies, only before they're borned."

"I don't believe it," said Willard.

"Well, it's true. The Sprague kid seen them and he says they ain't no bigger than this and they got little hands and feet and eyes."

"And hair?" Willard demanded.

"Well, the Sprague kid didn't say about hair."

"You should of asked him. I think he's a liar."

"You better not let him hear you say that," said Joey.

"Well, you can tell him I said it. I ain't afraid of him and I ain't afraid of you. I ain't afraid of anybody. You want to make something of it?" Joey didn't answer. "Well, do you?"

"No," said Joey. "I was thinkin', why don't we just go up and ask the guy if he's got babies in bottles? Maybe he'd show them to us, that is if he's got any."

"He ain't here," said Willard. "When he's here, his car's here. He's away some place. I think it's a lie. I think the Sprague kid is a liar. I think you're a liar. You want to make something of that?"

It was a lazy day. Willard was going to have to work hard to get up any excitement. "I think you're a coward, too. You want to make something of that?" Joey didn't answer. Willard changed his tactics. "Where's your old man now?" he asked in a conversational tone.

"He's dead," said Joey.

"Oh yeah? I didn't hear. What'd he die of?"

For a moment Joey was silent. He knew Willard knew but he couldn't let on he knew, not without fighting Willard, and Joey was afraid of Willard.

"He committed—he killed himself."

"Yeah?" Willard put on a long face. "How'd he do it?"

"He took rat poison."

Willard's voice shrieked with laughter. "What'd he think—he was a rat?"

Joey chuckled a little at the joke, just enough, that is.

"He must of thought he was a rat," Willard cried. "Did he go crawling around like this—look, Joey—like this? Did he wrinkle up his nose like this? Did he have a big old long tail?" Willard was helpless with laughter. "Why'n't he just get a rat trap and put his head in it?" They laughed themselves out on that one, Willard really wore it out. Then he probed for another joke. "What'd he look like when he took it—like this?" He crossed his eyes and opened his mouth and stuck out his tongue.

"He was sick all day," said Joey. "He didn't die 'til the middle of the night. It hurt him."

Willard said, "What'd he do it for?"

"He couldn't get a job," said Joey. "Nearly a year he couldn't get a job. And you know the funny thing? The next morning a guy come around to give him a job."

Willard tried to recapture his joke. "I guess he just figured he was a rat," he said, but it fell through even for Willard.

Joey stood up and put his hands in his pockets. He saw a little coppery shine in the gutter and walked toward it but just as he reached it Willard shoved him aside and picked up the penny.

"I saw it first," Joey cried. "It's mine."

"You want to try and make something of it?" said Willard. "Why'n't you go take some rat poison?"

27

Mack and the boys—the
Virtues, the Beatitudes, the Beauties. They sat in the
Palace Flophouse and they were the stone dropped in
the pool, the impulse which sent out ripples to all of
Cannery Row and beyond, to Pacific Grove, to Mon-
terey, even over the hill to Carmel.

"This time," said Mack, "we got to be sure he gets
to the party. If he don't get there, we don't give it."

"Where we going to give it this time?" Jones asked.

Mack tipped his chair back against the wall and
hooked his feet around the front legs. "I've give that a
lot of thought," he said. "Of course we could give it
here but it would be pretty hard to surprise him here.
And Doc likes his own place. He's got his music
there." Mack scowled around the room. "I don't know
who broke his phonograph last time," he said. "But if
anybody so much as lays a finger on it next time I
personally will kick the hell out of him."

"I guess we'll just have to give it at his place," said
Hughie.

People didn't get the news of the party—the knowledge of it just slowly grew up in them. And no one was invited. Everyone was going. October 27 had a mental red circle around it. And since it was to be a birthday party there were presents to be considered.

Take the girls at Dora's. All of them had at one time or another gone over to the laboratory for advice or medicine or simply for unprofessional company. And they had seen Doc's bed. It was covered with an old faded red blanket full of fox tails and burrs and sand, for he took it on all his collecting trips. If money came in he bought laboratory equipment. It never occurred to him to buy a new blanket for himself. Dora's girls were making him a patchwork quilt, a beautiful thing of silk. And since most of the silk available came from underclothing and evening dresses, the quilt was glorious in strips of flesh pink and orchid and pale yellow and cerise. They worked on it in the late mornings and in the afternoons before the boys from the sardine fleet came in. Under the community of effort, those fights and ill feelings that always are present in a whore house completely disappeared.

Lee Chong got out and inspected a twenty-five-foot string of firecrackers and a big bag of China lily bulbs. These to his way of thinking were the finest things you could have for a party.

Sam Malloy had long had a theory of antiques. He knew that old furniture and glass and crockery, which had not been very valuable in its day, had when time went by taken on desirability and cash value out of all proportion to its beauty or utility. He knew of one chair that had brought five hundred dollars. Sam collected pieces of historic automobiles and he was convinced that some day his collection, after making him very rich, would repose on black velvet in the best museums. Sam gave the party a good deal of thought and then he went over his treasures which he kept in a big locked box behind the boiler. He decided to give Doc one of his finest pieces—the connecting rod and piston from a 1916 Chalmers. He rubbed and polished this beauty until it gleamed like a piece of ancient armor. He made a little box for it and lined it with black cloth.

Mack and the boys gave the problem considerable thought and came to the conclusion that Doc always wanted cats and had some trouble getting them. Mack brought out his double cage. They borrowed a female in an interesting condition and set their trap under the cypress tree at the top of the vacant lot. In the corner of the Palace they built a wire cage and in it their collection of angry tom cats grew with every night. Jones had to make two trips a day to the canneries for fish heads to feed their charges. Mack considered and correctly that twenty-five tom cats would be as nice a present as they could give Doc.

"No decorations this time," said Mack. "Just a good solid party with lots of liquor."

Gay heard about the party clear over in the Salinas jail and he made a deal with the sheriff to get off that night and borrowed two dollars from him for a round trip bus ticket. Gay had been very nice to the sheriff who wasn't a man to forget it, particularly because election was coming up and Gay could, or said he could, swing quite a few votes. Besides, Gay could give the Salinas jail a bad name if he wanted to.

Henri had suddenly decided that the old-fashioned pincushion was an art form which had flowered and reached its peak in the Nineties and had since been neglected. He revived the form and was delighted to see what could be done with colored pins. The picture was never completed—you could change it by rearranging the pins. He was preparing a group of these pieces for a one-man show when he heard about the party and he instantly abandoned his own work and began a giant pincushion for Doc. It was to be an intricate and provocative design in green, yellow, and blue pins, all cool colors, and its title was Pre-Cambrian Memory.

Henri's friend Eric, a learned barber who collected the first editions of writers who never had a second edition or a second book, decided to give Doc a rowing machine he had got at the bankruptcy proceedings of a client with a three-year barber bill. The rowing machine was in fine condition. No one had rowed it much. No one ever uses a rowing machine.

The conspiracy grew and there were endless visits back and forth, discussion of presents, of liquor, of what time will we start and nobody must tell Doc.

Doc didn't know when he first became aware that something was going on that concerned him. In Lee Chong's, conversation stopped when he entered. At first it seemed to him that people were cold to him. When at least half a dozen people asked him what he was doing October 27 he was puzzled, for he had forgotten he had given this date as his birthday. Actually he had been interested in the horoscope for a spurious birth date but Mack had never mentioned it again and so Doc forgot it.

One evening he stopped in at the Halfway House because they had a draft beer he liked and kept it at the right temperature. He gulped his first glass and then settled down to enjoy his second when he heard a drunk talking to the bartender. "You goin' to the party?"

"What party?"

"Well," said the drunk confidentially, "you know Doc, down in Cannery Row."

The bartender looked up the bar and then back.

"Well," said the drunk, "they're givin' him a hell of a party on his birthday."

"Who is?"

"Everybody."

Doc mulled this over. He did not know the drunk at all.

His reaction to the idea was not simple. He felt a great warmth that they should want to give him a party and at the same time he quaked inwardly remembering the last one they had given.

Now everything fell into place—Mack's question and the silences when he was about. He thought of it a lot that night sitting beside his desk. He glanced about considering what things would have to be locked up. He knew the party was going to cost him plenty.

The next day he began making his own preparations for the party. His best records he carried into the back room where they could be locked away. He moved every bit of equipment that was breakable back there too. He knew how it would be—his guests would be hungry and they wouldn't bring anything to eat. They would run out of liquor early, they always did. A little wearily he went up to the Thrift Market where there was a fine and understanding butcher. They discussed meat for some time. Doc ordered fifteen pounds of steaks, ten pounds of tomatoes, twelve heads of lettuce, six loaves of bread, a big jar of peanut butter and one of strawberry jam, five gallons of wine and four quarts of a good substantial but not distinguished whiskey. He knew he would have trouble at the bank the first of the month. Three or four such parties, he thought, and he would lose the laboratory.

Meanwhile on the Row the planning reached a crescendo. Doc was right, no one thought of food but there were odd pints and quarts put away all over. The collection of presents was growing and the guest list, if there had been one, was a little like a census. At the Bear Flag a constant discussion went on about what to wear. Since they would not be working, the girls did not want to wear the long beautiful dresses which were their uniforms. They decided to wear street clothes. It wasn't as simple as it sounded. Dora insisted that a skeleton crew remain on duty to take care of the regulars. The girls divided up into shifts, some to stay until they were relieved by others. They had to flip for who would go to the party first. The first ones would see Doc's face when they gave him the beautiful quilt. They had it on a frame in the dining room and it was nearly finished. Mrs. Malloy had put aside her bedspread for a while. She was crocheting six doilies for Doc's beer glasses. The first excitement was gone from the Row now and its place was taken by a deadly cumulative earnestness. There were fifteen tom cats in the cage at the Palace Flophouse and their yowling made Darling a little nervous at night.

28

Sooner or later Frankie was bound to hear about the party. For Frankie drifted about like a small cloud. He was always on the edge of groups. No one noticed him or paid any attention to him. You couldn't tell whether he was listening or not. But Frankie did hear about the party and he heard about the presents and a feeling of fullness swelled in him and a feeling of sick longing.

In the window of Jacob's Jewelry Store was the most beautiful thing in the world. It had been there a long time. It was a black onyx clock with a gold face but on top of it was the real beauty. On top was a bronze group—St. George killing the dragon. The dragon was on his back with his claws in the air and in his breast was St. George's spear. The Saint was in full armor with the visor raised and he rode a fat, big-buttocked horse. With his spear he pinned the dragon to the ground. But the wonderful thing was that he wore a pointed beard and he looked a little like Doc.

Frankie walked to Alvarado Street several times a week to stand in front of the window and look at this beauty. He dreamed about it too, dreamed of running his fingers over the rich, smooth bronze. He had known about it for months when he heard of the party and the presents.

Frankie stood on the sidewalk for an hour before he went inside. "Well?" said Mr. Jacobs. He had given Frankie a visual frisk as he came in and he knew there wasn't 75 cents on him.

"How much is that?" Frankie asked huskily.

"What?"

"That."

"You mean the clock? Fifty dollars—with the group seventy-five dollars."

Frankie walked out without replying. He went down to the beach and crawled under an overturned rowboat and peeked out at the little waves. The bronze beauty was so strong in his head that it seemed to stand out in front of him. And a frantic trapped feeling came over him. He had to get the beauty. His eyes were fierce when he thought of it.

He stayed under the boat all day and at night he emerged and went back to Alvarado Street. While people went to the movies and came out and went to the Golden Poppy, he walked up and down the block. And he didn't get tired or sleepy, for the beauty burned in him like fire.

At last the people thinned out and gradually disappeared from the streets and the parked cars drove away and the town settled to sleep.

A policeman looked closely at Frankie. "What you doing out?" he asked.

Frankie took to his heels and fled around the corner and hid behind a barrel in the alley. At two-thirty he crept to the door of Jacob's and tried the knob. It was locked. Frankie went back to the alley and sat behind the barrel and thought. He saw a broken piece of concrete lying beside the barrel and picked it up.

The policeman reported that he heard the crash and ran to it. Jacob's window was broken. He saw the prisoner walking rapidly away and chased him. He didn't know how the boy could run that far and that fast carrying fifty pounds of clock and bronze, but the prisoner nearly got away. If he had not blundered into a blind street he would have got away.

The chief called Doc the next day. "Come on down, will you? I want to talk to you."

They brought Frankie in very dirty and frowzy. His eyes were red but he held his mouth firm and he even smiled a little welcome when he saw Doc.

"What's the matter, Frankie?" Doc asked.

"He broke into Jacob's last night," the chief said. "Stole some stuff. We got in touch with his mother. She says it's not her fault because he hangs around your place all the time."

"Frankie—you shouldn't have done it," said Doc. The heavy stone of inevitability was on his heart. "Can't you parole him to me?" Doc asked.

"I don't think the judge will do it," said the chief. "We've got a mental report. You know what's wrong with him?"

"Yes," said Doc, "I know."

"And you know what's likely to happen when he comes into puberty?"

"Yes," said Doc, "I know," and the stone weighed terribly on his heart.

"The doctor thinks we better put him away. We

couldn't before, but now he's got a felony on him, I think we better."

As Frankie listened the welcome died in his eyes. "What did he take?" Doc asked.

"A great big clock and a bronze statue."

"I'll pay for it."

"Oh, we got it back. I don't think the judge will hear of it. It'll just happen again. You know that."

"Yes," said Doc softly, "I know. But maybe he had a reason. Frankie," he said, "why did you take it?"

Frankie looked a long time at him. "I love you," he said.

Doc ran out and got in his car and went collecting in the caves below Pt. Lobos.

29

At four o'clock on October 27 Doc finished bottling the last of a lot of jellyfish. He washed out the formaline jug, cleaned his forceps, powdered and took off his rubber gloves. He went upstairs, fed the rats, and put some of his best records and his microscopes in the back room. Then he locked it. Sometimes an illuminated guest wanted to play with the rattlesnakes. By making careful preparations, by foreseeing possibilities, Doc hoped to make this party as non-lethal as possible without making it dull.

He put on a pot of coffee, started the *Great Fugue* on the phonograph, and took a shower. He was very quick about it, for he was dressed in clean clothes and was having his cup of coffee before the music was completed.

He looked out through the window at the lot and up at the Palace but no one was moving. Doc didn't know who or how many were coming to his party. But he knew he was watched. He had been conscious of it all day. Not that he had seen anyone, but someone or several people had kept him in sight. So it was to be a surprise party. He might as well be surprised. He would follow his usual routine as though nothing were happening. He crossed to Lee Chong's and bought two quarts of beer. There seemed to be a suppressed Oriental excitement at Lee's. So they were coming too. Doc went back to the laboratory and poured out a glass of beer. He drank the first off for thirst and poured a second one for taste. The lot and the street were still deserted.

Mack and the boys were in the Palace and the door was closed. All afternoon the stove had roared, heating water for baths. Even Darling had been bathed and she wore a red bow around her neck.

"What time you think we should go over?" Hazel asked.

"I don't think before eight o'clock," said Mack. "But I don't see nothin' against us havin' a short one to kind of get warmed up."

"How about Doc getting warmed up?" Hughie said. "Maybe I ought to just take him a bottle like it was just nothing."

"No," said Mack. "Doc just went over to Lee's for some beer."

'You think he suspects anything?" Jones asked.

"How could he?" asked Mack.

In the corner cage two tom cats started an argument and the whole cageful commented with growls and arched backs. There were only twenty-one cats. They had fallen short of their mark.

"I wonder how we'll get them cats over there?" Hazel began. "We can't carry that big cage through the door."

"We won't," said Mack. "Remember how it was

with the frogs. No, we'll just tell Doc about them. He can come over and get them." Mack got up and opened one of Eddie's wining jugs. "We might as well get warmed up," he said.

At five-thirty the old Chinaman flap-flapped down the hill, past the Palace. He crossed the lot, crossed the street, and disappeared between Western Biological and the Hediondo.

At the Bear Flag the girls were getting ready. A kind of anchor watch had been chosen by straws. The ones who stayed were to be relieved every hour.

Dora was splendid. Her hair freshly dyed orange was curled and piled on her head. She wore her wedding ring and a big diamond brooch on her breast. Her dress was white silk with a black bamboo pattern. In the bedrooms the reverse of ordinary procedure was in practice.

Those who were staying wore long evening dresses while those who were going had on short print dresses and looked very pretty. The quilt, finished and backed, was in a big cardboard box in the bar. The bouncer grumbled a little, for it had been decided that he couldn't go to the party. Someone had to look after the house. Contrary to orders, each girl had a pint hidden and each girl watched for the signal to fortify herself a little for the party.

Dora strode magnificently into her office and closed the door. She unlocked the top drawer of the rolltop desk, took out a bottle and a glass and poured herself a snort. And the bottle clinked softly on the glass. A girl listening outside the door heard the clink and spread the word. Dora would not be able to smell breaths now. And the girls rushed for their rooms and got out their pints. Dusk had come to Cannery Row, the gray time between daylight and street light. Phyllis Mae peeked around the curtain in the front parlor.

"Can you see him?" Doris asked.

"Yeah. He's got the lights on. He's sitting there like he's reading. Jesus, how that guy does read. You'd think he'd ruin his eyes. He's got a glass of beer in his hand."

"Well," said Doris, "we might as well have a little one, I guess."

Phyllis Mae was still limping a little but she was as good as new. She could, she said, lick her weight in City Councilmen. "Seems kind of funny," she said. "There he is, sitting over there and he don't know what's going to happen."

"He never comes in here for a trick," Doris said a little sadly.

"Lots of guys don't want to pay," said Phyllis Mae. "Costs them more but they figure it different."

"Well, hell, maybe he likes them."

"Likes who?"

"Them girls that go over there."

"Oh, yeah—maybe he does. I been over there. He never made a pass at me."

"He wouldn't," said Doris. "But that don't mean if you didn't work here you wouldn't have to fight your way out."

"You mean he don't like our profession?"

"No, I don't mean that at all. He probably figures a girl that's workin' has got a different attitude."

They had another small snort.

In her office Dora poured herself one more, swallowed it and locked the drawer again. She fixed her perfect hair in the wall mirror, inspected her shining red nails, and went out to the bar. Alfred the bouncer was sulking. It wasn't anything he said nor was his expression unpleasant, but he was sulking just the same. Dora looked him over coldly. "I guess you figure you're getting the blocks, don't you?"

"No," said Alfred. "No, it's quite all right."

That quite threw Dora. "Quite all right, is it? You got a job, Mister. Do you want to keep it or not?"

"It's quite all right," Alfred said frostily. "I ain't putting out no beef." He put his elbows on the bar and studied himself in the mirror. "You just go and enjoy yourself," he said. "I'll take care of everything here. You don't need to worry."

Dora melted under his pain. "Look," she said. "I don't like to have the place without a man. Some lush might get smart and the kids couldn't handle him. But a little later you can come over and you could kind of keep your eye on the place out the window. How would that be? You could see if anything happened."

"Well," said Alfred, "I would like to come." He was mollified by her permission. "Later I might drop over for just a minute or two. They was a mean drunk in last night. An' I don't know, Dora—I kind of lost my nerve since I bust that guy's back. I just ain't sure of myself no more. I'm gonna pull a punch some night and get took."

"You need a rest," said Dora. "Maybe I'll get Mack to fill in and you can take a couple of weeks off." She was a wonderful madam, Dora was.

Over at the laboratory, Doc had a little whiskey after his beer. He was feeling a little mellow. It seemed a nice thing to him that they would give him a

party. He played the *Pavane to a Dead Princess* and
felt sentimental and a little sad. And because of his
feeling he went on with *Daphnis and Chloe*. There was
a passage in it that reminded him of something else.
The observers in Athens before Marathon reported seeing a great line of dust crossing the Plain, and they
heard the clash of arms and they heard the Eleusinian
Chant. There was part of the music that reminded him
of that picture.

When it was done he got another whiskey and he
debated in his mind about the *Brandenburg*. That
would snap him out of the sweet and sickly mood he
was getting into. But what was wrong with the sweet
and sickly mood? It was rather pleasant. "I can play
anything I want," he said aloud. "I can play *Clair de
Lune* or *The Maiden with Flaxen Hair*. I'm a free
man."

He poured a whiskey and drank it. And he compro-
mised with the *Moonlight Sonata*. He could see the
neon light of La Ida blinking on and off. And then the
street light in front of the Bear Flag came on.

A squadron of huge brown beetles hurled themselves against the light and then fell to the ground and
moved their legs and felt around with their antennae.
A lady cat strolled lonesomely along the gutter looking
for adventure. She wondered what had happened to all
the tom cats who had made life interesting and the
nights hideous.

Mr. Malloy on his hands and knees peered out of
the boiler door to see if anyone had gone to the party
yet. In the Palace the boys sat restlessly watching the
black hands of the alarm clock.

30

The nature of parties has been imperfectly studied. It is, however, generally understood that a party has a pathology, that it is a kind of an individual and that it is likely to be a very perverse individual. And it is also generally understood that a party hardly ever goes the way it is planned or intended. This last, of course, excludes those dismal slave parties, whipped and controlled and dominated, given by ogreish professional hostesses. These are not parties at all but acts and demonstrations, about as spontaneous as peristalsis and as interesting as its end product.

Probably everyone in Cannery Row had projected his imagination to how the party would be—the shouts of greeting, the congratulation, the noise and good feeling. And it didn't start that way at all. Promptly at eight o'clock Mack and the boys, combed and clean, picked up their jugs and marched down the chicken walk, over the railroad track, through the lot across the street and up the steps of Western Biological. Everyone was embarrassed. Doc held the door open and Mack made a little speech. "Being as how it's your birthday, I and the boys thought we would wish you happy birthday and we got twenty-one cats for you for a present."

He stopped and they stood forlornly on the stairs.

"Come on in," said Doc. "Why—I'm—I'm surprised. I didn't even know you knew it was my birthday."

"All tom cats," said Hazel. "We didn't bring 'em down."

They sat down formally in the room at the left. There was a long silence. "Well," said Doc, "now you're here, how about a little drink?"

Mack said, "We brought a little snort," and he indicated the three jugs Eddie had been accumulating. "They ain't no beer in it," said Eddie.

Doc covered his early evening reluctance. "No," he said. "You've got to have a drink with me. It just happens I laid in some whiskey."

They were just seated formally, sipping delicately at the whiskey, when Dora and the girls came in. They presented the quilt. Doc laid it over his bed and it was beautiful. And they accepted a little drink. Mr. and Mrs. Malloy followed with their presents.

"Lots of folks don't know what this stuff's going to be worth," said Sam Malloy as he brought out the Chalmers 1916 piston and connecting rod. "There probably isn't three of these here left in the world."

And now people began to arrive in droves. Henri came in with a pincushion three by four feet. He wanted to give a lecture on his new art form but by this time the formality was broken. Mr. and Mrs. Gay came in. Lee Chong presented the great string of firecrack-

ers and the China lily bulbs. Someone ate the lily
bulbs by eleven o'clock but the firecrackers lasted
longer. A group of comparative strangers came in from
La Ida. The stiffness was going out of the party
quickly. Dora sat in a kind of throne, her orange hair
flaming. She held her whiskey glass daintily with her
little finger extended. And she kept an eye on the girls
to see that they conducted themselves properly. Doc
put dance music on the phonograph and he went to the
kitchen and began to fry the steaks.

The first fight was not a bad one. One of the group
from La Ida made an immoral proposal to one of Dora's
girls. She protested and Mack and the boys, outraged
at this breach of propriety, threw him out quickly and
without breaking anything. They felt good then, for
they knew they were contributing.

Out in the kitchen Doc was frying steaks in three
skillets, and he cut up tomatoes and piled up sliced
bread. He felt very good. Mack was personally taking
care of the phonograph. He had found an album of
Benny Goodman's trios. Dancing had started, indeed
the party was beginning to take on depth and vigor.
Eddie went into the office and did a tap dance. Doc
had taken a pint with him to the kitchen and he helped
himself from the bottle. He was feeling better and
better. Everybody was surprised when he served the
meat. Nobody was really hungry and they cleaned it
up instantly. Now the food set the party into a kind of
rich digestive sadness. The whiskey was gone and Doc
brought out the gallons of wine.

Dora, sitting enthroned, said, "Doc, play some of
that nice music. I get Christ awful sick of that juke
box over home."

Then Doc played *Ardo* and the *Amor* from an album
of Monteverdi. And the guests sat quietly and their
eyes were inward. Dora breathed beauty. Two newcomers crept up the stairs and entered quietly. Doc
was feeling a golden pleasant sadness. The guests
were silent when the music stopped. Doc brought out a
book and he read in a clear, deep voice:

Even now
If I see in my soul the citron-breasted fair one
Still gold-tinted, her face like our night stars,
Drawing unto her; her body beaten about with
    flame,
Wounded by the flaring spear of love,
My first of all by reason of her fresh years,
Then is my heart buried alive in snow.

Even now
If my girl with lotus eyes came to me again
Weary with the dear weight of young love,
Again I would give her to these starved twins of
    arms
And from her mouth drink down the heavy wine,
As a reeling pirate bee in fluttered ease
Steals up the honey from the nenuphar.

Even now
If I saw her lying all wide eyes
And with collyrium the indent of her cheek
Lengthened to the bright ear and her pale side
So suffering the fever of my distance,
Then would my love for her be ropes of flowers,
    and night
A black-haired lover on the breasts of day.

Even now
My eyes that hurry to see no more are painting,
    painting
Faces of my lost girl. O golden rings
That tap against cheeks of small magnolia leaves,
O whitest so soft parchment where
My poor divorcèd lips have written excellent
Stanzas of kisses, and will write no more.

Even now
Death sends me the flickering of powdery lids
Over wild eyes and the pity of her slim body
All broken up with the weariness of joy;
The little red flowers of her breasts to be my
    comfort
Moving above scarves, and for my sorrow
Wet crimson lips that once I marked as mine.

Even now
They chatter her weakness through the two bazaars
Who was so strong to love me. And small men
That buy and sell for silver being slaves
Crinkle the fat about their eyes; and yet
No Prince of the Cities of the Sea has taken her,
Leading to his grim bed. Little lonely one,
You clung to me as a garment clings; my girl.

Even now
I love long black eyes that caress like silk,
Ever and ever sad and laughing eyes,
Whose lids make such sweet shadow when they
    close
It seems another beautiful look of hers.

I love a fresh mouth, ah, a scented mouth,
And curving hair, subtle as a smoke,
And light fingers, and laughter of green gems.

Even now
I remember that you made answer very softly,
We being one soul, your hand on my hair,
The burning memory rounding your near lips:
I have seen the priestesses of Rati make love at
    moon fall
And then in a carpeted hall with a bright gold
    lamp
Lie down carelessly anywhere to sleep.[1]

Phyllis Mae was openly weeping when he stopped
and Dora herself dabbed at her eyes. Hazel was so
taken by the sound of the words that he had not listened to their meaning. But a little world-sadness had
slipped over all of them. Everyone was remembering a
lost love, everyone a call.

Mack said, "Jesus, that's pretty. Reminds me of a
dame—" and he let it pass. They filled the wine
glasses and became quiet. The party was slipping
away in sweet sadness. Eddie went out in the office
and did a little tap dance and came back and sat down
again. The party was about to recline and go to sleep
when there was a tramp of feet on the stairs. A great
voice shouted, "Where's the girls?"

Mack got up almost happily and crossed quickly to
the door. And a smile of joy illuminated the faces of
Hughie and Jones. "What girls you got in mind?"
Mack asked softly.

[1] "Black Marigolds," translated from the Sanskrit by E. Powys Mathers.

"Ain't this a whore house? Cab driver said they was one down here."

"You made a mistake, Mister." Mack's voice was gay.

"Well, what's them dames in there?"

They joined battle then. They were the crew of a San Pedro tuna boat, good hard happy fight-wise men. With the first rush they burst through to the party. Dora's girls had each one slipped off a shoe and held it by the toe. As the fight raged by they would clip a man on the head with the spike heel. Dora leaped for the kitchen and came roaring out with a meat grinder. Even Doc was happy. He flailed about with the Chalmers 1916 piston and connecting rod.

It was a good fight. Hazel tripped and got kicked in the face twice before he could get to his feet again. The Franklin stove went over with a crash. Driven to a corner the newcomers defended themselves with heavy books from the bookcases. But gradually they were driven back. The two front windows were broken out. Suddenly Alfred, who had heard the trouble from across the street, attacked from the rear with his favorite weapon, an indoor ball bat. The fight raged down the steps and into the street and across the lot. The front door was hanging limply from one hinge again. Doc's shirt was torn off and his slight strong shoulder dripped blood from a scratch. The enemy was driven half-way up the lot when sirens sounded. Doc's birthday party had barely time to get inside the laboratory and wedge the broken door closed and turn out the lights before the police car cruised up. The cops didn't find anything. But the party was sitting in the dark giggling happily and drinking wine. The shift changed at the Bear Flag. The fresh contingent raged in full of hell. And then the party really got going. The cops came back, looked in, clicked their tongues and joined it. Mack and the boys used the squad car to go to Jimmy Brucia's for more wine and Jimmy came back with them. You could hear the roar of the party from end to end of Cannery Row. The party had all the best qualities of a riot and a night on the barricades. The crew from the San Pedro tuna boat crept humbly back and joined the party. They were embraced and admired. A woman five blocks away called the police to complain about the noise and couldn't get anyone. The cops reported their own car stolen and found it later on the beach. Doc sitting cross-legged on the table smiled and tapped his fingers gently on his knee. Mack and Phyllis Mae were doing Indian wrestling on the floor. And the cool bay wind blew in through the broken windows. It was then that someone lighted the twenty-five-foot string of firecrackers.

31

A well-grown gopher took up residence in a thicket of mallow weeds in the vacant lot on Cannery Row. It was a perfect place. The deep green luscious mallows towered up crisp and rich and as they matured their little cheeses hung down provocatively. The earth was perfect for a gopher hole too, black and soft and yet with a little clay in it so that it didn't crumble and the tunnels didn't cave in. The gopher was fat and sleek and he had always plenty of food in his cheek pouches. His little ears were clean and well set and his eyes were as black as old-fashioned pin heads and just about the same size. His digging hands were strong and the fur on his back was glossy brown and the fawn-colored fur on his chest was incredibly soft and rich. He had long curving yellow teeth and a little short tail. Altogether he was a beautiful gopher and in the prime of his life.

He came to the place over land and found it good and he began his burrow on a little eminence where he could look out among the mallow weeds and see the trucks go by on Cannery Row. He could watch the feet of Mack and the boys as they crossed the lot to the Palace Flophouse. As he dug down into the coal-black earth he found it even more perfect, for there were great rocks under the soil. When he made his great chamber for the storing of food it was under a rock so that it could never cave in no matter how hard it rained. It was a place where he could settle down and raise any number of families and the burrow could increase in all directions.

It was beautiful in the early morning when he first poked his head out of the burrow. The mallows filtered green light down on him and the first rays of the rising sun shone into his hole and warmed it so that he lay there content and very comfortable.

When he had dug his great chamber and his four emergency exits and his waterproof deluge room, the gopher began to store food. He cut down only the perfect mallow stems and trimmed them to the exact length he needed and he took them down the hole and stacked them neatly in his great chamber, and arranged them so they wouldn't ferment or get sour. He had found the perfect place to live. There were no gardens about so no one would think of setting a trap for him. Cats there were, many of them, but they were so bloated with fish heads and guts from the canneries that they had long ago given up hunting. The soil was sandy enough so that water never stood about or filled a hole for long. The gopher worked and worked until he had his great chamber crammed with food. Then he made little side chambers for the babies who would inhabit them. In a few years there might be thousands of his progeny spreading out from this original hearthstone.

But as time went on the gopher began to be a little

impatient, for no female appeared. He sat in the entrance of his hole in the morning and made penetrating squeaks that are inaudible to the human ear but can be heard deep in the earth by other gophers. And still no female appeared. Finally in a sweat of impatience he went up across the track until he found another gopher hole. He squeaked provocatively in the entrance. He heard a rustling and smelled female and then out of the hole came an old battle-torn bull gopher who mauled and bit him so badly that he crept home and lay in his great chamber for three days recovering and he lost two toes from one front paw from that fight.

Again he waited and squeaked beside his beautiful burrow in the beautiful place but no female ever came and after a while he had to move away. He had to move two blocks up the hill to a dahlia garden where they put out traps every night.

32

Doc awakened very slowly and clumsily like a fat man getting out of a swimming pool. His mind broke the surface and fell back several times. There was red lipstick on his beard. He opened one eye, saw the brilliant colors of the quilt and closed his eye quickly. But after a while he looked again. His eye went past the quilt to the floor, to the broken plate in the corner, to the glasses standing on the table turned over on the floor, to the spilled wine and the books like heavy fallen butterflies. There were little bits of curled red paper all over the place and the sharp smell of firecrackers. He could see through the kitchen door to the steak plates stacked high and the skillets deep in grease. Hundreds of cigarette butts were stamped out on the floor. And under the fire-cracker smell was a fine combination of wine and whiskey and perfume. His eye stopped for a moment on a little pile of hairpins in the middle of the floor.

He rolled over slowly and supporting himself on one elbow he looked out the broken window. Cannery Row was quiet and sunny. The boiler door was open. The door of the Palace Flophouse was closed. A man slept peacefully among the weeds in the vacant lot. The Bear Flag was shut up tight.

Doc got up and went into the kitchen and lighted the gas water heater on his way to the toilet. Then he came back and sat on the edge of the bed and worked his toes together while he surveyed the wreckage. From up the hill he could hear the church bells ringing. When the gas heater began rumbling he went back to the bathroom and took a shower and he put on blue jeans and a flannel shirt. Lee Chong was closed but he saw who was at the door and opened it. He went to the refrigerator and brought out a quart of beer without being asked. Doc paid him.

"Good time?" Lee asked. His brown eyes were a little inflamed in their pouches.

"Good time!" said Doc and he went back to the laboratory with his cold beer. He made a peanut butter sandwich to eat with his beer. It was very quiet in the street. No one went by at all. Doc heard music in his head—violas and cellos, he thought. And they played cool, soft, soothing music with nothing much to distinguish it. He ate his sandwich and sipped his beer and listened to the music. When he had finished his beer, Doc went into the kitchen, and cleared the dirty dishes out of the sink. He ran hot water in it and poured soap chips under the running water so that the foam stood high and white. Then he moved about collecting all the glasses that weren't broken. He put them in the soapy hot water. The steak plates were piled high on the stove with their brown juice and their white grease sticking them together. Doc cleared a place on the table for the clean glasses as he washed them. Then he unlocked the

door of the back room and brought out one of his albums
of Gregorian music and he put a Pater Noster and Ag-
nus Dei on the turntable and started it going. The angelic, disembodied voices filled the laboratory. They
were incredibly pure and sweet. Doc worked carefully
washing the glasses so that they would not clash together and spoil the music. The boys' voices carried the
melody up and down, simply but with the richness that
is in no other singing. When the record had finished,
Doc wiped his hands and turned it off. He saw a book
lying half under his bed and picked it up and he sat
down on the bed. For a moment he read to himself but
then his lips began to move and in a moment he read
aloud—slowly, pausing at the end of each line.

Even now
I mind the coming and talking of wise men from
    towers
Where they had thought away their youth. And I,
    listening,
Found not the salt of the whispers of my girl,
Murmur of confused colors, as we lay near sleep;
Little wise words and little witty words,
Wanton as water, honied with eagerness.

In the sink the high white foam cooled and ticked as
the bubbles burst. Under the piers it was very high
tide and the waves splashed on rocks they had not
reached in a long time.

Even now
I mind that I loved cypress and roses, clear,
The great blue mountains and the small gray hills,

The sounding of the sea. Upon a day
I saw strange eyes and hands like butterflies;
For me at morning larks flew from the thyme
And children came to bathe in little streams.

Doc closed the book. He could hear the waves beat
under the piles and he could hear the scampering of
white rats against the wire. He went into the kitchen
and felt the cooling water in the sink. He ran hot water
into it. He spoke aloud to the sink and the white rats,
and to himself:

Even now,
I know that I have savored the hot taste of life
Lifting green cups and gold at the great feast.
Just for a small and a forgotten time
I have had full in my eyes from off my girl
The whitest pouring of eternal light—

He wiped his eyes with the back of his hand. And
the white rats scampered and scrambled in their
cages. And behind the glass the rattlesnakes lay still
and stared into space with their dusty frowning eyes.

OF MICE AND MEN

A few miles south of Soledad, the Salinas River drops in close to the hillside bank and runs deep and green. The water is warm too, for it has slipped twinkling over the yellow sands in the sunlight before reaching the narrow pool. On one side of the river the golden foothill slopes curve up to the strong and rocky Gabilan mountains, but on the valley side the water is lined with trees—willows fresh and green with every spring, carrying in their lower leaf junctures the debris of the winter's flooding; and sycamores with mottled, white, recumbent limbs and branches that arch over the pool. On the sandy bank under the trees the leaves lie deep and so crisp that a lizard makes a great skittering if he runs among them. Rabbits come out of the brush to sit on the sand in the evening, and the damp flats are covered with the night tracks of 'coons, and with the spread pads of dogs from the ranches, and with the split-wedge tracks of deer that come to drink in the dark.

There is a path through the willows and among the sycamores, a path beaten hard by boys coming down from the ranches to swim in the deep pool, and beaten hard by tramps who come wearily down from the highway in the evening to jungle-up near water. In front of the low horizontal limb of a giant sycamore there is an ash pile made by many fires; the limb is worn smooth by men who have sat on it.

Evening of a hot day started the little wind to moving among the leaves. The shade climbed up the hills toward the top. On the sand banks the rabbits sat as quietly as little gray, sculptured stones. And then from the direction of the state highway came the sound of footsteps on crisp sycamore leaves. The rabbits hurried noiselessly for cover. A stilted heron labored up into the air and pounded down river. For a moment the place was lifeless, and then two men emerged from the path and came into the opening by the green pool.

They had walked in single file down the path, and even in the open one stayed behind the other. Both were dressed in denim trousers and in denim coats with brass buttons. Both wore black, shapeless hats and both carried tight blanket rolls slung over their shoulders. The first man was small and quick, dark of face, with restless eyes and sharp, strong features. Every part of him was defined: small, strong hands, slender arms, a thin and bony nose. Behind him walked his opposite, a huge man, shapeless of face, with large, pale eyes, with wide, sloping shoulders; and he walked heavily, dragging his feet a little, the way a bear drags his paws. His arms did not swing at his sides, but hung loosely.

The first man stopped short in the clearing, and the

follower nearly ran over him. He took off his hat and wiped the sweat-band with his forefinger and snapped the moisture off. His huge companion dropped his blankets and flung himself down and drank from the surface of the green pool; drank with long gulps, snorting into the water like a horse. The small man stepped nervously beside him.

"Lennie!" he said sharply. "Lennie, for God' sakes don't drink so much." Lennie continued to snort into the pool. The small man leaned over and shook him by the shoulder. "Lennie. You gonna be sick like you was last night."

Lennie dipped his whole head under, hat and all, and then he sat up on the bank and his hat dripped down on his blue coat and ran down his back. "Tha's good," he said. "You drink some, George. You take a good big drink." He smiled happily.

George unslung his bindle and dropped it gently on the bank. "I ain't sure it's good water," he said. "Looks kinda scummy."

Lennie dabbled his big paw in the water and wiggled his fingers so the water arose in little splashes; rings widened across the pool to the other side and came back again. Lennie watched them go. "Look, George. Look what I done."

George knelt beside the pool and drank from his hand with quick scoops. "Tastes all right," he admitted. "Don't really seem to be running, though. You never oughta drink water when it ain't running, Lennie," he said hopelessly. "You'd drink out of a gutter if you was thirsty." He threw a scoop of water into his face and rubbed it about with his hand, under his chin and around the back of his neck. Then he replaced his hat, pushed himself back from the river, drew up his knees and embraced them. Lennie, who had been watching, imitated George exactly. He pushed himself back, drew up his knees, embraced them, looked over to George to see whether he had it just right. He pulled his hat down a little more over his eyes, the way George's hat was.

George stared morosely at the water. The rims of his eyes were red with sun glare. He said angrily, "We could just as well of rode clear to the ranch if that bastard bus driver knew what he was talkin' about. 'Jes' a little stretch down the highway,' he says. 'Jes' a little stretch.' God damn near four miles, that's what it was! Didn't wanta stop at the ranch gate, that's what. Too God damn lazy to pull up. Wonder he isn't too damn good to stop in Soledad at all. Kicks us out and says, 'Jes' a little stretch down the road.' I bet it was *more* than four miles. Damn hot day."

Lennie looked timidly over to him. "George?"

"Yeah, what ya want?"

"Where we goin', George?"

The little man jerked down the brim of his hat and scowled over at Lennie. "So you forgot that awready, did you? I gotta tell you again, do I? Jesus Christ, you're a crazy bastard!"

"I forgot," Lennie said softly. "I tried not to forget. Honest to God I did, George."

"O.K.—O.K. I'll tell ya again. I ain't got nothing to do. Might jus' as well spen' all my time tellin' you things and then you forget 'em, and I tell you again."

"Tried and tried," said Lennie, "but it didn't do no good. I remember about the rabbits, George."

"The hell with the rabbits. That's all you ever can

remember is them rabbits. O.K.! Now you listen and this time you got to remember so we don't get in no trouble. You remember settin' in that gutter on Howard street and watchin' that blackboard?"

Lennie's face broke into a delighted smile. "Why sure, George, I remember that . . . but . . . what'd we do then? I remember some girls come by and you says . . . you say . . ."

"The hell with what I says. You remember about us goin' into Murray and Ready's, and they give us work cards and bus tickets?"

"Oh, sure, George. I remember that now." His hands went quickly into his side coat pockets. He said gently, "George . . . I ain't got mine. I musta lost it." He looked down at the ground in despair.

"You never had none, you crazy bastard. I got both of 'em here. Think I'd let you carry your own work card?"

Lennie grinned with relief. "I . . . I thought I put it in my side pocket." His hand went into the pocket again.

George looked sharply at him. "What'd you take outa that pocket?"

"Ain't a thing in my pocket," Lennie said cleverly.

"I know there ain't. You got it in your hand. What you got in your hand—hidin' it?"

"I ain't got nothin', George. Honest."

"Come on, give it here."

Lennie held his closed hand away from George's direction. "It's on'y a mouse, George."

"A mouse? A live mouse?"

"Uh-uh. Jus' a dead mouse, George. I didn' kill it. Honest! I found it. I found it dead."

"Give it here!" said George.

"Aw, leave me have it, George."

"Give it here!"

Lennie's closed hand slowly obeyed. George took the mouse and threw it across the pool to the other side, among the brush. "What you want of a dead mouse, anyways?"

"I could pet it with my thumb while we walked along," said Lennie.

"Well, you ain't petting no mice while you walk with me. You remember where we're goin' now?"

Lennie looked startled and then in embarrassment hid his face against his knees. "I forgot again."

"Jesus Christ," George said resignedly. "Well— look, we're gonna work on a ranch like the one we come from up north."

"Up north?"

"In Weed."

"Oh, sure. I remember. In Weed."

"That ranch we're goin' to is right down there about a quarter mile. We're gonna go in an' see the boss. Now, look—I'll give him the work tickets, but you ain't gonna say a word. You jus' stand there and don't say nothing. If he finds out what a crazy bastard you are, we won't get no job, but if he sees ya work before he hears ya talk, we're set. Ya got that?"

"Sure, George. Sure I got it."

"O.K. Now when we go in to see the boss, what you gonna do?"

"I . . . I," Lennie thought. His face grew tight with thought. "I . . . ain't gonna say nothin'. Jus' gonna stan' there."

"Good boy. That's swell. You say that over two, three times so you sure won't forget it."

Lennie droned to himself softly, "I ain't gonna say

nothin' . . . I ain't gonna say nothin' . . . I ain't gonna say nothin'."

"O.K.," said George. "An' you ain't gonna do no bad things like you done in Weed, neither."

Lennie looked puzzled. "Like I done in Weed?"

"Oh, so ya forgot that too, did ya? Well, I ain't gonna remind ya, fear ya do it again."

A light of understanding broke on Lennie's face. "They run us outa Weed," he exploded triumphantly.

"Run us out, hell," said George disgustedly. "We run. They was lookin' for us, but they didn't catch us."

Lennie giggled happily. "I didn't forget that, you bet."

George lay back on the sand and crossed his hands under his head, and Lennie imitated him, raising his head to see whether he were doing it right. "God, you're a lot of trouble," said George. "I could get along so easy and so nice if I didn't have you on my tail. I could live so easy and maybe have a girl."

For a moment Lennie lay quiet, and then he said hopefully, "We gonna work on a ranch, George."

"Awright. You got that. But we're gonna sleep here because I got a reason."

The day was going fast now. Only the tops of the Gabilan mountains flamed with the light of the sun that had gone from the valley. A water snake slipped along on the pool, its head held up like a little periscope. The reeds jerked slightly in the current. Far off toward the highway a man shouted something, and another man shouted back. The sycamore limbs rustled under a little wind that died immediately.

"George—why ain't we goin' on to the ranch and get some supper? They got supper at the ranch."

George rolled on his side. "No reason at all for you. I like it here. Tomorra we're gonna go to work. I seen thrashin' machines on the way down. That means we'll be bucking grain bags, bustin' a gut. Tonight I'm gonna lay right here and look up. I like it."

Lennie got up on his knees and looked down at George. "Ain't we gonna have no supper?"

"Sure we are, if you gather up some dead willow sticks. I got three cans of beans in my bindle. You get a fire ready. I'll give you a match when you get the sticks together. Then we'll heat the beans and have supper."

Lennie said, "I like beans with ketchup."

"Well, we ain't got no ketchup. You go get wood. An' don't you fool around. It'll be dark before long."

Lennie lumbered to his feet and disappeared in the brush. George lay where he was and whistled softly to himself. There were sounds of splashings down the river in the direction Lennie had taken. George stopped whistling and listened. "Poor bastard," he said softly, and then went on whistling again.

In a moment Lennie came crashing back through the brush. He carried one small willow stick in his hand. George sat up. "Awright," he said brusquely. "Gi'me that mouse!"

But Lennie made an elaborate pantomime of innocence. "What mouse, George? I ain't got no mouse."

George held out his hand. "Come on. Give it to me. You ain't puttin' nothing over."

Lennie hesitated, backed away, looked wildly at the brush line as though he contemplated running for his freedom. George said coldly, "You gonna give me that mouse or do I have to sock you?"

"Give you what, George?"

"You know God damn well what. I want that mouse."

Lennie reluctantly reached into his pocket. His voice broke a little. "I don't know why I can't keep it. It ain't nobody's mouse. I didn't steal it. I found it lyin' right beside the road."

George's hand remained outstretched imperiously. Slowly, like a terrier who doesn't want to bring a ball to its master, Lennie approached, drew back, approached again. George snapped his fingers sharply, and at the sound Lennie laid the mouse in his hand.

"I wasn't doin' nothing bad with it, George. Jus' strokin' it."

George stood up and threw the mouse as far as he could into the darkening brush, and then he stepped to the pool and washed his hands. "You crazy fool. Don't you think I could see your feet was wet where you went acrost the river to get it?" He heard Lennie's whimpering cry and wheeled about. "Blubberin' like a baby! Jesus Christ! A big guy like you." Lennie's lip quivered and tears started in his eyes. "Aw, Lennie!" George put his hand on Lennie's shoulder. "I ain't takin' it away jus' for meanness. That mouse ain't fresh, Lennie; and besides, you've broke it pettin' it. You get another mouse that's fresh and I'll let you keep it a little while."

Lennie sat down on the ground and hung his head dejectedly. "I don't know where there is no other mouse. I remember a lady used to give 'em to me— ever' one she got. But that lady ain't here."

George scoffed. "Lady, huh? Don't even remember who that lady was. That was your own Aunt Clara. An' she stopped givin' 'em to ya. You always killed 'em."

Lennie looked sadly up at him. "They was so little,"

he said, apologetically. "I'd pet 'em, and pretty soon they bit my fingers and I pinched their heads a little and then they was dead—because they was so little.

"I wish't we'd get the rabbits pretty soon, George. They ain't so little."

"The hell with the rabbits. An' you ain't to be trusted with no live mice. Your Aunt Clara give you a rubber mouse and you wouldn't have nothing to do with it."

"It wasn't no good to pet," said Lennie.

The flame of the sunset lifted from the mountaintops and dusk came into the valley, and a half darkness came in among the willows and the sycamores. A big carp rose to the surface of the pool, gulped air and then sank mysteriously into the dark water again, leaving widening rings on the water. Overhead the leaves whisked again and little puffs of willow cotton blew down and landed on the pool's surface.

"You gonna get that wood?" George demanded. "There's plenty right up against the back of that sycamore. Floodwater wood. Now you get it."

Lennie went behind the tree and brought out a litter of dried leaves and twigs. He threw them in a heap on the old ash pile and went back for more and more. It was almost night now. A dove's wings whistled over the water. George walked to the fire pile and lighted the dry leaves. The flame cracked up among the twigs and fell to work. George undid his bindle and brought out three cans of beans. He stood them about the fire, close in against the blaze, but not quite touching the flame.

"There's enough beans for four men," George said.

Lennie watched him from over the fire. He said patiently, "I like 'em with ketchup."

"Well, we ain't got any," George exploded. "Whatever we ain't got, that's what you want. God a'mighty,
if I was alone I could live so easy. I could go get a job
an' work, an' no trouble. No mess at all, and when the
end of the month come I could take my fifty bucks and
go into town and get whatever I want. Why, I could
stay in a cat house all night. I could eat any place I
want, hotel or any place, and order any damn thing I
could think of. An' I could do all that every damn
month. Get a gallon of whisky, or set in a pool room
and play cards or shoot pool." Lennie knelt and looked
over the fire at the angry George. And Lennie's face
was drawn with terror. "An' whatta I got," George went
on furiously. "I got you! You can't keep a job and you
lose me ever' job I get. Jus' keep me shovin' all over
the country all the time. An' that ain't the worst. You
get in trouble. You do bad things and I got to get you
out." His voice rose nearly to a shout. "You crazy
son-of-a-bitch. You keep me in hot water all the
time." He took on the elaborate manner of little girls
when they are mimicking one another. "Jus' wanted to
feel that girl's dress—jus' wanted to pet it like it was a
mouse—— Well, how the hell did she know you jus'
wanted to feel her dress? She jerks back and you hold
on like it was a mouse. She yells and we got to hide in
a irrigation ditch all day with guys lookin' for us, and
we got to sneak out in the dark and get outta the
country. All the time somethin' like that—all the time.
I wisht I could put you in a cage with about a million
mice an' let you have fun." His anger left him suddenly. He looked across the fire at Lennie's anguished
face, and then he looked ashamedly at the flames.

It was quite dark now, but the fire lighted the trunks

of the trees and the curving branches overhead. Lennie crawled slowly and cautiously around the fire until he was close to George. He sat back on his heels. George turned the bean cans so that another side faced the fire. He pretended to be unaware of Lennie so close beside him.

"George," very softly. No answer. "George!"

"Whatta you want?"

"I was only foolin', George. I don't want no ketchup. I wouldn't eat no ketchup if it was right here beside me."

"If it was here, you could have some."

"But I wouldn't eat none, George. I'd leave it all for you. You could cover your beans with it and I wouldn't touch none of it."

George still stared morosely at the fire. "When I think of the swell time I could have without you, I go nuts. I never get no peace."

Lennie still knelt. He looked off into the darkness across the river. "George, you want I should go away and leave you alone?"

"Where the hell could you go?"

"Well, I could. I could go off in the hills there. Some place I'd find a cave."

"Yeah? How'd you eat. You ain't got sense enough to find nothing to eat."

"I'd find things, George. I don't need no nice food with ketchup. I'd lay out in the sun and nobody'd hurt me. An' if I foun' a mouse, I could keep it. Nobody'd take it away from me."

George looked quickly and searchingly at him. "I been mean, ain't I?"

"If you don' want me I can go off in the hills an' find a cave. I can go away any time."

"No—look! I was jus' foolin', Lennie. 'Cause I want you to stay with me. Trouble with mice is you always kill 'em." He paused. "Tell you what I'll do, Lennie. First chance I get I'll give you a pup. Maybe you wouldn't kill *it*. That'd be better than mice. And you could pet it harder."

Lennie avoided the bait. He had sensed his advantage. "If you don't want me, you only jus' got to say so, and I'll go off in those hills right there—right up in those hills and live by myself. An' I won't get no mice stole from me."

George said, "I want you to stay with me, Lennie. Jesus Christ, somebody'd shoot you for a coyote if you was by yourself. No, you stay with me. Your Aunt Clara wouldn't like you running off by yourself, even if she is dead."

Lennie spoke craftily, "Tell me—like you done before."

"Tell you what?"

"About the rabbits."

George snapped, "You ain't gonna put nothing over on me."

Lennie pleaded, "Come on, George. Tell me. Please George. Like you done before."

"You get a kick outta that, don't you? Awright, I'll tell you, and then we'll eat our supper. . . ."

George's voice became deeper. He repeated his words rhythmically as though he had said them many times before. "Guys like us, that work on ranches, are the loneliest guys in the world. They got no family. They don't belong no place. They come to a ranch an' work up a stake and then they go inta town and blow their stake, and the first thing you know they're poundin' their tail on some other ranch. They ain't got nothing to look ahead to."

Lennie was delighted. "That's it—that's it. Now tell how it is with us."

George went on. "With us it ain't like that. We got a future. We got somebody to talk to that gives a damn about us. We don't have to sit in no bar room blowin' in our jack jus' because we got no place else to go. If them other guys gets in jail they can rot for all anybody gives a damn. But not us."

Lennie broke in. *"But not us! An' why? Because . . . because I got you to look after me, and you got me to look after you, and that's why."* He laughed delightedly. "Go on now, George!"

"You got it by heart. You can do it yourself."

"No, you. I forget some a' the things. Tell about how it's gonna be."

"O.K. Someday—we're gonna get the jack together and we're gonna have a little house and a couple of acres an' a cow and some pigs and——"

"An' live off the fatta the lan'," Lennie shouted. "An' have *rabbits*. Go on, George! Tell about what we're gonna have in the garden and about the rabbits in the cages and about the rain in the winter and the stove, and how thick the cream is on the milk like you can hardly cut it. Tell about that, George."

"Why'n't you do it yourself? You know all of it."

"No . . . you tell it. It ain't the same if I tell it. Go on . . . George. How I get to tend the rabbits."

"Well," said George, "we'll have a big vegetable patch and a rabbit hutch and chickens. And when it rains in the winter, we'll just say the hell with goin' to work, and we'll build up a fire in the stove and set around it an' listen to the rain comin' down on the roof—Nuts!" He took out his pocket knife. "I ain't got time for no more." He drove his knife through the top of one of the bean cans, sawed out the top and passed the can to Lennie. Then he opened a second can. From his side pocket he brought out two spoons and passed one of them to Lennie.

They sat by the fire and filled their mouths with beans and chewed mightily. A few beans slipped out of the side of Lennie's mouth. George gestured with his spoon. "What you gonna say tomorrow when the boss asks you questions?"

Lennie stopped chewing and swallowed. His face was concentrated. "I . . . I ain't gonna . . . say a word."

"Good boy! That's fine, Lennie! Maybe you're gettin' better. When we get the coupla acres I can let you tend the rabbits all right. 'Specially if you remember as good as that."

Lennie choked with pride. "I can remember," he said.

George motioned with his spoon again. "Look, Lennie. I want you to look around here. You can remember this place, can't you? The ranch is about a quarter mile up that way. Just follow the river?"

"Sure," said Lennie. "I can remember this. Di'n't I remember about not gonna say a word?"

" 'Course you did. Well, look. Lennie—if you jus' happen to get in trouble like you always done before, I want you to come right here an' hide in the brush."

"Hide in the brush," said Lennie slowly.

"Hide in the brush till I come for you. Can you remember that?"

"Sure I can, George. Hide in the brush till you come."

"But you ain't gonna get in no trouble, because if you do, I won't let you tend the rabbits." He threw his empty bean can off into the brush.

"I won't get in no trouble, George. I ain't gonna say a word."

"O.K. Bring your bindle over here by the fire. It's gonna be nice sleepin' here. Lookin' up, and the leaves. Don't build up no more fire. We'll let her die down."

They made their beds on the sand, and as the blaze dropped from the fire the sphere of light grew smaller; the curling branches disappeared and only a faint glimmer showed where the tree trunks were. From the darkness Lennie called, "George—you asleep?"

"No. Whatta you want?"

"Let's have different color rabbits, George."

"Sure we will," George said sleepily. "Red and blue and green rabbits, Lennie. Millions of 'em."

"Furry ones, George, like I seen in the fair in Sacramento."

"Sure, furry ones."

" 'Cause I can jus' as well go away, George, an' live in a cave."

"You can jus' as well go to hell," said George. "Shut up now."

The red light dimmed on the coals. Up the hill from the river a coyote yammered, and a dog answered from the other side of the stream. The sycamore leaves whispered in a little night breeze.

The bunk house was a long, rectangular building. Inside, the walls were whitewashed and the floor unpainted. In three walls there were small, square windows, and in the fourth, a solid door with a wooden latch. Against the walls were eight bunks, five of them made up with blankets and the other three showing their burlap ticking. Over each bunk there was nailed an apple box with the opening forward so that it made two shelves for the personal belongings of the occupant of the bunk. And these shelves were loaded with little articles, soap and talcum powder, razors and those Western magazines ranch men love to read and scoff at and secretly believe. And there were medicines on the shelves, and little vials, combs; and from nails on the box sides, a few neckties. Near one wall there was a black cast-iron stove, its stovepipe going straight up through the ceiling. In the middle of the room stood a big square table littered with playing cards, and around it were grouped boxes for the players to sit on.

At about ten o'clock in the morning the sun threw a

bright dust-laden bar through one of the side windows, and in and out of the beam flies shot like rushing stars.

The wooden latch raised. The door opened and a tall, stoop-shouldered old man came in. He was dressed in blue jeans and he carried a big push-broom in his left hand. Behind him came George, and behind George, Lennie.

"The boss was expectin' you last night," the old man said. "He was sore as hell when you wasn't here to go out this morning." He pointed with his right arm, and out of the sleeve came a round stick-like wrist, but no hand. "You can have them two beds there," he said, indicating two bunks near the stove.

George stepped over and threw his blankets down on the burlap sack of straw that was a mattress. He looked into his box shelf and then picked a small yellow can from it. "Say. What the hell's this?"

"I don't know," said the old man.

"Says 'positively kills lice, roaches and other scourges.' What the hell kind of bed you giving us, anyways. We don't want no pants rabbits."

The old swamper shifted his broom and held it between his elbow and his side while he held out his hand for the can. He studied the label carefully. "Tell you what—" he said finally, "last guy that had this bed was a blacksmith—hell of a nice fella and as clean a guy as you want to meet. Used to wash his hands even *after* he ate."

"Then how come he got graybacks?" George was working up a slow anger. Lennie put his bindle on the neighboring bunk and sat down. He watched George with open mouth.

"Tell you what," said the old swamper. "This here blacksmith—name of Whitey—was the kind of guy that would put that stuff around even if there wasn't no bugs—just to make sure, see? Tell you what he used to do—At meals he'd peel his boil' potatoes, an' he'd take out ever' little spot, no matter what kind, before he'd eat it. And if there was a red splotch on an egg, he'd scrape it off. Finally quit about the food. That's the kinda guy he was—clean. Used ta dress up Sundays even when he wasn't going no place, put on a necktie even, and then set in the bunk house."

"I ain't so sure," said George skeptically. "What did you say he quit for?"

The old man put the yellow can in his pocket, and he rubbed his bristly white whiskers with his knuckles. "Why . . . he . . . just quit, the way a guy will. Says it was the food. Just wanted to move. Didn't give no other reason but the food. Just says 'gimme my time' one night, the way any guy would."

George lifted his tick and looked underneath it. He leaned over and inspected the sacking closely. Immediately Lennie got up and did the same with his bed. Finally George seemed satisfied. He unrolled his bindle and put things on the shelf, his razor and bar of soap, his comb and bottle of pills, his liniment and leather wristband. Then he made his bed up neatly with blankets. The old man said, "I guess the boss'll be out here in a minute. He was sure burned when you wasn't here this morning. Come right in when we was eatin' breakfast and says, 'Where the hell's them new men?' An' he give the stable buck hell, too."

George patted a wrinkle out of his bed, and sat down. "Give the stable buck hell?" he asked.

"Sure. Ya see the stable buck's a nigger."

"Nigger, huh?"

"Yeah. Nice fella too. Got a crooked back where a horse kicked him. The boss gives him hell when he's mad. But the stable buck don't give a damn about that. He reads a lot. Got books in his room."

"What kind of a guy is the boss?" George asked.

"Well, he's a pretty nice fella. Gets pretty mad sometimes, but he's pretty nice. Tell ya what—know what he done Christmas? Brang a gallon of whisky right in here and says, 'Drink hearty boys. Christmas comes but once a year.'"

"The hell he did! Whole gallon?"

"Yes sir. Jesus, we had fun. They let the nigger come in that night. Little skinner name of Smitty took after the nigger. Done pretty good, too. The guys wouldn't let him use his feet, so the nigger got him. If he coulda used his feet, Smitty says he woulda killed the nigger. The guys said on account of the nigger's got a crooked back, Smitty can't use his feet." He paused in relish of the memory. "After that the guys went into Soledad and raised hell. I didn't go in there. I ain't got the poop no more."

Lennie was just finishing making his bed. The wooden latch raised again and the door opened. A little stocky man stood in the open doorway. He wore blue jean trousers, a flannel shirt, a black, unbuttoned vest and a black coat. His thumbs were stuck in his belt, on each side of a square steel buckle. On his head was a soiled brown Stetson hat, and he wore high-heeled boots and spurs to prove he was not a laboring man.

The old swamper looked quickly at him, and then

shuffled to the door rubbing his whiskers with his knuckles as he went. "Them guys just come," he said, and shuffled past the boss and out the door.

The boss stepped into the room with the short, quick steps of a fat-legged man. "I wrote Murray and Ready I wanted two men this morning. You got your work slips?" George reached into his pocket and produced the slips and handed them to the boss. "It wasn't Murray and Ready's fault. Says right here on the slip that you was to be here for work this morning."

George looked down at his feet. "Bus driver give us a bum steer," he said. "We hadda walk ten miles. Says we was here when we wasn't. We couldn't get no rides in the morning."

The boss squinted his eyes. "Well, I had to send out the grain teams short two buckers. Won't do any good to go out now till after dinner." He pulled his time book out of his pocket and opened it where a pencil was stuck between the leaves. George scowled meaningfully at Lennie, and Lennie nodded to show that he understood. The boss licked his pencil. "What's your name?"

"George Milton."

"And what's yours?"

George said, "His name's Lennie Small."

The names were entered in the book. "Le's see, this is the twentieth, noon the twentieth." He closed the book. "Where you boys been working?"

"Up around Weed," said George.

"You, too?" to Lennie.

"Yeah, him too," said George.

The boss pointed a playful finger at Lennie. "He ain't much of a talker, is he?"

"No, he ain't, but he's sure a hell of a good worker. Strong as a bull."

Lennie smiled to himself. "Strong as a bull," he repeated.

George scowled at him, and Lennie dropped his head in shame at having forgotten.

The boss said suddenly, "Listen, Small!" Lennie raised his head. "What can you do?"

In a panic, Lennie looked at George for help. "He can do anything you tell him," said George. "He's a good skinner. He can rassel grain bags, drive a cultivator. He can do anything. Just give him a try."

The boss turned on George. "Then why don't you let him answer? What you trying to put over?"

George broke in loudly, "Oh! I ain't saying he's bright. He ain't. But I say he's a God damn good worker. He can put up a four hundred pound bale."

The boss deliberately put the little book in his pocket. He hooked his thumbs in his belt and squinted one eye nearly closed. "Say—what you sellin'?"

"Huh?"

"I said what stake you got in this guy? You takin' his pay away from him?"

"No, 'course I ain't. Why ya think I'm sellin' him out?"

"Well, I never seen one guy take so much trouble for another guy. I just like to know what your interest is."

George said, "He's my . . . cousin. I told his old lady I'd take care of him. He got kicked in the head by a horse when he was a kid. He's awright. Just ain't bright. But he can do anything you tell him."

The boss turned half away. "Well, God knows he

don't need any brains to buck barley bags. But don't you try to put nothing over, Milton. I got my eye on you. Why'd you quit in Weed?"

"Job was done," said George promptly.

"What kinda job?"

"We . . . we was diggin' a cesspool."

"All right. But don't try to put nothing over, 'cause you can't get away with nothing. I seen wise guys before. Go on out with the grain teams after dinner. They're pickin' up barley at the threshing machine. Go out with Slim's team."

"Slim?"

"Yeah. Big tall skinner. You'll see him at dinner." He turned abruptly and went to the door, but before he went out he turned and looked for a long moment at the two men.

When the sound of his footsteps had died away, George turned on Lennie. "So you wasn't gonna say a word. You was gonna leave your big flapper shut and leave me do the talkin'. Damn near lost us the job."

Lennie stared hopelessly at his hands. "I forgot, George."

"Yeah, you forgot. You always forget, an' I got to talk you out of it." He sat down heavily on the bunk. "Now he's got his eye on us. Now we got to be careful and not make no slips. You keep your big flapper shut after this." He fell morosely silent.

"George."

"What you want now?"

"I wasn't kicked in the head with no horse, was I, George?"

"Be a damn good thing if you was," George said viciously. "Save ever'body a hell of a lot of trouble."

"You said I was your cousin, George."

"Well, that was a lie. An' I'm damn glad it was. If I was a relative of yours I'd shoot myself." He stopped suddenly, stepped to the open front door and peered out. "Say, what the hell you doin' listenin'?"

The old man came slowly into the room. He had his broom in his hand. And at his heels there walked a dragfooted sheep dog, gray of muzzle, and with pale, blind old eyes. The dog struggled lamely to the side of the room and lay down, grunting softly to himself and licking his grizzled, moth-eaten coat. The swamper watched him until he was settled. "I wasn't listenin'. I was jus' standin' in the shade a minute scratchin' my dog. I jus' now finished swampin' out the wash house."

"You was pokin' your big ears into our business," George said. "I don't like nobody to get nosey."

The old man looked uneasily from George to Lennie, and then back. "I jus' come there," he said. "I didn't hear nothing you guys was sayin'. I ain't interested in nothing you was sayin'. A guy on a ranch don't never listen nor he don't ast no questions."

"Damn right he don't," said George, slightly mollified, "not if he wants to stay workin' long." But he was reassured by the swamper's defense. "Come on in and set down a minute," he said. "That's a hell of an old dog."

"Yeah. I had 'im ever since he was a pup. God, he was a good sheep dog when he was younger." He stood his broom against the wall and he rubbed his white bristled cheek with his knuckles. "How'd you like the boss?" he asked.

"Pretty good. Seemed awright."

"He's a nice fella," the swamper agreed. "You got to take him right."

At that moment a young man came into the bunk house; a thin young man with a brown face, with brown eyes and a head of tightly curled hair. He wore a work glove on his left hand, and, like the boss, he wore high-heeled boots. "Seen my old man?" he asked.

The swamper said, "He was here jus' a minute ago, Curley. Went over to the cook house, I think."

"I'll try to catch him," said Curley. His eyes passed over the new men and he stopped. He glanced coldly at George and then at Lennie. His arms gradually bent at the elbows and his hands closed into fists. He stiffened and went into a slight crouch. His glance was at once calculating and pugnacious. Lennie squirmed under the look and shifted his feet nervously. Curley stepped gingerly close to him. "You the new guys the old man was waitin' for?"

"We just come in," said George.

"Let the big guy talk."

Lennie twisted with embarrassment.

George said, "S'pose he don't want to talk?"

Curley lashed his body around. "By Christ, he's gotta talk when he's spoke to. What the hell are you gettin' into it for?"

"We travel together," said George coldly.

"Oh, so it's that way."

George was tense, and motionless. "Yeah, it's that way."

Lennie was looking helplessly to George for instruction.

"An' you won't let the big guy talk, is that it?"

"He can talk if he wants to tell you anything." He nodded slightly to Lennie.

"We jus' come in," said Lennie softly.

Curley stared levelly at him. "Well, nex' time you answer when you're spoke to." He turned toward the door and walked out, and his elbows were still bent out a little.

George watched him out, and then he turned back to the swamper. "Say, what the hell's he got on his shoulder? Lennie didn't do nothing to him."

The old man looked cautiously at the door to make sure no one was listening. "That's the boss's son," he said quietly. "Curley's pretty handy. He done quite a bit in the ring. He's a lightweight, and he's handy."

"Well, let him be handy," said George. "He don't have to take after Lennie. Lennie didn't do nothing to him. What's he got against Lennie?"

The swamper considered. . . . "Well . . . tell you what. Curley's like a lot of little guys. He hates big guys. He's alla time picking scraps with big guys. Kind of like he's mad at 'em because he ain't a big guy. You seen little guys like that, ain't you? Always scrappy?"

"Sure," said George. "I seen plenty tough little guys. But this Curley better not make no mistakes about Lennie. Lennie ain't handy, but this Curley punk is gonna get hurt if he messes around with Lennie."

"Well, Curley's pretty handy," the swamper said skeptically. "Never did seem right to me. S'pose Curley jumps a big guy an' licks him. Ever'body says what a game guy Curley is. And s'pose he does the same thing and gets licked. Then ever'body says the big guy oughtta pick somebody his own size, and maybe they gang up on the big guy. Never did seem right to me. Seems like Curley ain't givin' nobody a chance."

George was watching the door. He said ominously, "Well, he better watch out for Lennie. Lennie ain't no fighter, but Lennie's strong and quick and Lennie don't know no rules." He walked to the square table and sat down on one of the boxes. He gathered some of the cards together and shuffled them.

The old man sat down on another box. "Don't tell Curley I said none of this. He'd slough me. He just don't give a damn. Won't ever get canned 'cause his old man's the boss."

George cut the cards and began turning them over, looking at each one and throwing it down on a pile. He said, "This guy Curley sounds like a son-of-a-bitch to me. I don't like mean little guys."

"Seems to me like he's worse lately," said the swamper. "He got married a couple of weeks ago. Wife lives over in the boss's house. Seems like Curley is cockier'n ever since he got married."

George grunted, "Maybe he's showin' off for his wife."

The swamper warmed to his gossip. "You seen that glove on his left hand?"

"Yeah. I seen it."

"Well, that glove's fulla vaseline."

"Vaseline? What the hell for?"

"Well, I tell ya what—Curley says he's keepin' that hand soft for his wife."

George studied the cards absorbedly. "That's a dirty thing to tell around," he said.

The old man was reassured. He had drawn a derogatory statement from George. He felt safe now, and he spoke more confidently. "Wait'll you see Curley's wife."

George cut the cards again and put out a solitaire lay, slowly and deliberately. "Purty?" he asked casually.

"Yeah. Purty . . . but——"

George studied his cards. "But what?"

"Well—she got the eye."

"Yeah? Married two weeks and got the eye? Maybe that's why Curley's pants is full of ants."

"I seen her give Slim the eye. Slim's a jerkline skinner. Hell of a nice fella. Slim don't need to wear no high-heeled boots on a grain team. I seen her give Slim the eye. Curley never seen it. An' I seen her give Carlson the eye."

George pretended a lack of interest. "Looks like we was gonna have fun."

The swamper stood up from his box. "Know what I think?" George did not answer. "Well, I think Curley's married . . . a tart."

"He ain't the first," said George. "There's plenty done that."

The old man moved toward the door, and his ancient dog lifted his head and peered about, and then got painfully to his feet to follow. "I gotta be settin' out the wash basins for the guys. The teams'll be in before long. You guys gonna buck barley?"

"Yeah."

"You won't tell Curley nothing I said?"

"Hell no."

"Well, you look her over, mister. You see if she ain't a tart." He stepped out the door into the brilliant sunshine.

George laid down his cards thoughtfully, turned his piles of three. He built four clubs on his ace pile. The

sun square was on the floor now, and the flies whipped
through it like sparks. A sound of jingling harness and
the croak of heavy-laden axles sounded from outside.
From the distance came a clear call. "Stable Buck—
ooh, sta-able Buck!" And then, "Where the hell is that
God damn nigger?"

George stared at his solitaire lay, and then he
flounced the cards together and turned around to Lennie. Lennie was lying down on the bunk watching him.

"Look, Lennie! This here ain't no set up. I'm
scared. You gonna have trouble with that Curley guy. I
seen that kind before. He was kinda feelin' you out.
He figures he's got you scared and he's gonna take a
sock at you the first chance he gets."

Lennie's eyes were frightened. "I don't want no
trouble," he said plaintively. "Don't let him sock me,
George."

George got up and went over to Lennie's bunk and
sat down on it. "I hate that kinda bastard," he said. "I
seen plenty of 'em. Like the old guy says, Curley don't
take no chances. He always wins." He thought for a
moment. "If he tangles with you, Lennie, we're gonna
get the can. Don't make no mistake about that. He's
the boss's son. Look, Lennie. You try to keep away
from him, will you? Don't never speak to him. If he
comes in here you move clear to the other side of the
room. Will you do that, Lennie?"

"I don't want no trouble," Lennie mourned. "I never
done nothing to him."

"Well, that won't do you no good if Curley wants to
plug himself up for a fighter. Just don't have nothing to
do with him. Will you remember?"

"Sure, George. I ain't gonna say a word."

The sound of the approaching grain teams was louder, thud of big hooves on hard ground, drag of brakes and the jingle of trace chains. Men were calling back and forth from the teams. George, sitting on the bunk beside Lennie, frowned as he thought. Lennie asked timidly, "You ain't mad, George?"

"I ain't mad at you. I'm mad at this here Curley bastard. I hoped we was gonna get a little stake together—maybe a hundred dollars." His tone grew decisive. "You keep away from Curley, Lennie."

"Sure I will, George. I won't say a word."

"Don't let him pull you in—but—if the son-of-a-bitch socks you—let 'im have it."

"Let 'im have what, George?"

"Never mind, never mind. I'll tell you when. I hate that kind of a guy. Look, Lennie, if you get in any kind of trouble, you remember what I told you to do?"

Lennie raised up on his elbow. His face contorted with thought. Then his eyes moved sadly to George's face. "If I get in any trouble, you ain't gonna let me tend the rabbits."

"That's not what I meant. You remember where we slep' last night? Down by the river?"

"Yeah. I remember. Oh, sure I remember! I go there an' hide in the brush."

"Hide till I come for you. Don't let nobody see you. Hide in the brush by the river. Say that over."

"Hide in the brush by the river, down in the brush by the river."

"If you get in trouble."

"If I get in trouble."

A brake screeched outside. A call came, "Stable—Buck. Oh! Sta-able Buck."

George said, "Say it over to yourself, Lennie, so you won't forget it."

Both men glanced up, for the rectangle of sunshine in the doorway was cut off. A girl was standing there looking in. She had full, rouged lips and wide-spaced eyes, heavily made up. Her fingernails were red. Her hair hung in little rolled clusters, like sausages. She wore a cotton house dress and red mules, on the insteps of which were little bouquets of red ostrich feathers. "I'm lookin' for Curley," she said. Her voice had a nasal, brittle quality.

George looked away from her and then back. "He was in here a minute ago, but he went."

"Oh!" She put her hands behind her back and leaned against the door frame so that her body was thrown forward. "You're the new fellas that just come, ain't ya?"

"Yeah."

Lennie's eyes moved down over her body, and though she did not seem to be looking at Lennie she bridled a little. She looked at her fingernails. "Sometimes Curley's in here," she explained.

George said brusquely, "Well he ain't now."

"If he ain't, I guess I better look some place else," she said playfully.

Lennie watched her, fascinated. George said, "If I see him, I'll pass the word you was looking for him."

She smiled archly and twitched her body. "Nobody can't blame a person for lookin', " she said. There were footsteps behind her, going by. She turned her head. "Hi, Slim," she said.

Slim's voice came through the door. "Hi, Good-lookin'."

"I'm tryin' to find Curley, Slim."

"Well, you ain't tryin' very hard. I seen him goin' in your house."

She was suddenly apprehensive. " 'Bye, boys," she called into the bunk house, and she hurried away.

George looked around at Lennie. "Jesus, what a tramp," he said. "So that's what Curley picks for a wife."

"She's purty," said Lennie defensively.

"Yeah, and she's sure hidin' it. Curley got his work ahead of him. Bet she'd clear out for twenty bucks."

Lennie still stared at the doorway where she had been. "Gosh, she was purty." He smiled admiringly. George looked quickly down at him and then he took him by an ear and shook him.

"Listen to me, you crazy bastard," he said fiercely. "Don't you even take a look at that bitch. I don't care what she says and what she does. I seen 'em poison before, but I never seen no piece of jail bait worse than her. You leave her be."

Lennie tried to disengage his ear. "I never done nothing, George."

"No, you never. But when she was standin' in the doorway showin' her legs, you wasn't lookin' the other way, neither."

"I never meant no harm, George. Honest I never."

"Well, you keep away from her, 'cause she's a rat-trap if I ever seen one. You let Curley take the rap. He let himself in for it. Glove fulla vaseline," George said disgustedly. "An' I bet he's eatin' raw eggs and writin' to the patent medicine houses."

Lennie cried out suddenly—"I don' like this place, George. This ain't no good place. I wanna get outa here."

"We gotta keep it till we get a stake. We can't help it, Lennie. We'll get out jus' as soon as we can. I don't like it no better than you do." He went back to the table and set out a new solitaire hand. "No, I don't like it," he said. "For two bits I'd shove out of here. If we can get jus' a few dollars in the poke we'll shove off and go up the American River and pan gold. We can make maybe a couple of dollars a day there, and we might hit a pocket."

Lennie leaned eagerly toward him. "Le's go, George. Le's get outta here. It's mean here."

"We gotta stay," George said shortly. "Shut up now. The guys'll be comin' in."

From the washroom nearby came the sound of running water and rattling basins. George studied the cards. "Maybe we oughtta wash up," he said. "But we ain't done nothing to get dirty."

A tall man stood in the doorway. He held a crushed Stetson hat under his arm while he combed his long, black, damp hair straight back. Like the others he wore blue jeans and a short denim jacket. When he had finished combing his hair he moved into the room, and he moved with a majesty only achieved by royalty and master craftsmen. He was a jerkline skinner, the prince of the ranch, capable of driving ten, sixteen, even twenty mules with a single line to the leaders. He was capable of killing a fly on the wheeler's butt with a bull whip without touching the mule. There was a gravity in his manner and a quiet so profound that all talk stopped when he spoke. His authority was so great that his word was taken on any subject, be it politics or love. This was Slim, the jerkline skinner. His hatchet face was ageless. He might have been thirty-five or fifty. His ear heard more than was said to him, and his slow speech had overtones not of thought, but of understanding beyond thought. His hands, large and lean, were as delicate in their action as those of a temple dancer.

He smoothed out his crushed hat, creased it in the middle and put it on. He looked kindly at the two in the bunk house. "It's brighter'n a bitch outside," he said gently. "Can't hardly see nothing in here. You the new guys?"

"Just come," said George.

"Gonna buck barley?"

"That's what the boss says."

Slim sat down on a box across the table from George. He studied the solitaire hand that was upside down to him. "Hope you get on my team," he said. His voice was very gentle. "I gotta pair of punks on my team that don't know a barley bag from a blue ball. You guys ever bucked any barley?"

"Hell, yes," said George. "I ain't nothing to scream about, but that big bastard there can put up more grain alone than most pairs can."

Lennie, who had been following the conversation back and forth with his eyes, smiled complacently at the compliment. Slim looked approvingly at George for having given the compliment. He leaned over the table and snapped the corner of a loose card. "You guys travel around together?" His tone was friendly. It invited confidence without demanding it.

"Sure," said George. "We kinda look after each other." He indicated Lennie with his thumb. "He ain't bright. Hell of a good worker, though. Hell of a nice fella, but he ain't bright. I've knew him for a long time."

Slim looked through George and beyond him. "Ain't many guys travel around together," he mused. "I don't know why. Maybe ever'body in the whole damn world is scared of each other."

"It's a lot nicer to go around with a guy you know," said George.

A powerful, big-stomached man came into the bunk house. His head still dripped water from the scrubbing and dousing. "Hi, Slim," he said, and then stopped and stared at George and Lennie.

"These guys jus' come," said Slim by way of introduction.

"Glad ta meet ya," the big man said. "My name's Carlson."

"I'm George Milton. This here's Lennie Small."

"Glad ta meet ya," Carlson said again. "He ain't very small." He chuckled softly at his joke. "Ain't small at all," he repeated. "Meant to ask you, Slim— how's your bitch? I seen she wasn't under your wagon this morning."

"She slang her pups last night," said Slim. "Nine of 'em. I drowned four of 'em right off. She couldn't feed that many."

"Got five left, huh?"

"Yeah, five. I kept the biggest."

"What kinda dogs you think they're gonna be?"

"I dunno," said Slim. "Some kinda shepherds, I guess. That's the most kind I seen around here when she was in heat."

Carlson went on, "Got five pups, huh. Gonna keep all of 'em?"

"I dunno. Have to keep 'em a while so they can drink Lulu's milk."

Carlson said thoughtfully, "Well, looka here, Slim. I been thinkin'. That dog of Candy's is so God damn old he can't hardly walk. Stinks like hell, too. Ever' time he comes into the bunk house I can smell him for two, three days. Why'n't you get Candy to shoot his old dog and give him one of the pups to raise up? I can smell that dog a mile away. Got no teeth, damn near blind, can't eat. Candy feeds him milk. He can't chew nothing else."

George had been staring intently at Slim. Suddenly a triangle began to ring outside, slowly at first, and then faster and faster until the beat of it disappeared into one ringing sound. It stopped as suddenly as it had started.

"There she goes," said Carlson.

Outside, there was a burst of voices as a group of men went by.

Slim stood up slowly and with dignity. "You guys better come on while they's still something to eat. Won't be nothing left in a couple of minutes."

Carlson stepped back to let Slim precede him, and then the two of them went out the door.

Lennie was watching George excitedly. George rumpled his cards into a messy pile. "Yeah!" George said, "I heard him, Lennie. I'll ask him."

"A brown and white one," Lennie cried excitedly.

"Come on. Le's get dinner. I don't know whether he got a brown and white one."

Lennie didn't move from his bunk. "You ask him right away, George, so he won't kill no more of 'em."

"Sure. Come on now, get up on your feet."

Lennie rolled off his bunk and stood up, and the two of them started for the door. Just as they reached it, Curley bounced in.

"You seen a girl around here?" he demanded angrily.

George said coldly, " 'Bout half an hour ago maybe."

"Well what the hell was she doin'?"

George stood still, watching the angry little man. He said insultingly, "She said—she was lookin' for you."

Curley seemed really to see George for the first time. His eyes flashed over George, took in his height, measured his reach, looked at his trim middle. "Well, which way'd she go?" he demanded at last.

"I dunno," said George. "I didn't watch her go."

Curley scowled at him, and turning, hurried out the door.

George said, "Ya know, Lennie, I'm scared I'm gonna tangle with that bastard myself. I hate his guts. Jesus Christ! Come on. They won't be a damn thing left to eat."

They went out the door. The sunshine lay in a thin line under the window. From a distance there could be heard a rattle of dishes.

After a moment the ancient dog walked lamely in through the open door. He gazed about with mild, half-blind eyes. He sniffed, and then lay down and put his head between his paws. Curley popped into the doorway again and stood looking into the room. The dog raised his head, but when Curley jerked out, the grizzled head sank to the floor again.

Although there was evening brightness showing through the windows of the bunk house, inside it was dusk. Through the open door came the thuds and occasional clangs of a horseshoe game, and now and then the sound of voices raised in approval or derision.

Slim and George came into the darkening bunk house together. Slim reached up over the card table and turned on the tin-shaded electric light. Instantly the table was brilliant with light, and the cone of the shade threw its brightness straight downward, leaving the corners of the bunk house still in dusk. Slim sat down on a box and George took his place opposite.

"It wasn't nothing," said Slim. "I would of had to drowned most of 'em anyways. No need to thank me about that."

George said, "It wasn't much to you, maybe, but it was a hell of a lot to him. Jesus Christ, I don't know how we're gonna get him to sleep in here. He'll want to sleep right out in the barn with 'em. We'll have trouble keepin' him from getting right in the box with them pups."

"It wasn't nothing," Slim repeated. "Say, you sure was right about him. Maybe he ain't bright, but I never seen such a worker. He damn near killed his partner buckin' barley. There ain't nobody can keep up with him. God awmighty I never seen such a strong guy."

George spoke proudly. "Jus' tell Lennie what to do an' he'll do it if it don't take no figuring. He can't think of nothing to do himself, but he sure can take orders."

There was a clang of horseshoe on iron stake outside and a little cheer of voices.

Slim moved back slightly so the light was not on his face. "Funny how you an' him string along together." It was Slim's calm invitation to confidence.

"What's funny about it?" George demanded defensively.

"Oh, I dunno. Hardly none of the guys ever travel together. I hardly never seen two guys travel together. You know how the hands are, they just come in and get their bunk and work a month, and then they quit and go out alone. Never seem to give a damn about nobody. It jus' seems kinda funny a cuckoo like him and a smart little guy like you travelin' together."

"He ain't no cuckoo," said George. "He's dumb as hell, but he ain't crazy. An' I ain't so bright neither, or I wouldn't be buckin' barley for my fifty and found. If I was bright, if I was even a little bit smart, I'd have my own little place, an' I'd be bringin' in my own crops, 'stead of doin' all the work and not getting what comes up outa the ground." George fell silent. He wanted to talk. Slim neither encouraged nor discouraged him. He just sat back quiet and receptive.

"It ain't so funny, him an' me goin' aroun' together,"

George said at last. "Him and me was both born in Auburn. I knowed his Aunt Clara. She took him when he was a baby and raised him up. When his Aunt Clara died, Lennie just come along with me out workin'. Got kinda used to each other after a little while."

"Umm," said Slim.

George looked over at Slim and saw the calm, God-like eyes fastened on him. "Funny," said George. "I used to have a hell of a lot of fun with 'im. Used to play jokes on 'im 'cause he was too dumb to take care of 'imself. But he was too dumb even to know he had a joke played on him. I had fun. Made me seem God damn smart alongside of him. Why he'd do any damn thing I tol' him. If I tol' him to walk over a cliff, over he'd go. That wasn't so damn much fun after a while. He never got mad about it, neither. I've beat the hell outa him, and he coulda bust every bone in my body jus' with his han's, but he never lifted a finger against me." George's voice was taking on the tone of confession. "Tell you what made me stop that. One day a bunch of guys was standin' around up on the Sacramento River. I was feelin' pretty smart. I turns to Lennie and says, 'Jump in.' An' he jumps. Couldn't swim a stroke. He damn near drowned before we could get him. An' he was so damn nice to me for pullin' him out. Clean forgot I told him to jump in. Well, I ain't done nothing like that no more."

"He's a nice fella," said Slim. "Guy don't need no sense to be a nice fella. Seems to me sometimes it jus' works the other way around. Take a real smart guy and he ain't hardly ever a nice fella."

George stacked the scattered cards and began to lay out his solitaire hand. The shoes thudded on the

ground outside. At the windows the light of the evening still made the window squares bright.

"I ain't got no people," George said. "I seen the
guys that go around on the ranches alone. That ain't no
good. They don't have no fun. After a long time they
get mean. They get wantin' to fight all the time."

"Yeah, they get mean," Slim agreed. "They get so
they don't want to talk to nobody."

" 'Course Lennie's a God damn nuisance most of the
time," said George. "But you get used to goin' around
with a guy an' you can't get rid of him."

"He ain't mean," said Slim. "I can see Lennie ain't
a bit mean."

" 'Course he ain't mean. But he gets in trouble alla
time because he's so God damn dumb. Like what happened in Weed——" He stopped, stopped in the
middle of turning over a card. He looked alarmed and
peered over at Slim. "You wouldn't tell nobody?"

"What'd he do in Weed?" Slim asked calmly.

"You wouldn' tell? . . . No, 'course you wouldn'."

"What'd he do in Weed?" Slim asked again.

"Well, he seen this girl in a red dress. Dumb bastard like he is, he wants to touch ever'thing he likes.
Just wants to feel it. So he reaches out to feel this red
dress an' the girl lets out a squawk, and that gets
Lennie all mixed up, and he holds on 'cause that's the
only thing he can think to do. Well, this girl squawks
and squawks. I was jus' a little bit off, and I heard all
the yellin', so I comes running, an' by that time Lennie's so scared all he can think to do is jus' hold on. I
socked him over the head with a fence picket to make
him let go. He was so scairt he couldn't let go of that
dress. And he's so God damn strong, you know."

Slim's eyes were level and unwinking. He nodded very slowly. "So what happens?"

George carefully built his line of solitaire cards. "Well, that girl rabbits in an' tells the law she been raped. The guys in Weed start a party out to lynch Lennie. So we sit in a irrigation ditch under water all the rest of that day. Got on'y our heads sticking out from the side of the ditch. An' that night we scrammed outa there."

Slim sat in silence for a moment. "Didn't hurt the girl none, huh?" he asked finally.

"Hell, no. He just scared her. I'd be scared too if he grabbed me. But he never hurt her. He jus' wanted to touch that red dress, like he wants to pet them pups all the time."

"He ain't mean," said Slim. "I can tell a mean guy a mile off."

" 'Course he ain't, and he'll do any damn thing I——"

Lennie came in through the door. He wore his blue denim coat over his shoulders like a cape, and he walked hunched way over.

"Hi, Lennie," said George. "How do you like the pup now?"

Lennie said breathlessly, "He's brown an' white jus' like I wanted." He went directly to his bunk and lay down and turned his face to the wall and drew up his knees.

George put down his cards very deliberately. "Lennie," he said sharply.

Lennie twisted his neck and looked over his shoulder. "Huh? What you want, George?"

"I tol' you you couldn't bring that pup in here."

"What pup, George? I ain't got no pup."

George went quickly to him, grabbed him by the shoulder and rolled him over. He reached down and picked the tiny puppy from where Lennie had been concealing it against his stomach.

Lennie sat up quickly. "Give 'um to me, George."

George said, "You get right up an' take this pup back to the nest. He's gotta sleep with his mother. You want to kill him? Just born last night an' you take him out of the nest. You take him back or I'll tell Slim not to let you have him."

Lennie held out his hands pleadingly. "Give 'um to me, George. I'll take 'um back. I didn't mean no harm, George. Honest I didn't. I jus' wanted to pet 'um a little."

George handed the pup to him. "Awright. You get him back there quick, and don' you take him out no more. You'll kill him, the first thing you know." Lennie fairly scuttled out of the room.

Slim had not moved. His calm eyes followed Lennie out the door. "Jesus," he said. "He's jes' like a kid, ain't he."

"Sure he's jes' like a kid. There ain't no more harm in him than a kid neither, except he's so strong. I bet he won't come in here to sleep tonight. He'd sleep right alongside that box in the barn. Well—let 'im. He ain't doin' no harm out there."

It was almost dark outside now. Old Candy, the swamper, came in and went to his bunk, and behind him struggled his old dog. "Hello, Slim. Hello, George. Didn't neither of you play horseshoes?"

"I don't like to play ever' night," said Slim.

Candy went on, "Either you guys got a slug of whisky? I gotta gut ache."

"I ain't," said Slim. "I'd drink it myself if I had, an' I ain't got a gut ache neither."

"Gotta bad gut ache," said Candy. "Them God damn turnips give it to me. I knowed they was going to before I ever eat 'em."

The thick-bodied Carlson came in out of the darkening yard. He walked to the other end of the bunk house and turned on the second shaded light. "Darker'n hell in here," he said. "Jesus, how that nigger can pitch shoes."

"He's plenty good," said Slim.

"Damn right he is," said Carlson. "He don't give nobody else a chance to win——" He stopped and sniffed the air, and still sniffing, looked down at the old dog. "God awmighty, that dog stinks. Get him outa here, Candy! I don't know nothing that stinks as bad as an old dog. You gotta get him out."

Candy rolled to the edge of his bunk. He reached over and patted the ancient dog, and he apologized, "I been around him so much I never notice how he stinks."

"Well, I can't stand him in here," said Carlson. "That stink hangs around even after he's gone." He walked over with his heavy-legged stride and looked down at the dog. "Got no teeth," he said. "He's all stiff with rheumatism. He ain't no good to you, Candy. An' he ain't no good to himself. Why'n't you shoot him, Candy?"

The old man squirmed uncomfortably. "Well—hell! I had him so long. Had him since he was a pup. I herded sheep with him." He said proudly, "You wouldn't think it to look at him now, but he was the best damn sheep dog I ever seen."

George said, "I seen a guy in Weed that had an Airedale could herd sheep. Learned it from the other dogs."

Carlson was not to be put off. "Look, Candy. This ol' dog jus' suffers hisself all the time. If you was to take him out and shoot him right in the back of the head——" he leaned over and pointed, "——right there, why he'd never know what hit him."

Candy looked about unhappily. "No," he said softly. "No, I couldn' do that. I had 'im too long."

"He don't have no fun," Carlson insisted. "And he stinks to beat hell. Tell you what. I'll shoot him for you. Then it won't be you that does it."

Candy threw his legs off his bunk. He scratched the white stubble whiskers on his cheek nervously. "I'm so used to him," he said softly. "I had him from a pup."

"Well, you ain't bein' kind to him keepin' him alive," said Carlson. "Look, Slim's bitch got a litter right now. I bet Slim would give you one of them pups to raise up, wouldn't you, Slim?"

The skinner had been studying the old dog with his calm eyes. "Yeah," he said. "You can have a pup if you want to." He seemed to shake himself free for speech. "Carl's right, Candy. That dog ain't no good to himself. I wisht somebody'd shoot me if I got old an' a cripple."

Candy looked helplessly at him, for Slim's opinions were law. "Maybe it'd hurt him," he suggested. "I don't mind takin' care of him."

Carlson said, "The way I'd shoot him, he wouldn't feel nothing. I'd put the gun right there." He pointed with his toe. "Right back of the head. He wouldn't even quiver."

Candy looked for help from face to face. It was quite dark outside by now. A young laboring man came in. His sloping shoulders were bent forward and he walked heavily on his heels, as though he carried the invisible grain bag. He went to his bunk and put his hat on his shelf. Then he picked a pulp magazine from his shelf and brought it to the light over the table. "Did I show you this, Slim?" he asked.

"Show me what?"

The young man turned to the back of the magazine, put it down on the table and pointed with his finger. "Right there, read that." Slim bent over it. "Go on," said the young man. "Read it out loud."

" 'Dear Editor:' " Slim read slowly. " 'I read your mag for six years and I think it is the best on the market. I like stories by Peter Rand. I think he is a whing-ding. Give us more like the Dark Rider. I don't write many letters. Just thought I would tell you I think your mag is the best dime's worth I ever spent.' "

Slim looked up questioningly. "What you want me to read that for?"

Whit said, "Go on. Read the name at the bottom."

Slim read, " 'Yours for success, William Tenner.' " He glanced up at Whit again. "What you want me to read that for?"

Whit closed the magazine impressively. "Don't you remember Bill Tenner? Worked here about three months ago?"

Slim thought. . . . "Little guy?" he asked. "Drove a cultivator?"

"That's him," Whit cried. "That's the guy!"

"You think he's the guy wrote this letter?"

"I know it. Bill and me was in here one day. Bill had one of them books that just come. He was lookin' in it and he says, 'I wrote a letter. Wonder if they put it in the book!' But it wasn't there. Bill says, 'Maybe

they're savin' it for later.' An' that's just what they
done. There it is."

"Guess you're right," said Slim. "Got it right in the
book."

George held out his hand for the magazine. "Let's
look at it?"

Whit found the place again, but he did not sur-
render his hold on it. He pointed out the letter with his
forefinger. And then he went to his box shelf and laid
the magazine carefully in. "I wonder if Bill seen it,"
he said. "Bill and me worked in that patch of field
peas. Run cultivators, both of us. Bill was a hell of a
nice fella."

During the conversation Carlson had refused to be
drawn in. He continued to look down at the old dog.
Candy watched him uneasily. At last Carlson said, "If
you want me to, I'll put the old devil out of his misery
right now and get it over with. Ain't nothing left for him.
Can't eat, can't see, can't even walk without hurtin'."

Candy said hopefully, "You ain't got no gun."

"The hell I ain't. Got a Luger. It won't hurt him
none at all."

Candy said, "Maybe tomorra. Le's wait till tomorra."

"I don't see no reason for it," said Carlson. He went
to his bunk, pulled his bag from underneath it and
took out a Luger pistol. "Let's get it over with," he
said. "We can't sleep with him stinkin' around in
here." He put the pistol in his hip pocket.

Candy looked a long time at Slim to try to find some
reversal. And Slim gave him none. At last Candy said
softly and hopelessly, "Awright—take 'im." He did
not look down at the dog at all. He lay back on his

bunk and crossed his arms behind his head and stared at the ceiling.

From his pocket Carlson took a little leather thong. He stooped over and tied it around the old dog's neck. All the men except Candy watched him. "Come boy. Come on, boy," he said gently. And he said apologetically to Candy, "He won't even feel it." Candy did not move nor answer him. He twitched the thong. "Come on, boy." The old dog got slowly and stiffly to his feet and followed the gently pulling leash.

Slim said, "Carlson."

"Yeah?"

"You know what to do."

"What ya mean, Slim?"

"Take a shovel," said Slim shortly.

"Oh, sure! I get you." He led the dog out into the darkness.

George followed to the door and shut the door and set the latch gently in its place. Candy lay rigidly on his bed staring at the ceiling.

Slim said loudly, "One of my lead mules got a bad hoof. Got to get some tar on it." His voice trailed off. It was silent outside. Carlson's footsteps died away. The silence came into the room. And the silence lasted.

George chuckled, "I bet Lennie's right out there in the barn with his pup. He won't want to come in here no more now he's got a pup."

Slim said, "Candy, you can have any one of them pups you want."

Candy did not answer. The silence fell on the room again. It came out of the night and invaded the room. George said, "Anybody like to play a little euchre?"

"I'll play out a few with you," said Whit.

They took places opposite each other at the table under the light, but George did not shuffle the cards. He rippled the edge of the deck nervously, and the little snapping noise drew the eyes of all the men in the room, so that he stopped doing it. The silence fell on the room again. A minute passed, and another minute. Candy lay still, staring at the ceiling. Slim gazed at him for a moment and then looked down at his hands; he subdued one hand with the other, and held it down. There came a little gnawing sound from under the floor and all the men looked down toward it gratefully. Only Candy continued to stare at the ceiling.

"Sounds like there was a rat under there," said George. "We ought to get a trap down there."

Whit broke out, "What the hell's takin' him so long? Lay out some cards, why don't you? We ain't going to get no euchre played this way."

George brought the cards together tightly and studied the backs of them. The silence was in the room again.

A shot sounded in the distance. The men looked quickly at the old man. Every head turned toward him.

For a moment he continued to stare at the ceiling. Then he rolled slowly over and faced the wall and lay silent.

George shuffled the cards noisily and dealt them. Whit drew a scoring board to him and set the pegs to start. Whit said, "I guess you guys really come here to work."

"How do ya mean?" George asked.

Whit laughed. "Well, ya come on a Friday. You got two days to work till Sunday."

"I don't see how you figure," said George.

Whit laughed again. "You do if you been around these big ranches much. Guy that wants to look over a ranch comes in Sat'day afternoon. He gets Sat'day night supper an' three meals on Sunday, and he can quit Monday mornin' after breakfast without turning his hand. But you come to work Friday noon. You got to put in a day an' a half no matter how you figure."

George looked at him levelly. "We're gonna stick aroun' a while," he said. "Me an' Lennie's gonna roll up a stake."

The door opened quietly and the stable buck put in his head; a lean negro head, lined with pain, the eyes patient. "Mr. Slim."

Slim took his eyes from old Candy. "Huh? Oh! Hello, Crooks. What's'a matter?"

"You told me to warm up tar for that mule's foot. I got it warm."

"Oh! Sure, Crooks. I'll come right out an' put it on."

"I can do it if you want, Mr. Slim."

"No. I'll come do it myself." He stood up.

Crooks said, "Mr. Slim."

"Yeah."

"That big new guy's messin' around your pups out in the barn."

"Well, he ain't doin' no harm. I give him one of them pups."

"Just thought I'd tell ya," said Crooks. "He's takin' 'em outa the nest and handlin' them. That won't do them no good."

"He won't hurt 'em," said Slim. "I'll come along with you now."

George looked up. "If that crazy bastard's foolin' around too much, jus' kick him out, Slim."

Slim followed the stable buck out of the room.

George dealt and Whit picked up his cards and examined them. "Seen the new kid yet?" he asked.

"What kid?" George asked.

"Why, Curley's new wife."

"Yeah, I seen her."

"Well, ain't she a looloo?"

"I ain't seen that much of her," said George.

Whit laid down his cards impressively. "Well, stick around an' keep your eyes open. You'll see plenty. She ain't concealin' nothing. I never seen nobody like her. She got the eye goin' all the time on everybody. I bet she even gives the stable buck the eye. I don't know what the hell she wants."

George asked casually, "Been any trouble since she got here?"

It was obvious that Whit was not interested in his cards. He laid his hand down and George scooped it in. George laid out his deliberate solitaire hand— seven cards, and six on top, and five on top of those.

Whit said, "I see what you mean. No, they ain't been nothing yet. Curley's got yella-jackets in his drawers, but that's all so far. Ever' time the guys is around she shows up. She's lookin' for Curley, or she thought she lef' somethin' layin' around and she's lookin' for it. Seems like she can't keep away from guys. An' Curley's pants is just crawlin' with ants, but they ain't nothing come of it yet."

George said, "She's gonna make a mess. They's gonna be a bad mess about her. She's a jail bait all set on the trigger. That Curley got his work cut out for him. Ranch with a bunch of guys on it ain't no place for a girl, specially like her."

Whit said, "If you got idears, you ought ta come in town with us guys tomorra night."

"Why? What's doin'?"

"Jus' the usual thing. We go in to old Susy's place. Hell of a nice place. Old Susy's a laugh—always crackin' jokes. Like she says when we come up on the front porch las' Sat'day night. Susy opens the door and then she yells over her shoulder, 'Get yor coats on, girls, here comes the sheriff.' She never talks dirty, neither. Got five girls there."

"What's it set you back?" George asked.

"Two an' a half. You can get a shot for two bits. Susy got nice chairs to set in, too. If a guy don't want a flop, why he can just set in the chairs and have a couple or three shots and pass the time of day and Susy don't give a damn. She ain't rushin' guys through and kickin' 'em out if they don't want a flop."

"Might go in and look the joint over," said George.

"Sure. Come along. It's a hell of a lot of fun—her crackin' jokes all the time. Like she says one time, she says, 'I've knew people that if they got a rag rug on the floor an' a kewpie doll lamp on the phonograph, they think they're running a parlor house.' That's Clara's house she's talkin' about. An' Susy says, 'I know what you boys want,' she says. 'My girls is clean,' she says, 'an' there ain't no water in my whisky,' she says. 'If any you guys wanta look at a kewpie doll lamp an' take your own chance gettin' burned, why you know where to go.' An' she says, 'There's guys around here walkin' bow-legged 'cause they like to look at a kewpie doll lamp.'"

George asked, "Clara runs the other house, huh?"

"Yeah," said Whit. "We don't never go there. Clara

gets three bucks a crack and thirty-five cents a shot, and she don't crack no jokes. But Susy's place is clean and she got nice chairs. Don't let no goo-goos in, neither."

"Me an' Lennie's rollin' up a stake," said George. "I might go in an' set and have a shot, but I ain't puttin' out no two and a half."

"Well, a guy got to have some fun sometime," said Whit.

The door opened and Lennie and Carlson came in together. Lennie crept to his bunk and sat down, trying not to attract attention. Carlson reached under his bunk and brought out his bag. He didn't look at old Candy, who still faced the wall. Carlson found a little cleaning rod in the bag and a can of oil. He laid them on his bed and then brought out the pistol, took out the magazine and snapped the loaded shell from the chamber. Then he fell to cleaning the barrel with the little rod. When the ejector snapped, Candy turned over and looked for a moment at the gun before he turned back to the wall again.

Carlson said casually, "Curley been in yet?"

"No," said Whit. "What's eatin' on Curley?"

Carlson squinted down the barrel of his gun. "Lookin' for his old lady. I seen him going round and round outside."

Whit said sarcastically, "He spends half his time lookin' for her, and the rest of the time she's lookin' for him."

Curley burst into the room excitedly. "Any you guys seen my wife?" he demanded.

"She ain't been here," said Whit.

Curley looked threateningly about the room. "Where the hell's Slim?"

"Went out in the barn," said George. "He was gonna put some tar on a split hoof."

Curley's shoulders dropped and squared. "How long ago'd he go?"

"Five—ten minutes."

Curley jumped out the door and banged it after him.

Whit stood up. "I guess maybe I'd like to see this," he said. "Curley's just spoilin' or he wouldn't start for Slim. An' Curley's handy, God damn handy. Got in the finals for the Golden Gloves. He got newspaper clippings about it." He considered. "But jus' the same, he better leave Slim alone. Nobody don't know what Slim can do."

"Thinks Slim's with his wife, don't he?" said George.

"Looks like it," Whit said. " 'Course Slim ain't. Least I don't think Slim is. But I like to see the fuss if it comes off. Come on, le's go."

George said, "I'm stayin' right here. I don't want to get mixed up in nothing. Lennie and me got to make a stake."

Carlson finished the cleaning of the gun and put it in the bag and pushed the bag under his bunk. "I guess I'll go out and look her over," he said. Old Candy lay still, and Lennie, from his bunk, watched George cautiously.

When Whit and Carlson were gone and the door closed after them, George turned to Lennie. "What you got on your mind?"

"I ain't done nothing, George. Slim says I better not pet them pups so much for a while. Slim says it ain't good for them; so I come right in. I been good, George."

"I coulda told you that," said George.

"Well, I wasn't hurtin' 'em none. I jus' had mine in my lap pettin' it."

George asked, "Did you see Slim out in the barn?"

"Sure I did. He tol' me I better not pet that pup no more."

"Did you see that girl?"

"You mean Curley's girl?"

"Yeah. Did she come in the barn?"

"No. Anyways I never seen her."

"You never seen Slim talkin' to her?"

"Uh-uh. She ain't been in the barn."

"O.K.," said George. "I guess them guys ain't gonna see no fight. If there's any fightin', Lennie, you keep out of it."

"I don't want no fights," said Lennie. He got up from his bunk and sat down at the table, across from George. Almost automatically George shuffled the cards and laid out his solitaire hand. He used a deliberate, thoughtful, slowness.

Lennie reached for a face card and studied it, then turned it upside down and studied it. "Both ends the same," he said. "George, why is it both ends the same?"

"I don't know," said George. "That's jus' the way they make 'em. What was Slim doin' in the barn when you seen him?"

"Slim?"

"Sure. You seen him in the barn, an' he tol' you not to pet the pups so much."

"Oh, yeah. He had a can a tar an' a paint brush. I don't know what for."

"You sure that girl didn't come in like she come in here today?"

"No. She never come."

George sighed. "You give me a good whore house every time," he said. "A guy can go in an' get drunk and get ever'thing outa his system all at once, an' no messes. And he knows how much it's gonna set him back. These here jail baits is just set on the trigger of the hoosegow."

Lennie followed his words admiringly, and moved his lips a little to keep up. George continued, "You remember Andy Cushman, Lennie? Went to grammar school?"

"The one that his old lady used to make hot cakes for the kids?" Lennie asked.

"Yeah. That's the one. You can remember anything if there's anything to eat in it." George looked carefully at the solitaire hand. He put an ace up on his scoring rack and piled a two, three and four of diamonds on it. "Andy's in San Quentin right now on account of a tart," said George.

Lennie drummed on the table with his fingers. "George?"

"Huh?"

"George, how long's it gonna be till we get that little place an' live on the fatta the lan'—an' rabbits?"

"I don' know," said George. "We gotta get a big stake together. I know a little place we can get cheap, but they ain't givin' it away."

Old Candy turned slowly over. His eyes were wide open. He watched George carefully.

Lennie said, "Tell about that place, George."

"I jus' tol' you, jus' las' night."

"Go on—tell again, George."

"Well, it's ten acres," said George. "Got a little

win'mill. Got a little shack on it, an' a chicken run. Got a kitchen, orchard, cherries, apples, peaches, 'cots, nuts, got a few berries. They's a place for alfalfa and plenty water to flood it. They's a pig pen——"

"An' rabbits, George."

"No place for rabbits now, but I could easy build a few hutches and you could feed alfalfa to the rabbits."

"Damn right, I could," said Lennie. "You God damn right I could."

George's hands stopped working with the cards. His voice was growing warmer. "An' we could have a few pigs. I could build a smoke house like the one gran'pa had, an' when we kill a pig we can smoke the bacon and the hams, and make sausage an' all like that. An' when the salmon run up river we could catch a hundred of 'em an' salt 'em down or smoke 'em. We could have them for breakfast. They ain't nothing so nice as smoked salmon. When the fruit come in we could can it—and tomatoes, they're easy to can. Ever' Sunday we'd kill a chicken or a rabbit. Maybe we'd have a cow or a goat, and the cream is so God damn thick you got to cut it with a knife and take it out with a spoon."

Lennie watched him with wide eyes, and old Candy watched him too. Lennie said softly, "We could live offa the fatta the lan'."

"Sure," said George. "All kin's a vegetables in the garden, and if we want a little whisky we can sell a few eggs or something, or some milk. We'd jus' live there. We'd belong there. There wouldn't be no more runnin' round the country and gettin' fed by a Jap cook. No, sir, we'd have our own place where we belonged and not sleep in no bunk house."

"Tell about the house, George," Lennie begged.

"Sure, we'd have a little house an' a room to ourself. Little fat iron stove, an' in the winter we'd keep a fire goin' in it. It ain't enough land so we'd have to work too hard. Maybe six, seven hours a day. We wouldn't have to buck no barley eleven hours a day. An' when we put in a crop, why, we'd be there to take the crop up. We'd know what come of our planting."

"An' rabbits," Lennie said eagerly. "An' I'd take care of 'em. Tell how I'd do that, George."

"Sure, you'd go out in the alfalfa patch an' you'd have a sack. You'd fill up the sack and bring it in an' put it in the rabbit cages."

"They'd nibble an' they'd nibble," said Lennie, "the way they do. I seen 'em."

"Ever' six weeks or so," George continued, "them does would throw a litter so we'd have plenty rabbits to eat an' to sell. An' we'd keep a few pigeons to go flyin' around the win'mill like they done when I was a kid." He looked raptly at the wall over Lennie's head. "An' it'd be our own, an' nobody could can us. If we don't like a guy we can say, 'Get the hell out,' and by God he's got to do it. An' if a fren' come along, why we'd have an extra bunk, an' we'd say, 'Why don't you spen' the night?' an' by God he would. We'd have a setter dog and a couple stripe cats, but you gotta watch out them cats don't get the little rabbits."

Lennie breathed hard. "You jus' let 'em try to get the rabbits. I'll break their God damn necks. I'll . . . I'll smash 'em with a stick." He subsided, grumbling to himself, threatening the future cats which might dare to disturb the future rabbits.

George sat entranced with his own picture.

When Candy spoke they both jumped as though

they had been caught doing something reprehensible. Candy said, "You know where's a place like that?"

George was on guard immediately. "S'pose I do," he said. "What's that to you?"

"You don't need to tell me where it's at. Might be any place."

"Sure," said George. "That's right. You couldn't find it in a hundred years."

Candy went on excitedly, "How much they want for a place like that?"

George watched him suspiciously. "Well—I could get it for six hundred bucks. The ol' people that owns it is flat bust an' the ol' lady needs an operation. Say—what's it to you? You got nothing to do with us."

Candy said, "I ain't much good with on'y one hand. I lost my hand right here on this ranch. That's why they give me a job swampin'. An' they give me two hunderd an' fifty dollars 'cause I los' my hand. An' I got fifty more saved up right in the bank, right now. Tha's three hunderd, and I got fifty more comin' the end a the month. Tell you what——" He leaned forward eagerly. "S'pose I went in with you guys. Tha's three hunderd an' fifty bucks I'd put in. I ain't much good, but I could cook and tend the chickens and hoe the garden some. How'd that be?"

George half-closed his eyes. "I gotta think about that. We was always gonna do it by ourselves."

Candy interrupted him, "I'd make a will an' leave my share to you guys in case I kick off, 'cause I ain't got no relatives nor nothing. You guys got any money? Maybe we could do her right now?"

George spat on the floor disgustedly. "We got ten bucks between us." Then he said thoughtfully, "Look, if me an' Lennie work a month an' don't spen' nothing, we'll have a hunderd bucks. That'd be four fifty. I bet we could swing her for that. Then you an' Lennie could go get her started an' I'd get a job an' make up the res', an' you could sell eggs an' stuff like that."

They fell into a silence. They looked at one another, amazed. This thing they had never really believed in was coming true. George said reverently, "Jesus Christ! I bet we could swing her." His eyes were full of wonder. "I bet we could swing her," he repeated softly.

Candy sat on the edge of his bunk. He scratched the stump of his wrist nervously. "I got hurt four years ago," he said. "They'll can me purty soon. Jus' as soon as I can't swamp out no bunk houses they'll put me on the county. Maybe if I give you guys my money, you'll let me hoe in the garden even after I ain't no good at it. An' I'll wash dishes an' little chicken stuff like that. But I'll be on our own place, an' I'll be let to work on our own place." He said miserably, "You seen what they done to my dog tonight? They says he wasn't no good to himself nor nobody else. When they can me here I wisht somebody'd shoot me. But they won't do nothing like that. I won't have no place to go, an' I can't get no more jobs. I'll have thirty dollars more comin', time you guys is ready to quit."

George stood up. "We'll do her," he said. "We'll fix up that little old place an' we'll go live there." He sat down again. They all sat still, all bemused by the beauty of the thing, each mind was popped into the future when this lovely thing should come about.

George said wonderingly, "S'pose they was a carnival or a circus come to town, or a ball game, or any damn thing." Old Candy nodded in appreciation of the idea. "We'd just go to her," George said. "We wouldn't ask nobody if we could. Jus' say, 'We'll go to her,' an' we would. Jus' milk the cow and sling some grain to the chickens an' go to her."

"An' put some grass to the rabbits," Lennie broke in. "I wouldn't never forget to feed them. When we gon'ta do it, George?"

"In one month. Right squack in one month. Know what I'm gon'ta do? I'm gon'ta write to them old people that owns the place that we'll take it. An' Candy'll send a hunderd dollars to bind her."

"Sure will," said Candy. "They got a good stove there?"

"Sure, got a nice stove, burns coal or wood."

"I'm gonna take my pup," said Lennie. "I bet by Christ he likes it there, by Jesus."

Voices were approaching from outside. George said quickly, "Don't tell nobody about it. Jus' us three an' nobody else. They li'ble to can us so we can't make no stake. Jus' go on like we was gonna buck barley the rest of our lives, then all of a sudden some day we'll go get our pay an' scram outa here."

Lennie and Candy nodded, and they were grinning with delight. "Don't tell nobody," Lennie said to himself.

Candy said, "George."

"Huh?"

"I ought to of shot that dog myself, George. I shouldn't ought to of let no stranger shoot my dog."

The door opened. Slim came in, followed by Curley and Carlson and Whit. Slim's hands were black with tar and he was scowling. Curley hung close to his elbow.

Curley said, "Well, I didn't mean nothing, Slim. I just ast you."

Slim said, "Well, you been askin' me too often. I'm gettin' God damn sick of it. If you can't look after your own God damn wife, what you expect me to do about it? You lay offa me."

"I'm jus' tryin' to tell you I didn't mean nothing," said Curley. "I jus' thought you might of saw her."

"Why'n't you tell her to stay the hell home where she belongs?" said Carlson. "You let her hang around bunk houses and pretty soon you're gonna have som'-pin on your hands and you won't be able to do nothing about it."

Curley whirled on Carlson. "You keep outta this les' you wanta step outside."

Carlson laughed. "You God damn punk," he said. "You tried to throw a scare into Slim, an' you couldn't make it stick. Slim throwed a scare inta you. You're yella as a frog belly. I don't care if you're the best welter in the country. You come for me, an' I'll kick your God damn head off."

Candy joined the attack with joy. "Glove fulla vaseline," he said disgustedly. Curley glared at him. His eyes slipped on past and lighted on Lennie; and Lennie was still smiling with delight at the memory of the ranch.

Curley stepped over to Lennie like a terrier. "What the hell you laughin' at?"

Lennie looked blankly at him. "Huh?"

Then Curley's rage exploded. "Come on, ya big bastard. Get up on your feet. No big son-of-a-bitch is gonna laugh at me. I'll show ya who's yella."

Lennie looked helplessly at George, and then he

got up and tried to retreat. Curley was balanced and
poised. He slashed at Lennie with his left, and then
smashed down his nose with a right. Lennie gave a
cry of terror. Blood welled from his nose. "George,"
he cried. "Make 'um let me alone, George." He
backed until he was against the wall, and Curley
followed, slugging him in the face. Lennie's hands
remained at his sides; he was too frightened to defend
himself.

George was on his feet yelling, "Get him, Lennie.
Don't let him do it."

Lennie covered his face with huge paws and bleated
with terror. He cried, "Make 'um stop, George." Then
Curley attacked his stomach and cut off his wind.

Slim jumped up. "The dirty little rat," he cried,
"I'll get 'um myself."

George put out his hand and grabbed Slim. "Wait a
minute," he shouted. He cupped his hands around his
mouth and yelled, "Get 'im, Lennie!"

Lennie took his hands away from his face and
looked about for George, and Curley slashed at his
eyes. The big face was covered with blood. George
yelled again, "I said get him."

Curley's fist was swinging when Lennie reached for
it. The next minute Curley was flopping like a fish on
a line, and his closed fist was lost in Lennie's big
hand. George ran down the room. "Leggo of him, Lennie. Let go."

But Lennie watched in terror the flopping little man
whom he held. Blood ran down Lennie's face, one of
his eyes was cut and closed. George slapped him in
the face again and again, and still Lennie held on to
the closed fist. Curley was white and shrunken by

now, and his struggling had become weak. He stood crying, his fist lost in Lennie's paw.

George shouted over and over, "Leggo his hand, Lennie. Leggo. Slim, come help me while the guy got any hand left."

Suddenly Lennie let go his hold. He crouched cowering against the wall. "You tol' me to, George," he said miserably.

Curley sat down on the floor, looking in wonder at his crushed hand. Slim and Carlson bent over him. Then Slim straightened up and regarded Lennie with horror. "We got to get him in to a doctor," he said. "Looks to me like ever' bone in his han' is bust."

"I didn't wanta," Lennie cried. "I didn't wanta hurt him."

Slim said, "Carlson, you get the candy wagon hitched up. We'll take 'um into Soledad an' get 'um fixed up." Carlson hurried out. Slim turned to the whimpering Lennie. "It ain't your fault," he said. "This punk sure had it comin' to him. But—Jesus! He ain't hardly got no han' left." Slim hurried out, and in a moment returned with a tin cup of water. He held it to Curley's lips.

George said, "Slim, will we get canned now? We need the stake. Will Curley's old man can us now?"

Slim smiled wryly. He knelt down beside Curley. "You got your senses in hand enough to listen?" he asked. Curley nodded. "Well, then listen," Slim went on. "I think you got your han' caught in a machine. If you don't tell nobody what happened, we ain't going to. But you jus' tell an' try to get this guy canned and we'll tell ever'body, an' then will you get the laugh."

"I won't tell," said Curley. He avoided looking at Lennie.

Buggy wheels sounded outside. Slim helped Curley up. "Come on now. Carlson's gonna take you to a doctor." He helped Curley out the door. The sound of wheels drew away. In a moment Slim came back into the bunk house. He looked at Lennie, still crouched fearfully against the wall. "Le's see your hands," he asked.

Lennie stuck out his hands.

"Christ awmighty, I hate to have you mad at me," Slim said.

George broke in, "Lennie was jus' scairt," he explained. "He didn't know what to do. I told you nobody ought never to fight him. No, I guess it was Candy I told."

Candy nodded solemnly. "That's jus' what you done," he said. "Right this morning when Curley first lit intil your fren', you says, 'He better not fool with Lennie if he knows what's good for 'um.' That's jus' what you says to me."

George turned to Lennie. "It ain't your fault," he said. "You don't need to be scairt no more. You done jus' what I tol' you to. Maybe you better go in the wash room an' clean up your face. You look like hell."

Lennie smiled with his bruised mouth. "I didn't want no trouble," he said. He walked toward the door, but just before he came to it, he turned back. "George?"

"What you want?"

"I can still tend the rabbits, George?"

"Sure. You ain't done nothing wrong."

"I di'n't mean no harm, George."

"Well, get the hell out and wash your face."

Crooks, the negro stable buck, had his bunk in the harness room; a little shed that leaned off the wall of the barn. On one side of the little room there was a square four-paned window, and on the other, a narrow plank door leading into the barn. Crooks' bunk was a long box filled with straw, on which his blankets were flung. On the wall by the window there were pegs on which hung broken harness in process of being mended; strips of new leather; and under the window itself a little bench for leather-working tools, curved knives and needles and balls of linen thread, and a small hand riveter. On pegs were also pieces of harness, a split collar with the horsehair stuffing sticking out, a broken hame, and a trace chain with its leather covering split. Crooks had his apple box over his bunk, and in it a range of medicine bottles, both for himself and for the horses. There were cans of saddle soap and a drippy can of tar with its paint brush sticking over the edge. And scattered about the floor were a number of personal possessions; for, being alone, Crooks could leave his things about, and being a stable buck and a cripple, he was more permanent than the other men, and he had accumulated more possessions than he could carry on his back.

Crooks possessed several pairs of shoes, a pair of rubber boots, a big alarm clock and a single-barreled shotgun. And he had books, too; a tattered dictionary and a mauled copy of the California civil code for 1905. There were battered magazines and a few dirty books on a special shelf over his bunk. A pair of large gold-rimmed spectacles hung from a nail on the wall above his bed.

This room was swept and fairly neat, for Crooks was a proud, aloof man. He kept his distance and demanded that other people keep theirs. His body was bent over to the left by his crooked spine, and his eyes lay deep in his head, and because of their depth seemed to glitter with intensity. His lean face was lined with deep black wrinkles, and he had thin, pain-tightened lips which were lighter than his face.

It was Saturday night. Through the open door that led into the barn came the sound of moving horses, of feet stirring, of teeth champing on hay, of the rattle of halter chains. In the stable buck's room a small electric globe threw a meager yellow light.

Crooks sat on his bunk. His shirt was out of his jeans in back. In one hand he held a bottle of liniment, and with the other he rubbed his spine. Now and then he poured a few drops of the liniment into his pink-palmed hand and reached up under his shirt to rub again. He flexed his muscles against his back and shivered.

Noiselessly Lennie appeared in the open doorway and stood there looking in, his big shoulders nearly filling the opening. For a moment Crooks did not see him, but on raising his eyes he stiffened and a scowl came on his face. His hand came out from under his shirt.

Lennie smiled helplessly in an attempt to make friends.

Crooks said sharply, "You got no right to come in my room. This here's my room. Nobody got any right in here but me."

Lennie gulped and his smile grew more fawning. "I ain't doing nothing," he said. "Just come to look at my puppy. And I seen your light," he explained.

"Well, I got a right to have a light. You go on get outta my room. I ain't wanted in the bunk house, and you ain't wanted in my room."

"Why ain't you wanted?" Lennie asked.

" 'Cause I'm black. They play cards in there, but I can't play because I'm black. They say I stink. Well, I tell you, you all of you stink to me."

Lennie flapped his big hands helplessly. "Ever'body went into town," he said. "Slim an' George an' ever'-body. George says I gotta stay here an' not get in no trouble. I seen your light."

"Well, what do you want?"

"Nothing—I seen your light. I thought I could jus' come in an' set."

Crooks stared at Lennie, and he reached behind him and took down the spectacles and adjusted them over his pink ears and stared again. "I don't know what you're doin' in the barn anyway," he complained. "You ain't no skinner. They's no call for a bucker to come into the barn at all. You ain't no skinner. You ain't got nothing to do with the horses."

"The pup," Lennie repeated. "I come to see my pup."

"Well, go see your pup, then. Don't come in a place where you're not wanted."

Lennie lost his smile. He advanced a step into the room, then remembered and backed to the door again. "I looked at 'em a little. Slim says I ain't to pet 'em very much."

Crooks said, "Well, you been takin' 'em out of the nest all the time. I wonder the old lady don't move 'em someplace else."

"Oh, she don't care. She lets me." Lennie had moved into the room again.

Crooks scowled, but Lennie's disarming smile defeated him. "Come on in and set a while," Crooks said. " 'Long as you won't get out and leave me alone, you might as well set down." His tone was a little more friendly. "All the boys gone into town, huh?"

"All but old Candy. He just sets in the bunk house sharpening his pencil and sharpening and figuring."

Crooks adjusted his glasses. "Figuring? What's Candy figuring about?"

Lennie almost shouted, " 'Bout the rabbits."

"You're nuts," said Crooks. "You're crazy as a wedge. What rabbits you talkin' about?"

"The rabbits we're gonna get, and I get to tend 'em, cut grass an' give 'em water, an' like that."

"Jus' nuts," said Crooks. "I don't blame the guy you travel with for keepin' you outa sight."

Lennie said quietly, "It ain't no lie. We're gonna do it. Gonna get a little place an' live on the fatta the lan'."

Crooks settled himself more comfortably on his

bunk. "Set down," he invited. "Set down on the nail keg."

Lennie hunched down on the little barrel. "You think it's a lie," Lennie said. "But it ain't no lie. Ever' word's the truth, an' you can ast George."

Crooks put his dark chin into his pink palm. "You travel aroun' with George, don't ya?"

"Sure. Me an' him goes ever' place together."

Crooks continued. "Sometimes he talks, and you don't know what the hell he's talkin' about. Ain't that so?" He leaned forward, boring Lennie with his deep eyes. "Ain't that so?"

"Yeah . . . sometimes."

"Jus' talks on, an' you don't know what the hell it's all about?"

"Yeah . . . sometimes. But . . . not always."

Crooks leaned forward over the edge of the bunk. "I ain't a southern negro," he said. "I was born right here in California. My old man had a chicken ranch, 'bout ten acres. The white kids come to play at our place, an' sometimes I went to play with them, and some of them was pretty nice. My ol' man didn't like that. I never knew till long later why he didn't like that. But I know now." He hesitated, and when he spoke again his voice was softer. "There wasn't another colored family for miles around. And now there ain't a colored man on this ranch an' there's jus' one family in Soledad." He laughed. "If I say something, why it's just a nigger sayin' it."

Lennie asked, "How long you think it'll be before them pups will be old enough to pet?"

Crooks laughed again. "A guy can talk to you an' be sure you won't go blabbin'. Couple of weeks an' them pups'll be all right. George knows what he's about.

Jus' talks, an' you don't understand nothing." He leaned forward excitedly. "This is just a nigger talkin', an' a busted-back nigger. So it don't mean nothing, see? You couldn't remember it anyways. I seen it over an' over—a guy talkin' to another guy and it don't make no difference if he don't hear or understand. The thing is, they're talkin', or they're settin' still not talkin'. It don't make no difference, no difference." His excitement had increased until he pounded his knee with his hand. "George can tell you screwy things, and it don't matter. It's just the talking. It's just bein' with another guy. That's all." He paused.

His voice grew soft and persuasive. "S'pose George don't come back no more. S'pose he took a powder and just ain't coming back. What'll you do then?"

Lennie's attention came gradually to what had been said. "What?" he demanded.

"I said s'pose George went into town tonight and you never heard of him no more." Crooks pressed forward some kind of private victory. "Just s'pose that," he repeated.

"He won't do it," Lennie cried. "George wouldn't do nothing like that. I been with George a long time. He'll come back tonight——" But the doubt was too much for him. "Don't you think he will?"

Crooks' face lighted with pleasure in his torture. "Nobody can't tell what a guy'll do," he observed calmly. "Le's say he wants to come back and can't. S'pose he gets killed or hurt so he can't come back."

Lennie struggled to understand. "George won't do nothing like that," he repeated. "George is careful. He won't get hurt. He ain't never been hurt, 'cause he's careful."

"Well s'pose, jus' s'pose he don't come back. What'll you do then?"

Lennie's face wrinkled with apprehension. "I don' know. Say, what you doin' anyways?" he cried. "This ain't true. George ain't got hurt."

Crooks bored in on him. "Want me ta tell ya what'll happen? They'll take ya to the booby hatch. They'll tie ya up with a collar, like a dog."

Suddenly Lennie's eyes centered and grew quiet, and mad. He stood up and walked dangerously toward Crooks. "Who hurt George?" he demanded.

Crooks saw the danger as it approached him. He edged back on his bunk to get out of the way. "I was just supposin'," he said. "George ain't hurt. He's all right. He'll be back all right."

Lennie stood over him. "What you supposin' for? Ain't nobody goin' to suppose no hurt to George."

Crooks removed his glasses and wiped his eyes with his fingers. "Jus' set down," he said. "George ain't hurt."

Lennie growled back to his seat on the nail keg. "Ain't nobody goin' to talk no hurt to George," he grumbled.

Crooks said gently, "Maybe you can see now. You got George. You *know* he's goin' to come back. S'pose you didn't have nobody. S'pose you couldn't go into the bunk house and play rummy 'cause you was black. How'd you like that? S'pose you had to sit out here an' read books. Sure you could play horseshoes till it got dark, but then you got to read books. Books ain't no good. A guy needs somebody—to be near him." He whined, "A guy goes nuts if he ain't got nobody. Don't make no difference who the guy is, long's he's with you. I tell ya," he cried, "I tell ya a guy gets too lonely / an' he gets sick."

"George gonna come back," Lennie reassured himself in a frightened voice. "Maybe George come back already. Maybe I better go see."

Crooks said, "I didn't mean to scare you. He'll come back. I was talkin' about myself. A guy sets alone out here at night, maybe readin' books or thinkin' or stuff like that. Sometimes he gets thinkin', an' he got nothing to tell him what's so an' what ain't so. Maybe if he sees somethin', he don't know whether it's right or not. He can't turn to some other guy and ast him if he sees it too. He can't tell. He got nothing to measure by. I seen things out here. I wasn't drunk. I don't know if I was asleep. If some guy was with me, he could tell me I was asleep, an' then it would be all right. But I jus' don't know." Crooks was looking across the room now, looking toward the window.

Lennie said miserably, "George wun't go away and leave me. I know George wun't do that."

The stable buck went on dreamily, "I remember when I was a little kid on my old man's chicken ranch. Had two brothers. They was always near me, always there. Used to sleep right in the same room, right in the same bed—all three. Had a strawberry patch. Had an alfalfa patch. Used to turn the chickens out in the alfalfa on a sunny morning. My brothers'd set on a fence rail an' watch 'em—white chickens they was."

Gradually Lennie's interest came around to what was being said. "George says we're gonna have alfalfa for the rabbits."

"What rabbits?"

"We're gonna have rabbits an' a berry patch."

"You're nuts."

"We are too. You ast George."

"You're nuts." Crooks was scornful. "I seen hunderds of men come by on the road an' on the ranches, with their bindles on their back an' that same damn thing in their heads. Hunderds of them. They come, an' they quit an' go on; an' every damn one of 'em's got a little piece of land in his head. An' never a God damn one of 'em ever gets it. Just like heaven. Ever'body wants a little piece of lan'. I read plenty of books out here. Nobody never gets to heaven, and nobody gets no land. It's just in their head. They're all the time talkin' about it, but it's jus' in their head." He paused and looked toward the open door, for the horses were moving restlessly and the halter chains clinked. A horse whinnied. "I guess somebody's out there," Crooks said. "Maybe Slim. Slim comes in sometimes two, three times a night. Slim's a real skinner. He looks out for his team." He pulled himself painfully upright and moved toward the door. "That you, Slim?" he called.

Candy's voice answered. "Slim went in town. Say, you seen Lennie?"

"Ya mean the big guy?"

"Yeah. Seen him around any place?"

"He's in here," Crooks said shortly. He went back to his bunk and lay down.

Candy stood in the doorway scratching his bald wrist and looking blindly into the lighted room. He made no attempt to enter. "Tell ya what, Lennie. I been figuring out about them rabbits."

Crooks said irritably, "You can come in if you want."

Candy seemed embarrassed. "I do' know. 'Course, if ya want me to."

"Come on in. If ever'body's comin' in, you might just as well." It was difficult for Crooks to conceal his pleasure with anger.

Candy came in, but he was still embarrassed. "You got a nice cozy little place in here," he said to Crooks. "Must be nice to have a room all to yourself this way."

"Sure," said Crooks. "And a manure pile under the window. Sure, it's swell."

Lennie broke in, "You said about them rabbits."

Candy leaned against the wall beside the broken collar while he scratched the wrist stump. "I been here a long time," he said. "An' Crooks been here a long time. This's the first time I ever been in his room."

Crooks said darkly, "Guys don't come into a colored man's room very much. Nobody been here but Slim. Slim an' the boss."

Candy quickly changed the subject. "Slim's as good a skinner as I ever seen."

Lennie leaned toward the old swamper. "About them rabbits," he insisted.

Candy smiled. "I got it figured out. We can make some money on them rabbits if we go about it right."

"But I get to tend 'em," Lennie broke in. "George says I get to tend 'em. He promised."

Crooks interrupted brutally. "You guys is just kiddin' yourself. You'll talk about it a hell of a lot, but you won't get no land. You'll be a swamper here till they take you out in a box. Hell, I seen too many guys. Lennie here'll quit an' be on the road in two, three weeks. Seems like ever' guy got land in his head."

Candy rubbed his cheek angrily. "You God damn

right we're gonna do it. George says we are. We got the money right now."

"Yeah?" said Crooks. "An' where's George now? In town in a whore house. That's where your money's goin'. Jesus, I seen it happen too many times. I seen too many guys with land in their head. They never get none under their hand."

Candy cried, "Sure they all want it. Everybody wants a little bit of land, not much. Jus' som'thin' that was his. Somethin' he could live on and there couldn't nobody throw him off of it. I never had none. I planted crops for damn near ever'body in this state, but they wasn't my crops, and when I harvested 'em, it wasn't none of my harvest. But we gonna do it now, and don't make no mistake about that. George ain't got the money in town. That money's in the bank. Me an' Lennie an' George. We gonna have a room to ourself. We're gonna have a dog an' rabbits an' chickens. We're gonna have green corn an' maybe a cow or a goat." He stopped, overwhelmed with his picture.

Crooks asked, "You say you got the money?"

"Damn right. We got most of it. Just a little bit more to get. Have it all in one month. George got the land all picked out, too."

Crooks reached around and explored his spine with his hand. "I never seen a guy really do it," he said. "I seen guys nearly crazy with loneliness for land, but ever' time a whore house or a blackjack game took what it takes." He hesitated. ". . . If you . . . guys would want a hand to work for nothing—just his keep, why I'd come an' lend a hand. I ain't so crippled I can't work like a son-of-a-bitch if I want to."

"Any you boys seen Curley?"

They swung their heads toward the door. Looking in was Curley's wife. Her face was heavily made up. Her lips were slightly parted. She breathed strongly, as though she had been running.

"Curley ain't been here," Candy said sourly.

She stood still in the doorway, smiling a little at them, rubbing the nails of one hand with the thumb and forefinger of the other. And her eyes traveled from one face to another. "They left all the weak ones here," she said finally. "Think I don't know where they all went? Even Curley. I know where they all went."

Lennie watched her, fascinated; but Candy and Crooks were scowling down away from her eyes. Candy said, "Then if you know, why you want to ast us where Curley is at?"

She regarded them amusedly. "Funny thing," she said. "If I catch any one man, and he's alone, I get along fine with him. But just let two of the guys get together an' you won't talk. Jus' nothing but mad." She dropped her fingers and put her hands on her hips. "You're all scared of each other, that's what. Ever' one of you's scared the rest is goin' to get something on you."

After a pause Crooks said, "Maybe you better go along to your own house now. We don't want no trouble."

"Well, I ain't giving you no trouble. Think I don't like to talk to somebody ever' once in a while? Think I like to stick in that house alla time?"

Candy laid the stump of his wrist on his knee and rubbed it gently with his hand. He said accusingly, "You gotta husban'. You got no call foolin' aroun' with other guys, causin' trouble."

The girl flared up. "Sure I gotta husban'. You all seen him. Swell guy, ain't he? Spends all his time sayin' what he's gonna do to guys he don't like, and he don't like nobody. Think I'm gonna stay in that two-by-four house and listen how Curley's gonna lead with his left twict, and then bring in the ol' right cross? 'One-two' he says. 'Jus' the ol' one-two an' he'll go down.' " She paused and her face lost its sullenness and grew interested. "Say—what happened to Curley's han'?"

There was an embarrassed silence. Candy stole a look at Lennie. Then he coughed. "Why . . . Curley . . . he got his han' caught in a machine, ma'am. Bust his han'."

She watched for a moment, and then she laughed. "Baloney! What you think you're sellin' me? Curley started som'pin' he didn' finish. Caught in a machine—baloney! Why, he ain't give nobody the good ol' one-two since he got his han' bust. Who bust him?"

Candy repeated sullenly, "Got it caught in a machine."

"Awright," she said contemptuously. "Awright, cover 'im up if ya wanta. Whatta I care? You bindle bums think you're so damn good. Whatta ya think I am, a kid? I tell ya I could of went with shows. Not jus' one, neither. An' a guy tol' me he could put me in pitchers. . . ." She was breathless with indignation. "—Sat'iday night. Ever'body out doin' som'pin'. Ever'body! An' what am I doin'? Standin' here talkin' to a bunch of bindle stiffs—a nigger an' a dum-dum and a lousy ol' sheep—an' likin' it because they ain't nobody else."

Lennie watched her, his mouth half open. Crooks

had retired into the terrible protective dignity of the negro. But a change came over old Candy. He stood up suddenly and knocked his nail keg over backward. "I had enough," he said angrily. "You ain't wanted here. We told you you ain't. An' I tell ya, you got floozy idears about what us guys amounts to. You ain't got sense enough in that chicken head to even see that we ain't stiffs. S'pose you get us canned. S'pose you do. You think we'll hit the highway an' look for another lousy two-bit job like this. You don't know that we got our own ranch to go to, an' our own house. We ain't got to stay here. We gotta house and chickens an' fruit trees an' a place a hunderd time prettier than this. An' we got fren's, that's what we got. Maybe there was a time when we was scared of gettin' canned, but we ain't no more. We got our own lan', and it's ours, an' we c'n go to it."

Curley's wife laughed at him. "Baloney," she said. "I seen too many you guys. If you had two bits in the worl', why you'd be in gettin' two shots of corn with it and suckin' the bottom of the glass. I know you guys."

Candy's face had grown redder and redder, but before she was done speaking, he had control of himself. He was the master of the situation. "I might of knew," he said gently. "Maybe you just better go along an' roll your hoop. We ain't got nothing to say to you at all. We know what we got, and we don't care whether you know it or not. So maybe you better jus' scatter along now, 'cause Curley maybe ain't gonna like his wife out in the barn with us 'bindle stiffs.' "

She looked from one face to another, and they were all closed against her. And she looked longest at Lennie, until he dropped his eyes in embarrassment. Suddenly she said, "Where'd you get them bruises on your face?"

Lennie looked up guiltily. "Who—me?"

"Yeah, you."

Lennie looked to Candy for help, and then he looked at his lap again. "He got his han' caught in a machine," he said.

Curley's wife laughed. "O.K., Machine. I'll talk to you later. I like machines."

Candy broke in. "You let this guy alone. Don't you do no messing aroun' with him. I'm gonna tell George what you says. George won't have you messin' with Lennie."

"Who's George?" she asked. "The little guy you come with?"

Lennie smiled happily. "That's him," he said. "That's the guy, an' he's gonna let me tend the rabbits."

"Well, if that's all you want, I might get a couple rabbits myself."

Crooks stood up from his bunk and faced her. "I had enough," he said coldly. "You got no rights comin' in a colored man's room. You got no rights messing around in here at all. Now you jus' get out, an' get out quick. If you don't, I'm gonna ast the boss not to ever let you come in the barn no more."

She turned on him in scorn. "Listen, Nigger," she said. "You know what I can do to you if you open your trap?"

Crooks stared hopelessly at her, and then he sat down on his bunk and drew into himself.

She closed on him. "You know what I could do?"

Crooks seemed to grow smaller, and he pressed himself against the wall. "Yes, ma'am."

"Well, you keep your place then, Nigger. I could get you strung up on a tree so easy it ain't even funny."

Crooks had reduced himself to nothing. There was no personality, no ego—nothing to arouse either like or dislike. He said, "Yes, ma'am," and his voice was toneless.

For a moment she stood over him as though waiting for him to move so that she could whip at him again; but Crooks sat perfectly still, his eyes averted, everything that might be hurt drawn in. She turned at last to the other two.

Old Candy was watching her, fascinated. "If you was to do that, we'd tell," he said quietly. "We'd tell about you framin' Crooks."

"Tell an' be damned," she cried. "Nobody'd listen to you an' you know it. Nobody'd listen to you."

Candy subsided. "No . . ." he agreed. "Nobody'd listen to us."

Lennie whined, "I wisht George was here. I wisht George was here."

Candy stepped over to him. "Don't you worry none," he said. "I jus' heard the guys comin' in. George'll be in the bunk house right now, I bet." He turned to Curley's wife. "You better go home now," he said quietly. "If you go right now, we won't tell Curley you was here."

She appraised him coolly. "I ain't sure you heard nothing."

"Better not take no chances," he said. "If you ain't sure, you better take the safe way."

She turned to Lennie. "I'm glad you bust up Curley a little bit. He got it comin' to him. Sometimes I'd like to bust him myself." She slipped out the door and disappeared into the dark barn. And while she went through the barn, the halter chains rattled, and some horses snorted and some stamped their feet.

Crooks seemed to come slowly out of the layers of protection he had put on. "Was that the truth what you said about the guys come back?" he asked.

"Sure. I heard 'em."

"Well, I didn't hear nothing."

"The gate banged," Candy said, and he went on, "Jesus Christ, Curley's wife can move quiet. I guess she had a lot of practice, though."

Crooks avoided the whole subject now. "Maybe you guys better go," he said. "I ain't sure I want you in here no more. A colored man got to have some rights even if he don't like 'em."

Candy said, "That bitch didn't ought to of said that to you."

"It wasn't nothing," Crooks said dully. "You guys comin' in an' settin' made me forget. What she says is true."

The horses snorted out in the barn and the chains rang and a voice called, "Lennie. Oh, Lennie. You in the barn?"

"It's George," Lennie cried. And he answered, "Here, George. I'm right in here."

In a second George stood framed in the door, and he looked disapprovingly about. "What you doin' in Crooks' room. You hadn't ought to be in here."

Crooks nodded. "I tol' 'em, but they come in anyways."

"Well, why'n't you kick 'em out?"

"I di'n't care much," said Crooks. "Lennie's a nice fella."

Now Candy aroused himself. "Oh, George! I been figurin' and figurin'. I got it doped out how we can even make some money on them rabbits."

George scowled. "I though I tol' you not to tell nobody about that."

Candy was crestfallen. "Didn't tell nobody but Crooks."

George said, "Well you guys get outta here. Jesus, seems like I can't go away for a minute."

Candy and Lennie stood up and went toward the door. Crooks called, "Candy!"

"Huh?"

" 'Member what I said about hoein' and doin' odd jobs?"

"Yeah," said Candy. "I remember."

"Well, jus' forget it," said Crooks. "I didn' mean it. Jus' foolin'. I wouldn' want to go no place like that."

"Well, O.K., if you feel like that. Goodnight."

The three men went out of the door. As they went through the barn the horses snorted and the halter chains rattled.

Crooks sat on his bunk and looked at the door for a moment, and then he reached for the liniment bottle. He pulled out his shirt in back, poured a little liniment in his pink palm and, reaching around, he fell slowly to rubbing his back.

One end of the great barn was piled high with new hay and over the pile hung the four-taloned Jackson fork suspended from its pulley. The hay came down like a mountain slope to the other end of the barn, and there was a level place as yet unfilled with the new crop. At the sides the feeding racks were visible, and between the slats the heads of horses could be seen.

It was Sunday afternoon. The resting horses nibbled the remaining wisps of hay, and they stamped their feet and they bit the wood of the mangers and rattled the halter chains. The afternoon sun sliced in through the cracks of the barn walls and lay in bright lines on the hay. There was the buzz of flies in the air, the lazy afternoon humming.

From outside came the clang of horseshoes on the playing peg and the shouts of men, playing, encouraging, jeering. But in the barn it was quiet and humming and lazy and warm.

Only Lennie was in the barn, and Lennie sat in the hay beside a packing case under a manger in the end of the barn that had not been filled with hay. Lennie sat in the hay and looked at a little dead puppy that lay in front of him. Lennie looked at it for a long time, and then he put out his huge hand and stroked it, stroked it clear from one end to the other.

And Lennie said softly to the puppy, "Why do you got to get killed? You ain't so little as mice. I didn't bounce you hard." He bent the pup's head up and looked in its face, and he said to it, "Now maybe George ain't gonna let me tend no rabbits, if he fin's out you got killed."

He scooped a little hollow and laid the puppy in it and covered it over with hay, out of sight; but he continued to stare at the mound he had made. He said, "This ain't no bad thing like I got to go hide in the brush. Oh! no. This ain't. I'll tell George I foun' it dead."

He unburied the puppy and inspected it, and he stroked it from ears to tail. He went on sorrowfully, "But he'll know. George always knows. He'll say, 'You done it. Don't try to put nothing over on me.' An' he'll say, 'Now jus' for that you don't get to tend no rabbits!'"

Suddenly his anger arose. "God damn you," he cried. "Why do you got to get killed? You ain't so little as mice." He picked up the pup and hurled it from him. He turned his back on it. He sat bent over his knees and he whispered, "Now I won't get to tend the rabbits. Now he won't let me." He rocked himself back and forth in his sorrow.

From outside came the clang of horseshoes on the iron stake, and then a little chorus of cries. Lennie got up and brought the puppy back and laid it on the hay and sat down. He stroked the pup again. "You wasn't big enough," he said. "They tol' me and tol' me you wasn't. I di'n't know you'd get killed so easy." He worked his fingers on the pup's limp ear. "Maybe George won't care," he said. "This here God damn little son-of-a-bitch wasn't nothing to George."

Curley's wife came around the end of the last stall. She came very quietly, so that Lennie didn't see her. She wore her bright cotton dress and the mules with the red ostrich feathers. Her face was made up and the little sausage curls were all in place. She was quite near to him before Lennie looked up and saw her.

In a panic he shoveled hay over the puppy with his fingers. He looked sullenly up at her.

She said, "What you got there, sonny boy?"

Lennie glared at her. "George says I ain't to have nothing to do with you—talk to you or nothing."

She laughed. "George giving you orders about everything?"

Lennie looked down at the hay. "Says I can't tend no rabbits if I talk to you or anything."

She said quietly, "He's scared Curley'll get mad. Well, Curley got his arm in a sling—an' if Curley gets tough, you can break his other han'. You didn't put nothing over on me about gettin' it caught in no machine."

But Lennie was not to be drawn. "No, sir. I ain't gonna talk to you or nothing."

She knelt in the hay beside him. "Listen," she said. "All the guys got a horseshoe tenement goin' on. It's on'y about four o'clock. None of them guys is goin' to leave that tenement. Why can't I talk to you? I never get to talk to nobody. I get awful lonely."

Lennie said, "Well, I ain't supposed to talk to you or nothing."

"I get lonely," she said. "You can talk to people, but I can't talk to nobody but Curley. Else he gets mad. How'd you like not to talk to anybody?"

Lennie said, "Well, I ain't supposed to. George's scared I'll get in trouble."

She changed the subject. "What you got covered up there?"

Then all of Lennie's woe came back on him. "Jus' my pup," he said sadly. "Jus' my little pup." And he swept the hay from on top of it.

"Why, he's dead," she cried.

"He was so little," said Lennie. "I was jus' playin' with him . . . an' he made like he's gonna bite me . . . an' I made like I was gonna smack him . . . an' . . . an' I done it. An' then he was dead."

She consoled him. "Don't you worry none. He was jus' a mutt. You can get another one easy. The whole country is fulla mutts."

"It ain't that so much," Lennie explained miserably. "George ain't gonna let me tend no rabbits now."

"Why don't he?"

"Well, he said if I done any more bad things he ain't gonna let me tend the rabbits."

She moved closer to him and she spoke soothingly. "Don't you worry about talkin' to me. Listen to the guys yell out there. They got four dollars bet in that tenement. None of them ain't gonna leave till it's over."

"If George sees me talkin' to you he'll give me hell," Lennie said cautiously. "He tol' me so."

Her face grew angry. "Wha's the matter with me?" she cried. "Ain't I got a right to talk to nobody? Whatta they think I am, anyways? You're a nice guy. I don't know why I can't talk to you. I ain't doin' no harm to you."

"Well, George says you'll get us in a mess."

"Aw, nuts!" she said. "What kinda harm am I doin' to you? Seems like they ain't none of them cares how I gotta live. I tell you I ain't used to livin' like this. I coulda made somethin' of myself." She said darkly, "Maybe I will yet." And then her words tumbled out in a passion of communication, as though she hurried before her listener could be taken away. "I lived right in Salinas," she said. "Come there when I was a kid. Well, a show come through, an' I met one of the actors. He says I could go with that show. But my ol' lady wouldn' let me. She says because I was on'y fifteen. But the guy says I coulda. If I'd went, I wouldn't be livin' like this, you bet."

Lennie stroked the pup back and forth. "We gonna have a little place—an' rabbits," he explained.

She went on with her story quickly, before she should be interrupted. " 'Nother time I met a guy, an' he was in pitchers. Went out to the Riverside Dance Palace with him. He says he was gonna put me in the movies. Says I was a natural. Soon's he got back to Hollywood he was gonna write to me about it." She looked closely at Lennie to see whether she was impressing him. "I never got that letter," she said. "I always thought my ol' lady stole it. Well, I wasn't gonna stay no place where I couldn't get nowhere or make something of myself, an' where they stole your letters. I ast her if she stole it, too, an' she says no. So I married Curley. Met him out to the Riverside Dance Palace that same night." She demanded, "You listenin'?"

"Me? Sure."

"Well, I ain't told this to nobody before. Maybe I ought'n to. I don' *like* Curley. He ain't a nice fella." And because she had confided in him, she moved closer to Lennie and sat beside him. "Coulda been in the movies, an' had nice clothes—all them nice clothes like they wear. An' I coulda sat in them big hotels, an' had pitchers took of me. When they had them previews I coulda went to them, an' spoke in the radio, an' it wouldn'ta cost me a cent because I was in the pitcher. An' all them nice clothes like they wear. Because this guy says I was a natural." She looked up at Lennie, and she made a small grand gesture with her arm and hand to show that she could act. The fingers trailed after her leading wrist, and her little finger stuck out grandly from the rest.

Lennie sighed deeply. From outside came the clang of a horseshoe on metal, and then a chorus of cheers. "Somebody made a ringer," said Curley's wife.

Now the light was lifting as the sun went down, and the sun streaks climbed up the wall and fell over the feeding racks and over the heads of the horses.

Lennie said, "Maybe if I took this pup out and throwed him away George wouldn't never know. An' then I could tend the rabbits without no trouble."

Curley's wife said angrily, "Don't you think of nothing but rabbits?"

"We gonna have a little place," Lennie explained patiently. "We gonna have a house an' a garden and a place for alfalfa, an' that alfalfa is for the rabbits, an' I take a sack and get it all fulla alfalfa and then I take it to the rabbits."

She asked, "What makes you so nuts about rabbits?"

Lennie had to think carefully before he could come to

a conclusion. He moved cautiously close to her, until he was right against her. "I like to pet nice things. Once at a fair I seen some of them long-hair rabbits. An' they was nice, you bet. Sometimes I've even pet mice, but not when I could get nothing better."

Curley's wife moved away from him a little. "I think you're nuts," she said.

"No I ain't," Lennie explained earnestly. "George says I ain't. I like to pet nice things with my fingers, sof' things."

She was a little bit reassured. "Well, who don't?" she said. "Ever'body likes that. I like to feel silk an' velvet. Do you like to feel velvet?"

Lennie chuckled with pleasure. "You bet, by God," he cried happily. "An' I had some, too. A lady give me some, an' that lady was—my own Aunt Clara. She give it right to me—'bout this big a piece. I wisht I had that velvet right now." A frown came over his face. "I lost it," he said. "I ain't seen it for a long time."

Curley's wife laughed at him. "You're nuts," she said. "But you're a kinda nice fella. Jus' like a big baby. But a person can see kinda what you mean. When I'm doin' my hair sometimes I jus' set an' stroke it 'cause it's so soft." To show how she did it, she ran her fingers over the top of her head. "Some people got kinda coarse hair," she said complacently. "Take Curley. His hair is jus' like wire. But mine is soft and fine. 'Course I brush it a lot. That makes it fine. Here—feel right here." She took Lennie's hand and put it on her head. "Feel right aroun' there an' see how soft it is."

Lennie's big fingers fell to stroking her hair.

"Don't you muss it up," she said.

Lennie said, "Oh! That's nice," and he stroked harder. "Oh, that's nice."

"Look out, now, you'll muss it." And then she cried angrily, "You stop it now, you'll mess it all up." She jerked her head sideways, and Lennie's fingers closed on her hair and hung on. "Let go," she cried. "You let go!"

Lennie was in a panic. His face was contorted. She screamed then, and Lennie's other hand closed over her mouth and nose. "Please don't," he begged. "Oh! Please don't do that. George'll be mad."

She struggled violently under his hands. Her feet battered on the hay and she writhed to be free; and from under Lennie's hand came a muffled screaming. Lennie began to cry with fright. "Oh! Please don't do none of that," he begged. "George gonna say I done a bad thing. He ain't gonna let me tend no rabbits." He moved his hand a little and her hoarse cry came out. Then Lennie grew angry. "Now don't," he said. "I don't want you to yell. You gonna get me in trouble jus' like George says you will. Now don't you do that." And she continued to struggle, and her eyes were wild with terror. He shook her then, and he was angry with her. "Don't you go yellin'," he said, and he shook her; and her body flopped like a fish. And then she was still, for Lennie had broken her neck.

He looked down at her, and carefully he removed his hand from over her mouth, and she lay still. "I don't want ta hurt you," he said, "but George'll be mad if you yell." When she didn't answer nor move he bent closely over her. He lifted her arm and let it drop. For a moment he seemed bewildered. And then he whispered in fright, "I done a bad thing. I done another bad thing."

He pawed up the hay until it partly covered her.

From outside the barn came a cry of men and the double clang of shoes on metal. For the first time Lennie became conscious of the outside. He crouched down in the hay and listened. "I done a real bad thing," he said. "I shouldn't of did that. George'll be mad. An' . . . he said . . . an' hide in the brush till he come. He's gonna be mad. In the brush till he come. Tha's what he said." Lennie went back and looked at the dead girl. The puppy lay close to her. Lennie picked it up. "I'll throw him away," he said. "It's bad enough like it is." He put the pup under his coat, and he crept to the barn wall and peered out between the cracks, toward the horseshoe game. And then he crept around the end of the last manger and disappeared.

The sun streaks were high on the wall by now, and the light was growing soft in the barn. Curley's wife lay on her back, and she was half covered with hay.

It was very quiet in the barn, and the quiet of the afternoon was on the ranch. Even the clang of the pitched shoes, even the voices of the men in the game seemed to grow more quiet. The air in the barn was dusky in advance of the outside day. A pigeon flew in through the open hay door and circled and flew out again. Around the last stall came a shepherd bitch, lean and long, with heavy, hanging dugs. Halfway to the packing box where the puppies were she caught the dead scent of Curley's wife, and the hair rose along her spine. She whimpered and cringed to the packing box, and jumped in among the puppies.

Curley's wife lay with a half-covering of yellow hay. And the meanness and the plannings and the discontent and the ache for attention were all gone from her face. She was very pretty and simple, and her face was sweet and young. Now her rouged cheeks and her reddened lips made her seem alive and sleeping very lightly. The curls, tiny little sausages, were spread on the hay behind her head, and her lips were parted.

As happens sometimes, a moment settled and hovered and remained for much more than a moment. And sound stopped and movement stopped for much, much more than a moment.

Then gradually time awakened again and moved sluggishly on. The horses stamped on the other side of the feeding racks and the halter chains clinked. Outside, the men's voices became louder and clearer.

From around the end of the last stall old Candy's voice came. "Lennie," he called. "Oh, Lennie! You in here? I been figuring some more. Tell you what we can do, Lennie." Old Candy appeared around the end of the last stall. "Oh, Lennie!" he called again; and then he stopped, and his body stiffened. He rubbed his smooth wrist on his white stubble whiskers. "I di'n't know you was here," he said to Curley's wife.

When she didn't answer, he stepped nearer. "You oughten to sleep out here," he said disapprovingly; and then he was beside her and—"Oh, Jesus Christ!" He looked about helplessly, and he rubbed his beard. And then he jumped up and went quickly out of the barn.

But the barn was alive now. The horses stamped and snorted, and they chewed the straw of their bedding and they clashed the chains of their halters. In a moment Candy came back, and George was with him.

George said, "What was it you wanted to see me about?"

Candy pointed at Curley's wife. George stared.

"What's the matter with her?" he asked. He stepped closer, and then he echoed Candy's words. "Oh, Jesus Christ!" He was down on his knees beside her. He put his hand over her heart. And finally, when he stood up, slowly and stiffly, his face was as hard and tight as wood, and his eyes were hard.

Candy said, "What done it?"

George looked coldly at him. "Ain't you got any idear?" he asked. And Candy was silent. "I should of knew," George said hopelessly. "I guess maybe way back in my head I did."

Candy asked, "What we gonna do now, George. What we gonna do now?"

George was a long time in answering. "Guess . . . we gotta tell the . . . guys. I guess we gotta get 'im an' lock 'im up. We can't let 'im get away. Why, the poor bastard'd starve." And he tried to reassure himself. "Maybe they'll lock 'im up an' be nice to 'im."

But Candy said excitedly, "We oughtta let 'im get away. You don't know that Curley. Curley gon'ta wanta get 'im lynched. Curley'll get 'im killed."

George watched Candy's lips. "Yeah," he said at last, "that's right, Curley will. An' the other guys will." And he looked back at Curley's wife.

Now Candy spoke his greatest fear. "You an' me can get that little place, can't we, George? You an' me can go there an' live nice, can't we, George? Can't we?"

Before George answered, Candy dropped his head and looked down at the hay. He knew.

George said softly, "—I think I knowed from the very first. I think I knowed we'd never do her. He usta like to hear about it so much I got to thinking maybe we would."

"Then—it's all off?" Candy asked sulkily.

George didn't answer his question. George said, "I'll work my month an' I'll take my fifty bucks an' I'll stay all night in some lousy cat house. Or I'll set in some poolroom till ever'body goes home. An' then I'll come back an' work another month an' I'll have fifty bucks more."

Candy said, "He's such a nice fella. I didn' think he'd do nothing like this."

George still stared at Curley's wife. "Lennie never done it in meanness," he said. "All the time he done bad things, but he never done one of 'em mean." He straightened up and looked back at Candy. "Now listen. We gotta tell the guys. They got to bring him in, I guess. They ain't no way out. Maybe they won't hurt 'im." He said sharply, "I ain't gonna let 'em hurt Lennie. Now you listen. The guys might think I was in on it. I'm gonna go in the bunk house. Then in a minute you come out and tell the guys about her, and I'll come along and make like I never seen her. Will you do that? So the guys won't think I was in on it?"

Candy said, "Sure, George. Sure I'll do that."

"O.K. Give me a couple of minutes then, and you come runnin' out an' tell like you jus' found her. I'm going now." George turned and went quickly out of the barn.

Old Candy watched him go. He looked helplessly back at Curley's wife, and gradually his sorrow and his anger grew into words. "You God damn tramp," he said viciously. "You done it, di'n't you? I s'pose you're glad. Ever'body knowed you'd mess things up. You wasn't no good. You ain't no good now, you lousy tart." He sniveled, and his voice shook. "I could of

hoed in the garden and washed dishes for them guys."
He paused, and then went on in a singsong. And he
repeated the old words: "If they was a circus or a
baseball game . . . we would of went to her . . . jus'
said 'ta hell with work,' an' went to her. Never ast
nobody's say so. An' they'd of been a pig and chickens . . . an' in the winter . . . the little fat stove . . .
an' the rain comin' . . . an' us jus' settin' there." His
eyes blinded with tears and he turned and went weakly
out of the barn, and he rubbed his bristly whiskers
with his wrist stump.

Outside the noise of the game stopped. There was a
rise of voices in question, a drum of running feet and
the men burst into the barn. Slim and Carlson and
young Whit and Curley, and Crooks keeping back out
of attention range. Candy came after them, and last of
all came George. George had put on his blue denim
coat and buttoned it, and his black hat was pulled
down low over his eyes. The men raced around the last
stall. Their eyes found Curley's wife in the gloom, they
stopped and stood still and looked.

Then Slim went quietly over to her, and he felt her
wrist. One lean finger touched her cheek, and then his
hand went under her slightly twisted neck and his
fingers explored her neck. When he stood up the men
crowded near and the spell was broken.

Curley came suddenly to life. "I know who done it,"
he cried. "That big son-of-a-bitch done it. I know he
done it. Why—ever'body else was out there playin'
horseshoes." He worked himself into a fury. "I'm
gonna get him. I'm going for my shotgun. I'll kill the
big son-of-a-bitch myself. I'll shoot 'im in the guts.
Come on, you guys." He ran furiously out of the barn.
Carlson said, "I'll get my Luger," and he ran out too.

Slim turned quietly to George. "I guess Lennie done it, all right," he said. "Her neck's bust. Lennie coulda did that."

George didn't answer, but he nodded slowly. His hat was so far down on his forehead that his eyes were covered.

Slim went on, "Maybe like that time in Weed you was tellin' about."

Again George nodded.

Slim sighed. "Well, I guess we got to get him. Where you think he might of went?"

It seemed to take George some time to free his words. "He—would of went south," he said. "We come from north so he would of went south."

"I guess we gotta get 'im," Slim repeated.

George stepped close. "Couldn' we maybe bring him in an' they'll lock him up? He's nuts, Slim. He never done this to be mean."

Slim nodded. "We might," he said. "If we could keep Curley in, we might. But Curley's gonna want to shoot 'im. Curley's still mad about his hand. An' s'pose they lock him up an' strap him down and put him in a cage. That ain't no good, George."

"I know," said George. "I know."

Carlson came running in. "The bastard's stole my Luger," he shouted. "It ain't in my bag." Curley followed him, and Curley carried a shotgun in his good hand. Curley was cold now.

"All right, you guys," he said. "The nigger's got a shotgun. You take it, Carlson. When you see 'um, don't give 'im no chance. Shoot for his guts. That'll double 'im over."

Whit said excitedly, "I ain't got a gun."

Curley said, "You go in Soledad an' get a cop. Get Al

Wilts, he's deputy sheriff. Le's go now." He turned suspiciously on George. "You're comin' with us, fella."

"Yeah," said George. "I'll come. But listen, Curley. The poor bastard's nuts. Don't shoot 'im. He di'n't know what he was doin'."

"Don't shoot 'im?" Curley cried. "He got Carlson's Luger. 'Course we'll shoot 'im."

George said weakly, "Maybe Carlson lost his gun."

"I seen it this morning," said Carlson. "No, it's been took."

Slim stood looking down at Curley's wife. He said, "Curley—maybe you better stay here with your wife."

Curley's face reddened. "I'm goin'," he said. "I'm gonna shoot the guts outa that big bastard myself, even if I only got one hand. I'm gonna get 'im."

Slim turned to Candy. "You stay here with her then, Candy. The rest of us better get goin'."

They moved away. George stopped a moment beside Candy and they both looked down at the dead girl until Curley called, "You George! You stick with us so we don't think you had nothin' to do with this."

George moved slowly after them, and his feet dragged heavily.

And when they were gone, Candy squatted down in the hay and watched the face of Curley's wife. "Poor bastard," he said softly.

The sound of the men grew fainter. The barn was darkening gradually and, in their stalls, the horses shifted their feet and rattled the halter chains. Old Candy lay down in the hay and covered his eyes with his arm.

The deep green pool of the Salinas River was still in the late afternoon. Already the sun had left the valley to go climbing up the slopes of the Gabilan mountains, and the hilltops were rosy in the sun. But by the pool among the mottled sycamores, a pleasant shade had fallen.

A water snake glided smoothly up the pool, twisting its periscope head from side to side; and it swam the length of the pool and came to the legs of a motionless heron that stood in the shallows. A silent head and beak lanced down and plucked it out by the head, and the beak swallowed the little snake while its tail waved frantically.

A far rush of wind sounded and a gust drove through the tops of the trees like a wave. The sycamore leaves turned up their silver sides, the brown, dry leaves on the ground scudded a few feet. And row on row of tiny wind waves flowed up the pool's green surface.

As quickly as it had come, the wind died, and the clearing was quiet again. The heron stood in the shallows, motionless and waiting. Another little water

snake swam up the pool, turning its periscope head
from side to side.

Suddenly Lennie appeared out of the brush, and he
came as silently as a creeping bear moves. The heron
pounded the air with its wings, jacked itself clear of
the water and flew off down river. The little snake slid
in among the reeds at the pool's side.

Lennie came quietly to the pool's edge. He knelt
down and drank, barely touching his lips to the water.
When a little bird skittered over the dry leaves behind
him, his head jerked up and he strained toward the
sound with eyes and ears until he saw the bird, and
then he dropped his head and drank again.

When he finished, he sat down on the bank, with
his side to the pool, so that he could watch the trail's
entrance. He embraced his knees and laid his chin
down on his knees.

The light climbed on out of the valley, and as it
went, the tops of the mountains seemed to blaze with
increasing brightness.

Lennie said softly, "I di'n't forget, you bet, God
damn. Hide in the brush an' wait for George." He
pulled his hat down low over his eyes. "George gonna
give me hell," he said. "George gonna wish he was
alone an' not have me botherin' him." He turned his
head and looked at the bright mountain tops. "I can go
right off there an' find a cave," he said. And he continued sadly, "—an' never have no ketchup—but I
won't care. If George don't want me . . . I'll go away.
I'll go away."

And then from out of Lennie's head there came a
little fat old woman. She wore thick bull's-eye glasses
and she wore a huge gingham apron with pockets, and

she was starched and clean. She stood in front of Lennie and put her hands on her hips, and she frowned disapprovingly at him.

And when she spoke, it was in Lennie's voice. "I tol' you an tol' you," she said. "I tol' you, 'Min' George because he's such a nice fella an' good to you.' But you don't never take no care. You do bad things."

And Lennie answered her, "I tried, Aunt Clara, ma'am. I tried and tried. I couldn' help it."

"You never give a thought to George," she went on in Lennie's voice. "He been doin' nice things for you alla time. When he got a piece a pie you always got half or more'n half. An' if they was any ketchup, why he'd give it all to you."

"I know," said Lennie miserably. "I tried, Aunt Clara, ma'am. I tried and tried."

She interrupted him. "All the time he coulda had such a good time if it wasn't for you. He woulda took his pay an' raised hell in a whore house, and he coulda set in a pool room an' played snooker. But he got to take care of you."

Lennie moaned with grief. "I know, Aunt Clara, ma'am. I'll go right off in the hills an' I'll fin' a cave an' I'll live there so I won't be no more trouble to George."

"You jus' say that," she said sharply. "You're always sayin' that, an' you know sonofabitching well you ain't never gonna do it. You'll jus' stick around an' stew the b'Jesus outa George all the time."

Lennie said, "I might jus' as well go away. George ain't gonna let me tend no rabbits now."

Aunt Clara was gone, and from out of Lennie's head there came a gigantic rabbit. It sat on its haunches in front of him, and it waggled its ears and crinkled its nose at him. And it spoke in Lennie's voice too.

"Tend rabbits," it said scornfully. "You crazy bastard. You ain't fit to lick the boots of no rabbit. You'd forget 'em and let 'em go hungry. That's what you'd do. An' then what would George think?"

"I would *not* forget," Lennie said loudly.

"The hell you wouldn'," said the rabbit. "You ain't worth a greased jack-pin to ram you into hell. Christ knows George done ever'thing he could to jack you outa the sewer, but it don't do no good. If you think George gonna let you tend rabbits, you're even crazier'n usual. He ain't. He's gonna beat hell outa you with a stick, that's what he's gonna do."

Now Lennie retorted belligerently, "He ain't neither. George won't do nothing like that. I've knew George since—I forget when—and he ain't never raised his han' to me with a stick. He's nice to me. He ain't gonna be mean."

"Well he's sick of you," said the rabbit. "He's gonna beat hell outa you an' then go away an' leave you."

"He won't," Lennie cried frantically. "He won't do nothing like that. I know George. Me an' him travels together."

But the rabbit repeated softly over and over, "He gonna leave you, ya crazy bastard. He gonna leave ya all alone. He gonna leave ya, crazy bastard."

Lennie put his hands over his ears. "He ain't, I tell ya he ain't." And he cried, "Oh! George—George—George!"

George came quietly out of the brush and the rabbit scuttled back into Lennie's brain.

George said quietly, "What the hell you yellin' about?"

Lennie got up on his knees. "You ain't gonna leave me, are ya, George? I know you ain't."

George came stiffly near and sat down beside him. "No."

"I knowed it," Lennie cried. "You ain't that kind."

George was silent.

Lennie said, "George."

"Yeah?"

"I done another bad thing."

"It don't make no difference," George said, and he fell silent again.

Only the topmost ridges were in the sun now. The shadow in the valley was blue and soft. From the distance came the sound of men shouting to one another. George turned his head and listened to the shouts.

Lennie said, "George."

"Yeah?"

"Ain't you gonna give me hell?"

"Give ya hell?"

"Sure, like you always done before. Like, 'If I di'n't have you I'd take my fifty bucks——' "

"Jesus Christ, Lennie! You can't remember nothing that happens, but you remember ever' word I say."

"Well, ain't you gonna say it?"

George shook himself. He said woodenly, "If I was alone I could live so easy." His voice was monotonous, had no emphasis. "I could get a job an' not have no mess." He stopped.

"Go on," said Lennie. "An' when the enda the month come——"

"An' when the end of the month come I could take my fifty bucks an' go to a . . . cat house . . :" He stopped again.

Lennie looked eagerly at him. "Go on, George. Ain't you gonna give me no more hell?"

"No," said George.

"Well, I can go away," said Lennie. "I'll go right off in the hills an' find a cave if you don' want me."

George shook himself again. "No," he said. "I want you to stay with me here."

Lennie said craftily—"Tell me like you done before."

"Tell you what?"

" 'Bout the other guys an' about us."

George said, "Guys like us got no fambly. They make a little stake an' then they blow it in. They ain't got nobody in the worl' that gives a hoot in hell about 'em——"

"*But not us,*" Lennie cried happily. "Tell about us now."

George was quiet for a moment. "But not us," he said.

"Because——"

"Because I got you an'——"

"An' I got you. We got each other, that's what, that gives a hoot in hell about us," Lennie cried in triumph.

The little evening breeze blew over the clearing and the leaves rustled and the wind waves flowed up the green pool. And the shouts of men sounded again, this time much closer than before.

George took off his hat. He said shakily, "Take off your hat, Lennie. The air feels fine."

Lennie removed his hat dutifully and laid it on the ground in front of him. The shadow in the valley was bluer, and the evening came fast. On the wind the sound of crashing in the brush came to them.

Lennie said, "Tell how it's gonna be."

George had been listening to the distant sounds. For a moment he was business-like. "Look acrost the river, Lennie an' I'll tell you so you can almost see it."

Lennie turned his head and looked off across the pool and up the darkening slopes of the Gabilans. "We gonna get a little place," George began. He reached in his side pocket and brought out Carlson's Luger; he snapped off the safety, and the hand and gun lay on the ground behind Lennie's back. He looked at the back of Lennie's head, at the place where the spine and skull were joined.

A man's voice called from up the river, and another man answered.

"Go on," said Lennie.

George raised the gun and his hand shook, and he dropped his hand to the ground again.

"Go on," said Lennie. "How's it gonna be. We gonna get a little place."

"We'll have a cow," said George. "An' we'll have maybe a pig an' chickens . . . an' down the flat we'll have a . . . little piece alfalfa——"

"For the rabbits," Lennie shouted.

"For the rabbits," George repeated.

"And I get to tend the rabbits."

"An' you get to tend the rabbits."

Lennie giggled with happiness. "An' live on the fatta the lan'."

"Yes."

Lennie turned his head.

"No, Lennie. Look down there acrost the river, like you can almost see the place."

Lennie obeyed him. George looked down at the gun.

There were crashing footsteps in the brush now. George turned and looked toward them.

"Go on, George. When we gonna do it?"

"Gonna do it soon."

"Me an' you."

"You . . . an' me. Ever'body gonna be nice to you. Ain't gonna be no more trouble. Nobody gonna hurt nobody nor steal from 'em."

Lennie said, "I thought you was mad at me, George."

"No," said George. "No, Lennie. I ain't mad. I never been mad, an' I ain't now. That's a thing I want ya to know."

The voices came close now. George raised the gun and listened to the voices.

Lennie begged, "Le's do it now. Le's get that place now."

"Sure, right now. I gotta. We gotta."

And George raised the gun and steadied it, and he brought the muzzle of it close to the back of Lennie's head. The hand shook violently, but his face set and his hand steadied. He pulled the trigger. The crash of the shot rolled up the hills and rolled down again. Lennie jarred, and then settled slowly forward to the sand, and he lay without quivering.

George shivered and looked at the gun, and then he threw it from him, back up on the bank, near the pile of old ashes.

The brush seemed filled with cries and with the

sound of running feet. Slim's voice shouted, "George. Where you at, George?"

But George sat stiffly on the bank and looked at his right hand that had thrown the gun away. The group burst into the clearing, and Curley was ahead. He saw Lennie lying on the sand. "Got him, by God." He went over and looked down at Lennie, and then he looked back at George. "Right in the back of the head," he said softly.

Slim came directly to George and sat down beside him, sat very close to him. "Never you mind," said Slim. "A guy got to sometimes."

But Carlson was standing over George. "How'd you do it?" he asked.

"I just done it," George said tiredly.

"Did he have my gun?"

"Yeah. He had your gun."

"An' you got it away from him and you took it an' you killed him?"

"Yeah. Tha's how." George's voice was almost a whisper. He looked steadily at his right hand that had held the gun.

Slim twitched George's elbow. "Come on, George. Me an' you'll go in an' get a drink."

George let himself be helped to his feet. "Yeah, a drink."

Slim said, "You hadda, George. I swear you hadda. Come on with me." He led George into the entrance of the trail and up toward the highway.

Curley and Carlson looked after them. And Carlson said, "Now what the hell ya suppose is eatin' them two guys?"

TORTILLA FLAT

TO
SUSAN GREGORY
OF MONTEREY

CONTENTS

PREFACE

This is the story of Danny and of Danny's friends and of Danny's house. It is a story of how these three became one thing, so that in Tortilla Flat if you speak of Danny's house you do not mean a structure of wood flaked with old whitewash, overgrown with an ancient untrimmed rose of Castile. No, when you speak of Danny's house you are understood to mean a unit of which the parts are men, from which came sweetness and joy, philanthropy and, in the end, a mystic sorrow. For Danny's house was not unlike the Round Table, and Danny's friends were not unlike the knights of it. And this is the story of how that group came into being, of how it flourished and grew to be an organization beautiful and wise. This story deals with the adventuring of Danny's friends, with the good they did, with their thoughts and their endeavors. In the end, this story tells how the talisman was lost and how the group disintegrated.

In Monterey, that old city on the coast of California, these things are well known, and they are repeated and sometimes elaborated. It is well that this cycle be put down on paper so that in a future time scholars, hearing the legends, may not say as they say of Arthur and of Roland and of Robin Hood—"There was no Danny nor any group of Danny's friends, nor any house. Danny is a nature god and his friends primitive symbols of the wind, the sky, the sun." This history is designed now and ever to keep the sneers from the lips of sour scholars.

Monterey sits on the slope of a hill, with a blue bay below it and with a forest of tall dark pine trees at its back. The lower parts of the town are inhabited by Americans, Italians, catchers and canners of fish. But on the hill where the forest and the town intermingle, where the streets are innocent of asphalt and the corners free of street lights, the old inhabitants of Monterey are embattled as the Ancient Britons are embattled in Wales. These are the paisanos.

They live in old wooden houses set in weedy yards, and the pine trees from the forest are about the houses. The paisanos are clean of commercialism, free of the complicated systems of American business, and, having nothing that can be stolen, exploited, or mortgaged, that system has not attacked them very vigorously.

What is a paisano? He is a mixture of Spanish, Indian, Mexican, and assorted Caucasian bloods. His ancestors have lived in California for a hundred or two years. He speaks English with a paisano accent and Spanish with a paisano accent. When questioned concerning his race, he indignantly claims pure Spanish blood and rolls up his sleeve to show that the soft inside of his arm is nearly white. His color, like that of a well-browned meerschaum pipe, he ascribes to sunburn. He is a paisano, and he lives in the uphill district above the town of Monterey called Tortilla Flat, although it isn't a flat at all.

Danny was a paisano, and he grew up in Tortilla Flat and everyone liked him, but he did not stand out particularly from the screeching children of Tortilla Flat. He was related to nearly everyone in the Flat by blood or romance. His grandfather was an important man who owned two small houses in Tortilla Flat and was respected for his wealth. If the growing Danny preferred to sleep in the forest, to work on ranches, and to wrest his food and wine from an unwilling world, it was not because he did not have influential relatives. Danny was small and dark and intent. At twenty-five his legs were bent to the exact curves of a horse's sides.

Now when Danny was twenty-five years old, the war with Germany was declared. Danny and his friend Pilon (Pilon, by the way, is something thrown in when a trade is conducted—a boot) had two gallons of wine when they heard about the war. Big Joe Portagee saw the glitter of the bottles among the pines and he joined Danny and Pilon.

As the wine went down in the bottles, patriotism arose in the three men. And when the wine was gone they went down the hill arm in arm for comradeship and safety, and they walked into Monterey. In front of an enlistment station they cheered loudly for America and dared Germany to do her worst. They howled menaces at the German Empire until the enlistment sergeant awakened and put on his uniform and came into the street to silence them. He remained to enlist them.

The sergeant lined them up in front of his desk.

They passed everything but the sobriety test and then the sergeant began his questions with Pilon.

"What branch do you want to go in?"

"I don' give a god-damn," said Pilon jauntily.

"I guess we need men like you in the infantry." And Pilon was written so.

He turned then to Big Joe, and the Portagee was getting sober. "Where do you want to go?"

"I want to go home," Big Joe said miserably.

The sergeant put him in the infantry too. Finally he confronted Danny, who was sleeping on his feet. "Where do you want to go?"

"Huh?"

"I say, what branch?"

"What do you man, 'branch'?"

"What can you do?"

"Me? I can do anything."

"What did you do before?"

"Me? I'm a mule skinner."

"Oh, you are? How many mules can you drive?"

Danny leaned forward, vaguely and professionally. "How many you got?"

"About thirty thousand," said the sergeant.

Danny waved his hand. "String 'em up!" he said.

And so Danny went to Texas and broke mules for the duration of the war. And Pilon marched about Oregon with the infantry, and Big Joe, as shall be later made clear, went to jail.

1

HOW DANNY, HOME FROM THE WARS, FOUND HIMSELF AN HEIR, AND HOW HE SWORE TO PROTECT THE HELPLESS.

When Danny came home from the army he learned that he was an heir and an owner of property. The *viejo*, that is the grandfather, had died, leaving Danny the two small houses on Tortilla Flat.

When Danny heard about it he was a little weighed down with the responsibility of ownership. Before he ever went to look at his property he bought a gallon of red wine and drank most of it himself. The weight of responsibility left him then, and his very worst nature came to the surface. He shouted; he broke a few chairs in a poolroom on Alvarado Street; he had two short but glorious fights. No one paid much attention to Danny. At last his wavering bowlegs took him toward the wharf where, at this early hour in the morning, the Italian fishermen were walking down in rubber boots to go out to sea.

Race antipathy overcame Danny's good sense. He

menaced the fishermen. "Sicilian bastards," he called them, and "Scum from the prison island," and "Dogs of dogs of dogs." He cried, *"Chinga tu madre, Piojo."* He thumbed his nose and made obscene gestures below his waist. The fishermen only grinned and shifted their oars and said, "Hello, Danny. When'd you get home? Come around tonight. We got new wine."

Danny was outraged. He screamed, *"Pon un condo a la cabeza."*

They called, "Good-by, Danny. See you tonight." And they climbed into their little boats and rowed out to the lampara launches and started their engines and chugged away.

Danny was insulted. He walked back up Alvarado Street, breaking windows as he went, and in the second block a policeman took him in hand. Danny's great respect for the law caused him to go quietly. If he had not just been discharged from the army after the victory over Germany, he would have been sentenced to six months. As it was, the judge gave him only thirty days.

And so for one month Danny sat on his cot in the Monterey city jail. Sometimes he drew obscene pictures on the walls, and sometimes he thought over his army career. Time hung heavy on Danny's hands there in his cell in the city jail. Now and then a drunk was put in for the night, but for the most part crime in Monterey was stagnant, and Danny was lonely. The bedbugs bothered him a little at first, but as they got used to the taste of him and he grew accustomed to their bites, they got along peacefully.

He started playing a satiric game. He caught a bedbug, squashed it against the wall, drew a circle around it with a pencil and named it "Mayor Clough." Then he caught others and named them after the City Council. In a little while he had one wall decorated with squashed bedbugs, each named for a local dignitary. He drew ears and tails on them, gave them big noses and mustaches. Tito Ralph, the jailer, was scandalized; but he made no complaint because Danny had not included either the justice of the peace who had sentenced him or any of the police force. He had a vast respect for the law.

One night when the jail was lonely, Tito Ralph came into Danny's cell bearing two bottles of wine. An hour later he went out for more wine, and Danny went with him. It was cheerless in the jail. They stayed at Torrelli's, where they bought the wine, until Torrelli threw them out. After that Danny went up among the pines and fell asleep, while Tito Ralph staggered back and reported his escape.

When the brilliant sun awakened Danny about noon, he determined to hide all day to escape pursuit. He ran and dodged behind bushes. He peered out of the undergrowth like a hunted fox. And, at evening, the rules having been satisfied, he came out and went about his business.

Danny's business was fairly direct. He went to the back door of a restaurant. "Got any old bread I can give my dog?" he asked the cook. And while that gullible man was wrapping up the food, Danny stole two slices of ham, four eggs, a lamb chop, and a fly swatter.

"I will pay you sometime," he said.

"No need to pay for scraps. I throw them away if you don't take them."

Danny felt better about the theft then. If that was

the way they felt, on the surface he was guiltless. He
went back to Torrelli's, traded the four eggs, the lamb
chop, and the fly swatter for a water glass of grappa
and retired toward the woods to cook his supper.

The night was dark and damp. The fog hung like
limp gauze among the black pines that guard the land-
ward limits of Monterey. Danny put his head down and
hurried for the shelter of the woods. Ahead of him he
made out another hurrying figure; and as he narrowed
the distance, he recognized the scuttling walk of his
old friend Pilon. Danny was a generous man, but he
recalled that he had sold all his food except the two
slices of ham and the bag of stale bread.

"I will pass Pilon by," he decided. "He walks like a
man who is full of roast turkey and things like that."

Then suddenly Danny noticed the Pilon clutched his
coat lovingly across his bosom.

"Ai, Pilon, *amigo!*" Danny cried.

Pilon scuttled on faster. Danny broke into a trot.
"Pilon, my little friend! Where goest thou so fast?"

Pilon resigned himself to the inevitable and waited.
Danny approached warily, but his tone was enthusiastic. "I looked for thee, dearest of little angelic friends,
for see, I have here two great steaks from God's own
pig, and a sack of sweet white bread. Share my
bounty, Pilon, little dumpling."

Pilon shrugged his shoulders. "As you say," he
muttered savagely. They walked on together into the
woods. Pilon was puzzled. At length he stopped and
faced his friend. "Danny," he asked sadly, "how
knewest thou I had a bottle of brandy under my coat?"

"Brandy?" Danny cried. "Thou hast brandy? Perhaps it is for some sick old mother," he said naïvely.

"Perhaps thou keepest it for Our Lord Jesus when He comes again. Who am I, thy friend, to judge the destination of this brandy? I am not even sure thou hast it. Besides I am not thirsty. I would not touch this brandy. Thou art welcome to this big roast of pork I have, but as for thy brandy, that is thine own."

Pilon answered him sternly. "Danny, I do not mind sharing my brandy with you, half and half. It is my duty to see you do not drink it all."

Danny dropped the subject then. "Here in the clearing I will cook this pig, and you will toast the sugar cakes in this bag here. Put thy brandy here, Pilon. It is better here, where we can see it, and each other."

They built a fire and broiled the ham and ate the stale bread. The brandy receded quickly down the bottle. After they had eaten, they huddled near the fire and sipped delicately at the bottle like effete bees. And the fog came down upon them and grayed their coats with moisture. The wind sighed sadly in the pines about them.

And after a time a loneliness fell upon Danny and Pilon. Danny thought of his lost friends.

"Where is Arthur Morales?" Danny asked, turning his palms up and thrusting his arms forward. "Dead in France," he answered himself, turning the palms down and dropping his arms in despair. "Dead for his country. Dead in a foreign land. Strangers walk near his grave and they do not know Arthur Morales lies there." He raised his hands palms upward again. "Where is Pablo, that good man?"

"In jail," said Pilon. "Pablo stole a goose and hid in the brush; and that goose bit Pablo and Pablo cried out and so was caught. Now he lies in jail for six months."

Danny sighed and changed the subject, for he realized that he had prodigally used up the only acquaintance in any way fit for oratory. But the loneliness was still on him and demanded an outlet. "Here we sit," he began at last.

"—broken-hearted," Pilon added rhythmically.

"No, this is not a poem," Danny said. "Here we sit, homeless. We gave our lives for our country, and now we have no roof over our head."

"We never did have," Pilon added helpfully.

Danny drank dreamily until Pilon touched his elbow and took the bottle. "That reminds me," Danny said, "of a story of a man who owned two whorehouses—" His mouth dropped open. "Pilon!" he cried "Pilon! my little fat duck of a baby friend. I had forgotten! I am an heir! I own two houses."

"Whorehouses?" Pilon asked hopefully. "Thou art a drunken liar," he continued.

"No, Pilon. I tell the truth. The *viejo* died. I am the heir. I, the favorite grandson."

"Thou art the only grandson," said the realist Pilon. "Where are these houses?"

"You know the *viejo's* house on Tortilla Flat, Pilon?"

"Here in Monterey?"

"Yes, here in Tortilla Flat."

"Are they any good, these houses?"

Danny sank back, exhausted with emotion. "I do not know. I forgot I owned them."

Pilon sat silent and absorbed. His face grew mournful. He threw a handful of pine needles on the fire, watched the flames climb frantically among them and die. For a long time he looked into Danny's face with deep anxiety, and then Pilon sighed noisily, and again he sighed. "Now it is over," he said sadly. "Now the great times are done. Thy friends will mourn, but nothing will come of their mourning."

Danny put down the bottle, and Pilon picked it up and set it in his own lap.

"Now what is over?" Danny demanded. "What do you mean?"

"It is not the first time," Pilon went on. "When one is poor, one thinks, 'If I had money I would share it with my good friends.' But let that money come and charity flies away. So it is with thee, my once-friend. Thou art lifted above thy friends. Thou art a man of property. Thou wilt forget thy friends who shared everything with thee, even their brandy."

His words upset Danny. "Not I," he cried. "I will never forget thee, Pilon."

"So you think now," said Pilon coldly. "But when you have two houses to sleep in, then you will see. Pilon will be a poor paisano, while you eat with the mayor."

Danny arose unsteadily and held himself upright against a tree. "Pilon, I swear, what I have is thine. While I have a house, thou hast a house. Give me a drink."

"I must see this to believe it," Pilon said in a discouraged voice. "It would be a world wonder if it were so. Men would come a thousand miles to look upon it. And besides, the bottle is empty."

2

HOW PILON WAS LURED BY GREED OF POSITION TO FORSAKE DANNY'S HOSPITALITY.

The lawyer left them at the gate of the second house and climbed into his Ford and stuttered down the hill into Monterey.

Danny and Pilon stood in front of the paintless picket fence and looked with admiration at the property, a low house streaked with old whitewash, uncurtained windows blank and blind. But a great pink rose of Castile was on the porch, and grandfather geraniums grew among the weeds in the front yard.

"This is the best of the two," said Pilon. "It is bigger than the other."

Danny held a new skeleton key in his hand. He tiptoed over the rickety porch and unlocked the front door. The main room was just as it had been when the *viejo* had lived there. The red rose calendar for 1906, the silk banner on the wall, with Fighting Bob Evans looking between the superstructures of a battleship, the bunch of red paper roses tacked up, the strings of dusty red peppers and garlic, the stove, the battered rocking chairs.

Pilon looked in the door. "Three rooms," he said breathlessly, "and a bed and a stove. We will be happy here, Danny."

Danny moved cautiously into the house. He had bitter memories of the *viejo*. Pilon darted ahead of him and into the kitchen. "A sink with a faucet," he cried. He turned the handle. "No water. Danny, you must have the company turn on the water."

They stood and smiled at each other. Pilon noticed that the worry of property was settling on Danny's face. No more in life would that face be free of care. No more would Danny break windows now that he had windows of his own to break. Pilon had been right—he had been raised among his fellows. His shoulders had straightened to withstand the complexity of life. But one cry of pain escaped him before he left for all time his old and simple existence.

"Pilon," he said sadly, "I wished you owned it and I could come to live with you."

While Danny went to Monterey to have the water turned on, Pilon wandered into the weed-tangled back yard. Fruit trees were there, bony and black with age, and gnarled and broken with neglect. A few tent-like chicken coops lay among the weeds. A pile of rusty barrel hoops, a heap of ashes, and a sodden mattress. Pilon looked over the fence into Mrs. Morales' chicken yard, and after a moment of consideration he opened a few small holes in the fence for the hens. "They will like to make nests in the tall weeds," he thought kindly. He considered how he could make a figure-four trap in case the roosters came in too and bothered the hens and kept them from the nests. "We will live happily," he thought again.

Danny came back indignant from Monterey. "That company wants a deposit," he said.

"Deposit?"

"Yes. They want three dollars before they will turn on the water."

"Three dollars," Pilon said severely, "is three gallons of wine. And when that is gone, we will borrow a bucket of water from Mrs. Morales, next door."

"But we haven't three dollars for wine."

"I know," Pilon said. "Maybe we can borrow a little wine from Mrs. Morales."

The afternoon passed. "Tomorrow we will settle down," Danny announced. "Tomorrow we will clean and scrub. And you, Pilon, will cut the weeds and throw the trash in the gulch."

"The weeds?" Pilon cried in horror. "Not *those* weeds." He explained his theory of Mrs. Morales' chickens.

Danny agreed immediately. "My friend," he said, "I am glad that you have come to live with me. Now, while I collect a little wood, you must get something for dinner."

Pilon, remembering his brandy, thought this unfair. "I am getting in debt to him," he thought bitterly. "My freedom will be cut off. Soon I shall be a slave because of this Jew's house." But he did go out to look for some dinner.

Two blocks away, near the edge of the pine wood, he came upon a half-grown Plymouth Rock rooster scratching in the road. It had come to that adolescent age when its voice cracked, when its legs and neck and breast were naked. Perhaps because he had been thinking of Mrs. Morales' hens in a charitable vein, this little rooster engaged Pilon's sympathy. He walked slowly on toward the dark pine woods, and the chicken ran ahead of him.

Pilon mused, "Poor little bare fowl. How cold it must be for you in the early morning, when the dew falls, and the air grows cold with the dawn. The good God is not always so good to little beasts." And he thought, "Here you play in the street, little chicken. Some day an automobile will run over you; and if it kills you, that will be the best thing that can happen. It may only break your leg or your wing. Then all of your life you will drag along in misery. Life is too hard for you, little bird."

He moved slowly and cautiously. Now and then the chicken tried to double back, but always there was Pilon in the place it chose to go. At last it disappeared into the pine forest, and Pilon sauntered after it.

To the glory of his soul be it said that no cry of pain came from that thicket. That chicken, which Pilon had prophesied might live painfully, died peacefully, or at least quietly. And this is no little tribute to Pilon's technique.

Ten minutes later he emerged from the wood and walked back toward Danny's house. The little rooster, picked and dismembered, was distributed in his pockets. If there was one rule of conduct more strong than any other to Pilon, it was this: Never under any circumstances bring feathers, head or feet home, for without these a chicken cannot be identified.

In the evening they had a fire of cones in the airtight stove. The flames growled in the chimney. Danny and Pilon, well fed, warm, and happy, sat in the rocking chairs and gently teetered back and forth. At dinner they had used a piece of candle, but now only the light from the stove cracks dispelled the darkness of the room. To make it perfect, rain began to patter on the roof. Only a little leaked through, and that in places where no one wanted to sit anyway.

"It is good, this," Pilon said. "Think of the nights when we slept in the cold. This is the way to live."

"Yes, and it is strange," Danny said. "For years I had no house. Now I have two. I cannot sleep in two houses."

Pilon hated waste. "This very thing has been bothering me. Why don't you rent the other house?" he suggested.

Danny's feet crashed down on the floor. "Pilon," he cried. "Why didn't I think of it?" The idea grew more familiar. "But who will rent it, Pilon?"

"I will rent it," said Pilon. "I will pay ten dollars a month in rent."

"Fifteen," Danny insisted. "It's a good house. It is worth fifteen."

Pilon agreed, grumbling. But he would have agreed to much more, for he saw the elevation that came to a man who lived in his own house; and Pilon longed to feel that elevation.

"It is agreed, then," Danny concluded. "You will rent my house. Oh, I will be a good landlord, Pilon. I will not bother you."

Pilon, except for his year in the army, had never possessed fifteen dollars in his life. But, he thought, it would be a month before the rent was due, and who could tell what might happen in a month.

They teetered contentedly by the fire. After a while Danny went out for a few moments and returned with some apples. "The rain would have spoiled them anyway," he apologized.

Pilon, not to be outdone, got up and lighted the candle; he went into the bedroom and in a moment returned with a wash bowl and pitcher, two red glass vases, and a bouquet of ostrich plumes. "It is not good to have so many breakable things around," he said. "When they are broken you become sad. It is much better never to have had them." He picked the paper roses from the wall. "A compliment for Señora Torrelli," he explained as he went out the door.

Shortly afterward he returned, wet through from the rain, but triumphant in manner, for he had a gallon jug of red wine in his hand.

They argued bitterly later, but neither cared who won, for they were tired with the excitements of the day. The wine made them drowsy, and they went to sleep on the floor. The fire died down; the stove cricked as it cooled. The candle tipped over and expired in its own grease, with little blue protesting flares. The house was dark and quiet and peaceful.

3

HOW THE POISON OF POSSESSIONS WROUGHT WITH PILON, AND HOW EVIL TEMPORARILY TRIUMPHED IN HIM.

The next day Pilon went to live in the other house. It was exactly like Danny's house, only smaller. It had its pink rose of Castile over the porch, its weed-grown yard, its ancient, barren fruit trees, its red geraniums—and Mrs. Soto's chicken yard was next door.

Danny became a great man, having a house to rent, and Pilon went up the social scale by renting a house.

It is impossible to say whether Danny expected any rent, or whether Pilon expected to pay any. If they did, both were disappointed. Danny never asked for it, and Pilon never offered it.

The two friends were often together. Let Pilon come by a jug of wine or a piece of meat and Danny was sure to drop in to visit. And, if Danny were lucky or astute in the same way, Pilon spent a riotous night with him. Poor Pilon would have paid the money if he ever had any, but he never did have—not long enough to locate Danny. Pilon was an honest man. It worried him sometimes to think of Danny's goodness and his own poverty.

One night he had a dollar, acquired in a manner so astounding that he tried to forget it immediately for fear the memory might make him mad. A man in front of the San Carlos hotel had put the dollar in his hand, saying, "Run down and get four bottles of ginger ale. The hotel is out." Such things were almost miracles, Pilon thought. One should take them on faith, not worry and question them. He took the dollar up the road to give to Danny, but on the way he bought a gallon of wine, and with the wine he lured two plump girls into his house.

Danny, walking by, heard the noise and joyfully went in. Pilon fell into his arms and placed everything at Danny's disposal. And later, after Danny had helped to dispose of one of the girls and half of the wine, there was a really fine fight. Danny lost a tooth, and Pilon had his shirt torn off. The girls stood shrieking by and kicked whichever man happened to be down. At last Danny got up off the floor and butted one of the girls in the stomach, and she went out the door croaking like a frog. The other girl stole two cooking pots and followed her.

For a little while Danny and Pilon wept over the perfidy of women.

"Thou knowest not what bitches women are," Danny said wisely.

"I do know," said Pilon.

"Thou knowest not."

"I do know."

"Liar."

There was another fight, but not a very good one.

After that Pilon felt better about the unpaid rent. Had he not been host to his landlord?

A number of months passed. Pilon began again to worry about the rent. And as time went by the worry grew intolerable. At last in desperation he worked a whole day cleaning squids for Chin Kee and made two dollars. In the evening he tied his red handkerchief around his neck, put on his father's revered hat, and started up the hill to pay Danny the two dollars on account.

But on the way he bought two gallons of wine. "It is better so," he thought. "If I give him hard money, it does not express how warmly I feel toward my friend. But a present, now. And I will tell him the two gallons cost five dollars." This was silly, and Pilon knew it, but he indulged himself. No one in Monterey better knew the price of wine than Danny.

Pilon was proceeding happily. His mind was made up; his nose pointed straight toward Danny's house. His feet moved, not quickly, but steadily in the proper direction. Under each arm he carried a paper bag, and a gallon of wine was in each bag.

It was purple dusk, that sweet time when the day's sleeping is over, and the evening of pleasure and conversation has not begun. The pine trees were very black against the sky, and all objects on the ground were obscured with dark; but the sky was as mournfully bright as memory. The gulls flew lazily home to the sea rocks after a day's visit to the fish canneries of Monterey.

Pilon was a lover of beauty and a mystic. He raised his face into the sky and his soul arose out of him into the sun's afterglow. That not too perfect Pilon, who plotted and fought, who drank and cursed, trudged slowly on; but a wistful and shining Pilon went up to the sea gulls where they bathed on sensitive wings in the evening. That Pilon was beautiful, and his thoughts were unstained with selfishness and lust. And his thoughts are good to know.

"Our Father is in the evening," he thought. "These birds are flying across the forehead of the Father. Dear birds, dear sea gulls, how I love you all. Your slow wings stroke my heart as the hand of a gentle master strokes the full stomach of a sleeping dog, as the hand of Christ stroked the heads of little children. Dear birds," he thought, "fly to our Lady of Sweet Sorrows with my open heart." And then he said the loveliest words he knew, "*Ave Marie, gratia plena—*"

The feet of the bad Pilon had stopped moving. In truth the bad Pilon for the moment had ceased to exist. (Hear this, recording angel!) There was, nor is, nor ever has been a purer soul than Pilon's at that moment. Galvez' bad bulldog came to Pilon's deserted legs standing alone in the dark. And Galvez' bulldog sniffed and went away without biting the legs.

A soul washed and saved is a soul doubly in danger, for everything in the world conspires against such a soul. "Even the straws under my knees," says Saint Augustine, "shout to distract me from prayer."

Pilon's soul was not even proof against his own memories; for as he watched the birds, he remembered that Mrs. Pastano used sea gulls sometimes in her tamales, and that memory made him hungry, and hunger tumbled his soul out of the sky. Pilon moved on, once more a cunning mixture of good and evil.

Galvez' bad bulldog turned snarling and stalked back, sorry now that he had let go such a perfect chance at Pilon's legs.

Pilon hunched his arms to ease the weight of the bottles.

It is a fact verified and recorded in many histories that the soul capable of the greatest good is also capable of the greatest evil. Who is there more impious than a backsliding priest? Who more carnal than a recent virgin? This, however, may be a matter of appearance.

Pilon, just back from Heaven, was, although he did not know it, singularly receptive of every bitter wind, toward every evil influence that crowded the night about him. True, his feet still moved toward Danny's house, but there was neither intention nor conviction in them. They awaited the littlest signal to turn about. Already Pilon was thinking how stupendously drunk he could get on two gallons of wine, and more, how long he could stay drunk.

It was almost dark now. The dirt road was no longer visible, nor the ditches on either side. No moral conclusion is drawn from the fact that at this moment, when Pilon's impulses were balanced as precariously as a feather, between generosity and selfishness, at this very moment Pablo Sanchez happened to be sitting in the ditch at the side of the road, wishing he had a cigarette and a glass of wine.

Ah, the prayers of the millions, how they must fight and destroy each other on their way to the throne of God.

Pablo first heard footsteps, then saw a blurred figure, and then recognized Pilon. "Ai, *amigo*," he called enthusiastically. "What great burden is it thou carriest?"

Pilon stopped dead and faced the ditch. "I thought you were in jail," he said severely. "I heard about a goose."

"So I was, Pilon," Pablo said jocularly. "But I was not well received. The judge said the sentence did me no good, and the police said I ate more than the allowance for three men. And so," he finished proudly, "I am on parole."

Pilon was saved from selfishness. True, he did not take the wine to Danny's house, but instantly he invited Pablo to share it at the rented house. If two generous paths branch from the highroad of life and only one can be followed, who is to judge which is best?

Pilon and Pablo entered the little house joyfully. Pilon lighted a candle and produced two fruit jars for glasses.

"Health!" said Pablo.

"*Salud!*" said Pilon.

And in a few moments, "*Salud!*" said Pablo.

"Mud in your eye!" said Pilon.

They rested a little while. "*Su servidor,*" said Pilon.

"Down the rat-hole," said Pablo.

Two gallons is a great deal of wine, even for two paisanos. Spiritually the jugs may be graduated thus: Just below the shoulder of the first bottle, serious and concentrated conversation. Two inches farther down, sweetly sad memory. Three inches more, thoughts of old and satisfactory loves. An inch, thoughts of bitter loves. Bottom of the first jug, general and undirected sadness. Shoulder of the second jug, black, unholy de-

spondency. Two fingers down, a song of death or longing. A thumb, every other song each one knows. The
graduations stop here, for the trail splits and there is no
certainty. From this point on anything can happen.

But let us go back to the first mark, which says
serious and concentrated conversation, for it was at
that place that Pilon made his coup. "Pablo," he said,
"dost thou never get tired of sleeping in ditches, wet
and homeless, friendless and alone?"

"No," said Pablo.

Pilon mellowed his voice persuasively. "So *I*
thought, my friend, when I was a dirty gutter-dog. I
too was content, for I did not know how sweet a little
house is, and a roof, and a garden. Ah, Pablo, this is
indeed living."

"It's pretty nice," Pablo agreed.

Pilon pounced. "See, Pablo, how would you like to
rent part of my house? There would never be the cold
ground for you any more. Never the hard sand under
the wharf with crabs getting in your shoes. How would
you like to live here with me?"

"Sure," said Pablo.

"Look, you will pay only fifteen dollars a month!
And you may use all the house except my bed, and
all the garden. Think of it, Pablo! And if someone
should write you a letter, he will have some place to
send it to."

"Sure," said Pablo. "That's swell."

Pilon sighed with relief. He had not realized how
the debt to Danny rode on his shoulders. The fact that
he was fairly sure Pablo would never pay any rent did
not mitigate his triumph. If Danny should ever ask for
money, Pilon could say, "I will pay when Pablo pays."

They moved on to the next graduation, and Pilon remembered how happy he had been when he was a little boy. "No care then, Pablo. I knew not sin. I was very happy."

"We have never been happy since," Pablo agreed sadly.

4

HOW JESUS MARIA CORCORAN, A GOOD MAN,
BECAME AN UNWILLING VEHICLE OF EVIL.

Life passed smoothly on for
Pilon and Pablo. In the morning when the sun was up
clear of the pine trees, when the blue bay rippled and
sparkled below them, they arose slowly and thoughtfully from their beds.

It is a time of quiet joy, the sunny morning. When
the glittery dew is on the mallow weeds, each leaf
holds a jewel which is beautiful if not valuable. This is
no time for hurry or for bustle. Thoughts are slow and
deep and golden in the morning.

Pablo and Pilon in their blue jeans and blue shirts
walked in comradeship into the gulch behind the
house, and after a little time they returned to sit in the
sun on the front porch, to listen to the fish horns on
the streets of Monterey, to discuss in wandering,
sleepy tones the doings of Tortilla Flat; for there are a
thousand climaxes on Tortilla Flat for every day the
world wheels through.

They were at peace there on the porch. Only their toes wriggled on the warm boards when the flies landed on them.

"If all the dew were diamonds," Pablo said, "we would be very rich. We would be drunk all our lives."

But Pilon, on whom the curse of realism lay uneasily, added, "Everybody would have too many diamonds. There would be no price for them, but wine always costs money. If only it would rain wine for a day, now, and we had a tank to catch it in."

"But good wine," interjected Pablo. "Not rotgut swill like the last you got."

"I didn't pay for it," said Pilon. "Someone hid it in the grass by the dance hall. What can you expect of wine you find?"

They sat and waved their hands listlessly at the flies. "Cornelia Ruiz cut up the black Mexican yesterday," Pilon observed.

Pablo raised his eyes in mild interest. "Fight?" he asked.

"Oh, no, the black one did not know Cornelia got a new man yesterday, and he tried to come in. So Cornelia cut him."

"He should have known," Pablo said virtuously.

"Well, he was down in the town when Cornelia got her new man. The black one just tried to go in through the window when she locked the door."

"The black one is a fool," said Pablo, "Is he dead?"

"Oh, no. She just cut him up a little bit on the arms. Cornelia was not angry. She just didn't want the black one to come in."

"Cornelia is not a very steady woman," said Pablo.

"But still she has masses sung for her father, ten years dead."

"He will need them," Pilon observed. "He was a bad man and never went to jail for it, and he never went to confession. When old Ruiz was dying the priest came to give him solace, and Ruiz confessed. Cornelia says the priest was white as buckskin when he came out of the sickroom. But afterward that priest said he didn't believe half what Ruiz confessed."

Pablo, with a cat-like stroke, killed a fly that landed on his knee. "Ruiz was always a liar," he said. "That soul will need plenty of masses. But do you think a mass has virtue when the money for that mass comes out of men's pockets while they sleep in wine at Cornelia's house?"

"A mass is a mass," said Pilon. "Where you get two-bits is of no interest to the man who sells you a glass of wine. And where a mass comes from is of no interest to God. He just likes them, the same as you like wine. Father Murphy used to go fishing all the time, and for months the Holy Sacrament tasted like mackerel, but that did not make it less holy. These things are for priests to explain. They are nothing for us to worry about. I wonder where we could get some eggs to eat. It would be good to eat an egg now."

Pablo tilted his hat down over his eyes to keep the sun from bothering him. "Charlie Meeler told me that Danny is with Rosa Martin, that Portagee girl."

Pilon sat upright in alarm. "Maybe that girl will want to marry Danny. Those Portagees always want to marry, and they love money. Maybe when they are married Danny will bother us about the rent. That Rosa will want new dresses. All women do. I know them."

Pablo too looked annoyed. "Maybe if we went and talked to Danny—" he suggested.

"Maybe Danny has some eggs," said Pilon. "Those chickens of Mrs. Morales are good layers."

They put on their shoes and walked slowly toward Danny's house.

Pilon stooped and picked up a beer bottle cap and cursed and threw it down. "Some evil man has left it there to deceive people," he said.

"I tried it last night," said Pablo. He looked into a yard where the green corn was ripe and made a mental note of its ripeness.

They found Danny sitting on his front porch, behind the rose bush, wriggling his toes to keep the flies off.

"Ai, *amigos*," he greeted them listlessly.

They sat down beside him and took off their hats and their shoes. Danny took out a sack of tobacco and some papers and passed them to Pilon. Pilon looked mildly shocked, but made no comment.

"Cornelia Ruiz cut up the black Mexican," he said.

"I heard about it," said Danny.

Pablo spoke acidly. "These women, there is no virtue in them any more."

"It is dangerous to lie with them," said Pilon. I have heard that there is one young Portagee girl here on the Flat who can give a man something to remember her by, if he goes to the trouble to get it."

Pablo made disapproving clucking noises with his tongue. He spread his hands in front of him. "What is a man to do?" he asked. "Is there no one to trust?"

They watched Danny's face and saw no alarm appear there.

"This girl's name is Rosa," said Pilon. "I would not say her last name."

"Oh, you mean Rosa Martin," Danny observed with very little interest. "Well, what can you expect of a Portagee?"

Pablo and Pilon sighed with relief.

"How are Mrs. Morales' chickens getting along?" Pilon asked casually.

Danny shook his head sadly. "Every one of those chickens is dead. Mrs. Morales put up some string beans in jars, and the jars blew up, and she fed the beans to the chickens, and those chickens all died, every one."

"Where are those chickens now?" Pablo demanded.

Danny waved two fingers back and forth in negation. "Someone told Mrs. Morales not to eat those chickens or she would be sick, but we scraped the insides good and sold them to the butcher."

"Has anybody died?" Pablo asked.

"No. I guess those chickens would have been all right."

"Perhaps you bought a little wine with the money from those chickens?" Pilon suggested.

Danny smiled cynically at him. "Mrs. Morales did, and I went to her house last night. That is a pretty woman in some lights, and not so old either."

The alarm came back to Pablo and Pilon.

"My Cousin Weelie says she is fifty years old," Pilon said excitedly.

Danny spread his hands. "What is it how old in years she is?" he observed philosophically. "She is lively, that one. She owns her house and has two hundred dollars in the bank." Then Danny became a little embarrassed. "I would like to make a present to Mrs. Morales."

Pilon and Pablo regarded their feet and tried by strenuous mental effort to ward off what was coming. But their effort had no value.

"If I had a little money," said Danny, "I would buy her a box of big candy." He looked meaningly at his tenants, but neither one answered him. "I would need only a dollar or two," he suggested.

"Chin Kee is drying squids," Pilon observed. "Perhaps you could cut squids for half a day."

Danny spoke pointedly. "It would not look well for a man who owns two houses to cut squids. But perhaps if a little rent were ever paid——"

Pilon arose angrily. "Always the rent," he cried. "You would force us into the streets—into the gutters, while you sleep in your soft bed. Come, Pablo," Pilon said angrily, "we will get money for this miser, this Jew."

The two of them stalked off.

"Where will we get money?" Pablo asked.

"I don't know," said Pilon. "Maybe he won't ask again." But the inhuman demand had cut deep into their mental peace. "We will call him 'Old Jew' when we see him," said Pilon. "We have been his friends for years. When he was in need, we fed him. When he was cold, we clothed him."

"When was that?" Pablo asked.

"Well, we would have, if he needed anything and we had it. That is the kind of friends we were to him. And now he crushes our friendship into the ground for a box of big candy to give to an old fat woman."

"Candy is not good for people," said Pablo.

So much emotion had exhausted Pilon. He sat down in the ditch beside the road and put his chin in his hands and was disconsolate.

Pablo sat down too, but he only did it to rest, for his friendship with Danny was not as old and beautiful as Pilon's was.

The bottom of the ditch was choked with dry grass and bushes. Pilon, staring downward in his sorrow and resentment, saw a human arm sticking out from under a bush. And then, beside the arm, a half-full gallon bottle of wine. He clutched Pablo's arm and pointed.

Pablo stared. "Maybe he is dead, Pilon."

Pilon had got his breath and his fine clear vision again. "If he is dead, the wine will do him no good. He can't be buried with it."

The arm stirred, swept back the bushes, and disclosed the frowsy face and red stubble beard of Jesus Maria Corcoran. "Ai, Pilon. Ai, Pablo," he said hazily. "*Que tomas?*"

Pilon leaped down the bank on him. "*Amigo*, Jesus Maria! you are not well!"

Jesus Maria smiled sweetly. "Just drunk," he murmured. He rose to his knees. "Come have a drink, my friends. Drink deep. There is plenty more."

Pilon tilted the bottle over his elbow. He swallowed four times and over a pint left the jug. Then Pablo took the bottle from him, and Pablo played with it as a cat plays with a feather. He polished the mouth with his sleeve. He smelled the wine. He took three or four preliminary sips and let a few drops run all around his mouth, to tantalize himself. At last, "*Madre de Dios, que vino!*" he said. He raised the jug and the red wine gurgled happily down his throat.

Pilon's hand was out long before Pablo had to breathe again. Pilon turned a soft and admiring countenance to his friend Jesus Maria. "Hast thou discovered a treasure in the woods?" he asked. "Has some great man died and named thee in his will, my little friend?"

Jesus Maria was a humanitarian, and kindness was always in him. He cleared his throat and spat. "Give me a drink," he said. "My throat is dry. I will tell you how it was." He drank dreamily, like a man who has so much wine that he can take his time in drinking it, can even spill a little without remorse. "I was sleeping on the beach two nights ago," he said. "Out on the beach near Seaside. In the night the little waves washed a rowboat to the shore. Oh, a nice little rowboat, and the oars were there. I got in and rowed it down to Monterey. It was easily worth twenty dollars, but trade was slow, and I only got seven."

"Thou hast money left?" Pilon put in excitedly.

"I am telling you how it was," Jesus Maria said with some dignity. "I bought two gallons of wine and brought them up here to the woods, and then I went to walk with Arabella Gross. For her I bought one pair of silk drawers in Monterey. She liked them—so soft they were, and so pink. And then I bought a pint of whisky for Arabella, and then after a while we met some soldiers and she went away with them."

"Oh, the thief of a good man's money!" Pilon cried in horror.

"No," said Jesus Maria dreamily. "It was time she went anyway. And then I came here and went to sleep."

"Then thou hast no more money?"

"I don't know," said Jesus Maria. "I will see." He fished in his pocket and brought out three crumpled dollar bills and a dime. "Tonight," he said, "I will buy for Arabella Gross one of those little things that goes around higher up."

"You mean the little silk pockets on a string?"

"Yes," said Jesus Maria, "and not so little as you might think either." He coughed to clear his throat.

Instantly Pilon was filled with solicitude. "It is the night air," he said. "It is not good to sleep out in the open. Come, Pablo, we will take him to our house and cure this cold of his. The malady of the lungs has a good start, but we will cure it."

"What are you talking about?" said Jesus Maria. "I'm all right."

"So you think," said Pilon. "So Rudolfo Kelling thought. And you yourself went to his funeral a month ago. So Angelina Vasquez thought. She died last week."

Jesus Maria was frightened. "What do you think is the matter?"

"It is sleeping in this night air," Pilon said sagely. "Your lungs will not stand it."

Pablo wrapped the wine jug in a big weed, so disguising it that anyone passing would have been consumed with curiosity until he knew what that weed contained.

Pilon walked beside Jesus Maria, touching him now and then under the elbow to remind him that he was not a well man. They took him to their house and laid him on a cot, and although the day was warm, they covered him with an old comforter. Pablo spoke movingly of those poor ones who writhed and suffered with tuberculosis. And then Pilon pitched his voice to sweetness. He spoke with reverence of the joy of living in a little house. When the night was far gone, and all the talk and wine were gone, and outside the deadly mists clung to the ground like the ghosts of giant leeches, then one did not go out to lie in the sickly damp of a gulch. No, one got into a deep, soft, warm bed and slept like a little child.

Jesus Maria went to sleep at this point. Pilon and Pablo had to wake him up and give him a drink. Then Pilon spoke movingly of the mornings when one lay in one's warm nest until the sun was high enough to be of some use. One did not go shivering about in the dawn, beating one's hands to keep them from freezing.

At last Pilon and Pablo moved in on Jesus Maria as two silent hunting Airedales converge on their prey. They rented the use of their house to Jesus Maria for fifteen dollars a month. He accepted happily. They shook hands all around. The jug came out of its weed. Pilon drank deeply, for he knew his hardest task was before him. He said it very gently and casually, while Jesus Maria was drinking out of the bottle.

"And you will pay only three dollars on account now."

Jesus Maria put down the bottle and looked at him in horror. "No," he exploded. "I made a promise to Arabella Gross to buy one of those little things. I will pay the rent when it is time."

Pilon knew he had blundered. "When you lay on that beach at Seaside, God floated the little rowboat to you. Do you think the good God did it so you could buy silk drawers for a cannery slut? No! God did it so you would not die from sleeping on the ground in the cold. Do you think God is interested in Arabella's breasts? And besides, we will take a two-dollar deposit," he went on. "For one dollar you can get one of those things big enough to hold the udders of a cow."

Still Jesus Maria protested.

"I will tell you," Pilon went on, "unless we pay Danny two dollars we shall all be turned into the street, and it will be your fault. You will have it on your soul that we sleep in ditches."

Under so many shots, coming from so many directions, Jesus Maria Corcoran succumbed. He passed two of the crumpled bills to Pilon.

And now the tense feeling went out of the room, and peace and quiet and a warm deep comradeship took its place. Pilon relaxed. Pablo took the comforter back to his own bed, and conversation sprang up

"We must take this money to Danny."

Their first appetite over, they were sipping the wine out of fruit jars now.

"What is this great need Danny has for two dollars?" Jesus Maria asked.

Pilon grew confidential. His hands came into play like twin moths, restrained only by his wrists and arms from flying out the door. "Danny, our friend, is taking up with Mrs. Morales. Oh, don't think Danny is a fool. Mrs. Morales has two hundred dollars in the bank. Danny wants to buy a box of big candy for Mrs. Morales."

"Candy is not good for people," Pablo observed. "It makes their teeth ache."

"That is up to Danny," said Jesus Maria. "If he wants to ache Mrs. Morales' teeth, that is his business. What do we care for Mrs. Morales' teeth?"

A cloud of anxiety had settled on Pilon's face.

"But," he interposed sternly, "if our friend Danny takes big candy to Mrs. Morales, he will eat some too. So it is the teeth of our friend that will ache."

Pablo shook his head anxiously. "It would be a bad thing if Danny's friends, on whom he depends, should bring about the aching of his teeth."

"What shall we do then?" asked Jesus Maria, although he and everyone else knew exactly what they would do. They waited politely, each one for another, to make the inevitable suggestion. The silence ran on. Pilon and Pablo felt that the suggestion should not come from them, since, by some lines of reasoning, they might be considered interested parties. Jesus Maria kept silence in duty to his hosts, but when their silence made him aware of what was required of him, he came instantly into the breach.

"A gallon of wine makes a nice present for a lady," he suggested in a musing tone.

Pilon and Pablo were astonished at his brilliance. "We can tell Danny it would be better for his teeth to get wine."

"But maybe Danny will pay no heed to our warning. If you give money to that Danny, you can't tell what he will do with it. He might buy candy anyway, and then all of our time and worry are wasted."

They had made of Jesus Maria their feeder of lines, their opener of uneasy situations. "Maybe if we buy the wine ourselves and then give it to Danny there is no danger," he suggested.

"That is the thing," cried Pilon. "Now you have it."

Jesus Maria smiled modestly at being given credit for this. He felt that sooner or later this principle would have been promulgated by someone in the room.

Pablo poured the last little bit of wine into the fruit jars and they drank tiredly after their effort. It was a matter of pride to them that the idea had been arrived at so logically, and in such a philanthropic cause.

"Now I am hungry," said Pablo.

Pilon got up and went to the door and looked at the sun. "It is after noon," he said. "Pablo and I will go to Torrelli's to get the wine, while you, Jesus Maria, go into Monterey for something to eat. Maybe Mrs. Bruno, on the wharf, will give you a fish. Maybe you can get a little bread some place."

"I would rather go with you," said Jesus Maria, for he suspected that another sequence, just as logical, and just as inevitable, was beginning to grow in the heads of his friends.

"No, Jesus Maria," they said firmly. "It is now two o'clock, or about that. In an hour it will be three o'clock. Then we will meet you here and have something to eat. And maybe a little glass of wine to go with it."

Jesus Maria started for Monterey very reluctantly, but Pablo and Pilon walked happily down the hill toward Torrrelli's house.

5

HOW SAINT FRANCIS TURNED THE TIDE AND PUT A GENTLE PUNISHMENT ON PILON AND PABLO AND JESUS MARIA.

The afternoon came down as imperceptibly as age comes to a happy man. A little gold entered into the sunlight. The bay became bluer and dimpled with shore-wind ripples. Those lonely fishermen who believe that the fish bite at high tide left their rocks, and their places were taken by others, who were convinced that the fish bite at low tide.

At three o'clock the wind veered around and blew softly in from the bay, bringing all manner of fine kelp odors. The menders of nets in the vacant lots of Monterey put down their spindles and rolled cigarettes. Through the streets of the town, fat ladies, in whose eyes lay the weariness and the wisdom one sees so often in the eyes of pigs, were trundled in overpowered motorcars toward tea and gin fizzes at the Hotel Del Monte. On Alvarado Street, Hugo Machado, the tailor, put a sign in his shop door, "Back in Five Minutes," and went home for the day. The pines waved slowly and voluptuously. The hens in a hundred hen yards complained in placid voices of their evil lot.

Pilon and Pablo sat under a pink rose of Castile in Torrelli's yard and quietly drank wine and let the afternoon grow on them as gradually as hair grows.

"It is just as well that we do not take two gallons of wine to Danny," said Pilon. "He is a man who knows little restraint in drinking."

Pablo agreed. "Danny looks healthy," he said, "but it is just such people that you hear of dying every day. Look at Rudolfo Kelling. Look at Angelina Vasquez."

Pilon's realism arose mildly to the surface. "Rudolfo fell into the quarry above Pacific Grove," he observed in mild reproof. "Angelina ate a bad can of fish. But," he continued kindly, "I know what you mean. And there are plenty of people who die through abuse of wine."

All Monterey began to make gradual instinctive preparations against the night. Mrs. Guttierez cut little chiles into her enchilada sauce. Rupert Hogan, the seller of spirits, added water to his gin and put it away to be served after midnight. And he shook a little pepper into his early evening whisky. At El Paseo dancing pavilion, Bullet Rosendale opened a carton of pretzels and arranged them like coarse brown lace on the big courtesy plates. The Palace Drug Company wound up its awnings. A little group of men who had spent the afternoon in front of the post office, greeting their friends, moved toward the station to see the Del

Monte Express from San Francisco come in. The sea
gulls arose glutted from the fish cannery beaches and
flew toward the sea rocks. Lines of pelicans pounded
doggedly over the water wherever they go to spend the
night. On the purse-seine fishing boats the Italian men
folded their nets over the big rollers. Little Miss Alma
Alvarez, who was ninety years old, took her daily bouquet of pink geraniums to the Virgin on the outer wall
of the church of San Carlos. In the neighboring and
Methodist village of Pacific Grove the W.C.T.U. met
for tea and discussion, listened while a little lady described the vice and prostitution of Monterey with energy and color. She thought a committee should visit
these resorts to see exactly how terrible conditions
really were. They had gone over the situation so often,
and they needed new facts.

The sun went westering and took on an orange
blush. Under the rose bush in Torrelli's yard Pablo
and Pilon finished the first gallon of wine. Torrelli
came out of his house and passed out of the yard
without seeing his erstwhile customers. They waited
until he was out of sight on the way to Monterey;
whereupon Pablo and Pilon went into the house and,
with conscious knowledge of their art, cozened their
supper out of Mrs. Torrelli. They slapped her on the
buttocks and called her a "Butter Duck" and took little
courteous liberties with her person, and finally left
her, flattered and slightly tousled.

Now it was evening in Monterey, and the lights went
on. The windows glowed softly. The Monterey Theater
began to spell "Children of Hell—Children of Hell"
over and over with its lights. A small but fanatic group
of men who believe that the fish bite in the evening

took their places on the cold sea rocks. A little fog drifted through the streets and hung about the chimneys, and a fine smell of burning pine wood filled the air.

Pablo and Pilon went back to their rose bush and sat on the ground, but they were not as contented as they had been. "It is cool here," said Pilon, and he took a drink of wine to warm himself.

"We should go to our own house where it is warm," said Pablo.

"But there is no wood for the stove."

"Well," said Pablo, "if you will take the wine, I will meet you at the corner of the street." And he did, in about half an hour.

Pilon waited patiently, for he knew there are some things even one's friends cannot help with. While he waited, Pilon kept a watchful eye aimed down the street in the direction Torrelli had taken, for Torrelli was a forceful man to whom explanations, no matter how carefully considered nor how beautifully phrased, were as chaff. Moreover, Torrelli had, Pilon knew, the Italian's exaggerated and wholly quixotic ideal of marital relations. But Pilon watched in vain. No Torrelli came brutally home. In a little while Pablo joined him, and Pilon noticed with admiration and satisfaction that he carried an armful of pine sticks from Torrelli's wood pile.

Pablo made no comment on his recent adventure until they arrived at their house. Then he echoed Danny's words, "A lively one, that Butter Duck."

Pilon nodded his head in the dark and spoke with a quiet philosophy. "It is seldom that one finds all things at one market—wine, food, love, and firewood.

We must remember Torrelli, Pablo, my friend. There is a man to know. We must take him a little present sometime."

Pilon built a roaring fire in the cast-iron stove. The two friends drew their chairs close and held their fruit jars to the heat to warm the wine a little. This night the light was holy, for Pablo had brought a candle to burn for San Francisco. Something had distracted his attention before that sacred plan had been consummated. Now the little wax taper burned beautifully in an abalone shell, and it threw the shadows of Pablo and Pilon on the wall and made them dance.

"I wonder where that Jesus Maria has gone," Pilon observed.

"He promised he would come back long ago," said Pablo. "I do not know whether that is a man to trust or not."

"Perhaps some little thing happened to detain him, Pablo. Jesus Maria, with that red beard and that kind heart, is nearly always in some kind of trouble with ladies."

"His is a grasshopper brain," said Pablo. "He sings and plays and jumps. There is no seriousness in him."

They had no great time to wait. They had barely started their second fruit jar of wine when Jesus Maria staggered in. He held each side of the door to steady himself. His shirt was torn and his face was bloody. One eye showed dark and ominous in the dancing candlelight.

Pablo and Pilon rushed to him. "Our friend! He is hurt. He has fallen from a cliff. He has been run over by a train!" There was not the slightest tone of satire, but Jesus Maria knew it for the most deadly kind of satire. He glared at them out of the eye which still had some volition in such matters.

"Both thy mothers were udderless cows," he remarked.

They fell back from him in horror at the vulgarity of the curse. "Our friend is wandering in his mind."

"The bone of his head has been broken."

"Pour him a little wine, Pablo."

Jesus Maria sat morosely by the fire and caressed his fruit jar, while his friends waited patiently for an explanation of the tragedy. But Jesus Maria seemed content to leave his friends in ignorance of the mishap. Although Pilon cleared his throat several times, and although Pablo looked at Jesus Maria with eyes which offered sympathy and understanding, Jesus Maria sat sullenly and glared at the stove and at the wine and at the blessed candle, until at length his discourteous reticence drove Pilon to an equal discourtesy. Afterward he did not see how he could have done it.

"Those soldiers again?" he asked.

"Yes," Jesus Maria growled. "This time they came too soon."

"There must have been twenty of them to have used thee so," Pablo observed, for the good of his friend's spirit. "Everyone knows thou art a bad man in a fight."

And Jesus Maria did look a little happier then.

"They were four," he said. "Arabella Gross helped too. She hit me on the head with a rock."

Pilon felt a wave of moral resentment rising within him. "I would not remind thee," he said severely, "how thy friends warned thee against this cannery slob." He wondered whether he had warned Jesus Maria, and seemed to remember that he had.

"These cheap white girls are vicious, my friend," Pablo broke in. "But did you give her that little thing that goes around?"

Jesus Maria reached into his pocket and brought out a crumpled pink rayon brassiere. "The time had not come," he said. "I was just getting to that point; and besides, we had not come into the woods yet."

Pilon sniffed the air and shook his head, but not without a certain sad tolerance. "Thou hast been drinking whisky."

Jesus Maria nodded.

"Where did this whisky come from?"

"From those soldiers," said Jesus Maria. "They had it under a culvert. Arabella knew it was there, and she told me. But those soldiers saw us with the bottle."

The story was gradually taking shape. Pilon liked it this way. It ruined a story to have it all come out quickly. The good story lay in half-told things which must be filled in out of the hearer's own experience. He took the pink brassiere from Jesus Maria's lap and ran his fingers over it, and his eyes went to musing. But in a moment they shone with a joyous light.

"I know," he cried. "We'll give this thing to Danny as a gift to Mrs. Morales."

Everyone except Jesus Maria applauded the idea, and he felt himself hopelessly outnumbered. Pablo, with a delicate understanding of the defeat, filled up Jesus Maria's fruit jar.

When a little time had passed, all three men began to smile. Pilon told a very funny story of a thing that had happened to his father. Good spirits returned to the company. They sang. Jesus Maria did a shuffling dance to prove he was not badly hurt. The wine went down and down in the jug, but before it was gone the three friends grew sleepy. Pilon and Pablo staggered off to bed, and Jesus Maria lay comfortably on the floor, beside the stove.

The fire died down. The house was filled with the deep sounds of slumber. In the front room only one thing moved. The blessed candle darted its little spear-pointed flame up and down with incredible rapidity.

Later, this little candle gave Pilon and Pablo and Jesus Maria some ethical things to think about. Simple small rod of wax with a string through it. Such a thing, you would say, is answerable to certain physical laws, and to none other. Its conduct, you would think, was guaranteed by certain principles of heat and combustion. You light the wick; the wax is caught and drawn up the wick; the candle burns a number of hours, goes out, and that is all. The incident is finished. In a little while the candle is forgotten, and then, of course, it has never existed.

Have you forgotten that this candle was blessed? That in a moment of conscience or perhaps pure religious exaltation, it was designed by Pablo for San Francisco? Here is the principle which takes the waxen rod outside the jurisdiction of physics.

The candle aimed its spear of light at heaven, like an artist who consumes himself to become divine. The candle grew shorter and shorter. A wind sprang up outside and sifted through the cracks in the wall. The candle sagged sideways. A silken calendar, bearing the face of a lovely girl looking out of the heart of an American Beauty rose, floated out a little distance from the wall. It came into the spear of flame. The fire licked up the silk and raced toward the ceiling. A loose piece of wallpaper caught fire and fell flaming into a bundle of newspapers.

In the sky, saints and martyrs looked on with set and unforgiving faces. The candle was blessed. It belonged to Saint Francis. Saint Francis will have a big candle in its place tonight.

If it were possible to judge depth of sleep, it could be said with justice that Pablo, whose culpable action was responsible for the fire, slept even more soundly than his two friends. But since there is no gauge, it can only be said that he slept very very soundly.

The flames ran up the walls and found little holes in the roof, and leaked through into the night. The house filled with the roar of fire. Jesus Maria turned over uneasily and began, in his sleep, to take off his coat. Then a flaming shingle dropped in his face. He leaped up with a cry, and stood shocked at the fire that raged about him.

"Pilon!" he shrieked. "Pablo!" He ran into the other room, pulled his friends out of bed and pushed them out of the house. Pilon still grasped the pink brassiere in his fingers.

They stood outside the burning house and looked in the open fire-curtained door. They could see the jug standing on the table with a good two inches of wine in it.

Pilon sensed the savage incipient heroism of Jesus Maria. "Do not do it," he shouted. "It must be lost in the fire as a punishment on us for leaving it."

The cry of sirens came to them, and the roar of trucks climbing the hill in second gear from the fire house in Monterey. The big red fire vehicles drew near and their searchlights played among the pine trunks.

Pilon turned hastily to Jesus Maria. "Run and tell Danny his house is burning. Run quickly, Jesus Maria."

"Why don't you go?"

"Listen," said Pilon. "Danny does not know you are one who rents his house. He may be a little bit angry with Pablo and me."

Jesus Maria grasped this logic and raced toward Danny's house. The house was dark. "Danny," Jesus Maria cried.

"Danny, your house is on fire!" There was no answer. "Danny!" he cried again.

A window went up in Mrs. Morales' house next door. Danny sounded irritable. "What the hell do you want?"

"Your other house is on fire, the one Pablo and Pilon live in."

For a moment Danny did not answer. Then he demanded, "Is the fire department there?"

"Yes," cried Jesus Maria.

The whole sky was lighted up by now. The crackling of burning timbers could be heard. "Well," said Danny, "if the fire department can't do anything about it, what does Pilon expect me to do?"

Jesus Maria heard the window bang shut, and he turned and trotted back toward the fire. It was a bad time to call Danny, he knew, but then how could one tell? If Danny had missed the fire, he might have been angry. Jesus Maria was glad he had told him about it anyway. Now the responsibility lay on Mrs. Morales.

It was a little house, there was plenty of draft, the walls were perfectly dry. Perhaps not since old Chinatown had burned had there been such a quick and thorough fire. The men of the fire department took a look at the blazing walls and then began wetting the brush and the trees and the neighboring houses. In less than an hour the house was completely gone. Only then did the hoses play on the heap of ashes to put out the coals and sparks.

Pilon and Pablo and Jesus Maria stood shoulder to shoulder and watched the whole thing. Half the population of Monterey and all the population of Tortilla Flat except Danny and Mrs. Morales stood happily about and watched the fire. At last, when it was all over, when only a cloud of steam arose from the black heap, Pilon turned silently away.

"Where goest thou?" Pablo called.

"I go," said Pilon, "to the woods to have out my sleep. I counsel you to come too. It will be well if Danny does not see us for a little while." They nodded gravely and followed him into the pine forest. "It is a lesson to us," said Pilon. "By this we learn never to leave wine in a house overnight."

"Next time," Pablo said hopelessly, "you will take it outside and someone will steal it."

6

HOW THREE SINFUL MEN, THROUGH CONTRITION, ATTAINED PEACE. HOW DANNY'S FRIENDS SWORE COMRADESHIP.

When the sun was clear of the pines, and the ground was warm, and the night's dew was drying on the geranium leaves, Danny came out on his porch to sit in the sunshine and to muse warmly of certain happenings. He slipped off his shoes and wriggled his toes on the sun-warmed boards of the porch. He had walked down earlier in the morning and viewed the square black ashes and twisted plumbing which had been his other house. He had indulged in a little conventional anger against careless friends, had mourned for a moment over that transitory quality of earthly property which made spiritual property so much more valuable. He had thought over the ruin of his status as a man with a house to rent; and, all this clutter of necessary and decent emotion having been satisfied and swept away, he had finally slipped into his true emotion, one of relief that at least one of his burdens was removed.

"If it were still there, I would be covetous of the rent," he thought. "My friends have been cool toward me because they owed me money. Now we can be free and happy again."

But Danny knew he must discipline his friends a little, or they would consider him soft. Therefore, as he sat on his porch, warding off flies with a moving hand which conveyed more warning than threat to the flies, he went over the things he must say to his friends before he allowed them back into the corral of his affection. He must show them that he was not a man to be imposed upon. But he yearned to get it over and to be once more that Danny whom everyone loved, that Danny whom people sought out when they had a gallon of wine or a piece of meat. As the owner of two houses he had been considered rich, and he had missed a great many tidbits.

Pilon and Pablo and Jesus Maria Corcoran slept a long time on the pine needles in the forest. It had been a night of terrible excitement, and they were tired. But at length the sun shone into their faces with noonday ardor and the ants walked on them, and two blue jays stood on the ground near by, calling them all manner of sharp names.

What finished their sleep, though, was a picnic party which settled just on the other side of the bush from them and opened a big lunch basket from which moving smells drifted to Pilon and Pablo and Jesus Maria. They awakened; they sat up; and then the enormity of their situation burst upon them.

"How did the fire start?" asked Pablo plaintively, and no one knew.

"Perhaps," said Jesus Maria, "we had better go to

another town for a while—to Watsonville or to Salinas; those are nice towns."

Pilon pulled the brassiere from his pocket and ran his fingers over its pink smoothness. And he held it to the sunlight and looked through it.

"That would only delay matters," he decided. "I think it would be better to go to Danny and confess our fault, like little children to a father. Then he can't say anything without being sorry. And besides, have we not this present for Mrs. Morales?"

His friends nodded agreement. Pilon's eyes strayed through the thick brush to the picnic party, and particularly to that huge lunch basket from which came the penetrating odors of deviled eggs. Pilon's nose wrinkled a little, like a rabbit's. He smiled in a quiet reverie. "I am going to walk, my friends. In a little while I will meet you at the quarry. Do not bring the basket if you can help it."

They watched sadly as Pilon got up and walked away, through the trees, in a direction at right angles to the picnic and the basket. Pablo and Jesus Maria were not surprised, a few moments later, to hear a dog bark, a rooster crow, high shrill laughter, the snarl of a wild cat, a little short scream and a cry for help; but the picnic party was surprised and fascinated. The two men and two women left their basket and trotted away toward these versatile sounds.

Pablo and Jesus Maria obeyed Pilon. They did not take the basket, but always afterward their hats and their shirts were stained with deviled eggs.

At about three o'clock in the afternoon the three penitents walked slowly toward Danny's house. Their arms were loaded with offerings of reconciliation:

oranges and apples and bananas, bottles of olives and pickles, sandwiches of pressed ham, egg sandwiches, bottles of soda pop, a paper carton of potato salad, and a copy of the *Saturday Evening Post*.

Danny saw them coming, and he stood up and tried to remember the things he had to say. They lined up in front of him and hung their heads.

"Dogs of dogs," Danny called them, and "Thieves of decent folks' other house," and "Spawn of cuttlefish." He named their mothers cows and fathers ancient sheep.

Pilon opened the bag he held and exposed the ham sandwiches. And Danny said he had no more trust in friends, that his faith had been frostbitten and his friendship trampled upon. And then he began to have a little trouble remembering, for Pablo had taken two deviled eggs out of his bosom. But Danny went back to the grand generation and criticized the virtue of its women and the potency of its men.

Pilon pulled the pink brassiere from his pocket and let it dangle listlessly from his fingers.

Danny forgot everything then. He sat down on the porch and his friends sat down, and the packages came open. They ate to a point of discomfort. It was an hour later, when they reclined at ease on the porch, giving attention to little besides digestion, when Danny asked casually, as about some far-off object, "How did the fire start?"

"We don't know," Pilon explained. "We went to sleep, and then it started. Perhaps we have enemies."

"Perhaps," said Pablo devoutly, "perhaps God had a finger in it."

"Who can say what makes the good God act the way He does?" added Jesus Maria.

When Pilon handed over the brassiere and explained how it was a present for Mrs. Morales, Danny was reticent. He eyed the brassiere with some skepticism. His friends, he felt, were flattering Mrs. Morales. "That is not a woman to give presents to," he said finally. "Too often we are tied to women by the silk stockings we give them." He could not explain to his friends the coolness that had come to his relationship with Mrs. Morales since he was the owner of only one house; nor could he, in courtesy to Mrs. Morales, describe his own pleasure at that coolness. "I will put this little thing away," he said. "Some day it may be of use to someone."

When the evening came, and it was dark, they went into the house and built a fire of cones in the airtight stove. Danny, in proof of his forgiveness, brought out a quart of grappa and shared its fire with his friends.

They settled easily into the new life. "It is too bad Mrs. Morales' chickens are all dead," Pilon observed.

But even here was no bar to happiness. "She is going to buy two dozen new ones on Monday," said Danny.

Pilon smiled contentedly. "Those hens of Mrs. Soto's were no good," he said. "I told Mrs. Soto they needed oyster shells, but she paid no attention to me."

They drank the quart of grappa, and there was just enough to promote the sweetness of comradeship.

"It is good to have friends," said Danny. "How lonely it is in the world if there are no friends to sit with one and to share one's grappa."

"Or one's sandwiches," Pilon added quickly.

Pablo was not quite over his remorse, for he suspected the true state of celestial politics which had caused the burning of the house. "In all the world there are few friends like thee, Danny. It is not given to many to have such solace."

Before Danny sank completely under the waves of his friends, he sounded one warning. "I want all of you to keep out of my bed," he ordered. "That is one thing I must have to myself."

Although no one had mentioned it, each of the four knew they were all going to live in Danny's house.

Pilon sighed with pleasure. Gone was the worry of the rent; gone the responsibility of owing money. No longer was he a tenant, but a guest. In his mind he gave thanks for the burning of the other house.

"We will all be happy here, Danny," he said. "In the evenings we will sit by the fire and our friends will come in to visit. And sometimes maybe we will have a glass of wine to drink for friendship's sake."

Then Jesus Maria, in a frenzy of gratefulness, made a rash promise. It was the grappa that did it, and the night of the fire, and all the deviled eggs. He felt that he had received great gifts, and he wanted to distribute a gift. "It shall be our burden and our duty to see that there is always food in the house for Danny," he declaimed. "Never shall our friend go hungry."

Pilon and Pablo looked up in alarm, but the thing was said; a beautiful and generous thing. No man could with impunity destroy it. Even Jesus Maria understood, after it was said, the magnitude of his statement. They could only hope that Danny would forget it.

"For," Pilon mused to himself, "if this promise were enforced, it would be worse than rent. It would be slavery."

"We swear it, Danny!" he said.

They sat about the stove with tears in their eyes, and their love for one another was almost unbearable.

Pablo wiped his wet eyes with the back of his hand, and he echoed Pilon's remark. "We shall be very happy living here," he said.

7

HOW DANNY'S FRIENDS BECAME A FORCE FOR GOOD. HOW THEY SUCCORED THE POOR PIRATE.

A great many people saw the Pirate every day, and some laughed at him, and some pitied him; but no one knew him very well, and no one interfered with him. He was a huge, broad man, with a tremendous black and bushy beard. He wore jeans and a blue shirt, and he had no hat. In town he wore shoes. There was a shrinking in the Pirate's eyes when he confronted any grown person, the secret look of an animal that would like to run away if it dared turn its back long enough. Because of this expression, the paisanos of Monterey knew that his head had not grown up with the rest of his body. They called him the Pirate because of his beard. Every day people saw him wheeling his barrow of pitchwood about the streets until he sold the load. And always in a cluster at his heels walked his five dogs.

Enrique was rather houndish in appearance, although his tail was bushy. Pajarito was brown and curly, and these were the only two things you could see about him. Rudolph was a dog of whom passers-by said, "He is an American dog." Fluff was a Pug and Señor Alec Thompson seemed to be a kind of an Airedale. They walked in a squad behind the Pirate, very respectful toward him, and very solicitous for his happiness. When he sat down to rest from wheeling his barrow, they all tried to sit on his lap and have their ears scratched.

Some people had seen the Pirate early in the morning on Alvarado Street; some had seen him cutting pitchwood; some knew he sold kindling; but no one except Pilon knew everything the Pirate did. Pilon knew everybody and everything about everybody.

The Pirate lived in a deserted chicken house in the yard of a deserted house on Tortilla Flat. He would have thought it presumptuous to live in the house itself. The dogs lived around and on top of him, and the Pirate liked this, for his dogs kept him warm on the coldest nights. If his feet were cold, he had only to put them against the belly of Señor Alec Thompson. The chicken house was so low that the Pirate had to crawl in on his hands and knees.

Early every morning, well before daylight, the Pirate crawled out of his chicken house, and the dogs followed him, roughing their coats and sneezing in the cold air. Then the party went down to Monterey and worked along an alley. Four or five restaurants had their back doors on this alley. The Pirate entered each one, into a restaurant kitchen, warm and smelling of food. Grumbling cooks put packages of scraps in his hands at each place. They didn't know why they did it.

When the Pirate had visited each back door and had his arms full of parcels, he walked back up the hill to Munroe Street and entered a vacant lot, and the dogs excitedly swarmed about him. Then he opened the parcels and fed the dogs. For himself he took bread or a piece of meat out of each package, but he did not pick the best for himself. The dogs sat down about him, licking their lips nervously and shifting their feet while they waited for food. They never fought over it, and that was a surprising thing. The Pirate's dogs never fought each other, but they fought everything else that wandered the streets of Monterey on four legs. It was a fine thing to see the pack of five, hunting fox-terriers and Pomeranians like rabbits.

Daylight had come by the time the meal was over. The Pirate sat on the ground and watched the sky turn blue with the morning. Below him he saw the schooners put out to sea with deckloads of lumber. He heard the bell buoy ringing sweetly off China Point. The dogs sat about him and gnawed at the bones. The Pirate seemed to be listening to the day rather than seeing it, for while his eyes did not move about, there was an air of attentiveness in him. His big hands strayed to the dogs and his fingers worked soothingly in the coarse hair. After about half an hour the Pirate went to the corner of the vacant lot, threw the covering of sacks from his wheelbarrow, and dug up his ax out of the ground where he buried it every evening. Then up the hill he pushed the barrow, and into the woods, until he found a dead tree, full of pitch. By noon he had a load of fine kindling; and then, still followed by his dogs, he walked the streets until he had sold the load for twenty-five cents.

It was possible to observe all this, but what he did with the quarter, no one could tell. He never spent it. In the night, guarded from danger by his dogs, he went into the woods and hid the day's quarter with hundreds of others. Somewhere he had a great hoard of money.

Pilon, that acute man, from whom no details of the life of his fellows escaped, and who was doubly delighted to come upon those secrets that nestled deep in the brains of his acquaintances, discovered the Pirate's hoard by a logical process. Pilon reasoned thus: "Every day that Pirate has a quarter. If it is two dimes and a nickel, he takes it to a store and gets a twenty-five cent piece. He never spends any money at all. Therefore, he must be hiding it."

Pilon tried to compute the amount of the treasure. For years the Pirate had been living in this way. Six days a week he cut pitchwood, and on Sundays he went to church. His clothes he got from the back doors of houses, his food at the back doors of restaurants. Pilon puzzled with the great numbers for a while, and then gave it up. "The Pirate must have at least a hundred dollars," he thought.

For a long time Pilon had considered these things. But it was only after the foolish and enthusiastic promise to feed Danny that the thought of the Pirate's hoard gained any personal significance to Pilon.

Before he approached the subject at all, Pilon put his mind through a long and stunning preparation. He felt very sorry for the Pirate. "Poor little half-formed one," he said to himself. "God did not give him all the brain he should have. That poor little Pirate cannot look after himself. For see, he lives in filth in an old chicken house. He feeds upon scraps fit only for his dogs. His clothes are thin and ragged. And because his brain is not a good one, he hides his money."

Now, with his groundwork of pity laid, Pilon moved on to his solution. "Would it not be a thing of merit," he thought, "to do those things for him which he cannot do for himself? To buy him warm clothes, to feed him food fit for a human? But," he reminded himself, "I have no money to do these things, although they lie squirming in my heart. How can these charitable things be accomplished?"

Now he was getting somewhere. Like the cat, which during a long hour closes in on a sparrow, Pilon was ready for his pounce. "I have it!" his brain cried. "It is like this: The Pirate has money, but he has not the brain to use it. I have the brain! I will offer my brain to his use. I will give freely of my mind. That shall be my charity toward this poor little half-made man."

It was one of the finest structures Pilon had ever built. The urge of the artist to show his work to an audience came upon him. "I will tell it to Pablo," he thought. But he wondered whether he would dare do such a thing. Was Pablo strictly honest? Would he not want to divert some of this money to his own ends? Pilon decided not to take the chance, right then, anyway.

It is astounding to find that the belly of every black and evil thing is as white as snow. And it is saddening to discover how the concealed parts of angels are leprous. Honor and peace to Pilon, for he had discovered how to uncover and to disclose to the world the good that lay in every evil thing. Nor was he blind, as so many saints are, to the evil of good things. It must be admitted with sadness that Pilon had neither the stupidity, the self-righteousness, nor the greediness for reward ever to become a saint. Enough for Pilon to do good and to be rewarded by the glow of human brotherhood accomplished.

That very night he paid a visit to the chicken house where the Pirate lived with his dogs. Danny, Pablo, and Jesus Maria, sitting by the stove, saw him go and said nothing. For, they thought delicately, either a vapor of love had been wafted to Pilon or else he knew where he could get a little wine. In either case it was none of their business until he told them about it.

It was well after dark, but Pilon had a candle in his pocket, for it might be a good thing to watch the expression on the Pirate's face while he talked. And Pilon had a big round sugar cookie in a bag, that Susie Francisco, who worked in a bakery, had given him in return for a formula for getting the love of Charlie Guzman. Charlie was a Postal Telegraph messenger and rode a motorcycle; and Susie had a man's cap to put on backward in case Charlie should ever ask her to ride with him. Pilon thought the Pirate might like the sugar cookie.

The night was very dark. Pilon picked his way along a narrow street bordered with vacant lots and with weed-grown, neglected gardens.

Galvez' bad bulldog came snarling out of Galvez' yard, and Pilon spoke soothing compliments to him. "Nice dog," he said gently, and "Pretty dog," both of them palpable lies. They impressed the bulldog, however, for he retired into Galvez' yard.

Pilon came at last to the vacant property where the Pirate lived. And now he knew he must be careful, for the Pirate's dogs, if they suspected ill of anyone toward their master, were known to become defending furies. As Pilon stepped into the yard, he heard deep and threatening growls from the chicken house.

"Pirate," he called, "it is thy good friend Pilon, come to talk with thee."

There was silence. The dogs stopped growling.

"Pirate, it is only Pilon."

A deep surly voice answered him, "Go away. I am sleeping now. The dogs are sleeping. It is dark, Pilon. Go to bed."

"I have a candle in my pocket," Pilon called. "It will make a light as bright as day in thy dark house. I have a big sugar cookie for thee too."

A faint scuffling sounded in the chicken house. "Come then," the Pirate said. "I will tell the dogs it is all right."

As he advanced through the weeds, Pilon could hear the Pirate talking softly to his dogs, explaining to them that it was only Pilon, who would do no harm. Pilon bent over in front of the dark doorway and scratched a match and lighted his candle.

The Pirate was seated on the dirt floor, and his dogs were all about him. Enrique growled and had to be reassured again. "That one is not so wise as the others," the Pirate said pleasantly. His eyes were the pleased eyes of an amused child. When he smiled his big white teeth glistened in the candlelight.

Pilon held out the bag. "It is a fine cake for you," he said.

The Pirate took the bag and looked into it; then he smiled delightedly and brought out the cookie. The dogs all grinned and faced him, and moved their feet and licked their lips. The Pirate broke his cookie into seven pieces. The first he gave to Pilon, who was his guest. "Now, Enrique," he said. "Now, Fluff. Now, Señor Alec Thompson." Each dog received his piece and gulped it and looked for more. Last, the Pirate ate his and held up his hands to the dogs. "No more, you see," he told them. Immediately the dogs lay down about him.

Pilon sat on the floor and stood the candle on the ground in front of him. The Pirate questioned him self-consciously with his eyes. Pilon sat silently, to let many questions pass through the Pirate's head. At length he said, "Thou art a worry to thy friends."

The Pirate's eyes filled with astonishment. "I? To my friends? What friends?"

Pilon softened his voice. "Thou hast many friends who think of thee. They do not come to see thee because thou art proud. They think it might hurt thy pride to have them see thee living in this chicken house, clothed in rags, eating garbage with thy dogs. But these friends of thine worry for fear the bad life may make thee ill."

The Pirate was following his words with breathless astonishment, and his brain tried to realize these new things he was hearing. It did not occur to him to doubt them, since Pilon was saying them. "I have all these friends?" he said in wonder. "And I did not know it. And I am a worry to these friends. I did not know, Pilon. I would not have worried them if I had known." He swallowed to clear his throat of emotion. "You see, Pilon, the dogs like it here. And I like it because of them. I did not think I was a worry to my friends." Tears came into the Pirate's eyes.

"Nevertheless," Pilon said, "thy mode of living keeps all thy friends uneasy."

The Pirate looked down at the ground and tried to think clearly, but as always, when he attempted to cope with a problem, his brain grew gray and no help came from it, but only a feeling of helplessness. He looked to his dogs for protection, but they had gone back to sleep, for it was none of their business. And then he looked earnestly into Pilon's eyes. "You must tell me what to do, Pilon. I did not know these things."

It was too easy. Pilon was a little ashamed that it should be so easy. He hesitated; nearly gave it up; but then he knew he would be angry with himself if he did. "Thy friends are poor," he said. "They would like to help thee, but they have no money. If thou hast money hidden, bring it out into the open. Buy thyself some clothes. Eat food that is not cast out by other people. Bring thy money out of its hiding place, Pirate."

Pilon had been looking closely at the Pirate's face while he spoke. He saw the eyes droop with suspicion and then with sullenness. In a moment Pilon knew two things certainly; first, that the Pirate had money hidden; and second, that it was not going to be easy to get at it. He was pleased at the latter fact. The Pirate had become a problem in tactics such as Pilon enjoyed.

Now the Pirate was looking at him again, and in his eyes was cunning, and on top of that, a studied ingenuousness. "I have no money anywhere," he said.

"But every day, my friend, I have seen thee get a quarter for thy wood, and never have I seen thee spend it."

This time the Pirate's brain came to his rescue. "I give it to a poor old woman," he said. "I have no money anywhere." And with his tone he closed a door tightly on the subject.

"So it must be guile," Pilon thought. So those gifts, that in him were so sharpened, must be called into play. He stood up and lifted his candle. "I only thought to tell thee how thy friends worry," he said critically. "If thou wilt not try to help, I can do nothing for thee."

The sweetness came back into the Pirate's eyes. "Tell them I am healthy," he begged. "Tell my friends to come and see me. I will not be too proud. I will be glad to see them any time. Wilt thou tell them for me, Pilon?"

"I will tell them," Pilon said ungraciously. "But thy friends will not be pleased when they see thou dost nothing to relieve their minds." Pilon blew out his candle and went away into the darkness. He knew that the Pirate would never tell where his hoard was. It must be found by stealth, taken by force, and then all the good things given to the Pirate. It was the only way.

And so Pilon set himself to watch the Pirate. He followed him into the forest when he went to cut kindlings. He lay in wait outside the chicken house at night. He talked to him long and earnestly, and nothing came of it. The treasure was as far from discovery as ever. Either it lay buried in the chicken house or it was hidden deep in the forest and was only visited at night.

The long and fruitless vigils wore out the patience of Pilon. He knew he must have help and advice. And who could better give it than those comrades, Danny, Pablo, and Jesus Maria? Who could be so stealthy, so guileful? Who could melt to kindness with more ease?

Pilon took them into his confidence; but first he prepared them, as he had prepared himself: The Pirate's poverty, his helplessness, and finally—the solution. When he came to the solution, his friends were in a philanthropic frenzy. They applauded him. Their faces shone with kindness. Pablo thought there might be well over a hundred dollars in the hoard.

When their joy had settled to a working enthusiasm, they came to plans.

"We must watch him," Pablo said.

"But I have watched him," Pilon argued. "It must be that he creeps off in the night, and then one cannot follow too close, for his dogs guard him like devils. It is not going to be so easy."

"You've used every argument?" Danny asked.

"Yes. Every one."

In the end it was Jesus Maria, that humane man, who found the way out. "It is difficult while he lives in that chicken house," he said. "But suppose he lived here, with us? Either his silence would break under our kindness, or else it would be easier to know when he goes out at night."

The friends gave a good deal of thought to this suggestion. "Sometimes the things he gets out of restaurants are nearly new," mused Pablo. "I have seen him with a steak out of which only a little was missing."

"It might be as much as two hundred dollars," said Pilon.

Danny offered an objection. "But those dogs—he would bring his dogs with him."

"They are good dogs," said Pilon. "They obey him exactly. You may draw a line around a corner and say, 'Keep thy dogs within this line.' He will tell them, and those dogs will stay."

"I saw the Pirate one morning, and he had nearly half a cake, just a little bit damp with coffee," said Pablo.

The question settled itself. The house resolved itself into a committee, and the committee visited the Pirate.

It was a crowded place, that chicken house, when they all got inside. The Pirate tried to disguise his happiness with a gruff tone.

"The weather has been bad," he said socially. And, "You wouldn't believe, maybe, that I found a tick as big as a pigeon's egg on Rudolph's neck." And he spoke disparagingly of his home, as a host should. "It is too small," he said. "It is not a fit place for one's friends to come. But it is warm and snug, especially for the dogs."

Then Pilon spoke. He told the Pirate that worry was killing his friends; but if he would go to live with them, then they could sleep again, with their minds at ease.

It was a very great shock to the Pirate. He looked at his hands. And he looked to his dogs for comfort, but they would not meet his glance. At last he wiped the happiness from his eyes with the back of his hand, and he wiped his hand on his big black beard.

"And the dogs?" he asked softly. "You want the dogs too? Are you friends of the dogs?"

Pilon nodded. "Yes, the dogs too. There will be a whole corner set aside for the dogs."

The Pirate had a great deal of pride. He was afraid

he might not conduct himself well. "Go away now," he said pleadingly. "Go home now. Tomorrow I will come."

His friends knew how he felt. They crawled out of the door and left him alone.

"He will be happy with us, that one," said Jesus Maria.

"Poor little lonely man," Danny added. "If I had known, I would have asked him long ago, even if he had no treasure."

A flame of joy burned in all of them.

They settled soon into the new relationship. Danny, with a piece of blue chalk, drew a segment of a circle, enclosing a corner of the living room, and that was where the dogs must stay when they were in the house. The Pirate slept in that corner too, with the dogs.

The house was beginning to be a little crowded, with five men and five dogs; but from the first Danny and his friends realized that their invitation to the Pirate had been inspired by that weary and anxious angel who guarded their destinies and protected them from evil.

Every morning, long before his friends were awake, the Pirate arose from his corner, and, followed by his dogs, he made the rounds of the restaurants and the wharves. He was one of those for whom everyone feels a kindliness. His packages grew larger. The paisanos received his bounty and made use of it: fresh fish, half pies, untouched loaves of stale bread, meat that required only a little soda to take the green out. They began really to live.

And their acceptance of his gifts touched the Pirate more deeply than anything they could have done for him. There was a light of worship in his eyes as he watched them eat the food he brought.

In the evening, when they sat about the stove and discussed the doings of Tortilla Flat with the lazy voices of fed gods, the Pirate's eyes darted from mouth to mouth, and his own lips moved, whispering again the words his friends said. The dogs pressed in about him jealously.

These were his friends, he told himself in the night, when the house was dark, when the dogs snuggled close to him so that all might be warm. These men loved him so much that it worried them to have him live alone. The Pirate had often to repeat this to himself, for it was an astounding thing, an unbelievable thing. His wheelbarrow stood in Danny's yard now, and every day he cut his pitchwood and sold it. But so afraid was the Pirate that he might miss some word his friends said in the evening, might not be there to absorb some stream of the warm companionship, that he had not visited his hoard for several days to put the new coins there.

His friends were kind to him. They treated him with a sweet courtesy; but always there was some eye open and upon him. When he wheeled his barrow into the woods, one of the friends walked with him, and sat on a log while he worked. When he went into the gulch, the last thing at night, Danny or Pablo or Pilon or Jesus Maria kept him company. And in the night he must have been very quiet to have crept out without a shadow behind him.

For a week the friends merely watched the Pirate. But at last the inactivity tired them. Direct action was out of the question, they knew. And so one evening the subject of the desirability of hiding one's money came up for discussion.

Pilon began it. "I had an uncle, a regular miser, and he hid his gold in the woods. And one time he went to look at it, and it was gone. Someone had found it and stolen it. He was an old man, then, and all his money was gone, and he hanged himself." Pilon noticed with some satisfaction the look of apprehension that came upon the Pirate's face.

Danny noticed it too; and he continued, "The *viejo*, my grandfather, who owned this house, also buried money. I do not know how much, but he was reputed a rich man, so there must have been three or four hundred dollars. The *viejo* dug a deep hole and put his money in it, and then he covered it up, and then he strewed pine needles over the ground until he thought no one could see that anything had been done there. But when he went back, the hole was open, and the money was gone."

The Pirate's lips followed the words. A look of terror had come into his face. His fingers picked among the neck hairs of Señor Alec Thompson. The friends exchanged a glance and dropped the subject for the time being. They turned to the love life of Cornelia Ruiz.

In the night the Pirate crept out of the house, and the dogs crept after him; and Pilon crept after all of them. The Pirate went swiftly into the forest, leaping with sure feet over logs and brush. Pilon floundered behind him. But when they had gone at least two miles, Pilon was winded, and torn by vines. He paused to rest a moment; and then he realized that all sounds ahead of him had ceased. He waited and listened and crept about, but the Pirate had disappeared.

After two hours Pilon went back again, slowly and tiredly. There was the Pirate in the house, fast asleep among his dogs. The dogs lifted their heads when Pilon entered, and Pilon thought they smiled satirically at him for a moment.

A conference took place in the gulch the next morning.

"It is not possible to follow him," Pilon reported. "He vanished. He sees in the dark. He knows every tree in the forest. We must find some other way."

"Perhaps one is not enough," Pablo suggested. "If all of us should follow him, then one might not lose track of him."

"We will talk again tonight," said Jesus Maria, "only worse. A lady I know is going to give me a little wine," he added modestly. "Maybe if the Pirate has a little wine in him, he will not disappear so easily." So it was left.

Jesus Maria's lady gave him a whole gallon of wine. What could compare with the Pirate's delight that evening when a fruit jar of wine was put into his hand, when he sat with his friends and sipped his wine and listened to the talk? Such joy had come rarely into the Pirate's life. He wished he might clasp these dear people to his breast and tell them how much he loved them. But that was not a thing he could do, for they might think he was drunk. He wished he could do some tremendous thing to show them his love.

"We spoke last night of burying money," said Pilon. "Today I remembered a cousin of mine, a clever man. If anyone in the world could hide money where it would never be found, he could do it. So he took his money and hid it. Perhaps you have seen him, that poor little one who crawls about the wharf and begs fish heads to make soup of. That is my cousin. Someone stole his buried money."

The worry came back into the Pirate's face.

Story topped story, and in each one all manner of evil dogged the footsteps of those who hid their money.

"It is better to keep one's money close, to spend some now and then, to give a little to one's friends," Danny finished.

They had been watching the Pirate narrowly, and in the middle of the worst story they had seen the worry go from his face, and a smile of relief take its place. Now he sipped his wine and his eyes glittered with joy.

The friends were in despair. All their plans had failed. They were sick at heart. After all their goodness and their charity, this had happened. The Pirate had in some way escaped the good they had intended to confer upon him. They finished their wine and went moodily to bed.

Few things could happen in the night without Pilon's knowledge. His ears remained open while the rest of him slept. He heard the stealthy exit of the Pirate and his dogs from the house. He leaped to awaken his friends; and in a moment the four were following the Pirate in the direction of the forest. It was very dark when they entered the pine forest. The four friends ran into trees, tripped on berry vines; but for a long time they could hear the Pirate marching on ahead of them. They followed as far as Pilon had followed the night before, and then, suddenly, silence, and the whispering forest and the vague night wind. They combed the woods and brush patches, but the Pirate had disappeared again.

At last, cold and disconsolate, they came together and trudged wearily back toward Monterey. The dawn came before they got back. The sun was already shining on the bay. The smoke of the morning fires arose to them out of Monterey.

The Pirate walked out on the porch to greet them, and his face was happy. They passed him sullenly and filed into the living room. There on the table lay a large canvas bag.

The Pirate followed them in. "I lied to thee, Pilon," he said. "I told thee I had no money, for I was afraid. I did not know about my friends then. You have told how hidden money is so often stolen, and I am afraid again. Only last night did a way out come to me. My money will be safe with my friends. No one can steal it if my friends guard it for me. You would not believe it, but the last two nights someone followed me into the forest to steal my money."

Terrible as the blow was, Pilon, that clever man, tried to escape it. "Before this money is put into our hands, maybe you would like to take some out," he suggested smoothly.

The Pirate shook his head. "No. I cannot do that. It is promised. I have nearly a thousand two-bitses. When I have a thousand I will buy a gold candlestick for San Francisco de Assisi.

"Once I had a nice dog, and that dog was sick; and I promised a gold candlestick of one thousand days if that dog would get well. And," he spread his great hands, "that dog got well."

"Is it one of these dogs?" Pilon demanded.

"No," said the Pirate. "A truck ran over him a little later."

So it was over, all hope of diverting the money. Danny and Pablo morosely lifted the heavy bag of silver quarters, took it in the other room, and put it under the pillow of Danny's bed. In time they would take a certain pleasure in the knowledge that this money lay under the pillow, but now their defeat was bitter. There was nothing in the world they could do about it. Their chance had come, and it had gone.

The Pirate stood before them, and there were tears of happiness in his eyes, for he had proved his love for his friends.

"To think," he said, "all those years I lay in that chicken house, and I did not know any pleasure. But now," he added, "oh, now I am very happy."

8

HOW DANNY'S FRIENDS SOUGHT MYSTIC TREASURE ON SAINT ANDREW'S EVE. HOW PILON FOUND IT AND LATER HOW A PAIR OF SERGE PANTS CHANGED OWNERSHIP TWICE.

If he had been a hero, the Portagee would have spent a miserable time in the army. The fact that he was Big Joe Portagee, with a decent training in the Monterey jail, not only saved him the misery of patriotism thwarted, but solidified his conviction that as a man's days are rightly devoted half to sleeping and half to waking, so a man's years are rightly spent half in jail and half out. Of the duration of the war, Joe Portagee spent considerably more time in jail than out.

In civilian life one is punished for things one does; but army codes add a new principle to this—they punish a man for things he does not do. Joe Portagee never did figure this out. He didn't clean his rifle; he didn't shave; and once or twice, on leave, he didn't come back. Coupled with these shortcomings was a propensity Big Joe had for genial argument when he was taken to task.

Ordinarily he spent half his time in jail; of two years in the army, he spent eighteen months in jail. And he was far from satisified with prison life in the army. In the Monterey jail he was accustomed to ease and companionship. In the army he found only work. In Monterey only one charge was ever brought against him: Drunk and Disorderly Conduct. The charges in the army bewildered him so completely that the effect on his mind was probably permanent.

When the war was over, and all the troops were disbanded, Big Joe still had six months' sentence to serve. The charge had been: "Being drunk on duty. Striking a sergeant with a kerosene can. Denying his identity (he couldn't remember it, so he denied everything). Stealing two gallons of cooked beans. And going A.W.O.L. on the Major's horse."

If the Armistice had not already been signed, Big Joe would probably have been shot. He came home to Monterey long after the other veterans had arrived and had eaten up all the sweets of victory.

When Big Joe swung down from the train, he was dressed in an army overcoat and tunic and a pair of blue serge trousers.

The town hadn't changed much, except for prohibition; and prohibition hadn't changed Torrelli's. Joe traded his overcoat for a gallon of wine and went out to find his friends.

True friends he found none that night, but in Monterey he found no lack of those vile and false harpies and pimps who are ever ready to lead men into the pit. Joe, who was not very moral, had no revulsion for the pit; he liked it.

Before very many hours had passed, his wine was

gone, and he had no money; and then the harpies tried
to get Joe out of the pit, and he wouldn't go. He was
comfortable there.

When they tried to eject him by force, Big Joe, with
a just and terrible resentment, broke all the furniture
and all the windows, sent half-clothed girls screaming
into the night; and then, as an afterthought, set fire to
the house. It was not a safe thing to lead Joe into
temptation; he had no resistance to it at all.

A policeman finally interfered and took him in hand.
The Portagee sighed happily. He was home again.

After a short and juryless trial, in which he was
sentenced to thirty days, Joe lay luxuriously on his
leather cot and slept heavily for one-tenth of his
sentence.

The Portagee liked the Monterey jail. It was a place
to meet people. If he stayed there long enough, all his
friends were in and out. The time passed quickly. He
was a little sad when he had to go, but his sadness was
tempered with the knowledge that it was very easy to
get back again.

He would have liked to go into the pit again, but he
had no money and no wine. He combed the streets for
his old friends, Pilon and Danny and Pablo, and could
not find them. The police sergeant said he hadn't
booked them for a long time.

"They must be dead," said the Portagee.

He wandered sadly to Torrelli's, but Torrelli was not
friendly toward men who had neither money nor bar-
terable property, and he gave Big Joe little solace; but
Torrelli did say that Danny had inherited a house
on Tortilla Flat, and that all his friends lived there
with him.

Affection and a desire to see his friends came to Big Joe. In the evening he wandered up toward Tortilla Flat to find Danny and Pilon. It was dusk as he walked up the street, and on the way he met Pilon, hurrying by in a businesslike way.

"Ai, Pilon. I was just coming to see you."

"Hello, Joe Portagee." Pilon was brusque. "Where you been?"

"In the army," said Joe.

Pilon's mind was not on the meeting. "I have to go on."

"I will go with you," said Joe.

Pilon stopped and surveyed him. "Don't you remember what night it is?" he asked.

"No. What is it?"

"It is Saint Andrew's Eve."

Then the Portagee knew; for this was the night when every paisano who wasn't in jail wandered restlessly through the forest. This was the night when all buried treasure sent up a faint phosphorescent glow through the ground. There was plenty of treasure in the woods too. Monterey had been invaded many times in two hundred years, and each time valuables had been hidden in the earth.

The night was clear. Pilon had emerged from his hard daily shell, as he did now and then. He was the idealist tonight, the giver of gifts. This night he was engaged in a mission of kindness.

"You may come with me, Big Joe Portagee, but if we find any treasure I must decide what to do with it. If you do not agree, you can go by yourself and look for your own treasure."

Big Joe was not an expert at directing his own ef-

forts. "I will go with you, Pilon," he said. "I don't care
about the treasure."

The night came down as they walked into the forest.
Their feet found the pine-needle beds. Now Pilon
knew it for a perfect night. A high fog covered the sky,
and behind it the moon shone, so that the forest was
filled with a gauzelike light. There was none of the
sharp outline we think of as reality. The tree trunks
were not black columns of wood, but soft and unsub-
stantial shadows. The patches of brush were formless
and shifting in the queer light. Ghosts could walk
freely tonight, without fear of the disbelief of men; for
this night was haunted, and it would be an insensitive
man who did not know it.

Now and then Pilon and Big Joe passed other
searchers who wandered restlessly, zigzagging among
the pines. Their heads were down, and they moved
silently and passed no greeting. Who could say
whether all of them were really living men? Joe and
Pilon knew that some were shades of those old folk
who had buried the treasures; and who, on Saint Andrew's Eve, wandered back to the earth to see that
their gold was undisturbed. Pilon wore his saint's me-
dallion, hung around his neck, outside his clothes; so
he had no fear of the spirits. Big Joe walked with his
fingers crossed in the Holy Sign. Although they might
be frightened, they knew they had protection more
than adequate to cope with the unearthly night.

The wind rose as they walked, and drove the fog
across the pale moon like a thin wash of gray water
color. The moving fog gave shifting form to the forest,
so that every tree crept stealthily along and the bushes
moved soundlessly, like great dark cats. The treetops

in the wind talked huskily, told fortunes and foretold deaths. Pilon knew it was not good to listen to the talking of the trees. No good ever came of knowing the future; and besides, this whispering was unholy. He turned the attention of his ears from the trees' talking.

He began a zigzag path through the forest, and Big Joe walked beside him like a great alert dog. Lone silent men passed them and went on without a greeting; and the dead passed them noiselessly, and went on without a greeting.

The fog siren began its screaming on the Point, far below them; and it wailed its sorrow for all the good ships that had drowned on the iron reef, and for all those others that would sometime die there.

Pilon shuddered and felt cold, although the night was warm. He whispered a Hail Mary under his breath.

They passed a gray man who walked with his head down and who gave them no greeting.

An hour went by, and still Pilon and Big Joe wandered as restlessly as the dead who crowded the night.

Suddenly Pilon stopped. His hand found Big Joe's arm. "Do you see?" he whispered.

"Where?"

"Right ahead there."

"Yes—I think so."

It seemed to Pilon that he could see a soft pillar of blue light that shone out of the ground ten yards ahead of him.

"Big Joe," he whispered, "find two sticks about three or four feet long. I do not want to look away. I might lose it."

He stood like a pointing dog while Big Joe scurried off to find the sticks. Pilon heard him break two small dead limbs from a pine tree. And he heard the snaps as Big Joe broke the twigs from his sticks. And still Pilon stared at the pale shaft of nebulous light. So faint it was that sometimes it seemed to disappear altogether. Sometimes he was not sure he saw it at all. He did not move his eyes when Big Joe put the sticks in his hands. Pilon crossed the sticks at right angles and advanced slowly, holding the cross in front of him. As he came close, the light seemed to fade away, but he saw where it had come from, a perfectly round depression in the pine needles.

Pilon laid his cross over the depression, and he said, "All that lies here is mine by discovery. Go away, all evil spirits. Go away, spirits of men who buried this treasure, *In Nomen Patris et Filius et Spiritu Sancti,*" and then he heaved a great sigh and sat down on the ground.

"We have found it, oh my friend, Big Joe," he cried. "For many years I have looked, and now I have found it."

"Let's dig," said Big Joe.

But Pilon shook his head impatiently. "When all the spirits are free? When even to be here is dangerous? You are a fool, Big Joe. We will sit here until morning; and then we will mark the place, and tomorrow night we will dig. No one else can see the light now that we have covered it with the cross. Tomorrow night there will be no danger."

The night seemed more fearful now that they sat in the pine needles, but the cross sent out a warmth of holiness and safety, like a little bonfire on the ground.

Like a fire, however, it only warmed the front of them. Their backs were to the cold and evil things that wandered about in the forest.

Pilon got up and drew a big circle around the whole place, and he was inside when he closed the circle. "Let no evil thing cross this line, in the Name of the Most Holy Jesus," he chanted. Then he sat down again. Both he and Big Joe felt better. They could hear the muffled footsteps of the weary, wandering ghosts; they could see the little lights that glowed from the transparent forms as they walked by; but their protecting line was impregnable. Nothing bad from this world or from any other world could cross into the circle.

"What are you going to do with the money?" Big Joe asked.

Pilon looked at him in contempt. "You have never looked for treasure, Big Joe Portagee, for you do not know how to go about it. I cannot keep this treasure for myself. If I go after it intending to keep it, then the treasure will dig itself down and down like a clam in the sand, and I shall never find it. No, that is not the way. I am digging this treasure for Danny."

All the idealism in Pilon came out then. He told Big Joe how good Danny was to his friends.

"And we do nothing for him," he said. "We pay no rent. Sometimes we get drunk and break the furniture. We fight with Danny when we are angry with him, and we call him names. Oh, we are very bad, Big Joe. And so all of us, Pablo and Jesus Maria and the Pirate and I talked and planned. We are all in the woods tonight, looking for treasure. And the treasure is to be for Danny. He is so good, Big Joe. He is so kind; and we are so bad. But if we take a great sack of treasure to him, then he will be glad. It is because my heart is clean of selfishness that I can find this treasure."

"Won't you keep any of it?" Big Joe asked, incredulous. "Not even for a gallon of wine?"

Pilon had no speck of the Bad Pilon in him this night. "No, not one scrap of gold! Not one little brown penny! It is all for Danny, every bit."

Joe was disappointed. "I walked all this way and I won't even get a glass of wine for it," he mourned.

"When Danny has the money," Pilon said delicately, "it may be that he will buy a little wine. Of course I shall not suggest it, for this treasure is Danny's. But I think maybe he might buy a little wine. And then if you were good to him, you might get a glass."

Big Joe was comforted, for he had known Danny a long time. He thought it possible that Danny might buy a great deal of wine.

The night passed on over them. The moon went down and left the forest in muffled darkness. The fog siren screamed and screamed. During the whole night Pilon remained unspotted. He preached a little to Big Joe as recent converts are likely to do.

"It is worth while to be kind and generous," he said. "Not only do such actions pile up a house of joy in Heaven; but there is, too, a quick reward here on earth. One feels a golden warmth glowing like a hot enchilada in one's stomach. The Spirit of God clothes one in a coat as soft as camel's hair. I have not always been a good man, Big Joe Portagee. I confess it freely."

Big Joe knew it perfectly well.

"I have been bad," Pilon continued ecstatically. He was enjoying himself thoroughly. "I have lied and stolen. I have been lecherous. I have committed adultery and taken God's name in vain."

"Me too," said Big Joe happily.

"And what was the result, Big Joe Portagee? I have had a mean feeling. I have known I would go to Hell. But now I see that the sinner is never so bad that he cannot be forgiven. Although I have not yet been to confession, I can feel that the change in me is pleasing to God, for His grace is upon me. If you too would change your ways, Big Joe, if you would give up drunkenness and fighting and those girls down at Dora Williams' House, you too might feel as I do."

But Big Joe had gone to sleep. He never stayed awake very long when he was not moving about.

The grace was not quite so sharp to Pilon when he could not tell Big Joe about it, but he sat and watched the treasure place while the sky grayed and the dawn came behind the fog. He saw the pine trees take shape and emerge out of obscurity. The wind died down and the little blue rabbits came out of the brush and hopped about on the pine needles. Pilon was heavy-eyed but happy.

When it was light he stirred Big Joe Portagee with his foot. "It is time to go to Danny's house. The day has come." Pilon threw the cross away, for it was no longer needed, and he erased the circle. "Now," he said, "we must make no mark, but we must remember this by trees and rocks."

"Why don't we dig now?" Big Joe asked.

"And everybody in Tortilla Flat would come to help us," Pilon said sarcastically.

They looked hard at the surroundings, saying, "Now there are three trees together on the right, and two on the left. That patch of brush is down there, and here is a rock." At last they walked away from the treasure, memorizing the way as they went.

At Danny's house they found tired friends. "Did you find any?" the friends demanded.

"No," said Pilon quickly, to forestall Joe's confession.

"Well, Pablo thought he saw the light, but it disappeared before he got to it. And the Pirate saw the ghost of an old woman, and she had his dog with her."

The Pirate broke into a smile. "That old woman told me my dog was happy now," he said.

"Here is Big Joe Portagee, back from the army," announced Pilon.

"Hello, Joe."

"You got a nice place here," said the Portagee, and let himself down easily into a chair.

"You keep out of my bed," said Danny, for he knew that Joe Portagee had come to stay. The way he sat in a chair and crossed his knees had an appearance of permanence.

The Pirate went out and took his wheelbarrow and started into the forest to cut his kindlings; but the other five men lay down in the sunshine that broke through the fog, and in a little while they were asleep.

It was midafternoon before any of them awakened. At last they stretched their arms and sat up and looked listlessly down at the bay below, where a brown oil tanker moved slowly out to sea. The Pirate had left the bags on the table, and the friends opened them and brought out the food the Pirate had collected.

Big Joe walked down the path toward the sagging gate. "See you later," he called to Pilon.

Pilon anxiously watched him until he saw that Big Joe was headed down the hill to Monterey, not up toward the pine forest. The four friends sat down and dreamily watched the evening come.

At dusk Joe Portagee returned. He and Pilon conferred in the yard, out of earshot of the house.

"We will borrow tools from Mrs. Morales," Pilon said. "A shovel and pickax stand by her chicken house."

When it was quite dark they started. "We go to see some girls, friends of Joe Portagee's," Pilon explained. They crept into Mrs. Morales' yard and borrowed the tools. And then, from the weeds beside the road, Big Joe lifted out a gallon jug of wine.

"Thou hast sold the treasure," Pilon cried fiercely. "Thou art a traitor, oh dog of a dog."

Big Joe quieted him firmly. "I did not tell where the treasure was," he said with some dignity. "I told like this, 'We found a treasure,' I said, 'but it is for Danny. When Danny has it, I will borrow a dollar and pay for the wine.'"

Pilon was overwhelmed. "And they believed, and let you take the wine?" he demanded.

"Well—" Big Joe hesitated. "I left something to prove I would bring the dollar."

Pilon turned like lightning and took him by the throat. "What did you leave?"

"Only one little blanket, Pilon," Joe Portagee wailed. "Only one."

Pilon shook at him, but Big Joe was so heavy that Pilon only succeeded in shaking himself. "What blanket?" he cried. "Say what blanket it was you stole."

Big Joe blubbered. "Only one of Danny's. Only one.

He has two. I took only the little tiny one. Do not hurt me, Pilon. The other one was bigger. Danny will get it back when we find the treasure."

Pilon whirled him around and kicked him with accuracy and fire. "Pig," he said, "dirty thieving cow. You will get the blanket back or I will beat you to ribbons."

Big Joe tried to placate him. "I thought how we are working for Danny," he whispered. "I thought, 'Danny will be so glad, he can buy a hundred new blankets.'"

"Be still," said Pilon. "You will get that same blanket back or I will beat you with a rock." He took up the jug and uncorked it and drank a little to soothe his frayed sensibilities; moreover, he drove the cork back and refused the Portagee even a drop. "For this theft you must do all the digging. Pick up those tools and come with me."

Big Joe whined like a puppy and obeyed. He could not stand against the righteous fury of Pilon.

They tried to find the treasure for a long time. It was late when Pilon pointed to three trees in a row. "There!" he said.

They searched about until they found the depression in the ground. There was a little moonlight to guide them, for this night the sky was free of fog.

Now that he was not going to dig, Pilon developed a new theory for uncovering treasure. "Sometimes the money is in sacks," he said, "and the sacks are rotted. If you dig straight down you might lose some." He drew a generous circle around the hollow. "Now, dig a deep trench around, and then we will come *up* on the treasure."

"Aren't you going to dig?" Big Joe asked.

Pilon broke into a fury. "Am I a thief of blankets?" he cried. "Do I steal from the bed of my friend who shelters me?"

"Well, I ain't going to do all the digging," Big Joe said.

Pilon picked up one of the pine limbs that only the night before had served as part of the cross. He advanced ominously toward Big Joe Portagee. "Thief," he snarled. "Dirty pig of an untrue friend. Take up that shovel."

Big Joe's courage flowed away, and he stooped for the shovel on the ground. If Joe Portagee's conscience had not been bad, he might have remonstrated; but his fear of Pilon, armed with a righteous cause and a stick of pine wood, was great.

Big Joe abhorred the whole principle of shoveling. The line of the moving shovel was unattractive. The end to be gained, that of taking dirt from one place and putting it in another, was, to one who held the larger vision, silly and gainless. A whole lifetime of shoveling could accomplish practically nothing. Big Joe's reaction was a little more simple than this. He didn't like to shovel. He had joined the army to fight and had done nothing but dig.

But Pilon stood over him, and the trench stretched around the treasure place. It did no good to profess sickness, hunger, or weakness. Pilon was inexorable, and Joe's crime of the blanket was held against him. Although he whined, complained, held up his hands to show how they were hurt, Pilon stood over him and forced the digging.

Midnight came, and the trench was three feet down. The roosters of Monterey crowed. The moon sank behind the trees. At last Pilon gave the word to move in on the treasure. The bursts of dirt came slowly now; Big Joe was exhausted. Just before daylight his shovel struck something hard.

"Ai," he cried. "We have it, Pilon."

The find was large and square. Frantically they dug at it in the dark, and they could not see it.

"Careful," Pilon cautioned. "Do not hurt it."

The daylight came before they had it out. Pilon felt metal and leaned down in the gray light to see. It was a good-sized square of concrete. On the top was a round brown plate. Pilon spelled out the words on it:

UNITED STATES GEODETIC SURVEY +1915 +
ELEVATION 600 FEET

Pilon sat down in the pit and his shoulders sagged in defeat.

"No treasure?" Big Joe asked plaintively.

Pilon did not answer him. The Portagee inspected the cement post and his brow wrinkled with thought. He turned to the sorrowing Pilon. "Maybe we can take this good piece of metal and sell it."

Pilon peered up out of his dejection. "Johnny Pom-pom found one," he said with a quietness of great disappointment. "Johnny Pom-pom took the metal piece and tried to sell it. It is a year in jail to dig one of these up," Pilon mourned. "A year in jail and two thousand dollars' fine." In his pain Pilon wanted only to get away from this tragic place. He stood up, found a weed in which to wrap the wine bottle, and started down the hill.

Big Joe trotted after him solicitously. "Where are we going?" he asked.

"I don't know," said Pilon.

The day was bright when they arrived at the beach, but even there Pilon did not stop. He trudged along the hard sand by the water's edge until Monterey was far behind and only the sand dunes of Seaside and the rippling waves of the bay were there to see his sorrow. At last he sat in the dry sand, with the sun warming him. Big Joe sat beside him, and he felt that in some way he was responsible for Pilon's silent pain.

Pilon took the jug out of its weed and uncorked it and drank deeply, and because sorrow is the mother of a general compassion, he passed Joe's wine to the miscreant Joe.

"How we build," Pilon cried. "How our dreams lead us. I had thought how we would carry bags of gold to Danny. I could see how his face would look. He would be surprised. For a long time he would not believe it." He took the bottle from Joe Portagee and drank colossally. "All this is gone, blown away in the night."

The sun was warming the beach now. In spite of his disappointment Pilon felt a traitorous comfort stealing over him, a treacherous impulse to discover some good points in the situation.

Big Joe, in his quiet way, was drinking more than his share of the wine. Pilon took it indignantly and drank again and again.

"But after all," he said philosophically, "maybe if we had found gold, it might not have been good for Danny. He has always been a poor man. Riches might make him crazy."

Big Joe nodded solemnly. The wine went down and down in the bottle.

"Happiness is better than riches," said Pilon. "If we try to make Danny happy, it will be a better thing than to give him money."

Big Joe nodded again and took off his shoes. "Make him happy. That's the stuff."

Pilon turned sadly upon him. "You are only a pig and not fit to live with men," he said gently. "You who stole Danny's blanket should be kept in a sty and fed potato peelings."

They were getting very sleepy in the warm sun. The little waves whispered along the beach. Pilon took off his shoes.

"Even Stephen," said Big Joe, and they drained the jug to the last drop.

The beach was swaying gently, heaving and falling with a movement like a ground-swell.

"You aren't a bad man," Pilon said. But Big Joe Portagee was already asleep. Pilon took off his coat and laid it over his face. In a few moments he too was sleeping sweetly.

The sun wheeled over the sky. The tide spread up the beach and then retreated. A squad of scampering kildeers inspected the sleeping men. A wandering dog sniffed them. Two elderly ladies, collecting seashells, saw the bodies and hurried past lest these men should awaken in passion, pursue and criminally assault them. It was a shame, they agreed, that the police did nothing to control such matters. "They are drunk," one said.

And the other stared back up the beach at the sleeping men. "Drunken beasts," she agreed.

When at last the sun went behind the pines of the hill in back of Monterey, Pilon awakened. His mouth was as dry as alum; his head ached and he was stiff from the hard sand. Big Joe snored on.

"Joe," Pilon cried, but the Portagee was beyond call. Pilon rested on his elbow and stared out to sea. "A little wine would be good for my dry mouth," he thought. He tipped up the jug and got not a single drop to soothe his dry tongue. Then he turned out his pockets in the hope that while he slept some miracle had taken place there; but none had. There was a broken pocketknife for which he had been refused a glass of wine at least twenty times. There was a fish-hook in a cork, a piece of dirty string, a dog's tooth, and several keys that fit nothing Pilon knew of. In the whole lot was not a thing Torrelli would consider as worth having, even in a moment of insanity.

Pilon looked speculatively at Big Joe. "Poor fellow," he thought. "When Joe Portagee wakes up he will feel as dry as I do. He will like it if I have a little wine for him." He pushed Big Joe roughly several times; and when the Portagee only mumbled, and then snored again, Pilon looked through his pockets. He found a brass pants' button, a little metal disk which said "Good Eats at the Dutchman," four or five headless matches, and a little piece of chewing tobacco.

Pilon sat back on his heels. So it was no use. He must wither here on the beach while his throat called lustily for wine.

He noticed the serge trousers the Portagee was wearing and stroked them with his fingers. "Nice cloth," he thought. "Why should this dirty Portagee wear such good cloth when all his friends go about in jeans?" Then he remembered how badly the pants fitted Big Joe, how tight the waist was even with two fly-buttons undone, how the cuffs missed the shoe tops by inches. "Someone of a decent size would be happy in those pants."

Pilon remembered Big Joe's crime against Danny, and he became an avenging angel. How did this big black Portagee dare to insult Danny so! "When he wakes up I will beat him! But," the more subtle Pilon argued, "his crime was theft. Would it not teach him a lesson to know how it feels to have something stolen? What good is punishment unless something is learned?" It was a triumphant position for Pilon. If, with one action, he could avenge Danny, discipline Big Joe, teach an ethical lesson, and get a little wine, who in the world could criticize him?

He pushed the Portagee vigorously, and Big Joe brushed at him as though he were a fly. Pilon deftly removed the trousers, rolled them up, and sauntered away into the sand dunes.

Torrelli was out, but Mrs. Torrelli opened the door to Pilon. He was mysterious in his manner, but at last he held up the pants for her inspection.

She shook her head decisively.

"But look," said Pilon, "you are seeing only the spots and the dirt. Look at this fine cloth underneath. Think, señora! You have cleaned the spots off and pressed the trousers! Torrelli comes in! He is silent; he is glum. And then you bring him these fine pants! See how his eyes grow bright! See how happy he is! He takes you on his lap! Look how he smiles at you, señora! Is so much happiness too high at one gallon of red wine?"

"The seat of the pants is thin," she said.

He held them up to the light. "Can you see through them? No! The stiffness, the discomfort is taken out of them. They are in prime condition."

"No," she said firmly.

"You are cruel to your husband, señora. You deny him happiness. I should not be surprised to see him going to other women, who are not so heartless. For a quart, then?"

Finally her resistance was beaten down and she gave him the quart. Pilon drank it off immediately. "You try to break down the price of pleasure," he warned her. "I should have half a gallon."

Mrs. Torrelli was hard as stone. Not a drop more could Pilon get. He sat there brooding in the kitchen. "Jewess, that's what she is. She cheats me out of Big Joe's pants."

Pilon thought sadly of his friend out there on the beach. What could he do? If he came into town he would be arrested. And what had this harpy done to deserve the pants? She had tried to buy Pilon's friend's pants for a miserable quart of miserable wine. Pilon felt himself dissolving into anger at her.

"I am going away in a moment," he told Mrs. Torrelli. The pants were hung in a little alcove off the kitchen.

"Good-by," said Mrs. Torrelli over her shoulder. She went into her little pantry to prepare dinner.

On his way out Pilon passed the alcove and lifted down not only the pants, but Danny's blanket.

Pilon walked back down the beach, toward the place where he had left Big Joe. He could see a bonfire burning brightly on the sand, and as he drew nearer, a number of small dark figures passed in front of the flame. It was very dark now; he guided himself by the fire. As he came close, he saw that it was a Girl Scout wienie bake. He approached warily.

For a while he could not see Big Joe, but at last he discovered him, lying half covered with sand, speechless with cold and agony. Pilon walked firmly up to him and held up the pants.

"Take them, Big Joe, and be glad you have them back."

Joe's teeth were chattering. "Who stole my pants, Pilon? I have been lying here for hours, and I could not go away because of those girls."

Pilon obligingly stood between Big Joe and the little girls who were running about the bonfire. The Portagee brushed the cold damp sand from his legs and put on his pants. They walked side by side along the dark beach toward Monterey, where the lights hung, necklace above necklace against the hill. The sand dunes crouched along the back of the beach like tired hounds, resting; and the waves gently practiced at striking and hissed a little. The night was cold and aloof, and its warm life was withdrawn, so that it was full of bitter warnings to man that he is alone in the world, and alone among his fellows; that he has no comfort owing him from anywhere.

Pilon was still brooding, and Joe Portagee sensed the depth of his feeling. At last Pilon turned his head toward his friend. "We learn by this that it is great foolishness to trust a woman," he said.

"Did some woman take my pants?" Big Joe demanded excitedly. "Who was it? I'll kick the hell out of her!"

But Pilon shook his head as sadly as old Jehovah, who, resting on the seventh day, sees that his world is tiresome. "She is punished," Pilon said. "You might say she punished herself, and that is the best way. She had thy pants; she bought them with greed; and now she has them not."

These things were beyond Big Joe. They were mysteries it was better to let alone; and this was as Pilon wished it. Big Joe said humbly, "Thanks for getting my pants back, Pilon." But Pilon was so sunk in philosophy that even thanks were valueless.

"It was nothing," he said. "In the whole matter only the lesson we learn has any value."

They climbed up from the beach and passed the great silver tower of the gas works.

Big Joe Portagee was happy to be with Pilon. "Here is one who takes care of his friends," he thought. "Even when they sleep he is alert to see that no harm comes to them." He resolved to do something nice for Pilon sometime.

9

HOW DANNY WAS ENSNARED BY A VACUUM-CLEANER AND HOW DANNY'S FRIENDS RESCUED HIM.

Dolores Engracia Ramirez lived in her own little house on the upper edge of Tortilla Flat. She did housework for some of the ladies in Monterey, and she belonged to the Native Daughters of the Golden West. She was not pretty, this lean-faced paisana, but there was in her figure a certain voluptuousness of movement; there was in her voice a throatiness some men found indicative. Her eyes could burn behind a mist with a sleepy passion which those men to whom the flesh is important found attractive and downright inviting.

In her brusque moments she was not desirable, but an amorous combination came about within her often enough so that she was called Sweets Ramirez on Tortilla Flat.

It was a pleasant thing to see her when the beast in her was prowling. How she leaned over her front gate! How her voice purred drowsily! How her hips moved gently about, now pressing against the fence, now swelling back like a summer beach-wave, and then pressing the fence again! Who in the world could put so much husky meaning into *"Ai, amigo, a'onde vas?"*

It is true that ordinarily her voice was shrill, her face hard and sharp as a hatchet, her figure lumpy, and her intentions selfish. The softer self came into possession only once or twice a week, and then, ordinarily, in the evening.

When Sweets heard that Danny was an heir, she was glad for him. She dreamed of being his lady, as did every other female on Tortilla Flat. In the evenings she leaned over the front gate waiting for the time when he would pass by and fall into her trap. But for a long time her baited trap caught nothing but poor Indians and paisanos who owned no houses, and whose clothes were sometimes fugitive from better wardrobes.

Sweets was not content. Her house was up the hill from Danny's house, in a direction he did not often take. Sweets could not go looking for him. She was a lady, and her conduct was governed by very strict rules of propriety. If Danny should walk by, now, if they should talk, like the old friends they were, if he should come in for a social glass of wine; and then, if nature proved too strong, and her feminine resistance too weak, there was no grave breach of propriety. But it was unthinkable to leave her web on the front gate.

For many months of evenings she waited in vain, and took such gifts as walked by in jeans. But there are only a limited number of pathways on Tortilla Flat. It was inevitable that Danny should, sooner or later, pass the gate of Dolores Engracia Ramirez; and so he did.

In all the time they had known each other, there

had never been an occasion when it was more to
Sweets' advantage to have him walk by; for Danny had
only that morning found a keg of copper shingle nails,
lost by the Central Supply Company. He had judged
them jetsam because no member of the company was
anywhere near. Danny removed the copper nails from
the keg and put them in a sack. Then, borrowing the
Pirate's wheelbarrow, and the Pirate to push it, he
took his salvage to the Western Supply Company,
where he sold the copper for three dollars. The keg he
gave to the Pirate.

"You can keep things in it," he said. That made the
Pirate very happy.

And now Danny came down the hill, aimed with a
fine accuracy toward the house of Torrelli, and the
three dollars were in his pocket.

Dolores' voice sounded as huskily sweet as the
drone of a bumblebee. *"Ai, amigo, a'onde vas?"*

Danny stopped. A revolution took place in his
plans. "How are you, Sweets?"

"What difference is it how I am? None of my friends
are interested," she said archly. And her hips floated
in a graceful and circular undulation.

"What do you mean?" he demanded.

"Well, does my friend Danny ever come to see me?"

"I am here to see thee now," he said gallantly.

She opened the gate a little. "Wilt thou come in for
a tiny glass of wine in friendship's name?" Danny went
into her house. "What hast thou been doing in the
forest?" she cooed.

Then he made an error. He told vaingloriously of his
transaction up the hill, and boasted of his three
dollars.

"Of course I have only enough wine to fill two thimbles," she said.

They sat in Sweets' kitchen and drank a glass of wine. In a little while Danny assaulted her virtue with true gallantry and vigor. He found to his amazement a resistance out of all proportion to her size and reputation. The ugly beast of lust was awakened in him. He was angry. Only when he was leaving was the way made clear to him.

The husky voice said, "Maybe you would like to come and see me this evening, Danny." Sweets' eyes swam in a mist of drowsy invitation. "One has neighbors," she suggested with delicacy.

Then he understood. "I will come back," he promised.

It was midafternoon. Danny walked down the street, reaimed at Torrelli's; and the beast in him had changed. From a savage and snarling wolf it had become a great, shaggy, sentimental bear. "I will take wine to that nice Sweets," he thought.

On the way down, whom should he meet but Pablo, and Pablo had two sticks of gum. He gave one to Danny and fell into step. "Where goest thou?"

"It is no time for friendship," Danny said tartly. "First I go to buy a little wine to take to a lady. You may come with me, and have one glass only. I am tired of buying wine for ladies only to have my friends drink it all up."

Pablo agreed that such a practice was unendurable. For himself, he didn't want Danny's wine, but only his companionship.

They went to Torrelli's. They had a glass of wine out of the new bought gallon. Danny confessed that it was shabby treatment to give his friend only one little glass. Over Pablo's passionate protest they had another. Ladies, Danny thought, should not drink too much wine. They were apt to become silly; and besides, it dulled some of those senses one liked to find alert in a lady. They had a few more glasses. Half a gallon of wine was a bountiful present, especially as Danny was about to go down to buy another present. They measured down half a gallon and drank what was over. Then Danny hid the jug in the weeds in a ditch.

"I would like you to come with me to buy the present, Pablo," he said.

Pablo knew the reason for the invitation. Half of it was a desire for Pablo's company, and half was fear of leaving the wine while Pablo was at large. They walked with studied dignity and straightness down the hill of Monterey.

Mr. Simon, of Simon's Investment, Jewelry, and Loan Company, welcomed them into his store. The name of the store defined the outward limits of the merchandise the company sold; for there were saxophones, radios, rifles, knives, fishing-rods, and old coins on the counter; all secondhand, but all really better than new because they were just well broken-in.

"Something you would like to see?" Mr. Simon asked.

"Yes," said Danny.

The proprietor named over a tentative list and then stopped in the middle of a word, for he saw that Danny was looking at a large aluminum vacuum-cleaner. The dust-bag was blue and yellow checks. The electric cord was long and black and slick. Mr. Simon went to it and rubbed it with his hand and stood off and admired it. "Something in a vacuum-cleaner?" he asked.

"How much?"

"For this one, fourteen dollars." It was not a price so much as an endeavor to find out how much Danny had. And Danny wanted it, for it was large and shiny. No woman of Tortilla Flat had one. In this moment he forgot there was no electricity on Tortilla Flat. He laid his two dollars on the counter and waited while the explosion took place; the fury, the rage, the sadness, the poverty, the ruin, the cheating. The polish was invoked, the color of the bag, the extra long cord, the value of the metal alone. And when it was all over, Danny went out carrying the vacuum-cleaner.

Often as a *pasatiempo* in the afternoon, Sweets brought out the vacuum-cleaner and leaned it against a chair. While her friends looked on, she pushed it back and forth to show how easily it rolled. And she made a humming with her voice to imitate a motor.

"My friend is a rich man," she said. "I think pretty soon there will be wires full of electricity coming right into the house, and then zip and zip and zip! And you have the house clean!"

Her friends tried to belittle the present, saying, "It is too bad you can't run this machine." And, "I have always held that a broom and dust-pan, *properly* used, are more thorough."

But their envy could do nothing against the vacuum. Through its possession Sweets climbed to the peak of the social scale of Tortilla Flat. People who did not remember her name referred to her as "that one with the sweeping-machine." Often when her enemies passed the house, Sweets could be seen through the window,

pushing the cleaner back and forth, while a loud humming came from her throat. Indeed, after she had swept
her house every day, she pushed the cleaner about on
the theory that of course it would clean better with
electricity but one could not have everything.

She excited envy in many houses. Her manner became dignified and gracious, and she held her chin
high as befitted one who had a sweeping-machine. In
her conversation she included it. "Ramon passed this
morning while I was pushing the sweeping-machine";
"Louise Meater cut her hand this morning, not three
hours after I had been pushing the sweeping-machine."

But in her elevation she did not neglect Danny. Her
voice growled with emotion when he was about. She
swayed like a pine tree in the wind. And he spent
every evening at the house of Sweets.

At first his friends ignored his absence, for it is
the right of every man to have these little affairs. But
as the weeks went on, and as a rather violent domes-
tic life began to make Danny listless and pale, his
friends became convinced that Sweets' gratitude for
the sweeping-machine was not to Danny's best physical interests. They were jealous of a situation that
was holding his attention so long.

Pilon and Pablo and Jesus Maria Corcoran in turn
assaulted the nest of his affections during his absence;
but Sweets, while she was sensible of the compliment,
remained true to the man who had raised her position
to such a gratifying level. She tried to keep their
friendship for a future time of need, for she knew how
fickle fortune is; but she stoutly refused to share with
Danny's friends that which was dedicated for the time
being to Danny.

Wherefore the friends, in despair, organized a group, formed for and dedicated to her destruction.

It may be that Danny, deep in his soul, was beginning to tire of Sweets' affection and the duty of attendance it demanded. If such a change were taking place, he did not admit it to himself.

At three o'clock one afternoon Pilon and Pablo and Jesus Maria, followed vaguely by Big Joe Portagee, returned triumphant from three-quarters of a day of strenuous effort. Their campaign had called into play and taxed to the limit the pitiless logic of Pilon, the artistic ingenuousness of Pablo, and the gentleness and humanity of Jesus Maria Corcoran. Big Joe had contributed nothing.

But now, like four hunters, they returned from the chase more happy because their victory had been a difficult one. And in Monterey a poor puzzled Italian came gradually to the conviction that he had been swindled.

Pilon carried a gallon jug of wine concealed in a bundle of ivy. They marched joyfully into Danny's house, and Pilon set the gallon on the table.

Danny, awakened out of a sound sleep, smiled quietly, got up from bed, and laid out the fruit jars. He poured the wine. His four friends fell into chairs, for it had been an exhausting day.

They drank quietly in the late afternoon, that time of curious intermission. Nearly everyone in Tortilla Flat stops then and considers those things that have taken place in the day just past, and thinks over the possibilities of the evening. There are many things to discuss in an afternoon.

"Cornelia Ruiz got a new man this morning," Pilon

observed. "He has a bald head. His name is Kilpatrick. Cornelia says her other man didn't come home three nights last week. She didn't like that."

"Cornelia is a woman who changes her mind too quickly," said Danny. He thought complacently of his own sure establishment, built on the rock of the vacuum-cleaner.

"Cornelia's father was worse," said Pablo. "He could not tell the truth. Once he borrowed a dollar from me. I have told Cornelia about it, and she does nothing."

"Two of one blood. 'Know the breed and know the dog,' " Pilon quoted virtuously.

Danny poured the jars full of wine again, and the gallon was exhausted. He looked ruefully at it.

Jesus Maria, that lover of the humanities, spoke up quietly. "I saw Susie Francisco, Pilon. She said the recipe worked fine. She has been out riding with Charlie Guzman on his motorcycle three times. The first two times she gave him the love medicine it made him sick. She thought it was no good. But now Susie says you can have some cookies any time."

"What was in that potion?" Pablo asked.

Pilon became secretive. "I cannot tell all of it. I guess it must have been the poison oak in it that made Charlie Guzman sick."

The gallon of wine had gone too quickly. Each of the six friends was conscious of a thirst so sharp that it was a pain of desire. Pilon looked at his friends with drooped eyes, and they looked back at him. The conspiracy was ready.

Pilon cleared his throat. "What hast thou done, Danny, to set the whole town laughing at thee?"

Danny looked worried. "What do you mean?"

Pilon chuckled. "It is said by many that you bought a sweeping-machine for a lady, and that machine will not work unless wires are put into the house. Those wires cost a great deal of money. Some people find this present very funny."

Danny grew uncomfortable. "That lady likes the sweeping-machine," he said defensively.

"Why not?" Pablo agreed. "She has told some people that you have promised to put wires into her house so the sweeping-machine will work."

Danny looked even more perturbed. "Did she say that?"

"So I was told."

"Well, I will not," Danny cried.

"If I did not think it funny, I should be angry to hear my friend laughed at," Pilon observed.

"What will you do when she asks for those wires?" Jesus Maria asked.

"I will tell her 'no,'" said Danny.

Pilon laughed. "I wish I could be there. It is not such a simple thing to tell that lady 'no.'"

Danny felt that his friends were turning against him. "What shall I do?" he asked helplessly.

Pilon gave the matter his grave consideration and brought his realism to bear on the subject. "If that lady did not have the sweeping-machine, she would not want those wires," he said.

The friends nodded in agreement. "Therefore," Pilon continued, "the thing to do is to remove the sweeping-machine."

"Oh, she wouldn't let me take it," Danny protested.

"Then we will help you," said Pilon. "I will take the

machine, and in return you can take the lady a present of a gallon of wine. She will not even know where the sweeping-machine has gone."

"Some neighbor will see you take it."

"Oh, no," said Pilon. "You stay here, Danny. I will get the machine."

Danny sighed with relief that his problem was assumed by his good friends.

There were few things going on in Tortilla Flat that Pilon did not know. His mind made sharp little notes of everything that his eyes saw or his ears heard. He knew that Sweets went to the store at four-thirty every afternoon. He depended upon this almost invariable habit to put his plan into effect.

"It is better that you do not know anything about it," he told Danny.

In the yard Pilon had a gunny sack in readiness. With his knife he cut a generous branch from the rose bush and pushed it into the sack.

At Sweets' house he found her absent, as he had expected and hoped she would be. "It is really Danny's machine," he told himself.

It was a moment's work to enter the house, to put the vacuum-cleaner in the sack, and to arrange the rose branch artistically in the sack's mouth.

As he came out of the yard, he met Sweets. Pilon took off his hat politely. "I stepped in to pass the time," he said.

"Will you stop now, Pilon?"

"No. I have business in Monterey. It is late."

"Where do you go with this rose bush?"

"A man in Monterey is to buy it. A very fine rose bush. See how strong it is."

"Stop in some other time, Pilon."

He heard no cry of anger as he walked sedately down the street. "Perhaps she will not miss it for a while," he thought.

Half the problem was solved, but half was yet to be approached. "What can Danny do with this sweeping-machine?" Pilon asked himself. "If he has it, Sweets will know he has taken it. Can I throw it away? No, for it is valuable. The thing to do would be to get rid of it and still to reap the benefit of its value."

Now the whole problem was solved. Pilon headed down the hill toward Torrelli's house.

It was a large and shining vacuum-cleaner. When Pilon came again up the hill, he had a gallon of wine in each hand.

The friends received him in silence when he entered Danny's house. He set one jug on the table and the other on the floor.

"I have brought you a present to take to the lady," he told Danny. "And here is a little wine for us."

They gathered happily, for their thirst was a raging fire. When the first gallon was far gone, Pilon held his glass to the candlelight and looked through it. "Things that happen are of no importance," he said. "But from everything that happens, there is a lesson to be learned. By this we learn that a present, especially to a lady, should have no quality that will require a further present. Also we learn that it is sinful to give presents of too great value, for they may excite greed."

The first gallon was gone. The friends looked at Danny to see how he felt about it. He had been very quiet, but now he saw that his friends were waiting on him.

"That lady was lively," he said judiciously. "That lady had a very sympathetic nature. But God damn it!" he said, "I'm sick of it!" He went to the second jug and drew the cork.

The Pirate, sitting in the corner among his dogs, smiled to himself and whispered in admiration, " 'God damn it, I'm sick of it.' " That, thought the Pirate, was very fine.

They had not more than half finished the second jug, indeed they had sung only two songs, when young Johnny Pom-pom came in. "I was at Torrelli's," Johnny said. "Oh, that Torrelli is mad! He is shouting! He is beating on the table with his fists."

The friends looked up with mild interest. "Something has happened. It is probable Torrelli deserves it."

"Often he has refused his good customers a little glass of wine."

"What is the matter with Torrelli?" Pablo asked.

Johnny Pom-pom accepted a jar of wine. "Torrelli says he bought a sweeping-machine from Pilon, and when he hooked it up to his light wire, it would not work. So he looked on the inside, and it had no motor. He says he will kill Pilon."

Pilon looked shocked. "I did not know this machine was at fault," he said. "But did I not say Torrelli deserved what was the matter with him? That machine was worth three or four gallons of wine, but that miser Torrelli would give no more than two."

Danny still felt a glow of gratitude toward Pilon. He smacked his lips on his wine. "This stuff of Torrelli's is getting worse and worse," he said. "At its best it is swill the pigs leave, but lately it is so bad that Charlie Marsh even would not drink it."

They all felt a little bit revenged on Torrelli then.

"I think," said Danny, "that we will buy our wine some place else, if Torrelli does not look out."

10

HOW THE FRIENDS SOLACED A CORPORAL AND IN RETURN RECEIVED A LESSON IN PATERNAL ETHICS.

Jesus Maria Corcoran was a pathway for the humanities. Suffering he tried to relieve; sorrow he tried to assuage; happiness he shared. No hard nor haunted Jesus Maria existed. His heart was free for the use of anyone who had a use for it. His resources and wits were at the disposal of anyone who had less of either than had Jesus Maria.

He it was who carried José de la Nariz four miles when José's leg was broken. When Mrs. Palochico lost the goat of her heart, the good goat of milk and cheese, it was Jesus Maria who traced that goat to Big Joe Portagee and halted the murder and made Big Joe give it back. It was Jesus Maria who once picked Charlie Marsh out of a ditch where he lay in his own filth, a deed which required not only a warm heart, but a strong stomach.

Together with his capacity for doing good, Jesus

Maria had a gift for coming in contact with situations where good wanted doing.

Such was his reputation that Pilon had once said, "If that Jesus Maria had gone into the Church, Monterey would have had a saint for the calendar, I tell you."

Out of some deep pouch in his soul Jesus Maria drew kindness that renewed itself by withdrawal.

It was Jesus Maria's practice to go to the post office every day, first because there he could see many people whom he knew, and second because on that windy post office corner he could look at the legs of a great many girls. It must not be supposed that in this latter interest there was any vulgarity. As soon criticize a man who goes to art galleries or to concerts. Jesus Maria liked to look at girls' legs.

One day when he had leaned against the post office for two hours with very little success, he was witness to a pitiful scene. A policeman came along the sidewalk leading a young boy of about sixteen, and the boy carried a little baby wrapped in a piece of gray blanket.

The policeman was saying, "I don't care if I can't understand you. You can't sit in the gutter all day. We'll find out about you."

And the boy, in Spanish with a peculiar inflection, said, "But, señor, I do nothing wrong. Why do you take me away?"

The policeman saw Jesus Maria. "Hey, paisano," he called. "What's this *cholo* talking about?"

Jesus Maria stepped out and addressed the boy. "Can I be of service to you?"

The boy broke into a relieved flood. "I came here to

work. Some Mexican men said there would be work here, and there was none. I was sitting down resting when this man came to me and dragged me away."

Jesus Maria nodded and turned back to the policeman. "Has he done some crime, this little one?"

"No, but he's been sitting in the gutter on Alvarado Street for about three hours."

"He is a friend of mine," Jesus Maria said. "I will take care of him."

"Well, keep him out of the gutter."

Jesus Maria and his new friend walked up the hill. "I will take you to the house where I live. There you will have something to eat. What baby is this?"

"It is my baby," said the boy. "I am a *caporál*, and he is my baby. He is sick now; but when he grows up, he is going to be a *generál*."

"What is he sick from, Señor Caporál?"

"I don't know. He is just sick." He showed the baby's face, and it looked very ill indeed.

The sympathies of Jesus Maria mounted. "The house where I live is owned by my friend Danny, and there is a good man, Señor Caporál. There is one to appeal to when trouble is upon one. Look, we will go there, and that Danny will give us shelter. My friend Mrs. Palochico has a goat. We will borrow a little milk for the baby."

The corporal's face for the first time wore a smile of comfort. "It is good to have friends," he said. "In Torreón I have many friends who would make themselves beggars to help me." He boasted a little to Jesus Maria. "I have rich friends, but of course they do not know my need."

Pilon pushed open the gate of Danny's yard, and

they entered together. Danny and Pablo and Big Joe were sitting in the living room, waiting for the daily miracle of food. Jesus Maria pushed the boy into the room.

"Here is a young soldier, a *caporál*," he explained. "He has a baby here with him, and that baby is sick."

The friends arose with alacrity. The corporal threw back the gray blanket from the baby's face.

"He is sick, all right," Danny said. "Maybe we should get a doctor."

But the soldier shook his head. "No doctors. I do not like doctors. This baby does not cry, and he will not eat much. Maybe when he rests, then he will be well again."

At this moment Pilon entered and inspected the child. "This baby is sick," he said.

Pilon immediately took control. Jesus Maria he sent to Mrs. Palochico's house to borrow goat milk; Big Joe and Pablo to get an apple box, pad it with dry grass, and line it with a sheepskin coat. Danny offered his bed, but it was refused. The corporal stood in the living room and smiled gently on these good people. At last the baby lay in its box, but its eyes were listless and it refused the milk.

The Pirate came in, bearing a bag of mackerels. The friends cooked the fish and had their dinner. The baby would not even eat mackerel. Every now and then one of the friends jumped up and ran to look at the baby. When supper was over, they sat about the stove and prepared for a quiet evening.

The corporal had been silent, had given no account of himself. The friends were a little hurt at this, but they knew he would tell them in time. Pilon, to whom knowledge was as gold to be mined, made a few tentative drills into the corporal's reticence.

"It is not often that one sees a young soldier with a baby," he suggested delicately.

The corporal grinned with pride.

Pablo added, "This baby was probably found in the garden of love. And that is the best kind of babies, for only good things are in it."

"We too have been soldiers," said Danny. "When we die, we will go to the grave on a gun carriage, and a firing squad will shoot over us."

They waited to see whether the corporal would improve upon the opportunity they had offered. The corporal looked his appreciation. "You have been good to me," he said. "You have been as good and kind as my friends in Torreón would be. This is my baby, the baby of my wife."

"And where is your wife?" Pilon asked.

The corporal lost his smile. "She is in Mexico," he said. Then he grew vivacious again. "I met a man, and he told me a curious thing. He said we can make of babies what we will. He said, 'You tell the baby often what you want him to do, and when he grows up he will do that.' Over and over I tell this baby, 'You will be a *generál*.' Do you think it will be so?"

The friends nodded politely. "It may be," said Pilon. "I have not heard of this practice."

"I say twenty times a day, 'Manuel, you will be a *generál* some day. You will have big epaulets and a sash. Your sword will be gold. You will ride a palomino horse. What a life for you, Manuel!' The man said he surely will be a *generál* if I say it so."

Danny got up and went to the apple box. "You will be a *generál*," he said to the baby. "When you grow up you will be a great *generál*."

The others trooped over to see whether the formula had had any effect.

The Pirate whispered, "You will be a *generál*," and he wondered whether the same method would work on a dog.

"This baby is sick all right," Danny said. "We must keep him warm."

They went back to their seats.

"Your wife is in Mexico——" Pilon suggested.

The corporal wrinkled his brows and thought for a while, and then he smiled brilliantly. "I will tell you. It is not a thing to tell to strangers, but you are my friends. I was a soldier in Chihuahua, and I was diligent and clean and kept oil in my rifle, so that I became a *caporál*. And then I was married to a beautiful girl. I do not say that it was not because of the chevrons that she married me. But she was very beautiful and young. Her eyes were bright, she had good white teeth, and her hair was long and shining. So pretty soon this baby was born."

"That is good," said Danny. "I should like to be you. There is nothing so good as a baby."

"Yes," said the corporal, "I was glad. And we went in to the baptism, and I wore a sash, although the book of the army did not mention it. And when we came out of that church, a *capitán* with epaulets and a sash and a silver sword saw my wife. Pretty soon my wife went away. Then I went to that *capitán* and I said, 'Give me back my wife,' and he said, 'You do not value your life, to talk this way to your superior.' "

The corporal spread his hands and lifted his shoulders in a gesture of caged resignation.

"Oh, that thief!" cried Jesus Maria.

"You gathered your friends. You killed that *capitán*," Pablo anticipated.

The corporal looked self-conscious. "No. There was nothing to do. The first night, someone shot at me through the window. The second day a field gun went off by mistake and it came so close to me that the wind knocked me down. So I went away from there, and I took the baby with me."

There was fierceness in the faces of the friends, and their eyes were dangerous. The Pirate, in his corner, snarled, and all the dogs growled.

"We should have been there," Pilon cried. "We would have made that *capitán* wish he had never lived. My grandfather suffered at the hands of a priest, and he tied that priest naked to a post in a corral and turned a little calf in with him. Oh, there are ways."

"I was only a *caporál*," said the boy. "I had to run away." Tears of shame were in his eyes. "There is no help for a *caporál* when a *capitán* is against him; so I ran away, with the baby Manuel. In Fresno I met this wise man, and he told me I could make Manuel be what I wished. I tell that baby twenty times every day, 'You will be a *generál*. You will wear epaulets and carry a golden sword.' "

Here was drama that made the experiments of Cornelia Ruiz seem uninteresting and vain. Here was a situation which demanded the action of the friends. But its scene was so remote that action was impossible. They looked in admiration at the corporal. He was so young to have had such an adventure!

"I wish," Danny said wickedly, "that we were in Torreón now. Pilon would make a plan for us. It is too bad we cannot go there."

Big Joe Portagee had stayed awake, a tribute to the fascination of the corporal's story. He went to the apple box and looked in. "You going to be a general," he said. And then, "Look! This baby is moving funny." The friends crowded around. The spasm had already started. The little feet kicked down and then drew up. The hands crawled about helplessly, and then the baby scrabbled and shuddered.

"A doctor," Danny cried. "We must have a doctor." But he and everyone knew it was no use. Approaching death wears a cloak no one ever mistakes. While they watched, the baby stiffened and the struggle ended. The mouth dropped open, and the baby was dead. In kindness Danny covered the apple box with a piece of blanket. The corporal stood very straight and stared before him, so shocked that he could not speak nor think.

Jesus Maria laid a hand on his shoulder and led him to a chair. "You are so young," he said. "You will have many more babies."

The corporal moaned, "Now he is dead. Now he will never be a *generál* with that sash and that sword."

There were tears in the eyes of the friends. In the corner all the dogs whined miserably. The Pirate buried his big head in the fur of Señor Alec Thompson.

In a soft tone, almost a benediction, Pilon said, "Now you yourself must kill the *capitán*. We honor you for a noble plan of revenge. But that is over and you must take your own vengeance, and we will help you, if we can."

The corporal turned dull eyes to meet him. "Revenge?" he asked. "Kill the *capitán*? What do you mean?"

"Why, it was plain what your plan was," Pilon said. "This baby would grow up, and he would be a *generál*; and in time he would find that *capitán*, and he would kill him slowly. It was a good plan. The long waiting, and then the stroke. We, your friends, honor you for it."

The corporal was looking bewilderedly at Pilon. "What is this?" he demanded. "I have nothing to do with this *capitán*. He is the *capitán*."

The friends sat forward.

Pilon cried, "Then what was this plan to make the baby a *generál*? Why was that?"

The corporal was a little embarrassed then. "It is the duty of a father to do well by his child. I wanted Manuel to have more good things than I had."

"Is that all?" Danny cried.

"Well," said the corporal, "my wife was so pretty, and she was not any *puta*, either. She was a good woman, and that *capitán* took her. He had little epaulets, and a little sash, and his sword was only of a silver color. Consider," said the corporal, and he spread out his hands, "if that *capitán*, with the little epaulets and the little sash, could take my wife, imagine what a *generál* with a big sash and gold sword could take!"

There was a long silence while Danny and Pilon and Pablo and Jesus Maria and the Pirate and Big Joe Portagee digested the principle. And when it was digested, they waited for Danny to speak.

"It is to be pitied," said Danny at last, "that so few

parents have the well-being of their children at heart. Now we are more sorry than ever that the baby is gone, for with such a father, what a happy life he has missed."

All of the friends nodded solemnly.

"What will you do now?" asked Jesus Maria, the discoverer.

"I will go back to Mexico," said the corporal. "I am a soldier in my heart. It may be, if I keep oiling my rifle, I myself may be an officer some day. Who can tell?"

The six friends looked at him admiringly. They were proud to have known such a man.

11

HOW, UNDER THE MOST ADVERSE CIRCUMSTANCES, LOVE CAME TO BIG JOE PORTAGEE.

For Big Joe Portagee, to feel love was to do something about it. And this is the history of one of his love affairs.

It had been raining in Monterey; from the tall pines the water dripped all day. The paisanos of Tortilla Flat did not come out of their houses, but from every chimney a blue column of pinewood smoke drifted so that the air smelled clean and fresh and perfumed.

At five o'clock in the afternoon the rain stopped for a few moments, and Big Joe Portagee, who had been under a rowboat on the beach most of the day, came out and started up the hill toward Danny's house. He was cold and hungry.

When he came to the very edge of Tortilla Flat, the skies opened and the rain poured down. In an instant Big Joe was soaked through. He ran into the nearest house to get out of the rain, and that house was inhabited by Tia Ignacia.

The lady was about forty-five, a widow of long standing and some success. Ordinarily she was taciturn and harsh, for there was in her veins more Indian blood than is considered decent in Tortilla Flat.

When Big Joe entered she had just opened a gallon of red wine and was preparing to pour out a glass for her stomach's sake. Her attempt to push the jug under a chair was unsuccessful. Big Joe stood in her doorway, dripping water on the floor.

"Come in and get dry," said Tia Ignacia. Big Joe, watching the bottle as a terrier watches a bug, entered the room. The rain roared down on the roof. Tia Ignacia poked up a blaze in her airtight stove.

"Would you care for a glass of wine?"

"Yes," said Big Joe. Before he had finished his first glass, Big Joe's eyes had refastened themselves on the jug. He drank three glasses before he consented to say a word, and before the wolfishness went out of his eyes.

Tia Ignacia had given her new jug of wine up for lost. She drank with him as the only means to preserve a little of it to her own use. It was only when the fourth glass of wine was in his hand that Big Joe relaxed and began to enjoy himself.

"This is not Torrelli's wine," he said.

"No, I get it from an Italian lady who is my friend." She poured out another glass.

The early evening came. Tia Ignacia lighted a kerosene lamp and put some wood in the fire. As long as the wine must go, it must go, she thought. Her eyes dwelt on the huge frame of Big Joe Portagee with critical appraisal. A little flush warmed her chest.

"You have been working out in the rain, poor man,"
she said. "Here, take off your coat and let it dry."

Big Joe rarely told a lie. His mind didn't work
quickly enough. "I been on the beach under a rowboat, asleep," he said.

"But you are all wet, poor fellow." She inspected
him for some response to her kindness, but on Big
Joe's face nothing showed except gratification at being
out of the rain and drinking wine. He put out his glass
to be filled again. Having eaten nothing all day, the
wine was having a profound effect on him.

Tia Ignacia addressed herself anew to the problem.
"It is not good to sit in a wet coat. You will be ill with
cold. Come, let me help you to take off your coat."

Big Joe wedged himself comfortably into his chair.
"I'm all right," he said stubbornly.

Tia Ignacia poured herself another glass. The fire
made a rushing sound to counteract with comfort the
drumming of water on the roof.

Big Joe made absolutely no move to be friendly, to
be gallant, even to recognize the presence of his host-
ess. He drank his wine in big swallows. He smiled
stupidly at the stove. He rocked himself a little in the
chair.

Anger and despair arose in Tia Ignacia. "This pig,"
she thought, "this big and dirty animal. It would be
better for me if I brought some cow in the house out of
the rain. Another man would say some little friendly
word at least."

Big Joe stuck out his glass to be filled again.

Now Tia Ignacia strove heroically. "In a little warm
house there is happiness on such a night," she said.
"When the rain is dripping and the stove burns

sweetly, then is a time for people to feel friendly.
Don't you feel friendly?"

"Sure," said Big Joe.

"Perhaps the light is too bright in your eyes," she
said coyly. "Would you like me to blow out the light?"

"It don't bother me none," said Big Joe, "if you
want to save oil, go ahead."

She blew down the lamp chimney, and the room
leaped to darkness. Then she went back to her chair
and waited for his gallantry to awaken. She could hear
the gentle rocking of his chair. A little light came from
the cracks of the stove and struck the shiny corners of
the furniture. The room was nearly luminous with
warmth. Tia Ignacia heard his chair stop rocking and
braced herself to repel him. Nothing happened.

"To think," she said, "you might be out in this
storm, shivering in a shed or lying on the cold sand
under a boat. But no; you are sitting in a good chair,
drinking good wine, in the company of a lady who is
your friend."

There was no answer from Big Joe. She could
neither hear him nor see him. Tia Ignacia drank off
her glass. She threw virtue to the winds. "My friend
Cornelia Ruiz has told me that some of her best friends
came to her out of the rain and cold. She comforted
them, and they were her good friends."

The sound of a little crash came from the direction
of Big Joe. She knew he had dropped his glass, but no
movement followed the crash. "Perhaps he is ill," she
thought. "Maybe he has fainted." She jumped up,
lighted a match, and set it to the lamp wick. And then
she turned to her guest.

Big Joe was mountainously asleep. His feet stuck

out ahead of him. His head was back and his mouth wide open. While she looked, amazed and shocked, a tremendous rattling snore came from his mouth. Big Joe simply could not be warm and comfortable without going to sleep.

It was a moment before Tia Ignacia could move all her crowding emotions into line. She inherited a great deal of Indian blood. She did not cry out. No, shivering with rage although she was, she walked to her wood basket, picked out a likely stick, weighed it, put it down, and picked out another one. And then she turned slowly on Big Joe Portagee. The first blow caught him on the shoulder and knocked him out of the chair.

"Pig!" Tia Ignacia screamed. "Big dirty garbage! Out in the mud with you!"

Joe rolled over on the floor. The next blow made a muddy indentation on the seat of his pants. Big Joe was waking up rapidly now.

"Huh?" he said. "What's the matter? What you doing?"

"I'll show you," she screamed. She flung open her door and ran back to him. Big Joe staggered to his feet under the beating. The stick hammered at his back and shoulders and head. He ran out of the door, protecting his head with his hands.

"Don't," he pleaded. "Now don't do that. What's the matter?"

The fury followed him like a hornet, down the garden path and into the muddy street. Her rage was terrible. She followed him along the street, still beating him.

"Hey," he cried. "Now don't." He grabbed her and

held her while her arms struggled violently to be free to continue the beating.

"Oh, great garbage pig!" she cried. "Oh, cow!"

He could not let her go without more beating, so he held her tightly; and as he stood there, love came to Big Joe Portagee. It sang in his head; it roared through his body like a great freshet; it shook him as a tropical storm shakes a forest of palms. He held her tightly for a moment, until her anger relaxed.

In the night, in Monterey, a policeman patrols the streets on a motorcycle to see that good things come to no evil. Jake Lake rode about now, his slicker shining dully, like basalt. He was unhappy and uncomfortable. It was not so bad on the paved streets, but part of his route lay through the mud paths of Tortilla Flat, and there the yellow mud splashed nastily. His little light flashed about. The motor coughed with effort.

All of a sudden Jake Lake cried out in astonishment and stopped his motor. "What the devil! Say, what the hell is this?"

Big Joe twisted his neck. "Oh, is that you, Jake? Say, Jake, as long as you're going to take us to jail anyway, can't you just wait a minute?"

The policeman turned his motor around. "You get out of the street," he said. "Somebody'll come along and run over you."

His motor roared in the mud, and the flicker of his little headlight disappeared around the corner. The rain pattered gently among the trees of Tortilla Flat.

12

HOW DANNY'S FRIENDS ASSISTED THE PIRATE TO KEEP A VOW, AND HOW AS A REWARD FOR MERIT THE PIRATE'S DOGS SAW A HOLY VISION.

Every afternoon the pirate pushed his empty wheelbarrow up the hill and into Danny's yard. He leaned it against the fence and covered it with a sack; then he buried his ax in the ground, for, as everyone knows, it makes steel much harder to be buried. Last, he went into the house, reached into a Bull Durham bag which hung around his neck on a string, took out the day's quarter dollar, and gave it to Danny. Then Danny and the Pirate and any other of the friends who happened to be in the house went solemnly into the bedroom, stepping over the bedding that littered the floor. While the paisanos looked on, Danny reached under his pillow, brought out the canvas bag, and deposited the new quarter. This practice had continued for a long time.

The bag of money had become the symbolic center of the friendship, the point of trust about which the fraternity revolved. They were proud of the money, proud that they had never tampered with it. About the guardianship of the Pirate's money there had grown a structure of self-respect and not a little complacency. It is a fine thing for a man to be trusted. This money had long ceased, in the minds of the friends, to be currency. It is true that for a time they had dreamed of how much wine it would buy, but after a while they lost the conception of it as legal tender. The hoard was aimed at a gold candlestick, and this potential candlestick was the property of San Francisco de Assisi. It is far worse to defraud a saint than it is to take liberties with the law.

One evening, by that quick and accurate telegraph no one understands, news came in that a Coast Guard cutter had gone on the rocks near Carmel. Big Joe Portagee was away on business of his own, but Danny and Pablo and Pilon and Jesus Maria and the Pirate and his dogs joyfully started over the ridge; for if there was anything they loved, it was to pick up usable articles on the beach. This they thought the most exciting thing in the world. Although they arrived a little late, they made up for lost time. All night the friends scurried about the beach, and they accumulated a good pile of flotsam, a five-pound can of butter, several cases of canned goods, a water-soaked Bowditch, two pea jackets, a water barrel from a lifeboat, and a machine gun. When daylight came they had a goodly pile under guard.

They accepted a lump sum of five dollars for the lot from one of the spectators, for it was out of the question to carry all those heavy things over six miles of steep hillside to Tortilla Flat.

Because he had not cut his day's wood, the Pirate

received a quarter from Danny, and he put it in his
Bull Durham bag. Then they started tiredly, but with a
warm and expectant happiness, straight over the hills
to Monterey.

It was afternoon when they got back to Danny's
house. The Pirate ritualistically opened his bag and
gave the quarter to Danny. The whole squad trooped
into the other room. Danny reached under the pillow—
and his hand came out empty. He threw the pillow
back, threw the mattress back, and then he turned
slowly to his friends, and his eyes had become as
fierce as a tiger's eyes. He looked from face to face,
and on every one saw horror and indignation that could
not be simulated.

"Well," he said, "—well." The Pirate began to cry.
Danny put his arm around his shoulder. "Do not cry,
little friend," he said ominously. "Thou wilt have thy
money again."

The paisanos went silently out of the room. Danny
walked out into the yard and found a heavy pine stick
three feet long, and swung it experimentally. Pablo
went into the kitchen and returned bearing an ancient
can-opener with a vicious blade. Jesus Maria from
under the house pulled out a broken pick handle. The
Pirate watched them bewilderedly. They all came back
to the house and sat quietly down.

The Pirate aimed down the hill with his thumb.
"Him?" he asked.

Danny nodded slowly. His eyes were veiled and
deadly. His chin stuck out, and, as he sat in the chair,
his whole body weaved a little, like a rattlesnake aiming to strike.

The Pirate went into the yard and dug up his ax.

For a long time they sat in the house. No words were spoken, but a wave of cold fury washed and crouched in the room. The feeling in the house was the feeling of a rock when the fuse is burning in toward the dynamite.

The afternoon waned; the sun went behind the hill. The whole of Tortilla Flat seemed hushed and expectant.

They heard his footsteps on the street and their hands tightened on their sticks. Joe Portagee walked uncertainly up on the porch and in the front door. He had a gallon of wine in his hand. His eyes went uneasily from face to face, but the friends sat still and did not look directly at him.

"Hello," said Big Joe.

"Hello," said Danny. He stood up and stretched lazily. He did not look at Big Joe; he did not walk directly toward him, but at an angle, as though to pass him. When he was abreast, he struck with the speed of a striking snake. Fair on the back of Big Joe's head the stick crashed, and Big Joe went down, completely out.

Danny thoughtfully took a string of rawhide from his pocket and tied the Portagee's thumbs together. "Now water," he said.

Pablo threw a bucket of water in Big Joe's face. He turned his head and stretched his neck like a chicken, and then he opened his eyes and looked dazedly at his friends. They did not speak to him at all. Danny measured his distance carefully, like a golfer addressing the ball. His stick smashed on Big Joe's shoulder; then the friends went about the business in a cold and methodical manner. Jesus Maria took the legs, Danny

the shoulders and chest. Big Joe howled and rolled on
the floor. They covered his body from the neck down.
Each blow found a new space and welted it. The
shrieks were deafening. The Pirate stood helplessly
by, holding his ax.

At last, when the whole front of the body was one
bruise, they stopped. Pablo knelt at Big Joe's head
with his can-opener. Pilon took off the Portagee's
shoes and picked up his stick again.

Then Big Joe squalled with fear. "It's buried out by
the front gate," he cried. "For the love of Christ, don't
kill me!"

Danny and Pilon went out the front door and in a
few minutes they came back, carrying the canvas bag.
"How much did you take out?" Danny asked. There
was no inflection in his voice at all.

"Only four. Honest to God. I only took four, and I'll
work and put them back."

Danny leaned down, took him by the shoulder, and
rolled him over on his face. Then the friends went over
his back with the same deadly precision. The cries
grew weaker, but the work only stopped when Big Joe
was beaten into unconsciousness. Then Pilon tore off
the blue shirt and exposed the pulpy raw back. With
the can-opener he cross-hatched the skin so deftly that
a little blood ran from each line. Pablo brought the salt
to him and helped him to rub it in all over the torn
back. At last Danny threw a blanket over the unconscious man.

"I think he will be honest now," said Danny.

"We should count the money," Pilon observed. "We
have not counted it for a long time." They opened Big
Joe's gallon of wine and poured the fruit jars full, for

they were tired from their work, and their emotions were exhausted.

Then they counted the quarters out in piles of ten, and excitedly counted again. "Pirate," Danny cried, "there are seven over a thousand! Thy time is done! The day is come for thee to buy thy candlestick for San Francisco!"

The day had been too full for the Pirate. He went into the corner with his dogs, and he put his head down on Fluff and burst into hysterical sobs. The dogs moved uneasily about, and they licked his ears and pushed at his head with their noses; but Fluff, sensible of the honor of being chosen, lay quietly and nuzzled the thick hair on the Pirate's neck.

Danny put all the money back in the bag, and the bag under his pillow again.

Now Big Joe came to and groaned, for the salt was working into his back. The paisanos paid no attention to him until at last Jesus Maria, that prey to the humanities, untied Big Joe's thumbs and gave him a jar of wine. "Even the enemies of our Savior gave him a little comfort," he excused himself.

That action broke up the punishment. The friends gathered tenderly about Big Joe. They laid him on Danny's bed and washed the salt out of his wounds. They put cold cloths on his head and kept his jar full of wine. Big Joe moaned whenever they touched him. His morals were probably untouched, but it would have been safe to prophesy that never again would he steal from the paisanos of Danny's house.

The Pirate's hysteria was over. He drank his wine and his face shone with pleasure while he listened to Danny make plans for him.

"If we take all this money into town, to the bank, they will think we have stolen it from a slot machine. We must take this money to Father Ramon and tell him about it. Then he will buy the gold candlestick, and he will bless it, and the Pirate will go into the church. Maybe Father Ramon will say a word about him on Sunday. The Pirate must be there to hear."

Pilon looked distastefully at the Pirate's dirty, ragged clothes. "Tomorrow," he said sternly, "you must take the seven extra two-bitses and buy some decent clothes. For ordinary times these may be all right, but on such an occasion as this you cannot go into the church looking like a gutter rat. It will not be a compliment to your friends."

The Pirate beamed at him. "Tomorrow I will do it," he promised.

The next morning, true to his promise, he went down to Monterey. He shopped carefully and bargained with an astuteness that seemed to belie the fact that he had bought nothing in over two years. He came back to Danny's house in triumph, bearing a huge silk handkerchief in purple and green and also a broad belt studded profusely with colored glass jewels. His friends admired his purchases.

"But what are you going to wear?" Danny asked despairingly. "Two toes are out of your shoes where you cut holes to ease your bunions. You have only ragged overalls and no hat."

"We will have to lend him clothes," said Jesus Maria. "I have a coat and vest. Pilon has his father's good hat. You, Danny, have a shirt, and Big Joe has those fine blue pants."

"But then we can't go," Pilon protested.

"It is not our candlestick," said Jesus Maria. "Father Ramon is not likely to say anything nice about us."

That afternoon they convoyed the treasure to the priest's house. He listened to the story of the sick dog, and his eyes softened. "—And then, Father," said the Pirate, "there was that good little dog, and his nose was dry, and his eyes were like the glass of bottles out of the sea, and he groaned because he hurt inside. And then, Father, I promised the gold candlestick of one thousand days to San Francisco. He is really my patron, Father. And then there was a miracle! For that dog wagged his tail three times, and right away he started to get well. It was a miracle from San Francisco, Father, wasn't it?"

The priest nodded his head gravely. "Yes," he said. "It was a miracle sent by our good Saint Francis. I will buy the candlestick for thee."

The Pirate was very glad, for it is no little thing to have one's prayer answered with a true miracle. If it were noised about, the Pirate would have a higher station on Tortilla Flat. Already his friends looked at him with new respect. They thought no more of his intelligence than they had before, but they knew now that his meager wits were supplemented with all the power of Heaven and all the strength of the saints.

They walked back up to Danny's house, and the dogs walked behind them. The Pirate felt that he had been washed in a golden fluid of beatitude. Little chills and fevers of pleasure chased one another through his body. The paisanos were glad they had guarded his money, for even they took a little holiness

from the act. Pilon was relieved that he had not stolen
the money in the first place. What terrible things
might not have happened if he had taken the two-
bitses belonging to a saint! All of the friends were as
subdued as though they were in church.

The five dollars from the salvage had lain like fire
in Danny's pocket, but now he knew what to do with
it. He and Pilon went to the market and bought seven
pounds of hamburger and a bag of onions and bread
and a big paper of candy. Pablo and Jesus Maria went
to Torrelli's for two gallons of wine, and not a drop did
they drink on the way home either.

That night when the fire was lighted and two
candles burned on the table, the friends feasted themselves to repletion. It was a party in the Pirate's honor.
He behaved himself with a great deal of dignity. He
smiled and smiled when he should have been grave,
though. But he couldn't help that.

After they had eaten enormously, they sat back and
sipped wine out of the fruit jars. "Our little friend,"
they called the Pirate.

Jesus Maria asked, "How did you feel when it happened? When you promised the candlestick and the
dog began to get well, how did you feel? Did you see
any holy vision?"

The Pirate tried to remember. "I don't think so—
maybe I saw a little vision—maybe I saw San Francisco in the air and he was shining like the sun—"

"Wouldn't you remember that?" Pilon demanded.

"Yes—I think I remember—San Francisco looked
on me—and he smiled, like the good saint he is. Then
I knew the miracle was done. He said, 'Be good to
little doggies, you dirty man.'"

"He called you that?"

"Well, I was, and he is not a saint to be telling lies."

"I don't think you remember that at all," said Pablo.

"Well—maybe not. I think I do, though." The Pirate was drunk with happiness from the honor and attention.

"My grandmother saw the Holy Virgin," said Jesus Maria. "She was sick to death, and I myself heard her cry out. She said, 'Ohee. I see the Mother of God. Ohee. My dear Mary, full of grace.'"

"It is given to some to see these things," said Danny. "My father was not a very good man, but he sometimes saw saints, and sometimes he saw bad things. It depended on whether he was good or bad when he saw them. Have you ever seen any other visions, Pirate?"

"No," said the Pirate. "I would be afraid to see any more."

It was a decorous party for a long time. The friends knew that they were not alone this night. Through the walls and the windows and the roof they could feel the eyes of the holy saints looking down upon them.

"On Sunday your candlestick will be there," said Pilon. "We cannot go, for you will be wearing our clothes. I do not say Father Ramon will mention you by name, but maybe he will say something about the candlestick. You must try to remember what he says, Pirate, so you can tell us."

Then Pilon grew stern. "Today, my little friend, there were dogs all over Father Ramon's house. That was all right for today, but you must remember not to take them to the church on Sunday. It is not fitting that dogs should be in the church. Leave the dogs at home."

The Pirate looked disappointed. "They want to go," he cried. "How can I leave them? Where can I leave them?"

Pablo was shocked. "In this affair so far thou hast conducted thyself with merit, little Pirate. Right at the last do you wish to commit sacrilege?"

"No," said the Pirate humbly.

"Then leave thy dogs here, and we will take care of them. It will be a sacrilege to take them into the church."

It was curious how soberly they drank that night. It was three hours before they sang even an obscene song. And it was late before their thoughts strayed to light women. And by the time their minds turned to fighting they were almost too sleepy to fight. This evening was a great good marker in their lives.

On Sunday morning the preparation was violent. They washed the Pirate and inspected his ears and his nostrils. Big Joe, wrapped in a blanket, watched the Pirate put on his blue serge trousers. Pilon brought out his father's hat. They persuaded the Pirate not to wear his jewel-studded belt outside his coat, and showed him how he could leave his coat open so that the jewels flashed now and then. The item of shoes gave the most trouble. Big Joe had the only shoes big enough for the Pirate, and his were worse even than the Pirate's. The difficulty lay in the holes cut for the comfort of bunions, where the toes showed through. Pilon solved it finally with a little soot from the inside of the stove. Well rubbed into the skin, the soot made it quite difficult to see the bunion holes.

At last he was ready; Pilon's father's hat rakishly on his head, Danny's shirt, Big Joe's pants, the huge handkerchief around his neck, and, at intervals, the flashing of the jeweled belt. He walked, for the friends to inspect him, and they looked on critically.

"Pick up your feet, Pirate."

"Don't drag your heels."

"Stop picking at your handkerchief."

"Those people who see you will think you are not in the habit of good clothes."

At last the Pirate turned to his friends. "If those dogs could only come with me," he complained. "I would tell them they must not come in the church."

But the paisanos were firm. "No," said Danny. "They might get in some way. We will keep them here in the house for you."

"They won't like it," said the Pirate helplessly. "They will be lonely, maybe." He turned to the dogs in the corner. "You must stay here," he said. "It would not be good for you to go to church. Stay with my friends until I come back again." And then he slipped out and closed the door behind him. Instantly a wild clamor of barking and howling broke out in the house. Only his faith in the judgment of his friends prevented the Pirate's relenting.

As he walked down the street, he felt naked and unprotected without his dogs. It was as though one of his senses were gone. He was frightened to be out alone. Anyone might attack him. But he walked bravely on, through the town and out to the Church of San Carlos.

Now, before the service began, the swinging doors were open. The Pirate dipped Holy Water out of the marble font, crossed himself, genuflected before the Virgin, went into the church, did his duty to the altar, and sat down. The long church was rather dark, but the high altar was on fire with candles. And in front of the images at the sides, the votive lights were burning. The old and sweet incense perfumed the church.

For a time the Pirate sat looking at the altar, but it was too remote, too holy to think about very much, too unapproachable by a poor man. His eyes sought something warmer, something that would not frighten him. And there, in front of the figure of Saint Francis, was a beautiful golden candlestick, and in it a tall candle was burning.

The Pirate sighed with excitement. And although the people came in and the swinging doors were shut, and the service began and the Pirate went through the form, he could not stop looking at his saint and at the candlestick. It was so beautiful. He could not believe that he, the Pirate, had given it. He searched the face of the saint to see whether Saint Francis liked the candlestick. He was sure the image smiled a little now and then, the recurring smile of one who thinks of pleasant things.

At last the sermon began. "There is a new beauty in the church," Father Ramon said. "One of the children of the church has given a golden candlestick to the glory of Saint Francis." He told the story of the dog, then, told it rather badly on purpose. His eyes searched the faces of the parishioners until he saw little smiles appear. there. "It is not a thing to be considered funny," he said. "Saint Francis loved the beasts so much that he preached to them." Then Father Ramon told the story of the bad wolf of Gubbio and he told of the wild turtle doves and of the sister larks. The Pirate looked at him in wonder as the sermon went on.

Suddenly a rushing sound came from the door. A furious barking and scratching broke out. The doors swung wildly and in rushed Fluff and Rudolph, Enrique, Pajarito, and Señor Alec Thompson. They raised their noses, and then darted in a struggling squad to the Pirate. They leaped upon him with little cries and whinings. They swarmed over him.

The priest stopped talking and looked sternly down toward the commotion. The Pirate looked back helplessly, in agony. So it was in vain, and the sacrilege was committed.

Then Father Ramon laughed, and the congregation laughed. "Take the dogs outside," he said. "Let them wait until we are through."

The Pirate, with embarrassed, apologetic gestures, conducted his dogs outside. "It is wrong," he said to them. "I am angry with you. Oh, I am ashamed of you." The dogs cringed to the ground and whined piteously. "I know what you did," said the Pirate. "You bit my friends, you broke a window, and you came. Now stay here and wait, oh, wicked dogs; oh, dogs of sacrilege."

He left them stricken with grief and repentance and went back into the church. The people, still laughing, turned and looked at him, until he sank into his seat and tried to efface himself.

"Do not be ashamed," Father Ramon said. "It is no sin to be loved by your dogs, and no sin to love them. See how Saint Francis loved the beasts." Then he told more stories of that good saint.

The embarrassment left the Pirate. His lips moved. "Oh," he thought, "if the dogs could only hear this. They would be glad if they could know all this." When the sermon was over, his ears still rang with the stories. Automatically he followed the ritual, but he, did not hear the service. And when it was over, he rushed for the door. He was first out of the church. The dogs, still sad and diffident, crowded about him.

"Come," he cried. "I have some things to tell you."

He started at a trot up the hill toward the pine forest, and the dogs galloped and bounced about him. He came at last to the shelter of the woods, and still he went on, until he found a long aisle among the pines, where the branches met overhead, where the tree trunks were near together. For a moment he looked helplessly about.

"I want it to be the way it was," he said. "If only you could have been there and heard the father say it." He laid one big stone on top of another. "Now here is the image," he told the dogs. He stuck a little stick in the ground. "Right here is the candlestick, with a candle in it."

It was dusky in the glade, and the air was sweet with pine resin. The trees whispered softly in the breeze. The Pirate said with authority, "Now, Enrique, you sit here. And you, Rudolph, here. I want Fluff here because he is the littlest. Pajarito, thou great fool, sit here and make no trouble. Señor Alec Thompson, you may *not* lie down."

Thus he arranged them in two rows, two in the front line and three in the back.

"I want to tell you how it was," he said. "You are forgiven for breaking into the church. Father Ramon said it was no sacrilege this time. Now, attention. I have things to tell."

The dogs sat in their places and watched him earnestly. Señor Alec Thompson flapped his tail, until the Pirate turned to him. "Here is no place for that," he said. "Saint Francis would not mind, but I do not like you to wag your tail while you listen. Now, I am going to tell you about Saint Francis."

That day his memory was inspired. The sun found interstices in the foliage and threw brilliant patterns on the pine-needle carpet. The dogs sat patiently, their eyes on the Pirate's lips. He told everything the priest had told, all the stories, all the observations. Hardly a word was out of its place.

When he was done, he regarded the dogs solemnly. "Saint Francis did all that," he said.

The trees hushed their whispering. The forest was silent and enchanted.

Suddenly there was a tiny sound behind the Pirate. All the dogs looked up. The Pirate was afraid to turn his head. A long moment passed.

And then the moment was over. The dogs lowered their eyes. The treetops stirred to life again and the sunlight patterns moved bewilderingly.

The Pirate was so happy that his heart pained him. "Did you see him?" he cried. "Was it San Francisco? Oh! What good dogs you must be to see a vision."

The dogs leaped up at his tone. Their mouths opened and their tails threshed joyfully.

13

HOW DANNY'S FRIENDS THREW THEMSELVES TO THE AID OF A DISTRESSED LADY.

Señora Teresina Cortez and her eight children and her ancient mother lived in a pleasant cottage on the edge of the deep gulch that defines the southern frontier of Tortilla Flat. Teresina was a good figure of a mature woman, nearing thirty. Her mother, that ancient, dried, toothless one, relict of a past generation, was nearly fifty. It was long since any one had remembered that her name was Angelica.

During the week work was ready to this *vieja's* hand, for it was her duty to feed, punish, cajole, dress, and bed down seven of the eight children. Teresina was busy with the eighth, and with making certain preparations for the ninth.

On Sunday, however, the *vieja*, clad in black satin more ancient even than she, hatted in a grim and durable affair of black straw, on which were fastened two true cherries of enameled plaster, threw duty to the wind and went firmly to church, where she sat as motionless as the saints in their niches. Once a month, in the afternoon, she went to confession. It would be interesting to know what sins she confessed, and where she found the time to commit them, for in Teresina's house there were creepers, crawlers, stumblers, shriekers, cat-killers, fallers-out-of-trees; and each one of these charges could be trusted to be ravenous every two hours.

Is it any wonder that the *vieja* had a remote soul and nerves of steel? Any other kind would have gone screaming out of her body like little skyrockets.

Teresina was a mildly puzzled woman, as far as her mind was concerned. Her body was one of those perfect retorts for the distillation of children. The first baby, conceived when she was fourteen, had been a shock to her; such a shock, that she delivered it in the ball park at night, wrapped it in newspaper, and left it for the night watchman to find. This is a secret. Even now Teresina might get into trouble if it were known.

When she was sixteen, Mr. Alfred Cortez married her and gave her his name and the two foundations of her family Alfredo and Ernie. Mr. Cortez gave her that name gladly. He was only using it temporarily anyway. His name, before he came to Monterey and after he left, was Guggliemo. He went away after Ernie was born. Perhaps he foresaw that being married to Teresina was not going to be a quiet life.

The regularity with which she became a mother always astonished Teresina. It occurred sometimes that she could not remember who the father of the impending baby was; and occasionally she almost grew convinced that no lover was necessary. In the time when she had been under quarantine as a diphtheria carrier she conceived just the same. However, when a question became too complicated for her mind to unravel, she usually laid that problem in the arms of the Mother of Jesus, who, she knew, had more knowledge of, interest in, and time for such things than she.

Teresina went often to confession. She was the despair of Father Ramon. Indeed he had seen that while her knees, her hands, and her lips did penance for an old sin, her modest and provocative eyes, flashing under drawn lashes, laid the foundation for a new one.

During the time I have been telling this, Teresina's ninth child was born, and for the moment she was unengaged. The *vieja* received another charge; Alfredo entered his third year in the first grade, Ernie his second, and Panchito went to school for the first time.

At about this time in California it became the stylish thing for school nurses to visit the classes and to catechize the children on intimate details of their home life. In the first grade, Alfredo was called to the principal's office, for it was thought that he looked thin.

The visiting nurse, trained in child psychology, said kindly, "Freddie, do you get enough to eat?"

"Sure," said Alfredo.

"Well, now. Tell me what you have for breakfast."

"Tortillas and beans," said Alfredo.

The nurse nodded her head dismally to the principal. "What do you have when you go home for lunch?"

"I don't go home."

"Don't you eat at noon?"

"Sure. I bring some beans wrapped up in a tortilla."

Actual alarm showed in the nurse's eyes, but she controlled herself. "At night what do you have to eat?"

"Tortillas and beans."

Her psychology deserted her. "Do you mean to

stand there and tell me you eat nothing but tortillas and beans?"

Alfredo was astonished. "Jesus Christ," he said, "what more do you want?"

In due course the school doctor listened to the nurse's horrified report. One day he drove up to Teresina's house to look into the matter. As he walked through the yard the creepers, the crawlers, and the stumblers were shrieking one terrible symphony. The doctor stood in the open kitchen door. With his own eyes he saw the *vieja* go to the stove, dip a great spoon into a kettle, and sow the floor with boiled beans. Instantly the noise ceased. Creepers, crawlers, and stumblers went to work with silent industry, moving from bean to bean, pausing only to eat them. The *vieja* went back to her chair for a few moments of peace. Under the bed, under the chairs, under the stove the children crawled with the intentness of little bugs. The doctor stayed two hours, for his scientific interest was piqued. He went away shaking his head.

He shook his head incredulously while he made his report. "I gave them every test I know of," he said, "teeth, skin, blood, skeletons, eyes, co-ordination. Gentlemen, they are living on what constitutes a slow poison, and they have from birth. Gentlemen, I tell you I have never seen healthier children in my life!" His emotion overcame him. "The little beasts," he cried. "I never saw such teeth in my life. I *never* saw such teeth!"

You will wonder how Teresina procured food for her family. When the bean threshers have passed, you will see, where they have stopped, big piles of bean chaff. If you will spread a blanket on the ground, and, on a windy afternoon, toss the chaff in the air over the blanket, you will understand that the threshers are not infallible. For an afternoon of work you may collect twenty or more pounds of beans.

In the autumn the *vieja* and those children who could walk went into the fields and winnowed the chaff. The landowners did not mind, for she did no harm. It was a bad year when the *vieja* did not collect three or four hundred pounds of beans.

When you have four hundred pounds of beans in the house, you need have no fear of starvation. Other things, delicacies such as sugar, tomatoes, peppers, coffee, fish, or meat, may come sometimes miraculously, through the intercession of the Virgin, sometimes through industry or cleverness; but your beans are there, and you are safe. Beans are a roof over your stomach. Beans are a warm cloak against economic cold.

Only one thing could threaten the lives and happiness of the family of the Señora Teresina Cortez; that was a failure of the bean crop.

When the beans are ripe, the little bushes are pulled and gathered into piles, to dry crisp for the threshers. Then is the time to pray that the rain may hold off. When the little piles of beans lie in lines, yellow against the dark fields, you will see the farmers watching the sky, scowling with dread at every cloud that sails over; for if a rain comes, the bean piles must be turned over to dry again. And if more rain falls before they are dry, they must be turned again. If a third shower falls, mildew and rot set in, and the crop is lost.

When the beans were drying, it was the *vieja*'s custom to burn a candle to the Virgin.

In the year of which I speak, the beans were piled

and the candle had been burned. At Teresina's house, the gunny sacks were laid out in readiness.

The threshing machines were oiled and cleaned.

A shower fell.

Extra hands rushed to the fields and turned the sodden hummocks of beans. The *vieja* burned another candle.

More rain fell.

Then the *vieja* bought two candles with a little gold piece she had kept for many years. The field hands turned over the beans to the sun again; and then came a downpour of cold streaking rain. Not a bean was harvested in all Monterey County. The soggy lumps were turned under by the plows.

Oh, then distress entered the house of Señora Teresina Cortez. The staff of life was broken; the little roof destroyed. Gone was that eternal verity, beans. At night the children cried with terror at the approaching starvation. They were not told, but they knew. The *vieja* sat in church, as always, but her lips drew back in a sneer when she looked at the Virgin. "You took my candles," she thought. "Ohee, yes. Greedy you are for candles. Oh, thoughtless one." And sullenly she transferred her allegiance to Santa Clara. She told Santa Clara of the injustice that had been done. She permitted herself a little malicious thought at the Virgin birth. "You know, sometimes Teresina can't remember either," she told Santa Clara viciously.

It has been said that Jesus Maria Corcoran was a great-hearted man. He had also that gift some humanitarians possess of being inevitably drawn toward those spheres where his instinct was needed. How many times had he not come upon young ladies when they needed comforting. Toward any pain or sorrow he was irresistibly drawn. He had not been to Teresina's house for many months. If there is no mystical attraction between pain and humanitarianism, how did it happen that he went there to call on the very day when the last of the old year's beans was put in the pot?

He sat it Teresina's kitchen, gently brushing children off his legs. And he looked at Teresina with polite and pained eyes while she told of the calamity. He watched, fascinated, when she turned the last bean sack inside out to show that not one single bean was left. He nodded sympathetically when she pointed out the children, so soon to be skeletons, so soon to die of starvation.

Then the *vieja* told bitterly how she had been tricked by the Virgin. But upon this point Jesus Maria was not sympathetic.

"What do you know, old one?" he said sternly. "Maybe the Blessed Virgin had business some place else."

"But four candles I burned," the *vieja* insisted shrilly.

Jesus Maria regarded her coldly. "What are four candles to Her?" he said. "I have seen one church where She had hundreds. She is no miser of candles."

But his mind burned with Teresina's trouble. That evening he talked mightily and piteously to the friends at Danny's house. Out of his great heart he drew a compelling oratory, a passionate plea for those little children who had no beans. And so telling was his speech that the fire in his heart ignited the hearts of his friends. They leaped up. Their eyes glowed.

"The children shall not starve," they cried. "It shall be our trust!"

"We live in luxury," Pilon said.

"We shall give of our substance," Danny agreed. "And if they needed a house, they could live here."

"Tomorrow we shall start," Pablo exclaimed. "No more laziness! To work! There are things to be done!"

Jesus Maria felt the gratification of a leader with followers.

Theirs was no idle boast. Fish they collected. The vegetable patch of the Hotel Del Monte they raided. It was a glorious game. Theft robbed of the stigma of theft, crime altruistically committed—what is more gratifying?

The Pirate raised the price of kindlings to thirty cents and went to three new restaurants every morning. Big Joe stole Mrs. Palochico's goat over and over again, and each time it went home.

Now food began to accumulate in the house of Teresina. Boxes of lettuce lay on her porch, spoiled mackerel filled the neighborhood with a strong odor. And still the flame of charity burned in the friends.

If you could see the complaint book at the Monterey Police Department, you would notice that during this time there was a minor crime wave in Monterey. The police car hurried from place to place. Here a chicken was taken, there a whole patch of pumpkins. Paladini Company reported the loss of two one-hundred-pound cases of abalone steaks.

Teresina's house was growing crowded. The kitchen was stacked high with food. The back porch overflowed with vegetables. Odors like those of a packing house permeated Tortilla Flat. Breathlessly the friends

dashed about at their larcenies, and long they talked
and planned with Teresina.

At first Teresina was maddened with joy at so much
food, and her head was turned by compliment. After a
week of it, she was not so sure. The baby was down
with colic. Ernie had some kind of bowel trouble,
Alfredo's face was flushed. The creepers and crawlers
cried all the time. Teresina was ashamed to tell the
friends what she must tell them. It took her several
days to get her courage up; and during that time there
arrived fifty pounds of celery and a crate of canta-
loupes. At last she had to tell them. The neighbors
were beginning to look at her with lifted brows.

She asked all of Danny's friends into her kitchen,
and then she informed them of the trouble, modestly
and carefully, that their feelings might not be hurt.

"Green things and fruit are not good for children,"
she explained. "Milk is constipating to a baby after it
is weaned." She pointed to the flushed and irritable
children. See, they were all sick. They were not getting the proper food.

"What is the proper food?" Pilon demanded.

"Beans," she said. "There you have something to
trust, something that will not go right through you."

The friends went silently away. They pretended to
themselves to be disheartened, but they knew that the
first fire of their enthusiasm had been lacking for several days.

At Danny's house they held a conference.

This must not be told in some circles, for the charge
might be serious.

Long after midnight four dark forms who shall be
nameless moved like shadows through the town. Four

indistinct shapes crept up on the Western Warehouse
Company platform. The watchman said, afterward,
that he heard sounds, investigated, and saw nothing.
He could not say how the thing was done, how a lock
was broken and the door forced. Only four men know
that the watchman was sound asleep, and they will
never tell on him.

A little later the four shadows left the warehouse,
and now they were bent under tremendous loads. Pant-
ings and snortings came from the shadows.

At three o'clock in the morning Teresina was awakened by hearing her back door open. "Who is there?"
she cried.

There was no answer, but she heard four great
thumps that shook the house. She lighted a candle and
went to the kitchen in her bare feet. There, against the
wall, stood four one-hundred-pound sacks of pink
beans.

Teresina rushed in and awakened the *vieja*. "A miracle!" she cried. "Come look in the kitchen."

The *vieja* regarded with shame the plump full sacks.
"Oh, miserable dirty sinner am I," she moaned. "Oh,
Holy Mother, look with pity on an old fool. Every
month thou shalt have a candle, as long as I live."

At Danny's house four friends were lying happily in
their blankets. What pillow can one have like a good
conscience? They slept well into the afternoon, for
their work was done.

And Teresina discovered, by a method she had
found to be infallible, that she was going to have a
baby. As she poured a quart of the new beans into the
kettle, she wondered idly which one of Danny's friends
was responsible.

14

OF THE GOOD LIFE AT DANNY'S HOUSE, OF A GIFT PIG, OF THE PAIN OF TALL BOB, AND OF THE THWARTED LOVE OF THE VIEJO RAVANNO.

Clocks and watches were not used by the paisanos of Tortilla Flat. Now and then one of the friends acquired a watch in some extraordinary manner, but he kept it only long enough to trade it for something he really wanted. Watches were in good repute at Danny's house, but only as media of exchange. For practical purposes, there was the great golden watch of the sun. It was better than a watch, and safer, for there was no way of diverting it to Torrelli.

In the summer when the hands of a clock point to seven, it is a nice time to get up, but in winter the same time is of no value whatever. How much better is the sun! When he clears the pine tops and clings to the front porch, be it summer or winter, that is the sensible time to get up. That is a time when one's hands do not quiver nor one's belly quake with emptiness.

The Pirate and his dogs slept in the living room,

secure and warm in their corner. Pilon and Pablo and Jesus Maria and Danny and Big Joe Portagee slept in the bedroom. For all his kindness, his generosity, Danny never allowed his bed to be occupied by anyone but himself. Big Joe tried it twice, and was smacked across the soles of the feet with a stick; so that even he learned the inviolable quality of Danny's bed.

The friends slept on the floor, and their bedding was unusual. Pablo had three sheepskins stitched together. Jesus Maria retired by putting his arms through the sleeves of one old overcoat and his legs through the sleeves of another. Pilon wrapped himself in a big strip of carpet. Most of the time Big Joe simply curled up like a dog and slept in his clothes. Big Joe, while he had no ability to keep any possession for very long, had a well-developed genius for trading everything that came into his hands for some little measure of wine. Thus they slept, noisily sometimes, but always comfortably. On one cold night Big Joe tried to borrow a dog for his feet, and got well bitten, for the Pirate's dogs were not lendable.

No curtains covered the windows, but a generous Nature had obscured the glass with cobwebs, with dust, and with the neat marks of raindrops.

"It would be nice to clean that window with soap and water," Danny said one time.

Pilon's sharp mind leaped to the problem with energy, but it was too easy for him. It did not require a decent quota of his powers. "More light would get in," he said. "We would not spend so much time out in the air if it were light in here. And at night, when the air is poisonous, we have no need for light."

Danny retired from the field, for if one little mention

brought such clear and quick refutation of his project, what crushing logic would insistence bring forth? The window remained as it was; and as time passed, as fly after fly went to feed the spider family with his blood and left his huskish body in the webs against the glass, as dust adhered to dust, the bedroom took on a pleasant obscurity which made it possible to sleep in a dusky light even at noonday.

They slept peacefully, the friends; but when the sun struck the window in the morning and, failing to get in, turned the dust to silver and shone on the iridescence of the blue-bottle flies, then the friends awakened and stretched and looked about for their shoes. They knew the front porch was warm when the sun was on the window.

They did not awaken quickly, nor fling about nor shock their systems with any sudden movement. No, they arose from slumber as gently as a soap bubble floats out from its pipe. Down into the gulch they trudged, still only half awake. Gradually their wills coagulated. They built a fire and boiled some tea and drank it from the fruit jars, and at last they settled in the sun on the front porch. The flaming flies made halos about their heads. Life took shape about them, the shape of yesterday and of tomorrow.

Discussion began slowly, for each man treasured the little sleep he still possessed. From this time until well after noon, intellectual comradeship came into being. Then roofs were lifted, houses peered into, motives inspected, adventures recounted. Ordinarily their thoughts went first to Cornelia Ruiz, for it was a rare day and night during which Cornelia had not some curious and interesting adventure. And it was an unusual adventure from which no moral lesson could be drawn.

The sun glistened in the pine needles. The earth smelled dry and good. The rose of Castile perfumed the world with its flowers. This was one of the best of times for the friends of Danny. The struggle for existence was remote. They sat in judgment on their fellows, judging not for morals, but for interest. Anyone having a good thing to tell saved it for recounting at this time. The big brown butterflies came to the rose and sat on the flowers and waved their wings slowly, as though they pumped honey out by wing power.

"I saw Albert Rasmussen," said Danny. "He came from Cornelia's house. What trouble that Cornelia has. Every day some trouble."

"It is her way of life," said Pablo. "I am not one to cast stones, but sometimes I think Cornelia is a little too lively. Two things only occur to Cornelia, love and fighting."

"Well," said Pilon. "What do you want?"

"She never has any peace," Jesus Maria said sadly.

"She doesn't want any," said Pilon. "Give peace to that Cornelia, and she will die. Love and fighting. That is good, what you said, Pablo. Love and fighting, and a little wine. Then you are always young, always happy. What happened to Cornelia yesterday?"

Danny looked in triumph at Pilon. It was an unusual thing for Pilon not to know everything that happened. And now Danny could tell by the hurt and piqued look on Pilon's face that he did not know this one.

"All of you know Cornelia," he began. "Sometimes men take presents to Cornelia, a chicken or a rabbit or a cabbage. Just little things, and Cornelia likes those things. Well, yesterday Emilio Murietta took to Cornelia a little pig, only so long; a nice little pink pig. Emilio found that pig in the gulch. The sow chased him when he picked it up, but he ran fast, and he came to Cornelia's house with that pig.

"This Emilio is a great talker. He said to Cornelia, 'There is nothing nicer to have than a pig. He will eat anything. He is a nice pet. You get to love that little pig. But then that pig grows up and his character changes. That pig becomes mean and evil-tempered, so that you do not love him any more. Then one day that pig bites you, and you are angry. And so you kill that pig and eat him.' "

The friends nodded gravely, and Pilon said, "In some ways Emilio is not a dull man. See how many satisfactions he has made with his pig—affection, love, revenge, and food. I must go to talk with Emilio sometime." But the friends could see that Pilon was jealous of a rival logician.

"Go on with this pig," said Pablo.

"Well," said Danny, "Cornelia took that little pig, and she was nice to Emilio. She said that when the time came, and she was angry at that pig, Emilio could have some of it to eat. Well, then Emilio went away. Cornelia made a little box for that pig to sleep in, by the stove.

"Some ladies came in to see her then, and Cornelia let them hold the little pig and pet it. After a while Sweets Ramirez stepped on that pig's tail. Oh! It squealed like a steam whistle. The front door was open. That big sow she came in for her little pig again. All the tables and all the dishes were smashed. All the chairs, they were broken. And that big sow bit Sweets Ramirez and pulled off Cornelia's skirt, and then, when those ladies were in the kitchen and the door locked, the sow went away, and that little pig went too. Now Cornelia is furious. She says she will beat Emilio."

"There it is," said Pablo. "That is the way life goes, never the way you planned. It was that way when Tall Bob Smoke went to kill himself."

The faces of the friends swung appreciatively toward Pablo.

"You will know Bob Smoke," Pablo began. "He looks the way a vaquero should look, long legs, thin body; but he cannot ride very well. At the rodeo he is often in the dust. Now this Bob is one who wants to be admired. When there is a parade he likes to carry the flag. When there is a fight he wants to be referee. At the show he is always the first to say 'Down in front!' Yes, there is a man who wants to be a great man, and to have people see him, and admire him. And something you do not know, perhaps, he wants people to love him too.

"Poor unfortunate one, he is a man born to be laughed at. Some people pity him, but most of them just laugh at him. And laughter stabs that Tall Bob Smoke.

"Maybe you remember that time in the parade when he carried the flag. Very straight Bob sat, on a big white horse. Right in front of the place where the judges sat that big stupid horse fainted from the heat. Bob went flying right over that horse's head, and the flag sailed through the air like a spear and stuck in the ground, upside down.

"That is how it is with him. Whenever he tries to be a great man, something happens and everybody laughs. You remember when he was poundmaster he tried all afternoon to lasso a dog. Everybody in town came to see. He threw the rope and the dog squatted down and the rope slipped off and the dog ran away. Oh, the people laughed. Bob was so ashamed that he thought, 'I will kill myself, and then people will be sad. They will be sorry they laughed.' And then he thought, 'But I will be dead. I will not know how sorry they are.' So he made this plan, 'I will wait until I hear someone coming to my room. I will point my pistol at my head. Then that friend will argue with me. He will make me promise not to shoot myself. The people will be sorry then that they drove me to kill myself.' That is the way he thought it.

"So he walked home to his little house, and everybody he passed called out, 'Did you catch the dog, Bob?' He was very sad when he got home. He took a pistol and put cartridges in it, and then he sat down and waited for someone to come.

"He planned how it would be, and he practiced it with a pistol. The friend would say, 'Ai, what you doing? Don't shoot yourself, poor fellow.' Then Bob would say how he didn't want to live any more because everyone was so mean.

"He thought about it over and over, but no one came. And the next day he waited, and no one came. But that next night Charlie Meeler came. Bob heard him on the porch and put the pistol to his head. And he cocked it to make it look more real. 'Now he will argue with me, and I will let him persuade me,' Bob thought.

"Charlie Meeler opened the door. He saw Bob holding that pistol to his head. But he did not shout; no, Charlie Meeler jumped and grabbed that gun and that gun went off and shot away the end of Bob's nose. And then the people laughed even more. There were pieces in the paper about it. The whole town laughed.

"You have all seen Bob's nose, with the end shot off. The people laughed; but it was a hard kind of laughing, and they felt bad to laugh. And ever since then they let Tall Bob carry the flag in every parade there is. And the city bought him a net to catch dogs with.

"But he is not a happy man, with his nose like that." Pablo fell silent and picked up a stick from the porch and whipped his leg a little.

"I remember his nose, how it was," said Danny. "He is not a bad one, that Bob. The Pirate can tell you when he gets back. Sometimes the Pirate puts all his dogs in Bob's wagon and then the people think Bob has caught them, and the people say, 'There is a poundman for you.' It is not so easy to catch dogs when it is your business to catch dogs."

Jesus Maria had been brooding, with his head back against the wall. He observed, "It is worse than whipping to be laughed at. Old Tomas, the rag sucker, was laughed right into his grave. And afterward the people were sorry they laughed.

"And," said Jesus Maria, "there is another kind of laughing too. The story of Tall Bob is funny; but when you open your mouth to laugh, something like a hand squeezes your heart. I know about old Mr. Ravanno who hanged himself last year. And there is a funny story too, but it is not pleasant to laugh at."

"I heard something about it," said Pilon, "but I do not know that story."

"Well," said Jesus Maria. "I will tell you that story, and you will see if you can laugh. When I was a little boy, I played games with Peter Ravanno. A good quick little boy, that Petey, but always in trouble. He had two brothers and four sisters, and there was his father, Old Pete. All that family is gone now. One brother is in San Quentin, the other was killed by a Japanese gardener for stealing a wagonload of water-melons. And the girls, well, you know how girls are; they went away. Susy is in Old Jenny's house in Salinas right now.

"So there was only Petey and the old man left. Petey grew up, and always he was in trouble. He went to reform school for a while, then he came back. Every Saturday he was drunk, and every time he went to jail until Monday. His father was a kind of a friendly man. He got drunk every week with Petey. Nearly always they were in jail together. Old man Ravanno was lonely when Petey was not there with him. He liked that boy Petey. Whatever Petey did, that old man did, even when he was sixty years old.

"Maybe you remember that Gracie Montez?" Jesus Maria asked. "She was not a very good girl. When she was only twelve years old the fleet came to Monterey, and Gracie had her first baby, so young as that. She was pretty, you see, and quick, and her tongue was sharp. Always she seemed to run away from men, and men ran fast after her. And sometimes they caught her. But you could not get close to her. Always that Gracie seemed to have something nice that she did not give to you, something in back of her eyes that said, 'If

I really wanted to, I would be different to you from any woman you ever knew.'

"I know about that," said Jesus Maria, "for I ran after Gracie too. And Petey ran after her. Only Petey was different." Jesus Maria looked sharply into his friends' eyes to emphasize his point.

"Petey wanted what Gracie had so much that he grew thin, and his eyes were as wide and painted as the eyes of one who smokes marihuana. Petey could not eat, and he was sick. Old Man Ravanno went over and talked to Gracie. He said, 'If you are not nice to Petey, he will die.' But she only laughed. She was not a very good one. And then her little sister 'Tonia came into the room. 'Tonia was fourteen years old. The old man looked at her and his breath stopped. 'Tonia was like Gracie, with that funny thing that she kept away from men. Old Man Ravanno could not help it. He said, 'Come to me, little girl.' But 'Tonia was not a little girl. She knew. So she laughed and ran out of the room.

"Old Man Ravanno went home then. Petey said, 'Something is the matter with thee, my father?'

" 'No, Petey,' the old man said, 'only I worry that you do not get this Gracie, so you can be well again.'

"Hot-blooded, all those Ravannos were!

"And then what do you think?" Jesus Maria continued. "Petey went to cut squids for Chin Kee, and he made presents to Gracie, big bottles of Agua Florida and ribbons and garters. He paid to have her picture taken, with colors on the picture too.

"Gracie took all the presents and she ran away from him and laughed. You should have heard how she laughed. It made you want to choke her and pet her at the same time. It made you want to cut her open and

get that thing that was inside of her. I know how it
was. I ran after her, and Petey told me too. But it
made Petey crazy. He could not sleep any more. He
said to me, 'If that Gracie will marry me in the church,
then she will not dare to run away any more, because
she will be married, and it will be a sin to run away.'
So he asked her. She laughed that high laugh that
made you want to choke her.

"Oh! Petey was crazy. He went home and put a rope
over a rafter and he stood on a box and put the rope
around his neck and then he kicked out the box. Well,
Petey's father came in then. He cut the rope and called
the doctor. But it was two hours before Petey opened his
eyes, and it was four days before he could talk.'"

Jesus Maria paused. He saw with pride that his
friends were leaning in toward the story. "That was the
way of it," he said.

"But Gracie Montez married that Petey Ravanno,"
Pilon cried excitedly. "I know her. She is a good
woman. She never misses mass, and she goes once a
month to confession."

"So it is now," Jesus Maria agreed. "Old man Ravanno was angry. He ran to Gracie's house, and he
cried, 'See how you murder my boy with your foolishness. He tried to kill himself for you, dung-heap
chicken.'

"Gracie was afraid, but she was pleased too, because it is not many women who can make a man go so
far. She went to see Petey where he was in bed with a
crooked neck. After a little while they were married.

"It turned out the way Petey thought it would, too.
When the church told her to be a good wife, she was a
good wife. She didn't laugh to men any more. And she

didn't run away so they chased her. Petey went on cutting squids, and pretty soon Chin Kee let him empty the squid boxes. And not long after that he was the mayordomo of the squid yard. You see," said Jesus Maria, "there is a good story. It would be a story for a priest to tell, if it stopped there."

"Oh yes," said Pilon gravely. "There are things to be learned in this story."

The friends nodded appreciatively, for they liked a story with a meaning.

"I knew a girl in Texas like that," said Danny. "Only she didn't change. They called her the wife of the second platoon. 'Mrs. Second Platoon,' they said."

Pablo held up his hand. "There is more to this story," he said. "Let Jesus Maria tell the rest."

"Yes, there is more. And it is not such a good story, in the ending. There was the *viejo*, over sixty. And Petey and Gracie went to live in another house. The Viejo Ravanno was lonely, for he had always been with Petey. He didn't know how to take up his time. He just sat and looked sad, until one day he saw 'Tonia again. 'Tonia was fifteen, and she was prettier, even, than Gracie. Half the soldiers from the Presidio followed her around like little dogs.

"Now as it had been with Petey, so it was with the old man. His desire made him ache all over. He could not eat or sleep. His cheeks sunk in, and his eyes stared like the eyes of a marihuana smoker. He carried candy to 'Tonia, and she grabbed the candy out of his hands and laughed at him. He said, 'Come to me, little dear one, for I am thy friend.' She laughed again.

"Then the *viejo* told Petey about it. And Petey laughed too. 'You old fool,' Petey said. 'You've had

enough women in your life. Don't run after babies.'
But it did no good. Old Man Ravanno grew sick with
longing. They are hot-blooded, those Ravannos. He
hid in the grass and watched her pass by. His heart
ached in his breast.

"He needed money to buy presents, so he got a job
in the Standard Service Station. He raked the gravel
and watered the flowers at that station. He put water in
the radiators and cleaned the windshields. With every
cent he bought presents for 'Tonia, candy and ribbons
and dresses. He paid to have her picture taken with
colors.

"She only laughed more, and the *viejo* was nearly
crazy. So he thought, 'If marriage in the church made
Gracie a good woman, it will make 'Tonia a good
woman too.' He asked her to marry him. Then she
laughed more than ever. She flung up her skirts to
worry him. Oh, she was a devil, that 'Tonia."

"He was a fool," said Pilon smugly. "Old men
should not run after babies. They should sit in the
sun."

Jesus Maria went on irritably. "Those Ravannos are
different," he said, "so hot-blooded."

"Well, it was not a decent thing," said Pilon. "It
was a shame on Petey."

Pablo turned to him. "Let Jesus Maria go on. It is
his story, Pilon, not thine. Sometime we will listen to
thee."

Jesus Maria looked gratefully to Pablo. "I was
telling.

"The *viejo* could not stand it any more. But he was
not a man to invent anything. He was not like Pilon.
He could not think of anything new. The Viejo Ra-

vanno thought like this: 'Gracie married Petey because he hanged himself. I will hang myself, and maybe 'Tonia will marry me.' And then he thought, 'If no one finds me soon enough, I will be dead. Someone must find me.'

"You must know," said Jesus Maria, "at that service station there is a tool house. Early in the morning the *viejo* went down and unlocked the tool house and raked the gravel and watered the flowers before the station opened. The other men came to work at eight o'clock. So, one morning, the *viejo* went into the tool house and put up a rope. Then he waited until it was eight o'clock. He saw the men coming. He put the rope around his neck and stepped off a work bench. And just when he did that, the door of the tool shed blew shut."

Broad smiles broke out on the faces of the friends. Sometimes, they thought, life was very, very humorous.

"Those men did not miss him right away," Jesus Maria went on. "They said, 'He is probably drunk, that old one.' It was an hour later when they opened the door of that tool shed." He looked around.

The smiles were still on the faces of the friends, but they were changed smiles. "You see," Jesus Maria said, "it is funny. But it squeezes in you too."

"What did 'Tonia say?" Pilon demanded. "Did she read a lesson and change her living?"

"No. She did not. Petey told her, and she laughed. Petey laughed too. But he was ashamed. 'Tonia said, 'What an old fool he was,' and 'Tonia looked at Petey that way she had.

"Then Petey said, 'It is good to have a little sister like thee. Some night I will walk in the woods with thee.' Then 'Tonia laughed again and ran away a little. And she said, 'Do you think I am as pretty as Gracie?' So Petey followed her into the house."

Pilon complained, "It is not a good story. There are too many meanings and too many lessons in it. Some of those lessons are opposite. There is not a story to take into your head. It proves nothing."

"I like it," said Pablo. "I like it because it hasn't any meaning you can see, and still it does seem to mean something, I can't tell what."

The sun had turned across noon, and the air was hot.

"I wonder what the Pirate will bring to eat," said Danny.

"There is a mackerel run in the bay," Pablo observed.

Pilon's eyes brightened. "I have a plan that I thought out," he said. "When I was a little boy, we lived by the railroad. Every day when the train went by, my brothers and I threw rocks at the engine, and the fireman threw coal at us. Sometimes we picked up a big bucketful of coal and took it in to our mother. Now I thought maybe we could take rocks down on the pier. When the boats come near, we will call names, we will throw rocks. How can those fishermen get back at us? Can they throw oars, or nets? No! They can only throw mackerel."

Danny stood up joyfully. "Now there is a plan!" he cried. "How this little Pilon of ours is our friend! What would we do without our Pilon? Come, I know where there is a great pile of rocks."

"I like mackerel better than any other fish," said Pablo.

15

HOW DANNY BROODED AND BECAME MAD. HOW THE DEVIL IN THE SHAPE OF TORRELLI ASSAULTED DANNY'S HOUSE.

There is a changeless quality about Monterey. Nearly every day in the morning the sun shines in the windows on the west sides of the streets; and, in the afternoons, on the east sides of the streets. Every day the red bus clangs back and forth between Monterey and Pacific Grove. Every day the canneries send a stink of reducing fish into the air. Every afternoon the wind blows in from the bay and sways the pines on the hills. The rock fishermen sit on the rocks holding their poles, and their faces are graven with patience and with cynicism.

On Tortilla Flat, above Monterey, the routine is changeless too; for there is only a given number of adventures that Cornelia Ruiz can have with her slowly changing procession of sweethearts. She has been known to take again a man long since discarded.

In Danny's house there was even less change. The friends had sunk into a routine which might have been monotonous for anyone but a paisano—up in the morning, to sit in the sun and wonder what the Pirate would bring. The Pirate still cut pitchwood and sold it in the streets of Monterey, but now he bought food with the quarter he earned every day. Occasionally the friends procured some wine, and then there was singing and fighting.

Time is more complex near the sea than in any other place, for in addition to the circling of the sun and the turning of the seasons, the waves beat out the passage of time on the rocks and the tides rise and fall as a great clepsydra.

Danny began to feel the beating of time. He looked at his friends and saw how with them every day was the same. When he got out of his bed in the night and stepped over the sleeping paisanos, he was angry with them for being there. Gradually, sitting on the front porch, in the sun, Danny began to dream of the days of his freedom. He had slept in the woods in summer, and in the warm hay of barns when the winter cold was in. The weight of property was not upon him. He remembered that the name of Danny was a name of storm. Oh, the fights! The flights through the woods with an outraged chicken under his arm! The hiding places in the gulch when an outraged husband proclaimed feud! Storm and violence, sweet violence! When Danny thought of the old lost time, he could taste again how good the stolen food was, and he longed for that old time again. Since his inheritance had lifted him, he had not fought often. He had been drunk, but not adventurously so. Always the weight of the house was upon him; always the responsibility to his friends.

Danny began to mope on the front porch, so that his friends thought him ill.

"Tea made from yerba buena will be good," Pilon suggested. "If you will go to bed, Danny, we will put hot rocks to your feet."

It was not coddling Danny wanted, it was freedom. For a month he brooded, stared at the ground, looked with sullen eyes at his ubiquitous friends, kicked the friendly dogs out of his way.

In the end he gave up to his longing. One night he ran away. He went into the pine woods and disappeared.

When in the morning the friends awakened and found him missing, Pilon said, "It is some lady. He is in love."

They left it there, for every man has a right to love. The friends went on living as they had. But when a week passed with no sign of Danny, they began to worry. In a body they went to the woods to look for him.

"Love is nice," said Pilon. "We cannot blame any man for following a girl, but a week is a week. It must be a lively girl to keep Danny away for a week."

Pablo said, "A little love is like a little wine. Too much of either will make a man sick. Maybe Danny is already sick. Maybe this girl is too lively."

Jesus Maria was worried too. "It is not like the Danny we know to be gone so long. Some bad thing has happened."

The Pirate took his dogs into the woods. The friends advised the dogs, "Find Danny. He may be sick. Somewhere he may be dead, that good Danny who lets you sleep in his house."

The Pirate whispered to them, "Oh, evil, ungrateful dogs, find our friend." But the dogs waved their tails happily and sought out a rabbit and went kyoodling after it.

The paisanos ranged all day through the woods, calling Danny's name, looking in places they themselves might have chosen to sleep in, the good hollows between the roots of trees, the thick needle beds, encircled by bushes. They knew where a man would sleep, but they found no sign of Danny.

"Perhaps he is mad," Pilon suggested. "Some secret worry may have turned his wit."

In the evening they went back to Danny's house and opened the door and went in. Instantly they became intense. A thief had been busy. Danny's blankets were gone. All the food was stolen. Two pots were missing.

Pilon looked quickly at Big Joe Portagee, and then he shook his head. "No, you were with us. You didn't do it."

"Danny did it," Pablo said excitedly. "Truly he is mad. He is running through the woods like an animal."

Great care and worry settled on Danny's house. "We must find him," the friends assured one another. "Some harm will fall upon our friend in his craziness. We must search through the whole world until we find him."

They threw off their laziness. Every day they looked for him, and they began to hear curious rumors. "Yes, Danny was here last night. Oh, that drunk one! Oh, that thief! For see, Danny knocked down the *viejo* with a fence picket and he stole a bottle of grappa. What kind of friends are these who let their friend do such things?"

"Yes, we saw Danny. His eye was closed, and he was singing. 'Come into the woods and we will dance, little girls,' but we would not go. We were afraid. That Danny did not look very quiet."

At the wharf they found more evidence of their friend. "He was here," the fishermen said. "He wanted to fight everybody. Benito broke an oar on Danny's head. Then Danny broke some windows, and then a policeman took him to jail."

Hot on the path of their wayward friend, they continued. "McNear brought him in last night," the sergeant said. "Some way he got loose before morning. When we catch him, we'll give him six months."

The friends were tired of the chase. They went home, and to their horror they found that the new sack of potatoes that Pilon had found only that morning was gone.

"Now it is too much," Pilon cried. "Danny is crazy, and he is in danger. Some terrible thing will happen to him if we do not save him."

"We will search," said Jesus Maria.

"We will look behind every tree and every shed," Pablo guaranteed.

"Under the boats on the beach," Big Joe suggested.

"The dogs will help," the Pirate said.

Pilon shook his head. "That is not the way. Every time we come to a place after Danny has gone. We must wait in some place where he will come. We must act as wise men, not as fools."

"But where will he come?"

The light struck all of them at once. "Torrelli's! Sooner or later Danny will go to Torrelli's. We must go there to catch him, to restrain him in the madness that has fallen upon him."

"Yes," they agreed. "We must save Danny."

In a body they visited Torrelli, and Torrelli would not let them in. "Ask me," he cried through the door, "have I seen Danny? Danny brought three blankets and two cooking pots, and I gave him a gallon of wine. What, did that devil do then? My wife he insulted and me he called bad names. My baby he spanked, my dog he kicked! He stole the hammock from my porch." Torrelli gasped with emotion. "I chased him to get my hammock back, and when I returned, he was with my wife! Seducer, thief, drunkard! That is your friend Danny! I myself will see that he goes to penitentiary."

The eyes of the friends glinted. "Oh Corsican pig," Pilon said evenly. "You speak of our friend. Our friend is not well."

Torrelli locked the door. They could hear the bolt slide, but Pilon continued to speak through the door. "Oh, Jew," he said, "if thou wert a little more charitable with thy wine, these things would not happen. See that thou keepest that cold frog which is thy tongue from dirtying our friend. See thou treatest him gently, for his friends are many. We will tear thy stomach out if thou art not nice to him."

Torrelli made no sound inside the locked house, but he trembled with rage and fear at the ferocity of the tones. He was relieved when he heard the footsteps of the friends receding up the path.

That night, after the friends had gone to bed, they heard a stealthy step in the kitchen. They knew it was Danny, but he escaped before they could catch him. They wandered about in the dark, calling disconsolately, "Come, Danny, our little sugar friend, we need thee with us."

There was no reply, but a thrown rock struck Big Joe in the stomach and doubled him up on the ground. Oh, how the friends were dismayed, and how their hearts were heavy!

"Danny is running to his death," they said sadly. "Our little friend is in need, and we cannot help him."

It was difficult to keep house now, for Danny had stolen nearly everything in it. A chair turned up at a bootlegger's. All the food was taken, and once, when they were searching for Danny in the woods, he stole the airtight stove; but it was heavy, and he abandoned it in the gulch. Money there was none, for Danny stole the Pirate's wheelbarrow and traded it to Joe Ortiz for a bottle of whisky. Now all peace had gone from Danny's house, and there was only worry and sadness.

"Where is our happiness gone?" Pablo mourned. "Somewhere we have sinned. It is a judgment. We should go to confession."

No more did they discuss the marital parade of Cornelia Ruiz. Gone were the moralities, lost were the humanities. Truly the good life lay in ruins. And into the desolation came the rumors.

"Danny committed partial rape last night."

"Danny has been milking Mrs. Palochico's goat."

"Danny was in a fight with some soldiers the night before last."

Sad as they were at his moral decay, the friends were not a little jealous of the good time Danny was having.

"If he is not crazy, he will be punished," said Pilon. "Be sure of that. Danny is sinning in a way which, sin for sin, beats any record I ever heard of. Oh, the penances when he wants to be decent again! In a few weeks Danny has piled up more sins than Old Ruiz did in a lifetime."

That night Danny, unhindered by the friendly dogs, crept into the house as silently as the moving shadow of a limb under a street light, and wantonly he stole Pilon's shoes. In the morning it did not take Pilon long to understand what had happened. He went firmly to the porch and sat down in the sun and regarded his feet.

"Now he has gone too far," Pilon said. "Pranks he has played, and we were patient. But now he turns to crime. This is not the Danny we know. This is another man, a bad man. We must capture this bad man."

Pablo looked complacently down at his shoes. "Maybe this is only a prank too," he suggested.

"No," Pilon said severely. "This is crime. They were not very good shoes, but it is a crime against friendship to take them. And that is the worst kind of crime. If Danny will steal the shoes of his friends, there is no crime he will stop at."

The friends nodded in agreement. "Yes, we must catch him," said Jesus Maria of the humanities. "We know he is sick. We will tie him to his bed and try to cure him of the sickness. We must try to wipe the darkness from his brain."

"But now," said Pablo, "before we catch him, we must remember to put our shoes under our pillows when we sleep."

The house was in a state of siege. All about it raged Danny, and Danny was having a wonderful time.

Seldom did the face of Torrelli show any emotions but suspicion and anger. In his capacity as bootlegger, and in his dealings with the people of Tortilla Flat, those two emotions were often called into his heart, and their line was written on his face. Moreover, Torrelli had never visited anyone. He had only to stay at home to have everyone visit him. Consequently, when Torrelli walked up the road toward Danny's house in the morning, his face suffused with a ferocious smile of pleasure and anticipation, the children ran into their yards and peeked through the pickets at him; the dogs caressed their stomachs with their tails and fled with backward, fearful looks; men, meeting him, stepped out of his path and clenched their fists to repel a madman.

This morning the fog covered the sky. The sun, after a number of unsuccessful skirmishes, gave up and retired behind the gray folds. The pine trees dripped dusty dew on the ground; and in the faces of the few people who were about, the day was reflected with somber looks and gray skins. There were no hearty greetings. There was none of that human idealism which blandly hopes this day will be better than all other days.

Old Roca, seeing Torrelli smiling, went home and told his wife, "That one has just killed and eaten his children. You will see!"

Torrelli was happy, for in his pocket there was a folded, precious paper. His fingers sought his coat again and again, and pressed until a little crackling sound assured Torrelli that the paper was still there. As he walked through the gray morning, he muttered to himself.

"Nest of snakes," he said. "I will wipe out this pestilence of Danny's friends. No more will I give wine for goods, and have the goods stolen again. Each man alone is not so bad, but the nest of them! Madonna, look down how I will cast them out into the street! The toads, the lice, the stinging flies! When they sleep in the woods again, they will not be so proud.

"I would have them know that Torrelli has triumphed. They thought to cheat me, despoil my house of furniture and my wife of virtue! They will see that Torrelli, the great sufferer, can strike back. Oh, yes, they will see!"

Thus he muttered as he walked, and his fingers crackled the paper in his pocket. The trees dripped mournful drops into the dust. The sea gulls circled in the air, screaming tragically. Torrelli moved like gray Fate on Danny's house.

In Danny's house there was gloom. The friends could not sit on the porch in the sunshine, for there was no sunshine. No one can produce a better reason for gloom. They had brought back the stolen stove from the gulch and set it up. They clustered to it now, and Johnny Pom-pom, who had come to call, told the news he had.

"Tito Ralph," he said, "is no longer the jailer down at the city jail. No, this morning the police judge sent him away."

"I liked Tito Ralph," said Pilon. "When a man was in jail, Tito Ralph would bring him a little wine. And he knew more stories than a hundred other men. Why did he lose his job, Johnny Pom-pom?"

"That is what I came to tell. Tito Ralph, you know, was often in jail, and he was a good prisoner. He knew how a jail should be run. After a while he knew more about the jail than anyone. Then Daddy Marks, the old jailer, died, and Tito Ralph took his place. Never has there been such a good jailer as Tito Ralph. Everything he did just right. But he has one little fault.

When he drinks wine, he forgets he is the jailer. He escapes, and they have to catch him."

The friends nodded. "I know," said Pablo. "I have heard he is hard to catch too. He hides."

"Yes," continued Johnny Pom-pom, "except for that, he is the best jailer they ever had. Well, this is the thing that I came to tell. Last night Danny had enough wine for ten men, and he drank it. Then he drew pictures on windows. He was very rich, he bought eggs to throw at a Chinaman. And one of those eggs missed the Chinaman and hit a policeman. So, Danny was in jail.

"But he was rich. He sent Tito Ralph out to get some wine, and then some more wine. There were four men in the jail. They all drank wine. And at last that fault of Tito Ralph's came out. So he escaped, and all the others escaped with him. They caught Tito Ralph this morning and told him he could not be jailer any more. He was so sad that he broke a window, and now he is in jail again."

"But Danny," Pilon cried. "What about Danny?"

"Oh, Danny," said Johnny Pom-pom, "he escaped too. They did not catch him."

The friends sighed in dismay.

"Danny is getting bad," Pilon said seriously. "He will not come to a good end. I wonder where he got the money."

It was at this moment that the triumphant Torrelli opened the gate and strode up the path. The Pirate's dogs got up nervously from their corner and moved toward the door, snarling. The friends looked up and questioned one another with their eyes. Big Joe picked up the pick handle that had so lately been used on him. The heavy confident step of Torrelli pounded on the porch. The door flew open, and there stood Torrelli, smiling. He did not bluster at them. No, he approached as delicately as a house cat. He patted them kindly, as a house cat pats a cockroach.

"Oh, my friends," he said gently, at their looks of alarm. "My dear good friends and customers. My heart is torn that I must be a carrier of bad news to those whom I love."

Pilon leaped up. "It is Danny. He is sick, he is hurt. Tell us."

Torrelli shook his head daintily. "No, my little ones, it is not Danny. My heart bleeds, but I must tell you that you cannot live here any more." His eyes gloated at the amazement his words wrought. Every mouth dropped open, every eye went blank with astonishment.

"That is foolish," Pablo cried. "Why can't we live here any more?"

Torrelli's hand went lovingly into his breast pocket, and his fingers brought out the precious paper and waved it in the air. "Imagine my suffering," Torrelli went on. "Danny does not own this house any more."

"What!" they cried. "What do you mean? How does not Danny own his house any more? Speak, O Corsican Pig."

Torrelli giggled, a thing so terrible that the paisanos stepped back from him. "Because," he said, "the house belongs to me. Danny came to me and sold me his house for twenty-five dollars last night." Fiendishly he watched the thoughts crowd on their faces.

"It is a lie," their faces said. "Danny would not do such a thing." And then, "But Danny has been doing many bad things lately. He has been stealing from us. Maybe he has sold the house over our heads."

"It is a lie," Pilon cried aloud. "It is a dirty wop lie."

Torrelli smiled on and waved the paper. "Here I have proof," he said. "Here is the paper Danny signed. It is what we of business call a bill of sale."

Pablo came to him furiously. "You got him drunk. He did not know what he did."

Torrelli opened the paper a little bit. "The law will not be interested in that," he said. "And so, my dear little friends, it is my terrible duty to tell you that you must leave my house. I have plans for it." His face lost its smile then, and all the cruelty came back into it. "If you are not out by noon, I will send a policeman."

Pilon moved gently toward him. Oh, beware, Torrelli, when Pilon moves smiling on you! Run, hide yourself in some iron room and weld up the door. "I do not understand these things," Pilon said gently. "Of course I am sad that Danny should do a thing like this."

Torrelli giggled again.

"I never had a house to sell," Pilon continued. "Danny signed this paper, is that it?"

"Yes," Torrelli mimicked him, "Danny signed this paper. That is it."

Pilon blundered on, stupidly. "That is the thing that proves you own this house?"

"Yes, O little fool. This is the paper that proves it."

Pilon looked puzzled. "I thought you must take it down and have some record made."

Torrelli laughed scornfully. Oh, beware, Torrelli! Do you not see how quietly these snakes are moving? There is Jesus Maria in front of the door. There is

Pablo by the kitchen door. See Big Joe's knuckles white on the pick handle.

Torrelli said, "You know nothing of business, little hobos and tramps. When I leave here I shall take this paper down and——"

It happened so quickly that the last words belched out explosively. His feet flew up in the air. He landed with a great thump on the floor and clawed at the air with his fat hands. He heard the stove lid clang.

"Thieves," he screamed. The blood pressed up his neck and into his face. "Thieves, oh, rats and dogs, give me my paper!"

Pilon, standing in front of him, looked amazed.

"Paper?" he asked politely. "What is this paper you speak of so passionately?"

"My bill of sale, my ownership. Oh, the police will hear of this!"

"I do not recall a paper," said Pilon. "Pablo, do you know what is this paper he talks about?"

"Paper?" said Pablo. "Does he mean a newspaper or a cigarette paper?"

Pilon continued with the roll. "Johnny Pom-pom?"

"He is dreaming, maybe, that one," said Johnny Pom-pom.

"Jesus Maria? Do you know of a paper?"

"I think he is drunk," Jesus Maria said in a scandalized voice. "It is too early in the morning to be drunk."

"Joe Portagee?"

"I wasn't here," Joe insisted. "I just came in now."

"Pirate?"

"He don't have no paper," the Pirate turned to his dogs, "do he?"

Pilon turned back to the apoplectic Torrelli. "You are mistaken, my friend. It is possible that I might have been wrong about this paper, but you can see for yourself that no one but you saw this paper. Do you blame me when I think that maybe there was no paper? Maybe you should go to bed and rest a little."

Torrelli was too stunned to shout any more. They turned him about and helped him out of the door and sped him on his way, sunk in the awfulness of his defeat.

And then they looked at the sky, and were glad; for the sun had fought again, and this time won a pathway through the fog. The friends did not go back into the house. They sat happily down on the front porch.

"Twenty-five dollars," said Pilon. "I wonder what he did with the money."

The sun, once its first skirmish was won, drove the fog headlong from the sky. The porch boards warmed up, and the flies sang in the light. Exhaustion had settled on the friends.

"It was a close thing," Pablo said wearily. "Danny should not do such things."

"We will get all our wine from Torrelli to make it up to him," said Jesus Maria.

A bird hopped into the rose bush and flirted its tail. Mrs. Morales' new chickens sang a casual hymn to the sun. The dogs, in the front yard, thoughtfully scratched all over and gnawed their tails.

At the sound of footsteps from the road, the friends looked up, and then stood up with welcoming smiles. Danny and Tito Ralph walked in the gate, and each of them carried two heavy bags. Jesus Maria darted into the house and brought out the fruit jars. The friends noticed that Danny looked a little tired when he set his jugs on the porch.

"It is hot climbing that hill," Danny said.

"Tito Ralph," cried Johnny Pom-pom, "I heard you were put in jail."

"I escaped again," Tito Ralph said wanly. "I still had the keys."

The fruit jars gurgled full. A great sigh escaped from the men, a sigh of relief that everything was over.

Pilon took a big drink. "Danny," he said, "that pig Torrelli came up here this morning with lies. He had a paper he said you signed."

Danny looked startled. "Where is that paper?" he demanded.

"Well," Pilon continued. "We knew it was a lie, so we burned that paper. You didn't sign it, did you?"

"No," said Danny, and he drained his jar.

"It would be nice to have something to eat," observed Jesus Maria.

Danny smiled sweetly. "I forgot. In one of those bags are three chickens and some bread."

So great was Pilon's pleasure and relief that he stood up and made a little speech. "Where is there a friend like our friend?" he exclaimed. "He takes us into his house out of the cold. He shares his good food with us, and his wine. Ohee, the good man, the dear friend."

Danny was embarrassed. He looked at the floor. "It is nothing," he murmured. "It has no merit."

But Pilon's joy was so great that it encompassed the world, and even the evil things of the world. "We must do something nice some time for Torrelli," he said.

16

OF THE SADNESS OF DANNY. HOW THROUGH SACRIFICE DANNY'S FRIENDS GAVE A PARTY. HOW DANNY WAS TRANSLATED.

When Danny came back to his house and to his friends after his amok, he was not conscience-stricken, but he was very tired. The rough fingers of violent experience had harped upon his soul. He began to live listlessly, arising from bed only to sit on the porch, under the rose of Castile; arising from the porch only to eat; arising from the table only to go to bed. The talk flowed about him and he listened, but he did not care. Cornelia Ruiz had a quick and superb run of husbands, and no emotion was aroused in Danny. When Big Joe got in his bed one evening, so apathetic was Danny that Pilon and Pablo had to beat Big Joe for him. When Sammy Rasper, celebrating a belated New Year with a shotgun and a gallon of whisky, killed a cow and went to jail, Danny could not even be drawn into a discussion of the ethics of the case, although the arguments raged about him and although his judgment was passionately appealed to.

After a while it came about that the friends began to worry about Danny. "He is changed," said Pilon. "He is old."

Jesus Maria suggested, "This Danny has crowded the good times of a life into a little three weeks. He is sick of fun."

In vain the friends tried to draw him from the cavern of his apathy. In the mornings, on the porch, they told their funniest stories. They reported details of the love life of Tortilla Flat so penetratingly that they would have been of interest to a dissection class. Pilon winnowed the Flat for news and brought home every seedling of interest to Danny; but there was age in Danny's eyes and weariness.

"Thou art not well," Jesus Maria insisted in vain. "There is some bitter secret in thine heart."

"No," said Danny.

It was noticed that he let flies crawl on his feet a long time, and that when he did slap them off there was no art in his stroke. Gradually the high spirits, the ready laughter went out of Danny's house and tumbled into the dark pool of Danny's quietness.

Oh, it was a pity to see him, that Danny who had fought for lost causes, or any other kind; that Danny who could drink glass for glass with any man in the world; that Danny who responded to the look of love like an aroused tiger. Now he sat on his front porch in the sunlight, his blue-jeaned knees drawn up against his chest, his arms hanging over, his hands dangling from limp wrists, his head bent forward as though by a heavy black thought. His eyes had no light of desire nor displeasure nor joy nor pain.

Poor Danny, how has life left thee! Here thou sittest

like the first man before the world grew up around
him; and like the last man, after the world has eroded
away. But see, Danny! Thou art not alone. Thy friends
are caught in this state of thine. They look at thee from
their eye-corners. They wait like expectant little dogs
for the first waking movement of their master. One
joyful word from thee, Danny, one joyful look, and
they will bark and chase their tails. Thy life is not
thine own to govern, Danny, for it controls other lives.
See how thy friends suffer! Spring to life, Danny, that
thy friends may live again!

This, in effect, although not in words so beautiful,
was what Pilon said. Pilon held out a jar of wine to
Danny. "Come on," he said. "Get up off your can."

Danny took the jar and drained it. And then he settled back and tried to find again his emotional Nirvana.

"Do you hurt any place?" Pilon asked.

"No," said Danny.

Pilon poured him another jar of wine and watched
his face while the wine disappeared. The eyes lost
their lackluster. Somewhere in the depths, the old
Danny stirred to life for a moment. He killed a fly with
a stroke that would have done justice to a master.

Slowly a smile spread over Pilon's face. And later
he gathered all the friends, Pablo and Jesus Maria and
Big Joe and the Pirate and Johnny Pom-pom and Tito
Ralph.

Pilon led them all into the gulch behind the house.
"I gave Danny the last of the wine, and it did him
good. What Danny needs is lots of wine, and maybe a
party. Where can we get wine?"

Their minds combed the possibilities of Monterey
like rat terriers in a barn, but there were no rats.

These friends were urged on by altruism more pure than most men can conceive. They loved Danny.

Jesus Maria said, finally, "Chin Kee is packing squids."

Their minds bolted, turned with curiosity and looked at the thing, crept stealthily back and sniffed it. It was several moments before their shocked imaginations could become used to the thing. "But after all, why not?" they argued silently. "One day would not be so bad—only one day."

Their faces showed the progress of the battle and how they were defeating their fears in the interest of Danny's welfare.

"We will do it," Pilon said. "Tomorrow we will all go down and cut squid, and tomorrow night we will give a party for Danny."

When Danny awakened the next morning, the house was deserted. He got up from his bed and looked through the silent rooms. But Danny was not a man to brood very long. He gave it up as a problem, and then as a thought. He went to the front porch and listlessly sat down.

Is it premonition, Danny? Do you fear the fate that is closing in on you? Are there no pleasures left? No. Danny is as sunk in himself as he had been for a week.

Not so Tortilla Flat. Early the rumor flew about. "Danny's friends are cutting squids for Chin Kee." It was a portent, like the overthrow of government, or even of the solar system. It was spoken of in the street, called over back fences to ladies who were just then hurrying to tell it. "All of Danny's friends are down cutting squids."

The morning was electric with the news. There must be some reason, some secret. Mothers instructed their children and sent them running toward Chin Kee's squid yard. Young matrons waited anxiously behind their curtains for later news. And news came.

"Pablo has cut his hand with a squid knife."

"Chin Kee has kicked the Pirate's dogs."

Riot.

"The dogs are back."

"Pilon looks grim."

A few small bets were laid. For months nothing so exciting had happened. During one whole morning not a single person spoke of Cornelia Ruiz. It was not until the noon hour that the real news leaked out, but then it came with a rush.

"They are going to give a big party for Danny."

"Everyone is going."

Instructions began to emerge from the squid yard. Mrs. Morales dusted her phonograph and picked out her loudest records. Some spark flared, and Tortilla Flat was tinder. Seven friends, indeed, to give a party for Danny! It is as though to say Danny had only seven friends! Mrs. Soto descended upon her chicken yard with a cleaver. Mrs. Palochico poured a bag of sugar into her largest cooking pot to make dulces. A delegation of girls went into the Woolworth store in Monterey and bought the complete stock of colored crepe paper. Guitars and accordions cried experimentally through the Flat.

News! More news from the squid yard. They are going to make it. They are firm. They will have at least fourteen dollars. See that fourteen gallons of wine are ready.

Torrelli was overwhelmed with business. Everyone wanted to buy a gallon to take to Danny's house. Torrelli himself, caught in the fury of the movement, said to his wife, "Maybe we will go to Danny's house. I will take a few gallons for my friends."

As the afternoon passed, waves of excitement poured over the Flat. Dresses unworn in a lifetime were unpacked and hung to air. Shawls the moths had yearned for during two hundred years hung from porch railings and exuded the odor of moth balls.

And Danny? He sat like a half-melted man. He moved only when the sun moved. If he realized that every inhabitant of Tortilla Flat had passed his gate that afternoon, he gave no sign. Poor Danny! At least two dozen pairs of eyes watched his front gate. At about four o'clock he stood up, stretched, and sauntered out of his yard, toward Monterey.

Why, they hardly waited until he was out of sight. Oh, the twisting and stringing of green and yellow and red crepe paper! Oh, the candles shaved, and the shavings thrown on the floor! Oh, the mad children who skated the wax in evenly!

Food appeared. Basins of rice, pots of steaming chicken, dumplings to startle you! And the wine came, gallons and gallons of it. Martinez dug up a keg of potato whisky from his manure pile and carried it to Danny's house.

At five-thirty the friends marched up the hill, tired and bloody, but triumphant. So must the Old Guard have looked when they returned to Paris after Austerlitz. They saw the house, bristling with color. They laughed, and their weariness fell from them. They were so happy that tears came into their eyes.

Mama Chipo walked into the yard followed by her two sons who carried a washtub of salsa pura between them. Paulito, that rich scamp, rushed the fire under a big kettle of beans and chili. Shouts, songs broken off, shrieks of women, the general turmoil of excited children.

A carful of apprehensive policemen drove up from Monterey. "Oh, it is only a party. Sure, we'll have a glass of wine. Don't kill anybody."

Where is Danny? Lonely as smoke on a clear cold night, he drifts through Monterey in the evening. To the post office he goes, to the station, to the pool rooms on Alvarado Street, to the wharf where the black water mourns among the piles. What is it, Danny? What makes you feel this way? Danny didn't know. There was an ache in his heart like the farewell to a dear woman; there was vague sorrow in him like the despair of autumn. He walked past the restaurants he used to smell with interest, and no appetite was aroused in him. He walked by Madam Zuca's great establishment, and exchanged no obscene jests with the girls in the windows. Back to the wharf he went. He leaned over the rail and looked into the deep, deep water. Do you know, Danny, how the wine of your life is pouring into the fruit jars of the gods? Do you see the procession of your days in the oily water among the piles? He remained motionless, staring down.

They were worried about him at Danny's house, when it began to get dark. The friends left the party and trotted down the hill into Monterey. They asked, "Have you seen Danny?"

"Yes, Danny walked by here an hour ago. He walked slow."

Pilon and Pablo hunted together. They traced their friend over the route he had followed, and at last they saw him, on the end of the dark pier. He was lighted by a dim electric wharf light. They hurried out to him.

Pablo did not mention it then, but ever afterward it was his custom, when Danny was mentioned, to describe what he saw as he and Pilon walked out on the wharf toward Danny. "There he stood," Pablo always said. "I could just see him, leaning on the rail. I looked at him, and then I saw something else. At first it looked like a black cloud in the air over Danny's head. And then I saw it was a big black bird, as big as a man. It hung in the air like a hawk over a rabbit hole. I crossed myself and said two Hail Marys. The bird was gone when we came to Danny."

Pilon did not see it. Moreover, Pilon did not remember Pablo crossing himself and saying the Hail Marys. But he never interfered with the story, for it was Pablo's story.

They walked rapidly toward Danny; the wharf boards drummed hollowly under their feet. Danny did not turn. They took him by the arms and turned him about.

"Danny! What is wrong?"

"Nothing. I'm all right."

"Are you sick, Danny?"

"No."

"Then what is it that makes you so sad?"

"I don't know," said Danny. "I just feel this way. I don't want to do anything."

"Maybe a doctor could do something for you, Danny."

"I tell you I am not sick."

"Then look," Pilon cried. "We are having a party for you at your house. Everybody in Tortilla Flat is there, and music and wine and chicken! There are maybe twenty or thirty gallons of wine. And bright paper hanging up. Don't you want to come?"

Danny breathed deeply. For a moment he turned back to the deep black water. Perhaps he whispered to the gods a promise or a defiance.

He swung around again to his friends. His eyes were feverish.

"You're goddam right I want to go. Hurry up. I am thirsty. Any girls there?"

"Lots of girls. All the girls."

"Come on, then. Hurry up."

He led them, running up the hill. Long before they arrived they could hear the sweetness of the music through the pines, and the shrill notes of excited happy voices. The three belated ones arrived at a dead run. Danny lifted his head and howled like a coyote. Jars of wine were held out to him. He took a gulp from each one.

That was a party for you! Always afterward when a man spoke of a party with enthusiasm, someone was sure to say with reverence, "Did you go to that party at Danny's house?" And, unless the first speaker were a newcomer, he had been there. That was a party for you! No one ever tried to give a better one. Such a thing was unthinkable, for within two days Danny's party was lifted out of possible comparison with all other parties that ever were. What man came out of that night without some glorious cuts and bruises? Never had there been so many fights; not fights between two men, but roaring battles that raged through whole clots of men, each one for himself.

Oh, the laughter of women! Thin and high and brittle as spun glass. Oh, the ladylike shrieks of protest from the gulch. Father Ramon was absolutely astounded and incredulous at the confessions the next week. The whole happy soul of Tortilla Flat tore itself from restraint and arose into the air, one ecstatic unit. They danced so hard that the floor gave way in one corner. The accordions played so loudly that always afterward they were windbroken, like foundered horses.

And Danny—just as this party knew no comparison, so Danny defied emulation as a celebrant. In the future let some squirt say with excitement, "Did you see me? Did you see me ask that nigger wenches for a dance? Did you seen us go 'round and 'round like a tom cats?" and some old, wise, and baleful eye would be turned on him. Some voice, sated with having known the limit of possibilities, would ask quietly, "Did you see Danny the night of the party?"

Sometime a historian may write a cold, dry, fungus-like history of The Party. He may refer to the moment when Danny defied and attacked the whole party, men, women, and children, with a table-leg. He may conclude, "A dying organism is often observed to be capable of extraordinary endurance and strength." Referring to Danny's superhuman amorous activity that night, this same historian may write with unshaking hand: "When any living organism is attacked, its whole function seems to aim toward reproduction."

But I say, and the people of Tortilla Flat would say, "To hell with it. That Danny was a man for you!" No one kept actual count, and afterward, naturally, no lady would willingly admit that she had been ignored; so that the reputed prowess of Danny may be somewhat overstated. One tenth of it would be an overstatement for anyone in the world.

Where Danny went, a magnificent madness followed. It is passionately averred in Tortilla Flat that Danny alone drank three gallons of wine. It must be remembered, however, that Danny is now a god. In a few years it may be thirty gallons. In twenty years it may be plainly remembered that the clouds flamed and spelled DANNY in tremendous letters; that the moon dripped blood; that the wolf of the world bayed prophetically from the mountains of the Milky Way.

Gradually a few of those whose stuff was less stern than Danny's began to wilt, to sag, to creep out from under foot. Those who were left, feeling the lack, shouted the louder, fought the more viciously, danced the harder. In Monterey the motors of the fire trucks were kept running, and the firemen, in their red tin hats and raincoats, silently sat in their places and waited.

The night passed quickly, and still Danny roared through the party.

What happened is attested by many witnesses, both men and women. And although their value as witnesses is sometimes attacked on the ground that they had drunk thirty gallons of wine and a keg of potato whisky, those people are sullenly sure of the major points. It took some weeks to get the story into line; some said one thing, some another. But gradually the account clarified into the reasonable form it now has and always will have.

Danny, say the people of Tortilla Flat, had been
rapidly changing his form. He had grown huge and
terrible. His eyes flared like the headlights of an automobile. There was something fearsome about him.
There he stood, in the room of his own house. He held
the pine table-leg in his right hand, and even it had
grown. Danny challenged the world.

"Who will fight?" he cried. "Is there no one left in
the world who is not afraid?" The people were afraid;
that table-leg, so hideous and so alive, had become a
terror to them all. Danny swung it back and forth. The
accordions wheezed to silence. The dancing stopped.
The room grew chill, and a silence seemed to roar in
the air like an ocean.

"No one?" Danny cried again. "Am I alone in the
world? Will no one fight with me?" The men shuddered before his terrible eyes, and watched, fascinated, the slashing path of the table-leg through the
air. And no one answered the challenge.

Danny drew himself up. It is said that his head just
missed touching the ceiling. "Then I will go out to The
One who can fight. I will find The Enemy who is
worthy of Danny!" He stalked to the door, staggering a
little as he went. The terrified people made a broad
path for him. He bent to get out of the door. The
people stood still and listened.

Outside the house they heard his roaring challenge.
They heard the table-leg whistle like a meteor through
the air. They heard his footsteps charging down the
yard. And then, behind the house, in the gulch, they
heard an answering challenge so fearful and so chill
that their spines wilted like nasturtium stems under
frost. Even now, when the people speak of Danny's

Opponent, they lower their voices and look furtively about. They heard Danny charge to the fray. They heard his last shrill cry of defiance, and then a thump. And then silence.

For a long moment the people waited, holding their breaths lest the harsh rush of air from their lungs should obscure some sound. But they listened in vain. The night was hushed, and the gray dawn was coming.

Pilon broke the silence. "Something is wrong," he said. And Pilon it was who first rushed out of the door. Brave man, no terror could restrain him. The people followed him. Back of the house they went, where Danny's footsteps had sounded, and there was no Danny. They came to the edge of the gulch, where a sharp zigzag path led down to the bottom of that ancient watercourse wherein no stream had flowed for many generations. The following people saw Pilon dart down the path. They went after him, slowly. And they found Pilon at the bottom of the gulch, leaning over a broken and twisted Danny. He had fallen forty feet. Pilon lighted a match. "I think he is alive," he shrieked. "Run for a doctor. Run for Father Ramon."

The people scattered. Within fifteen minutes four doctors were awakened, dragged from their beds by frantic paisanos. They were not allowed that slow deliberateness by which doctors love to show that they are no slaves to emotion. No! They were hustled, rushed, pushed, their instrument cases were shoved into their hands by men hopelessly incapable of saying what they wanted. Father Ramon, dragged from his bed, came panting up the hill, uncertain whether it was a devil to drive out, a newborn baby to baptize before it died, or a lynching to attend. Meanwhile

Pilon and Pablo and Jesus Maria carried Danny up the hill and laid him on his bed. They stood candles all about him. Danny was breathing heavily.

First the doctors arrived. They glanced suspiciously at one another, considered precedence; but the moment of delay brought threatening looks into the eyes of the people. It did not take long to look Danny over. They were all through by the time Father Ramon arrived.

I shall not go into the bedroom with Father Ramon, for Pilon and Pablo and Jesus Maria and Big Joe and Johnny Pom-pom and Tito Ralph and the Pirate and the dogs were there; and they were Danny's family. The door was, and is, closed. For after all there is pride in men, and some things cannot decently be pried into.

But in the big room, crowded to suffocation with the people of Tortilla Flat, there was tenseness and a waiting silence. Priests and doctors have developed a subtle means of communication. When Father Ramon came out of the bedroom his face had not changed, but at sight of him the women broke into a high and terrible wail. The men shifted their feet like horses in a box stall, and then went outside into the dawning. And the bedroom door remained closed.

17

HOW DANNY'S SORROWING FRIENDS DEFIED THE CONVENTIONS. HOW THE TALISMANIC BOND WAS BURNED. HOW EACH FRIEND DEPARTED ALONE.

Death is a personal matter, arousing sorrow, despair, fervor, or dry-hearted philosophy. Funerals, on the other hand, are social functions. Imagine going to a funeral without first polishing the automobile. Imagine standing at a graveside not dressed in your best dark suit and your best black shoes, polished delightfully. Imagine sending flowers to a funeral with no attached card to prove you had done the correct thing. In no social institution is the codified ritual of behavior more rigid than in funerals. Imagine the indignation if the minister altered his sermon or experimented with facial expression. Consider the shock if, at the funeral parlors, any chairs were used but those little folding yellow torture chairs with the hard seats. No, dying, a man may be loved, hated, mourned, missed; but once dead he becomes the chief ornament of a complicated and formal social celebration.

Danny was dead, two days dead; and already he had ceased to be Danny. Although the faces of the people were recently and mournfully veiled with gloom, there was excitement in their hearts. The government has promised a military funeral to all of its ex-soldier sons who wish it. Danny was the first of Tortilla Flat to go, and Tortilla Flat was ready critically to test the government promises. Already the news had been sent to the Presidio and Danny's body had been embalmed at government expense. Already a caisson was newly painted and waiting in the artillery shed with a neat new flag folded on top of it. Already orders of the day for Friday were made out:

TEN TO ELEVEN A.M., FUNERAL. ESCORT, SQUADRON A, 11th CAVALRY, 11th CAVALRY BAND, AND FIRING SQUAD.

Were these not things to set every woman in Tortilla Flat window shopping at the National Dollar Store in Monterey? During the day dark children walked the streets of Monterey, begging flowers from the gardens for Danny's funeral. And at night the same children visited the same gardens to augment their bouquets.

At the party, the finest clothes had been worn. During the two-day interval, those clothes had to be cleaned, washed, starched, mended, and ironed. The activity was frantic. The excitement was decently intense.

On the evening of the second day, Danny's friends were gathered in Danny's house. The shock and the wine had worn off; and now they were horror-stricken, for in all Tortilla Flat they, who had loved Danny

most, who had received the most from his hands, they,
the paisanos, were the only ones who could not attend
Danny's funeral. Through the murk of the headaches
they had been conscious of this appalling tragedy, but
only on this evening had the situation become so concrete that it must be faced. Ordinarily their clothes
were unspeakable. The party had aged their jeans and
blue shirts by years. Where was the trouser knee un-
burst? Where the shirt unripped? If anyone else had
died, they could have borrowed clothes; but there was
no person in Tortilla Flat who was not going to wear
his good clothes to the funeral. Only Cocky Riordan
was not going, but Cocky was in quarantine for small-
pox, and so were his clothes. Money might be begged
or stolen to buy one good suit, but money for six suits
was simply impossible to get.

You may say, did they not love Danny enough to go
to his funeral in rags? Would you go in rags when your
neighbors were dressed in finery? Would not the disre-
spect to Danny be more if they went in rags than if
they did not go at all?

The despair that lay on their hearts was incalcu-
lable. They cursed their fate. Through the front door
they could see Galvez parading by. Galvez had bought
a new suit for the funeral, and he had it on twenty-four
hours in advance. The friends sat, chin in hand,
crushed by their ill fortune. Every possibility had been
discussed.

Pilon, for once in his life, descended to absurdity.
"We might go out tonight and each one steal a suit,"
he suggested. He knew that was silly, for every suit
would be laid on a chair beside a bed that night. It
would be death to steal a suit.

"The Salvation Army sometimes gives suits," said Jesus Maria.

"I have been there," Pablo said. "They have fourteen dresses this time, but no suits."

On every side Fate was against them. Tito Ralph came in with his new green handkerchief sticking out of his breast pocket, but the hostility he aroused made him back apologetically out of the room.

"If we had a week, we could cut squids," Pilon said heroically. "The funeral is tomorrow. We must look in the eye at this thing. Of course we can go to the funeral all right."

"How?" the friends demanded.

"We can go on the sidewalk, while the band and the people march in the street. It is all grass around the cemetery fence. We can lie there in the grass and see everything."

The friends looked at Pilon gratefully. They knew how his sharp wits had been digging over possibilities. But it was only half, less than half, to see the funeral. Being seen at the funeral was the most important half. This was the best that could be done.

"In this we learn a lesson," said Pilon. "We must take it to heart that we should always have a good suit of clothes laid by. We can never tell what may happen."

There they left it, but they felt that they had failed. All through the night they wandered in the town. What yard then was not plundered of its finest blooms? What flowering tree remained standing? In the morning the hole in the cemetery that was to receive Danny's body was almost hidden by a mound of the finest flowers from the best gardens in Monterey.

It is not always that Nature arranges her effects with good taste. Truly, it rained before Waterloo; forty feet of snow fell in the path of the Donner Party. But Friday turned out a nice day. The sun arose as though this were a day for a picnic. The gulls flew in across a smiling bay to the sardine canneries. The rock fishermen took their places on the rocks for the ebbing tide. The Palace Drug Company ran down its awnings to protect the red hot-water bottles in its windows from the chemical action of the sun. Mr. Machado, the tailor, put a sign in his window, Back In Ten Minutes, and went home to dress for the funeral. Three purse seiners came in, loaded with sardines. Louie Duarte painted his boat, and changed its name from Lolita to The Three Cousins. Jake Lake, the cop, arrested a roadster from Del Monte and turned it loose and bought a cigar.

It is a puzzle. How can life go on its stupid course on such a day? How can Mamie Jackson hose off her front sidewalk? How can George W. Merk write his fourth and angriest letter to the water company? How can Charlie Marsh be as dirtily drunk as usual? It is sacrilege. It is outrage.

Danny's friends awakened sadly and got up off the floor. Danny's bed was empty. It was like the riderless charger of an officer which follows its master to his grave. Even Big Joe Portagee had cast no covetous glance at Danny's bed. The sun shone enthusiastically through the window and cast the delicate shadows of spider webs on the floor.

"Danny was glad on mornings like this," said Pilon.

After their trip to the gulch the friends sat for a while on the front porch and celebrated the memory of their friend. Loyally they remembered and proclaimed Danny's virtues. Loyally they forgot his faults.

"And strong," said Pablo. "He was as strong as a mule! He could lift a bale of hay."

They told little stories of Danny, of his goodness, his courage, his piety.

All too soon it was time to go to the church, to stand across the street in their ragged clothes. They blushed inwardly when luckier people went into the church, dressed so beautifully, smelling so prodigally of Agua Florida. The friends could hear the music and the shrill drone of the service. From their vantage point they saw the cavalry arrive, and the band with muffled drums, and the firing squad, and the caisson with its three pairs of horses, and a cavalryman on the near horse of each pair. The mournful clop-clop of shod horses on asphalt put despair in the hearts of the friends. Helplessly they watched the casket carried out and laid on the caisson, and the flag draped over it. The officer blew his whistle, raised his hand and threw it forward. The squadron moved, the firing squad dropped its rifles. The drums thundered their heart-breaking, slow rhythm. The band played its sodden march. The caisson moved. The people walked majestically behind, men straight and stern, women daintily holding their skirts up out of the indelible trail of the cavalry. Everyone was there, Cornelia Ruiz, Mrs. Morales, Galvez, Torrelli and his plump wife, Mrs. Palochico, Tito Ralph the traitor, Sweets Ramirez, Mr. Machado, everyone who amounted to anything on Tortilla Flat, and everyone else, was there.

Is it any wonder that the friends could not stand the

shame and misery of it? For a little while they slunk along the sidewalk, bolstered with heroism.

Jesus Maria broke down first. He sobbed with shame, for his father had been a rich and respected prize-fighter. Jesus Maria put down his head and bolted; and the five other friends followed, and the five dogs bounded behind them.

Before the procession was in sight, Danny's friends were lying in the tall grass that edged the cemetery. The service was short and military. The casket was lowered; the rifles cracked; the bugle sang taps, and at the sound Enrique and Fluff, Pajarito and Rudolph and Señor Alec Thompson laid back their heads and howled. The Pirate was proud of them then!

It was over too soon; the friends walked hurriedly away so that the people would not see them.

They had to pass Torrelli's deserted house anyway, on the way home. Pilon went in through a window and brought out two gallons of wine. And then they walked slowly back to Danny's quiet house. Ceremoniously they filled the fruit jars and drank.

"Danny liked wine," they said. "Danny was happy when he had a little wine."

The afternoon passed, and the evening came. Each man, as he sipped his wine, roved through the past. At seven o'clock a shamed Tito Ralph came in with a box of cigars he had won on a punch board. The friends lighted the cigars and spat, and opened the second gallon. Pablo tried a few notes of the song "Tuli Pan," to see whether his voice was gone for good.

"Cornelia Ruiz was alone today," Pilon said speculatively.

"Maybe it would be all right to sing a few sad songs," said Jesus Maria.

"But Danny did not like sad songs," Pablo insisted. "He liked the quick ones, about lively women."

They all nodded gravely. "Yes, Danny was a great one for women."

Pablo tried the second verse to "Tuli Pan," and Pilon helped a little, and the others joined in toward the end.

When the song was done, Pilon puffed at his cigar, but it had gone out. "Tito Ralph," he said, "why don't you get your guitar so we can sing a little better?" He lighted his cigar and flipped the match.

The little burning stick landed on an old newspaper against the wall. Each man started up to stamp it out; and each man was struck with a celestial thought, and settled back. They found one another's eyes and smiled the wise smiles of the deathless and hopeless ones. In a reverie they watched the flame flicker and nearly die, and sprout to life again. They saw it bloom on the paper. Thus do the gods speak with tiny causes. And the men smiled on as the paper burned and the dry wooden wall caught.

Thus must it be, O wise friends of Danny. The cord that bound you together is cut. The magnet that drew you has lost its virtue. Some stranger will own the house, some joyless relative of Danny's. Better that this symbol of holy friendship, this good house of parties and fights, of love and comfort, should die as Danny died, in one last glorious, hopeless assault on the gods.

They sat and smiled. And the flame climbed like a snake to the ceiling and broke through the roof and roared. Only then did the friends get up from their chairs and walk like dreaming men out of the door.

Pilon, who profited by every lesson, took what was left of the wine with him.

The sirens screamed from Monterey. The trucks roared up the hill in second gear. The searchlights played among the trees. When the Department arrived, the house was one great blunt spear of flame. The hoses wet the trees and brush to keep the flames from spreading.

Among the crowding people of Tortilla Flat, Danny's friends stood entranced and watched until at last the house was a mound of black, steaming cinders. Then the fire trucks turned and coasted away down the hill.

The people of the Flat melted into the darkness. Danny's friends still stood looking at the smoking ruin. They looked at one another strangely, and then back to the burned house. And after a while they turned and walked slowly away, and no two walked together.